Friends in High Places

Friends in High Places

A NOVEL

LUCIANNE GOLDBERG
SONDRA TILL ROBINSON

RICHARD MAREK PUBLISHERS
NEW YORK

Library of Congress Cataloging in Publication Data

Goldberg, Lucianne.
    Friends in high places.

    I. Robinson, Sondra Till, joint author. II. Title.
PZ4.G61919Fr [PS3557.03579] 813'.5'4 78-26187
ISBN 0-399-90039-X

PRINTED IN THE UNITED STATES OF AMERICA

Prologue

May 1965

Washington, D.C., was not what they had promised.

She had been there for eight months and had yet to be a conscious part of participatory democracy at work. That was what the FBI recruiter had said to the students in her political science class at the University of Chicago. "You will be a direct participant in your government." She had listened, in awe, to the exciting opportunities the man offered, and she had signed up immediately after graduation.

Three months later she strode out of the great, gray Justice Department Building, resigning after her supervisor requested that she sort out the big paper clips from the little paper clips in all the containers.

She and her roommate ate a celebratory feast that night. A tuna fish noodle casserole topped with crumbled Krispy Crackers—the Government Girl Special. They washed it down with Champale. Then she had a good cry and went out for the early edition of the morning want ads.

The opaque glass door on the tenth floor of the National Press Building read: Jane Connor and Associates, Inc., Consultants.

Oh, my God. A woman. The ad hadn't said anything about the consultant being a woman. She could visualize her: probably fifty,

fifty-five; mottled gray and brown hair in a washerwoman jumble on top of her head; thick woolen suits and orthopedic shoes; the kind of woman her sister had warned her she would become, if she hung around Washington too long. She had already discovered there were few decent men in Washington. *Time* magazine had recently reported the ratio of men to women as one to five.

She turned to walk back to the elevator, sorry that she had given her name when she phoned. Then she remembered the grim Mrs. Rosenwald, her landlady, who had held the bounced rent check like a dead thing earlier that morning, her voice high and shrill with threats of eviction.

She swiveled back toward the glass door. Before she could turn the knob, a shadow behind the glass pulled it open.

"Hello, there," a very pretty young woman said, smiling at her. She was pretty like her English lit teacher back at Evanston High School. Youngish and blond; nice clothes and a big, friendly smile.

"I'm Jane Connor. Are you the Beth who called?"

"Uh, yes. I was answering your ad for a secretary?" she said tentatively.

"Come on in," the woman said, and stood aside and gestured toward a small anteroom office. There seemed to be a larger office beyond, and a window that looked right smack out on the Washington Monument.

As soon as they were seated in the larger office, Jane Connor told her that she was a lobbyist.

"The 'consultant' designation is an inside joke. Lobbyist is a dirty word to most people. Well, I'm a lobbyist, but I'm pretty straight. Oh, a contribution to a deserving public servant from time to time . . ." She rolled her eyes toward the ceiling and they both laughed.

Beth liked this lady. She didn't understand the setup, but she liked Jane Connor. Maybe in her office she would see some of what they had been talking about in poli sci. Maybe here she could find out what made this sleepy, square, boring town what it was said to be.

Now it was four fifty-five on a Tuesday in May. Beth half dozed over a copy of *Look*, pondering the comfort versus the expense of taking a cab to Clyde's in Georgetown for a drink and a chance encounter with a man, or just going home to her walk-up. Between the GS-5 typists and the stone-broke CIA secretaries, the competition at Clyde's was always cutthroat. In nine months the best she had managed had been a night on the town with a married correspondent for a Kansas City daily, and one dinner with an earnest but limp young SEC lawyer she never saw again.

From her desk Jane studied her secretary's sagging posture. Beth was beginning to look like so many of them. And Beth had been in town less than a year. Jane gave her another six months in which to discover that the males in Washington were either married, alimony-ridden retreads or on the make for a rich girl with an important family name.

"Hon," Jane called to her secretary, "you might as well go home. I'll see you tomorrow."

"Okay, thanks, Jane. Have a nice evening." She was out the door in a minute and a half.

Jane shrugged when the door slammed shut. She couldn't complain. She was lucky to have found Beth at all. Damn few girls would work for a woman in Washington. It reduced the odds of meeting a man if one worked for a woman. A woman wouldn't take her secretary to lunch or up to the Press Club bar or invite her along to dinner with a client. Jane had run her ad for a week and received only three responses. The first two applicants had been housewives with no experience. Beth was smart and knew how to type and track her down by phone when she needed to be contacted.

Her phone buzzed. "Jane Connor and Associates."

"Senator Pratt is on the line for Miss Connor," a female voice whined.

"This is she. Put him on." Jane lit a cigarette. "Hello, Bill. Yes, I *can* have a drink."

"Wish that was the reason for my call, kind lady."

The Senator's heavy voice reminded Jane that he was the one who told knock-knock jokes. The Senator outlined his problem in terse, rapid language. She listened and jotted notes on a yellow legal pad. After agreeing to get back to him as soon as possible, she hung up.

"Crap. Couldn't call me at nine in the morning. Waits until closing time." She then realized she was talking to an empty office.

This would be a sticky one. She swiveled around and stared out

7

the window that faced south. A steady stream of traffic crawled bumper to bumper down Fourteenth Street. Bureaucrats headed toward bedroom Washington across the river in Virginia. It depressed her. She watched a particular red convertible inch its way toward the Fourteenth Street Bridge. She lit a fresh cigarette and considered Senator Pratt's current problem.

His eighteen-year-old daughter had been working on more than her backhand with the married tennis instructor at Mount Vernon Seminary, and was now in need of a doctor to get her out of trouble. The Senator had turned to Jane for assistance, and while she found the assignment repellent, she knew that Senator Pratt's position of seniority on the Immigration and Naturalization Committee was crucial to a chemical company she represented in Washington.

The chief engineer of the company's Midwestern laboratory was a chemist from New Delhi. The man's services were highly valued. The Immigration Bureau had been harassing him and making deportation noises. The company brass had appealed to Jane to press for a special naturalization bill. Jane had managed to get another Senator to sponsor a private bill, and it was to come before the committee that Pratt controlled in three weeks.

Damn his eyes!

Jane smashed out her cigarette and began to dial. She called a woman she knew in Senator Smathers' office who had a contact with the Cuban doctors who had flooded Florida since the revolution. Her friend said she would get back with a name as soon as she could. Within an hour Jane had the name of a man to contact in Miami, reservations for a flight to Miami and the name of a hotel and a date for the Pratt girl to check in.

Senator Pratt was grateful for Jane's speed and efficiency. There was no need for him to mention her pending business before his committee. Just as there was no need for Jane to mention the little white envelope she had slid across his desk weeks ago, an envelope passed to her at dinner by the East Coast public relations director of the chemical company.

Jane had had few illusions about what she would be doing when she set up her office in the Press Building. She had been around Washington for a long time.

At thirty-two, Jane Carleton Connor was the antithesis of a political cartoonist's version of a Washington lobbyist. She sat at her desk looking cucumber cool in a beautifully tailored suit, her blond hair softly pulled back into a French twist.

She was a nice-looking woman, nothing spectacular: wide-spaced blue eyes, mobile mouth, bones that would serve her well long after she passed through menopause.

Her appearance was not the explanation for her success. Not that she was ever the least reluctant to use her femininity, when and if it was required. Rather, Jane always maintained self-control. Always. And Jane's reading of people was keenly accurate.

She was on a first-name basis with most of the important people in Washington. She was personally close to a few, and those few she valued highly. Her closest female friend was Ann Hawkins Adams of the *Washington Herald*, who, at that moment, was propped up in a bed at George Washington University Hospital making life lively for the staff there, and talking nonstop on two telephones. Jane's evening plans for the past weeks had included a drink at Ann's bedside. Each day they discussed Ann's test results and gossip they had gleaned from dozens of conversations each had held with sources high *and* low around the city.

The two women valued each other enormously. Their friendship was based on utter trust.

Ann Hawkins Adams was not *just* a reporter. A month before, she had won a Pulitzer Prize, and now she was scheduled to be the subject of a *Time* magazine cover story. Jane had been delighted to learn that she herself would be included in a sidebar story to Ann's profile, which was to be a roundup of influential Washington women.

The Senator Pratt matter dispatched, the phone quiet at last, Jane picked up her bag and briefcase and headed toward the Press Building elevators and out onto Fourteenth Street to hail a northbound cab to the hospital.

Jane's high heels clinked rhythmically down the familiar wide, waxed hall to Ann's room on the top floor of the hospital. Tentatively, she opened the door and stuck her head in. Ann had a receiver cradled against one shoulder. She waved the other receiver in a gesture of welcome, motioning Jane to come in.

Ann's room was not institutional white or even public-building green; rather, a pale soft apricot. The rumor was that it had been furnished for a former Cabinet member who had insisted on

9

transforming the room at his own expense. It was a prized accommodation, and usually booked months in advance. The hospital board had made it available to Ann after a call from her publisher. In addition to Ann's two phones, there were three television sets that she could operate by remote control.

Each of the three television sets was tuned to a different network, but the sound was off. Momentarily.

"Why, hell, honey," she said to someone at the other end, "I am deeeelighted about it. Nobody ever said I didn't have an ego." Ann pointed Jane's attention to a picture of J. Edgar Hoover on the front page of the evening paper at her side and held up two fingers, a language indicating, Jane assumed, that she was talking to Hoover's number two at the FBI, Clyde Tolson. She handed the second receiver to Jane, signaling that she should hang it up. Jane shrugged and did as Ann wanted.

Then Ann pointed toward the little bar that was a part of the large hospital room and made a drinking gesture with her free hand.

Jane removed ice from the small refrigerator and placed the cubes in two Baccarat tumblers. She poured bourbon into one glass and premixed brandy Alexander into the other. She whisked away the overflowing ashtray next to Ann, emptied it and replaced it. Then she handed Ann her drink.

"Clyde, you are a honey lamb to call. I want you to buy five hundred copies of *Time* and send them around to the boys for target practice." Ann roared her big Tennessee gut laugh. She was having a good time. "Sometime next month, they tell me. But, I'll be out of here long before that, so we can party." She paused and took a sip of her brandy Alexander. "Just dumb old tests, honey, that's all. 'Bout as much fun as slaughtering hogs. Come see me, ya hear?"

She hung up and turned to Jane "Hi, precious." She leaned forward and gave Jane a brushing kiss on the cheek. "As you no doubt gathered, that was Tolson down at the Bureau." Ann let up on her thick, hill-country accent. "Don't you know those *Time* boys came sniffing around looking for my file? Clyde thought I'd get a kick out of that."

"Why is *Time* digging around like that?"

"Oh, you know how those eager beaver *Time* staffers are. I kind of feel sorry for whoever has to do my life story. I ain't barely

10

moved outa a fifty-block square since I got to this town back in the forties. Won't make for thrilling reading."

"Come on, Annie. Stop putting yourself down. What are they doing about the cover?"

"The paper is taking care of that, thank goodness. I'm in no shape to have any pictures taken at the moment." She patted her bright red hair; the white-streaked roots were beginning to show.

Jane had seldom seen Ann bareheaded. Ann was given to wearing enormous, brightly colored hats at all times. Jane half expected her to wear one in bed.

Even hatless and hospitalized, Ann Adams was not to be overlooked. Her lanky frame was draped in flowing, red satin Chinese pajamas, the same shade as the polish on her long fingernails and the toenails of her bare feet.

At forty-three, Ann was not a beautiful woman, and obviously never had been. She did possess a certain presence that was, in its way, more alluring than simple, perfect beauty. Behind the snapping brown eyes and the freckles on her cheeks, crackled a vitality that most people found irresistible. Ann Hawkins Adams knew precisely who she was in what she considered to be the great scheme of things. Jane had once heard an editor at Ann's paper describe her simply as a "no bullshit lady," and felt that summed her up better than the boys at *Time* ever could.

Jane loved her dearly, and she was not alone.

"Anybody come by today?" she asked.

Ann nodded. "Billie Claire Hutchins, to name one. She walked over from the West Wing with my button. See my button?" Ann picked up an enamel pin with a picture of Snoopy, head pointed toward the sky, whirling around with his eyes shut. The caption read, 'To Live Is to Dance.' "I'd wear it but I don't want to rip my new peejays." She reached up and pinned it to the silk lampshade.

"How is Billie Claire making out with the LBJ crowd?" Jane asked as she rattled the ice in her empty glass.

"Going nuts. She spends most of her time trying to figure out where Johnson is going to jump next. He's not like Kennedy. He tells them nothing in the pressroom. Just ups and does. Drives them all half-crazy. Billie's convinced he hates the press. I'm not so sure she's wrong. She's kinda cozied up to Jack Valenti recently. He's the big man's valet and pants presser, but I guess he's as good a source as any."

Ann turned up the sound on one of her sets and they listened to Walter Cronkite be concerned about cheating at the Air Force Academy. After a minute she turned off Walter and found Howard K. Smith's voice. Jane refreshed their drinks and Smith drawled on about Bogalusa, Louisiana. Ann turned off his sound and said, "You know, honey, these guys have it easy. You don't see Walter or Howard or David doing the ankle express after hard news. They come in all cool and spiffy in their custom-made suits, and read the stuff that the Billie Claire Hutchins types around here sweat their tails off for every day."

"Give a cheer, Melon's here!" sang a voice from the direction of the door.

Ann flashed a quick glance at Jane, who rolled her eyes heavenward and then turned to see Mary Ellen Bowersox bounce into the room, her arms encircling a huge, flat grease-stained box.

"Jesus! Pizza!" Ann bellowed and bounced up and down on the bed. "Melon, you are a pussycat. Gimme! Gimme!"

Melon Bowersox dropped the big box at the foot of Jane's chaise and embraced Ann. "How are you, hon? Got to get you *out* of here. This place is a drag."

"I want pizza. I want pizza," Ann chanted, still bouncing.

Jane grabbed up the greasy box to prevent it from staining the chaise. It was still hot. "Wait a goddamn minute, Adams. Are you supposed to eat this crap? I rather doubt it."

"Goddamn straight I can have it. Nothing, nowhere, nohow says 'don't give patient pizza.' You know I love it. Give it to me!" she demanded.

"Don't be a party poop." Melon tugged at the box. "She sits around swilling brandy and cream and smoking two packs a day and the doctors let her get away with *that*. Give her the fucking pizza."

Melon Bowersox was tiny. She had a high, sharp and brittle voice that served her well as the *Washington Inquirer*'s new feature writer. Hers was a voice that could pierce and intimidate the most reticent news source.

Jane released the box to Melon. "Okay, I give up. Melon, you want a drink?" Melon nodded. She had already begun to tear off a huge hunk of pizza for herself. "Your usual death ball?"

Melon nodded again, her mouth full of pizza. Melon drank Manhattans with olives. "God, have I had a day. God! I get an interview with Billy Moyers, right? Exclusive. Just him and me." She spoke with machine-gun speed, moving the pizza around to make room for the words. "Right? Right?" Melon chewed.

"For God's sake, Melon. You sit there chowing down the pizza you brought Ann, and not even offering her a bite!" Jane walked to the pizza box and removed it from Melon's side of the bed. She walked around and put it on the night table next to Ann, out of Melon's reach.

"Anyway, anyway," Melon began again. "I spent four hours in the morgue yesterday reading up on Bill Moyers. All about how he's the son of a minister, how *he's* a minister. All that shit. Guess what? He doesn't show! Sends word he's busy. How could he be so busy? I'm a top feature writer with a circulation of over two hundred thousand in the Nation's capital, and he's busy. So there I am without a story for tomorrow."

"So what did you do?" Jane asked, knowing a cue when she heard one.

"So . . ." Melon settled back, taking up half of Ann's bed. Ann was happily devouring the rest of the pizza. "So, I had to have lunch on the Hill anyway. So, I stopped by Ev Dirksen's office after lunch to see who's sitting around. And guess what?"

"What, Melon?" Jane said flatly.

"That loony lady? You know the one who's been lobbying to make the marigold the national flower for the last ten years? Well. You know Dirksen lets her sit around his office. He likes the idea of having the marigold be the national flower for some crazy reason. Anyway, she goes 'Psst,' at me. Just like that. 'Pssst.' I went over to her and she says she knows who I am and she wants to give me some really dynamite information. Going to blow the roof off the Capitol Building. She proceeds to tell me that there is this giant *daffodil* lobby. A virtual flower cartel that has gotten Bird to fling all those daffodils all over town. Now think about this for a minute. Makes sense. First Lady's got this beautification gimmick worked out. Great idea. Great press. Why not daisies? or carnations? or roses? No. She chooses *daffodils.* Why?" Melon stopped to take a breath.

Ann's mouth was stuffed with pizza. Jane had been sitting staring at Melon, sipping her drink. They looked at each other. In singsong unison they both asked, "Why, Melon?"

"A daffodil lobby!" she shrieked. "Great lead! Great story."

Again the two women answered in unison. "No, Melon."

Melon was angry. "Why not, for Christ's sake? I think it's terrific."

Ann swallowed the last of the pizza. "Well, number one, that marigold lady has been around since Millard Fillmore. She's not hot news, nor is she a particularly good source, considering the fact that Lady Bird didn't decide to plant *forty million marigolds*. Second, there *is* no daffodil lobby, because Lady Bird got all those flowers for free as a gift to the Government of the You Ess of A."

Melon looked crestfallen. "Shit. Now what am I gonna do?"

"Have you got a date tonight?" Jane asked.

"Yes. As a matter of fact, I have two dates tonight. For drinks and then for dinner. Why?"

"Because my hunch is that you'll have a story by morning."

"She won't be able to print it, Janey," Ann hooted.

"Hey, lay off, you guys." Melon produced her best little-girl pout. She stared up at Jane through her curly bangs. She consciously used her perfect Walt Disney eyes to draw attention away from her not quite successful Walt Disney mouth. A mouth that had never fully matured. Her slight overbite gave her lips a look that Marilyn Monroe used to enormous advantage. They almost formed the shape of a kiss, and a great many people were fascinated by Melon Bowersox's mouth. They had been hypnotized by the seemingly endless flow of bitchy anecdotes she delivered in a crisp, slightly nasal voice.

Jane and Ann, who were her friends, knew Melon was driven by energy enough for them all. For the most part, her drive was focused; her ears and eyes were attuned to what in any other American city would be called pure gossip. In Washington, though, gossip wasn't *printed*. But it was a coin of considerable social and professional value. A tidbit, succulent and unprintable, could often be used in trade for something that could be used in the next day's paper.

Permitting fifteen seconds of silence, Melon said, "Jane, has *Time* interviewed you yet?"

"No, not really. Jean Franklin called from the Washington Bureau, and we had a giggle. She already knows as much about me as I care to have printed."

"Yeah, she called me, too. Hot damn! I hope they use a decent picture of me."

14

"Melon, Jesus! What makes you think they'll use a picture?"

"They have to, they just have to!" Melon wailed. "What's the good of being in a national magazine if people can't *see* you?" She was speaking around her second olive, which she had pierced with the nail of her index finger.

"Melon, you are hopeless," Ann laughed from the bed.

Melon started to rise, glanced at Jane and sat back down. "I'll bet Billie Claire gets *her* picture in. I'll bet Helen Thomas and Fran Lewine and Marianne Means and Nancy . . ."

Jane moaned and fell back against the back of the chaise.

Melon made a face at Jane. "And what about Miss Allegra Farr? You can bet they'll use a picture of Washington's answer to Grace Kelly. Count on it!"

"Well, that's a fact, Mel," Ann said. "Allegra called yesterday to say they'd already been up to the house in Georgetown. Took pictures of her in every dress in her wardrobe."

"Ha! That makes one thousand pictures—even." Melon moved toward the bar, pouting. "I just hope she didn't open her beautiful trap about who *bought* those rags."

"Careful, Melon," warned Jane.

"Wadda ya mean, 'careful.'" Melon mimicked Jane as she splashed liquor into her glass. "Everyone knows she's Seth Hathaway's mistress, including *Jeannine* Magnuson Hathaway. That that's *his* house and his antiques and his jewelry she clanks around in. 'Prominent Washington hostess,' my ass!"

"Allegra doesn't clank. She glides," Jane corrected.

"She glides, right, just like a swan through the life of *your* publisher, Ann." She pointed a menacing finger at the bedridden redhead.

"Allegra and Seth and Jeannine are all handling it," Ann yawned, smoothing her red pajama top.

"I hope you're right. Gotta go." She tossed back her drink. "My first tonight is a really groovy guy who was on Bobby's staff at Justice. Says he can give me some new stuff on that old Jenkins mess."

While Melon was in the bathroom humming and fluffing her hair, Jane said, "Still no change in Del, Annie?"

"Nope. My formerly distinguished husband is still Dr. Dalton's prize pickled vegetable. I tell you, between the tubes and machines, the poor man doesn't have a chance to get better. I think it's time for them to just let him be. What good is it doing?"

15

"You never know."

"Bullshit. I know. Del's had it." Ann's voice was sad and bitter.

"How do I look?" Melon stood in the doorway to the tiny bathroom.

"Umm. Good enough for any Justice Department hotshot," Jane smiled. "I have to admire your tolerance for boredom."

"We can't all have suave Wall Street lawyers in our humble lives," Melon said pointedly, and walked over to kiss Ann goodbye. "You staying, Jane?"

"For a minute."

"Where *is* Mr. Wonderful, anyway?"

"Paul's on the coast this week."

"I don't mean him, love; where's that dishy guy from *Newsweek?* What's his name? Irving? Sheldon?"

"Sam," Jane said, lowering her eyebrows and voice. "He was coming down on the six o'clock shuttle tonight, but I've got these textile guys in town sweating out a Tariff Commission ruling. Couldn't shake them."

"Sounds thrilling. See you two." She blew kisses around the room.

Both Jane and Ann blew out sighs instead, after Melon was safely down the hall.

"Why is it that that woman wears me out? With Melon, it's not a hunger for attention, it's an addiction."

Jane smiled over at Ann, who was waving her empty glass. "You want another?"

"Yep. It will either kill me or cure me."

Jane winced. "Cut that out, Annie. You're going to be fine."

"What's going on with you and Sam, anyway?" Ann asked, thereby changing the subject.

"I don't know for sure. He's an exciting guy after three years with good, old, reliable, married-man Paul." Jane handed Ann a fresh drink and settled back on the chaise.

"I hope you aren't forgetting that good, old, reliable, married-man Paul put you in the lobbying business. That's got to count for something."

"It does, of course. But I've paid him back all the money he loaned me. That was a business deal."

"He may not think so. How's he going to take to you seein' a snappy young fella from Noo Yawk City?" Ann drawled.

16

"I'll deal with that when the time comes. At the moment I've got to figure out how I can get next to a certain Senator from Maine. Know anyone I can call, Annie?"

"You 'consultants' are all business, aren't you?"

"You can call me a lobbyist. I don't mind."

Ann reached for her address book. "Ed Zemsky lobbies the Maine delegation on both sides of the House. Let me give him a call for you. Set up an introduction."

Jane waved her hand dismissingly. "Not now. You're tired. I'm tired. It can wait until the end of the week. I've got a hellish day tomorrow and the next. Meetings all morning tomorrow, then lunch with the new man in the press office at Interior. I've got a three o'clock conference call coming into the office that's going to run at least an hour."

"Maybe you could stop by for a drink when your ear's gone numb?"

"Fine. Shall I call first?"

"I'm not going anywhere." Ann studied her glass. "You know, that doctor of mine says something's wrong with my liver. Last night he stopped in and he joined me for a drink. Didn't say one word about me drinking with him. Does that seem odd to you?"

"Not necessarily. Maybe he thinks a couple of drinks are good for what ails you."

"Well, it's my liver that seems to be ailing. That's what all these tests show. You don't think he knows something about the state of my liver that I don't know, do you?"

"Hey, come on! Don't start sagging now. You've only had the Pulitzer under your belt for a month, and in a few weeks your face will be plastered all over the country—the world."

Ann watched her silent animated screens. "When I turned in my copy for that plane crash–kickback series, I was pretty certain I'd at least get a nomination. Seth is terrific about pushing on that sort of thing. *Time*, though, that wasn't part of the picture. Those people dearly love to dig around."

"So? Let them dig. This isn't a cover on Melon. It's on Ann Hawkins Adams. What have *you* got to hide?"

Almost inaudibly, Ann said, "You'd be surprised."

"Don't pull a mystery act on me, Annie. You're so clean, you make my life look like Tallulah Bankhead's. And if you are worried about them saying anything about Del, they'll simply say your

17

husband is seriously ill. You know how these things are handled. 'Del Porterfield, former Washington columnist for the Hartford chain is unable to share his wife's triumph.' Something like that. Don't sweat it."

"Jane, I'm sweating it." Ann stared at her friend, her eyes clouded with concern.

"Why, for heaven's sake? Ann, want to tell me something?"

"Remember when you came in, I was talking to Clyde Tolson?"

Jane nodded.

"What I didn't tell you was that someone is scratching around, looking into how I got onto the plane crash story that got me the damn prize. Not so much the plane crash, the rest of it."

"What's the difference? You got it."

"It would make a difference if it were someone else's story, first. Someone, like, say, Del Porterfield."

"But, Ann, Del was hospitalized more than two months before your plane crash series was published. I didn't think he even knew you were working on it. And he hasn't been . . . well, *aware* of much of anything since he was carried out of the Press Club."

Ann watched a middle-aged female quiz show contestant jump up and down and hug the master of ceremonies on one of her silent TV sets. "Well, I hope to hell they're *not* onto anything. For your sake, as well as mine."

"My sake, Ann? What do I have to do with your Pulitzer?"

"You're going to be in *Time* because I won the Pulitzer," Ann said factually, without ego.

"Sure. Without that there wouldn't have been a peg for the story."

"Well?"

"Well, what?" Jane scanned Ann's profile. "What are you getting at?"

"Suppose some *Time* researcher came upon, ah, say, something a little irregular about my series on the plane crash and the money and all those big names?"

"Irregular, how?"

"It wasn't exactly an original story."

"What do you mean? *You* broke the story."

"It wasn't my story."

"For God's sake, whose *was* it?"

18

"Del's."

"How could it be Del's? You covered the crash. Then you picked up the rest of the story later, did the legwork and wrote it. Didn't you?"

"That's not quite how it was. Except for the plane crash, the story was Del's."

"But *you wrote* the series!"

"No, I *rewrote* it from Del's notes. *After* he'd been carried out of the Press Club. He'd kept this one very close to the vest."

"Oh, shit, Annie." Jane leaned forward, frowning, searching what she could see of Ann's face for an explanation. "What have you *done?*"

"I've screwed myself, that's what I've done. And, what's paining me so right this minute is that you and Melon and Billie Claire and Allegra have been screwed in the process." Ann closed her eyes.

Jane straightened and briskly lit a cigarette. "Let me see if I have this straight. Before Del went on his final bender, he'd made the right connections between the money and the plane crash and the kickbacks and that poor greedy guy they killed."

"That is correct. That is why he went off the wagon. He was celebrating."

"Who else knows this?"

"If I thought anyone else knew about it, do you think I would have done what I did?"

"What about Seth?"

Ann groaned. "He guessed. But he went ahead with the series."

"So that's one. Seth. You both must have been certain Del hadn't told anyone else about what he was working on."

"We were. But when you came in tonight I was being told some *Time* people are digging in my file, or trying to. If they, or some other smart folks in town, ask the right questions of the right people . . ."

"The timing," Jane murmured.

"That is correct, my friend. The timing. Del began on a hunch. He was also afraid, so the people he interviewed didn't realize they were being interviewed. That was in his notes. When *I* covered the same ground, I had the whole story from the first, and asked questions I already knew the answers to."

19

Jane stubbed out her cigarette and immediately lit another. "A lot of men in this town remember Del Porterfield before he became a falling-down drunk. And I'm sure you're aware that some of them are quite comfortable laying the blame on you, Ann."

She gave a slow nod. "Oh, yes. Ann Adams's success is the cause of Del Porterfield's decline. Melon Bowersox is a good feature writer because men just naturally can't resist her nice blue eyes. Jane Connor had made it big here *only* because she's got connections. Billie Claire is covering the White House because she has big boobs and is friendly. Allegra Farr has hypnotized my otherwise rational publisher, and in the process managed to become the most celebrated hostess in town. Do you want me to expand on the list?"

"That isn't necessary. Do you want me to give you a list of men within ten miles of this hospital whose self-opinion would be greatly expanded if they could shoot you down? or me? or about ten other women I could instantly name?"

"You have the picture." Ann held out her glass. "I'm going to need another of these, plus whatever those nurses think puts me to sleep."

Jane refilled their glasses in the silence.

"I'm scared," she said when she handed Ann her drink.

"I've been scared for a year. After I found out about *Time,* I became terrified. Not so much for myself, not any longer for myself." She encompassed the hospital room with a broad, lazy sweep of her free hand. "I've put my *friends* in jeopardy, goddammit. I don't have all that many friends, but the ones I do mean more to me than six consecutive Pulitzers."

"We couldn't have survived very long here without each other. And we *know* it, old pal." Jane cleared her throat. "Okay, then. As far as you know, at this moment, there are three of us who know the truth—you and Seth and me. *Time* is just nosing around?"

"As far as I know. You have it figured out—if I'm exposed, all those sharks out there will go crazy from the smell of blood. They'll go after any of us so-called 'influential women' with so much as an itty-bitty hangnail."

"Most of us have a helluva lot more than a *hangnail!* I certainly do. God knows Melon does. Billie and Allegra . . . Oh, Christ . . ."

20

"Yes, ma'am, Miss Connor. We're the skeletons in our own closets and the doorknobs are rattling."

A nurse entered and took Ann's temperature and blood pressure. No one spoke. The nurse stared balefully at Ann's full ashtray and the drinks in the hands of both women.

After the door was closed Jane sighed. "I can't believe the irony of this! In sixty-three you had a Pulitzer in your pocket for your Martin Luther King piece. *No* one was betting against you."

"But then our President was murdered and *that* blotted out everything else. I did love that man."

Again, the silence rose like a wall of fog.

Finally, Jane said, "You have to tell the truth to your friends. It comes down to that."

"Yep. I've just now begun with you." She turned away. "I don't know whether I can do this three more times. Especially Billie Claire."

"She's a big girl. She is also in a very good position to pick up any chitchat about you that's going around. So are Melon and Allegra. Once they've been told the facts, they'll be in a position to try to counteract what will be only rumors to your male colleagues."

"I'd be grateful if you'll explain everything to them."

"Of course I will. We've all been in the soup together before, haven't we?"

"But this time it's not soup. It's molten lava. A whole volcano's worth."

One

Chapter One

Jane

At age four, Jane fully accepted the direct simplicity of magic. Her favorite story was the Shoemaker and the Elves. The helpful elves who made marvelous shoes while the shoemaker and his wife slept the deep sleep of good honest folk.

Jane's inflexible and humorless mother did not think the comfort her daughter derived from the words, "Once upon a time," was in any way beneficial. Survival, in Mrs. Connor's eyes, depended on complete objectivity. All forms of survival: physical, economic, intellectual and emotional.

At age seven Jane no longer believed in magic.

As the years passed, she sometimes remembered the feeling of her lost belief, much the way one remembers the aura of a pleasant dream without recalling a single detail or image.

By the time she was twenty-eight she had earned a degree in journalism from one of the most respected universities in the country (and performed a seemingly endless number of odd jobs to pay for much of the tuition and expenses), put in five years as a reporter for one of the nation's influential daily papers, left the paper to work in the presidential primary of one of the most powerful men in the U.S. Senate. She had also made a silly, stupid mistake when she was nineteen, and she was still paying for it.

The Senator for whom Jane worked eighteen hours a day at double her reporter's salary (plus expenses), a man for whom she felt little affection but great respect, was not, in the end, nominated for the Presidency by his party. He was selected, instead, to run as his party's vice presidential candidate.

At this point, having demonstrated her ability to function efficiently without losing her sense of humor after only four hours sleep, her capacity to maintain a good-natured composure in times of daily crisis, plus her constant objectivity, Jane was asked to continue as a member of the party's campaign press relations staff. After one of the closest elections in the history of the Republic, the Senator became Vice President of the United States and a handsome, younger Senator became the President.

The accounting of dues commenced.

Funny little trolls in torchlit caves did not dance about as they divided the piles of solid gold coins.

A small group of men with a Boston drag to their vowels poured over complex lists of names and sheets of organization charts.

And so it happened that on a sunny day in April, Jane Connor walked up to a uniformed and armed man standing guard before a small white cubicle beside an imposing iron gate.

"Visitors can't enter through this gate, ma'am," the man said brusquely.

"I'm not a visitor. I work here," Jane said, not quite believing her own words.

The guard caught her hesitancy. "Move along, miss." He wasn't kidding.

"This is my first day." She felt foolish saying the words.

"ID?"

"Oh, of course. Just a minute."

Jane began to fumble through her purse for that special little card she had been given containing her name, her thumbprint and a picture of the White House.

"I'm a bit late," she said as she pawed through cigarettes, make-up, loose bills and envelopes. "Why don't you phone in and verify me? I'm with Mr. Sorensen's office."

"I'll have to have some identification from you, ma'am." He didn't move.

A middle-aged man in a pin-striped suit flashed his open wallet at the guard as he strode through the gate.

"Good morning, sir."

Two sets of husband-and-wife tourists were firmly but politely turned away. Jane began to sweat. Dammit, this is ridiculous. Seven months ago I used the bathroom in Jack Kennedy's hotel suite, now I can't set foot on his front lawn.

Ah! She pulled the card from the envelope in which it had arrived at her apartment. A White House envelope.

"Here." She shoved her thumbprint under the guard's chin.

He drew back and studied it. Instantly his demeanor changed. "Oh, yes. Miss Connor. We were expecting you this morning. Sorry to have held you up. You didn't give me your name. Go right ahead." He came close to standing at attention. Just like that? Well, all right.

She started briskly up the crescent driveway, but as the immaculate white mansion loomed closer, she slowed.

There were no guards or fences between her and a door to the most powerful human being in the world. She knew that man only slightly. She knew his sisters and brothers and their wives and husbands only slightly. She knew some of his closest advisers better. The Irish Mafia. She had sat in bars with them during the final days of the campaign at 3:00 A.M.—men in rumpled shirts, half-smashed and exhausted, stubble on their chins, bloodshot eyes. Driving themselves to the next morning, the next airport. Dragging and being dragged by their candidate. Focused on the dream of winning the right to reside in the gleaming mansion and all the power such a residency possessed.

Halfway between the gate and the White House, Jane stopped and stood, staring at the sparkling windows like some housewife from Arizona about to receive a specially arranged tour. It always surprised her that she could see people walking around inside. First-floor windows. The Oval Office itself was on the first floor.

The "magic feeling" filled her as it hadn't in years. And this time she knew the source: a combination of two stimuli.

The Jack Kennedy who had thought, fought and bought his way to the Democratic nomination was now John F. Kennedy, President of the United States. He was the handsomest, most glamorous, dynamic politician Jane had ever encountered, an opinion shared by many jaded Washington observers three times Jane's age. The grandfather President had been replaced by the young prince, the magnetic and virile hero of ancient mythology.

The man in the Oval Office was Choate and Harvard. He was as at ease in top hat and tails at his Inauguration as he was in Bermudas on a sailboat off Hyannis Port. His wit was urbane and spontaneous. He had known the power of money and the verities of politics all his life. The fairy tale had become a reality.

There was definitely a quality of magic about the man. Whether positive or negative, it was impossible not to react to him.

Still standing alone, Jane savored the moment in her own life. Now she too possessed a degree of power. She could taste it on her tongue and feel it through the soles of her shoes. Jane Connor, Presidential Consultant.

She had taken pleasure from seeing her name on a column of news because that gave her satisfaction at being paid in both money and prestige for her work. But, as a young reporter, she had seen nothing intrinsically powerful about a by-line for a story in which, by adhering to the rules of journalism, she had written less than half the truth.

Since elementary school Jane had been keenly aware of the question, "What do you do?" Her mother, on the few occasions when she was asked, replied through clenched teeth, "I'm the wife of Professor Emett Connor. He is a historian." Or, "I am Mrs. Emett Connor of Chantry Farms."

The wife of, the mother of, the daughter of, the secretary of . . .

Jane had decided during her freshman year in college that she would never be defined by a man. Helped by a man, even used by a man. But never defined.

That was why she was drawn to jobs designated by a specific title.

Her first job description at the *Herald* had been Copygirl. Not the most prestigious label, but one she was certain would lead to that genderless classification, Reporter. Holders of working press passes weren't lined up and given a physical before being admitted.

Then she had been Jane Connor, Press Aide, Lyndon Baines Johnson for President Committee. Followed by Jane Connor,

Democratic National Committee Press Office. After that, Jane Connor, John F. Kennedy Inaugural Committee. All of which led to Jane Connor, Presidential Consultant.

She hadn't the remotest idea how she was to be consulted or if such consultation would provide someone with something that they could otherwise find for themselves. Possibly her job would have to do with the Kennedy women and the Johnson women.

Someone had needed to take care of that aspect of the candidates' images during the campaign. A campaign fraught with friction brought about by trying to mix Boston and Austin life-styles and backgrounds. She had put in her time trying to mollify and mediate the frequent mix-ups between the two groups. Always seeing that the presidential candidate's family received the most advantageous exposure while protecting the interests of her mentor, the man from Texas.

God knew Presidential wives were of increasing interest to the public. Before Jackie and Lady Bird appeared, there had been Mamie and her intriguing "rests" at Elizabeth Arden's farm, and Pat with her Republican cloth coat and her rigid, almost shell-shocked loyalty to the father of Tricia and Julie during various political traumas.

The Eisenhower-Nixon women, to say nothing of the men themselves, were pallid copy in comparison to the tribes from Massachusetts and Texas.

The Kennedy women, whether actual Kennedy family or old chums of Jackie's or wives of old school ties of Jack's were a handsome lot. Chic women who always wore the right clothes to the right event. They were polished, well-bred women who gave beautiful parties and stimulating little dinners in their homes, whether it was Georgetown, Manhattan or Cambridge. Most of them had spent their junior years at the Sorbonne or in Italy or London, had played hockey at Miss Porter's School and tennis at the Palm Beach Racquet Club.

The sun streaks in their thick, casually styled hair were legitimate, acquired while sailing, skiing or on a tennis court. Even at their worst, the Kennedy women possessed style.

At their best, the Texas women were "fashionable," but by far less demanding standards. The women attached to the men attached to the Vice President spoke with a nasal twang, wore beehive hairdos and pale pink or green polyester pants suits that were invariably too short or too tight or both. Those who hadn't been Homecoming Queen at the University of Texas had been, at least, members of a precision drill team. They were proud, rather sweet women who retained vestiges of Old South mannerisms that were still evident after four generations of hardscrabble frontier life. They were proud of their men; they had been raised to marry men of whom they could be proud.

During the campaign in 1960 Jane had been called in to soften disagreements between the women associated with the camps of two dynamic, imperious men. The press wanted a Kennedy or a Kennedy surrogate, rather than a lady with an LBJ brand. The Kennedys made better copy. A women's group in the Midwest (knowing they couldn't get Jackie because she had discreetly opted out of the campaign to be delicately pregnant) asked for Ethel or Eunice or Jean Kennedy Smith. It took a lot of talking on Jane's part to get the group to accept a teenaged Lynda Bird as a substitute. The women's editor of every publication from *Ladies' Home Journal* to the *Moosejaw Morning News* wanted to print a recipe for one of Jackie's delicate French sauces (they assumed she actually cooked). Often they had to settle for Lady Bird's pickled okra. Jane could recite it in her sleep and in four languages and was convinced that it must have been the nastiest dish ever served.

In her mid-twenties Jane had become a well-paid and effective member of the Democratic National Committee press staff because she was more than a single-minded reporter questing after Truth. Back in Austin, as well as on the Hill, the men behind the man were of the sort who didn't mind a woman moving around in a man's world, as long as she wasn't one of their own. They saw a political wife as a woman who stood mute and bright-eyed beside her husband, an asset in many other ways. But working was something someone else's wife did. As the campaign machinery cranked itself into high gear for the final run, they became aware that it simply wouldn't do to have a man dealing with the female press on the subject of their women, and Jane's newspaper experience and reputation for diplomacy filled their requirements. She knew almost everyone in the Washington press corps, men and women who not only covered for the local papers and television outlets, but also for every major daily paper and national magazine. They required careful handling and gentle manipulation. Someone was needed to bridge the gap between what was so, and what was written.

The Texas women trusted Jane because she had worked for their man in the primary, even though she had graduated from One of Those Eastern Schools. The Boston women were comfortable with her because she knew which fork to use and didn't speak with that hated Texas twang that they considered a dead giveaway to an unacceptable social class.

On the Inaugural Committee, Jane was careful to see that those in the press who had made it through the exhausting campaign without attacking the candidates, or consistently losing their luggage, were given special consideration: extra tickets, leftover Presidential Medallions, invitations to parties where they would find the most distinguished and newsworthy Important People. A great deal of John Kennedy's success with the press during the campaign had been the result of his clever use of social clout. If one behaved one was included. It was a tricky juggling act for Jane, among others, and it did not go unnoticed.

All of which had, after several months of transition, resulted in her presence on the White House lawn on an April morning.

She became aware that her kid gloves were becoming clammy with perspiration and that men striding along the drive were glancing at her over their shoulders.

She gave the vista what she hoped was a casual once-over and headed toward the West Wing.

Just inside the door a pleasant man in a conservative suit (whose very fingernails announced a Boston connection) smiled at her from behind the desk.

"Miss Connor?"

"Yes."

"Good morning. Pleasant day after that rain, isn't it?"

"Ah, yes." Miss Connor? She felt flattered. The guard must have phoned ahead.

"Mr. Sorensen's secretary asked me to direct you to your office in the Executive Office Building," he said, handing her a slip of paper on which he had written, Room 240/E.O.B. "It's just across the drive to your left as you . . ."

"Thank you, I know where it is."

The old War Department Building which now housed the overflow personnel connected with the operation of the White House stood immediately west of the mansion and was in stately architectural contrast to the surrounding buildings. Its turrets, balconies and high-peaked windows set it apart from the newer buildings along Pennsylvania Avenue.

She crossed the drive that separated the two buildings, passed another sentry who nodded, "Good morning, Miss Connor." Up the steps to face yet another uniformed guard who wished her good morning.

My God, this makes me feel good! She said, "Hello, I'm looking for Room two forty. Nice day, isn't it?"

"Yes, it is, Miss Connor. Just take the first elevator to the second floor."

Another guard was seated at a desk beside the elevator on the second floor. "Fourth door on your right, Miss Connor."

Suddenly Jane understood that certain lack of a sense of reality she had observed in White House personnel.

She opened the massive oak door decorated only by three gold numerals—240.

The huge, high-ceilinged room contained four imposing desks. One of the desks was bare. Behind each of the others a man was bent over stacks of papers. In a small alcove to her left sat a young woman who seemed to be the communal secretary. Each desk held a push-button phone, but no one was talking on a phone, none of the phones was ringing.

The room was silent.

As Jane entered, the three men looked up.

Each of the men was familiar. She couldn't recall their names but she instantly recognized the short, stocky man as a staffer from Senator Humphrey's office on the Hill. The tall, sandy-haired man had been a Stevenson staffer. She had dozed next to him on a campaign plane going to some forgotten place on some forgotten night. And the other man was a Smathers worker she remembered as one of the people around Bobby Baker's crowd.

"Welcome aboard," the Humphrey man said and waved her toward the gleaming empty desk.

Jane moved toward the desk, wondering if one had to work for a losing candidate to qualify for a desk in this room.

"The phone's connected to the White House switchboard, but if

32

you want to place a call on an outside line, just dial nine," the Smathers man said.

Jane sat down in the leather executive chair. "What number do you dial for information?"

The Humphrey man chuckled and bent over a thick report in a neutral beige binder.

"I suppose we're all here consulting together?"

"Mmm," the Smathers man said and returned to his papers.

The Stevenson man yawned, swiveled and after selecting a newspaper from the pile on his desk, fastidiously placed his well-shod feet on his blotter.

Jane was poking through her desk drawers when a woman walked through a door that had been well-concealed by the oak paneling.

"Miss Connor? Mr. Franklin will see you now."

"Franklin? Norman Franklin? I didn't know he was working over here."

"This way, please."

Jane followed the woman into a pleasant anteroom off the cavernous four-desk office. "I'm to be working for Norm Franklin? I thought I'd be under Ted Sorensen."

The woman smiled the universally cryptic Good Secretary's smile and ushered Jane into a large cluttered office filled with bookcases and file cabinets and piles of paperbound documents. A rumpled Norman Franklin was talking into his phone. "Yes, yes. I told you I'd have someone on it this week." He looked up. "She just walked in." He slammed the phone down. "Hi, Jane." He stood and extended his hand with genuine warmth.

"Hi, Norm." She perused the chaos. "What are you doing way over here? I didn't know you were in tight with the Jackie end of things."

"We don't have anything to do with the Jackie operation."

"Oh. I just assumed I'd be part of her press arrangements."

"No. Pam Turnure has that covered."

"Then what *will* I be doing?"

He studied her for a long moment. "Jane, this is an entirely different setup here. We have some special projects lined up for you. Something more suited to your talents."

"What sort of projects, Norm?"

"Well, as far as your friends in the *press* are concerned, we call what we do here 'research.'"

"Then I actually will be part of Sorensen's staff!" She lowered herself into the visitor's chair beside Norman's desk. "Is that what my roommates out there are doing? Research for Presidential speeches? Norm, sorting through statistics isn't exactly my strong suit."

"For the moment you needn't concern yourself with what those men are doing. You'll be reporting only to me."

"Reporting *what* only to you?"

For a few minutes Norm addressed himself to the lighting of his pipe. "As you know, right now we have a very high profile with the press. Lippmann might as well be our PR man; even old Henry Luce has been going easy."

"Yes?"

"We want to be certain it stays that way."

"Naturally. But isn't that somewhat beyond Presidential control?"

"Jane, I can see you have something to learn about the 'parameters of power,' as they say."

"In other words, you want the honeymoon to last."

"Exactly. No President has even gotten the kind of coverage Kennedy has. If Caroline sneezes it's front-page stuff. We want to, shall we say—sculpture the public's insatiable need to know."

"So how do I fit into that?"

"Jane, it would be extremely beneficial for us if we can receive early warnings when the natives become restless. We've had excellent reports on you. You know the press, they like and trust you. You can be very valuable to us. We'd like you to keep right on living the life you do now: seeing the same people, hitting the Press Club and the various watering holes, embassy parties, freeloads. Just keep you ears and eyes open. Chat up the columnists, the White House press corps, give us feedback about their thinking about matters of concern to us."

"You want me to spy," she said flatly.

"No. You won't be spying. You'll be doing objective reporting. To me."

"I don't see the difference, evidently." Jane lit her own cigarette. Norm may have been a man who spent five minutes seeing that his pipe drew properly, but it would never occur to him to lean over his desk with a lit match for a woman's cigarette. There were a lot of Norms in Washington, and they were often the most interesting men. Interesting in terms of their work, not socially. She had noticed more of them in the past few months than ever before. The Camelot Commandos seemed to be divided into two distinct types. There were the roiling Irishmen, witty, quick, great drinking companions. The other group was composed of men like Norm, men who had the educational edge, wore that grim facial expression that said someone somewhere was boring them. They could be unendurably arrogant. Washington was a place of long memories and long knives. Men like Norman Franklin would be neither forgotten nor forgiven. They would accomplish things in their political lives that would whirl back and one day catch them smack in the back of the head. Jane wondered, but only for a moment, if she would someday be caught herself, in another's boomerang.

"We think you see the difference, Jane, or, let me say, we think you can *find* a difference. You'll be on the payroll here. A White House staffer with all the proper credentials." He looked directly at her eyes; his own were expressionless. "We want to know what's on their minds . . . before it's printed. As often as we can."

She didn't look away. "I see. But I can't begin to cover everyone."

"We know that. There will be others. No reason for you to know who they are."

"Okay. I'll mingle. But what *am* I?"

"Just say you're working for Sorensen. That should handle any questions. You will also be expected to show up here, of course." He gestured toward the high-ceilinged room beyond his door. "I want you to keep track of what's being printed in selected dailies. We'll provide a list of which columnists you're to keep track of. The secretary out there will have the material on your desk every morning. Go over it and write a daily report on the entries on your list. Let me know how what's being written compares with what you know personally, and also if you find a trend beginning with specific columnists or with editorial policy on a particular paper."

"That's it?"

"Right." Norm stood. "There's nothing sinister in our small operation here."

35

"I didn't say there was."

"But you do understand this is to be confidential. Totally."

"Of course, Norm."

When she returned to her desk she found a folder containing lists of key reporters and columnists. Attached to the list of selected newspapers was a note: Read the unsigned editorials carefully.

The Stevenson and Humphrey men were both busy at typewriters now. The Smathers man grinned at her when she turned to see what he was doing. Jane grinned back and then began to read the editorials from that day's *Boston Globe*.

She held mixed feelings about her job. On the one hand the operation seemed like overkill. The President was an idol of heroic proportions. For the moment many people who had voted against him were prepared to forgive him his father, his religion, his youth and his liberal positions. Then again, there were areas in politics that she knew she had not yet discovered, and even though she now found herself neatly stuffed into one of them, she realized that she was, perhaps, just another victim of the media hype that surrounded the President. Everyone in Washington was saturated with it, and the stories filed by the press went far beyond the Potomac. Norm Franklin's operation seemed a bit paranoid, but she was able to rationalize it. Kennedy's positions on civil rights and Communism faced rough going, and evidently the Presidential advisers wanted to have whatever advance knowledge they could get in order to deflect attacks that were certain to come. Even a few hours' warning would permit preparation of a public defense. Still, Jane decided, it would be exciting to be part of the Room 240 operation.

During the remainder of the day Jane learned that Carl, the Stevenson man, was monitoring radio and televison news scripts. Leonard, the Humphrey man, was keeping track of the periodicals. And Ben, the Smathers man, was in charge of the Southern media. Evidently none of them mingled. Jane wondered who else was out there mingling.

At five thirty Norm's secretary collected the sheaves of reports stacked on the four desks.

Jane took a liesurely stroll past Treasury and down F Street to the Press Club.

Since it was now after six, she headed for the Main Lounge. She would probably have gone there after work whether she was being paid to or not. She was accepted there, not only because she was an attractive young woman—Washington was bulging with attractive young women. Rather, Jane knew the rules of the game and played it very well. She was an expert at suffering bores amiably. And two out of three men in the club were full-time bores.

She never paid for a drink in the Main Lounge. Sometimes she groaned to herself when she thought of the cumulative hours she had spent listening to dull men who bought her bourbon.

A woman was tolerated in the solidly male atmosphere of the Press Club if she didn't talk too much. When she did say something, she was expected to contribute her share of gossip and amusing anecdotes or wisecracks, but never at a man's expense. Now, though, her job would make access to inside material difficult. Until she worked out a system, her role would have to be that of thoughtful and interested listener. She could manage that.

"Hey, Janey," Jack Warren, the AP man who covered the House, moved crablike up the bar, the color of his eyes and nose indicating his presence at the club since lunch. "What are you drinking?"

Jane turned to face him, leaning to take the weight off her three-inch heels. She was, as usual, unaware that in doing so, in moving as she had thousands of times before at bars, her left upper arm pressed her breast upward, creating a visible cleavage under her silk shirtwaist.

She smiled. "Hello, Jack. Bourbon, thanks." She said it loud enough for Harry, the bartender and social critic, to hear. "What's new?"

"Ahh. Filed four takes on the Cuba stuff before lunch and that's about it. You're the one with something new. What the hell are you doing over at the White House? I thought you were a cowboy loyalist."

"Well, I guess they thought they'd spread some of it around." She eyed her thanks to Harry for the drink he slid in front of her with a wink.

"Whose office are you with?" he asked, not uninterested.

"Ted Sorensen's," she said, wondering what Ted Sorensen would say if the AP man ever inquired about her at some party. Not to mention whether Sorensen even knew of the existence of Room 240.

"Sorensen? You mean speech stuff? Are you writing?"

"Not really. Memos, mostly. Research. Pretty dull."

Anyone on the White House staff was a potential news source for a reporter and they were therefore treated with deference. Celebrated staffers were fawned over. Not only could such a person provide a juicy tidbit from which to swing an entire story, but they were expense account gold back at the home office. One White House staffer was good for at least two phantom lunches a week and one night on the town. She knew her name would appear prominently in Jack's expense account by Friday at the latest.

"No kidding," Jack said with false enthusiasm. "We should have lunch soon."

"Sure." Jane knew that lunch would never be eaten—by her, at any rate.

By the time she had reached the ice cubes in her first drink, a small but growing band had gathered around her end of the bar. She accepted congratulations and tried hard to ask questions that would start each of the men talking before he could ask her anything penetrating about her job.

By eight thirty the group with whom Jane was drinking had collected a lobbyist with an open-ended expense account and was heading toward Georgetown and the Carriage House for dinner.

Four or five nights a week, as had been her custom, Jane drank at the Press Club, and later ate dinner with the reporters, lobbyists and correspondents she found herself with when someone finally suggested food. Other times she left the Executive Office Building to spend an entire evening with one man.

Her first affair had resulted in tragedy.

Jane had finished her first year as a full-time student at George Washington University, and holder of three part-time jobs, one with the *Washington Herald*.

She fell in love with Sean O'Melveny, a handsome, happy-go-lucky graduate student at Georgetown University. Jane and Sean thought they were Zelda and Scott Fitzgerald. He was rebelling against his strict Catholic upbringing and she was rebelling against the world. A week after they met, Sean told Jane he needed to put in six months in the service in Texas.

Off they went to Texas in his convertible. Speeding and half drunk down in Bayou country, Sean smashed the car into a weeping willow. Three days later they made it into San Antonio. Jane's nose was broken, Sean had put his lower teeth through his lip. They and the car were a mess.

Sean parked Jane in a rooming house and went off to Lackland Air Force Base for his flight training. He phoned every evening long distance to proclaim his undying love. Every weekend he came into town and they spent two days drinking Carta Blanca in Mexican bars and making love in the big old brass bed in the rooming house.

Jane wangled a job as a copygirl on the *San Antonio Light*, a newspaper published, she was shortly convinced, for the sole purpose of wrapping tacos. She even suspected that some Mexicans smoked it.

When she missed her first period, she was too preoccupied with being in love for the first time to notice. She missed a second and became alarmed. By the time she missed the third and couldn't close her waistband, she panicked and told her carefree lieutenant. He suddenly became white-faced and serious. He was truly sorry as hell, but there wasn't anything he could do. Sean had somehow forgotten to tell Jane that there was *another* Zelda back in Washington to whom he was not only married, but with whom he shared a year-old daughter.

While the two of them were trying to figure out what to do, Sean's commanding officer, also a Catholic, informed the lieutenant he was being thrown out of the Air Force on a vague morals charge. Sean's records indicated he was married, and not to the blonde he was cavorting about San Antonio with.

She felt she had no choice but to return to Chantry Farms, Leesburg, Virginia, and face her mother's triumphant, "This was to have been expected, of course."

Mrs. Connor made all of the arrangements through her church. When the time came, a "nice Christian couple" was to come to the Leesburg hospital, where Jane would be registered under a false name, and pick up their lovely new baby.

Jane's baby, however, was a most imperfect baby boy. None of the nice Christian couples within miles of Leesburg were interested in adopting a seriously retarded infant. There were no couples of *any* denomination willing to adopt Nathaniel.

After Mrs. Connor saw Nathaniel for the first time, she marched into Jane's hospital room and announced, "*That* was also to be expected, of course."

Mrs. Connor gave Jane a few thousand dollars from her grandmother's trust. Jane used the money to pay for a foster home for her son and went back to her old job at the *Herald* and her classes at George Washington University. When Nat was three, she could no longer find foster parents who were willing to take him on. She was, though, able to place him in the excellent Adela Whelan Home for Children in Baltimore. Their fees were considerably higher than those of a good foster home, but Jane felt she had no other choice.

Now Nat was eight years old, and although she visited him at least twice a month, he did not know she was his mother. He did not know who anyone was. His mental age was less than that of a child of three.

No one in Washington knew of Nat's existence—not even Sean knew he had sired a child. What would have been gained by telling him? What would be gained by telling anyone? Pity? Sympathy? Jane wanted neither, under any circumstances.

There had been other men in her life after Sean. She always needed to feel that she and a man she slept with were deeply involved emotionally as well as physically. It didn't matter if the man was single or married. Jane guarded and valued her independence, even when she was in love, and she assumed her current man did also.

After Sean, for the most part she had been fortunate in her affairs. Only once had she been the recipient of an apologetic phone call. For her part, she rapidly learned that a man must be let down gently enough so that he could salvage his pride; men could be bitchier than women when hurt. Then, too, the fewer enemies a woman had in Washington, the better.

For three and a half months Jane read columns, unattributed editorials and news at her desk in the E.O.B., Room 240. She had lunch with as many members of the press as she could arrange. She typed her reports and the reports were carried through the door leading to Norman Franklin's office. She did not know what was done with them. She could discern no direct effect from her efforts. Not even an indirect effect. She felt she was working in a vacuum. All Norm said was, "Good work. Keep it coming." He never mentioned an issue, a personality, nothing at all of substance.

Yet, the papers were filled with the Bay of Pigs disaster, the embarrassments of Paris and Vienna. A great deal was written that was extremely negative, and many columnists pointed the blame at Bobby Kennedy's influence on his brother, because some found him easy to hate. Jackie's popularity during the European trip helped deflect some of the serious and thoughtful press reports.

Jane had picked up the information that the press knew that Dr. Max Jacobson, a New York physician who specialized in amphetamine injections for "beautiful people," was somehow involved in these diplomatic fiascos, and also about the President's inability to handle crusty old DeGaulle and Khrushchev, himself. She had learned this during a long lunch with a female *New York Times* reporter who had visited Jacobson the fall before, and who had dropped twenty pounds, seemingly overnight. Jane had included the information under the heading: General.

During the second week of July, at three thirty in the afternoon, Jane was seated at her desk reading an editorial in the *Atlanta Constitution* when the hall door was flung open and in walked Mary Ellen Bowersox of the *Washington Herald*.

Jane's heart dropped into her stomach.

"So *here* you are," Melon called and ambled toward Jane, smiling at Leonard, Carl and Ben. Quite clearly, Melon enjoyed the four dropped jaws. "Janey, love, just you and three men in here without a chaperone?" She scrutinized Carl. "I know you," she said, pressing a long red nail to her lips. "Weren't you gladly for Adlai somewhere back in fifty-six?" She passed over Leonard and studied Ben. All she said was, "Hmm."

"Why, Melon . . ." Jane rose, clearing her throat and trying to keep her voice even. "What are you doing over in the E.O.B.?"

Melon sat on the corner of Jane's cluttered desk. "Oh, I had to interview the new Physical Fitness Committee chairman down the hall and, well . . . I just asked around. A receptionist down there said she knew everyone on the hall except the people in Room two forty, and she hadn't heard of any Jane Connor. And . . . you know how unmarked doors intrigue me."

Jane lit a cigarette as calmly as she could. "This is only a temporary office, Melon. They just stuck us in here until Sorensen's given more space."

"Haven't you been here since April?" Melon said as she picked

41

up a typewritten report on a column by James Reston. "I didn't know the President used *his* ideas in his speeches."

"Ted likes to know what everyone's thinking." Jane carefully lifted the report from Melon's fingers and turned it facedown on the desk.

"Jane," Melon leaned toward her, whispering, "I knew Ben Alexander from a Sunday piece I did on Rosemary Smathers. What's he doing here? What kind of operation is this, really?"

"Jane!" Norman Franklin was standing in the door to his office. "Will you step into my office for a moment?" His face was maroon.

"Ben," Jane said, "Melon here says she's an old friend of yours. Says she met you with the Senator. Say hello. Excuse me, Melon."

Melon had begun to riffle through the newsprint and typed copy on Jane's desk. Suavely, Ben walked over and extended his hand to Melon, leading her to an adjoining chair. With Southern courtliness he maneuvered her so that she was sitting with her back to his desk.

The moment Norm Franklin's door was closed, he turned to Jane. His cheeks were mottled-purple and a vein was visibly pulsing in the side of his neck.

"What the hell is Melon Bowersox doing in this office?"

"Norm, she just burst in here out of nowhere. She's doing an interview down the hall and the receptionist told her she didn't know who was in this room. Melon put two and two together. I'm sorry as hell, but you know Melon. She's been pestering me for weeks to find out what I'm doing over here." Jane sagged onto Norm's sofa, pushing aside half a dozen file folders. "Christ!"

"You're damn right I know Melon Bowersox. I don't want her anywhere near this place. What have you told her about your job here?"

"Virtually nothing. Nothing she could run with, anyway. But she knows my background. She knows I wouldn't settle for some dusty research job with no visibility. That's why she's such a damn good reporter—her bitchy nosiness and intuition."

"Damn it all! Well, I guess it was inevitable." His face had become pale, but the vein in his neck was still pulsing. "Okay, get her the hell out of here. Say you've finished for the day. What's she doing out there now?"

"It's okay. Ben is oozing Southern all over her."

"Then take her to Duke's and get her sloshed while you go over

42

your cover with her until she gets it straight or becomes so confused she won't dare write a word about you. And, Jane, don't come back here in the morning."

"Just a damn minute. I didn't invite her into that room."

"She is your friend, isn't she?"

"Yes, she's my friend. But, Norm, this is my *job*." She tried to keep her voice down.

"Melon Bowersox is the *Herald*'s resident big mouth. You know that and you should have been more careful."

"*More* careful! I'd have had to stop breathing! Now, if I don't come back here in the morning, she'll really become suspicious. And also more fatheaded. Look what Melon brought about!"

"Don't worry, we'll find new space for you. I'll have Francie see what she can come up with down at Commerce. Even if I wanted to I couldn't fire you at your level. Well," he began gouging the bowl of his pipe with what looked like a surgical instrument, "there will be other assignments for you after Bowersox has forgotten about Room two forty. For the moment, get that woman out of here, fast!"

Jane did her best to close the door quietly. She walked to her desk and stacked all the papers in one pile. Melon was laughing at one of Ben's down-home stories, her hand lightly brushing his knee. Jane knew she was watching her at the same time. As Melon excused herself to Ben she whispered something that sounded like, "Eight o'clock, then," and moved toward Jane.

"Long day," Jane said. "I'm pooped. Let's go find a drink."

As they were walking down the hall to the elevator, Melon said, "Just what in hell is going on in that room, Jane?"

"Just what I've told you. Research for Sorensen."

"Come off it, Jane. Ben Alexander was one of the hotshot strategists for Smathers. You were one of the LBJ interpreters." She lifted her eyebrow toward the room they had just left. "None of that figures. A bunch of Georgetown grad students would do what you call research for free. What you've been telling everyone is research, that is."

Jane tried a subject Melon invariably found interesting, her effect on men. "I think ol' Ben has a thing for you. Why don't you follow it up?"

"It will be followed up. My number's now in his little alligator book."

43

"Shall we hit Duke's? See who's there?"

The late afternoon crowd was already assembled when they pushed their way to the long, dark bar at Duke Ziebert's. Melon was the resident star, and five minutes after her arrival had accumulated a satisfying audience. She was always good for a string of true, but unprintable, tales that would require five drinks in the telling.

Jane slipped away to use the phone.

The switchboard operator in her building rattled off several messages. Miss Connor was told that her dry cleaning was ready to be picked up. And Jerry Kelley had called three times. The last time to say he would be waiting for her at Alfredo's at six thirty.

Jane sagged against the wall. A combination of fatigue and anger sent tiny jabs of pain through her forehead.

Goddamn Melon.

Goddamn Norm Franklin.

Goddamn herself.

She thanked the operator and hung up.

That job was a matter of pride, and Norm knew it. She had managed herself as tightly as she could. A person like Melon was always a threat, friend or not. Norm had been expecting her to do the impossible. The town was too small, the people in it were too tuned into what everyone else was doing, to keep Norm's foursome invisible long.

She had been the one listening intently to some pompous wordsmith over a lousy lunch. *She* had been the one getting a bad liver and a worse complexion from night after night of rich food and bourbon, to say nothing of the tiresome company. Not the men in Room 240. They went home to Bethesda or Alexandria and fell into their beds by 11:00 P.M.—while she was on her second after-dinner stinger, dodging clammy paws under the table.

Her hand was still on the reservations phone Duke usually let her use, when it rang. She jumped and moved away from it. Now she had a view of Melon at the bar. She had launched into something Pierre Salinger might or might not have told her. "He said he'd kill me if I used it, but . . ."

God, where did the woman find the energy?

Jane thought about Jerry Kelley. He'd been taking her out to dinner for weeks. A six-foot-two, black Irish lawyer for the Justice Department. A friend of a friend of a Kennedy cousin. Thirty-

44

four, married, with two kids back in Brookline. A very nice, very funny man who didn't drink himself into a stupor.

She walked to the ladies' room in the back of the restaurant to repair her hair and makeup. She didn't really have much to do: the Washington singles life required that she dress for an eighteen-hour day. One was seldom slowed down by having to "dress for dinner"—unless it was a black-tie affair. But then, it was the wives who went to the black-tie affairs.

Yes. Jerry might be just what she needed at this moment. He was the only man she had been seeing regularly. But not as regularly as he would have liked.

He was waiting at a side table as usual. Broad shoulders, thick but tamed black hair, a deep and gently controlled lawyer's voice, large and surprisingly agile and graceful hands. An extremely calm and reassuring man.

After the second drink, while he was telling her about some antitrust case that she only vaguely understood, Jane decided to heed her body's several signals. She would invite him up to her apartment for a "nightcap": their code word after their third date. Jerry never pushed, but he never declined, either.

Jane never went to a man's apartment—let *him* go out with a wilted shirt the next morning; she would never wear the same outfit two mornings in a row.

Jane needed to control as many aspects of her life as possible. And that included a sex life on her own grounds—exclusively.

And so now here was Jerry. Jane liked his responses to her. He enjoyed her, her conversation, her mundane problems, her ideas. And he never pressed for the details of her job.

Yes. This nice, slightly naive and appreciative married man across from her could take care of matters in a lovely and uncomplicated way.

She'd phone Norm around ten to see if he'd found her a temporary hideout.

She did not want to go to sleep alone. She wanted to wake up beside a warm, relaxed body. Bacon and eggs and orange juice were in the refrigerator. Breakfast with Jerry would be comfortable and pleasant.

A married man was always so utterly and genuinely grateful the next morning.

45

Jerry accepted the offer of a nightcap.

When Jane phoned Norm at ten thirty in the morning, he told her he had found an office for her at the Weather Bureau on M Street.

She smashed out her cigarette and said, "Swell!"

He said, "That's the best we could come up with."

"Am I supposed to be doing anything there, Norm? Or should I bring along my needlepoint?"

"They need a brochure done for the press office."

"Norm, if Melon was wondering what I was doing in Room two forty, she'll really have fun with the Weather Bureau."

"That's why you're writing a brochure. That won't be for long. Then, as I understand, you'll be assigned elsewhere. With an agency the President is setting up."

"Perhaps the Small Business Administration regional office in Nome, Alaska? Jesus, Norm, I'm taking heat I don't deserve."

"Look, Jane. Your credibility has to be reestablished. You're sorry, I'm sorry, we're *all* sorry about Melon. Your next assignment, after the Weather Bureau, will be a good one, one you can handle. The people I spoke with this morning said you'd be perfect for this other job."

Jane slammed down the receiver before she said, "I think I've heard that one before."

Jerry had left his PT-109 tie clasp on the night table, a personal gift from JFK during the campaign.

She knew he would be leaving it there again during the next months.

At least there was *that* to look forward to.

Chapter Two

Ann

Ann Adams's green metal desk was the tidiest green metal desk in the *Washington Herald's* city room. Her desk, with all the others, held a typewriter, a telephone, a stock of copy paper and heavy black carbon paper piled neatly next to it and an ashtray. That was it. No drooling bottles of rubber cement, no stacks of last week's issues, no overflowing out-box. Nothing else.

When she was seated at her desk only a stenographer's notebook lay open beside the typewriter. Even the notebook's contents were spare and neat. It contained dates, names and short cryptic phrases that only she could decipher. The rest was in her head.

Anyone standing at the door to the city room noticed Ann immediately. The long rows of gray-green desks occupied by shirt-sleeved reporters and copy readers was abruptly punctuated by the presence of Ann Hawkins Adams. Her ramrod posture as she hammered away at an old Remington noiseless, her enormous and vividly colored hats and matching shifts, always seemed out of place amidst the colorless chaos. She interrupted her typing only to turn a page in the notebook or flick ashes, when she remembered, from the cigarette that dangled from her mouth. The city room was filled with the sound of wire machines, typewriters and agitated voices. A "civilian" usually wondered how anyone could

47

survive under such circumstances, let alone work with the cool detachment of Ann Adams, star reporter and, grudgingly, one of the boys. But she was more than one of the boys, she was better than any of them. They knew it and so did she.

On a muggy day in July, Ann arrived in the block-long city room on the dot of 10:00 A.M. Her passage from the elevator to her desk required fifteen minutes. She stopped or was stopped at every desk en route. Greetings, jokes, questions asked and answered. Ann was popular with everyone.

As she seated herself a copyboy materialized at her side.

"Some coffee, Miss Adams?"

"God, yes, Tom," she said, securing the mustard-colored cartwheel atop her flame-red hair. "I've got a hangover you could drive a truck through, honey. Make it hot, black and fast."

"Yes, ma'am!" He sprinted for the coffee machine in the outer hall.

She settled in her chair, laid out her cigarettes and matches, opened her notebook and rolled copy paper and carbon into her machine. She sat staring at the blank sheet in the machine for ninety seconds, and then, with a pounce, attacked the keys.

She didn't look up when Tom set a container of hot black coffee beside her phone.

The day before she had interviewed Attorney General Robert F. Kennedy for two hours. She had then interviewed five of his top lieutenants. Returning to the city room after dark she telephoned over a dozen political figures known to harbor some disaffection for the young brother of the President. From dates, names, events and comments, she compiled an in-depth picture of the Attorney General and his impact on the new Administration. Her writing was crisp, straightforward and well-balanced. The article was complete in a little over two hours. During that time she never looked up, spoke to no one, nor did anyone dare speak to her. Her working habits were a legend and only the greenest copy kid would dare to put a call through to her while she was typing. An editor never called Ann back to ask her to explain her copy, nor did he change a word. Occasionally a semicolon was replaced by a comma, or vice versa.

Ann had been collecting a *Herald* paycheck for eighteen of her thirty-eight years. She had been tough, tireless and thoroughly professional when she was hired, and she had become more polished with time. Few knew anything about Ann's past, and among those who speculated on her future, the question was—which would Ann get first, cirrhosis of the liver or the Pulitzer Prize.

Ann didn't talk about her pre-Washington years, not because she was ashamed of them, but because they were in the past and the past was painful. It was as though she believed sheer physical and mental assertion would burn away the years before she walked into the *Herald* and talked her way into a job.

Bristol, Tennessee, straddles the Tennessee-Virginia border. In the Depression its best-known contribution to the arts was a postcard sold to strayed tourists. It depicted a hillbilly on a donkey straddling the state line with the caption reading: Farmer in Tennessee with His Ass in Virginia. The postcard sold on the Virginia side reversed both the donkey and the caption. The postcard and Ann Hawkins Adams were both born in Bristol.

In the Adams clapboard house beside the Southern Pacific tracks, no one actually had his or her own bed. There were several beds, but they never seemed to belong to anyone in particular. If no one was sleeping in a bed, it was yours for the night. Meals were provided in much the same way, and were usually consumed standing in front of the old gas refrigerator or over the sink. Catch-as-catch-can.

"It isn't as though he's no-'count," Lally Adams told her older daughter when Ann began to notice that her father was seldom home, and was usually drunk when he was. "He just has to wander. A railroad man's a wanderin' man, Annie. Don't marry up with one 'less you need him only sometimes."

Lally Adams was rawboned and red-haired. She was a shy, quiet woman who seemed to exist in a slightly withdrawn, once-removed state when her husband was away. It was as if some vital part of her psyche was activated only by his physical presence. Her pleasure and escape were Coca-Cola, Lucky Strikes and *True Romance* magazine. The skinny, redheaded Adams girls, Ann and Hester, learned early to move silently through the house when Lally was in her chair, smoking, sipping Coke and reading her magazines. If they interrupted to ask a question or converse, she laid down her *True Romance* and gazed at them as if she weren't clear about just who they were.

49

However, when Matt Adams appeared, the little four-room house sprang to life. He always arrived exuberantly drunk. A special meal was prepared, the oilcloth on the kitchen table was scrubbed and the cats were shooed out into the yard. By midnight Matt reached the bottom of the Southern Comfort bottle and lay snorting and snoring on the rump-sprung couch on the porch. Lally sat beside her husband in the porch rocker and told him about her thoughts and the plots of the love stories she had read. She knew he didn't hear her, but it didn't seem to matter.

There was always a fight, though, the next morning, and one of the most frequent subjects was Ann. On one eventful morning, from where she sat reading on the kitchen stoop, Ann could clearly hear the voices.

"Girl's always got her nose in some book, Lally."

"That's not so bad, is it? She's a smart one. Too skinny, but she's real smart."

"She's gettin' fancy ideas, Lally. This town's got no room for fancy ideas. Comin' from a girl, especially. Whenever I'm here she's always reading or writing down things in her notebooks. What's she expect to do with all that reading and those notebooks in this hillbilly town?"

"Then can't we move on, Matt? This ain't no place to be raising girls. Can't we move someplace bigger? Richmond, maybe?"

"Goddammit, woman, be patient. Don't *push* me!" He shoved his chair away from the table and belched.

By nine that evening he was gone, and Lally was in her overstuffed chair in the front room with the half-full smoking stand beside her and a glass of Coke in her hand.

"Annie," her mother said, "I'm to be patient. I can't think of another way to be, excepting patient. That don't mean *you* need to wait around. Your daddy don't like the idea of you reading them books you do. Honey, you keep right on. You're going to read and write yourself to someplace other than Bristol. You hear?"

Ann nodded. Never before had she heard her mother talk that way. Lally even stared right into her eyes as she spoke. After she'd finished speaking, Lally continued to peer intently at Ann. She's trying to tell me something with her eyes, because she doesn't have the proper words, Ann knew it. Lally was frowning, giving her head an occasional tiny shake, never taking her eyes from Ann's.

50

"Annie, you figure out how to get it right. You hear? You do that and you'll have a life of your own."

"Yes, Momma. I'll try."

Ann remembered that day and both her parents' words. Her father's words were the last she ever heard him speak. Matt Adams took his lunch pail and his small suitcase and left to catch the nine twenty-eight from Lynchburg. He never came back.

Lally found a part-time job at the People's Drug Store soda counter. Her earnings, plus an occasional money order from Matt, helped them get by. She began to lace her Cokes with sour mash "because of the coughing," she said. By the summer Ann was fifteen, the coughing was bad enough to send Lally to the county hospital. When Ann and Hester visited her, she lay pale and hollow-eyed and silent, but for wracking coughs.

One afternoon Ann visited her alone. She sat beside her mother's white-painted iron bed and held her cold, limp hand.

"Momma, don't go away."

Lally Adams opened her eyes and stared straight up at the ceiling. "You get it right, now. You hear?"

"Yes, Momma."

Lally closed her eyes.

Later that afternoon, old Dr. Wilkins came to get Ann at the Bristol Public Library. He told her her mother had passed away in her sleep.

Things did not change much.

Ann had already assumed most of the household chores years before, and Hester wasn't much of a problem to anyone. After a halfhearted fuss by the local child welfare authorities, it was decided it would be safe for the girls to stay alone in the clapboard house. Ann was tall for her age and people had stopped thinking of her as a child long ago. Lally's sister, Aunt Hallie Hawkins, was up the road and could look in on them, although Ann knew she never would. Aunt Hallie's husband was also a railroad man. While Uncle William was away, Aunt Hallie spent her time scrubbing, scouring and polishing her small house, tending her renowned kitchen garden and sleeping with a parade of men who delivered everything from eggs to coal. Aunt Hallie washed her bed sheets every day, rain or shine. A childless woman, she had never had any interest in Lally's daughters. There was no reason to think she would begin to be interested with Lally dead. The ar-

51

rangement suited Ann. There was a small check every month from the county which she augmented with a part-time job at King's Department Store.

By the summer her mother died, Ann had read her way through five of the twelve shelves in the Bristol Public Library. A floor manager at King's had a sister who was a librarian up at Sullins College on the hill that overlooked the smoky town. Miss Poster let Ann use the library on Sunday afternoons when she was unlikely to be noticed. There she spent the hours with her closest friends: the sisters Brontë, the Brothers Karamazov and F. Scott Fitzgerald.

She had read the Bible, both Old and New Testaments, before she was ten, and an entire set of *World Book Encyclopedia* before she was eleven. She was fascinated by history and biographies and autobiographies. At night, after she had cleaned up the few dishes and gotten Hester to bed, she would sit on the porch with her journals (which were stacked by dates and subject matter beside the old Motorola in the sitting room). The entries were written in a tight small hand in ink. Nothing was ever crossed out on the neat pages.

In the months before Ann wore out the local public library, she had to spend her time reading at one of the two scratched oak tables in the single room. A new lending policy had been instituted: no one could check out more than three books at a time. Ann herself had brought about the rule change by staggering away from the aging brick building once a week with as many as fifteen thick tomes in her spindly arms.

Mr. Horace Fuller did not institute the new policy because Ann damaged his books or returned them late or even because she didn't read every book she carried home. He announced the limitation because, "The city of Bristol is blessed with so many enthusiastic readers that this is the only fair way to make certain none of our readers is ever deprived."

The real reason for the rule was that Mr. Fuller didn't much care for that tall, red-haired and strangely attractive Ann Adams who lived alone with her sister in a virtual hovel beside the tracks. She didn't fit in with his idea of the order of things.

Another of Mr. Fuller's policies was that "certain material" could not be checked out by anyone under eighteen unless the person bore a note from one of his parents. Ann won in a confrontation over whether she could or could not take home Mr. Fuller's copy of *Madame Bovary*. Mr. Fuller did not take the defeat lightly.

Miss Poster up at Sullins was more open-minded and also fascinated by Ann's insatiable appetite for books. She even managed to locate a copy of Joyce's *Ulysses*, which she wrapped in a manila envelope, telling Ann (for both their sakes) not to open until she got it home.

Ann treasured her long Sunday afternoons in the high, paneled Sullins library. She hated to leave when darkness began to settle. On her way home she passed young couples strolling along the tree-shaded campus walkways. The tea dances at Sullins finished at five, then the girls would stroll arm in arm with their handsome young men, the boys dashing in their white linen trousers and white shoes and bowlers, and the girls giggling and covering their mouths in the way proper Southern young ladies were taught to do at proper Southern finishing schools. Ann scurried past them, her worn gabardine coat pulled around her bony frame. She couldn't imagine what it would be like to talk to one of those golden young men with names like Wentworth and Chapin. Occasionally a Virginia Polytechnic Institute cadet would pass, walking briskly in his high-necked and skintight uniform, his officer's cap pulled down to the bridge of his nose. In addition to the friends and lovers who rose up from the pages of books, there were real boys in Ann's life. There was Bobby John with the adenoids from the stockroom at King's. He took her for a drive in his father's pickup truck out to the lake and tried to put his tongue in her mouth. And there was Eddy from Birdie's Lunchette who told her ways she could get him to give her free lunches. She could handle them. She simply quoted Elizabeth Barrett Browning at them and they backed off as if she were a Martian.

It was Horace Fuller at the library who was the first man to touch her body. It happened several months after the *Madam Bovary* incident. Horace Fuller had had two years at East Tennesse State University and he couldn't understand, let alone, enjoy the books this orphaned daughter of a railroad brakeman was pouring over.

He would watch her from a high stool in back of the reference stack as she bashed through the swinging gates into the reading room, rusty-colored curls clinging to her forehead, arms full of books to return. He would peek between the volumes and watch as she sat at a table and read. Here he was, thirty-six, stuck in this awful gritty town with a wife and three children and a night job at the canning plant. And there she was, a gawky and unfinished girl, telling him, as he stamped expiration dates into her three books, that she read all those books "because something's out there, Mr. Fuller. And I figure all these words will help me find out what it is and how to get it."

He envied her. He hated her. And he desired her in silent, confused torment until he could stand it no longer and waited until closing time one winter night. As Ann pushed through the swinging gate, he moved up behind her and reached up under her sweater, his hands wild and trembling. Ann whirled on him with one strong, swift motion. Her eyes were angry slits. She stood two inches taller than his five foot six. He lowered his hand and stood frozen.

"Mr. Fuller," she said evenly, "I don't have a daddy who can whup you and I don't have a mama who can go to the police. But you touch me again and I'll kick your skinny tail to Kingston." She hefted her books and marched down the steps.

Flushed and muttering, Horace Fuller watched her go.

The following year Ann finished high school. She had skipped two grades. Hester turned sixteen and overnight became pretty in that short-term way of certain hill women. By twenty-five, no matter how she cared for herself, her skin would be taut, the deep lines around her mouth and eyes would be distinct and her hair would be skimpy and dry.

Hester's wedding was held in Aunt Hallie's parlor, a room that smelled of furniture polish and Evening in Paris. Frederick Wheelock, nine years older than Hester's sixteen and a half, stood holding his bride's hand, the shiny seat of his good blue suit sagging noticeably. Hester's dress had been mail-ordered from the big Penney's store in Lynchburg. Ann and Aunt Hallie were splitting the cost.

A week after Hester and Frederick left for Knoxville, Ann quit her job at King's, packed her mother's cardboard suitcase that had been under her bed since her death and closed the door to her house for the last time. No sense trying to sell the thing; it wasn't a time when anyone would pay cash for a tilting clapboard shack beside the railroad tracks.

Sitting in the back of the bus, she counted her assets. One black gabardine suit and two white shirtwaists. One pair of good shoes, a flannel nightgown, a first-edition Tennyson she had found at the Salvation Army Thrift Shop and her precious journals. And eighty-three dollars left after she had bought a one-way ticket to Winston-Salem, North Carolina.

She found a room near the university campus, bought a schedule of classes and found a seven-to-noon job as a waitress in a busy diner that catered to students. Without registering, Ann began to attend afternoon classes she had carefully selected. After a year, she was able to buy a battered '36 Ford and then persuade the editor of the weekly *Piedmont Gazette* to take her on to sell advertising. Part of her deal with Orville Randall was that he would also let her do some reporting.

Four months after she began to work for the *Gazette*, Ann had produced eleven articles. Mr. Randall raised her salary to ten dollars a week and gave her three afternoons a week during which she could audit classes.

As far as the university was concerned, Ann Hawkins Adams didn't exist. She had never registered or taken an examination. She listened to the lectures and read the assigned books (that she bought used and sold as soon as she was finished with them). She never asked questions or participated in class discussions for fear of calling attention to herself. But whenever she could find the time, she joined a group of political science majors that could always be found in a café called Uncle Andy's. Usually she was the only female at the table.

Ann didn't flirt. She didn't know how. She would watch the co-eds who occasionally came into the café giggle and tease the young men. They were already experts in the rituals Southern mamas handed down to their daughters. "Let him chase you till you catch him." Ann simply couldn't and wouldn't play the game. When a boy told a story she didn't think was funny, she did not laugh. The other girls collapsed with mirth, pressing their hands to their faces, finally sighing, "Oh, Lester, you are just the most *fun!*" or "Jimmy Joe, I do believe you are the smartest *thing.*" Ann would sit quietly until the games were over. A Southern woman was supposed to serve as a mirror in which her man could preen himself. Ann saw the logic in such behavior if one wanted a man all her own. But Ann wanted a lot more than a man of her very own.

Her friends at Uncle Andy's accepted her as Annie Adams, the original oddball. She was attractive enough, in a unique and intimidating way, but because she didn't observe the conventions, the young men were unable to deal with her as a woman. They, too, had been groomed. They had been taught by their daddies.

The rally for Congressman Allen G. Hicks, candidate for the United States Senate, was held under the cottonwood trees in a downtown park. Ann had scurried over from the university to cover his speech and write it up for the *Gazette*. As she walked along the rows of card tables groaning with fried chicken and spareribs, she felt someone touch her elbow. Tall as she was, Congressman Hicks towered over her.

"I noticed you taking notes earlier," he said, putting down his paper plate.

"I'm Ann Hawkins Adams, with the *Piedmont Gazette*. You'd be doing me a big favor if you'd answer some questions."

He gestured toward the milling people, the bunting and the card tables. "I'm tied up right now. Why don't you come over to my office in Greensboro tomorrow around four and we'll chat?"

The interview with the forty-eight-year-old legislator began promptly at four the next day in his district office, and continued in a small hotel in Martinsville, just across the border in Virginia.

Hicks was so overwhelmed by Ann's mind and her virginity that he canceled four campaign appearances in order to spend thirty-eight uninterrupted hours with her.

Although Ann had no means for comparison, Allen Hicks was one of those men who is an enthusiastic but awkward lover. His wife, a former belle, had turned cold and bitter when he entered politics. He was seldom home anyway, and his sexual activities were limited to furtive one-night stands. For a woman with a bottomless intellect (compared to the women he knew), Ann was almost childlike in bed. He took her sexual education upon himself. By the time they left Martinsville, Ann was deftly moving her body to Allen's complete satisfaction. She had even begun to take some pleasure from their lovemaking. If Allen Hicks had known more about female anatomy he could have easily brought her to orgasm. As it was, Ann was more excited when she and a genuine United States Congressman talked and drank twelve-year-old bourbon than she was by the hours they tumbled together on the hotel bed. She was fascinated by his knowledge of worlds she had never glimpsed.

During the months preceding the election, Hicks and Ann spent at least one night a week together. Such encounters were difficult for a highly visible and hardworking senatorial candidate. After Allen Hicks was elected to the United States Senate, he asked Ann to come to Washington with him. He would make her a member of his staff and they could continue to see each other— with less inconvenience in Washington.

Once more the battered cardboard suitcase was carefully packed, and with only a few more possessions than when she had arrived in Winston-Salem.

Ann passed the night on the Greyhound bus to Washington, D.C., fitfully trying to untangle her thoughts and feelings. Was it the man? Was it the job? The new life in the new place? She was almost nauseated by excitement and anticipation.

"I'm getting out, Mr. Fuller, I'm getting out," she said softly to the dark window.

With part of the five hundred dollars Allen had given her, Ann rented a furnished room on R Street. Three flights up in an old brownstone. Her room was at the rear of a long, paint-chipped hallway, over the kitchen of a Chinese restaurant.

On her first morning in Washington, Ann awoke with a start, utterly confused by her surroundings and the odd smells wafting through her open window. After only a minute she stretched, laughed out loud and said, "Why, I am *here!*" She quickly showered and dressed for the day.

At seven o'clock that night she returned to her room. She had walked from the run-down brownstone on R Street straight up Pennsylvania Avenue to Capitol Hill, from the Hill to the Washington Monument, around the White House again and back up to Georgetown. She had stopped in a drugstore for coffee and a sandwich some time during the afternoon. When she climbed into the creaking single bed that night, she realized that she wasn't the least bit tired from the miles and miles of walking all day in the early autumn sun. She savored every block, lying there inhaling smells from the Chinese restaurant. The streets had been full of

57

uniforms of every shade and rank, as befit the capital of a nation at war. Young, and to Ann, beautiful girls, had rushed by, laughing. Trolleys had clanged and lurched at many intersections, and most cars on the broad avenues bore priority gas rationing stickers.

A week after Ann arrived in Washington, as she was stepping out of her floor's communal shower, the pay phone midway down the hall rang. A secretary who worked at the War Department answered it and yelled, "Anyone named Adams here?"

Allen Hicks knocked at her door forty-five minutes later. He slowly lowered himself into the single easy chair in the room and stared at Ann as she recounted her first days in Washington, all of the sights and sounds and her own excitement.

"Allen, I don't believe I'm here! Yesterday I went on the Capitol Building tour and I actually sat in the gallery of the United States Senate. Everything here seems so important. And just about everyone *looks* important."

As Hicks looked at Ann and listened to her, everything in him sagged. The steam of the campaign must have affected his senses. Perched on the edge of the studio bed was, quite simply, a gawky, redheaded country girl. God, was she country. Her speech, her mannerisms, the cheap cotton dress that had so intrigued him in Winston-Salem embarrassed him now. The body and face that had aroused such passion in that little hotel back in Martinsville now looked rawboned and underfed. She sounded like a babbling tourist stopping by his office for an autographed picture. Sure she was smart, smart as hell. But, sweet Jesus, it didn't *show*. What showed was hillbilly. The lobbyists and politicians who frequented his office would most surely not be impressed by him *or* his staff. Down-home or not, Ann simply wouldn't do.

Senator Hicks was not a man capable of subtlety. Ann stopped talking and watched him. His eyes were darting about, looking at everything in the room but her. She waited.

Finally he spoke. "Annie, honey, you didn't pay much in advance on this place, did you?"

Ann froze. At that moment she knew what Allen was seeing and thinking—all of it. But she remained silent and waited to see how he would deal with it.

Her silence made him more uncomfortable. "Annie, I'm going

to have to change some of my plans. Plans regarding my staff here. Ann, you know how politics are . . . Well, sometimes things can't be the way you'd like them to be."

Was he hoping she would say something helpful? She didn't.

"What I'm trying to tell you is that some of my most important supporters are putting on pressure to have me hire their friends and relations. I guess I made some promises along the way, the way you do. I assumed . . . Well, Annie, the hog's been slaughtered and now some folks want their share of the fatback. Annie, what I want to say is that I can't hire you for my staff. I don't think I can get you anything on one of the committees, either. Women are pouring into town by the thousands because of the man shortage and there just aren't enough decent jobs to go around. Listen, honey, why don't you let me get you a train ticket back to Winston-Salem? That bus ride is too rough. A Pullman. I'm sure I can manage Pullman for you."

She was sitting very straight, her hands close to her thighs, fists clenched. But when she spoke, her voice did not betray the anger welling in her chest.

"Too country, eh, Senator?"

"What . . .?"

"I'm too country for you, aren't I, Mr. Senator of the U.S. of A.?"

"Now, just a minute here, girl . . ."

"No, sir, you wait a minute. I may be country. No, I *am* country. What did you expect? I've never been north of Martinsville before. I know I don't look like the women here. I know I probably don't talk right. But I can outthink any one of them. I'm here and I'm staying. And I'm grateful to you for bringing me."

Now Allen Hicks was clutching the arms of the grease-stained chair. "Annie, listen. You don't understand the way things are here. A man in my position . . ."

"I know what your position is, Allen. I've never been one to impose. I want to say thank you for what you've done so far. And now I want you to get your fat ass out of here."

"Annie, honey, let's start this conversation all over." He tried his campaign smile, but couldn't quite arrange his face properly. "Maybe Senator Ryer's got something over at Public Works. You type good, right?"

"Do you need your five hundred back now or can you wait until I save it up?"

"Annie, please . . ."

"When you close my door over there, close it like a gentleman."

Allen Hicks moved toward the door. There was something almost menacing about this woman. He didn't want a scene. God knew what kind of people lived in the firetrap. He closed the door quietly.

During the time she had been in Washington, Ann had absorbed more than the monuments and statues. Even the September air itself carried a constant vitality. All the people here seemed to come from someplace else. Just as she had.

Ann did not waste time feeling betrayed and abandoned.

She had no job and everything about her screamed bumpkin. She knew that if she could get someone at least to let her say something, that person would forget the way she looked. She had never given much thought to her appearance. She knew she wore her hair in a careless way. Clean, but not what one would call stylish. Her clothes were cheap. It hadn't *mattered* before.

She had a little over three hundred dollars of Hicks's money left. The clothes and hair could be transformed by money. But that wouldn't be enough. In this place you had to know somebody—contacts—she'd learned that from Allen. Everything here was done through contacts. And the only person she knew was a chicken junior Senator from North Carolina who was embarrassed by her. She couldn't even use him as a reference, not after she'd shoved him out her door.

It occurred to her that in a town whose major industry was politics and people, what might set a person apart from the wheeling and dealing would be directness and honesty. Maybe that would get some attention.

The *Washington Herald* wasn't hard to find. It crouched ten stories high, a crumbling pile of limestone on M Street. Carved gargoyles protruded at the corners of its roof.

At nine two mornings later she presented herself to the wheezing old lady at the marble counter in the lobby.

"Who is the managing editor of this paper?" she asked briskly.

"Danny Waites," the old woman said, not looking up from the crossword puzzle she was working.

"Where can I locate Mr. Waites?"

"City room. Top floor. Elevator over to the right there."

"Thank you most kindly."

At that the woman glanced up. But only for a moment.

Danny Waites's secretary was harassed. One phone receiver was draped over her left shoulder and she was holding another to her ear.

"My name is Ann Hawkins Adams and I would like to see Mr. Danny Waites, please."

The secretary was astonished.

"Do you have an appointment, Miss Adams?"

"No. I have just arrived in town. I don't have an appointment. It's very important that I have a few moments of his time."

"What does this concern?" the secretary said, hanging up the phone at her ear and ignoring the one resting on her shoulder.

"It is a matter of some importance. I'd prefer to speak to him personally."

Danny Waites's secretary remembered the day when a seedy-looking man walked in unannounced and asked to see the editor. He was kept waiting for two and a half hours. When he finally saw Danny, he had handed him documents in Japanese later proving that the Japanese had succeeded in breaking the secret code used by the Allies. Ann knew what the woman must be thinking. This rangy, redheaded kid with the South in her mouth seemed to have the confidence of a countess. She would probably turn out to be a nuisance. But she wasn't a nut. Maybe she came bearing a formula for making explosives out of peanut shells.

"Just a minute," the secretary said.

Danny Waites was leaning back in his swivel chair, his glasses pushed up on the rim of his receding hairline. When he spotted Ann standing in his door, he quickly righted his chair and pulled himself into an erect position.

"Yes?" he said, startled.

"Mr. Waites," she said, pronouncing it Way-yuts.

He smiled. She was like nothing he had ever seen before. A twenty-year-old redhead—green shoes, matching green two-piece suit, green eye makeup, all topped by a staggeringly high green felt hat. The great legs are real, at least, he thought.

"Sit down, Miss Adams. How can I help you?"

61

"You can hire me, Mr. Waites."

"What can you do, Miss Adams?" It was early. He wasn't busy yet. This might be fun for a few minutes.

"I can sell ads, write copy, crop pictures, set type, write heads that count out to the letter. I can tell a California case from a turtle. I can handle hot lead and spell. I do features, sidebars, obits and editorials. I know what a dangling participle is and the difference between will and shall. If you don't have openings in those departments and you are not too tied up with the union, I can fold, stack, wire-bale and deliver your bulldog edition faster than a scalded dog."

Danny Waites was dumbfounded. He caught his pipe as it dropped from his ordinarily clenched teeth.

"Holy Mother of . . . Where did you come from?"

"Bristol, Tennessee, by way of Winston-Salem, North Carolina. I have done two years on the *Piedmont Gazette* and if they had a job there that I didn't do it must have been going on in the men's room."

Waites was fascinated. "How in the world did you get to Washington, D.C.? You didn't just pick up and come here cold, did you?"

"No, sir. I came in, you might say . . . hot. A gentleman friend in a considerably high position in this town offered me a job. Unfortunately, ours was a personal relationship and by the time I got here, while *I* might not have cooled off entirely, *he* had."

"I see."

She hoped she had convinced him that she was not the average Washington camp follower, a girl who didn't pick up and go anyplace on whim or a burst of passion.

"Well now, Miss Adams. I'm sorry to tell you we don't have any jobs right now. I can see that you're qualified, but . . ."

"Mr. Waites, I have exactly one hundred and forty-three dollars and carfare left of my traveling money. That's since buying this outfit and paying another two weeks' rent on my room on R Street. I can live on that for time enough. I'd like you to try me out here for two weeks. You don't have to pay me. If in two weeks you think I can be of some value to this newspaper, perhaps you will be able to find room for me. I have no references except the gentleman who invited me to your city. For obvious reasons I

62

don't care to use his name. You can write to my editor down in Winston-Salem, though."

"Miss Adams, I don't need to write to your editor. I'm sure you're a skillful and competent worker. But we can't let you work here for nothing. It just isn't done."

Ann Hawkins Adams started her job as copygirl after lunch that day, wearing the green outfit, hat and all. Six months later she was promoted to general assignment reporter. At that time she was given a desk and a by-line. She had kept both for eighteen years.

After Ann finished her article on Bobby Kennedy, she pulled the last sheets from her typewriter, separated the carbons and neatly stacked the papers. Without proofing the pages, Ann wound her way toward the circle of editors' desks in the center of the city room.

As she passed the desk of a young reporter she had befriended, Ann paused. "How's Montgomery County's star investigative reporter doing, Billie Claire?"

"God, Ann," Billie Claire groaned, "this beat is going to send me screaming up the wall. There's only so much anyone can milk from a meeting of a county sewage committee, outraged or not."

"Courage, honey. Everyone's got to start somewhere. There are worse assignments than Montgomery County. Why don't you get out and do some digging into that dentist who shot himself out there last week?"

"I began yesterday. Ann, would you have a few minutes to . . .?"

"Not now. I'm rushing, honey. How about tomorrow? In the afternoon, if I'm in? I'm late for lunch."

"Okay. Tomorrow. Thanks."

Ann dropped her story in the in-box on the copy desk and pointed herself in the direction of the Hay-Adams Hotel and the table near the rear of the hotel's elegant dining room.

Del. Del. Del.

Rumpled, brilliant, suave Del Porterfield.

Tender, intense Del who listened to her words and explored her body as if he could never learn all of it. Del who finally completed the job that Senator Allen G. Hicks had begun so many

63

years before. Del who had finally brought Ann to fulfilled womanhood.

Del was from another world. Fourth-generation old money, now gone, but no matter. Yale. Patrician. She never knew when he would stop her in midsentence, lean toward her and say, "Ann, I love you." It had taken her a long time to find Del and she hadn't even realized she had been looking.

She was thirty-eight and in love for the first time in her life.

Ann didn't feel silly. She felt grateful. But, she couldn't help it, she was also puzzled.

Ann Hawkins Adams and Del Porterfield?

Much of Washington was also puzzled.

The closer people were to both Ann and Del, the greater their mystification. Whatever it was the two of them had going for almost two months obviously wasn't a casual flirtation.

Everyone in metropolitan Washington knew who Ann Adams was. A grainy photograph of her distinctive freckled face accompanied her regular column in the *Herald*'s Sunday "think section."

Just about everyone in the country who watched Sunday TV knew who Del Porterfield was, or at least recognized his face as one of the participants on political discussion panels like *Meet the Press*. His column, "Capital Outlook," appeared three times a week in papers owned by the Hartford chain—sixty-three newspapers printed daily in every state except North Dakota. Sixty-three newspapers owned and held in the powerful, opinionated grip of Cynthia Critchell Hartford, widow of Charles Madill Hartford.

Every day one copy of each of the chain's newspapers was delivered to Mrs. Hartford's pale pink office on the tenth floor of Chicago's Merchandise Mart. She perused each one, and with a long, crimson-nailed forefinger, slashed through columns that did not please her. They were returned by messenger to the writer or the writer's editor. She seldom slashed "Capital Outlook."

Mrs. Hartford held strong opinions, pro and con, regarding certain issues and public figures.

For the most part Del could write around her revered or abhored issues and public figures. But occasionally they couldn't be ignored by a political columnist of Del's stature. When confronted with this fact of his life, Del poured a tumbler of Scotch, drank half with his eyes closed. Then, clenching his teeth, he began to type. After he pulled the last sheet from his typewriter, he finished the Scotch, slammed down the glass and said, "There you are, Dragon Lady, another slice of my balls."

An hour after Del filed his copy he had put the periodic obligatory column from his mind, before he fell in love with Ann and afterward—for a time.

Cynthia Hartford was simply carrying out the political legacy of the Hartford chain. Del had known Charles Madill Hartford's positions when he signed on to write "Capital Outlook." Old Hartford's political views had once been dismissed by Scotty Reston as being slightly to the right of George III. Del considered himself a moderate-liberal, but he was confident he could maintain his integrity without too many painful compromises. In press-preoccupied Washington the prestige of having one's own nationwide column relieved considerable pain.

Del had been more than comfortable during the Eisenhower Administrations.

He had been writing "Capital Outlook" for three years when Ike came to power. The men around the new President courted the suave, forty-four-year-old journalist who wrote the literate and evenhanded columns that reached approximately two million households three times a week. He wasn't *granted* interviews, he was invited to join golf and bridge weekends at Augusta, Palm Springs and Camp David with the Presidential party. He was asked to Washington's prestigious Burning Tree Country Club by Cabinet members and senior Senators. When Jim Hagerty, Ike's press secretary, occasionally "suggested" a question, Del could be counted upon to ask it at a Presidential press conference.

For eight years of the Eisenhower Administration Del Porterfield interpreted events in Washington with easy authority. His aphorisms were quoted in the columns of other writers, in news broadcasts and weekly journals. His columns were thoughtful observations of events and trends, according to those who agreed with him, and stuffy, middle-brow ruminations to those who did not.

For eight years Del Porterfield's political and social clout was only surpassed by Stewart Alsop and Walter Lippmann.

In 1958 a small, but distinguished New York publisher brought out a collection of forty "Capital Outlooks," each accompanied by an appropriate political cartoon.

Ann Adams bought a copy—three years before Del first asked her to dine with him.

Critical decisions emanate from Washington so frequently that its residents, to say nothing of the rest of the country, are unable to absorb them fully, grasp the broad implications, before another shattering incident sweeps in to replace them. In order to maintain a degree of sanity, politicians and members of the press develop a once-removed sensibility. The sharp points of specifics are dealt with and dismissed. What remains is the flow of enduring problems and people: taxes, poverty, inflation, crime, Defense budgets, Presidents, Cabinet appointments, powerful Senators and Congressmen . . . and influential members of the press.

Ann and Del were part of the enduring flow, and in small, almost imperceptible ways could alter minute rivulets.

Few people not in touch with the unfolding events directly related to Washington and its satellite communities were familiar with the name Ann Hawkins Adams. Her beat was the city itself. She was the consummate reporter. She stalked and sniffed, asked questions and set down the answers. One day she dug through musty Congressional files, another, she walked the sweltering streets of a northeast Washington ghetto interviewing fire victims. She never used the words, "I," or "In my opinion." The who, what, where and when were always there, but she often ached to write her personal WHY. But Seth Hathaway was not paying her to editorialize. The Del Porterfields of Washington did that.

The only thing Del stalked was a golf ball he'd sliced into the rough. He left the leather chair in his comfortable Press Building office during the week to lunch with a senior Senator in the Senate Dining Room, or to mingle with colleagues in the Press Club Tap Room.

While Del analyzed the implications of price support extensions for cotton, wheat and grain sorghum, Ann was calling everyone named Johnson in the D.C., Maryland and Virginia phone books to see if she could locate a relative of the man who had killed six people in a Rexall Drug Store the night before.

Although Del enjoyed his position, he felt something was lacking. He yearned to *break* a big story. Not place what most people already knew in a different context.

More than anything else, Del wanted a Pulitzer Prize, and he knew he'd never earn one being thoughtful and reasoned.

More than anything else, Ann wanted a Pulitzer. She did not see it as just a benchmark in her career. It was the Grail. She compulsively drove herself toward its attainment.

They discussed the Pulitzer with each other on their second date. Neither had ever before spoken the words to anyone else.

The Hay-Adams's maître d' led Ann to the table she and Del favored in the large-paneled dining room. Less than a minute after she was seated a waiter set a glass of Jack Daniels on the rocks before her and said, "Will Mr. Porterfield be joining you, Miss Adams?"

"God willing and the creek don't rise," she smiled.

The waiter handed her a folded slip of paper. "The captain asked me to give you this," he said as he whisked away the single butt in her ashtray.

Ann read, "Darling, running about a half hour late. Sit tight."

"That's class," she murmured as she studied Del's looping, aristocratic writing.

Washington restaurants did not encourage an unescorted woman to occupy a table—unless she was over sixty-five. Maître d's seated solitary women behind posts or in corners so that their presence would not "disturb" the other diners. Realizing this, Del had taken the time to send a note. And Ann was seated where she was because the maître d' had glanced at Del's message.

Such a small evidence of Del's thoughtfulness. Only one of many. Graceful, tactful acts, often overlapping. No one had ever shown her such attention before. Now she could entrust her long-suppressed womanliness to a man, because this one would appreciate and cherish it.

The high-ceilinged dining room was filling. Several White House staffers had taken seats around a big oval table in the corner. Senator Hartke and his administrative assistant, Mace Brodie, sat huddled a few tables from Ann, glancing in her direction, nodding, lowering their voices.

From where she was sitting, Ann saw only three people she was unable to identify by name and title. One was an attractive, beautifully groomed young woman seated with an Assistant Secretary of Agriculture. She held a daiquiri in one hand and delicately lifted a single peanut from a crystal dish with the other.

"Hmm," Ann said, trying to remember where she'd seen the young woman before.

Then she laughed and everyone turned.

Now she remembered.

It had been in the lobby of the Mayflower at 2:30 A.M., the first time she and Del had slept together. The blonde had been standing in the ornate lobby with a junior Congressman from California. Ann had thought it rather amusing and less than discreet for the Congressman to be there at that hour, but, then, she herself was there for the same reason.

After the Congressman and his friend received their key, Del, well-tanked and flustered, approached the front desk.

"Mr. and Mrs. John Brown," Del told the effete desk clerk.

"How long will you be with us?"

"Ah, just for tonight."

The clerk raised one eyebrow. "Your luggage, Mr., uh, Brown?"

Del began to stammer contradictory explanations about the absence of luggage.

Del Porterfield, only two years divorced, was unaccustomed to the casual sadism of hotel night clerks. He had spent his newly single years squiring ladies ten years his senior to concerts at Constitution Hall or to embassy dinners, and then handing them over to their chauffeurs at evening's end.

For her part, Ann had consented to sleep with few men in the years since Allen Hicks had scuttled away from her furnished room.

Neither of them was accustomed to standing before the desk of a midtown hotel at 2:30 in the morning. But a hotel room it had to be. Ann's apartment was a capitulation she was unwilling to make. Del felt his furnished bachelor rooms unworthy of this woman.

"I'm sorry, Mr. Brown," the clerk peered at Ann and Del through his pink-tinted glasses, "we can't register guests without luggage."

"Lost," Del blurted. "Airport baggage handling's trying to find . . ."

"I see. Then I'll need some identification. A credit card?"

"Listen here, honey." Ann pushed Del aside and slammed her purse on the polished desk. "You all want identification. Here's identification." She pulled her District of Columbia Police Press ID from her purse and held it under the clerk's nose.

"Ah, yes." The clerk backed away. "Sorry, Miss Adams. You know how it is." He grabbed a key and handed it to the red-faced Del. "Room six seventeen."

In the confusion, no one signed the register.

After the door was closed and locked, Del stared at Ann. Ann stared back. Then they both began to laugh. They fell onto the bed, holding tightly to each other and laughing so hard their tears ran into each other's mouth. Finally they fell silent. Amazed.

And so it began.

Ann did not realize she was smiling from the memory when she caught sight of Del weaving his tall, graceful body between the tables. He spoke as briefly as possible to men who greeted him as he passed by.

"You got my message?" he said as he slid onto the banquette beside her, ignoring the facing chair. "Sorry, darling, couldn't be helped. A dry Rob Roy, Johnny."

In less than a minute the waiter was back with Del's drink and a fresh Jack Daniels for Ann.

"You look fine to me, early or late." She placed her hand on the crook of his elbow, needing to touch him. "What held you?"

"That panel for the ASNE convention at the Statler Hilton. I damned near forgot about it. Pete Lisagor, Max Friedman, Jake and I had at Salinger on the Kennedy press conferences."

"How did Pierre handle it?"

"He just sat there puffing on that damn cigar. He was taking a pounding and didn't even feel it."

"That's what he's paid to do."

Del nodded. "Pete was amusing and sarcastic. Max was urbane and diplomatic. Jake went right for the jugular and asked why the electronic people are consistently receiving the advantage over us pencil pushers. Of course he knew the answer. I suppose he wondered if he could get a small squirm out of Pierre. A good question for the American Society of Newspaper Editors. But a hell of a lot of good it did. God damn, what a farce." Del took a large gulp of his drink.

"Del, honey, what is this? You know the pencil press didn't get Kennedy elected. Why should he change horses now? The man's a realist."

"Frustration, darling, kindergarten frustration." He gestured to the waiter. "Sure he plays his press conferences to TV. Is CBS going to throw a three-minute question from a rumpled Cleveland reporter at its six o'clock news viewers?" He downed half of his fresh drink and laid his long, cool, aristocratic fingers on Ann's wrist. "God, I can't believe how much I love you. I love the way your mind works. I love the way you make me feel."

"Del, I suspect that panel has you more than frustrated."

"Maybe I've been at it too long, Annie. This town has changed. I don't like the manipulation. Not that Ike's people didn't have their little tricks. But with them I could talk frankly and openly with policy people. Privately. I was trusted. If someone said, 'Off the record,' it was off the record. Now I feel as if I were lost in a fog of cotton candy."

Ross Mark, bureau chief of the *London Express,* stopped at their table. "It's looking very good, Del. Close, but very good for you."

Del was one of the candidates for president of the Press Club.

Ann watched Del as he spoke with Ross.

Two nights ago that man with the cultivated voice and manner had asked her to marry him. That man who mesmerized her with his minilectures on everything from the second law of thermodynamics to the sex life of Jesus to the courting customs of an obscure Mayan tribe. Her catch-as-catch-can education had not prepared her for Del's erudition.

Two nights ago, having just finished his brandy and a monologue on Agrippa von Nettiesheim's concept of a world soul, he leaned across the table and said, "Ann, marry me. You've got to."

Startled, Ann slowly said, "I can't say no, because we both know I love you. I can't say yes, because I'm not too clear about what a wife is, and that's what I'd like to be. I need to think about it."

While Del talked club politics with Ross, she was still considering.

Del was fifty-three. Since his divorce he had been living in a grubby, two-room furnished apartment and eating at the club.

His ex-wife back in Massachusetts, accurately counting on Del's sense of honor, had ended up with the house in suburban Brookline, the cottage in Chatham, custody of the girls, the checking and savings accounts and three-quarters of his salary. Most of the monthly crunch was to end soon: Ellen Porterfield was marrying the smart lawyer who had paved Del's way to near poverty. However, getting his two daughters through school and summers in God-knew-where would continue for another five years.

Money wasn't the problem. Ann was well-paid and comfortable in her spacious and, as her friends said, "uniquely decorated" apartment at Cathedral Towers.

There was her independence. She had been on her own, completely, for twenty-three of her thirty-eight years. She was successful and damn proud of it. Ann had succeeded by way of brains, drive and self-discipline, occasionally lessened, but never suspended, after the better part of a fifth of Jack Daniels.

There was her practicality.

In this summer of 1961 Del Porterfield was one of the dozen or so distinguished resident Washington columnists and opinion molders. But now he lacked the influence he had enjoyed when Eisenhower was President. The new Administration had brought with it a quite different style and bestowed significant information where it would be most beneficial to itself. Just as Ike's people had done. The senior political analyst for the Hartford chain was not considered an especially useful vehicle for advancing the programs of JFK and his brother. In addition, there were political dues to be paid and knuckles to be rapped. Cynthia Hartford had supported Richard Nixon. Delman George Porterfield III, was her Washington standard-bearer.

The Hartford chain could not be ignored, but it did not need to be stroked.

So, while Del's stature had been lessened during the past six months, Ann's hadn't.

She had to admit that Del's status mattered to her. She had come too far not to "marry up," as they said back home.

Which was why her decision about whether or not to marry Del hung on the *actual* voting for president of the National Press Club, not the straw votes Del and Ross were discussing.

Right now Del needed the prestige accompanying the position of president of the club. In times past some of the dreariest news hacks in Washington had been elevated to a level of local godliness while they had been president of the Press Club. They had walked with kings and other heads of state.

If Del became president he would be the man who entertained and escorted guest speakers to the podium for a National Press Club luncheon and press conference.

If she were his wife she could join Del when he dined with a Supreme Court Justice, with Charles De Gaulle, with Khrushchev. If not she would sit in the exile of the Tampax Room, where members of the men only club had their female guests wait for them.

The voting would begin in three days.

Del was aware of the importance of the voting to Ann. It had never been discussed. There was no need.

"Say, Ann," Ross said, "is Salinger seeing Melon Bowersox?"

"Who knows? Pierre makes friends with the press any way he can. And you know Melon."

"Last night she was going strong with that crowd of lushes who hang about Pete Williams's office." Ross smiled and shook his head. "She had everyone riveted by a story about Jane Connor."

"That tall blonde who used to be at the DNC with the Johnsons?" Del asked.

"Right. From what I was able to make out, Melon found her hidden away in an unlabeled office at the E.O.B. acting very furtive."

Ann shook her head. "Jane's gonna strangle Melon if she messes up something important she had going."

Ross headed for another table and Johnny appeared before them with fresh drinks.

"Would you like to see a menu now, Mr. Porterfield?"

Ann and Del nodded their heads in unison.

Chapter Three

Melon

A strip of sunlight slid up Melon's cheek and passed over her left eyelid. She held that eye closed and half-opened her right eye. She was then able to determine that she was flat on her back on the pull-out couch in her apartment. She further determined that within the past eight hours she had been vigorously screwed: her pubic bone felt bruised and her vagina ached.

Very slowly, she turned her head away from the closed but askew venetian blinds. Now her cheek lay on the fringed black velvet pillow decorated with a portrait of President John F. Kennedy under crossed American flags, and she felt an additional discomfort. She was still wearing one earring. Melon slid her hand between her neck and the pillow. As she was pulling off the earring she observed that she was wearing her bra and a sleeveless black blouse.

"Oh, Christ," she groaned and opened both eyes.

Hanging from the gooseneck lamp on her desk was one stocking, a clip from her black garter belt still attached. She raised her head. A mistake, she realized instantly, as a brilliant pain pierced her right temple. Before she lowered her head she saw the other stocking, twisted around her ankle.

"Shit, my last pair," she muttered just as a loud and unmistakable reverberation occurred behind the closed bathroom door.

She froze. Swell! He's still here, whoever *he* is.

Mary Ellen Bowersox seldom brought men to her apartment. She was seldom there herself.

The only time Jane Connor had ever been in it she had slowly taken in the chaos and said, "What is this? Ground zero at Alamogordo?"

Melon had ignored the sarcasm and casually pushed an empty bottle of Budweiser and one Capezio under the permanently pulled-out couch.

She resided in a large single room contained within a dull modern building near the Capitol in southwest Washington. Her bathroom was tiny and splattered with mascara, underarm spray and hardening toothpaste. The bathroom mirror was studded with half a dozen false eyelashes, pasted there for safekeeping. A solitary towel, with various stains by Elizabeth Arden, either hung over the edge of the basin or lay on the floor in a damp heap. Mildew was well established in the corners of the shower.

Clothes fell from the drawers of a dresser and from hangers in the walk-in closet.

A teakettle and one enamel pan, containing the remains of a can of Campbell's soup, rested on the two-burner stove in the pullman kitchen. Seven glasses of assorted sizes, plus caked bowls and plates lay in the sink. The refrigerator under the counter held one doggie bag from the Golden Parrot in which the greater part of a once rare filet mignon was turning iridescent. The sour cream in an untouched baked potato was furred with mold. Beside the doggie bag lay an unwrapped wedge of Brie displaying perfect teeth marks. On the lower shelf an open can of Budweiser leaned against the wall (for Melon's hair), and draped over the rest of the shelf were three pairs of black lace panties ("because they feel so *good* on these awful mornings").

The single room was covered by an acrylic tweed wall-to-wall carpet spotted with random mysterious dark stains, and was furnished with the couch bed upon which Melon lay, trying to put together the night before. She could not remember when the couch had been properly closed, with the cushions in place. Along one wall was a bookcase made of bricks and unpainted plywood, and an unpainted kneehole desk upon which rested a white telephone. A bullfight poster was scotch-taped to the wall above the desk. Telephone numbers were scribbled over the lower half of

74

the poster. The only other piece of furniture was a canvas butterfly chair ripped at one corner and unusable except as a place upon which to throw clothes.

Melon raised herself up on her elbows and surveyed the room for a clue. A dark brown suit coat and trousers and large, wing-tipped shoes were on the floor beside the chair.

Now the toilet was being flushed and the shower was turned on full force.

That would give her from three to five minutes.

Holding her head, she sat up, swung her feet to the floor and stood up shakily. Taking a step, she lurched violently backward, her left heel sliding out from under her and sending her crashing against the hard metal couch frame.

"What the hell?"

Frowning at her foot she recognized her diaphragm cupped firmly to her heel, with the help of Ortho Jelly. She peeled it off and threw it toward the pullman sink.

Terrific, she thought. I wonder if it popped out or if I ever had it in?

Melon drove her friends slightly mad once a month with hysterical phone calls in the middle of the night announcing that she was pregnant. She never was, but to anyone who cared to listen it meant the entire litany of "Does hot gin really work?" "Do you know someone who isn't a butcher?" to "Where will I get the money?" On and on until finally she would rush to the ladies' room of some restaurant and return beaming and manic because she had once more been saved from that fate worse than death. Melon could never find her notebook, her black cashmere sweater, her checkbook or her diaphragm, and when she did find the latter, she either forgot to use it or got it in wrong. She once found it in a manila envelope in her mailbox. The chivalrous man had not included his name or address.

She padded to the closet and grabbed a wrinkled skirt and her raincoat.

God, she was hungry. Her teeth felt as if they were encased in felt. She had to get out of there before "he" came out. She hated morning-after small talk, and it was her experience that morning-after men were generally horny. Melon did not like sex in daylight, if it could be avoided.

Her watch read 8:45.

75

Crap!

Last night's blouse tucked into the mismatched skirt, bare feet forced into high-heeled pumps, her raincoat over her arm and purse in hand, Melon opened the apartment door and silently shut it behind her.

At the corner drugstore she asked for two glazed doughnuts and a large lemon Coke which she carried to the phone booth near the door.

Halfway through the first doughnut and one digit away from completing a call to the *Washington Herald* city desk, she saw a White House car glide to a stop in front of her building. She depressed the cradle and heard her dime fall as a tall, powerfully built young man with a still-damp head of dark hair walked briskly to the car. He gave the driver a curt nod and slid into the back seat. From her perch in the phone booth she could not see his face. The dark brown suit, though, had last been seen on her tweed rug.

Pensively, Melon finished the doughnut and Coke.

She and Jane Connor had begun the previous evening at Duke Ziebert's and Jane had done one of her disappearing acts. Then she and Mac Kilduff and Pierre had gone up to the Rotunda and started sloshing it with Senator Williams's crowd. She remembered trading sexual cutenesses with a terrific-looking guy and kidding him about being from some place called Swampscott, which had seemed terribly funny at the time. After that there were gaps and spaces. The last clear image was of herself and a tall, faceless man doing a furious twist at some subterranean dump in Georgetown.

Whoever he was he could swing a White House car in less than five minutes. Damn! Only God knew what goodies he had imparted to her during the wee hours of the morning.

She shrugged.

Onward.

She looked at her watch. 9:10.

Melon had a nine-thirty assignment to interview an aging comedian who wasn't making people laugh much at the Shoreham Blue Room that week.

Dumb assignment. He probably snorts coke for breakfast and ends every sentence with "But, seriously, folks." How come she always got the crap assignments?

76

"Because you're good, Melon, that's why," she had been told by her city editor when she had violently complained about having to interview an eighteen-year-old starlet who spoke one line in a B movie and never left the back of a Harley-Davidson. "Melon, you could interview a glacier on the subject of speed and make it sound interesting."

This didn't mollify her one bit. She was tired of being the city room cutie pie, the deadline fluffball with the clever leads.

There was no way Melon could show up at the Fairfax Hotel where Manny Manning was staying without a decent pair of hose and makeup. In the full light of day she could see that the raincoat hadn't been a great idea: a few days before she had used the office staple gun to tack up the ripped-out hem. Reflected sunlight bounced off the large, copper-colored staples.

Shit!

She could have faked it at the city room by grabbing a pair of stockings from the dispenser in the ladies' room and done her face from whatever was rattling around in the bottom of her handbag. But, the shiny staples were too much.

Nine thirteen.

Melon dialed the Fairfax and was put through to Manny Manning's suite. Her reputation for being a genius with a telephone was deserved.

In two minutes she had switched the interview from his suite at nine thirty to a corner table in the Jockey Club downstairs for one o'clock. She then quickly called Wally McCardle, the assigned photographer, and told him to meet her before lunch for a quick shot or two of the comedian in his suite.

Next she called the city room. A bored dictationist answered the phone.

"This is Melon. Ernie around?"

While she was on hold, she ran her tongue over her teeth. Blahh! At some point the night before she must have switched to banana daiquiris. Never again, dear Lord. I'll be good.

"Where the hell are you, Melon. You've got a nine-thirty assignment," the perpetually harassed Ernie Prescott roared into the phone.

"Ernie, that bastard comedian switched the interview to one," she moaned to the city editor.

"Then get your little tail in here, damn it!"

"Ernie, wait. I have a toothache that's taking off the top of my head. I was going to see the dentist on my lunch hour, but when Manning switched I was able to get an appointment for this morning. I've been up all night with it."

"Sure, Melon, sure," Ernie growled, familiar with Melon's incredible repertoire of excuses. "You just be here five minutes after that interview. We've promised it all week. I need it for the split page tomorrow. You had better have it on my desk by four, babe."

He slammed down his receiver so hard Melon's ear popped.

She leaned her head against the cool glass of the phone booth door and finished the second doughnut.

Humming now, Melon returned to her apartment, removed her clothes, tossed them onto the floor of her closet and stepped into the still-dripping shower.

The water pounded her short dark hair. She let the water run into her mouth and swished it around her teeth with her tongue.

Only nine thirty. Over three hours.

Goody.

She shaved her legs and armpits, rinsed off the soap and shampooed her hair. She then propped herself on the edge of the washbasin and began to apply the day's makeup. Moisturizer, Touch n' Glow, eyeliner, electric blue shadow, then lipliner and hot pink lipstick. She twisted her hair into pin curls, slipped on a frayed man's shirt and flopped onto the unmade couch.

It was now ten o'clock.

She phoned Gino's and ordered a double pepperoni pizza and a six-pack of Pepsi. While she waited she paced. Melon found being alone and unoccupied so uncomfortable she became panicky after five minutes.

Her only true and trusted friend was the telephone, and it was to the phone that she turned in times of need, and boredom.

Still niggling around in her head was the memory of Jane Connor in the E.O.B. the day before. Melon knew Jane had left the Democratic National Committee after the inauguration and had taken off with some gorgeous Italian correspondent for a couple of weeks. When she had run into her at the Press Club a month or so ago, Jane was vague and offhand about what she was doing in the new Administration. Vagueness bothered Melon. Melon felt

78

that *everything* was her business; whether anyone else agreed was beside the point. What if someone was doing something she wasn't a part of, in *some* way? Unbearable.

Melon also smelled a story in Jane's new occupation. Jane Connor was one of the most direct people she knew. She would answer any question, no matter how personal, with a flat, no-nonsense statement and go on about her business. So why had she been so cagey when Melon appeared in her office? Shuffling all those papers around, turning them facedown, hustling her out and down the hall?

Maybe Jane was doing something more interesting and exciting than Melon was. If she was Melon had to know. And, in any case, Melon hated secrets of all kinds. Ann Adams once told Jane that it was stupid for anyone to spend money on advertising in Washington when they could simply tell Melon and get much wider coverage. Everyone had laughed, including Melon.

However it occurred, intuition or desperation, Melon invariably found the right rock to turn over. That was half of it, sensing the significant rock or slab of human cement from among the many. The other half was assimilating what lay under the slab and knowing how best to use what she found. She was not above inventing embellishments. Poetic licentiousness, she called it.

Melon Bowersox's great fear that she might miss something provided her with extraordinary peripheral vision and hearing.

To many people, Melon Bowersox was an A 1, blue-ribbon pain in the ass.

She was also, however, a skillful writer who consistently managed to write "clever" rather than "cute" stories. She was very good at what she did.

A year before, Melon had been given her own by-lined feature column. Not bad for twenty-five.

But the column wasn't enough, because she had to fill it with what she considered inconsequential little pieces, dripping with color, bathos and nostalgia; Smokey the Bear's birthday party at the zoo; crippled kids on a ward at Children's Hospital saving pennies to get a new leg for a friend; an interview with the parents of two teenagers who had formed a suicide pact and walked into the surf of Rehobeth, never to be seen again; the courage with which a Senator's wife was dealing with Parkinson's disease.

Melon handled the material beautifully and her column received attention. People who did not know her wanted to pat Mary Ellen Bowersox on the head or squeeze her cheek or hug her. As far as management was concerned, she was a circulation builder, and for that she was forgiven a great deal.

She hated it. She hated being the quintessential "baby girl." She wanted to be taken seriously, to have clout and power, to influence something more important than whether or not the Heart Fund met its quota or some ghetto kids got back their destroyed playground equipment. And she intended to have power. She didn't care who she had to take over the side with her in order to get it. She knew the target—power, and with it, prestige, but she hadn't quite figured out the logistics for the assault. She was certain, though, that if she kept moving, kept digging, kept the action going, somehow it would fall in her lap.

No one who knew Melon was betting against her.

It was when she couldn't get what she wanted through stealth, manipulation and cuteness that she fell back on native intelligence and hard work.

And hers was an intelligence that had earned her a four-year scholarship at Smith.

Melon never talked to anyone about the first eighteen years of her life. Not the real life. Depending on which scenario appealed to her and which impression she was trying to make, she had been born in Paris of a jazz musician father and a concert singer mother and brought up in boarding schools she would rather not discuss. After four Manhattans and if the company was attentive, she was born out of wedlock to a famous Hollywood star and a politician's daughter. Some thought she was an orphan, others thought she was the youngest of fourteen children. No one ever got the straight story. The straight story was painful to Mary Ellen Bowersox.

The only part of her pre-Washington life she would talk about honestly was the four years at Smith. It had social and economic cachet.

Melon had been born in California. When forced honestly to admit her place of birth, she would say only, Southern California. If further pressed, she said, The Valley, which was easy enough in

80

Washington. No one knew much about California, and, good God, there were hundreds of valleys in the state.

Melon's mother had not been overcome with joy when she learned she was pregnant with her first child. Noreen Moore was sixteen years old and the daughter of a Glendale optometrist, going steady with Billy Bowersox, all-league halfback at Glendale Hoover.

Noreen and Bill eloped to Yuma after Noreen missed her second period and moved in with the Moores for five months while Bill finished his senior year of high school. They moved into a bungalow court on Ventura Boulevard in Van Nuys when Noreen was eight months along and Bill had been named "Best Build" in the senior class poll. After graduation he found a job as a plumber's helper.

Mary Ellen was born on the sixth day of one of the worst Santa Anas on record. When Noreen went into labor the temperature was 115 degrees and the San Fernando Valley lay under a thick cloud of brown smoke from an out-of-control brushfire in the hills above Burbank.

Bill was fascinated by his tiny daughter.

Noreen not only resented her virile young husband's fascination, she regarded the baby as the embodiment of the mess she was in. Bill worked fourteen-hour days and did penance to Noreen in every way he could.

When Mary Ellen was eleven months old, Bill moved his family into a pleasant, two-bedroom duplex and Noreen emerged from her lattice of self-pity.

Now little Melon no longer smelled of sour milk and ammonia. Bill was doing very well, better than many men twice his age in the Depression year of 1937.

The duplex gleamed with wax and polish. The curtains from the May Company were always crisp and white. The windows sparkled.

Melon became the darling of the neighborhood. Strangers stopped Noreen as she pushed her around the market in her stroller and commented on her looks. "Just like a brunette Shirley Temple!" "Adorable! She ought to be in the movies!" Noreen began to dress Melon with more care and spend more time with her, encouraging her to strike poses and repeat cute little expressions. She did "I'm a Little Teapot" endlessly, complete with a theatrical flourish and a flash of ruffled panties under her dotted-swiss dress.

By the time she was four Melon was a shrewd little ham. She had been taken over Cahuenga Pass to a talent agent's studio where she tap danced, sang "On the Good Ship Lollipop" and "Yankee Doodle Dandy." Expensive photographs were taken for a portfolio. Noreen phoned the talent agent once a week for over a year before she abandoned the idea that Melon was not the new Shirley Temple or Jane Withers.

At about the time Noreen was convinced Melon was not destined for child stardom, friends and strangers began to tell her that Melon was an unusually bright child. She spoke so clearly and used such big words. Why, maybe she had the makings of an Edna Ferber or Margaret Mitchell or Edna St. Vincent Millay.

Melon had no difficulty playing the role of prodigy her mother now assigned her. For a year she read and was read to, and learned how to print on pads of lined paper. Noreen sought indications of what she called, "sensitivity and temperament," in her daughter. Melon soon figured out what her mother was after and, without enthusiasm, spent hours being a high-strung bookworm while the other kids in the neighborhood ran through sprinklers or rode homemade scooters.

Her father didn't treat her as if she were an interesting new major appliance. He loved her the way she really was and talked to her the way he always had. He told her about his work. He made plumbing sound like an adventurous occupation. Melon loved to listen to her father, and he always responded to her attention.

After a year, when Melon didn't produce tangible evidence of brilliance, Noreen lost interest in her daughter as a potential genius. And, without a concrete designation, child actress or child prodigy, Noreen was unclear about just how to react to a five-and-half-year-old daughter.

Melon was relieved. Now she could make her own scooter and play with the other children.

The economy was picking up as a result of the war. Noreen bought a used car and drove it over the hills to browse in the shops along Wilshire and in Beverly Hills.

Bill Bowersox remained the same.

In February 1942, her mother told Melon a new baby would be coming to live with them, but not in the duplex. Her father was going to find a whole separate house for them. It would have three bedrooms and a rumpus room.

Before Bill Bowersox found the big new house he was drafted into the United States Army.

Melon's mother cried. One night she screamed. She made phone calls and wrote letters. The draft board was sorry, but, no.

Bill packed a small suitcase, talked quietly with Melon about how she would need to be a big help to Mommy and the new baby.

And then he was gone.

Charlie was born and her mother went into such a depression the three of them had to stay with Grandma and Grandpa Moore. On the day after Thanksgiving, Grandma Moore collapsed from exhaustion.

Melon's mother got out of bed and took her daughter and four-month-old son back to the duplex.

The next two years were a blur for Melon. Her mother became addicted to radio serials, root beer floats, long telephone conversations and long naps. Noreen's face grew puffy and her stomach looked the way it had before Charlie was born. She was no longer pretty.

Then everything changed.

Charlie caught measles and became so sick he had to be taken to the Childrens Hospital. Melon was sent over to stay with Mr. and Mrs. Cartwright, who lived in the other half of the duplex, so Noreen could stay at the hospital with Charlie.

After Charlie's crisis was over Noreen sat in the middle of the Cartwright's mohair love seat. She was thinner and didn't look dopey and bored. She spoke crisply and decisively.

"The measles have affected Charlie's vision," she said.

"Oh, my God," Mrs. Cartwright said. "How badly?"

"The doctors don't think he'll be completely blind. He'll need special training and special glasses, though."

"Oh, my God!"

During Charlie's last days in the hospital, Melon's mother thoroughly cleaned the duplex for the first time since her husband had gone off to war. She listened only to hourly news broadcasts, and when she talked on the phone it was to different people and in a new voice. Melon thought of it as her new fake-brave, bright voice.

Melon was afraid the day Charlie was brought home. She was afraid he'd be all withered and feeble and his eyes would be opaque and gray like those of the old collie down the street.

Noreen carried Charlie into the spotless house in her arms.

Melon gasped. Charlie looked healthier than he'd ever looked before. But he was wearing dark glasses held in place by a strip of elastic.

Noreen carefully set him down next to the sofa where Melon was sitting with her hands clenched on her coveralls. She held her breath. Poor little baby. Poor little Charlie.

But Charlie walked directly to Melon and climbed onto her lap. "Melon, Melon, Melon." He put his arms around her neck.

"Hi, Charlie. I missed you."

"Missed you."

Charlie slid down and ran into their bedroom and returned clutching his Popeye doll.

"Mommy," Melon said, "he's *not* blind! He can see! His Popeye doll wasn't where he usually keeps it. He *saw* it!"

"Of course he isn't *blind*. He has what a doctor called impaired vision." She lowered her voice. "He'll never be normal. He needs extraspecial care." She turned and looked through the window at some point in the distance. "I will see that he gets it."

While their mother was in the kitchen Melon lifted Charlie's dark glasses. His eyes looked exactly the way they had before he caught the measles. He looked straight at Melon and stuck his finger on the tip of her nose, just the way he usually did.

After Charlie had fallen asleep, Melon said, "Mommy, I think the doctor made a mistake. I think Charlie can see okay. All he does is knock his blocks over. But he did that before."

Noreen slapped Melon's face so hard her neck made a cracking sound. She grabbed the back of Melon's hair and held her face a foot from her own. "Charlie is *not* okay. Don't you ever say that again. You're just a jealous little bitch!"

By the time Charles Bowersox was three years old he was a spoiled, demanding brat who could do nothing for himself.

For the first time, Noreen was contented, poised and purposeful. She had finally found an identity for herself: The Mother of a Handicapped Child.

Melon was furious. Not because her mother paid little attention to her. The only times she *had* hadn't been much fun. Melon was angry because her mother was making a cripple out of Charlie. And she was having a marvelous time acting all martyred and brave. She even wrote her husband every week now.

Melon remembered her father in only a dreamlike form. She had stared at the enlarged snapshot of a young enlisted man on the mantel of the fake fireplace for so long she no longer saw the person in it, not as a real person. When life became most difficult she sat alone and talked out loud to him.

"Daddy, he doesn't *need* those dark glasses she keeps strapped on his head all the time."

Melon was doing well in school without trying. After school she changed into boy's jeans and polo shirt. She ran with a rowdy gang of six boys and two other girls who managed to get themselves barred from the local movie theater for their escapades during Saturday matinees.

When her father returned from the war Melon was almost ten.

His eyes were still gentle, but now they held a sadness.

He didn't know how to be with a fragile son he'd never before seen. And Charlie was terrified by the man who had come to live in their duplex.

Melon and her father sat together on the sofa, just as they had before he went away. He asked what she was doing these days and she was afraid to tell him. The flesh-and-blood man reacted in a variety of ways, often unpredictably. The face in the photograph had always seemed to respond as she expected and needed.

Once, during the night, Melon wakened and heard her mother moaning and then saying in a loud, frightened voice, "Stop it, Bill! You're hurting me! What's happened to you? Get off, goddammit!"

Then she heard her father's voice. She couldn't make out the words, but she could tell he was crying. In the soft darkness of her bed she felt no fear about her mother being hurt. It was the sound of her father crying that caused her stomach to go into a spasm.

Every night after dinner, while Noreen had her "Special quiet

85

time with Charlie," Melon sat as close to her father as she could. Sometimes he sat silently. Sometimes he talked about the crummy plumbing he was installing in the new tract houses. And sometimes his eyes took on a marvelous excitement and intensity, and he talked about his plans for going into business for himself. He drew Melon against his great chest and gave her a happy hug. "You just wait, honey. Man, oh, man. One of these days!" He would work with good architects and contractors who *cared,* and he would install copper pipes and beautiful Scandinavian faucets and handles.

By the time Melon entered junior high, her father's "One of these days," evenings occurred about once in three or four months.

She had counted on her father. She had shared his dreams and he had betrayed her by being weak and giving up.

Now Melon hated The Valley. She saw it as some kind of dusty enemy. She hated her house that was almost identical to every other house within blocks. She couldn't bear to watch her mother and Charlie. Her father staring.

She hated junior high. She hated the giggling girls in their Spaulding saddle shoes and cashmere sweater sets. She didn't want to be a tomboy any longer, but she couldn't get the hang of acting casually feminine.

Melon decided to invent a personality for herself, something eccentric. The problem was—eccentric, how?

She settled on being an intense liberal-intellectual. The idea came to her one Saturday afternoon in a deli in Westwood Village while she was eating a cheeseburger. She was able to observe four students from UCLA. They were intently discussing names like Marx and Sartre and Camus and Spengler. The young women wore neither saddle shoes nor hose; their feet were encased in heavy leather sandals. Their hair was in neither a pageboy nor a pompadour. Melon could detect no makeup of any sort. The young men, both of whom were good-looking, paid serious attention when either of the young women spoke. Melon memorized their appearance and manner. Before she finished the pickle on her plate she knew she had found an identity for herself.

She persuaded her mother to let her buy a pair of heavy sandals. She stopped wearing the small amount of lipstick she had been using and took to carrying a canvas book bag.

Her fellow students had no idea what Melon was doing or being. Her reputation preceded her to North Hollywood High, and by then Melon was hooked on the attention her new persona drew to her. She became more and more sure of herself in the role of brilliant oddball in a society of conformers. She never realized how close she came to being considered just plain weird. She was always saved by her genuinely witty sense of humor and her quick, often bitchy reactions. By her junior year she had assembled a small crew of students who could be counted upon to hang on her every word. Melon was smart. Melon was fast. Melon was unflappable.

In her senior year she sailed through her college boards with the highest scores ever recorded by a student at her school. Her counselor was ecstatic when she poured over the offers from colleges around the country.

Mrs. Keene, the counselor, studied the petite, alert young woman. "You've had acceptances from the best of the lot. What are your goals?"

"I'll need a full scholarship, Mrs. Keene."

"I'm sure that won't be a problem."

"Okay, then, my first goal is to get as far away from the San Fernando Valley as I can. Then I'll consider the next ones."

Smith College assigned Diana Hathaway of Georgetown, Washington, D.C. (winters), and Lyford Cay, the Bahamas (summers), and Mary Ellen Bowersox of North Hollywood, California, as roommates for their freshman year. Diana had done her junior and senior high-school years in Lausanne and had wanted very much to bring her bay gelding, Seraglio, to Smith with her. Her father objected. After all, as the publisher of one of Washington's two liberal morning newspapers, it wouldn't look right for his daughter to receive special privileges. No matter that she had lived a life of nothing *but* special privilege. It was now time for Diana Hathaway to begin to learn a little self-discipline and humility.

Melon found her new roommate buried in a heap of cashmere sweaters of every conceivable hue in front of three steamer trunks, open and spewing their contents over the floor of their se-cond-story room.

Silk scarves, heavy pleated skirts of the most elegant wool, rid-ing breeches, boots with brass spurs, satin evening skirts were heaped on one bed. Melon felt as if an elegant Wilshire Boulevard boutique had exploded around her. She had never before seen such personal material splendor. Almost all of it was obviously brand-new.

Diana herself was draped across the other bed, running her long graceful hands through her wheat-colored hair, a mass of gold bracelets jingling.

"Oh, thank God!" she said when she saw Melon. "You look civi-lized."

Melon set down the two heavy pieces of Samsonite her mother had given her before she left, frozen with the prospect of unpack-ing her meager wardrobe in the presence of such opulence.

"Well, thanks. You look . . . rich."

Diana waved a crash of clanking gold at the array. "Mummy goes berserk every time she faces getting rid of me for another year. I'll never use half this stuff. Hope you can. We aren't the same size. But anyone can wear a lot of this junk." She tossed Mel-on a heavy cashmere sweater.

"Sure, if my name was Delon Howersox," she said, tossing it back after she had noted the small triangular monogram on the front.

Diana grinned. She was going to like this strange, dark little girl. She was different.

"What do you think your major will be?" Diana asked, rolling off the bed and sitting cross-legged on the rug. She started absent-mindedly to sort through a pile of exotic lingerie the color and texture of whipping cream.

"I asked for world beating, but it looks as if I'll be stuck with poli sci. How about you?"

"Oh, God, who cares? It boils down to men. Mummy's got this incredible debut planned for the Sulgrave Club in Washington for Christmas where I'm supposed to be auctioned off to some chinless wonder. I want to get as much mileage out of my life as I can before I'm sold into Boredom Bondage."

Plans for Diana's debut seemed to permeate their first fall

together at Smith. There were nightly screaming sessions from the pay phone down the hall over everything from invitations to the merits of Meyer Davis versus some obscure jazz combo Diana wanted. It was expected of her, and as a daughter of a family of position and wealth, she knew better than to be totally uncooperative.

Diana's fondness for her smoothed over a great many social problems Melon might have otherwise encountered. Melon's clothes weren't right. She had that hard, flat California clip to her speech, and her sarcastic wisecracking did not endear her to most of her classmates. Being the best pal of tawny, long-legged Diana Hathaway was pure luck. And Diana was amused by defending Melon to irate "insultees."

Melon had instantly known that it would be impossible to compete with Diana. She simply possessed too much, she knew all about a world Melon had only read about. Had Diana been closer to her own background Melon would have locked horns with her immediately and tried to cut her down to size. But she had seen at their first meeting this would be impossible. She also saw that the heavy sandals had to go, as did some of her stated radical views—they sounded foolish and would do nothing for her here. This was a different planet and called for a *new* identity, and until she could carve it out of the thin, crisp air of the Connecticut Valley or form it from the waters of Paradise Pond, she would have to keep her mouth shut, stand back and wait.

For the first time in her life she began carefully to read and analyze books: determine what the words actually meant, rather than memorize and confidently spout selected phrases.

Still, Melon craved the limelight. She knew it shone on girls like Diana—automatically. The fine old family name, the aura evoked by her father's power and wealth, and the *appearance*. Diana had no need to extend herself the way Melon did: her teeth were so straight and translucent you could candle eggs through them; her hair, eyes, skin—her whole body seemed to radiate a golden glow. She was in absolute contrast to the small, dark, gauche girl from California.

Diana Hathaway and Melon Bowersox held one thing in common besides their mutual fascination with each other's difference. They were both slobs. Diana's sloppiness was born of eighteen years of certainty that someone would pick up after her, and ignorance of how to do anything for herself except wash her own hair. Melon was unkempt because she saw it as a form of rebellion, and a cover: people, she assumed, would not be able to tell the difference between a cheap wrinkled skirt and an expensive wrinkled one. So she maintained an "I don't give a shit" attitude toward her belongings, as well as everyone else's. And she would not be a freak for her mother or a Scandinavian sink fixture for her father. More than once the housemother had to report Diana and Melon. Something about the school's aversion to dirt. Diana assumed if the mess became bad enough someone would come in and clean it up. Melon didn't give a damn. She was certain that anything she owned beyond the contents of her head was worthless.

The Christmas holidays loomed ominously in both their lives. Diana dreaded the tedious social rounds awaiting her in Washington. Melon knew there was no way in hell she could afford a trip home to California. And if she had had the fare, she had no desire to spend ten days staring at her father staring or to listen to Charlie whining and her mother playing cheerful martyr.

"Come with me, Mel," Diana began pleading shortly after Thanksgiving.

"You've got to be kidding. What do I know about that group of yours? I don't have the right clothes. I'd feel weird."

"Mel, for God's sake. You'd be a smash. Mummy would think you were from Mars, but Daddy would eat you up. He loves free souls. And don't worry about clothes. I have a charge at Garfinkel's, and we can clean them out in three hours before we even go home. Daddy always sends a car to the airport and we'll just have Crandall stop us off on F Street and lay waste to the place."

"Do you really think I could get away with it?"

"We'll kill 'em," her roommate said.

Until that Christmas, the vague hunger in Melon had been painful and undefined. Those two weeks in Diana's world not only crystallized her personality, they sealed into the crevices of her psyche a need so overwhelming that it was to govern her life from then on.

Diana felt her parents' friends and associates and their offspring were dull, pretentious snobs who could be counted

90

upon to do absolutely nothing interesting or unexpected. Everyone would wear the proper clothes, use the proper phrases and gestures. Diana was grateful to Melon for accompanying her south. "God, I know you'll be bored to death. I really appreciate this."

Melon was not bored.

She was not bored when the Hathaways' chauffeur, Crandall, deposited their suitcases and a dozen dove-gray Garfinkel boxes in the front hall of Diana's home. The Federal-style mansion had been decorated for the season. Great, thick garlands of evergreens twisted up the winding banister. Tiny red and white velvet birds perched among the crystal droplets of the enormous Williamsburg chandelier that dominated the center hall. Off to her left, through high polished doors, reposed the most enormous and symmetrical Christmas tree she had ever seen. It was laden with what appeared to be thousands of sparkling jewels. Gifts were heaped beneath it, each carefully wrapped in either red or white lacquered paper and great red satin bows.

"Dee, pinch me. I've died and gone to heaven," Melon gasped.

Diana shrugged and handed her coat to a waiting maid. "Come on, Mel, I'll show you around after we dress. Daddy is a fiend about everyone being on time for drinks. Crandall, will you see that Miss Bowersox's luggage and the boxes get up to my room?"

Melon was introduced to Diana's family at cocktails in the library before dinner. The Hathaways always dressed for dinner, and Diana had carefully selected a simple A-line cocktail dress of deep blue shantung for Melon. Melon had to admit she looked wonderful.

Diana's mother, a slim, patrician blonde whose hair, eyes, skin and teeth all seemed to be the same color, was polite, but just a shade patronizing. "Any friend of our Dee Dee's . . ."

Diana's father was pleasant and direct with Melon. If he was disappointed in his daughter's choice of houseguest, Melon could not detect it. Seth Hathaway exuded self-confidence and authority, even when he was seated in a brocade armchair silently observing the women over the rim of his glass. And when he spoke! The timbre and inflections of his words conveyed one proclamation— power. A strong man possessed of true power.

Melon had never before encountered elemental power.

91

Then she realized Mrs. Hathaway, in her own way, also possessed power.

During the next days she saw, felt and heard evidence of power from the time she awoke until she fell asleep.

The Hathaways lived in a mansion in Georgetown, the house where Jeannine Magnuson Hathaway had been born. It did not contain Scandinavian bathroom appliances; rather, heavy, ornate, hand-cast brass fixtures that gleamed from daily scrubbings and polishings. In the morning she was served breakfast from a tray set with silver and china as she sat propped between cool Porthault sheets. She gazed at the single long-stemmed rose on her tray and poured her coffee from a Limoges carafe. Melon did not know the linen was Porthault or the china Limoges, but she knew it was special and used as "everyday." No one was trying to impress her.

The first week was a blur.

Dinners in the soft glow of polished mahogany where she was seated, one evening, between a Supreme Court Justice and a dynamic young Senator from Michigan. Parties in other mansions where she danced with young men who breathed in her ear and tried to paw her in darkened libraries and sitting rooms. The young men from the various corners of the Ivy League became a hazy forest of dark suits, straight teeth and identical faces.

On Christmas Eve, after a "family dinner," after the grandfather clock had struck midnight, Seth Hathaway took Melon by the hand as she was about to lift her fifth Dom Perignon from the butler's tray. He led her out onto the icy, moonlit terrace. The Potomac River below was a ribbon of black ice.

"Miss Bowersox, Mrs. Hathaway and I are so pleased you could be with us for Christmas. Diana's written a great deal about you."

"Mr. Hathaway, thank you for having me." She slurred the last three words and reached for the marble railing.

"Please call me Seth. I'll be more comfortable."

"Call you Seth?" She weaved a bit to steady herself and found her face against the tucked front of his dress shirt.

"If it weren't for you, Melon, I don't think Diana would have stayed at Smith for a month. And I suppose that's because you're different from the girls and young women she's known all her life. How do *you* like being at a Seven Sisters school?"

"I'm afraid all I'm going to get out of Smith is a fantastic education."

The publisher smiled. "Diana is extremely fond of you. She thinks you're one of the most clever and ambitious young people she's ever encountered. Of course, most of her contemporaries are singularly unclever and unambitious."

Four glasses of champagne caused Melon to interpret a mild swipe at Diana as an insult to herself.

"Mr. Hathaway," she said evenly, "I *am* clever and I *am* ambitious, and I'm sick of sitting in classrooms filled with a bunch of spoiled brats who've been given a blank check on the world. All I've gotten out of one semester in a college I probably shouldn't be in is my friendship with Dee. The rest's been bullshit. I'll tell you what I've deduced in three months. Wordsworth wasn't a great nature poet. He had clammy hands and no sense of humor. Rousseau didn't bring nearly as much reform to education as he did hatred to intelligent women. The Age of Elegance wasn't all wit and charm, but some Whig duchess telling her footman to stop rubbing his great greasy belly against the back of her chair. If there was one thing I brought to Smith that's been reinforced there, it's that you have to kick through the shit of life if you want to see what's underneath. Once you do that, it's yours, if you want what's there badly enough." Melon hiccuped, surprised by her outburst, but higher on this encounter than on the champagne.

Seth Hathaway raised one eyebrow, then smiled.

"So where does that insight leave you, Melon?"

"Well, at least I know I want to be head shitkicker."

"Melon, let me tell you something," he said softly, laying a massive hand over her wrist. In the moonlight she could see the reddish-blond hairs on his fingers and the back of his hand, and the brilliant white of his cuffs against the black velvet of his dinner jacket. She was astonished by the power and eroticism of that hand, the heat flowing from it. "Don't push so hard against life. People see more than you think they do. Be a bit more generous with them."

"Why? So they'll like me?"

"Don't you want people to like you?"

"I gave that up when I discovered it wasn't going to happen."

"Then what do you want people to feel about you?"

93

"I want them to be afraid of me."

The pressure of Seth Hathaway's hand increased. Melon felt he could crush her bones if he wished to. Then, slowly he released his grip and slowly slid both hands up her arms. He let his hands rest for a moment on her shoulders, cupping them, before dropping them to his sides.

"Melon, come and see me after you've finished with Smith. Whenever that is."

After the "Merry Christmases" and "good nights" were said, Melon went to her room and slid between the wonderful sheets.

She did not sleep. She stared at the darkness and saw Seth Hathaway's hands. She felt them moving over her body, her face, through her hair, touching every part of her, hurting her.

Those hands possessed power.

Her nipples hardened, her groin ached, heat flowed down her thighs.

He was the man she wanted.

She had met dynamic, successful men since she had been in the capital. Of them all, Seth alone possessed true power.

Oh, yes. Power flowed through the man's hands. It was measurable. She would never forget, now that she knew.

Melon saw little of Seth Hathaway during the remainder of her stay in Washington.

He saw Diana and Melon to the airport in his limousine when they left for Boston. During the drive the three of them chatted and laughed about the past two weeks.

As Melon slid through the door Crandall was holding open, Seth caught her wrist gently.

"Miss Bowersox," he said quietly, "if you really want people to be afraid of you, you've made a formidable beginning."

Flustered, Melon said, "Who's afraid of me?"

"I am," the publisher replied.

Melon asked Seth Hathaway for an appointment on the day she received her diploma from Smith. She had neither seen nor spoken with him privately since the January morning at the airport three and a half years before. After the end of their freshman year, Melon and Diana had found different friends and enthusiasms.

She was not granted the appointment. She was notified, instead, by Ernie Prescott, that she could begin work as a reporter in one week. She was to report directly to him.

When Melon occasionally saw Seth Hathaway in the Herald Building, she received a polite nod. After she had been with the paper for five months, he phoned her at her apartment.

"Melon," he said, "I want to give you my private number. I want you to phone me when you have something that might be of special interest to me."

"How will I know, Seth?"

"You'll know."

She wanted to beg him to come over and crush her with his hands and mouth. Instead she said, "Yes, I'll know."

He had given her the number and hung up.

She had called him exactly six times.

Each time he had said, "Thank you, Melon."

On this warm morning in July 1961 Melon wondered if pursuit of the Jane Connor presence in the E.O.B. could lead to a special Seth call. Between bites of pizza she dialed eight numbers. No one knew a thing about Jane Connor's job. She slammed down the receiver after the last call.

"Crap!"

Manny Manning would be worth exactly zero to Seth. But she had to interview the man.

Wally took his pictures.

Melon laughed at Manny's stories over an expensive lunch at the Jockey Club. When he got to the, "But, seriously, now . . ." Melon listened with a show of intense interest, jotting in her notebook.

The man had lived through a rough life. And he was still trim and vigorous at fifty-five. He was a friend and gin rummy companion to some of the biggest names in show business.

"Tell me about the real Frank Sinatra and Bob Hope," she said as she laid her hand, palm down, on his upper thigh. Melon felt the Italian silk fabric of his trousers tighten.

"Why don't we go up to my room for another drink and I'll tell you all about Frank and Bob and Johnny and Ed and even Marlon, if you can believe that."

Manny told her about Frank and Bob and Sammy and even Marlon as they walked from the restaurant to the elevator.

They didn't bother to close the drapes or pull back the bed-spread.

Manny was virile and eager.

In the midst, Melon flipped him over so that she was astride. For a moment Manny paused and studied Melon's face. Then he smiled a smile of almost frightening comprehension and grabbed her hips and buttocks. "It's that way, huh?" His thrusts were more forceful than before. Melon met them, her head flopping like a rag doll's.

The pain increased, the rhythm speeded. Melon caught her lower lip in her teeth and tried to watch Manny's face. With one final, agonizing plunge Manny ejaculated and Melon almost screamed. His eyes rolled upward and the lids closed as his mouth fell open and slack.

Melon didn't know if what she felt at that moment was an orgasm. It was deep pleasure of a sort.

Chapter Four

Billie Claire

Billie Claire plopped a second can of Campbell's mushroom soup into the Dansk casserole simmering on the front burner and watched the pale soup ooze down over the browning chicken.

Miles Buford had especially requested her favorite Single Girl Friday Night Special. She had been relieved. It was one of only three dishes she did well for company. In fifteen minutes the casserole would be finished and ready for the refrigerator, affording her plenty of time to get to the city room by nine.

Nice, peaceful, funny Miles. She felt completely at ease with him. He had been the *Herald*'s culture vulture for seventeen years, and it looked as if he was set up there for life, attending screenings, plays and concerts and writing thorough, thoughtful reviews.

He had come to dinner in her comfortable one-bedroom apartment four times now. And he had given Billie Claire astute and tactful suggestions about how she could nicely decorate it on her *Herald* salary. He told her to throw out all those knickknacks that "scream I'm single and broke." He helped her pick out a big deep green rug and arrange the time payments. Miles had recommended such artful groupings of baskets and plants that the place looked much larger than it was. He had found, he wouldn't say where, an enormous Peacock chair, and made her throw out the two backbreaking, Danish-modern, foam-rubber ones. Then he had her pile batik pillows everywhere.

Now Billie Claire had a chic apartment and she kept it spotless.

When she and Miles were together for dinner they discussed plays and movies they had seen or wanted to see, the shows at the Corcoran and the National Gallery. He came to her apartment to watch the Miss America Pageant and they made themselves almost sick laughing and wisecracking. They made an irrevocable date to watch the Academy Awards together.

Miles was lonely. His lover of three years had left his job with the State Department and gone to work for a San Francisco decorating firm. Miles had been devastated. "Coming out meant more to him than I did," he said with a catch in his sonorous bass voice.

Miles Buford talked to Billie Claire about Edward as he had to no one else. Billie Claire realized this was a necessity and a relief. She listened intently, first from curiosity, and finally with tears of sympathy in her own eyes.

Love was such a mystery. The sex of the lovers was beside the point.

Her own experiences had been, without exception, briefly joyful, then bewilderingly painful. She could only imagine the desolation Miles was experiencing. Over three years with one lover! The men she fell in love with seemed to disappear in less than a month.

Love was a mystery, but sex wasn't.

Sex was more natural and beautiful than eating. Anyone could sit down at a table and be served marvelous delicacies. Ah, but when two naked bodies came together, a person could *give*. The possibilities for giving were limitless. That was the delight. Hands, tongue, breath, lips, mouth. The scent of physical excitement.

The night before, Joe from the Promotion Department had lain on her bed, flat on his back as if being crucified. In the course of arousing a man, she became aroused. Joe, like most men, enjoyed fondling and suckling her breasts. Her huge, firm breasts. Breasts her mother told her were impossible and vulgar.

Billie Claire gave an involuntary shiver as she thought about all she and Joe had done last night. She almost cut herself as she sliced liver into tiny cubes for her cat, Phideaux, thinking of Joe, waiting for the casserole.

98

She would never sleep with Miles. She did vaguely understand his desire for a male body. The firm muscles, the erect penis, excited her also. Why shouldn't it excite another man? She had no difficulty figuring out how men could have sex together and how they could love each other, want to be close, share their lives. She also realized how difficult such a relationship could be. Especially in Washington, D.C.

Miles didn't need to tell her to respect his sexuality and not to try to "convert" him. He enjoyed her as a special person, as a friend. And that was a comfort.

She knew their relationship would never result in connection. Fusion. The obliteration, for a moment, of loneliness.

Billie Claire was at her desk in the *Herald* city room ten minutes early that morning. She waited until Ernie Prescott put down both of the phones he had been listening to simultaneously as he handed out assignments to *senior* reporters. The story she had worked so hard on, her three pages on a report of the Montgomery County Sewage Committee had been pared down to one ten-line paragraph and placed on the fifth page of the second section of that day's edition. It was completely missing from the following editions.

Two years out of Columbia Journalism School and here she sat writing up "citz" meetings and watching the world go by. But at least she was here drawing a paycheck. At least she had graduated from copygirl and its attendant humiliations.

She approached the city editor's desk.

"Mr. Prescott, remember that dentist who shot himself recently out in Montgomery County? Well, I've got a lead on it. It seems that wasn't a simple suicide. I'd like to follow the story up."

"What the hell do you want from me, Hutchins? I've got three veteran reporters who can do that stuff. Besides, it was probably just that, simple suicide, or we'd have gotten the word here by now."

"Yes, sir. But you see, a friend of mine had an abortion by that guy and from what I've learned I'm almost certain he was involved in gambling as well as abortions. I'd really like to follow it up."

She had made him angry now. She knew she was being presumptuous. Damn it, though, she had to *try*.

"Hutchins, we're short on the dictation bank for the early shift.

You take over." He dismissed her and turned to take a jangling phone.

"But, Mr. Prescott . . ."

"Beat it, honey," he growled around his cigar. "Who the hell does she think she is?" he muttered to no one in particular.

Billie Claire felt her cheeks burn. Sweat formed on her upper lip. Who the hell did she think she was? Those terrible words. She hadn't heard them for years and she was surprised they could still evoke the same old response—uncertainty and panic.

Boiling with rage now and knowing she was pushing her luck, she persisted. She waited until he slammed down the phone again and said, "Mr. Prescott, I told Ann Adams about my lead and she said I should . . ."

Ernie Prescott had had it. "You listen to me, goddammit. Ann Adams doesn't hand out assignments around here. I do! Now, I want you over in Chevy Chase to cover a board of realtors luncheon by noon. There will be two speakers, one from the board and one from the Urban League."

"Yes, sir. But after I turn in my copy on the luncheon, then can I look into the dentist thing and his . . .?"

"NO!" Ernie Prescott closed his eyes, inhaled deeply and sat back in his chair. "Hutchins, I realize you aren't stimulated by most of your assignments. Very few reporters are stimulated by their assignments. The great Ann Adams is seldom stimulated by her assignments. But stimulating or not, certain events and people must be covered. What we assign you is based on experience and information not available to you." He was mouthing each word separately, as if he were talking to a slow child. "Now, move it! I need your copy before three. You can phone it in. Meantime, get on the bank and give Shirley a hand before those phones come off the wall."

Billie Claire walked to the dictation bank and placed the headset around her head. She sat glumly for half an hour taking only two calls and typing out the copy read to her by reporters out around the city. She ripped the last sheet from the typewriter and glanced at the clock at the end of the room. One hour to make it out over the District line. God, this was tedious. When would she ever get a shot at something she could put her name to?

She returned to her own desk to gather up her notebook and purse.

100

Ernie Prescott was right. She knew he was. There were priorities on a metropolitan daily. She had never held any illusions about being a reporter. She knew it wouldn't be like *Front Page.* Dammit, though, all she wanted was *one break.*

The elevator doors slid open and Ann Adams strode forth, bouncing off a pensive Billie Claire.

Ann adjusted her wide-brimmed lavender hat and frowned down at the young reporter. "Say there, Billie Claire, are you coming or going or just standing around?"

"I'm sorry, Ann. I suppose I wasn't paying attention."

"Having problems?"

"Prescott just laid into me. I guess I pushed him too hard on that dentist's suicide."

"What did he do, give you another Montgomery County thriller?"

Billie Claire nodded. "Not only *that,* he also told me to lay off the dentist story. I've got a sneaking feeling he may assign one of the big guns to it, now that I've tipped him off that there may be more to the original story. Damn it, Ann, when am I going to get a shot at something that will make a difference around here?"

"Where are you headed?"

"Chevy Chase. Some board of realtors lunch with an Urban Leaguer coming to yell and scream to no avail, I suppose."

"They won't start talking until after one thirty. Let me drop something off at my desk and we can grab a quick cup of coffee. I'm a little shaggy around the edges this morning."

"Okay. Thanks. I'll meet you in the ladies' room."

Billie Claire scurried past the city room front doors and pushed through the double doors to the rest room.

Ann's undeclared sponsorship and friendship, as usual, took away some of the frustrations of working for Ernie Prescott.

"Who do I think I am, indeed!" Billie Claire spoke to the washroom mirror. "I'm a twenty-five-year-old reporter on one of the country's biggest and best dailies and I'm having coffee with Ann Hawkins Adams in the *Herald*'s cafeteria before going out on assignment—that's who I am, goddammit."

The face in the mirror mocked the brave assertion.

The face in the mirror, she had been told often enough, was *plain.* Not ugly, without *distinction.* The eyes were a shade too small, the mouth a bit too wide and full, the nose too flat. The skin tended to be overly oily in the summer and dry and chapped in the winter—no matter what makeup she tried. The smile crinkles at the corners of her eyes and a deep dimple in one cheek never showed in Billie Claire's mirror because when she gazed at her face she was invariably frowning and searching for all the flaws her mother had matter-of-factly listed.

Consuela Grenville Hutchins held no such feelings when she gazed into her mirrors. Her mirrors reflected back an image so exquisite that Mrs. Hutchins' dressing table was her favorite place for deep contemplation.

It was there that Billie Claire had found her mother one morning when she was five years old. She had watched her mother carefully applying the creams and emollients that seemed to be unnecessary to her already dazzling beauty.

"Mommy, does that creamy stuff make you beautiful?"

"No, Billie Claire, it just helps keep me this way."

Not satisfied, Billie Claire waited until her mother had left on one of her mysterious "appointments" and took her place on the satin-cushioned stool. For hours she played with the creams, the pencils, the brushes, the vivid paints. Digging her fingers deep into magnificently scented jars, smearing, tasting, painting, until she had attained the appearance of a tiny circus clown. She was just finishing the application of a fourth coat of dark brown mascara to her stubby lashes when she heard her mother screaming.

"Get out! Get out! What are you doing, you hideous child?"

Billie Claire was immobilized.

Her mother grasped her by her thin, unruly hair and pulled her to the floor, then she brought her hand with its large, emerald-cut diamond slashing across Billie Claire's face.

"How dare you touch my things! How dare you! Who do you think you are?" her mother shrieked.

She received the blows without a word and curled into a small ball on the bedroom rug until her mother became exhausted. Finally, she felt herself being lifted to the edge of the bed. Her mother was bent over her, her long fingernails biting into her upper arms.

"You listen to me, Billie Claire Hutchins. You are never to

touch my things again. Nothing is going to make you look like anything but what you are. Plain, plain, plain. You are a plain child. You will be a plain woman."

She was impaled by her mother's eyes until her mother chose to release her. Until she was dismissed.

Consuela Hutchins dismissed people with an Olympian flick. Consuela Hutchins saw herself as royalty.

She was an aristocrat, American-style. Her grandfather had made a fortune in textile and land speculation. Her father had graduated from Princeton and married the belle of Baltimore and set her up in a town house in Manhattan, then he bought himself a seat on the New York Stock Exchange. Consuela's coming-out party was held at the Waldorf-Astoria in 1925. In January of 1930 Thomas Grenville shot himself, unable to face the consequences of the Crash the year before. When he died, all that remained of his fortune was the town house on East Sixty-eighth Street. Consuela's mother managed to sell the lovely building to a diamond merchant who had been untouched by events on Wall Street.

Consuela Grenville, bewildered and extraordinarily beautiful, possessed a pleasant alto voice, and like some other young women of good breeding who had fallen victim to the times, found a job singing in a small but smart supper club in the East Forties.

At the end of the second week of her engagement there Thaddeus Hutchins (né Horthy) sat at a table less than six feet from the hem of Consuela's black-sequined evening gown.

Thaddeus was forty-two years old. He had been too busy making money in, first, demolition, and then construction, to give much thought to women. When he had, he sought flashy show girls.

Consuela Grenville was the most exquisite woman he had ever seen. She was a real *lady*.

Thaddeus bought an eight-carat diamond with two baguettes on either side. He had Van Cleef & Arpels put it in a small morocco leather box and pushed the box across the table at "21" the following night, after Consuela had finished at her club. It took Consuela five days to accept the ring and Thaddeus as her husband.

The man was a short, muscular peasant. He had not even completed high school. Even so, Thaddeus had worked hard and he was very, very rich. His parents preferred to continue to live in a small, two-story house in Queens where Mr. Horthy owned a butcher shop.

Thaddeus idolized the dainty blonde with large, lavender eyes and a regal voice and bearing. He would give her whatever she desired. Anything. Even a separate bedroom. Champagne for breakfast, if she wished.

Consuela adored champagne.

She said yes.

After a brief honeymoon in Paris (because Thaddeus could spare only two weeks), Consuela settled into the ten-bedroom house Thaddeus bought in Tarrytown and began planning parties.

Thaddeus was not a sensitive or gentle lover. Consuela's moans did not arise from ecstasy as her husband assumed.

But there *was* champagne for breakfast, and tiny packages from Van Cleef & Arpels and Tiffany's hidden under her napkin.

And then there was the birth of Nicholas.

When he was a year old the world could see he was a Grenville. Nicky was bright and quick and his face was a tiny duplicate of his mother's own perfect oval.

Consuela's second pregnancy was difficult from the first.

The product was a daughter. And she was a Horthy. A miniature peasant. Consuela didn't object when her husband named the child Billie Claire (after the dim memory of a show girl who had once done the most amazing things with her tongue). As far as Consuela was concerned, the child's name wouldn't matter.

Billie Claire loved her beautiful mother and her gruff and forthright father. She grew up loving her handsome brother also, but she was never certain how any of them felt about her.

Her father was seldom home. She knew he was busy working in New York City or in New Jersey or Connecticut. Her mother was seldom home either, but her whereabouts were often a mystery to Billie Claire and Nicky. The household help seemed to know where she went all dressed up at odd hours, and she had once heard Stella, the cook, muttering, "Mr. Fredlow, supposed to be the family lawyer, he's gonna mess up this home."

She did observe that her mother frequently went out at night in beautiful, long dresses and tiny silver sandals, or spent a lot of time at the country club to which the Hutchinses held membership. She also noticed that many of the parties that were held in the big house when Thaddeus was away seemed to have a number of unattached men around who paid a great deal of attention to Consuela. Once a week Consuela put on her black Christian Dior coat with the tucked waist and the big puffy sleeves, a tiny black velvet hat with a tight veil drawn across her high cheekbones and drove the Packard into the city, not to return until late the following day.

One evening Billie Claire was invited to a slumber party at Liz Sweeley's house. At 1:00 A.M. she developed a fever and was bundled home by Mr. Sweeley. On her way past her mother's bedroom she heard strange noises and peeped through the slit between the hinges. She saw the back of her mother's silver-blond head moving rhythmically up and down. As Billie Claire leaned closer she saw that her mother's mouth was firmly affixed to the penis of a young man who was a complete stranger. The sight baffled her: she had never before seen her mother exerting so much energy on anything.

While Consuela was cool and abrupt with Billie Claire, she was openly flirtatious with Nicky. The boy was obsessed with his mother. He would beg to brush her long hair while she was dressing to go out. He sat in the room for hours when she was entertaining a guest. He spied on her after she finally told him to leave the room and close the door. He listened to her phone conversations on the library extension. He read her mail and pawed through her purse. He held wineglasses to the wall and tried to use two mirrors to see under closed and locked doors. And he teased and made insinuating remarks to his mother. Rather than flying into a rage as she would have had Billie Claire attempted such flippancy, she hugged the boy and tousled his hair and kissed his face with little pecking kisses until he squealed and squirmed with excitement.

Consuela and Nicky had a special way of talking with each other. A way of communicating that made Billie Claire feel utterly left out. And whenever she tried to emulate them, she said the wrong words with the wrong inflections. Nicky would fall silent and her mother would fix her eyes on Billie Claire and say, "How dare you say such a thing to me. Who do you think you are?"

"I'm Billie Claire," she would say, feeling desperate and confused. "I'm your little girl."

Consuela's response to those words depended on the time of day, her mood, where she had been the night before, where she was going, and with whom.

"You certainly are your *father's* child," was her most frequent response. Seldom, far too seldom, she said, "Of course you're my little girl. Come let me give you a big squeeze."

Billie Claire yearned for those times when her mother, her beautiful mother, opened her arms to her.

She became so adept at reading her mother's moods that she could tell by a quick glance at Consuela's profile whether she dared to speak to her or not. Her life became a perpetual vigil in which she tried to judge her mother's needs and wants and moods and the best way to respond to them. She knew it was a chancy, ruleless game, but she continued to try to play it. The biggest obstacle to staying in was that what pleased her mother one day would not necessarily please her the next.

The only way to deal with her mother, Billie Claire finally realized, was to be always calm, even-voiced, direct and patient. She tried to overcome Consuela's inconsistency with total consistency of her own. Nicky could be sarcastic, sullen and demanding. Her father could shout, slam doors and threaten. The cook could pout and lecture. Consuela permitted it all.

For reasons she could never understand, Billie Claire could never complain or demonstrate anger, even impatience, toward her mother. Occasionally even Nicky asked why she put up with it.

"Because I know, deep down, she really loves me, and she's only the way she is with me because of the way I look," she told her thirteen-year-old brother.

"Oh, come on, Billie, you're not so bad," Nicky said, embarrassed.

"But it's true. She's never forgiven me for not being beautiful."

"Well," Nicky shrugged, "she should be thankful not to have the competition."

Nicky went away to prep school when he was fourteen. Billie Claire stayed in Tarrytown. Nicky made friends, did very well with his studies and after a short time was the center of the school's most select clique. The boys at Exeter knew nothing about Consuela Grenville Hutchins' "friends" or Grandfather Horthy's butcher shop. They could see Nick Hutchins had plenty of money and he had a style and bearing that made him one of them.

106

The students at Billie Claire's day school heard their parents' gossip. No one was mean to her. She simply wasn't included in nonschool activities.

Her friends, the few girls she ate lunch with, accepted her as a kind, plodding, unassuming presence. She listened attentively and asked no favors.

By the time she was twelve and a half, Billie Claire had sprouted pubic hair and her breasts had begun to form. By the time she was thirteen and a half she was wearing a 34 D bra and her world began to change. She noticed it first on the streets: remarks under the breath from men, sometimes loud shouts from trucks. She was elated. Could no one, suddenly, see her plain face? Could they see nothing but her blossoming chest? She didn't care. Those men saw something they liked about her and they were letting her know it.

Meanwhile, Consuela was outraged by Billie Claire's breasts. "The only hope for you was the right clothes. But designers don't *design* for big bosoms. They never have and they never will."

Ironically, as the breasts began to bring her the first positive attention she had ever received, she developed acne—acne so repellent that even the Manhattan dermatologist Consuela dragged her to would shake his head, defeated.

In her senior year she was accepted by Barnard. She had never been asked out by a boy, although many had stopped by her locker to chat briefly and attempt to rub up against her breasts. Once a group of them at the country club had grabbed her in the pool and twisted off her bathing suit top. But not one of them had ever asked her out.

She did know about sex, though, and it fascinated her. The pleasure she learned to derive from masturbation was her one secret joy.

She had listened to teachers in physical education and senior life classes allude to self-abuse and autoeroticism as something natural, or unnatural, depraved, or "just a phase." Taking her usual complete notes, Billie Claire observed and noted that every teacher who touched on the subject of sex was distinctly uncomfortable. They whizzed through schematic drawings of vaginas, penises (never erect), fallopian tubes, dropping eggs and desperate tadpole sperms.

Evidently sexual intercourse between a man and a woman was

107

normal; between a husband and wife who loved each other, to be sure. Because terrible anguish lay waiting for a girl, especially, if one of those miniature tadpoles connected with one of the giant eggs.

You must wait.

The mysteries will be revealed at the proper time.

After courtship, after college, after a good solid job and a bridal shower. Then it would be okay to explore parts of one's body or to have someone, one's husband, explore them with one.

In her own systematic and thorough way, Billie Claire had already discovered and explored those easily accessible parts of her body. And she found, with no difficulty at all, that if properly touched and manipulated (it was instinct), an exquisite tension built and was followed by a wondrous release.

She could achieve this alone, in bed, in the bathroom or leaning hard against the washing machine in the laundry room.

She felt no guilt, no sense of self-loathing.

But she did feel a kind of sadness.

How much better to be doing and being done to with another person. The closeness of another body.

The only evil Billie Claire perceived was aloneness.

However, if one was a plain-faced, shy, enormous-breasted sixteen year old, one found pleasure and release as best one could.

Better that, she felt, than to lie awake, arms stiff, fists clenched, staring at the darkness for hours because a withered gym teacher mumbled about the possibilities of "harming one's body." Billie Claire knew what she was doing harmed nothing and no one. If anything, it made her body feel better.

The first man who made love to Billie Claire was the Hutchins' three-times-a-week gardener-handyman.

He was hardly Lady Chatterley's virile Mellors. Luther Metz was an arthritic gnome of fifty-five whose fingernails were permanently dirty from thirty years of mulching rosebushes.

The seduction of Billie Claire Hutchins didn't warrant the word. When, in the large, dimly lit garage, Luther first brushed against and then began to nuzzle her breasts, Billie Claire reached for his crotch as if it were as natural as scratching a mosquito bite.

They completed the act in the back seat of Consuela's Packard. Sweating and silent. They were both grateful. What was there to say?

Billie Claire and Luther made love daily, even during her menstrual period, for three months, until she left for New York City and Barnard.

At no time did they speak about what they did together or anything else. The old man suckled at her breasts like a famished child and the girl examined his penis and testicles, fascinated.

How marvelously simple and straightforward sex was.

During the days before Billie Claire left home for college, her mother's moods swung between rare bursts of maternal solicitude to long manic phone conversations to lying in bed with astringent-soaked pads on her eyes to tearful requests for her daughter to tell her the ways she had been a good mother.

"I'm going to be all alone, all alone. Nicky's off at Yale and now you're going. Why can't you stay here? You could get a part-time job."

"I want to be somebody, Mother."

Consuela rose from her lace-trimmed elbow pillows. "Well, who? Everyone's somebody."

"I want people to respect me for what I can do in life."

"*Respect* you?"

"Yes. For what I do and what I am."

Consuela's eyes closed to slits and she spat, "Just who do you think you are, anyway? Are you trying to tell me people don't respect me for who and what I am?"

"No, Mother"—patiently—"I didn't say that. I was talking about myself, not about you."

"Oh, go away. Just go away. You've never cared about me or what I want. Now when I need a daughter you're deserting me. Go away. My head's splitting."

Billie Claire went back to her room and her packing.

Less than five minutes later she could hear her mother talking on the phone. She was laughing and flirting. The person at the other end of the line could have been a man or a woman. Consuela told most people she loved them. It seemed to reassure her to say it.

Thaddeus drove Billie Claire to the station.

"One day," he said, "you'll meet a good man and settle down with your children. That is my wish for you, Billie."

"Thank you, Father."

She knew it made little sense to tell him the last thing she had in

109

mind as a life goal was a husband and babies. She didn't know specifically what she wanted from life. All she knew was that she wanted to be accepted and respected for herself—whatever that self was. And through that respect and acceptance, perhaps do something someday that would make a difference in the world.

At college, Billie Claire was a hardworking, methodical student. Her lecture notes were so thorough some students didn't bother to attend lectures. Billie Claire shared everything she had.

Whenever she could, she went to coffeehouses in the Village to pick up men. A tight sweater or a clinging blouse eventually brought a man to her table. She had a succession of brief affairs as a freshman and sophomore. She never spoke of them to her fellow students at Barnard, who assumed, if they bothered to make any assumptions about her, that Billie Claire spent her free time studying and going to museums and concerts.

Billie Claire was considered sweet, serious, guileless and utterly without style. A good kid.

Beginning with her junior year, in her dogged and systematic way, she investigated the *real* opportunities available to women in a number of professions. She observed, asked questions and intently listened to answers. The truth she heard in the year 1957 was that in almost no occupations were women equal, but that in several they were more equal than others. One of those fields was journalism. With hard work, brains and enterprise, a woman reporter could make a difference, be effective, achieve recognition. Columbia Journalism School accepted her application.

She was ecstatic.

Finally, the focus on a specific goal.

Billie Claire Hutchins, Political Reporter.

Someday soon people would read a column of print by Billie Claire Hutchins and judge her by her words, her ideas, not by her face, or the size of her breasts.

After a segment of her master's thesis was published in the *Columbia Journalism Review* she received a short, crisp letter from the managing editor of the *Washington Herald*.

He liked what he had read. Would she be interested in a job as a copygirl, to start, with a good chance at a staff job within a year? She phoned him.

Yes. Yes. Yes.

Billie Claire was hired as a copygirl and told, master's or no master's, she'd be working her way up just like everyone else—male or female. That suited her just fine.

Within the year she had made staff reporter on the dullest beat outside the Department of Agriculture, the county beat. But it was a start.

Ann Adams flung open the door to the ladies' room. "Let's go."

Billie Claire hurried after the tall redhead, today dressed in vivid shades of lavender.

"Now then, honey, aside from Montgomery County, what's the trouble?"

Billie Claire poured sugar into her coffee. "It's very frustrating, doing this damn stuff that doesn't mean anything."

"Well, the truth is, honey, that those meetings over there do mean something. Everything they assign means something, and you've got to get your feet wet somewhere. Your chance'll come. You just hang on and keep doin' what you're doin'."

"Oh, I know you're right. But people like you occasionally get to write what you want to."

"Wrong, I get to write what Ernie tells me to write."

"You know what I mean, Ann. You have clout. People know that if you're writing a story, it's important enough to read."

"Sure, sure, but I've been around here for a coon's age, Billie. I didn't start at the top. Nobody does. You've got to come up with something that will knock their eyes out. But on your own time. Don't expect them to hand it to you."

"Well, dammit, I've been trying. I have a great lead into that dentist story, but Ernie won't even consider letting me develop it."

"Listen, you have to go out on the assignments Ernie gives you. But you don't have to give a small shit about what Ernie won't let you do. Do it. Follow this lead on your own. Write up the story and slap it under his nose. But don't go beggin' him to assign it to you, 'cause he sure as hell ain't gonna do it."

"Do you think I could get away with that?" Billie Claire said incredulously. "I don't want him to can me. I can't afford it."

"Nobody can afford to get canned. Just be sure you have every detail of that story backed up with at least two sources. Incidentally, how are you managing on the piddling money they pay around here?"

"Not too well, really. When I first came here my father was

111

helping me with the rent. But he had a heart attack some months back, and while he was sick they audited his books. It seems he didn't have nearly the money we all thought he had in these last years. Now there's needed to be a lot of cutting back. My mother isn't taking it very well, the cutting back. Anyway, I'm really stretching to make the rent on my apartment at 2500 Q Street."

"Wow, that's a pretty fancy address for a gal alone on your salary, Daddy's money or not."

Billie Claire blushed. "Well, when I took it I *had* the money to handle it. I assumed I'd be making better money here by now."

"How would you feel about sharing your apartment?"

"Gee, I've never thought about it."

"You won't have any trouble finding someone, not with that address."

"I wouldn't want just anyone."

"Tell you what, hon. You type up a notice and stick it up on the bulletin board in the city room. You'll have more offers than you can handle. And you can always be selective. You let me know how you're getting along, ya hear?"

And off she went, a dramatic swirl of lavender linen.

Billie Claire returned to her desk and quickly typed a note on a blank file card and tacked it up on the bulletin board before she left for her assignment. It read, Roommate wanted. Female. One-bedroom apartment. 2500 Q Street. Share rent. KL5-1159. B.C. Hutchins—City Room.

The two after-lunch speakers spoke. The realtor was affirmative about housing negatives and the Urban League man cited laws and court decisions and salaries and educational levels, all the while trying to keep the bitterness and frustration from breaking through in his voice.

Billie Claire briefly interviewed both men and headed back to the *Herald* to meet her four o'clock deadline. The story would run to four pages and she knew she'd be lucky to see an inch of it in the next day's paper.

At a quarter of four as she was tapping the keys of her typewriter a copyboy hurried up to her desk. He cleared his throat and leaned close to her. "Billie, you're wanted up in Mr. Hathaway's office. Right away."

She stared at him. "Eddie, are you trying to give me a heart attack?"

"No. I mean it. They just phoned down. He wants to see you. Now."

"But why? I mean, oh, God, what have I done?"

The copyboy shrugged and backed away, not a little impressed. Cub reporters didn't need to go to the publisher to get reamed out. Something must be up.

She was unable to move. Clammy sweat broke out on her face and the palms of her hands. Her lips were numb and she could feel her heart beating in her throat.

She managed to cross the city room on knees she was certain would give with each step. By the time she reached the publisher's inner office on the tenth floor, her brain was so flooded with fear she couldn't think.

A hard-faced, middle-aged woman scowled at Billie Claire from behind a large mahogany desk. "Oh, yes, Miss Hutchins. Mr. Hathaway is expecting you."

The receptionist pointedly took in Billie Claire's bust, gave a cluck of disgust and pressed a lever on the intercom. Seth Hathaway's personal secretary answered. "A Miss Hutchins is here."

"Send her in, please," said a metallic voice from the box.

Billie Claire had some difficulty maneuvering the thick Chinese rug in the inner office. Mr. Hathaway's secretary greeted her with a stiff smile and gestured toward the large oak doors at the end of the room. She somehow reached them as the secretary walked a few paces in front of her and silently opened the doors.

"Mr. Hathaway, Miss Hutchins," she intoned.

Billie Claire found herself standing a long distance away from a large man wearing half-glasses. He was immaculately dressed. He stood.

"Miss Hutchins, thank you for coming so promptly. Please have a seat." He gestured to a large, leather wing-backed chair at the side of the most gigantic desk Billie Claire had seen since her mother had taken her to see that fancy Park Avenue dermatologist many years before. She sat on the very edge of the leather chair and stared at this man she had only seen from a distance, or in pictures. He was roughly handsome, with a great shock of sandy-red hair and the most piercing blue eyes she had ever seen.

They never left her face, and she felt that this was the way he always dealt with people. The powerful don't apologize. The powerful can also afford to look you straight in the eye because it is of no consequence to them whether they are lying or not. They control the situation. He squeezed a filter cigarette into a short ormolu holder.

Dear God, dear God, what can this man want with me? her nerves screamed at her. What in bloody hell have I done to get myself here?

"Well, now, Billie Claire. I may call you Billie Claire, may I not?"

"Of course. Sure. Yes, of course," she stammered.

"I've been receiving some very good reports about you from downstairs."

"Really?"

"Your co-workers seem to feel you've fit right in here at the *Herald*. That you are willing and accurate. Those are the qualities of a good reporter."

"Not to mention not being afraid to make an ass of yourself," she blurted, then blushed, astonished at herself.

The publisher grinned. The ice was broken. Then he laughed out loud. "Where did you hear that?"

"From you. You spoke at my commencement at Columbia and I've never forgotten what you said."

The man was delighted. "You *are* a good reporter. One with a damn fine memory."

"Thank you, sir."

"Discretion," he said firmly. "That's another quality I look for in people. Discretion. The ability to keep things to one's self."

"Yes, sir. I suppose I'm not a very good gossip."

"Billie Claire, let me get right to the point. The White House, as you're obviously aware, has taken on an entirely different light since the Kennedys' arrival. An aura, one might say. We have two men over there now and they're having a very hard time just keeping up. One area we're taking a beating on from the *Post* is the family coverage. The entire Jackie, Caroline, hamsters, dogs side of things. To say nothing of the sisters and brothers and parents and in-laws. We need more color, more human interest. People are fascinated by that stuff and we've got to start giving more of it to them."

114

Shit, did he really call me up here to talk about Caroline's hamsters?

"You're good, you're quick, you're quiet. You're also a good, solid writer. How would you like a corner of the White House beat? Features, interviews, Sunday paper stuff? It wouldn't be *all* color. But I'd like you to concentrate on that for starters."

She couldn't answer immediately. The *White House!* She couldn't believe what she was hearing.

"Mr. Hathaway, what can I say? Of course. Of course, I want it. And I'm certain I can handle it."

"So am I, or I wouldn't have made the assignment."

"Well, I'm simply flabbergasted and very grateful. Thank you."

"Then I'll speak to Ernie Prescott."

She made a move to go and the publisher shifted his weight slightly, indicating he had something further to say.

"Incidentally, my secretary saw a notice on the city room bulletin board this afternoon. You're looking for a roommate?" he said, releasing her eyes and focusing at something over her shoulder.

"Why, yes." She was flattered by such a personal inquiry.

Seth Hathaway made a steeple of his fingers and rested his chin on it. "I have a rather personal matter to discuss with you."

"Yes, sir?" Good Lord, what's coming now? You never get anything for nothing.

"Perhaps you could do me a kindness. The daughter of an old Yale chum, Bob Farr, has asked if Mrs. Hathaway and I could be of help finding his daughter a place to stay. She needs to come to Washington periodically, sometimes on the spur of the moment, and rather dislikes hotels. We thought, Mrs. Hathaway and I, that a much more acceptable arrangement might be the part-time sharing of an apartment with another young lady. Your situation seems tailor-made. I'm sure there would be no problem with her picking up half the rent, even though she wouldn't be there much of the time."

"Certainly, that would be terrific. What's she like?"

"Lovely person. Lovely young woman. Finest background. Someone I'm confident you could get along with." He cleared his throat. "Incidentally, she has a young man. Someone in the government. For some reason, her family doesn't approve of the fellow. Mrs. Hathaway and I have been rather siding with the young people in the matter. She'd like an occasional weekend alone with him. Would that present any difficulties for you?"

"You mean, they'd want to . . . use my apartment for the whole weekend? Alone?"

"Well, yes. Occasionally, as I said."

Billie Claire thought for a moment. She didn't object to someone using her apartment for a rendezvous. It was the idea of needing to find somewhere to park herself for an entire weekend on short notice that didn't sound too terrific. But she realized the discomfort of occasionally sleeping on a friend's couch would be a small price to pay for the White House assignment.

"I don't see any problems. Although there's a gorgeous vacant apartment down the hall from mine." She was trying to be helpful. "I mean, you know how hard a good apartment in that area is to find. I peeked in the other day when the painters had the door open. I'm pretty sure it hasn't been taken yet."

He shook his head. "No, an apartment in her name could create difficulties. You understand," he said vaguely.

"It all sounds rather Montague and Capulet," she said, smiling.

"Yes. Exactly. Leave it to our new White House reporter to come up with the perfect summation." He rose. "I'm sure I can count on you to keep this confidential. Her family's well-known, and you know Washington gossips. I'll ask Allegra to phone you."

"Allegra? All right."

"Lovely name, isn't it?"

Billie Claire moved toward the door. "Mr. Hathaway, you have made my day, if not possibly my life."

"Not at all. You're being most accommodating. I'm sure the arrangement will be satisfactory to everyone concerned."

She finished her Chevy Chase story just on deadline, and yelled, "Copy," at a harassed young man who was whizzing by her desk, and slapped the pages into his outstretched hand.

This was no day to face the sweating masses on the R-20 up P Street to her apartment. She hailed a cab on the corner of Sixteenth and L, dizzy with elation. Thoughts tumbled through her head like Ping-Pong balls in a wind tunnel. She leaned back against the seat and tried to sort out what had just happened to her.

Billie Claire, like everyone else in Washington who paid attention to such things, had heard the rumors about Seth Hathaway's extracurricular activities. The fact that he was a ladies' man was common knowledge around the city room. In no way would he get himself *seriously* involved, however. Not with his wife, Jeannine, sitting on all that Magnuson money and the ultimate control of the paper. Billie Claire had once seen Jeannine Hathaway in the elevator, and she had been awed by the woman's cool elegance. As far as anyone knew, she stayed home, raised her children, and did good works such as sponsoring the National Symphony Ball and pouring Pimm's Cup at the Warrenton Gold Cup Hunt every year. A formidable lady who probably "screws through her girdle," as she had once overheard Melon Bowersox say.

The "old school chum's" daughter with the unacceptable romance story simply didn't wash. There was a lot more to it and she bet it involved the use of her place as a trysting spot by the old man himself. Billie Claire didn't care. Visions of Air Force One appeared before her. The man could screw the entire chorus line of *Camelot* on her couch for all she cared.

It's happened! It's finally happened to Billie Claire Hutchins! The big time. Name in lights. The top. Twenty-five, a reporter for a great newspaper, assigned to cover the most exciting Administration in modern history, inside the most awesome house in the world. She squeezed her eyes together hard. It was like being made chief historian to Marie Antoinette's court.

"I deserve it, I deserve it," she whispered to herself.

Monday morning a subdued Ernie Prescott told Billie Claire she was to report to the Secret Service office to be fingerprinted and then to Pierre Salinger's office to pick up her credentials.

"All the arrangements seem to have been made upstairs," he sniffed. He preferred to determine personnel changes, then he maintained direct control of his people.

The news of Billie Claire's new assignment crackled through the city room like a flash fire. A steady stream of reporters, editors, copyboys and clerks stopped at her desk to congratulate her, tease her and generally wish her well. Ann Adams was the most effusive.

"Dahlin' baby girl," she called when she spotted Billie Claire in the hall. "What's this I hear? How marvelous for you." She threw her orange-clad arms around Billie Claire and gave her a twirl.

"Oh, God, Ann, I'm so thrilled." She added hastily, "I'm scared stiff, too. I don't know *anything* about the White House. Do you think we could have a cup of coffee after work?"

"Tell you what, meet me at the Jefferson around four thirty. The first one will be on me."

They met under the canopy. As they walked across the hotel lobby, Melon Bowersox emerged from an elevator, hurrying, patting her hair into place. She did not see her two colleagues. Ann grabbed Billie Claire's arm as she started to move toward Melon.

"Not now, hon."

"I wasn't going to gloat. But I did want to tell her. She wasn't in this morning."

"I know you wouldn't gloat. But I think it's best if she hears about your assignment from someone else."

Billie Claire frowned. "Melon wouldn't resent my new job, would she? I mean, she's such a good feature writer. She wouldn't want to be limited to the White House, would she?"

"As a matter of fact, she just might." They were seated at a small table against the wall. "About two weeks ago Melon told me she thought the *Herald* ought to have a reporter covering the First Family full time. She also told Ernie. And she felt she should be the one."

Billie Claire slumped down. "Oh, God. I'm glad you stopped me. I like Melon. She's been very nice to me . . . when she has time."

"Melon's tough as whang leather. She'll get over it."

The waiter took their orders.

"But, until then?"

"Why then she'll be the way she always is with you. If you don't pick yourself up in a hurry around here, people figure you're just part of the crosswalk."

"I'll try to remember that."

"You'd better." Ann drank deeply

Billie Claire nodded thoughtfully and sipped her vodka and tonic. "I started making some preliminary calls today just to get a feeling of things over there."

"What did you pick up?"

Ann signaled the waiter.

"Well, I was able to get to Pam Turnure just to tell her I'd be

118

over. But I think she's just some sort of showcase press secretary for Jackie. That woman doesn't know where the ladies' room is. Maybe there aren't any for the press. I have a strong feeling that Tish Baldridge is the pipeline to the First Lady and I'm going to have my problems. There seem to be about three fences around Jackie. I wonder what they're so afraid of."

"After you find out, you probably won't be able to write about it." The waiter placed fresh drinks before them. Billie Claire was only a third into her first. "But good luck, anyway." Ann lifted her second glass. "And here's to you and the horse you rode in on."

Chapter Five

Allegra

"Your regular booth, Miss Farr," the uniformed attendant murmured.

Allegra lay back in the adjustable couch. Another attendant arranged a downy blanket over her. "May I get you some mint tea, Miss Farr?" she asked.

"Umm. Thank you, Anise. I need *something* this morning."

The treatment booths of the Vivienne Laurent Salon of Fifth Avenue, in midtown Manhattan, were separated by shoulder-high partitions, which provided clients with a degree of privacy during their hour under the unsparing lights.

Allegra Farr cuddled herself further under the blanket that protected patrons from the air conditioner, and closed her eyes. From the adjoining booth she could clearly hear the rasping voice of her neighbor.

"If you could do something to make me look like the girl who just slid into booth three you could change my life."

"The good Lord does that kind of work, Mrs. Shiskin," a heavily accented voice purred. "There is nothing we can do here at Laurent's but maintain what you were given."

"Oh, well. Give her another five years and she'll need more than mint tea. Like the rest of us."

Laurent clients were not secretaries or shop clerks or the wives of bank branch managers. For Laurent's regular clients their weekly visits were pilgrimages. The promise, *never* stated as such, was Eternal Youth, and the price Mme. Laurent exacted was high.

The soft leather chaise on which Allegra relaxed was surrounded by pastel machines and cabinets and mysteriously hissing tubes.

Her hair was enveloped in a loose, pale green cap that matched the gown she wore over her bra and panties. Soothing, moist pads were placed over her eyes. Now bright lights illuminated her face as Laurent specialists set to work. A large magnifying glass was swung into place and every centimeter of her face, neck and décolletage was examined for flaws. The light was merciless.

Allegra Farr's skin required no mercy.

"Are you comfortable?" a soft voice asked from beyond the back of Allegra's head.

"Yes. Thank you, Eglantine."

The Tuesday morning regulars envied Allegra more than the condition of her pores. She always got Eglantine, Mme. Laurent's resident wizard.

Vivienne Laurent (née Anya Homulka) possessed a gift for selling her "secret" creams and hope. She had built an international beauty business from it. She also had a talent for finding and underpaying gifted illegal aliens whom she trained in the ways of beauty. Her apprentices were in no position to complain about their low pay and fourteen-hour days, not without the Green Card of a registered alien. The few who survived the training were adept at handling people, as well as skin, and among the regulars, Eglantine was known as a worker of miracles.

Allegra was in no need of a miracle.

Eglantine's fingers, dipped in warm, scented oils, began to stroke her face. The forehead and temples were first.

Allegra tried to give herself over to the sensuous massage. She couldn't. She was thinking, considering, analyzing.

At six thirty the preceding Friday, Seth Hathaway phoned her suite at the Hampshire House. He had found an apartment for her in Washington. It wasn't to be her apartment, though. She was to "have the complete and unlimited use of the lovely apartment of a *Herald* reporter." Allegra could occupy the place whenever she came to Washington. She wouldn't ever need to *see* the other woman. Seth had made all the arrangements. Discretion *was* important. Nonetheless, Allegra was not pleased with the offer.

Access to another woman's apartment was hardly a full commitment from Seth, and she found the idea of using another person's things offensive. The man could easily afford an apartment exclusively for her.

Allegra was playing a game of great complexity and consequence.

The moment her forehead furrowed into a frown of concentration, Eglantine's fingers were there, smoothing, caressing. "No, no, no, no," she cooed. "Only thoughts of velvet and cool water flowing over marble."

"Mmm," Allegra said, and consciously relaxed the muscles of her face.

She knew a great deal about Seth Hathaway. But no one knew anything about Allegra she didn't want known.

Her mother had taught her to be very, very careful and never trust any one person with all the pieces. "While others may see you as, ah, enigmatic, you must always see your actions and choices for what they are. Above all," Deena Farr said, "keep your life as simple as possible; make lists. A woman guards her privacy, dear."

Seth Hathaway was a public figure. He was the source of endless speculation and gossip, as are all powerful figures. Excluding embellishments, the stories about the man were consistent. Allegra had compiled a biography from such sources as *Who's Who*, slick magazines, firsthand word of mouth and her own careful observations. This is what Allegra knew about the man. For, as Deena Farr insisted, "Knowledge of others is power."

Seth Lowell Hathaway was the improper son of the very proper Hathaways of Maryland's Eastern Shore. By the time he was eighteen he had become such a rebelliously free spirit he had been thrown out of five prep schools. His banker father issued an ultimatum. With a shrug, Seth capitulated and strode up the gangway of a merchant marine freighter. "I went to sea to see the world and never even saw the sky," he later joked at dinner parties. A year and a half later he entered Yale, where, four tumultuous years later he graduated, a member of the bottom quarter of his class.

That fall he married Jeannine Claymore Magnuson. Mr. and Mrs. Raleigh Magnuson were not happy about their only child's choice of a handsome, cocky playboy who had been described as "a street fighter in white tie." In addition to other holdings, Raleigh Magnuson owned and was publisher of Washington's tabloid *Herald,* a third-rate morning paper devoted to race results, comic strips, controversial syndicated columnists of every persuasion and thorough reporting off the police blotter.

With elevated blood pressure and clenched teeth, Mr. Magnuson hired his son-in-law.

Seth served his apprenticeship on the *Herald* with an enthusiasm that startled everyone. He had found his calling. Mr. Magnuson turned over more and more responsibility to Seth. When Seth was thirty, the old man reluctantly named him publisher and removed himself to Florida.

Under Seth's guidance the paper dropped the sleazy tabloid format, went to eight columns and began a slow but steady rise to journalistic respectability. The challenge, and he always needed a challenge, became his determination to make the *Herald* into a better paper than the *Post.* The competition was cutthroat, and the nuances of the battle between Seth Hathaway and Phillip Graham, the *Post*'s publisher, became a kind of parlor game among Washington insiders.

Seth's personal rise to power directly paralleled the *Herald's* ascent. By way of his newspaper, its publisher manipulated the careers and fortunes of an ever-widening circle of people. What he lacked in style he made up with flair; what he lacked in taste he made up for in *joie de vivre.* When he was *up* he would charter a jet to Las Vegas or London or tip an elevator man. When he was *down* he could have terrified a mass murderer. He had decided who and what he was and felt no further need for introspection. He terrified weak and uncertain men, and simultaneously charmed and infuriated the strong and self-assured.

During the first months of the Kennedy Administration, it was natural for people close to the President to cultivate the publisher of an important liberal Washington newspaper, regardless of his personality.

The icy intellects of the JFK brain trust were uneasy about Seth. They regarded him as an anti-intellectual, but one who was awesomely shrewd in his understanding of the uses of power. He could not be controlled. He was invariably bursting with ideas, and in his verbal rushes to articulate them he drowned out thoughtful objections.

The more playful Kennedys saw him as their kind of man. If Seth couldn't do it he could fake it, and there was little he couldn't do: play squash or tennis, scuba, sail, dance, ride, drink and make love.

Ah, yes. Seth Hathaway and women.

Allegra's knowledge of Seth's sexuality came from two sources: accounts by women whom he had bedded, and her own intuition and observation.

For all his macho thrust, he truly enjoyed and respected women. He took pleasure in women as can only the most self-assured men. He hired, paid and promoted women ahead of any other newspaper. The *Herald* was the first Washington paper to have a woman on the police beat, and on its editorial board. He had elevated the talented and tough Ann Hawkins Adams to a showcase position on the metropolitan staff and was prepared to further her career.

Then there were Seth Hathaway's affairs.

Allegra had no reason to doubt a quip currently making the rounds to the effect that Seth Hathaway had lost count after a thousand.

Eglantine began to apply an aromatic mask.

Allegra had first encountered Seth ten years before. She vividly recalled the meeting, but was certain Seth didn't. Her father had brought the publisher home to the Farr's enormous North Shore apartment in Chicago after Seth had delivered a speech to Dr. Farr's club. As a member of the university's board of regents whose other hobbies were the financial backing of politicians (Democratic) and the acquisition of money, Bob Farr frequently entertained important people. From Allegra's thirteen-year-old vantage point, most of those important people were boring beyond belief. But not this dynamic and arrogant publisher with his faint Southern drawl. Allegra gracefully sat in a corner sipping a Coke during cocktails, running the tip of her tongue over her braces, watching men who never shut up, as a rule, hanging on the publisher's *jokes*, and women moistening their lips and assuming seductive stances, crossing and recrossing their legs. Before the adults passed into the dining room, the publisher paused before her. "You'd better watch this one, Robert, She's going to break a lot of hearts one day." That was the first time she had recognized that odd expression in some women's eyes for what it was—jealousy.

She smiled at the memory.

Eglantine gasped. "No, no, no, no, Miss Farr! The face must remain absolutely still for the mask."

Allegra acknowledged the caution with a little hum and resumed her speculations.

Seth's love affairs were short and sweet and generally ended with the delivery of a bauble—never accompanied by a card. Once he had thoroughly explored and used a woman's body, and picked her brain, the challenge was over. A year before, Allegra had heard a beautiful and rather drunk Broadway actress musing, "I've been with a couple of other men like Seth Hathaway. Only a couple. When the big moment arrives, he's totally alone. Like a surfer or a glider pilot or a deep-sea diver. He's alone and he's free. Odd, isn't it?" her voice trailed off.

Allegra considered that bit of information beyond price. She had been carefully utilizing it for the past three months—by so far refusing him her body.

And after those solo flights of his? He always went home to his comfortable house in Georgetown. To Jeannine. Jeannine and Seth Hathaway made a ritual of having breakfast together, crisp copies of the *Herald* and the *Post* beside their coffee cups. A set for each.

The *Washington Herald* bound Seth Hathaway to his wife more inexorably than a feudal marriage performed by the Pope.

Before he died in 1958, Raleigh Magnuson willed his newspaper to his only child and named his two lawyer-brothers and their lawyer-sons trustees of his estate. Jeannine gave her husband all the space he wanted, and he wanted and needed a great deal of space. Whenever an uncle or a cousin began to move in too close-ly, Jeannine waved him off.

As the eucalyptus-scented steam seeped over her, gently dissolving the crusty mask, Allegra felt a buzz of excitement in her stomach.

That was the challenge.

To extricate the publisher of the *Herald* from his frostily beautiful, serene and proper wife, the *owner* of the newspaper that was his baby, his joy, at times his Frankenstein monster, for over thirty-five years the most important thing in his life.

She wanted Seth Hathaway, publisher of the *Washington Herald*, and along with the man, she wanted those little translucent cards from Tiffany's with the dark blue engraving that said, "Mrs. Seth Lowell Hathaway." She wanted the monogram inside her horizontally worked Black Diamond mink to read, in regal script, "A.F.H."

Amazing, Eglantine's tender skill as she removed the last of the mask with moist puffs of cotton.

". . . don't see the *point* of shooting those men up in rockets," Mrs. Shiskin was saying. "Do you realize how much this nonsense is costing . . . ?"

Allegra tuned out the voice, shut off the pleasure of Eglantine's fingers. She needed to concentrate on that evening.

Seth's plane would be arriving at LaGuardia at six thirty. He would be driven from the airport to a political dinner at the Waldorf. He promised to be at her apartment at exactly eleven thirty. His promises to her, which he always kept, meant more to him than they did to her. She had patience. Whether he arrived at the Hampshire House at eleven thirty or one thirty was not as important as his undisguised passion to be there as soon as he possibly could.

Tonight's meeting would determine the course of their relationship, and the next ten years of her life.

The objective was to become Seth Hathaway's mistress. How much more exciting to be the acknowledged mistress of one of the most powerful men in Washington than the wife of say, a staid Wall Street lawyer. *Openly acknowledged* mistress. She had not turned down marriage proposals from millionaires to sit alone waiting for a phone call or a knock on the door at 3:00 A.M.

For the present, the Tiffany cards and the monograms would have to wait. Jeannine could do nothing, *would* do nothing, because she was a lady. Jeannine would act as if Allegra Farr didn't exist, and she would be gracefully patient while her husband "comes to his senses." She would hold off the uncles and cousins. Seth's name would remain on the masthead while Jeannine bided her time until "he gets over *this* silly infatuation."

Allegra knew something Jeannine Hathaway didn't. Seth was a man obsessed. For the first time in his life, Seth Lowell Hathaway was in love. Crazily, raptly, utterly in love with Miss Allegra Farr of Evanston, Illinois, and New York City.

Eglantine's fingers moved down her throat, rhythmically stroking, down to her décolletage. "Ah, such perfection," she murmured.

Allegra smiled at the words; Eglantine's eyes and hands, educated by years of touching and scrutinizing every kind of skin, could not be deceived.

As a professional, a connoisseur, Eglantine cherished Allegra. The young woman was living, smiling, autonomous perfection. As such, she was a freak of sorts. Eglantine had ministered to many beautiful women; in some way each was marred. Not so Allegra Farr. Eglantine had searched. Finally, she accepted, and like an entomologist in possession of a rare, flawlessly mounted butterfly, Eglantine rejoiced in Allegra.

Seth was baffled to the point of rage.

How could such loveliness *be?* Every sort of grace. Symmetry. Poise. A speaking voice so mellifluous, even over the phone long distance, that as she spoke sweat formed on his upper lip and the palms of his hands. His loins ached.

He wanted her. He always got what he wanted. Always. Until Allegra. She didn't say no, but she wouldn't say yes, either.

He thought of her during the mandatory daily editorial conferences held around the large table in the paneled room next to his office. He dreamed of her. He phoned her four, five times a day, and became enraged when the Hampshire House switchboard operator asked if she could take a message. He ordered tiny, exquisite gifts sent to her, only to have everything except flowers and perfume returned. He schemed to get to New York City. She would not come to him in Washington. He found he could make the 11:00 A.M. shuttle, and by bellowing at the driver of the waiting limousine, be seated with her at "21" for lunch by twelve forty-five. Then back in the car, another shuttle, and at his desk for the conference. Friends with private planes headed north to La-Guardia automatically called Seth.

This frenzy had been going on for months and it was affecting his health and newspaper.

Allegra was only twenty-three, but she understood exactly what fifty-seven-year-old Seth Hathaway was experiencing. The man had permitted himself to become mindlessly vulnerable in his pursuit of what, in essence, was a symbol. But she was not in the least jeopardy, because she saw Seth and herself with cool objectivity. On that warm morning in July she felt the thrill of the gambler with the winning cards whose only problem is to keep the other player in and betting.

Tonight was the night when the cards would be laid on the table, face up.

Eglantine removed the loose cap and held a mirror before Allegra

She searched her reflection. All was well. No evidence of the night before.

"Thank you, Eglantine."

That had been so stupid, last night. But she had been bored and just a little anxious.

She had accepted a dinner invitation from Hank Bellamy. He was always a marvelous companion: tanned and handsome, immaculately groomed, witty, suave and, as a very hot press agent with three current Broadway hits, known by everyone who mattered in Manhattan. And although Allegra had never heard even a tentative rumor, she assumed Hank was homosexual. In six months of squiring her around town he hadn't made a single pass. Extricating one's self from a determined man without damaging his self-esteem required finesse—and time. Evenings with Hank could be counted upon to end without these complications by one thirty or two.

Their table at "21" was strategically located. Charlie always saw that they were seated where everyone could see them. They had been on their second cocktail when the place was suddenly flooded by an opening-night crowd. Joey and Cindy Adams, the Earl

Wilsons, Lemoyne Billings up from Washington with the Stephen Smiths. They all stopped at Hank's table to discuss what apparently was a turkey.

"I came out humming the scenery," Cindy said when she swept up to the table.

"You can stop humming, Cindy," Aaron Hayden, the producer, called after her. "They're striking the scenery right now. The notice went up backstage after the second act."

His words evoked a scattering of groans. Some people had lost a great deal of money.

Hank flashed perfectly capped Chiclet-sized teeth at Allegra. "Sure glad this one wasn't mine. The only thing that beats winning is watching the competition lose."

"Umm." She ran a long red nail along the edge of her glass.

Cindy moved on to the next table.

Joey lingered. "Do ya know my wife's cooking is so bad the oven flushes?"

Hank roared and the two men slapped backs.

Allegra sipped her wine. This was what she wanted Seth to take her away from, these people whom she had thought so fascinating six months ago. Before Seth and his almost offhand accounts of his friendship with the *President of the United States.* About how the President enjoyed the company of newspaper people because "they know what's going on." Seth said the President loved unprintable gossip, the inside dope. She knew Seth was not overplaying his association with the President and his relations and close friends. Allegra carefully studied magazine and newspaper photographs of Seth Hathaway on the deck of the Kennedy family yacht, *Marlin,* wind tousling his thick hair; Seth Hathaway whispering into the ear of an attentive Jackie at a black-tie dinner in the East Room; Seth in Tennis whites at the compound at Hyannis. She read columnists' speculations about the possibility of the *Herald's* publisher being appointed an Under Secretary of State, or of Navy, or Ambassador to England or France. Seth was a *national* figure, possibly international. The Kennedys, those ebullient Kennedys, had rewritten the definitions of Beautiful People. Seth had been anointed by them and he was *in.*

Allegra went through the practiced motions of displaying interest in the talk of actors and actresses, who was sleeping with whom, which producers were taking flyers on what and why.

God, it sounded so inconsequential. She wanted to be taken home. But at the checkroom Hank told her they were going on to El Morocco, and before she could protest, Allegra was squeezed into the back of a limousine headed across to the East Side. When Hank waved for the second round at "Elmo's," she tried to plead a headache. He said, "Not yet, please, Allegra. Do me a favor. It's business." She nodded. She owed him a favor for introducing her to men and women she had considered (before Seth) the most glamorous in the country.

Next, Hank's group headed downtown to Trude Heller's in the Village. She no longer knew who was navigating, but she did know that after they got there the smoke and noise would destroy anyone sober.

An impatient crowd was shuffling about on the sidewalk when their cars stopped at the curb. Hank pushed to the front of the line and pressed some bills into the hand of the gorilla blocking the door. Their party was led to a table beside the tiny dance floor.

Vibrations approximating music blasted from the gigantic speakers. Strobe lights flashed and whirled over the pumping rhythm of "Jim Dandy to the Rescue."

Cut off from the sight of the highest fashion and the sound of famous names shot forth, juggled and dropped, Allegra felt herself pulsing to the primal beat.

She rose from the table, and with one graceful movement was in Hank's arms on the crowded floor. After a few moments they drew apart and broke into a stationary twist.

Her body moved in perfect, instinctual time to the repetitive rhythm; the muscles of her pelvis tightened as she thrust her hips forward, around and around. Oh, God, how good it *felt,* the throbbing, up through the floor, coursing up her legs to explode in the exact center of her body. A quite tangible point around which she swung her hips. Every nerve and muscle was focused on the exultation of her essence. Her dance became a celebration of herself.

When she became aware that the other dancers had pushed back to the edges of the small floor, she felt an even deeper excitement. She was alone in the darkness, broken now only by a pink baby spotlight that played over her face and body.

Several feet away, a young black man in skintight black satin pants was matching her dance, as if he were a mirror. His expressionless black eyes were fused with hers. He was a devil, taunting her, encouraging her. He was reading her body. He could see she was close to an orgasm, and was helping her build to it.

Oh, yes. Oh, yes. Oh, yes.

Allegra stopped, froze, as the paroxysm caught her, burst and then spread. Her head fell back and her eyes slid away from the black man's. He alone had seen and he alone knew. She felt rage at the ah, cool, baby, cool, message in his eyes. The bastard. Everyone else was oblivious. All they saw was her beauty and abandon. Yelling, stomping and applause almost drowned out the music. She felt herself being lifted into the air by a black-haired man in a tux.

"Jesus Christ, you're gorgeous," he moaned into her neck. "Marry me or I'll kill myself. I'll give you anything you want."

"I'll take a brandy and soda," she said coolly, as she pulled herself free and retrieved a spaghetti strap that had slipped down her arms.

"Who in the name of God are you? My name is Allen Boxer. I'm an attorney. I live at Sixty-eight East End Avenue. I'm divorced. I have around one hundred thousand in savings and double that in stock and I'm in love with you." He stopped, completely out of breath.

Allegra heard him out, her hand motionless in her long, damp hair. Then she brushed it back from her forehead, laughed and turned back to the group at her table. As she sat down she noticed the spike heel of her silver slipper was giving way. The man with all the money followed.

"Allegra, do you know Allen, here?" Hank beamed. "He's the hottest criminal lawyer in town. What he can't take he gives to Roy Cohn. Allegra, Allen Boxer, Allen, Allegra Farr."

A response to the introduction over the din was impossible. They smiled and shook their heads. He reached for her hand and propelled her back onto the floor, aware that all eyes were on the beautiful blonde who had just provided the floor show. What would she do next? He pulled her tight against himself. The man's intensity was overwhelming.

After a moment she pushed him away.

"What's wrong?" he shouted over the noise.

"I don't feel like dancing," she screamed and pushed through the jerking bodies.

She certainly didn't feel like dancing with a man, no matter who he was, who was pressing an erection hard against her inner thigh. That sort of attention wasn't flattering, it was demeaning, insulting.

The young lawyer, chastened and solicitous, insisted on taking Allegra, Hank, Aaron and the rest of the group to his favorite late night spot in Little Italy. From the signals Hank was sending her she knew he thought they should accept the offer. God knew what convoluted business Hank was cooking up with Aaron Hayden and this Allen Boxer. She nodded. As long as she had hung on this long, she might as well see the night through. To do otherwise would be awkward.

Umberto's Clam House at 3:00 A.M. was filled with men trying to look like mafiosi and hookers trying to look like show girls. Allegra was too sleepy to eat the cannelloni, and after forty-five minutes she and Hank crawled into the waiting limo.

When the car halted before the Hampshire House at four thirty, Hank was asleep and the driver too punchy with fatigue to beat the early doorman to Allegra's side of the car. Hank didn't wake up when she kissed his cheek.

"Good morning, Miss Farr." The doorman touched his cap, smiling.

"Good morning, Willie." The grinning old man would have some gossip to spread backstairs later over coffee laced with gin. "Willie, will you see that some coffee gets up to me as soon as possible?" She fished a five-dollar bill from her evening bag and pressed it into his gloved had.

"Yes, Miss Farr. Certainly, Miss Farr. Is the all-night on Seventh okay?"

"Umm." Allegra nodded and moved through the revolving door Willie had set in motion for her.

The maid had turned down her bed hours before and left the

133

bed lamp on. She ignored the pile of pink telephone messages beside the phone—she knew they were all from Seth—and reached for her Gucci appointment book to see what was scheduled for Tuesday. Through the pain in her pounding head she realized Tuesday was Today.

9:30 — massage — Pablo — here.

"Oh, damn, only five hours sleep. And tonight *Seth*." She read on.

10:30 — facial — Eglantine — leg wax, pedicure
11:45 — color — Marco — shampoo, set
          Patti-Nails (ask for polish to match new wine shoes)
1:15 — makeup — Eloise
1:45 — fitting — 375 Madison — Craig
5:00 — Palm Court — Diana Hathaway
6:00 — Wally F. Gallery opening — Diana Hathaway
          Dinner — here
11:30 — Seth!!!!!!

The exclamation marks after Seth's name were followed by a tiny heart with a smile. She had dotted her i's that way until her mother had told her it was babyish and tasteless.

God, what a day! She would make every appointment, though. She had to.

The timing of Seth's arrival was excellent. She had discussed it with her mother, long distance, the day before and had taken notes. A Tuesday night couldn't be better. Tuesdays were always given over to the maintenance of Allegra's beauty. She had been told it was a gift, something precious which should never be neglected—or she would lose it. Her mother had early instilled in her a no-nonsense awareness of her responsibility for herself. "You must never neglect yourself, dear. Always remember you are beautiful and beautiful things happen to people who are beautiful."

Allegra Farr grew to womanhood never questioning her physical appearance. She was able to fascinate and manipulate people because she never sought their confirmation or approval. It was assumed. If she needed occasional reassurance, she received it

134

from certifiably objective sources: Eglantine and Pablo, salesladies at Saks and Bergdorf's, cabdrivers and delivery boys and head-waiters—and her own magnified mirror. There was no reason to waste energy competing, because there was no competition.

She set her alarm for nine, then called the door and told Willie he could drink the coffee, thanks anyway.

After she stripped off her clothes, she carefully laid them on the other bed for her maid to handle. She dropped the silver sandals into the tiny wastebasket next to the Louis XVI desk, giggling to herself at the prospect of two-hundred-pound Lillian trying to wear them.

Makeup off, nightgown on, Allegra slipped between the cool sheets and was asleep in less than a minute.

Worry caused people to frown, her mother said, creating wrinkles. Wrinkles were a sign of inner turmoil, and beautiful women should never show inner turmoil.

Allegra didn't worry for more than cosmetic reasons. Her mother had trained her not to trouble herself about matters over which she had no control, and to attend systematically to particulars she could govern.

For example, her two-and-a-half-room suite in the Hampshire House. The address on Central Park South was excellent, the security system intimidating and the restaurant off the lobby was a proper place for a lady to dine alone—if the need should ever arise.

However, Allegra's windows did not overlook the park; they gave onto a view of an apartment building a few feet to the east. Lack of a vista was of no concern; she used her suite only to bathe, dress, sleep, eat room service breakfasts and a rare supper in front of the television. The problem was lighting. There was no natural light in which to apply her daytime makeup.

Mrs. Farr had seen to the installation of an elaborate lighting system over her daughter's dressing table. Just as she had seen to the furnishing and decor of the suite, always patiently explaining every decision.

Deena Farr had been methodically explaining everything from footwear to menus to the interpretation of newspaper engagement announcements since Allegra was four years old. Mrs. Farr was always frank about money.

135

"Your father is an extremely skilled and successful physician. But his world is larger than medicine."

Allegra's suite at the Hampshire House was annually leased by one of the many corporations Dr. Farr served as a member of the board of directors. The limousine made available to her, should she need it, was leased to a company owned by a heavy contributor to the Democratic National Committee. The man's son had been miraculously delivered from a severe case of hepatitis by the genius of Dr. Robert Farr. A clever use of tax shelters for Dr. Farr's holdings was provided by attorneys who played squash with him at the New York Athletic Club when he visited Manhattan. And Allegra's trips to Europe were graciously sponsored by the managing director of a conglomerate who had recuperated from a gall bladder removal at Bob and Deena Farr's Upper Peninsula lodge.

Dr. and Mrs. Robert Farr were invited to John F. Kennedy's inaugural festivities not simply because Bob Farr openly supported JFK. He had contributed money that paid for most of the handbills, radio and television advertising and car rentals during the cutthroat West Virginia primary that had left a weeping Hubert Humphrey wondering what had hit him.

Allegra adored her distinguished father, but it was her mother she needed. With her mother she could shop, gossip, giggle, confess and scheme. For Deena, Allegra was an extension and continuation of herself. She was born again and lived through her daughter. Even if Allegra had not been beautiful, she would have seen to it that she was striking. By the time their daughter was ten the Farrs realized there was not going to be a Seven Sisters college in Allegra's future. But did brilliance really matter? She simply needed to be "finished."

Finch in New York City was the answer. A true finishing school. Not that Allegra had not been thoroughly buffed and polished by the time she graduated from Miss Porter's; she needed work on her conversational French, a solid foundation in art from the sixteenth century on and the fundamentals of economics, literature and history.

By her last year at Finch, Allegra's frenetic social life left little time for classes. But, after all, that was what the school was there for. Her body, its every movement, was now as calculated and

136

controlled as a ballerina's. The difference was, Allegra was on from the moment she opened her eyes in the morning until she closed them at night.

After her graduation, which was followed by a sit-down dinner for fifty at the St. Regis and a summer in the Hamptons, Bob Farr decided the time had come for Allegra to do some meaningful work. A holding-pattern job until she received the most advantageous offer.

Simply because "everyone else" was working at *Vogue* or *Harper's Bazaar*, Allegra agreed to submit to a rigged interview. She was hired, as an assistant to the beauty editor's assistant. During the two months she lasted at *Vogue*, Allegra shared a cubicle with the more ambitious Diana Hathaway. Diana became one of Allegra's few female friends. It was a loose friendship, based primarily on a shared interest in clothes.

Tuesday morning Allegra woke before the alarm went off. She was into her fifteenth deep knee bend when Pablo rang the buzzer.

"You need music, darling," he said as he closed the door to the corridor. He brought forth a tape recorder from his large Hermes duffel bag, punched a button and the suite was filled by the soft strains of "Blue Moon." Zippered into the compartments of Pablo's bag were the accouterments of his trade: a large rubber dildoe for some, special oils for others and for practically all, a rainbow assortment of uppers, downers, tranks and vitamins, glycerine for nails and hair and a stash of pot and coke. Miss Farr needed only the exercise music and a little palm oil. In Pablo's opinion, she didn't even need them, or him, yet.

Later, glowing from her session with Eglantine, Allegra walked the block and a half to Marco's. She was not satisfied with the particular shade of dark blond he had produced during her last visit. Too monochromatic. He had the skill to achieve the color she wanted: a natural honey-champagne.

She emptied her mind of everything but the piped-in music while Marco set to work. First emerging darkish roots were stripped and a butter-wheat toner was infused into the exposed strands. Then the hair about the face and temples was pulled through tiny holes in a tight plastic cap, never more than one or two strands at a time, and bleached and toned to the proper shades. The effect was exactly what she had sought.

After Eloise performed her makeup artistry, Allegra tolerated two grueling hours of standing, turning, pinning and trying on and taking off at M. Craig's. Eventually the fit of an emerald green silk hostess gown was perfect and delivery was promised before six that day.

Diana Hathaway was waiting for her at the corner table of the Palm Court at the Plaza. The string quartet that arrived at four stood under a bending potted palm playing show tunes. Diana was looking pensive.

Seth Hathaway's tawny daughter smiled as her friend approached. "Darling, you look gorgeous."

"I should. I'm down about five hundred dollars and eight hours." She bent and kissed the air near Diana's cheek. "What's happening among the dinosaurs at *Vogue*? I don't know how you've stood it this long."

Diana sipped her dry Rob Roy as the waiter took Allegra's order for dry vermouth with a twist on the rocks.

"Well?" Allegra prompted after the waiter left. Diana was acting oddly still.

"Oh, Farrsy, between the fags and the mummies I sometimes think I'll lose my mind. Today's big fight was over Regina's wanting to run an article about abortion. The old ladies are threatening to commit suicide by staple gun."

"I think something controversial is a good idea. Shake everyone up a little."

"They probably won't do it. Abortion's too touchy." She finished her drink and gestured to the waiter for another. "Have you ever had one, Allegra?"

"Pardon?" She felt a flush rising from her neck.

"Have you ever had an abortion?"

"Well, yes. But, *really!*"

"No offense. I'm just curious about what one would be like, now."

"Ghastly. Diana, are you trying to tell me something?"

"Who, me? No, it's just that if the article goes through I may have to edit it and I'd like to know more about the subject."

138

"Okay. It was my sophomore year at Finch. Mummy called her o.b. here in New York and it was all over in an hour. I hated the whole experience. I felt like a side of beef. Debased. Ugly. I don't know how girls who have theirs done by the local pharmacist, or whoever, stand it."

Diana stirred her drink. "Tell me, did you enjoy getting pregnant? By that, I mean, do you enjoy screwing?"

"What *is* this?" Allegra was truly shocked. "Are you on some kind of sex kick?"

"When did you become Mrs. Norman Vincent Peale? You just finished telling me you had an abortion. That means you were there when you were laid. Furthermore, old pal, this in one hell of a small town when you know the right people. And those 'right' people are telling a nasty little story about you and a certain relative of mine. It has to do with the subject of fucking."

"What are you talking about?" Allegra said menacingly.

"I'm talking about my inadvertent and disgusting role as pimp on your behalf."

Now she could see that Diana's unusual sour mood was really barely suppressed fury. She had been set up. "What the bloody hell are you trying to say?"

"You seem to forget, *dear friend,* that I was the one who called you a few months ago to ask if you'd baby-sit my father for dinner because I had a date and didn't know he'd be in town that night." She was almost shouting now. "You also seem to forget that my father is one of the most recognizable men in the Western Hemisphere."

"Diana . . ."

"Also, dear *friend,* you've been seen with him *frequently* at the Colony and "21" and the Pierre and several hot bed motels in Jersey, for all I know."

"*That* is a lie," Allegra said softly. "I have had dinner with your father, yes. Is that a Federal offense? But motels in Jersey? My *God!*"

"No? And bears don't shit in the woods." She slammed down her glass.

"Diana, I am not sleeping with your father. You should pray I was only having an affair with him, because then it would be over and done with, like that." She snapped her fingers. "Despite your vulgarity, I think you can understand what I'm about to tell you." She paused. "I am in love with your father."

With one graceful motion, Allegra pulled a ten-dollar bill from her purse, threw it on the table and rose.

People at nearby tables watched, fascinated.

Diana threw back her head and emitted a loud, harsh laugh. "There's a name for women like you, Allegra Farr."

"Yes," Allegra said evenly before she walked to the lobby, "in your case, it may soon be Mother."

Damn, Allegra thought as she walked the block from the Plaza to the Hampshire House, she had really wanted to attend the Findlay opening. Now she had four hours to kill.

Well, the Diana aspect's over with. And the irony was that she *hadn't* slept with Seth. She'd miss doing gallery and museum openings with Diana. Oh, well, there are museums in Washington and there were knowledgeable and stimulating people in the nation's capital. She'd have Seth introduce her to the *Herald*'s man who wrote the reviews. He was good—a Miles Something.

Halfway across her lobby to the elevator a stab of fear struck her stomach. What if Diana was able to reach her father and go into hysterics before he came to her apartment later? Impossible. He would be on the plane now, and he was going directly to the Waldorf, and then straight to the Hampshire House.

She was still in control.

Allegra hated loose ends.

An hour later room service set out her dinner of two pink lamb chops, asparagus and fresh raspberries with a small pitcher of whole cream. Before she began to eat, Allegra lifted her glass of Perrier water in the general direction of Chicago.

Mother, if I bring this off it won't be the Cole Porter musical you had in mind. It will be Giuseppe Verdi on opening night at the Met. Sold out!

The refrigerator in the kitchenette held Dom Perignon and two jars of beluga. The bar had been set up exactly as she had requested the day before. Shaved ice: Seth was partial to Cutty Sark over shaved ice. By eleven fifteen she had eaten, bathed (being careful not to steam out Marco's set) and slipped into her new hostess gown and matching mules.

140

Seth had taken her to a performance of *Carnival,* with Anna Maria Alberghetti. She had bought the album and three bottles of Cutty Sark the next day. She started the record after Security rang to tell her a Mr. Hathaway was in the lobby.

"Send him up, thank you." A flutter rose in her stomach. She willed it away.

And there he was. "Hello, beautiful." He shut the door and stood for a moment, half-frowning, half-smiling as he looked at her. "God, you look good." He reached for her waist and gently pulled her to him. Just as gently, she pushed herself away, grazing his cheekbone with her lips.

"Darling, you're drenched. Let me have your coat."

"No, barely damp." He handed her his light raincoat. "Thanks. I let my driver go. So I walked from the Waldorf. Thought the rain would hold off."

"Drink?"

"Thanks. I could use one. Damn dull bunch. Couldn't wait to get out of there." He heaved himself onto the couch, leaning his head back, but watching her as she moved to the bar to fill two glasses.

"Did you eat anything?" she asked with a tiny frown of concern.

"The same veal look-alike they always serve. Just pushed it around on my plate. Speaking of food," he said as she handed him his drink, "you look like emerald ice cream."

"Impossible," she laughed.

"*You're* impossible," he said, smoothly pulling her down next to him. He cupped her face in one great, tender hand. "Beautiful, beautiful, child-woman. Hand me my coat, there."

She did as he asked. He pulled a small, robin's-egg blue box tied with a white ribbon from a deep pocket.

Allegra instantly recognized the Tiffany box, and she also knew, from the shape and size, it contained a bracelet. It would be, she was certain, a diamond bracelet. He had already offered her emeralds—to match her eyes. She had not accepted them. She would not accept this gift either.

"Seth, darling, I've asked you not to. I can't take valuable gifts from you." She said it sadly, but firmly, as a mother would to an impetuously generous child.

141

"You can't accept a little bracelet from the man you tell people you love?" The corners of his mouth curved up in a smile, but his eyes were pleading.

Allegra searched his face, panic rising in her throat. "Seth, I've never told a living . . ."

"Diana called me."

She carefully, slowly set down the box, giving the act her full attention. Oh, no! "How? I mean, when . . .?"

"On the way in from LaGuardia, on the mobile phone. I could barely hear through the static and she was her usual harebrained, agitated self. I couldn't make out anything but," he turned her face toward his, "that you told her you love me. Damn near ordered the driver to keep going past the Waldorf . . . straight to you. Allegra, you told her that? You meant it?"

Allegra was completely alert, her mind clear. Dammit. Goddamn Diana. She looked down into her lap. She knew light from the table lamp was creating an aureole around her hair. She had practiced with every light in the suite.

"Seth, I was afraid to tell you myself. This afternoon she asked me point-blank. I couldn't pretend any longer. Not even to Diana."

"Then it's true?"

He didn't wait for her to answer. It happened so fast she was unable to remove the large satin pillow caught under the small of her back. Seth's mouth was clamped over hers; his chest pressed her backward. While his right hand held her, his left ripped open the top of her gown. She heard the buttons popping. He was on top of her fully clothed, heavy, straining against her.

"Stop, Seth. Stop for a minute, please," she mumbled against his tongue and teeth.

"My sweet darling, don't stop me. You *love* me."

"No, not this way." She struggled to extricate herself. His whiskers were doing something irreparable, she was sure, to Eglantine's work. Marco's masterpiece would be next, and how in God's name would she explain to Craig the damage to his gown? "Wait!" she said, and rolled free.

Seth sat up, his tie twisted, hair disheveled. He looked like a man who had had too many drinks, but Allegra knew he wasn't drunk.

She stood before him and reached to the shoulders of the gown. With a flick it dropped to the floor. Seth gasped.

"Oh, look, your ice has melted." Allegra picked up his drink and walked slowly to the bar, fully aware that what she was doing could cause coronary arrest in men younger than Seth. The lamp on the bar had been equipped with a pink light bulb in anticipation of this moment. She knew how the light was falling across her thigh and buttocks. She also knew that if she stood at a certain angle he could see her left breast and a tuft of pubic hair. She turned her back for an instant and rapidly squeezed both nipples until she felt the pain. They stood hard and erect as she slowly walked back to Seth.

"What are you doing to me, woman?" he croaked as he reached for her and buried his face between her legs.

She managed to set down the glass without spilling a drop of Cutty sark over shaved ice.

"Now, Seth. Now. Because I love you."

She maneuvered him into the bedroom, where Seth made love to her for three and a half hours. There was no aspect of a woman's sensuality he did not understand and attend to. There was no part of his own body that had not been skillfully caressed and manipulated before. In the physical particulars of their encounter there was nothing novel, no mysteries were revealed. The magic was in his mind. He was transcended. He experienced himself as his most perfect self, as he dreamed of being, mirrored in this woman. Through her, he flew, walked on water, possessed the world. Through her.

The wide closet door with its full-length mirror stood three feet from the bed. Allegra had opened it the precise two and one third inches before Seth's arrival, the exact angle to reflect the bed. The lamps were also adjusted. From her position under Seth she was able to see her body in the mirror through partially closed eyes. Seth's body, over hers, was a large, amorphous dark shadow. Each time his passion built she moved faster, the reflection of her body's motion released moisture from her skin, her eyes and, most importantly, her vagina. Seth was not mistaken; Allegra achieved those orgasms.

Finally exhausted, they lay quietly, exchanging small, brushing kisses.

143

When Allegra went to the kitchenette, Seth watched her. "Oh, my God," he moaned.

Trembling, she managed to remove the cork from a well-chilled bottle of Dom Perignon and prepare a tray a beluga and thinly sliced brown bread.

They ate and drank in the hour before the first lightening of dawn.

Seth poured dribbles of champagne over her stomach. Allegra laughed as she tried to wipe it off with a sheet before he could go after it with his tongue. And they fed each other caviar.

On her way back for the second bottle of champagne, Allegra pushed closed the mirrored closet door.

"Allegra," Seth said, groggy now from champagne and his walk on water.

"Yes, darling?" She lay back, resting her glass on her stomach.

"I don't think that Billie Claire Hutchins arrangement in Washington will work."

Allegra sat up. "Why, love? It sounds acceptable to me. We can see each other on weekends. I'm sure Miss Hutchins and I can find things to do Saturday nights if you're tied up."

"No. It won't work," he said flatly and firmly.

"Oh, Seth, don't disappoint me. I love seeing you here, but I know you have terrible time problems. You simply can't continue to run up to New York so often. You're too important. Your work's too important."

"No, you don't understand. I don't want to share you."

"But you wouldn't be sharing me. I'd be with you anytime you'd like, when I'm in Washington."

"Damn it, you *still* don't understand what I'm telling you, you incredible, beautiful fool." He grabbed her pubic hair and gave it a gentle squeeze.

"Ouch! Seth Hathaway!"

He laughed and swung his feet over the side of the bed and picked up the pale green phone.

"May I help you?" came a nasal voice from somewhere in the warrens beneath the Hampshire House.

"Credit card call, please—339-220-20M3. Calling Washington, D.C., KL5-7999. Thank you."

He buried his face between her breasts. She stroked his hair

144

with one hand and reached for her champagne glass on the night table with the other.

"Helen? Sorry to wake you. Yes, thanks, it went very well . . . Yes, Rostow was there . . . yes, McNamara, also . . . Mmm, I'll be giving you a lot of dictation when I get back. But, Helen, first thing, I want you to get hold of Billie Claire Hutchins in the city room. You remember her, the one we just assigned to the White House? Tell her, and get this exactly, tell her to lease that vacant apartment at 2500 Q Street. She'll know what you mean. Tell her to lease it in her name." There was a long pause as Seth's secretary spoke. "No, don't worry. She'll know what to do. Just tell her to lease the goddamned apartment *this morning*. Month's security, month's advance, whatever. Send a blank check down to her. Thanks, Helen."

The blissful smile Allegra gave Seth as he spoke on the phone was genuine.

After he replaced the receiver she gently pushed him down. He lay absolutely still, afraid that if he moved she would stop doing whatever she was doing with the very tips of her long fingernails and her tongue.

Two

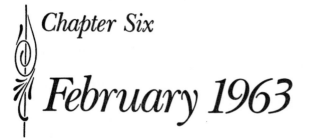

Chapter Six

February 1963

The snow had been predicted for after midnight Monday. The first tiny, crisp crystals began to fall early Tuesday afternoon.

In general, Melon thought of Washington as a white marble city. But during and after a snowfall the stately public buildings could more easily be seen in their true subtle pastels: greens, pinks, grays. As her cab passed the National Gallery of Art on Pennsylvania Avenue she marveled at its delicate soft apricot.

Melon did not marvel long over the color of walls.

She was on her way to the Longworth Building for an interview with Congressman Carson Peck. She had dressed carefully that morning, taking unusual pains selecting a clinging angora turtleneck and a full, soft wool skirt that could be arranged to show at least her knees. The predicted snow had shot down the possibility of sexy high-heeled pumps.

Melon had been asking questions about the Congressman from Tennessee ever since she had seen him seated with a beautiful woman at the piano bar of the Carriage House two weeks before. How in hell had she missed him until then? He was gorgeous. Tall, lean, early forties, with the thick Kennedyesque hair and strong jawline.

The first person she had quizzed had been Jane Connor who knew everyone in the White House *and* in Congress.

"Melon, stay away from that," had been Jane's immediate response. "He's slick, slippery and has a brain the size of a pea."

"His brain isn't exactly the part of his body I'm curious about, Janey," she murmured into the phone.

"Look, Melon, stick to your Secret Service guys. This man is not only married, he pokes everything that walks."

"The woman I saw him with was no pincushion. She was gorgeous. And I'll bet you she wasn't charging him a fee."

"Take a friend's advice for a change," Jane said wearily. "Leave Peck alone. He's *too* handsome, and he's very ambitious. You don't need that combination."

"Hmm. Thanks, Jane."

She hung up, her appetite thoroughly whetted now, and phoned Ann Adams. Ann was from Peck's part of the country. She did know about Carson Peck's background, and she also cautioned Melon to look elsewhere.

But there was no way to discourage Melon once she had begun to stalk.

Within two days she possessed a skimpy dossier on the Congressman. Nothing in it provided a handle for an interview, though. Then, a week after she first spotted him at the Carriage House, the wires carried the story of his announcement that he would seek the seat held by the aging Senator from Tennessee, Talbot Sowerby. A perfect peg!

Ernie Prescott was not enthusiastic.

"Christ, Melon, what do you want to do him for?" he said without looking up from the sked sheet he was furiously rearranging. "He's just another glamour-boy Congressman from nowhere. You horny for the guy or something?"

"Ernie!" She was furious. "He's one of the hottest men on the Hill! He's a Kennedy man! He's at the best parties! He has a powerful old man who used to be a friend of Joe's back in the bootleg days! And now he's announced for the Senate! Any combination of two is enough of a peg!" She was yelling, her eyes flooding with tears.

"Okay, okay. I don't give a shit. Go interview the jerk and let me get some work done. And don't bawl. It gives me the creeps."

"Thank you, Ernie." Melon turned and walked back to her desk. The tears were gone before she sat down.

The Congressman's office in the Longworth Building looked

150

just like all the other offices that opened onto the long marble corridors. As a second-term member, he was entitled to a slightly larger space, and more plants from the Botanic Garden. Melon sat on a two-seater couch in the anteroom and wriggled her chilled toes.

She had been very warmly greeted by a platinum blonde with perfect, inch-long fingernails. Melon understood the effusion. Reporters from the Washington bureaus of the large Tennessee papers were one thing, a columnist from a Washington daily was another matter. The staff had been alerted.

"The Congressman will be with you in just a minute, Miss Bowersox. May I get you some coffee? Tea? A Coke? I love your boots. What an unusual umbrella handle."

"I found the umbrella in a cab last week." God, the woman's a nervous half-wit. "Ah, how do you type with those nails?" she said pleasantly.

"It's not easy," the blonde smiled. "That's a wonderful coat. I love fleece lining."

"Have you worked for the Congressman long?"

"About six months," the receptionist said. "I just love it here. The work is so exciting."

"What's the Congressman like to work for?"

"Great. Just great."

I'll bet, Melon thought. She wouldn't be learning anything of use from this one.

She examined the framed photographs on the room's walls. Eight-by-ten glossies of Carson Peck shaking the hands of important constituents. Carson Peck cutting ribbons at supermarket openings. Carson Peck listening to or talking with Tennessee dignitaries. One picture, larger than the others, of Carson Peck and John F. Kennedy on the same bunting-draped platform. A beautiful, Grace Kelly–type blonde was demurely seated at the Congressman's left.

"That's a great picture of Mr. Peck and Jack Kennedy. Who's the lovely blond lady with them?"

Before the bewildered receptionist could answer, the inner office door opened.

"The Congressman will see you now, Miss Bowersox," a perky redhead said in the breathy Jackie manner. She was also wearing a Jackie A-line dress.

151

Jesus, another one, she thought. No wonder they're called Peck's Pussy Posse. She felt as if she were backstage at a Miss Universe contest.

As Melon followed the cute redhead down a short hallway, she reviewed the little she had been able to learn about Carson Peck. He was the son of Judge Leroy Peck, a formidable old machine politician back home. The judge had evidently masterminded his only son's campaigns by relying heavily on Carson's good looks, television appeal and an implied family connection with the Kennedys. And while the Kennedy-Johnson ticket had not taken Tennessee by a landslide in 1960, it had carried Carson Peck and his perfect teeth into the United States Congress by a tidy margin. As a freshman, he had kept the traditional "new boy" low silhouette in the House.

But it was his true connection with the Kennedys and his after-hours activities that interested Melon.

"Miss Bowersox." The tall, sunlamp-tanned Congressman moved out from behind his huge mahogany desk and took her hand in both of his. "I am most sorry you have been kept waiting." He spoke in a mellow drawl and his brow was furrowed, ever so slightly, with concern.

"That's all right, Congressman," she said briskly. "The Eighty-eighth Congress comes first." My God, the man's even handsomer in the daylight!

"I was speaking with George Morris from the *Commercial Appeal* about my announcement to run. They've been Sowerby supporters for years and don't take kindly to my opposing him in the primary. Party squabbling, that sort of thing."

"I understand." Melon folded her skirt for maximum effect when she seated herself in a straight-backed chair opposite him.

Suddenly, Peck rose. "Miss Bowersox, I'd like you to meet my A.A., Marshall Austin." He gestured toward a wiry, rather tired-looking man who had just entered the room. "He will be joining us for our, ah, chat."

It was a very bad move. Melon wondered why he needed a baby-sitter. After two years in Congress, surely he knew the ground rules for an interview. His administrative assistant's presence was unsettling.

"How do you do?" she said coolly and opened her spiral notebook and pulled a pencil from the wire binding. "I'm sure you're

152

familiar with my column, Congressman. I leave the political thinking to Mary McGrory at the *Star*. I like to know the man behind the politician. My readers want to know what makes people tick."

"I'd be pleased if you'd call me Carson." He flashed another toothpaste commercial smile. "Yes, of course. I'd never think of missing your column. Starts my day. Wonderful piece you did on the PT-109 tie clips. Very witty. I have one myself." He lifted his Countess Mara tie. "This is a fourteen-karat clip. Not one of those, ah, shall we say, souvenir imitations that were given away by the Democratic National Committee during the campaign."

"I take it the President gave you that tie clip?"

Peck glanced at his A.A., who had quietly seated himself in a corner beside the bookshelves.

"Yes. Yes, I've known Jack for a long time. Our families knew each other."

"Will the President be campaigning for you in Tennessee?"

"Wellll, the President's a very busy man. And he'll be very much involved in his own reelection come 1964."

The Congressman's responses and the A.A.'s presence were beginning to irritate Melon.

For starters, he was blowing her lead. She had intended to tie him to the Kennedy clout and write him into a blackstrap molasses version of the Irish Mafia. But he was giving her nothing she couldn't find in the *Herald*'s morgue, and he was insulting her by having his A.A. chaperon the interview. It was difficult to interpret whatever electricity was passing between them with that tired fish sitting behind her. Okay, time for a zinger. Check the old reflexes.

"Around town, gossip has it that you're something of a ladies' man," she said and gave him a bright smile.

Peck blinked several times, then pushed himself back in his leather executive chair and laughed, a warm, boyish laugh that crinkled the taut, tanned skin at the corners of his eyes. "Well, now, Miss Bowersox . . ."

"Melon."

"Well, now, Melon, I'm a happily married man."

"To a former Miss Tennessee, I understand."

"Yes, that's right. Martha's a wonderful girl. And a fine mother. We have three wonderful sons."

Before she could ask another question, Carson Peck launched into a twenty-minute monologue sprinkled with anecdotes about his days at the University of Tennessee Law School. His barefoot boyhood in rural Tennessee. His love of horses and his devotion to free speech and the elevation of the downtrodden. Melon felt her toes going numb again. He finished up with his three years in the Marine Corps and his fondness for fly casting. The whole recitation had the authentic ring of an expensive Madison Avenue PR firm. Or Marshall Austin. Although, she didn't yet know how the A.A. spoke. So far he hadn't opened his mouth.

Now was the time for her most effective device.

Melon said, "Thank you very much, Carson," folded her notebook, stuck the pencil back in the wire binding and assumed a "well, that's finished," position.

"I can't tell you how enjoyable this has been." The Congressman stood.

"Incidentally," Melon said casually, "I was going to come over and introduce myself at the Carriage House the other night, but you appeared to be rather involved so I . . ."

"The Carriage House? Oh, yes . . ." His eyes flicked toward his A.A. for an instant. "You should have, Melon, then I would have had the honor of meeting you sooner." He stood beside her and lightly touched her shoulder. A hesitant graze. Too hesitant.

"That piano bar can get pretty wild later in the evening. That's one of the many good things about this Administration, the night life has certainly picked up."

"Certainly has. Have you been to the Rotunda since they redecorated? Quite a lovely place now."

She could hear Marshall Austin stirring in his corner. Melon wondered how or if he would insert himself.

The roll call bell clanged.

Shit!

"Excuse us, Miss Bowersox. Congressman, there's the bell." The aide's voice was surprisingly deep and cultivated.

Carson Peck reached for her hand. "Please forgive me, Melon. I have to hurry to the floor to vote. If you have further questions, please feel free to ask Marshall. He may know more about me than I do."

Damn. She wanted to know more about the restaurants he preferred and how often he visited them.

"Thank you, I have enough now," she said curtly and made it to the door before Peck.

Out in the marble corridor Melon glanced at her watch. Five past four. She would have loved to pop into the Carroll Arms and check out the scene. A little after four was the best time to catch the really long lunchers. A great deal could often be learned by one quick drink there at this hour. Oh, well.

She was on deadline. And worse, she had gotten nothing at all from Carson Peck. Swell. After she'd begged and screamed at Ernie.

In a cab headed down the hill she felt the old panic welling up in her throat.

"Dumb idea, Melon."

"Huh?" the driver said.

"Oh, nothing," she said to the snow outside the window. "I'm just pissed at myself for setting up an interview with a guy just because he's good-looking, who had absolutely nothing to say. Where am I going to find eight hundred words on a guy who loves fly casting and fucking?"

"Huh?" The driver swiveled around. "You a reporter at the *Herald*, lady?"

"I might not be by this time tomorrow," she said as she handed him the fare.

Melon didn't take off her coat when she sat at her desk. She rolled a sheet of copy paper into the machine and stared straight ahead for several minutes. Then she began to type.

From the smoke-filled air, the clatter of keys and bells, the babble and the occasional shouts, Melon pulled forth the hardscrabble, subsistence-level life along the narrow river valleys and forested foothills of East Tennessee. The life of a freckle-faced boy in tattered pants with a fishing pole on his shoulder and the dream in his heart of making democracy work for everyone. A willowy lad with the blood of the once-proud Chickamaugas coursing through his veins, whittling and gazing up at clouds that formed the profiles of his heroes—Andy Jackson and Davy Crockett. How, as a young state Senator, by allying himself with the reform forces of Estes Kefauver against the evil Crump machine, he had started his ascent to political stardom. A man with a mission. The lean backwoods boy making it in politics with his principles intact, the living example of new politics in the New Frontier.

155

It was pure bullshit and she knew it. By the time she typed "end" at the bottom of the fourth page she half expected an American flag to pop out of her old Underwood.

That ought to do it. Set Mr. Wonderful on his ear.

"Copy?" she screamed at a passing copyboy.

Let old Talbot Sowerby eat his heart out tomorrow morning over this one. The column was guaranteed to elicit at *least* a phone call from Congressman Peck.

Now what she needed was several pounds of Mac's Manhattans with two olives apiece. She knew the Press Club bar would be dead now, so instead headed west toward Duke Ziebert's, turning up her collar against the snow and shoving her hands deep into her pockets.

She was finishing her third Manhattan and regaling the crowd at Duke's long bar with a highly embellished description of Peck's Pussy Posse when, dripping melted snow, Bob Brattle from the picture desk pushed through the double doors that faced on L Street. He approached the crowd at the bar with a whoop, waving the bulldog edition of the *Herald*.

"Great stuff here, Melon. Terrific. Makes me want to find a parade to march in."

"Hi, Bobby." Melon swung around on the tall barstool. "What are you jabbering about?"

"Tomorrow's column, babe. Terrific. This guy sounds like a corn-pone Kennedy for sure." He brandished the dripping paper in her face.

It was folded to the split page where her column appeared full length down the left-hand side of the page. Some headline genius had slugged it FROM HILL COUNTRY TO CAPITOL HILL; An American Odyssey.

Melon's mailbox at the lobby desk of her apartment building held three pink slips. Jane Connor had called. A press agent for the National Theater was peddling some touring B actor. And, one, "C. Peck at KL 5-4353. Please call when you get in."

It had worked. Her heart began to thud. She checked her watch. It was only eleven fifteen. He must have picked up the early edition. She wondered about the phone number. Would he leave his home number?

She raced to her apartment and rummaged for her Blue Book,

which contained the home numbers of everyone in Congress. The one on the message slip didn't match the number in the Blue Book. Holding her breath, she dialed KL 5-4353.

"The Rotunda. Mr. Carl speaking."

Melon hesitated.

"Hello. The Rotunda. Carl speaking."

"Carl? This is Melon Bowersox."

"Why, hello, Miss Bowersox. How are you this evening?"

"Carl, I have a message here to call Congressman Peck at this number. Is he there?"

"Yes he is, Miss Bowersox. He left word to put you through to his table if you called. Just a moment, please."

"Wait, Carl."

"Yes, ma'am?"

"Who is he with? Who else is at his table?"

"I believe he's with a young lady. Yes, I can see them from here. A young lady and a gentleman."

"What color is the young lady's hair, Carl?"

"I think reddish. Yes, red."

Aha. And she would bet her new long-lash mascara that the "gentleman" was good, old, faithful Marshall Austin doing a beard number for his boss. Riding shotgun for Peck and the girl in the Jackie getup. No wonder the A.A. looked so tired.

"Should I put you through, Miss Bowersox?"

Melon paused. "Ah, no, Carl. I won't bother him right now. But, Carl . . ."

"Yes?"

"Take my number, please. I'd like you to call me when the Congressman leaves and tell me who he leaves with."

"Certainly, ma'am. Incidentally, Miss Bowersox, thank you so much for the mention of our redecoration in your column last week. We're getting all the regulars back."

"You're welcome, Carl."

Jane's phone rang four times before she answered.

"Are you with someone or can you talk?" Melon said.

"No, I'm here with the Third Division of the Yugoslav Army. Wait a minute, I'm just finishing off this here sergeant. Ooooo, ahhhh, ummmm," Jane groaned into the phone. "Christ on a crutch, Melon, I'm asleep. What the hell do you want?"

"Funny lady, funny, funny," Melon said flatly. Then, brighten-

157

ing, "Jane, I'm in love. The most delicious, fascinating man. Listen."

Jane groaned. "Melon, you talk so much to so many people you forget who you tell what. If you're about to do a half hour on Carson Pecker again, I'm hanging up."

"*Peck*, not Pecker! Don't be such a smart-ass. Anyway, I have just got to have that man. Now!" She rolled over on her pull-out couch and began unzipping her boots.

"You already have, Melon. You fucked him sideways in twenty-four-point type in that column. It is destined to become his ultimate campaign brochure. What are you trying to pull?" Melon could hear the click of Jane's cigarette lighter.

"You've already read it? God, doesn't anyone in this town wait for the morning editions?"

"Melon, I know this Peck is this week's toy-toy, but I told you before and I'll say it again. Peck is a certifiable shit. It's very easy to locate Carson Pecker; just follow the trail of torn-up Fredericks of Hollywood lingerie. Why add yourself to that list?"

"Who's counting? I think he's very handsome."

"Oh, God, Melon. I'm going back to sleep."

Her phone went dead. Immediately, it rang. She whipped up the receiver.

"Yes?"

"Miss Bowersox, this is Carl. Your friend just left with the young lady."

"Did the other man go with him?" she asked, already knowing the answer.

"No, ma'am. Mr. Austin saw them to the car and asked me to call him a taxi."

158

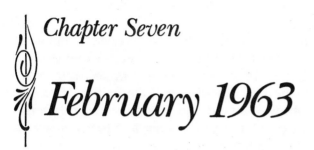

Chapter Seven

February 1963

Wednesday morning the snow was six inches deep.

Jane had called a cab before she stepped into her shower, familiar with the effects of snow on Washington traffic. She was damned if she'd walk the six long blocks to the Executive Office Building in this weather. The desk rang her an hour later to announce the cab's arrival.

Damn Melon. After she'd phoned, Jane had been unable to find sleep again until after two.

Ah, Melon. Even though she drove Jane slightly mad on occasion, she couldn't imagine life without her. Jane could not bear the company of bores. Melon was many things, but she was never, never boring. Knowing Melon was like knowing the lead in a blue soap opera. Melon fell in love every Tuesday and was out of love by Sunday afternoon. She took risks Jane would never consider, and created action and excitement by sheer will and energy. Even so, Jane felt protective about Melon, rather like caring for an adorable pet monkey that demolished one's life in an amusing, irresistible way. Melon was impossible to insult, although one could momentarily bruise her feelings. Momentarily.

Jane scanned her *New York Times* in the taxi. She carefully parceled her must reading by picking up the morning *Herald* and *Post* the night before, and having *The New York Times* delivered to her door in the morning. Wicker was moaning about Cubans, Reston puffed on about the awful state of the economy. Nothing new or earthshaking this morning.

Jane Connor resided at 1515 Massachusetts Avenue in a modest, one-bedroom apartment that appeared far more expensively furnished than it was. She had found every item greatly reduced at a good store, or on the first day of an affluent church's rummage sale. Her wardrobe was not extensive, and it, like her furniture, had been carefully selected for excellence and that timeless-classic look from inventory clearances and seconds racks.

The rates for her retarded child at the Adela Whelan Home rose as rapidly as her salary.

The one extravagance she permitted herself was taxis. Cab rates in Washington were regulated by Congress, for the convenience of Congressmen, and were a bargain by New York standards.

With a GS-15 rating she had approximately $13,000 as income after taxes. The home charged four hundred a month for Nat's care.

She seldom paid for a meal out or for an evening's entertainment. And after her brief, involuntary exile from the E.O.B. (thanks to the insatiable curiosity of Miss Mary Ellen Bowersox), it had been good to return. She had been welcomed back to her original designation as consultant by a somewhat begrudging Norm Franklin. He knew a political appointment when he saw one. And his complaints to Ted Sorensen that he didn't have the budget to take her back had been quickly shot down when an unfilled GS-15 slot miraculously developed at the Weather Bureau. Jane's papers were processed in an incredible three days, "temporarily assigning" the bureau's new GS-15 to the White House. No one argued. Done was done. Jane reported to Norm as she had before. Whoever he reported to was his business. Jane had learned to ask no questions in Washington, even before those months in purgatory writing Weather Bureau brochures.

She hurried up the steps of the Executive Office Building, nodding to the smiling guards.

Of the original occupants of Room 240 only Leonard remained. Ben had been replaced by another Deep South expert, and Carl was back up on the Hill, safe in the less tenuous employ of the Foreign Policy Committee.

160

She had left an unfinished "working memo" on the wire service coverage of Jackie and the children on her desk the night before and was not enthusiastic about the prospect of digging back in her notes.

Essentially, she was responsible for monitoring media coverage in six major Eastern daily papers and compiling think piece memos on how the First Family was being treated in print. That was in addition to her own input about what she was able to pick up from "mingling" with the press corps. Their interests, gripes, persuasions, likes and dislikes. What she was doing seemed somewhat amorphous and pointless, but she also realized that her little job was part of the great mosaic which made up the Administration's extremely deft handling and manipulation of the press.

About the only new item she had picked during the past twelve hours was that one wire service reporter's romance with a rival wire service reporter was having rough going. She had witnessed a boozy lovers' quarrel early the evening before at the Rive Gauche. Overturned wine-glasses, tears, the lady stomping out on an embarrassed table of diners. The single-girl-in-love-with-a-married-man-and-fed-up-with-it scene. She had puzzled over how to put it all in the proper language for an in-house report during the hours she had lain awake the night before. This was the sort of thing Norm wanted. That didn't mean she was comfortable about it.

Leonard was already at his desk nursing what appeared to be a monumental hangover.

"Morning, Len. Anyone else survive the explosion?"

"Only me and Henry Simmons. *Newsweek* guys always survive. I spent several weeks in the East Lounge last night."

"You look it. Want some coffee?" She went to the automatic coffee maker in the alcove outside the office.

"No, thanks. I take cream and I couldn't take the sound of it going into the cup. How are you?"

"Okay, considering a half-hour cab ride to go six blocks. Len, what do you know about Carson Peck?" She sat down in front of his desk, placing her coffee cup carefully on a thick-lined legal pad.

"Jesus, Janey, not you, too? You aren't going to break that nice, button-down Wall Street lawyer's heart, are you?"

"No, no, not me. A friend of mine has a bad case of the toasties

161

for him. Everything I know about him is bad. If you know anything good I could at least pass it on to ease the pain."

"When I hear something good about Carson Peck, other than
his looks, I'll pass it on. He's all flash and dash. The real creep in
that office is his A.A., Marshall Austin. From what I hear he's just
one notch higher than a hit man. He's old Judge Peck's man, and
Carson doesn't take a leak unless Marshall says 'go.' Which one of
that gang of yours wants a shot at ol' Carson? Melon Bowersox, I'll
bet, after reading this morning's column."

Jane sighed. "Just this week, Len. You know Melon."

"Christ, she plays games in that column of hers."

"But she's good. You or I should be so good."

Jane went to her own desk and riffled through the pages of the
unfinished memo. Waiting in her in-basket were notes she had
scribbled on the Johnson office infighting. Nothing delighted
Norm more than memos on the goings-on in the Vice President's
office. God knew where they ended up, but it was clear he had orders to pass on *any* morsel. She was getting depressed.

By twelve fifteen she had finished the wire service reporters
memo and handed it to Norm's secretary. She stepped into the
outer corridor to check the three tickers that were eternally
pounding out information. The UP machine was moving a dull
voter registration story. Equally uninteresting stuff was coming
from the AP ticker. The Reuters ticker was momentarily still.
Back at her desk, she dialed the *Herald's* extension in the White
House pressroom. Billie Claire Hutchins answered the first ring.

"Pressroom, Hutchins."

"Hi, Billie. Are you freed up yet?"

"Janey, hi. Yes. My editor had about fifteen queries after
Pierre's briefing this morning and I've just finished up. I have a
call in to Pam Turnure, but I know she won't get back to me before four. A dull day everywhere. The only moment of excitement this morning was when Gwen Gibson and I tried to sit in the
same chair at the briefing."

"I know what you mean about dull. I just checked the wires
here. Blah. Nothing. Must be the snow. Want to grab some
lunch?"

"Love to. Shall we go to the White House mess?"

"Billie, I could use a drink. I can't have one in the mess. Are you
up to hoofing it over to the East Lounge?"

"Sure. Meet you at the East Gate in ten minutes."

The three-block walk through the snow left both of them invigorated. The East Lounge of the Press Club was jammed. The snowy day gave the correspondents who worked in the building an excuse to stake out an all-day spot at the bar. The two women found a relatively quiet table near the window and ordered drinks.

Billie Claire and Jane were friends, yet both were fully aware that Jane, as a White House staffer, was considered a source to Billie Claire. A fine line had to be drawn between what she could and could not use from her conversations with Jane. They both understood the situation and never discussed or abused it. Billie Claire could ask Jane certain questions; Jane understood that was her job. It was up to Jane to draw the guidelines about the use of the information she provided.

They both took a sip of their drinks.

"God, that tastes good," Jane said.

"A little of the hair of the dog, as Ann Adams says." Billie Claire lit a cigarette. "Stop me if I'm out of line, but one of the queries Ernie had me chasing around this morning had to do with a Dr. Max Jacobson. What do you know about him?"

"He's a fancy New York speed doctor, Billie. You know that," Jane replied flatly.

"Well, what I know and what I can print are two different things, as we all say. Can you give me any leads at all? We all know he was with Kennedy on the Vienna trip and he's been down to Palm Beach."

"Maybe that's how Jackie stays so skinny."

"And maybe that's how Jack stays so up, what with Addison's disease, and all that cortisone he walks around with."

"Billie, if I knew anything, I'd tell you. For the record I don't know any more than you do. But, if it were my problem, I would have someone check out the doctor through New York. If it will help, I'll ask Paul who a good source there would be."

"Thanks. I think Ernie just likes gossip. You know the *Herald* would never print anything like that. But they need to have it on file to protect themselves in case some conservative paper breaks something on it."

"I'm surprised Ernie would even ask you to run it down, Billie. What happened to your paper's interest in matters of state?" Jane smiled, and changed the subject. "Are you going to Allegra's party next Wednesday?"

"For Ann and David Brinkley? Yes, I hope we get an early lid that day. I wouldn't want to miss it. You know she didn't ask Melon and she's livid."

Jane reached across the table and gave Billie Claire's wrist a squeeze. "Don't worry about Melon. She's tracking a new man this week."

"It's got to be Carson Peck, from her column this morning. Really, she's outrageous. How does she get away with a puff piece like that?"

"Billie, she gets away with it because she's a superb writer. You and I and everyone else who is plugged into this town knows Peck's a toad. But if you read that column without knowing him you'd have to admit it was excellent. Melon makes beautiful use of the English language."

"I guess you're right. Is she having an affair with him?"

"I don't think anyone has taken off his or her clothes yet. But if you want to get in on the pool, take sometime after two thirty next Saturday as the winning number."

Billie Claire giggled. "Have you talked with Ann this week?"

"She doesn't say anything, but it's obvious that Del is really back on the bottle again. She gets that pinched look when his name comes up. Dammit, they're so crazy about each other. And his drinking is tearing them both apart. The fights have gone public recently. Some pretty bad scenes."

"I know. I stopped by the office to pick up some material this morning. She's wearing sunglasses."

"Sunglasses? In a blizzard? What the hell for?"

"I don't know," Billie Claire said. "But if I'd been crying all night, I'd probably wear sunglasses the next day."

"Or if you had a black eye."

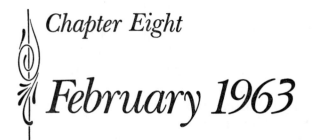

Chapter Eight

February 1963

Ann required fifteen minutes and half a tube of Erase.

Studying her eye carefully in the mirror of the *Herald*'s ladies' room, she had to admit she had done one hell of a job. The puff remained, but she had managed to cover the discoloration, which this morning had turned a yellowish magenta.

"There, that ought to do it," she muttered, gathering up her handbag and coat. She had made several trips to the ladies' room for touch-ups during the day and so far her enormous shiner had gone undetected.

"Hubba-hubba," the night city editor called out as she strolled past his desk. Randy Klopman was given to using phrases from the happiest time of his life, which happened to be World War II. "Nothing like a good war to make a man out of you," he often said.

"If that hubba-hubba is for me, I thank you kindly, sir." Ann bowed in a mock curtsy. "Like my outfit? I've got a heavy date."

"Anything newsworthy?"

"Not for you. For me it's a five-star extra. Del's driving me out to the Olney Inn for dinner."

"You gotta be nuts. Why go all the way out there in a blizzard?"

"Because it's romantic, Randy. And right now I need a shot of romance real bad. I checked, and River Road is clear." She slipped into her coat. "And with this weather, we'll have the place to ourselves."

Klopman ran a hand over his close-cropped gray hair. "How's Del these days? I haven't seen as much of him as I used to."

"My husband has his ups and downs." Ann tucked in her scarf. "As you damn well know, Randy."

"Don't get on your high horse, Annie. Del's an old buddy of mine. I'm just interested in his welfare."

"Sorry. We've been having some rough times lately."

"So I see," he said, gazing up over his half-glasses.

Ann touched her hand to her eye. "It shows, huh?"

"No, not really. It's just that you haven't spent so much time in the ladies' room since you came back from that vacation in Mexico. And you weren't wearing sunglasses then."

"Don't be tacky." She reached across and flipped the editor's tie into his face. "I bid you good night now, sir."

Ann walked to the elevator, head high. She stood under the canopy waiting for Del's car to crawl around the block in the creeping traffic.

She knew today's big topic of conversation around town had been their shoving match at Clyde's the night before. She had wanted to go home and Del had wanted another for the road. She had tried to wrestle the car keys out of his pocket, and when he had pushed her away, she had slipped and hit her cheekbone against the corner of the bar. Del had immediately sobered. He had become contrite and apologetic. But anyone standing four feet away would have sworn he had slugged her. She was too angry to speak and had stormed out to hail a cab on M Street, after yelling at him from the doorway not to come home. He hadn't. At dawn she had called the Willard Hotel, knowing he would have holed up there. They had then spent thirty weeping minutes on the phone, swearing undying love and offering apologies.

Dinner at the Olney Inn had been Del's idea. He loved her. He was switching to beer. He promised. And why didn't they have a quiet evening at the Olney and start over again?'

The lovely converted coach house out along the old C & O Canal held nothing but pleasant memories for them both. The low-beamed ceilings and roaring fireplace made it an ideal lovers' hideaway. And it had been there that Del had officially asked Ann to marry him. They hadn't been there for months. It was the perfect spot. She had accepted immediately.

"I'll pick you up at seven, sharp. I love you, Annie."

"I love you, too, darling." She had dabbed carefully at her swollen eye. "Seven. Perfect."

Once past Glen Echo the traffic thinned. While the snow was deeper in the hilly countryside, the road was remarkably clear, and they pulled into the parking lot in less than an hour.

A fire blazed in the rough stone fireplace. Ellie was guarding their favorite chairs by the hearth. Not that it was necessary. The place was deserted. Ann ordered a martini and gazed into the fire.

He loves me and that's not easy. She gently bit her lower lip. *I* can't change the way I work *or* drink. So why should I expect him to? I know I threaten him professionally, and there's nothing to be done about that. Goddammit, there has to be a way for an accommodation without either of us compromising.

"Any more heat from old Cynthia Hartford?" she asked gently when he returned from the checkroom and joined her.

Del sighed heavily. "I don't know. I stayed under cover today. What I don't know won't hurt me."

The day before Ann had dug a terrific story out of Wilbur Mills and Ernie had front-paged it. When she had met Del at the Press Club bubbling with her good news, he had handed her a crumpled memo from Mrs. Hartford, complaining about the recent decline in the quality of his columns. He had missed two deadlines in the last month and had repeated himself in three columns. Del had sulked at the bar while Ann tried to shush the enthusiastic late arrivals who had seen her piece in the early edition. She could see it was going to be a bad night and had eased him out of the club.

Stopping at Clyde's had been a bad idea. There, they had gotten into a career argument, and she had said a lot of words she couldn't take back. She had no intention of letting up on her own work because Del was finding his old sources drying up and new ones harder to unzip. They simply had to be more open and honest about their problem. Del's term as president of the Press Club hadn't been enough.

Now, sober and sitting by the fire, Del politely declined the waiter's request for his drink order for a second time. He sat smoking a thin cigar, the light from the fire playing on his thick white hair and high cheekbones.

She sat beside him, resisting the urge to touch the side of his face. *God, I love that man.*

She felt her insides turning soft and receptive, and tears began to fill her eyes.

"You look like the Ambassador to the Court of St. James's," she smiled, blinking away the moisture.

He was wearing the tweed suit he wore when he appeared as one of the panel of reporters on *Meet the Press.*

"And you look frozen and beautiful. Maybe I'll skip the menu and have you for dinner."

"Maybe we could run out and turn on the heater in the car and steam up the windows?"

Del laughed. "Outrageous, wanton hussy." He pushed his hand under the hem of her skirt. She playfully removed it, looking around the room.

"Annie, I'm lost without you. You know that. It's the old devil booze. Poison. Turns us all into beasts. I quit. Dry as a bone." He held both his hands in the air as if to prove there wasn't a glass hidden up his sleeves.

"Excuse me," the waiter said softly, "Miss Adams you have a phone call."

"Tear it up," she said, not taking her eyes away from Del's face.

"The gentleman says it's important, ma'am."

"What gentleman?" she impatiently asked the waiter.

"A Mr. Klopman from the *Herald.*"

"Goddamn. All right. Where's the phone?"

"This way, ma'am."

"Darling, I'll be right back. I can't imagine what this is about."

"How the hell did he know where to find you?"

"Oh, he was on the desk when I left to meet you. Wanted to know where I was going all done up. By the way, you didn't mention my new dress."

"Did I have to? How can I see your clothes when I want what's underneath so badly. Go on, darling, get rid of him. Probably wants to know how to spell something." He half rose and kissed her lightly. "Go do your stuff, but hurry."

"Annie," Randy's voice barked into the receiver. "Sorry as hell to do this to you. I know it's a big night, but we've got a hot one out near where you are."

"Out here!" she shouted into the phone. "There's nothing but jackrabbits and pine trees out here. What the hell are you talking about?"

"Plane just went down about three miles up River Road from the Inn. I'm strapped. There's no one here. Even if there were we couldn't get him out there fast enough."

"Damn. What kind of plane?" Ann dug into her purse for her notebook. An automatic reflex.

"Private craft. A small twin engine. Seems it just left Butler Aviation at National Airport in this snowstorm and smacked down into the trees about fifteen minutes ago. We just got a call from the Maryland state troopers. I want you to get out there and see who was in the plane before the Feds mess up the site."

"Shit, Randy. That's not my beat. I'm standing here in a pair of eighty-dollar suede boots and a hundred-dollar dress, and you want me to make like Nanook of the North in the pitch-dark . . ."

"Ann, don't do this to me. I can't get anyone out there in less than an hour. We can replate the final with the story before the *Post* can get anyone there. Please. I'll make it up to you."

Ann sighed. "Okay, Randy, okay. How the hell do I find the wreck? I assume the plane didn't have the consideration to go down in the middle of a well-lit highway."

"There should be a state trooper arriving at the inn any minute. I asked Sergeant Malachi to pick you up."

Through the leaded glass window of the inn, Ann could see a red flasher swiveling from the roof of a Maryland State Police car.

"They're here now, Randy. Don't worry, I've got you covered." She slammed down the phone.

She sat down beside Del. "Darling, that was the desk. A private plane has gone down a few miles up the road. They've sent the troopers to take me to the site. I'll just go have a look-see and run right back and file from here. Won't take me more than an hour."

"Fuck all, Annie. Why you . . . ?" Del stood up.

"I'm the only one close enough to get there fast. Randy wants to make the final with the story." Ann was struggling into her coat, which the waiter had hurriedly brought.

"Do you want me to go with you?" He started to get up.

169

"No, darling. I want you to stay put right by the fire. I'll feel better knowing you're here and warm. I won't be long." She grabbed her scarf and raced for the door, blowing him a kiss over her shoulder.

Ann could see the auxilliary lights the police had set up as the car approached the site. The plane had gone down about fifty yards from the main road. With several "goddammit all to hells," she left the car and plunged into the deep snow. "Good-bye, boots," she muttered.

She stumbled through snow and underbrush, simultaneously trying to hold on to the burly trooper, her handbag and her footing. An emergency vehicle had made it through the snow and underbrush; its flashing light was turning the silent, falling snow the color of fresh blood. Two blanket-covered bodies lay about forty feet from the crumpled plane.

A gigantic trooper in a fur-lined parka and bright yellow rubber boots approached her.

"I'm Ann Hawkins Adams. *Washington Herald*." She extended her gloved hand.

"Yes, I know, Miss Adams."

"You want to fill me in?" She took out her notebook, scanning the scene.

"Maybe you better talk to the Federal Aviation man."

"Which one is he?"

"The one in the tuxedo over there." The trooper smiled as he pointed to a man crouched near the open door of the wrecked plane, peering intently inside. "He came flying out here like a bat out of hell. Maybe he's worried about his job."

"Okay, I'll talk to him. What's your name, officer?"

"Reynolds, ma'am."

"Were you the first one here?"

"Well, yeah. Me and my partner. Billy Kelly over there."

"Good. I'll want to talk to you both in a minute. Stay put."

She approached the FAA inspector and introduced herself. The man did not look pleased, but told her his name was Clarence Quackenbusch.

"The *Herald*, huh? You're going to freeze out here. And there really isn't much I can tell you. I just got here myself. Pulled away from a dinner party." He indicated his tuxedo under his topcoat.

170

"Who was in the plane, Mr. Quackenbusch? I see two bodies laid out."

"Can't give you that, Miss Adams. We have to follow procedure here and notify the next of kin first."

"But you know who they were? Men? Women? What?"

"Miss Adams, I know you have a job to do, and I admire your spunk being out here in this weather and all, but rules are . . ."

"I had a nice interview last week with your administrator over at the FAA," she said pointedly. "Fine man. Talk with him quite often."

Her point was not lost on the flustered civil servant.

"Look, all I know is that Washington tower got a distress call about ten minutes after this plane took off. He said he'd lost power and was going down. They got two maydays and then the air went dead. Those two troopers," he pointed, "saw the plane skimming the trees along the river. I haven't had time to check who filed the flight plan at Butler, so there's no way I can tell you who these men were or where they were headed."

"Men? Thank you." She scribbled in her notebook.

"We should have the information on the craft's owner shortly." He smiled wearily, but Ann sensed he was rather nervous. "Now, if you'll excuse me, Miss Adams, I've got work to do." Quackenbusch turned and resumed his examination of the plane's doorway.

Ann walked to the two mounds under blankets. After a moment, a trooper came up beside her as she started to bend down.

"I'm sorry, Miss Adams. The inspector, Mr. Quackenbusch, has just closed the area. You'll have to leave. Sergeant Reynolds will take you back to the Inn. You must be pretty uncomfortable out in this weather."

"Not as uncomfortable as I'm going to be when I call my editor with all this wonderfully helpful information," she said sarcastically.

Her trip back to the Inn produced no further information from Sergeant Reynolds, who could only tell her what she already knew about the plane going down over the trees.

She pushed through the door of the Olney Inn at exactly eleven thirty. She could no longer feel her feet. Del was still seated before the fire. The blaze had been reduced to a bed of embers. He was

171

holding an empty old-fashioned glass, staring into the dying coals.

His eyes were open, but he was seeing nothing.

Ann shook her head and headed for the pay phone. She dictated what little she had to night rewrite.

"A Cessna twin-engine, privately owned aircraft carrying the pilot and one male passenger crashed in a wooded section of Montgomery County at approximately ten P.M. last night. According to two Maryland state troopers who witnessed the accident, the plane experienced possible engine failure and crashed on contact. Both the pilot and the passenger were declared dead at the scene by Federal Aviation Inspector Clarence Quackenbusch, who arrived within minutes of the crash. Federal officials are withholding the identity of the two men pending notification of next of kin."

Pretty skimpy stuff for an eighty-dollar pair of boots. But, she couldn't file blue sky, and that was the best she could do.

She returned to the dying fire. She watched Del slowly, very slowly, lift his glass to his mouth without realizing it was empty.

"Annie, ol' girl," he slurred, blinking up at her. "My Brenda Starr is back. Come here, darling." He lurched toward her, trying to wrap his arms around her waist, but falling back into the chair instead. "Oh, lookee, you've ruined your nice new boots and dress," he said with mock pity.

Ann stared straight ahead, not looking at her husband's sagging face. "That's all right. I'll put it on my expense account," she said absently.

She sat down across from her husband as he tried to raise his empty glass to his lips again. "But, some things have no price, Del."

His eyes were closed now. Over his silver head she watched the snow silently falling beyond the old leaded windows.

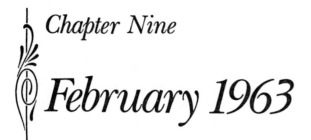

Chapter Nine

February 1963

"I don't *care* how much it costs, darling. I want celery. Yes, celery. That's the exact color. It's a very special shade of icy green. It will pick up the small floral design in the chintz drapes. And that chair is to go right beside the
. . . No, darling, *velvet*."

Allegra watched Chu enter the bedroom with her breakfast tray. "No, Kenneth, love, flat, not crushed." She shifted the receiver to her right ear in order to adjust the lace elbow pillows. "But, love, of *course* you can find the fabric. And if you can't, then you can have your little elves weave it."

Chu set the footed tray over her thighs and stood back, waiting for Allegra to finish her call. "Bring the swatches over next week. Let's see, today is Thursday. Wednesday? No, I'm busy all day next Wednesday. Dinner party for the Brinkleys. Thursday, then." She poured coffee from a Spode carafe. "Bye, darling."

Allegra set the receiver in the cradle and handed the phone to Chu. "God, what one has to take from an incompetent faggot!"

"Yes, miss," the uniformed Formosan said. "Chu open the drapes?"

Allegra tapped the top of her soft-boiled egg. "All right. Is it still snowing?"

"Yes, miss. It stop tonight on radio."

Allegra scooped a bit of the opened egg into the cup and lightly sprinkled salt on it. "Chu, if Chai is in the kitchen when you go downstairs, tell him Mr. Hathaway and I will be dining alone this evening, rather late. He has to go to a reception at the White House with Mrs. Hathaway. Here, I'll write it down." She wrote on a pale blue pad with a gold pencil. "Lobster bisque. Arugala, fresh fruit and cheese. The Vacherin will be perfect. We will dine in the library. Tell him to lay the fire around nine, but not to light it. He can select the wine."

Chu drew open the pale green brocade drapes, then took the slip of paper from the night table.

Allegra pensively sipped Chai's excellent French breakfast coffee. The Tiffany invitations for next Wednesday's dinner party stated that *Miss Allegra Farr* requested the pleasure of certain people's company. She smiled over the rim of her cup.

How marvelous! How deliciously ironic. The woman whose Tiffany calling cards read, "Mrs. Seth Lowell Hathaway," was paying for next Wednesday's food and wine and flowers, to say nothing of the silver service, the crystal and the china.

Over in her much larger Georgetown mansion, Jeannine Hathaway knew this. Everyone who received invitations from Miss Allegra Farr knew whose money paid for the paper, the engraving, the envelopes and even the postage stamps.

Happily, Allegra stretched. "Chu, hand me the *Herald*. It's there on the foot of the chaise."

Chu picked up the still-folded paper and placed it beside Allegra on the king-sized canopied bed.

"Umm." Allegra skimmed the front page for several moments as she finished her egg and unbuttered, crustless toast. Below the fold she spotted Ann Adams's by-line. "Oh, Ann Adams made the front page again. Good heavens. A plane crash out in the woods. What in the world was she doing out there on a night like last night?"

Ann Adams was special to Allegra. She was one of the very few people who was openly friendly with both Mrs. Seth Hathaway and Miss Allegra Farr, and made no apologies for it. Seth had introduced them, and Allegra had been inviting Ann to her parties ever since. She liked Ann and followed her by-line closely. She

174

read every story of Ann's that appeared, whether they were on the front page or not.

Allegra had never been happier. In addition to Seth, the beautiful house and her raved-about dinner parties, she now had interesting friends of her *own*. Billie Claire had introduced her to Miles Buford, and Miles always caught and appreciated the most subtle nuances of clothes and decor. Through Billie Claire she had also met Melon Bowersox, and through Ann, Jane Connor. She had never before known such lively, amusing women. The night before, she, Melon and Miles had stayed far too late at a new Georgetown disco. She smiled at the memory. Yes, life was certainly good.

Although Allegra did not know it, Ann's story had grown considerably during the night, as more information became available to the rewrite man who pursued it after Ann filed her first lead. By the late city edition, the names of the two dead men had been revealed.

She read the entire story. A pilot from New Jersey named Elmo Sherry and a lawyer from a New York law firm had been aboard and had died instantly. Allegra paused at the name of the lawyer's firm. "Prouty, Langtry and Boxer. Hmm."

"Pardon, miss?" Chu was accustomed to her muttering and generally ignored it unless she detected an order of some kind.

"Nothing, Chu. Oh, ask Chai to order some cherrywood logs from Neam's for tonight. They burn longer and have such a lovely fragrance."

"Yes, miss."

She studied Ann's story for several moments after she had finished reading it, then reached for the phone and dialed the *Herald*'s number.

"Miss Adams, please," she told the switchboard operator.

An instant later Ann came on the line. "Adams."

"Ann, Allegra Farr."

"Hello, Allegra. I'm sorry I haven't responded to your invitation for Wednesday night. I've been swamped. You know I'll be there."

"Marvelous, but that's not why I called. I just saw your story on that plane crash last night."

"Oh, God, don't remind me. My feet are still blue."

"You poor darling. You do get all the good assignments, don't you? Listen, Ann, what do you know about the passenger that was killed? His name was Boxer. I remember that name from somewhere, but I can't place it and it's driving me mad."

"Hell, I don't know who he was. The desk is going to follow up on that story today. Someone said he was a criminal lawyer from New York down here on routine business. Some fat-cat client must have owned the plane. The thing just stalled out in that rotten weather. Bang. Crash. Dead. That's all there was to it."

"Oh, *now* I remember who Allen Boxer was. When I was living in New York, I met him through a press agent friend of mine. How could I have forgotten him? The creep made advances on the dance floor at Trude Heller's one night."

"Well, I'm happy to have jogged your memory, darlin'. I've got to scoot. Got an assignment halfway across town and I'm running late. See you Wednesday."

Allegra did two extra deep knee-bends and walked nude into her pink and beige bathroom. "Allen Boxer. Hummmm. Wonder who he left all that stock to? Chu," she called over the running water, "lay out my Chanel please. Then call the Jockey Club and book two for twelve thirty, regular table." She began to cream her face.

"Yes, miss."

The *Herald's* first edition the next day had moved the follow-up on the crash back to page seven with no by-line. *The New York Times* ran a small obit on Allen Boxer.

Chapter Ten

July 1963

At nine fifteen in the evening of July second, Billie Claire crawled into the bed she had wondered if she would ever see again. Her apartment was exactly as she had left it, except for a pile of mail and magazines her thoughtful neighbor had stacked on the coffee table. Her hair was stiff with dirt, her ordinarily well-manicured nails were chipped and grimy, every inch of bone and muscle ached. She collapsed onto the quilted bedspread, too tired to pull it farther down than the pillows. She ignored the bedside alarm and closed her eyes, but she was so exhausted she was unable to fall into that deep, blank state of healing sleep.

During the preceding eleven days, dozing upright in noisy, smoke-filled buses, in the press plane that followed Air Force One from country to country, and in lumpy foreign hotel beds she had fantasized her quiet apartment, the firm, familiar bed. She had existed on a diet of Bloody Marys and cellophane-wrapped packages of RyKrisp and processed cheese. She thought she had taken enough American cigarettes, but she had run out and had smoked only Gauloises during the last three days. Her mouth felt swollen, her gums raw.

Three weeks earlier, Ernie Prescott had told her she would be assigned to cover the President's trip to Europe. She had needed to sit down quickly on the chair by her cluttered desk in the White

House pressroom. The previous week she had done nothing but file a feature on Caroline's damn pony and she was beginning to think Seth had put her in the West Wing only to pay her off for Allegra.

"Ernie! Thank you!" she had said, holding the receiver with both hands to make sure she was hearing him correctly. "Thank God!"

"You may well be asking Him to forgive me, B.C. Better take some uppers and a good pair of sneakers. I expect you to outrun both Helen Thomas and Fran Lewine."

"What do I cover, Ernie? I mean, Jackie isn't going and that's my beat." For a moment, bewilderment moderated her excitement.

"No, but Eunice and Jean are, and so is Lee Radziwill. You've got the 'sister beat.'"

"But what if something happens to Jackie? She's pretty pregnant, almost seven months. What if she has the baby?"

"Don't worry about it; nothing's going to happen to Jackie we can't cover. Doesn't take any time at all to hustle someone up to Hyannis. Anyway, she's not due until mid-September."

"Oh, Ernie, this is terrific. I've never been to Europe." Billie Claire pawed frantically through the pile of crumpled copy paper trying to locate a pack of cigarettes. When she found one she lit the filter end.

"You deserve it, kid. Two years over there rates something better than local out-and-back trips. Better put a green ribbon in your Olivetti, though. I want copy out of Ireland that will make Hathaway's half-Irish heart weep." He had lapsed into an Irish brogue laced with Brooklynese.

"I'll get the schedule from Pierre's office right away. He should know what the sisters will be up to." Billie Claire coughed and mashed out the melting filter.

"That's the idea, kid. Leave the heavy stuff to the Lisagors and Restons. Besides the sisters, I want schmaltz, color, the mood of the masses, little kids, flags waving."

When she replaced the phone she sat quietly for a moment, letting it all sink in. At Pierre's briefing that morning the questions from the reporters who crammed his small office had focused mostly on the upcoming trip. Salinger and Kenny O'Donnell had advanced the President's trip on a dry run a month earlier, plotting his every move. Billie Claire had stood at the back of the room feeling mildly jealous of the questioners, knowing most of them would be going.

Now she was one of them.

She knew it would mean sitting with the Secret Service men in the back of the chartered press plane that followed Air Force One, the worst hotel rooms along the route, having to scurry around trying to get information and being generally treated like excess baggage. None of that mattered. She would be traveling with the official entourage of one of the most exciting Presidents in the nation's history. She knew the *Boston Globe* and *Newsweek* and *The New York Times* would get the good stuff, and even be invited to ride with the Presidential party on Air Force One, and that she would be left to hold her own in the rampaging pack that followed. But, more importantly, she knew what the professional prestige of being on even the second plane would do for her.

In 1961 Bill Lawrence of *The Times* had quit because his paper didn't assign him to a Presidential trip. At the time she had thought him foolish. Now she understood.

Her last two years covering the White House had been the most exciting time of her life. Everything a Kennedy said or did was front-page copy. Craggy old Eddie Folliard, the *Washington Post*'s senior White House man, had taken her under his wing her first month in the West Wing and patiently explained to her that everything that happened there held significance. He cautioned her about not letting Kennedy officials whisper questions in her ear to ask the President at his press conferences.

"Ask your own questions, kiddo. There are enough whores around here for them to plant stuff with."

Sure enough, a staffer tried it with her the second week on the job, and sure enough, someone else asked the identical question during the ensuing press conference.

Billie Claire was seldom recognized at the conferences, not because she didn't try, or because John Kennedy didn't like her, but because she simply was too ladylike to assert herself. She just wasn't a performer. Sarah McClendon could croak, "Mr. President, Mr. President," over and over, until he had no choice but to recognize her. He knew she would have a tough question, but he seemed to enjoy coming up with an answer. Helen Thomas always got a front-row seat and she was hard to ignore. Then, there were the television guys. The President knew that if he recognized a CBS White House man he would make the six o'clock news. That man's question, and his answer, would be seen and heard by millions. Such was not the case with May Craig and her little paper in Maine.

Most importantly, Eddie had warned her of the dangers of being "stroked." Being stroked meant being invited to a White House reception as a guest. Being stroked meant having a White House official leak a bit of juicy information to you, personally. Being stroked meant being seduced into the Kennedy inner circle, and Eddie had warned her about how intoxicating that could be . . . and dangerous, dangerous to her job and her ability to keep her thinking straight, her copy evenhanded.

He need not have worried. After two years, no one had even blown in her ear.

Billie Claire punched at one of her sweat-dampened down pillows, then turned it over, trying to erase the jumble of sounds and images of the last few exhilarating days.

Think of the beach, she told herself. Think of the gang sitting around Ann's and Del's deck at Rehobeth drinking and laughing. A long Fourth of July weekend in the company of good friends, good talk. The rental of a beach house had been Jane's idea, really, and Ann and Del had been more than happy to chip in and share. Their timing for a big Fourth of July bash was perfect, just what she needed to clear her head.

As soon as she fell into half-sleep, the anticipated ocean waves of her imagination became overlaid by the sound of half-hysterical massed voices, cheering, screaming, waving flags and handkerchiefs, flinging flowers and constantly chanting, "Ken-ah-dee, Ken-ah-dee, Ken-ah-dee." Her head pulsed with the memory of Berlin crowds advancing on the press bus, pressing against it until it rocked. It was not a menacing crowd, but one driven by worship of the young American emperor. After the bus had been parked four blocks from the platform on which Kennedy was to speak, it had taken her ten minutes to get out the door. She had managed to claw her way around to the front of the bus where anonymous hands had lifted her onto the bumper, and then up onto the sagging hood. From there she had been able to see over the heads of what looked to be at least a million Germans. She had found herself hanging onto the tweed sleeve of a man already firmly in place against the windshield. He had seemed totally oblivious to her clutching. The crowd continued to sweep forward. It surged ahead like a giant protoplasm, trying to climb onto and over the hood and roof of the bus toward John F. Kennedy.

Her high heels began to slide on the slick surface and she felt herself pitching forward. She plummeted into a sea of arms and shoulders and backs. As she felt two strong hands lifting her upright, out of the chaos, she knew the terror of mindless panic for the first time in her life. Her breath left her, she could hear her heart beating in her ears as she looked into the face of a pleasant, sandy-haired man in his mid-forties. His hair and skin and eyebrows all seemed to be the same color. He was struggling with all his strength to keep her from falling back into the crowd again. They were both carried forward in the crush. She told herself that if she ever got out of this alive, let alone a simple cripple, she would find a safer, saner occupation.

Her rescuer, now the color of raw meat, and perspiring in the afternoon heat, managed to get her back up onto the sidewalk and safely against a brick building.

"Jack Schoonover, *Time*, Bonn Bureau," he said, gasping for air. He still firmly held her arm. "A body can get killed that way. Never seen anything like this."

"I think you just saved my life," she said, pushing wet tendrils of hair back behind her ears.

"Don't tell me you're trying to cover this?" He gestured toward her open note pad.

"At first I was. Then I was just trying to stay with the traveling press on that bus. . . . I'm sorry. I'm Billie Claire Hutchins, *Washington Herald*."

"So I see," he smiled and flicked the press pass dangling from the chain around her neck. "I think we've met."

"You've got to be kidding."

"No. I used to work with Bob Smith and Hank Suydam in the Washington *Time-Life* Bureau."

"Oh, for God's sake. Small world. Of course I remember you." She didn't, but he was very good-looking.

"We'll never get back to the bus from here. Let's duck in somewhere and I'll buy you a beer. They're famous for that stuff over here."

They spent the rest of the afternoon together, his arm firmly, reassuringly, around her, steadying her as more crowds mauled and pushed to views of Kennedy at the Brandenburg Gate, at Checkpoint Charlie, at City Hall. Then, sitting beside her on the press bus as it crept through traffic. Schoonover proved to be a marvelous guide and a superior sprinter, virtually dragging her behind him, teasing her about her ridiculous shoes.

"I know," she panted, climbing the steps of a building the color of old chewing gum opposite an open plaza, again jammed with mobs. "My editor told me to wear sneakers. I thought he was just trying to be cute."

They found an empty office on the second floor. From the window they could see the mass of people and almost hear the President.

"These people have a hero problem," he said as he pulled her down beside him on the wide windowsill. "Remember how they turned out for Hitler?"

"Don't be obscene."

"Oh, you think there's no comparison?" He put his arm around her. "A leader who can produce this kind of mass response could be dangerous."

"Good God, there's nothing remotely dangerous about Jack Kennedy. He's the most overwhelmingly popular political figure alive."

"Yeah, but I don't trust leaders who can make people go berserk. Look at him. He could tell them to charge those machine guns at The Wall, and damn if they wouldn't do it. They're mindless right now. It's like orgasm."

Billie Claire absently reached for his thigh.

He immediately pushed closed the door with his foot and began to unzip her shift and unfasten her bra.

"Do you have any idea how much I've been wanting to do this?" he said as he pressed her down on a cluttered desk and clamped his mouth to her breast.

He moaned and eased her to the floor amidst a cascade of index cards and magazine clippings. He was an eager and efficient lover From the open window, somewhere over her head, she heard a great roar, and in her head rang the clipped, nasal voice, high-pitched and resonant, ". . . Ich bin ein Berliner . . ." afterward, she could sense that Jack Schoonover, *Time* Bonn Bureau, was a bit unsettled by the vigor of her response.

Billie Claire lifted her head from the topmost of the hot damp pillows and squinted at the luminous hands of her bedside clock. One fifteen A.M. She sighed, pondered half a Seconal, then realized she had taken them all on the trip and lay back.

She smiled sleepily to herself as she remembered Ireland.

It was from Dublin that she had filed her best copy of the trip. After that she felt she had earned her seat on the press plane. She had also taken the notes for a long Sunday feature and carried them home with her.

The President had made an unscheduled stop at Waddington Royal Air Force Base in England. He had gone from there to visit his sister Kathleen's grave. He had watched his sister Jean place red and white Irish roses beneath the headstone inscribed, "Joy she gave—Joy she found." The press had been barred from covering what had been a private occasion, but Billie Claire had pieced together the information from picking the brains of those who were there. If Ernie wanted schmaltz, he was going to have it for the Sunday feature. Big, smeared splotches on her notes reminded her of how she had felt rereading the pages, curled up in the back of the press plane on the flight back home.

The next day, after the laundry, the bath, the shampoo, the nails and shaving the hairy legs, she would type up the feature for Ernie.

The beautiful Irish-American President had been almost manic about being on "the sod" as he had called it to more vast and hysterical crowds. Men held small children above their heads to provide them with a glimpse of him. Women sobbed and screamed, "Bless you," as he moved along O'Connell Street in Dublin. At Mary Kennedy Ryan's cottage on the old Kennedy farm at Dunganstown, Billie Claire had slipped in the mud trying to keep up with the frenzied members of the press, clawing at any morsel of speech uttered between the President and the swarm of love-crazed cousins who greeted him. She had managed to squeeze herself between a man from UPI and a *Life* photographer beside the tiny cottage. Through the window she could see the President and his cousins gathered around a bright turf fire. A silver pot of tea and a tray of brown bread and salmon were laid out on a white linen tablecloth. She saw someone pass David Powers a slug of Irish whiskey. That detail she didn't put in her story of the scene.

She turned in her feature piece at eight in the evening of the following day and returned home. She felt wonderfully clean and relaxed. Billie Claire read for a while and yawned deeply as she set her alarm for 7::00 A.M.

When Miles knocked at her door the next morning she was stepping into a crisp, sleeveless shift and sandals.

She opened the apartment door to Miles's outstretched arms.

"Ahhh, Brenda Starr returns!" he shouted and kissed her on both cheeks. "Just in time for the birthday of our country."

"Oh, Miles, take me away—fast." She handed him her canvas overnight bag.

"I want to hear every juicy detail. What does it feel like to travel with the leader of the Free World?"

"I don't know yet, I'm still numb. I think I'll just sleep on it for the next three days. I've never been so exhausted."

Miles looked truly handsome. His tan was already well begun, contrasting nicely with his beautifully groomed dark hair that was graying at the temples. The tailored white ducks and blue button-down shirt he wore set off his trim physique. Out in the hallway he tilted his head toward a door between Billie Claire's apartment and the elevator.

"Who's living in the Contessa Allegra's apartment now? I invariably forget to ask."

"Being bitchy this morning, darling? It was taken by an absolutely *adorable* window dresser at Farnsworth-Reed who seems to have a taste for men in leather jackets and chains. Want to meet him?"

"Now, now. Talk about bitchy. In that case, he probably doesn't appreciate the mauve silk walls. God, she was only there three months. Poor old Seth. It's a good thing he has a bundle."

"Oh? How do you know about the mauve walls, Miles? You were never in that apartment when Allegra was there." Billie Claire held open the elevator door with her thigh.

"When the call goes out for one hundred and twenty-seven yards of mauve watered silk in this town, those of us with an interest in interior design are bound to hear." He gave her a boyish smile. "Actually, a friend of mine who works for Millicent Greer told me."

After stowing her bag in the tiny trunk and settling behind the wheel of his MG, he said, "Now then, my beauty, you must tell me all about Europe."

Traffic on the streets of the capital was almost nonexistent at that early hour on a holiday weekend. In only minutes they had crossed town and were on the Annapolis highway.

Billie Claire sketched the trip, giving him only the highlights.

"I haven't really digested any of it yet." She patted his wrist. "And what have you been up to? How are Liz and Dick? Did you get to the *Cleopatra* screening? Is it really a bomb?"

"Bomb, darling, it is a technicolor turd. She looks like fifteen puppies fighting in a sack. But Burton . . . ahh. I'd kick Eddie Fisher out of bed for that anytime!"

Miles rattled on about the movies he had seen, either at critics' screenings or on the late shows. He knew every line of dialogue in every Bette Davis movie. While she was gone he had seen *Dark Victory* for the sixteenth time. That film reminded him of a long, convoluted anecdote involving the goings-on at Rezzonico, the palazzo on the Grand Canal taken by Cole Porter for a masked ball at which Tallulah Bankhead had said something outrageous. Billie Claire had heard the story several times before, but she would never think of interrupting him. Besides, it kept her from having to discuss the exhausting events of the past days. As they traversed the great arc of the Chesapeake Bay Bridge she could see the tiny sailboats far below skittering about in a light breeze. Once over the long bridge and onto the flat expanse of Route 301 heading east into a blazing morning sun, Miles said gently,

"Come now, my Venus, you're not yourself. Tell kindly old Miles what's bothering you."

"Nothing, dear." She tried to smile, but she really wanted to flop over the gearshift, lay her cheek on his thigh and sob. "I'm just very, very tired."

"You're more than tired."

"No, honestly."

"All right, love, you'll tell me in time. Oh, I know what I forgot to tell you. Cliff Robertson is going to play Kennedy in *PT-109.*"

Sweet Miles, he never pushed; he was the most perceptive person she knew. The constant chatter, his self-deprecating humor, covered a great deal of pain. He was sensitive and vulnerable and she loved him more at that moment than she could ever tell him.

185

Why did she need sex? she wondered. If she didn't want it, crave it, sometimes, here would be the perfect man. They could be children together forever, holding hands, going to the movies, giggling at life.

"Cliff Robertson? Great Scott, he doesn't even look like Kennedy. People simply won't believe it."

"Well, if they'll swallow that PT-109 story, they'll swallow Cliff Robertson. No pun intended."

She ignored his remark. She always felt uncomfortable during any prolonged discussion of Miles's sex life and never encouraged one. "I know you aren't exactly a Kennedy fan, Miles, but if you had seen what I just saw in Germany and Ireland and Italy . . . as the man says, 'you had to be there.'"

"It isn't that I'm not a fan, Billie. I'm just suspicious of hero worship. This country's always wanted a movie star for President, and now they have one. He *is* very sexy."

"Even the old pros on the trip had to admit they had never seen anything like it. He's magic."

"Well, those crowds I saw on the tube had to be real. Those weren't precinct workers who'd been turned out with the promise of a couple of bucks and a beer blast at the union hall."

"Don't be so cynical. Those people loved him. It was almost sexual, the passion, the adoration . . ."

"Ah, speaking of such lofty emotions, I'd better fill you in on our host and hostess."

"Yes. What's up with Del? His absence on the press plane was duly noted."

"Seems Cynthia Hartford had him pulled and sent someone from her Chicago bureau. Del went on a real bender and got himself thrown out of the Press Club, suspended. Fortunately, he's no longer president. According to Melon, it was quite a scene. He's been doing the A.A. bit for the past few weeks. He might be a little fragile this weekend, darling, so I wouldn't go on about your trip when he's around. Just might set old D.P. three off. That wouldn't be fair to Ann."

Billie Claire could now smell the clean scent of the ocean. The sea's first scent always startled her; it implied such a confusion of simple joys and obscure menaces. "I'm sorry, Miles. What about Ann?"

186

"His drinking is pretty hard on her. She's mad for him. As far as I'm concerned, that's Annie's only flaw."

"He's quite handsome, isn't he?" she said. "I mean, in an Eric Sevareid sort of way. Rather a remembered handsomeness, if you know what I mean."

"Precisely, and that's the problem. Everyone remembers the way he was. In Ann's case, the way she *thought* he was." Miles glanced at Billie Claire, tobacco fields flashing past her profile, and gave her a sad smile. "Mark my words, sweetie pie, those two are star-crossed."

She poked him in the ribs. "You see too many bad old movies."

"No, really. I see a definite drama in that coupling. I remember Ann when she first came to the *Herald*. She was bright-eyed and bushy-tailed, but she had hick written all over her. She was smart, though. Coon-dog smart, as she would say. When she married Del she thought she had shagged a cross between Descartes and Cornelius Vanderbilt; not that there was any Porterfield money left. Anyway, she didn't care about the dough, only the elegance she thought it produced in him. How was the poor woman to know she had married a social moth who writes with his elbows?"

"I think you're being too harsh, Miles. Del can write very well, and you know it. Besides, Ann adores him and he needs her terribly."

He nodded. "Someday, darling, you will, perhaps, learn that the strong always fail to take into account the terrible strength of the weak. It destroys them. It will destroy Ann."

"Miles! Look at the ocean!" She leaned toward the windshield.

"Sorry, Billie, didn't mean to dish. It's most ungracious of me, considering I'm freeloading off them this weekend."

"Did Ann tell you who was coming besides us?"

"Let's see, there's the King and Mrs. Windsor, Lady Diana Cooper and the Maharaja of Gwalior, for starters. Perhaps a meretricious Jew. You know how Del is."

"Miles, you're vile!"

"Seriously, I don't know. Probably the entire Congress since Melon's agreed to come for a whole weekend."

"I wonder how she'll get along with Nicky?" Billie Claire struck her forehead. "Miles, I forgot to tell you. There was a note from my brother along with all the bills and throwaway stuff. He's staying in Ocean City for the holiday. I phoned him and he's going to drive up for the party tonight. I hope no one will mind."

"We're finally going to meet your brother?" Miles raised his eyebrows. "He's going to actually visit his little sister?"

"Nicky's very busy. He's working hard being a lawyer. He's also the most-sought-after ladies' man on Wall Street, the Hamptons and all those chic in islands in the Caribbean all winter."

"In that case, Melon can have him for dessert."

"He can handle Melon, but my guess is he'll bring his own dessert."

"That's never stopped Melon. You know she loves competition. And since she's split up with the Honorable Carson Pecker, I'd bet she's getting randy."

"You've been talking with Jane! It's *Peck*. I'm glad she's not seeing him anymore. My information is that that Marshall Austin creep leaned on him to dump Melon. She, of course, files a different story."

Miles glanced into the space behind the seat. "I hope our pâté isn't turning green."

"What pâté? Honestly, Miles, sometimes I have a hard time following you."

"I picked up a hamper at Neam's. The last batch of pâté I got at Macgruder's tasted like camel ka-ka."

"What did you get? Yum." Billie Claire leaned over the seat and pawed through the packages in the large wicker hamper.

"Usual stuff one bears to a freebee weekend. The pâté, some pickled artichokes, cheese, some great Brie, it's crawling, some black bread and those tiny green peppercorns in case Del wants to cremate a steak. I got a vat of baba au rhum for Ann's sweet tooth."

"I'll bet no one else shows up with more than a six-pack of Miller High Life."

"I got two quarts of Virginia Gentleman you can take credit for if you promise to love me forever and ever, forsaking all others." He reached across and smoothed the back of her head.

She settled back, leaning her head against the soft leather seat. How lovely it was out here. The ocean. Good friends. Peace.

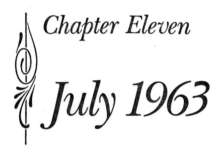

Chapter Eleven

July 1963

He didn't startle her at all when he crept up behind her and slid his hands gently around her waist, then up to cup her small breasts. This was not an effort at seduction, rather, a wordless expression of love by a man whose trade was words.

Ann gazed down at the tanned, heavily veined hands covering the front of her red-checked work shirt. She grazed a kiss at his chin resting on her shoulder.

"Officer, I was mindin' my own business, when up comes this here man smellin' of day-old fish, and he commits a rudeness on my person. Oh, Del, honey . . ."

She turned in his arms, laid her damp hands on his neck and shoulders and kissed his mouth.

"Hussy," he murmured after a pleasant mingling of lips and tongues. "Down, girl. The blues are running and they'll smell woman on me."

"No!" She pushed her knee between his legs.

"'Once, when I loved I would enlace,'" he began to quote into her loose red hair, "'Breast, eyelids, hands, feet, form and face. Of her I loved, in one embrace.' Including this soft little thing you have down here."

He made a grab for the fly of her old white jeans and she

pushed him away. "Rape! And shame on you. Mr. Brownin' didn't write dirty things like that."

He pulled her back and encircled her with his arms. "Oh, Annie, do you think we'll have had enough by the end of August?"

"No, never enough." She sighed and laid her cheek against the stubble of his day-old beard. "But right now I can't fun with you, sir."

Ann turned back to the sink to finish hulling a mound of strawberries.

"Don't know why you invited all those people out here tonight," he grumbled and popped a strawberry in his mouth.

"Don't be such a grouch. It will be fun. Besides we owe everyone in Washington from last winter."

"Well, if you plan to feed that rat pack I'd better go and wake up Beautiful Buns Bowersox, Porterfield-style." He leered.

"Leave her sleep, lecher. Go on back and threaten your nasty fish. People aren't due till six. I can manage. Now go on."

Ann watched him cross the deck, barefooted, old khaki pants rolled to his knees, a tattered straw hat with Montego Bay printed across the crown. She laughed as he turned toward the kitchen window and pulled both sides of his trousers out and executed a deep curtsy.

"Big hambone," she called through the screen.

"For your information, madam, *Gentleman's Quarterly* loved this outfit. Said I'll be on the cover." He picked up his pole and creel and headed down the steps to the beach.

He disappeared for a moment, then reappeared on the dunes beneath the house. She moved to the picture window in the living room. Del was the only adult to be seen on the beach. Some children were already digging in the sand and romping in the shallow water. Del ambled up the shoreline carrying his fishing pole like a lance, squinting out at the bright ocean, his raggedy hat set down on his forehead. He hadn't touched liquor for three and a half weeks, not since he had gone on a four-day drunk after Cynthia Hartford phoned from Chicago to inform him casually that she was assigning Ed Harley to cover the President's trip for the Hartford papers. Del had told Ann that the wave of nausea that had swept over him had been overwhelming. After he had hung up, the nausea had congealed into rage. Cynthia Hartford had given no reason. She simply said his "services" would be better used right in Washington and "young (that really stung) Harley could handle the assignment nicely."

To be deprived of the camaraderie, to suffer the humiliation of being pulled off such an assignment when he rightfully should have been there, infuriated him beyond endurance and he had headed straight for the Men's Bar at the Press Club.

Now Del was a speck in the distance. He was himself again. His color was good. His hand was steady. He had been writing better columns in the past few weeks than he had in ages.

This was the first time since the early, heady and blissful weeks of their marriage that *both* of them were fully satisfied with their work. Ann did not need to downplay her work; she could talk about it without holding back. Share the good and bitch about the problems. The professional balance between them was perfect.

Lord, Lord, Momma, if only you could have lived to share all this with me. You see, sometimes things *do* work out.

She wanted to run up the beach and sit on the sand several yards from Del. Just silently watch him. But, no. He needed privacy and she had all these damn strawberries to get soaking in the brandy.

Jane would be back from her bike ride in a few minutes. Billie Claire and Miles would be arriving soon. She had promised Melon she would wake her before noon. She would then want an eye-opener and Ann would join her. No problem there. Del was down on the beach, so they wouldn't be rubbing it in. She was truly looking forward to the party. Their apartment in town wasn't large enough for such a crowd, and it would be so easy to entertain out on the big deck. The only people who had declined had done so with genuine disappointment, and had elicited promises from the Porterfields to be given a rain check and a full account of the proceedings.

Ann walked through the quiet house. Maybe it wasn't the most sumptuous summer house at Rehobeth, but it was perfect for their purposes. The huge beamed living room rose two stories. At one end stood a raised stone fireplace, its mantel a tangle of beachcombed driftwood. The furnishings were typical beach-modern, lacquered bamboo couches and low tables. The ceiling had been draped with fishnet and glass floats, giving the place the

191

look of a boat more than a house. The five bedrooms each had its own bath and an entrance from the deck. The kitchen was part of the main room, separated by a bar counter which was surrounded by high bamboo stools. They had paid a premium for being right on the water, but with Jane chipping in part of the rent everything had worked out. It would be a great summer.

"Hellooo, anybody home?" Billie Claire called from the wide back deck. "Where's the front door?"

"Welcome to Hyannis South." Ann swept open one of the doors that opened onto the weathered deck that surrounded the house on three sides.

"Ann, what a wonderful *house!*" Billie Claire was so busy taking in the space and the view from the large windows, she tripped over the doorsill. "Oops."

Miles caught her before she fell. "No house could do justice to our hostess. Ann, you look marvelous!" He set the big hamper down on the counter.

"Miles, you darlin' man. Goodies! All mine? Billie, I'm putting you in the second bedroom with Melon. She's in there suffering from narcolepsy at the moment; don't wake her up yet," she said, gesturing down the long hall off the living room. "You look a little peaked, honey. How was the trip?" Not waiting for an answer she began to open packages in the hamper.

"Where do you want me?" Miles asked.

"Last door at the end of the hall. Jump into your suit and get comfortable, then I'll make you something cool."

"A cold beer for me, thanks, Annie." Miles was already halfway down the hall.

"How about you, Billie? A little hair of the dog?"

"It's a little early for me. Just coffee, if you have it."

"Coming up."

The late morning sun fell across the redwood chaises on the deck. Billie Claire had changed into a flowing muumuu and Miles into his bathing suit and a terry-cloth robe. He stretched out on a deck chair and Billie Claire was seated on the side of a chaise. Ann pushed through the screen door backwards, carrying a tray of coffee and beer. She had made herself a tall screwdriver.

"Ann, this is heaven," Billie Claire said, squinting into the sun.

"Heaven it is. We finally found it." Ann flopped full length on a chaise.

"You'll pardon me, please, if I do not move from this place for the rest of my life." Billie Claire wriggled back into the soft cushions and closed her eyes. "Where's Del?"

"Down on the beach doing his famous fishing act. If he actually caught one we'd have to frame it. Frankly, I think he's out there to keep out of the line of fire. Throwing parties isn't his idea of relaxation."

"What time are people coming," Billie Claire asked without opening her eyes.

"Sixish."

"Who's coming besides the usual?"

"Well, I think I got carried away. I asked everyone who's down here for the Fourth. Our esteemed leader will be here without Jeannine. She's still recovering from her hysterectomy up at Henlopen Acres. Jane Wheeler's coming. Don't know who she's bringing, but it should be interesting. The Paul Fays. Bob Loftus is bringing Ellen Simmons. Ann and David Brinkley. Myra MacPherson and Maurie Siegel, and knowing them, the last ten people they run into on the way over. Joanne and Frank Wilson *and* the dogs, God help us. Steve and Ada Cushing and two house guests. Let's see who else. Jerry and Maria O'Leary and Les Whitten."

"And the fabulous Jane Carleton Connor, breaker of a thousand hearts, Washington's foremost home wrecker," came a voice from the screen door.

"Janey!" Billie Claire and Miles called in unison.

Jane stepped onto the deck wearing white tennis shorts and a halter that amply displayed her honey-brown tan. Her long, gold-streaked hair was pulled back into a ponytail; her face was shaded by a tennis visor.

"You look like three consumptives taking the cure," she said as she pulled up a rattan stool and placed a can of beer on the deck beside it.

"Golden Goddess! When did you get out?" Miles said, swinging his feet over the side of his chair and reaching up to give Jane a kiss on the nose.

193

"Last night. I've spent the morning working off last night's calories. I must have pedaled a hundred miles and I'm pooped."

"Then relax awhile, darlin'. The groceries came. The beer's icing in the locker. I've drowned the strawberries in a gallon of Remy Martin. There's nothing to do for hours."

"Are you going to have time to run over and see Jeannine?" Jane asked Ann.

"I promised, as I told you, and I really must. And I want to."

"I don't know how you do it, Ann," Billie Claire yawned, "knowing Jeannine all these years and now being so friendly with Allegra. Must get sticky sometimes."

"No, not really. I know when to hush my mouth. What Seth Hathaway does is his business. Anyway, I like all of them."

Ann waved and set out up the road. The Hathaways' summer home in exclusive Henlopen Acres evoked, for Ann, the word "estate." The main house had been erected on the top of a small rise, giving it a commanding view of the sea. The house was surrounded by a vast carpet of lawn, maintained on sandy soil at enormous expense by Japanese gardeners. From Memorial Day until Labor Day the house and the two guest cottages were fully staffed. During the winter a caretaker and one gardener stayed on. The house stood two stories high and was adorned with white pillars and a gabled roof. It contained ten bedrooms, enclosed porches, a formal dining room, butler's pantry, two kitchens and a forty-foot-long drawing room. One of its more recent additions was a magnificent solarium near the pool for nude sunbathing.

As she approached the front of the house Ann wondered how women like Jeannine and Allegra could be so comfortable and competent with servants. She never quite knew how to act with the woman who came to their apartment in town twice a week to clean and tend to the laundry. Was Hattie an inferior because she did Ann's dirty laundry? Was Hattie superior because she did those things Ann was unwilling to do? Or were they equals because they were both working to survive?

An ebony-skinned man in immaculate dark trousers and a short jacket that matched his gleaming hair answered her ring at the massive front door.

194

"Yes, Mrs. Porterfield, Mrs. Hathaway is expecting you," he said, and led her through the drawing room to a large screened porch shaded by the thick, shiny leaves of an enormous magnolia tree in full bloom. Jeannine was propped up on a double-sized white chaise lounge surrounded by pale blue satin pillows. The porch was furnished with white filigreed, wrought-iron-and-glass tables and chairs and couches covered with white leather.

Seth's wife wore her customary subdued yet obvious makeup. Her skin was almost translucent. Her graying blond hair glistened from brushing and fell loosely about the shoulders of a white lace robe tied with blue satin ribbons. Ann had never before seen Jeannine's hair free. Her legs were covered by a white summer blanket. A large lapis lazuli jardiniere filled with magnolia blossoms sat on the glass table next to the lounge.

The atmosphere was so cool and muted Ann felt grossly conspicuous in her loudly flowered beach shift.

Jeannine held out her hand while the butler placed a filigreed chair beside the lounge.

"Ann. How kind of you to come. Please . . ." She gestured toward the chair. "Let Roger get you something cool. Is it too early for a drink?"

"Jeannine, you look beautiful. A mite drawn, but beautiful. Thank you, I will have something. A gin and tonic?" She glanced up at the waiting butler.

"Thank you, Roger, a gin and tonic for Mrs. Porterfield and iced tea for me, please."

"Yes, ma'am." The butler disappeared into the cool, dark house.

"What are you doing out of bed?"

"This is my first day downstairs. Elsie and Roger helped me down. I must say it felt rather odd to be upright. But I do love this spot, so cool. Smell the magnolia. They'll be gone soon." She looked out toward the tree. Beyond it Ann could see a sliver of the sea at the bottom of the sweeping lawn.

"How do you feel? Is everything mending properly?"

"What an incredibly undignified bit of business. A hysterectomy is a sort of milestone, I suppose. Like losing one's virginity or having a baby—only they're positive. This is so negative. It seems to accomplish nothing."

195

"Doctors don't do it for sport, Jeannine. There are usually reasons."

"Sometimes I wonder," she said wistfully, then, firmly, "Enough! I don't want to talk about my health. I bore myself."

"Are you the only Hathaway staying in this little cottage of yours?"

"No. Diana and her husband are here. They brought two other couples down from New York. Nice young people, although I've hardly seen them. They've been down at the tennis courts since dawn."

"Did Seth get away for the weekend?"

"He's driving out this afternoon. He was out to see Phil Graham last night. Tragic situation. We're all sick about it."

Ann lifted a frosted crystal glass from the silver tray held by Roger.

"Here's to your plumbing, Jeannine. Oops, sorry. That was a bit crude of me."

Jeannine laughed. "Don't be silly. That's what I like about you. You're always you. Here's to my plumbing, absolutely!" She raised her glass to her lips, sipped and grimaced. "Roger, I have decided against tea. Bring me what Mrs. Porterfield is having." She returned the iced tea glass to the tray.

"Certainly, Mrs. Hathaway. A gin and tonic."

"There. I really wanted a drink all along. I should never try and pretend with you. Do you realize you're the only person I feel comfortable enough with to be completely open?"

"Why thank you." Ann looked at her friend with great affection, the kind of affection two women share that makes explanations unnecessary.

"I trust you. I know I can talk to you. Ann, I don't need to tell you I have my pride."

"No, you don't. I know about pride." Ann looked down into her glass.

Roger returned, silently placed another frosted glass on the table next to Jeannine and departed.

"How's Del?"

"Better. Two of the men at the club got him to A.A. He's been going regularly, and he hasn't touched a drop for three weeks." She felt her body tensing, the muscles in her neck and shoulders

196

becoming taut. There was no reason to be uncomfortable with Jeannine, especially as her anguish was for Del, not for herself. Having people know he was flawed was excruciating. She felt her face reddening. Jeannine's eyes were fixed on her and they contained both pain and compassion. Ann didn't want compassion from anyone. "Have you been reading his column lately?"

"Yes, I have. Brilliant. Your Del has a remarkable mind." She reached under one of the satin pillows and pressed a mother-of-pearl bell pull attached to a cord that disappeared under the white sisal rug. Almost immediately Roger materialized in the doorway.

"Roger, please bring me another of these, and another for Mrs. Porterfield." She held out her already empty glass.

Ann watched Jeannine place her glass on the table beside her lounge. The rattling sound caused her to notice that Jeannine's hand was trembling. A flash of sunlight caught in a large diamond solitaire sent shimmering shards of blue light into the shady porch.

Jeannine trembling? Must be some medication, Ann thought.

"Ann, tell me about her."

So! It's not medicine. It's Allegra. She's finally brought up the subject. Ann took a deep breath. "What would you like to know?"

"I wouldn't *like* to know anything about Miss Farr, but I suppose I ought to know more about her than I do. I have my sources, of course, but there are some things that, shall we say, professional information-gatherers can't tell one. Will she be out this weekend?"

"Not to my knowledge. I certainly would not have invited her. Not under the circumstances."

"What circumstances? You mean my being out here, too? Good Lord, Ann, she lives four blocks away from me in Georgetown. What's the difference?"

"I just wouldn't have done it. It would have been—" Ann paused—"tacky."

"Yes, tacky. That's a good word. She spends a great deal of my husband's money—mine, too, if one cares to look at it that way. That big house, the car, the servants. It is tacky, isn't it?"

Ann could not respond. Clearly Jeannine wanted to do the talking. Perhaps it was best just to sit and listen.

"She's quite beautiful, but of course you know that. I see her

197

lunching at Rive Gauche occasionally and she was at the Corcoran Ball. Exquisite young woman. I suppose I should be thankful for that. She's only in her mid-twenties and Seth is fifty-nine. I'm fifty-three and an enormous chunk of our resources is going for the maintenance of a woman younger than our daughter. Are you aware that Diana introduced her father to Miss Farr?"

Ann shook her head. "I'd never heard how they met."

"Diana hates her to the point of white rage. Such strong negative feelings, when unexpressed, are quite destructive. I've tried to explain that to my daughter. Ann, I know a great deal about Miss Farr. I have paid a great deal of money for that information, but there are some things I have been unable to learn." Jeannine's eyes were blue ice.

"What are you talking about? Detectives?"

"If you will," she said, trying to appear offhanded.

"Oh, dear. Well, what do you want to know, then?"

A very long silence filled the magnolia-scented porch.

"What do they do in bed together, Ann? What does she do to him, for him? This man who has been my life since the moment I met him. This man whose body and mind are as familiar to me as my own. Is it young flesh he wants? Firmer breasts? Youth for its own sake?" Her voice was trembling from rage.

"Good God in heaven, Jeannine, I never took you for a masochist. How in Christ's name would I know details like that? I'm not in bed with them. And what if I did know? What if Allegra had given me a detailed description of their sex life? How could I tell you? How could you listen? This is pornographic, Jeannine." Now Ann was angry, yet filled with pity for this elegant, graceful woman whose suffering Ann could only imagine.

Jeannine lay back silently for a long while. The sound of a power lawn mower could be heard manicuring some distant part of the grounds. Finally she spoke. "I'm sorry. Please forgive me." She reached for her friend's hand and clutched it so hard Ann could feel fingernails biting into her flesh. "Ann, help me. I'm losing him."

When Ann returned to the rented house she found Jane and Miles performing a hilarious ballet to Ravel's *Boléro*. Two stereo speakers had been rigged on the deck, and she had heard the music before she had turned the car into the gravel driveway at the rear of the house. Billie Claire was asleep in the hammock Del had slung under the raised deck. Melon, in a bikini, was spread-eagled on a chaise, her skin beginning to turn the color of the Bloody Mary in her hand. Del was singing "Mad Dogs and Englishmen" in the outdoor shower. No one was paying attention to the ringing phone.

"Hell! I leave the asylum for an hour and the inmates go berserk," Ann shouted, banging the screen door behind her and racing for the phone.

Laughing, Ann said, "Hello, there."

"I must have the right number from the sound of things. This is Nick Hutchins. Are you, by any chance, harboring my sister?"

"Harboring is right. She's the only one here with the good grace to be asleep. Let me fetch her before she gets a second-degree burn."

"Don't wake her. I just wanted to tell her I'll be able to make it to the party this evening. Are you our esteemed hostess?"

"Yes, indeed."

"How do you do, Ann. Billie's spoken nothing but wonders about you. Thank you for having me over."

"Not at all, Nicky. We're all looking forward to meeting you."

"I'm certainly looking forward to meeting *you*. I hear you are one of the best in the business."

Charming. Ann smiled over the mouthpiece. "How you *do* go on, Mr. Hutchins. Are you sure you aren't a Southern boy?" She could hear him chuckling at the other end of the line.

"But I'm not kidding. I see the *Herald* from time to time. I caught your piece on that plane crash and remarked about it to my sister. She told me how you slogged through a blizzard to cover it. That's what I call intrepid!"

"Oh, *that*. Don't give me too much credit. My husband and I just happened to be having dinner out that way. Cost me a hot meal and a brand-new pair of boots," she laughed.

"Whatever happened to that story? I never saw a follow-up."

"There wasn't any, really."

Nick Hutchins said, "Hmm. That's odd, isn't it?"

"Not really. It was one of those one-day deals. The bodies were identified and the FAA was satisfied with the cause of the crash.

199

Engine failure, I think. The two men killed were out-of-towners."

"Yes, I know. I knew the lawyer, Allen Boxer."

"No kidding!" Ann watched Jane and Miles glide along the deck, arms straight out and cheek to cheek, in an exaggerated tango. They were really quite good.

"Not well. I met him at a few parties in the Hamptons one summer. I must say I've heard more about him since he died than I did when he was alive."

"Oh, what are you hearing?"

Nick Hutchins chuckled again. "Off the record or on?"

"Off, of course. I'm on vacation."

"Well, it's nothing I can put my finger on. Boxer ran with a pretty wild bunch, and even though he was a partner in his firm, he still had a very big bundle of money to throw around. A Maserati, four-hundred-dollar suits . . . and the dames, phew!"

"There's not much of a high life in Washington. What do you suppose he was doing down here?" Ann pawed through the drawer of the bamboo telephone stand searching for a match for her cigarette.

"He spent a lot of time in D.C., but I haven't a clue what business he had there. No one else does either."

"Well, whatever it was he was doing, he sure must have wanted to get out of town bad. Taking off in a little plane like that in a snowstorm doesn't seem too bright to me." Through the open door she could see Del tiptoeing up behind Melon's chaise with a full bucket of water. "Say, Nick, I can see I'd better go back out and turn over a couple of broiled bodies . . ."

"Of course. Sorry to keep you. You must have a lot to do before your party. All right if I bring a date?"

"Of course. See you when you get here."

Ann hung up the phone a split second before the cold water landed. Melon's scream obliterated all other sounds within a quarter of a mile of the house.

During the remainder of the afternoon the contents of Miles's hamper were consumed. By six thirty the deck was filled to capacity. Along one shaded wall stood a redwood picnic table laden with the two huge salads Melon had made, with Jane's crocks of baked beans and Billie Claire's garlic bread. The only food Ann had permitted to be store bought was a dozen tubs of fried chicken that had been sent in from a restaurant in town. Three bartenders had arrived and set up bars at either end of the deck.

Ann had stationed herself at one corner of the deck, having given up trying to greet people at the door. By nine, a third of the party had overflowed down onto the sand beneath the deck.

The two basic subjects of conversation for the evening seemed to be who had gone to Hyannis with the President for the long weekend and the President's trip. Ann observed that Billie Claire was careful not to be within earshot of Del when she answered questions about Europe. Most of the other guests also seemed to sense the problem and were discreet.

Melon had chosen to wear a see-through, floor-length cotton gown over a matching bikini, and was the center of male attention.

"This is the smash of the season," Melon said as she squeezed onto the chaise between Miles and Emerson Beauchamp of the *Star*. "I should be taking notes. What are you two dishing about?" She winked up at Ann.

"We, dear Melon, are dishing about Phil Graham," Miles said, putting his arm around her. "And you are going to get yourself attacked in that outfit."

"Promise? What about Phil? Still in the loony bin? What's to tell?"

"There's a rumor that his girlfriend was paid off and sent packing," Emerson said.

"I don't believe it," Melon said casually.

"You don't believe it because you didn't already know about it." Miles gave her a playful slap on the wrist.

"Even if I knew about it, I couldn't print it. He and Seth are big buddies." She wiggled free and moved off into the crowd.

"You see that?" Miles said to Ann. "Want to bet she's off to pick brains about what she just heard. She'll be back in half an hour telling us about her big scoop on Phil Graham."

Ann had seen it coming for over an hour. Del had stopped laughing at jokes and clever stories told by his well-oiled guests. He had been leaning on the deck railing, long legs stretched out, hands in his trouser pockets, frowning and listening for twenty minutes. The paper bags weighted with sand and holding burning candles that lined the deck were now the only light, and they

cast a flickering light across his glowering face. He had been barely civil when Billie Claire's suave and handsome brother tried to
engage him in conversation. Martha Cole was in the middle of a
funny story when Ann glanced over her guest's shoulder just in
time to see Del walk to the bar, and, ignoring the bartender, pour
himself a tumbler of Scotch. She tried to excuse herself, but it was
too late. He downed the first glass and was pouring another.

". . . and if I hadn't called him on it I think Pierre would
have . . . What's the matter, Annie?" Martha's face held concern.

"Nothing." She turned away. "Just everything, that's all."

"What's up, kiddo?" Jane materialized at Ann's elbow, as she
felt her eyes filling.

Ann gestured weakly toward the bar where Del stood, drink in
hand, having an animated one-sided conversation with Brian Corcoran from Scoop Jackson's office.

"Oh, shit," Jane said softly.

Ann forced herself to move around the deck, trying to chat with
her guests, but she was unable to concentrate on what anyone was
saying. Melon had proposed a nocturnal dip in the ocean. Ann
knew that meant naked bodies running up and down in the dark
in front of her house, but she was too miserable to care. Several
guests disappeared onto the darkened beach. At the back door, as
she was saying good night to Hildy Bornstein and her date, she
heard him.

"Bunch of fuckin' Commie rat-finks!" Del bawled.

"Excuse me, Gerry. Thanks for comin', darlin'. Come see us
soon." She whirled and hurried toward the deck.

"Del, honey, don't you want to . . ."

"Assholes!" Del lurched across the now silent deck. "I want to
propose a toast," he bellowed. "Listen up, assholes. To my favorite
hypocrites! To all of you. To my favorite, fuckin', asshole hypocrites."

"Come on, fella. You can't flatter us," Frank Wilson called and
embarrassed laughter rose in a collective spasm.

"I'll flatter you all right," he said, steadying himself against the
deck railing. "Bunch of shits, all of you."

"Hey, Del, we've got critics from all four papers here. We don't
need another one," called Steve Cushing.

"Yeah, Del, this is a party."

202

"Absolutely!" Del swept glasses and bowls of nuts and Fritos from the picnic table. Then, with the surreal coordination and grace of drunks and clowns, he managed to mount the table by way of a tilted wrought-iron stand.

"A toast! I think a toast is in order here." He surveyed the up-turned faces. "Here's to the one hundred and eighty-seventh anniversary of the Declaration of Independence! Here's to the Constitution of the You Ess of A."

"Bet your 'A,' Del," someone called, trying to humor him.

"My friends and colleagues," he continued, his glass raised over his head, "I mention the Constitution to you this evening because, as you may recall, that is the document that will not abridge freedom of the press."

"Oh, Christ," someone moaned.

Billie Claire was standing next to Ross Mark of the *London Express*. "Jesus, Ross," she whispered, "get him down from there. This is awful."

"If you think I want a fistfight with the eminent Del Porterfield, you're wrong," he hissed in a clipped Australian accent.

"I would like to address my remarks to my colleagues who have just triumphantly returned from a whirlwind Presidential tour. I want to give all of you an award, a toast, a tribute. To the White House Suck-Asses! To the Brown Nose Brigade of the West Wing. Fuck you all!"

Ann slowly lowered herself into a rattan chair and watched people turn their backs on Del and resume their conversations. Someone had turned up the stereo as high as it would go. Billie Claire stood her ground for a moment, transfixed by the angry drunk who only a few hours before had been happily singing in the shower. Then she moved toward the table, now a mess of over-turned salad and greasy chicken. She reached up and took Del's hand and helped him down. It was a mistake, Ann could see that.

She was the only one left, so she had become the target.

"So, Billie. How do you like covering your movie star President?" Del yelled into her face. "Have they got you snowed by now? Next thing you know you'll be out there at Hickory Hill playing touch football."

"Come off it, Del. You're embarrassing Ann. It's her party, too."

"Heard you saw Dave Powers take a slug of whiskey on government time and didn't file it. They're getting to you, kid. Keep it up and you can become a professional Kennedy leak like Charlie Bartlett."

"Better a leak than a drunk, Del." Suddenly Billie Claire appeared very sober and very serious.

"Oh, my wife's little protégé turns smart-ass critic? My, my, Billie Claire, how the meek´do inherit. What did the young emperor do, Billie, grab your ass? An occasional feel from Pierre and you'll be filing fluff like all the rest. I always heard you did it for free." Del lowered himself onto the long bench beside the table and pulled Billie Claire down beside him.

Ann could see her wince. From her rattan chair in the shadows she felt nausea rising. "Billie, get away from him. Stop listening. He's gone mad," she whispered. She looked around helplessly for someone to break it up. But if she signaled anyone she would be calling more attention to the awful situation. She could stand it no longer. She rose from her chair and walked toward the pair.

"Billie, darlin', Nicky is asking for you in the house." She flashed a menacing look at Del, who stared up at her, his head bobbing slowly back and forth.

"Okay, Ann." Billie Claire stood. "Your esteemed husband seems to feel I've sold out, that my journalistic credentials have been blemished," she said it looking straight at Del.

"You're damn right," Del said, weaving.

Billie Claire stood directly in front of him, her arms straight at her sides. "Del Porterfield, I don't argue with drunks, but if you are capable of absorbing anything at this point, let me simply tell you that John F. Kennedy makes me feel good. He makes me feel proud. He makes me think this world isn't such a shit hole after all."

"Billie!" Ann was astonished by Billie Claire's cool determination.

"That's all right, Ann, I'm almost finished." She turned back to Del, who was staring at her, his mouth hanging loose. "Del, you leave my journalistic performance to me. I know I'll never be a big shot like you. I know millions of readers will never hang on my every pronouncement the way they do yours. But I can tell you what I'm going to tell my grandchildren. I'm going to tell them that John F. Kennedy smiled at me." The tears were now pouring down her cheeks.

204

"Come on, honey." Ann put her arm around Billie Claire and gently pulled her toward the house.

"I'm sorry, Ann. I've ruined your party."

Ann led her to the kitchen. "Oh, Billie." She leaned her forehead against the cool enamel of the refrigerator door, where she had stood that morning. How far away and false that morning was now.

"Can I do anything?" Billie Claire stood before her, looking bewildered and helpless. "Whatever I did, I'm sorry."

"Please, Billie, honey, stop apologizing."

"But I don't understand. What's the matter with Del? Why did he attack me that way?"

"He wasn't on that plane and you were. So were a dozen other people here tonight. Surely you must know what that means to a man like Del?"

"You're defending what he was saying?" She was incredulous.

Ann leaned back against the refrigerator and folded her arms. She looked straight at Billie Claire. "I love him. His heart is broken and I love him."

"What about you, Ann? What about your heart?"

Ann looked away, staring over Billie Claire's shoulder out through the kitchen window toward the black sea. "He is my heart, honey."

Chapter Twelve

July 1963

Damn faggoty Miles.

Melon tapped her long fingernails against the side of her glass while Miles, of all people, explained to gorgeous, bronze-blond Nick Hutchins why their host had been carried off to the master bedroom barely conscious, and babbling about Air Force One.

Billie Claire's brother attentively listened to a capsule history of Del Porterfield and Ann Adams, sympathetically presented by the *Herald's* drama critic.

Melon had spotted him from her bathroom window as she was tardily dressing for the party. She had seen the little silver Porsche whip into the curved driveway as she stepped out of the shower. "Hot damn!" she had said aloud. Right then she had decided on the see-through caftan. "Fresh stuff. Gonna get me some," she had hummed, applying yet another coat of mascara. She had done her best during the early evening coolly to arrange an introduction, and later, to strike her most enticing cocktail party pose—that of "fascinated listener." Nicky Hutchins had been absolutely charming and obviously interested in her, but people had continually interrupted, dragging him off, dragging her off. She had kept an eye on him all evening and now that goddamned Miles Buford was monopolizing him.

She had been studying Nicky, trying to determine how the Hutchins' genes had been so unfairly distributed. No wonder Billie Claire had a galloping inferiority complex. Plain, plain, boringly plain little sister with this Adonis big brother who got all the cheekbones and teeth.

During the afternoon Billie Claire had warned her that her brother would be bringing some Eastern Shore beauty, as if to caution her. But he had ignored his date all evening. Now she was nowhere in sight.

Melon put a cigarette to her lips. An arm extended over her shoulder from the semidarkness on the deck. A gold Dunhill lighter flashed upward toward her cigarette.

"Ah," she said, startled. Then she sat up and pushed out her breasts. "Nicky, thank you. I see you've met Miles. Charming and amusing, isn't he? Absolutely the best in the business." Flashing a four-star smile, she swung her legs to one side to allow room for him at the foot of the chaise.

"Things seem to be slowing down. Did you swim?" he said, ignoring the seat.

"Umm. Too cold. I'm still freezing." She hugged herself through the thin cloth of her dress. "You could do me a kindness as well as warm me up."

"Oh, how's that?"

"Let's dance. I love Ella Fitzgerald." She slithered off the chaise and extended both arms to Nick Hutchins.

"At your service, madame." Nick placed his arm around her waist and they moved into the center of the deck where three other couples were shuffling about to "A Foggy Day in London Town."

She placed both arms around his neck. She knew they looked good together: she, tiny and dark, her well-proportioned body moving sensuously beneath her thin dress; he, tall, sinewy-muscular, blond and tan. She pressed her hips toward him.

Nothing.

He couldn't have used it all up in Ocean City. That move had always been foolproof. She could feel his thighs and belly. Flat and taut. She would have picked up the tiniest twitch.

Nada.

Abruptly the music changed. "Hey baba re bop . . . "

An old boogie-woogie record blasted into the night. Nicky moved away from her, sliding his hand down her arm, then moving toward her to place a firm hand around her waist. Like a matched set they moved, gliding, sliding around the deck. His step exactly matched hers. Jesus he's sexy; look at the way he moves. He was making her look terrific, she thought, as he caught her hand just in time to bring her back and swing her around him.

"Go, Melon!" a man shouted from the sidelines. Someone in the kitchen flipped on a floodlight that shone on the center of the deck, bathing them in a pool of light.

"Floor show time!" came a female voice from the bar area.

Melon threw back her head and said, "Whee!"

Suddenly she became aware of someone pulling at her shoulder. She glanced back and saw Arnie Welsh from the AP.

"Cut-in time," he said, grinning drunkenly.

"Shit, I really need this," she muttered through clenched teeth. She could see a well-advanced erection under his loose aloha shirt. She gave the intruder a grim smile. "Arnie, beat it or you're a dead man."

The music ended with eight slow beats, during which Nicky dramatically bent her over backward in a frozen finale. Applause.

"A dip! I don't believe it. A dip. I haven't done that since high school," she said as they walked to the railing, her arm around Nick's slender back.

"Nostalgia time, pretty lady." He returned her to a chaise. "May I get you a drink?"

"Please."

"What are you drinking, Melon?"

She didn't answer. She had glanced toward the main door onto the deck. Ann was greeting Seth Hathaway with a big hug.

"Sorry to be so late, Ann," he said after he brushed her cheek with his lips and surveyed the deck.

"You're never late, Seth. I'm afraid the food's been pretty well picked over, but the bar's open-ended. What can I get you?"

"Whiskey and ice, thanks. Why, hello, Melon." He ambled toward her, while Ann headed for the bar.

Melon scrambled to her feet and smoothed her dress. "Hello, Seth, and welcome." She was flustered and didn't like it.

She had attended only two parties in town when Seth was present. Both at Allegra's, both formal. She had never before seen the man wearing anything but dinner clothes or a suit—not even in the ancient past during those glorious Christmas holidays with Diana. Now here he was looking even more attractive than Nick Hutchins. His white sharkskin trousers were sharply creased. His black LaCoste sport shirt was open at the neck, revealing a deep tan and a surprisingly hairy chest.

Seth moved around the deck, greeting everyone by name. A soft buzz of recognition rippled through the remaining guests. Clearly, the star of the evening had arrived. Seth had made Ann's party a success by his mere presence. The spirit of the early evening revived. People ten yards away from Seth Hathaway became animated. The weary bartenders sprang to life and began to tidy up. New blood, Melon thought. Just what this sagging party needed.

Nicky had completely disappeared. She searched.

Shit. She suddenly felt very depressed. Fourth of July. Sexy outfit. And she had been unable to snag Nick Hutchins. Every other man there was either drunk or not worth the effort. "I'm going to bed," she muttered to herself. Maybe she could scratch up some action tomorrow at the Carousel. She started toward her room and then remembered seeing Billie Claire in deep conversation with the guy from *Newsweek*. She walked down the hall. Their bedroom door was firmly locked. Double shit. She walked back toward the living room. Well, make the best of it. At least Seth's here. Maybe she could get in a few brownie points with the great man. Say something brilliant within his hearing.

"Melon," Jane called, "come join us. You know Vic Munsing? He's just back from covering Profumo."

Melon sat down on the raised hearth next to Jane and a rather tired-looking Englishman. "Hi, I'm Melon Bowersox," she said and extended her hand to him.

He didn't take it or even rise. Jerk, she thought. Typical English journalist, thinks women are either whores or mothers. Oh, well, there was nothing better to do, might as well give him a hard time.

"What fascinates me about the Profumo case, *Mr.* Munsing," she said as she lowered her thick-lashed eyes and looked straight at his crotch, "is that it shows that your upper classes are into fucking as well as your lower classes. Refreshing."

"My dear lady, *we* started it."

"We? I didn't realize Fleet Street recruited their hacks from Burke's Peerage." Whenever she felt threatened by a man she went for the most available major vein.

"Melon . . . " Jane said menacingly.

"I wasn't aware that an American female journalist would know what Burke's Peerage was," he said, staring down the front of her dress.

Melon felt the blood flash to her face. "From looking at you, I'm surprised *you* know about *fucking*." She felt a hand on her shoulder and turned. Seth Hathaway was standing at her left, holding a drink and smiling down at her.

"Now, Melon, don't anger them. They're vicious when cornered. Hello, Vic. How's Lord Beaverbrook treating you?"

Vic Munsing immediately rose, embarrassed by being caught in a catfight by a man of Seth Hathaway's prestige.

"Fine, sir. Nice to see you again," he fumbled, drying his drinking hand on his chinos and offering it to Seth.

The older man took it firmly and looked straight at Munsing. "I see you have met our *star* reporter. Miss Bowersox's work is an excellent example of fine American journalism. Pity you Fleet Streeters are not yet advanced enough to assign more women to responsible positions."

Munsing shuffled from one foot to the other.

"Melon, if you have a minute I'd like to introduce you to an interesting couple. He's the chairman of the Riggs Bank and a good contact for you. Good evening, Munsing. Jane, as usual, you make the stars blush with envy."

Melon walked out onto the deck with Seth. "Whew, you saved my life, Seth. That man was obnoxious."

"I know you can handle all comers, my dear, but you looked as if you needed a hand. Actually the man from Riggs Bank left ten minutes ago." They both laughed. "Let's get a fresh drink, and then will you join me for a walk?"

"Sure." Melon was delighted. The rage was gone, the boredom and depression she had felt just a few minutes ago had vanished. Mary Ellen Bowersox being escorted on a walk by Seth Hathaway! Melon believed in luck, but only when it took a turn in her favor.

They walked silently along the dark beach, the ice in their plastic glasses rapidly melting in the warm, humid night. Seth paused at the water's edge, rolled up his white slacks and slipped off his Gucci loafers.

"Oh, that feels good," he said when his bare feet sank in the sand. "Here, hand me your sandals."

Melon slid off her sandals and handed them to Seth. In the distance, beyond the dunes, they could see an occasional firework rising briefly to illuminate the sky.

They walked side by side on the uneven sand. She felt the warmth of his body as it brushed hers.

"Seems I missed some sort of fracas," he said.

"Fracas, indeed," she said, imitating him. "Del really tied one on and made a speech from the picnic table that had everyone squirming."

"So I heard. How did Ann take it? I'm more worried about her than I am about Porterfield. He can be a bit of an ass. Ann's special."

"She's all right, I guess. There was nothing she could do to stop him. She's a tough lady, but she doesn't deserve all this."

"No, she doesn't. You're a bit of a tough lady yourself, Melon. It's not like you to get into a pissing match with a lightweight like Munsing. Is anything wrong?" He put his arm loosely around her waist.

She jumped slightly from his touch. She liked it.

"Oh, I'm okay, I guess. I usually get a little jumpy when I'm temporarily manless." She shrugged. "It's really nothing, and I don't want to bore you."

"I'm not bored in the slightest. Tell me."

"Oh, I've been seeing a certain member of Congress and . . . "

"Well, that I knew about. As you know, people talk."

Melon was embarrassed. The thought of people talking about her personal life with Seth Hathaway made her feel childish. "Oh."

"Peck isn't for a woman like you, Melon. That fellow is bad news. I suppose women find him attractive, but I would assume someone like you would be a bit more . . . demanding. You're always so demanding of yourself, I'd think you'd be the same with the man in your life."

She was unable to respond. She felt as she had when her father had looked at her report card and found her math grades wanting. He would always tell her she was better than she was, and was letting him down by not living up to it. It was nice to have a man doing that to and for her now.

"I do get involved with some odd types, I suppose," she said after a long pause. "But I've never had anything to do with a man like Carson Peck before. Seth, do you know Carson ?"

"I know *something* about every Congressman and Senator. I have to."

"What do you know about him?"

"He's glib, handsome, well backed from his home district, but not very hardworking or well informed." He tilted his head thoughtfully. "Interesting question, Melon. On the one hand, I see him as a very shallow, ineffectual man without any substance whatsoever."

"Yes?"

"On the other hand, he's . . . quite effective in certain areas. Frankly, I can't put together my personal appraisal, and his accomplishments in the House."

"Yes?"

He smiled down at her. "Why don't you tell me what you think of the Congressman?"

Melon slowed and made a figure eight in the damp sand with her toe. For months she had dated almost no one but Carson Peck. She supposed this was general knowledge, but she had never discussed him with anyone but Jane, and then, only at the beginning. That in itself was unusual. "Carson's almost a cliché. More or less what you just said. He's very handsome and has lots of money. But that isn't the point. Do you know his A.A., Marshall Austin?"

"I seem to have heard of him. Why?"

"Because he gives me the creeps. Carson doesn't make a move without him. It's a very weird relationship. It's as if Austin has complete control over Carson."

"Perhaps you exaggerate a bit, my dear. An A.A.'s function is to protect the Congressman. Ease his work load, keep the time-wasters away. Maybe this Austin is especially good at his job."

"I'll say, *good*! He's practically got a leash around Carson's neck. It was always, 'I don't know, I'll have to check with Marshall.' 'Don't ask me, ask Marshall.' I mean, who won that election anyway? And, besides, Carson acts as if he's afraid of the man. He doesn't ask him for advice, he asks him for *permission*, for Christ's sake! That's one of the main reasons I stopped seeing Carson. I mean, really, Seth. I got the feeling when I asked him if he was going to come he'd reach for the phone and ask Marshall Austin if it was all right."

Seth's great head shot back against his shoulders and he let out a roaring laugh. "Why, Melon, how indelicate of you."

Melon pouted. "Don't laugh at me, Seth. It was miserable. Austin was like some sort of specter floating around, all white and pasty, and with those tiny, little, ratlike hands. Blah! It just wasn't worth it. I don't know why I put up with both of them as long as I did. I was plain stupid."

"I think perhaps you sell yourself short at times. You are a sensitive, vulnerable woman and, I might add, a lovely one." He stopped and looked down at her.

She could feel her heart thumping. And, even in this light, she could see his blue eyes.

"Come on, let's go sit up there in the dunes. I'll show you the Big Dipper." He laughed happily and took the glass from her hand and threw it into the lapping water with his own.

They climbed up the beach into the softly rising dunes. He guided her, holding her firmly until they found a cup in the sand midway between the wet beach and the now-darkened summer cottages. He pulled off his shirt to spread for her. But, for a time, he held her head against his chest. They were both silent. She had never felt so completely safe, so calm.

"Seth . . . " she said against the thick, warm hair of his chest.

"Shh." He placed a finger under her chin and lifted her face. "Do you trust me?"

"Of course. You're the only man I've ever trusted."

He did not begin with her breasts. First, her back, long, gentle strokes. His great head, silhouetted against the night sky, bent down to gaze at her. Gently he eased her down onto the sand. She lay back and gave herself over to the deliberate curiosity of his hands and mouth. Mindless, mindless. With the most natural motion of her life, she reached for the hem of her long dress and pulled it over her head. The night air covered her flesh with tingling gooseflesh. She pulled off her bikini as he hurriedly removed his trousers. Instantly, they came together. Stroking, kissing, rolling in the soft, warm sand.

She was a graceful, submerged sea plant, languidly undulating to the perfect rhythm of the ocean. And what was happening to her was beyond anything so mundane as trust and fear.

On and on it went, the tender, elegant lesson, until she thought she would burst.

She could not believe that this man, this idol, this person so far removed from any aspect of her personal and sexual life could at that moment want her so totally. Seth Hathaway was untouchable. He was a challenge so great that she had never even let herself dream about it, and at this moment he was pressing his swollen penis gently against her thigh. She had done nothing to encourage him, nothing to indicate anything physical was possible between them. *He* had begun it. *He* wanted *her*.

And when he finally entered her, she did not clench her teeth and force the cadence. This was no duel, no thrust for conquest that drove her to manipulate the rhythm of her body for a response. A force unknown to her had taken control of her mind and her body. They were in ecstatic accord.

He is doing this to me. . . . He is doing this for me and I want it all now, yes, yes . . . oh, yes.

Her mouth was open and a small humming moan was coming from deep in her throat. She had felt the unresolved tensions and anguish of her lifetime converge, grow unendurably vast and then become transformed into a joy that increased until it had slowly collapsed upon itself.

They lay together, silently, sweetly, for a long time. She felt she might have slept. She propped herself on one elbow and looked into his face.

"Seth, that never happened to me before." She spoke in an awed whisper.

"Now, my dear girl, that's not necessary." He brushed the dark, damp hair from her face.

"No, I mean it. I never came before."

"Well, now you know what all the fuss has been about." Obviously, he thought she was kidding him.

She sat up, her nipples still erect. It was important she convince him, make him realize what he had just done. "Seth, all this time, never. Never before."

He must have seen the sincerity in her eyes and heard it in her almost pleading voice. "Good Lord, Melon. I'm flattered, of course, if what you're saying is true. But, I find it . . . shall we say, implausible?" He chuckled deep in his throat. "I mean, a woman of your . . . sophistication . . . your obvious physical . . . attributes . . . You *have* involved yourself with the wrong men."

"Oh, don't blame the men. It's been *me*. I think now that I must have been waiting for you. For years, and I didn't realize it."

"Now, Melon." He gently tugged his crumpled shirt out from under them and, after shaking the sand from it, slipped it on. "We're two healthy people. The night is warm and wonderful. The wine was plentiful."

"Don't tease me, Seth." Melon felt the tears brimming.

Both of them were standing now, and again he raised her face and looked into her eyes.

"My God, you aren't kidding, are you?"

"No," she whispered, and the tears streamed down her face.

He put his arms around her small naked body and pulled her to him. "My darling little girl," he said against her hair, "my baby. I'm so glad I was able to do this for you. Call it my masculine pride, but it pleasures me no end, what you're telling me."

"I'm not telling you this to 'pleasure' you," she said angrily. "Don't you *hear* me? I love you, Seth. I've loved you all these years . . . or this wouldn't have happened."

"But, of course, I'm delighted. I couldn't even claim a first like that with Allegra."

"Allegra!" Melon stared at him. How could he mention her here on this beach that was *theirs*?

"I know I can trust you to be discreet, Melon. I know you're a close friend of hers, but . . . well, she isn't too tolerant of my occasional lapses."

Melon's cheeks were blazing now. "Occasional lapses! Jesus Christ on a crutch! I've just told you I *love* you. I just told you you've given me the first orgasm of my life and you're pleading your mistress's sensitivity!"

216

"I'm sorry, Melon." He reached for her hands. "I'm being a boor. That was thoughtless of me. Perhaps I'm a little shaken by your . . . reactions here. I don't, I didn't, mean to start something difficult, or to make things uncomfortable for you."

She jerked away from him. "You told me to trust you."

"Have I given you any reason not to trust me?"

"No. But, you see, I thought . . . "

He tenderly brushed sand from her back and shoulders. Then he knelt and picked up the two twisted strings that had been her bikini, and next her gown. "Here, put these on, the wind's up. Come on, I'll walk you back to your cottage."

Numbly, Melon dressed.

Allegra.

Why had he mentioned her? She was the most beautiful woman Melon had ever known. But evidently even Allegra wasn't enough for an incredible man like Seth Hathaway, or none of what had just happened would have happened. She had just made love, been made love to, by Allegra's lover. Seth was a man numberless women desired, but couldn't touch. But he had made love to her. That was *real*. He had desired *her*.

They trudged along the beach toward the house, holding hands like children. She would make him want her again.

The beach house was in almost complete darkness. One dim lamp was lit in the living room. There wasn't a soul in sight. The party was over. An offshore breeze had come up and was pushing several empty plastic cups and paper plates around the deck.

Melon tried to regain her composure.

"Seth," she said brightly, "when will I see you again?"

"Well, with luck, Tuesday."

"Tuesday?"

"Unless you have a better offer. I know they'd love to have you at the *Inquirer*. Are you trying to tell me something?"

"I mean, when will we see each *other*?"

He pulled her firmly against his chest and rested his chin on the top of her head. "Darling girl, you mustn't complicate your life. You were truly delicious tonight. I'm a lucky man to have had so much of you and your time. Let's leave it at this, all right?"

She walked him to his white Mercedes and stood silently as he started the engine. He reached through the open window and laid his hand on her cheek for an instant. "Good night, pretty thing. Sleep well."

She watched the tail lights of the car move up the dune road. She watched until the faint red lights disappeared around the last curve.

Tuesday?

Probably in the city room under the fluorescent lights, amid all the noise and confusion.

She felt her way up the steps to the deck.

Oh, shit.

Empty glasses, overflowing ashtrays, plates and bowls of congealed food.

She closed the door and shivered. Suddenly she felt quite cold.

"Mel? Is that you?" Jane sat, half hidden in a high-backed wicker chair, her bare feet propped on the glass coffee table between an empty fifth of vodka and three tilting paper plates of watermelon rinds.

"You're still up?"

"Can't sleep. I'm contemplating the size and dimension of tomorrow's hangover. Want a nightcap?" Jane started to get up.

"Don't. I'll fix it." Melon went to the kitchen bar counter and picked up the first bottle she found, a jug of red wine. She located a clean coffee mug. "Christ, the last clean anything in the house." She filled the mug with the tepid wine and flopped onto the couch.

"Great party until the shit hit the fan," Jane said and lit a fresh cigarette from the stub of her old one.

Melon stared blankly into the cold fireplace. "Jane," the words seemed to issue forth of their own accord, because she certainly didn't intend to say them, "I love him."

"Me, too, Melon. He's the dishiest man I've ever known."

Melon turned to look at her friend, her jaw tense from determination. "No, I mean, I *love* him. *I am in love with him.*"

"Oh, Melon, cut it," Jane said wearily. "I saw you padding off down the beach with Seth, chatting away. Now here you are, two hours later, telling me you're in love with the man. Just exactly how does that work?"

"I don't know. Something happened on the beach. I mean,

something happened, really important, to my head as well as my body."

"Your *body*? Oh, goody! You mean you actually screwed old Seth? In the sand? Melon, I love it! You are such a rabbit." Jane whooped with glee.

"Stop it!" Melon said furiously. "It wasn't like that at all." Again, hot tears welled and spilled down her cheeks. She had not felt so helpless for many, many years.

"Oh, Jesus, you're *serious*." Jane dropped her feet to the floor. "I'm sorry. Damn! What a mess."

"What am I going to do, Jane?"

"Maybe it will look better in the morning, hon." Her voice held concern.

"It won't change in the morning. I am hooked."

"Oh, honey! That's big trouble. He's the Boss! How in hell are you going to squeeze in between the most beautiful wife in the world and the most beautiful mistress in the world? That man barely has time to pee!"

"Jane, I'm going to bed. I have to do some serious thinking." Melon slowly rose from the couch.

"I'll say!"

Melon paused at the edge of the fireplace. "You know, men have been known to leave both their wives and mistresses. Men have been known to change their entire lives . . . for the . . . right woman. Good night."

"Night, Melon." Jane was shaking her head very slowly.

Chapter Thirteen

July 1963

Jane stared out over the deck toward the ocean. The morning light was just beginning to brighten a sliver of the horizon. The house reeked from the overflowing ashtrays and stale drinks sitting on every horizontal surface in sight. She had wandered onto the deck for better air and to ponder Melon's confession.

Damn. Seth in the sand. Surprising he would stick it in the company ink. Why not her? He knew *she* was uncomplicated, and she certainly wouldn't have minded a sandy fling with Seth Hathaway. He had looked particularly good, too. All tanned, flashing those bright blue eyes and glistening teeth, tilting that great fiery head.

Jane sighed and dropped onto a deck chair. She was mystified by Seth taking a poke at Melon, of all people. And, poor Melon, skulking after Billy Claire's dreamy brother all evening. Seth had hardly accomplished a seduction. All he had probably done was tap her on the shoulder.

Few women would or could have resisted sex with Seth. It was certainly nothing to get emotional about. He was a lost cause and everyone knew it. How could Melon be so *vulnerable?* Melon, of all people? Seth Hathaway had gotten to Mary Ellen Bowersox.

Jane set down her grimy glass and rubbed her temples, trying to erase the remembered pain in Melon's voice, the wide, suddenly defenseless eyes. Melon could be bitchy and insensitive, but she only deliberately went after a small and select group of individuals who had deeply offended her or someone she liked. After Jane had been temporarily banished from E.O.B. 240, Melon had been so contrite she had called Jane six times a day for weeks. Occasionally Jane saw flickers of the vulnerability Melon so desperately tried to camouflage, and those glimpses caused Jane to feel protective of her friend. Many were the times when Jane had picked up the bits of flesh and broken bone Melon had strewn all over Washington and its suburbs. She had logged long hours on barstools listening as one man after another attempted to sort out what Melon had done to him. And all-hours calls from Melon. But this one was different. She had never heard Melon say she actually loved any of them. "I'm crazy about him," or, "This new one is gorgeous," or, "Have I got a dandy this time," or "Hot stuff, Janey." But never, "I love him." Never.

The sea had turned an irresistible lavender, but the air held chilly moisture. She pulled on one of Del's old Windbreakers from a hook on the side of the house before she descended the steps and walked slowly over the dunes in the faint, pink light.

No doubt Paul was preparing to get up and dress for his 6:00 A.M. tennis match with his oldest son, leaving the big double bed to his sleeping wife in their beach house in East Hampton.

At the beginning of their love affair Paul had given her his exact schedule when they were apart, as if to reassure her that he was with her in spirit, no matter what else he was doing. It had helped. He spent a lot of time with his three boys, not just out of duty, but because he loved them and he was proud of each of them. She often wondered if they had any idea that their father's trips to Washington always included some very intimate hours with a certain female member of the White House staff. She also wondered what it would be like to share *anything* with a child of one's own.

Weekends and holidays were the worst, but she endured them for the pleasant days each month that they did have together in Washington, or when she could get up to New York.

She had never resented Paul's wife, only the time it took him to be married to her. He had been forthright about their relationship from the first. He never made a pretense of being single or not wanting to stay married—to his way of life—if not to Eleanor.

Jane and Paul enjoyed each other immensely. They respected

222

each other's minds. Their senses of humor balanced nicely. Their lovemaking was satisfying, and never forced. Perhaps in another relationship, with another man, at another time, the many missing pieces in her emotional life would be filled. But for now, she supposed, this was the best that could be expected.

A few yards to her left, over a rise in the dune, she heard a rustle and a moan.

She glanced in the direction of the noise.

Yikes! She had almost stepped on two bodies in the tall beach grass, hidden in the purple morning shadows.

One body belonged to Nick Hutchins. She recognized the silver-blond hair immediately. He was lying on his back, his eyes closed, his face contorted by ecstasy. The other body belonged to a very busy Miles Buford, who lifted his head when Jane gasped.

"Excuse *me,* gentlemen," she said, embarrassed, and stumbled back the way she had come.

Miles Buford she knew about. But Billy Claire's lady-killer brother? The scourge of the Mid-Atlantic States? Phew. What did sand *do* to people? Del getting plastered and making a total ass of himself, almost killing Ann with mortification. Melon letting herself get steamrolled by Seth. And now this awkward tableau.

Jane had had it.

She found a piece of typing paper and scribbled: "Call Coroner If Not Seen Before Monday. Otherwise, LEAVE ME ALONE." She was asleep two minutes after thumbtacking it on her door.

The thump of a Frisbee against the screen of her bedroom window woke her at one thirty in the afternoon of July fifth.

"Go get it, butterfingers," she heard Miles call from the far side of the deck.

She stood under the shower for ten minutes, then wrapped a towel around her long, wet hair and pulled on a pair of jeans and a denim work shirt.

"Good morning, Glory," Billie Claire said brightly as Jane emerged from the dark back hall. Billie Claire was struggling toward the kitchen with a full tray of dirty glasses. "You're the fourth survivor. Coffee or a Bloody? I made a medicinal pitcherful."

"Blah! Yeah, I'll have a Bloody, but pour it very slooowly. God, it reeks out here!" She climbed onto a barstool and held her head.

Billie Claire poured the thick red drink into a coffee mug

marked Washington Redskins, then turned to the sink and began washing out a big ashtray. "I figured if I moved veeery slowly I'd get some help with this mess. I want to make a dent in it before Ann comes out."

"Here, I'll give you a hand." Jane took a deep swallow of her drink and started piling paper plates on top of each other. Everything was covered by a cold layer of chicken grease. She found an empty carton and began to fill it. "Come on, B.C., you wash and I'll dry. I'll put all this crap away if I can figure out where it's supposed to go."

The two women stood side by side at the sink. They could see Miles and Nicky throwing the Frisbee on the sand out beyond the deck.

"What's Nicky doing here?" Jane asked.

"Oh, his date took off last night. She's probably crying her eyes out in some motel in Ocean City. He slept on the beach, of all places." Billie Claire scraped the remains of avocado dip into the trash. "Yuk. Nothing like black avocado the morning after. I may barf."

"After*noon* after. Where's Melon?"

"She's still in our room. What's the matter with her anyway? I heard her crying last night and padded over to see what I could do. All she would say was, 'I don't want to talk about it.' Somebody at the party must have told her she was gaining weight."

"Maybe she's just upset in general." Jane was carefully noncommittal.

"Melon doesn't get upset, she gets even."

Crack! The Frisbee hit the glass of the big picture window. "Jesus, those two are going to decapitate somebody," Jane said.

"I know, they've been at it for hours. What do you think of my handsome brother?"

"Ah . . . he's, ah, as you say, very handsome, Billie. Hand me the rest of that potato salad, I'm going to toss it. Must be crawling with ptomaine by now. Oh, crap. Someone put out a cigarette in the bowl." Jane stared with disgust at the big wooden bowl.

"Nicky's going to be some catch for someone."

"Were the two of you close when you were growing up?" Jane asked as she ran hot water into the bowl.

"No, not really. He went away to boarding school when he was around fourteen. He was just always my weird big brother."

224

"Weird? How, weird?"

"Oh, always playing detective. Spying on people. Going through everyone's dresser drawers. Especially our mother's." She sniffed a glass bowl of brandied strawberries, judged them unsafe and poured them on top of the potato salad. "He was awfully sneaky, cute, but sneaky. And bright. He made the *Review* at Yale. Got hired by Renfrew and Parker right after graduation. Big Wall Street firm."

"I know," Jane smiled. "I am not without some Wall Street connections."

"Oh, right. Paul. Well, someday Nicky will have that kind of clout. I'm absolutely certain about it. If only he'd stop chasing women so devotedly. One of these days he's going to get himself shot."

"Shot?" Jane rinsed the strawberry bowl.

"He seems to have a taste for married women. I can't prove it, of course, but occasionally I get a call from some very upset men who are looking for him. They'd have to be really frantic to phone his little sister. I figure they're the irate husbands and just act dumb."

Jane glanced at her everlastingly cheerful friend. My God, she has no idea. Irate husbands, indeed! "Well, that's that. We can see the actual floor of the Augean stables at last." She took one final swipe at the countertop with a sponge and dropped it into the sink.

Miles and Nick came pounding onto the deck. Jane called through the window. "Your timing is exquisite, fellas. We just finished cleaning up. Thanks a bunch."

Nick pressed his face against the window screen. "You girls are lucky. You get to stay in the nice cool house while we sweat our brains out trying to prevent a wild Frisbee from attacking you."

Jane flicked water at him through the screen. Nothing in his expression betrayed their shared knowledge of his activities on the dunes at dawn.

"Hey, B.C.," he called to his sister, "Miles has offered to drive me down to Ocean City. That crazy broad's probably cracked up my car by now."

Billie Claire pushed open the door to the deck. "Nicky, are you nuts? Why did you sleep on the beach? I'm surprised the mosquitoes didn't eat you alive."

225

"Hell, it was great. Clears the head." He did a little jogging step around the deck.

"What did you do to that girl to send her off in such a snit?" Billie Claire giggled. She had told Jane she hadn't particularly liked the woman Nick had brought to the party.

"Damned if I know," he puffed. "Guess she got bored. I was having a perfectly civilized conversation with Miles and she got pissed off and stomped out. Got any cold beer, B.C.?"

Miles stood by the screen door stripping off a sweat-soaked T-shirt. "Jane, would you tell Ann I'm going to run Nicky to Ocean City, and I'll be back in time for dinner. Need anything?"

Jane was finishing her Bloody Mary on a tall stool. "Ann's asleep, so I don't really know. Some more beer, probably."

"Okay, then. I'll see you in a couple of hours." He hurried toward his room to change.

We won't count on it, Jane thought, and poured the last of the Bloody Mary into her mug. Playing it a little broadly, Miles. Better watch it.

"Janey, I'm going for a swim. Want to come?"

"No, thanks, Billie. As they say down home, don't touch water, fish fuck in it. You go ahead. I'm going to sit in the shade and read my Ian Fleming."

Billie Claire laughed. "Is that official White House staff policy? You *will* read what the President reads?"

"Something like that." Jane flopped into a deck chair out of the blazing sun.

Later, at the sound of ice cubes dropping into the steel sink, Jane looked up from the James Bond thriller. Through the kitchen window she could see the back of Ann's shiny, carrot-colored head.

"Hey, there," she called, "if it isn't Pearl Mesta."

"Pearl Messed Up is more like it. Where is everybody?"

"Billie went for a swim to wash off the chicken grease. Melon is zonked and Miles drove Nicky Hutchins over to Ocean City."

"Nicky? What's he doing here?"

"It's complicated." Jane put down her book.

"Damn, this place wasn't this clean when we rented it." Ann looked around the kitchen. "Who hoed it out?"

"Kind and loving gremlins."

"I'll say. I thought if I just stayed in bed long enough it would go away or catch fire." Ann stepped out onto the deck. "Arrgh! Sunlight!"

"I know. Awful stuff, but at these prices we'd better use it."

Ann sat down on the deck chair next to Jane's and held her palms against the sides of her head. "I'm glad Billie Claire isn't around. I don't think I can face her right now."

"Oh, Annie, she's forgotten last night. You know Billie Claire. She's the most understanding person alive."

"All the more reason. I am officially not speaking to Del for his behavior, particularly to Billie." Ann pulled a big red straw hat down over her eyes. "Anybody eat?"

"Bloodies."

"Well, that may be food to you, but I've got to eat something. My tummy's been giving me fits lately." Ann felt her way back to the kitchen and returned to the deck five minutes later with a plate of cold leftover beans, a slab of brown bread and butter and a Jack Daniels on the rocks.

Jane observed her over the tops of her sunglasses. "How can you eat that stuff? Throw it away."

Ann stared down at the food on the plate for a long moment. "You're right." She pushed the plate under the deck chair and took a sip of her drink. "Maybe later, after it stops moving."

"The food?" Jane chuckled.

"No, the universe."

"Why? You didn't drink that much last night."

"My hangover is emotional, honey." She leaned back into the cushion and pulled her hat over her face. "You know who I'm thinkin' about?"

"Tab Hunter?"

"Kay Graham. I'm thinkin' about Kay Graham and what she must be going through."

"Del's not a lunatic, he's a drunk."

Ann winced. "Drunk. Crazy. It's all the same. You gotta be crazy to drink like that and cause such a fuss."

"Del's going to be all right. He took a terrible thumping from old Cynthia. But he'll get over it."

"Sure, sure, after he's lost his liver and his job and all our friends."

"Buck up, Annie, it's going to be all right."

"Jane, you don't know what troubles are," she sighed. "I'll bet your biggest problem right now is whether we ever recognize Red China."

"I wouldn't say that," Jane said quietly over the lip of her mug.

"Come on, honey. You are the original golden girl. Look at you. Great skin, nice, streaky blond hair, long legs and not yet thirty. You've got the world by the tail."

Jane laughed. "The grass is always greener . . ."

"No, I mean it. You don't have a mark on you, outside or inside. I come from hardscrabble and grits. You come from those slick Southern boarding schools and that fancy, horsey family. You're class, honey, and people with class don't get heartache like us poor folks. You got money and looks and a dream job and I don't know a man who wouldn't faint dead away if you crooked your little finger at him."

Jane twisted her head around to look over her shoulder. "Who are you talking about? I don't see anyone here but you and me."

"Well, I don't know much about your bringin' up but I always could tell shit from sunshine, and you are sunshine, Jane Connor."

"I thank you for the compliments about my looks, but you are way off base about the rest. For instance, what in the world makes you think I have money?"

"Why, the way you dress and the way you've fixed up your apartment. I don't know, everything about you says buckets of fine old money to me."

"Well, just for the record, Ann, I buy my clothes on sale or at Seventh Avenue showrooms through a connection of Paul's. The stuff in my apartment came mostly from other people's castoffs and Goodwill Industries. Haven't you ever noticed that I don't own a car? I don't have any jewelry. I never take a vacation. I didn't want to say anything, but I had to borrow a grand from Paul to take this house."

"But you make a damn good salary. Where does it all go?"

"It goes."

"Sorry. I didn't mean to pry . . ."

"That's okay, Annie. Fortunately it was you who brought this up, because you're also the only person I could tell the truth to. Certainly none of the others. Billie is too sensitive. I'm not that

228

close to Miles. And Melon . . . well, forget it. She's a one-woman public-address system."

"Just a sec, I don't want to miss anything." Ann rose from her chair. "You want something from the kitchen?" She shook the ice in the bottom of her empty glass.

"Thanks. A cold beer. This Bloody isn't working."

Ann returned a few moments later with a tray containing a fresh Jack Daniels, a bottle of Heineken's and a paper plate of cold fried chicken. "You better eat somethin', honey."

Jane picked up a wing and took a nibble, then put it down. "Ann, practically everything I make goes to the Adela Whelan Home in Baltimore."

"The Adela Whelan . . . but that's a home for . . ."

"You've got it. His name is Nathaniel. He's ten years old chronologically, but you'd never know it. He can't talk, he can't even stand up, and he shits in his pants. It takes two people to feed him—one to hold his head and another to scrape the food off his chin. That's on the good days. On the bad days he doesn't eat, he screams and throws things and tries to kill the attendants."

"I'll be whipped!" Ann stared at her. "Is he your child?"

"No. I adopted him to satisfy a perverted maternal instinct," she said sarcastically. "Of course, he's mine."

"Jane, I never knew you were married!"

"Didn't anyone ever tell you you don't have to get married to have a baby?"

"You poor darlin'." Ann's eyes were wide with sympathy. "How in the world did you manage?"

"I didn't, really. When I found out I was really pregnant it was too late. Besides, 'nice girls' didn't get abortions." With her eyes closed behind her sunglasses, Jane told Ann about Sean and Texas and the birth of Nathaniel.

"Lordy, you poor darlin'! What did your folks do? What happened?"

"Well, as Queen Elizabeth would say, I got the shit kicked out of me." Jane pulled a towel over Ann's ankles. "You are turning into one big freckle. The sun's moved, and you ought to too, love."

Ann moved her chair back under the eaves of the house.

"My mother was a minister's daughter. How about that? Only her father wasn't like the gentle, liberal men of the cloth who join the Reverend Doctor King on his marches. Oh, no. The Right

Reverend Jennings Moncure—Episcopal—was the second-to-last authentic Puritan. His only child is the last. And she's my mother. If you asked her what the word 'fun' meant she honestly couldn't tell you. She's convinced that even eating is somehow suspect. A possible worldly pleasure. Such a dilemma, since one *needs* to partake of nourishment."

"Sounds like a real beauty." Ann slowly shook her head.

"Complete with Old Testament gloom. My mother perceives God as a demanding, judgmental presence. He tolerates nothing in excess. If everything is done in moderation He will provide. My mother defined the excesses and the moderations. My mother, to this day, is a remarkable woman. Everyone says so. 'Mrs. Connor is a remarkable woman!'"

Grace Moncure Connor stood six feet tall in her stocking feet. Jane could never remember her mother's hair in anything but a tight bun at the back of her neck. It had been coal-black hair until she was well past fifty.

While Jane heard her mother referred to as stately and refined and, of course, remarkable, she thought of her as intimidating and sullen.

Grace had been born and raised in Boston. When she was twenty, Reverend Moncure had accepted the rectorate of St. Clement's in Charlottesville. His daughter and wife were greatly relieved. Down in Virginia they were a comfortable distance from rowdy Irish Catholics and intense intradenominational bickering. The pace in the South was gentler and the people more genteel.

Five years later Grace's parents began to worry that their stern and statuesque daughter would never find a man who could meet her high standards. Almost every young man who attended social functions at St. Clement's was shorter than Grace. The few men who were comfortably taller were boring football fanatics or boisterous fraternity men or a combination of both.

Dudley Connor attended his first Wednesday Evening Social Evening at St. Clement's rectory a week after he came to the University of Virginia as an assistant professor in the History Department.

He was six foot five and wore a vest as if he were more comfortable with it than without it. He carried his rangy body with an unathletic stoop. His neatly combed hair was whitish-blond, as were his eyebrows and eyelashes. His high cheekbones and long, thin nose emphasized his deep-set pale blue eyes.

Dudley Connor, Ph.D., exuded the authentic aristocracy of the Old South.

Grace decided she would marry him after they had exchanged tentative pleasantries while she poured his tea. She assumed it was God's will, rather than what some people called "instinct"—an offensive term. Within moments she *knew* he would make an excellent husband. During the following months she was continually amazed by God's good sense and her capacity to perceive it.

Dudley Connor was the firstborn son of an old northern Virginia family that took its pride from being one of the First Families of Virginia. One evening he explained to Grace that F.F.V. was more a state of mind than history. For, while, on paper, the Connor bloodlines could be traced back to Roanoke Colony, the *fact* that those settlers had disappeared without a trace was seen to be irrelevant. Grace and Dudley had a good chuckle over that.

Even so, Dudley did possess formidable credentials.

Seven generations of Connors had owned three thousand acres of gently rolling hills outside of Leesburg that had been called Chantry Farms since long before the War Between the States. He had grown to manhood on land where some of the best quarter horses in the country were bred and raised.

Chantry Farms, Virginia.

It meant nothing to him.

He had been sent to prep school at Staunton Military Academy in Waynesboro and then "north" to Princeton, where he stayed as long as possible. He had no desire to be a gentleman horse breeder like his father, and his father's father, or his younger brothers. The study of history, the past, was more symmetrical and predictable.

Grace Moncure and Dudley Connor shared a distaste for conventional social intercourse, and, more importantly, an aspiration toward excellence—in all things.

"My mother used the word 'excellent' only slightly more often than she used the word 'disgusting,'" Jane said, gazing out toward a two-masted schooner on the horizon. "Everything that was ever done in that enormous house was done to my mother's standards of excellence—which, incidentally, had a way of changing from day to day, depending on her mood."

231

"You mean you grew up on the place? But you said your father hated it."

"Yes, that was the irony. Here was my father who hated horses, hated anything to do with the land—heir to all that prime real estate and a string of quarter horses he didn't give a damn about. But Chantry Farms had been in the Connor family a *long* time, and, no matter what, a Connor held onto it. They fought off Union soldiers who tried to burn it. After that war, Connorses stayed there and almost starved. The land was sacred. When my father's parents died, his two brothers were too busy chasing fast women and slow horses and spending their shares of the inheritance to want to be strapped with all those boring details like upkeep of a breeding farm and taxes. My father was duty-bound to give up teaching and go back and run Chantry. He was, remember, the oldest son."

"But how could he if he'd never been interested?" Ann hunched her shoulders, shook her head and squinted intently.

"As it turned out, my mother ran it. Very strange, my mother and Chantry Farms. She was passionate about the place. I was born in the big four-poster bed in my mother's bedroom. File that fact. My father's bedroom was about five miles down the hall and in another wing. I'm not sure how they conceived me, let alone my three brothers. With four kids, I figure they got together four times in all."

No one ever knew what Dudley Connor did ten hours a day in his library on the second floor of the old plantation house. Whatever he did, Jane's mother referred to it as "your father's work." Jane assumed his "work" was some endless historical tract of cosmic importance. She was never to intrude on his inner sanctum in the darkened room on the second floor. On the rare occasions when she was invited to enter, she was awed by the hundreds of leather-bound books that lined the walls, and the wonderful musty smell mingled with pipe tobacco. Whatever his "work" was, it kept him removed from the horses and Grace's relentless demands.

He would emerge from the library thirty minutes before the evening meal and take his sherry with Grace in the drawing room on the lower floor. In the winter they would sit facing each other before the fire. In the summer they would sit on the west portico that overlooked the long sweep of lawn that stretched down to the banks of the Potomac, where weeping willow trees dipped into the tranquil water. Grace never took sherry. She considered spirits of any kind to be "addlers of the mind." Jane never once saw her father without a necktie and a starched collar.

Dudley Connor was a twice-removed element in his only daughter's life. Jane knew almost nothing about him—except his pedigree—nothing of what he thought or felt or even *did*. One thing she did know, though, her father hated the very breeze that wafted the smell of horses from the stables toward the house.

Grace Connor, upon arriving at Chantry Farms, became an excellent rider within an astonishingly short time. Every morning at daybreak, regardless of the weather, she tacked and groomed her mare, Weather Prophet, and set out for the wooded trails and the open, rolling hills. Jane could watch her mother from the dormered window of her third-floor bedroom. Jane could *see* her mother's exhilaration, the expression on her face under the visor of her hunt cap, the way she held herself. But, by eight she would be back in the huge old kitchen, her cheeks bright red and the sweat stains visible on the front of her ratcatcher. She would be tormenting the cook with demands and complaints for a few minutes, and then Grace Moncure Connor went off to bathe and change. For the remainder of the day she was her reserved, brusque self.

"I think the horses were her only release," Jane continued, still pacing the deck. Ann, her audience of one, remained completely silent, her eyes never leaving Jane's face. "Looking back, I think she used those horses as a substitute for things lost, rather, never found—a career, romantic love, sex, fun. And, you know, Ann, she could and did muck the stalls and shoe brood mares. I never saw anyone take a fence with the ease and control she had. She was enormously intelligent and could have done or been anything she set her mind to, but there was something about her that prevented conscious enjoyment. There was no laughter in the woman. When I was fifteen, she permitted me to go out alone with the son of the doctor in Leesburg. He spent four hours mauling me in the back of a Nash Rambler. When I wouldn't put out, he said, 'What are you saving it for?' I thought about that question a lot. Not just concerning sex. I often wondered what the hell my mother was saving *it* for. Heaven, probably." Jane leaned against the railing.

233

"Want one?" Ann rattled her dying ice cubes.

"Oh, hell, yes. I've started this saga, I might as well finish it."

"You damn well better! Wait a sec. Don't say a word." Ann swept into the kitchen and returned immediately with a full bottle of Miles's Virginia Gentleman and two clean glasses. "This is appropriate. Fuck the ice. It doesn't last anyway." Ann slopped bourbon almost to the rims of the glasses and handed one to Jane. "Okay, shoot."

"I've always felt there's something weird about people who love the country," Jane said, taking a long pull at her drink. "Granted, it's beautiful to look at, but if I never saw another blade of grass or a tree or vine it wouldn't bother me. I think it's my remembrance of the loneliness. That terrible, gnawing *loneliness*. I didn't realize I *was* lonely, really, not in a conscious way. But I knew something was wrong, something bewildering in that half-bright way small animals feel pain."

Jane lived in a dormitory at Miss Madiera's during the week, and returned home for weekends. She dreaded going home. There was no one to talk with except old Early, the handyman, or Alma, the cook. Her mother was either riding or working in the little office off the kitchen doing the books, keeping the breeding register and paying feed bills. Her father was almost never to be seen, and her brothers were always off doing whatever it was country boys do. The only brother she was close to was Tommy, the eldest by two years. Leander and Brady, the two younger boys, were simply little blond people covered with jelly and scabs, their pockets full of frogs.

The one bright moment of the weekend was Saturday morning when old Mr. McCabe, who drove their RFD route, pulled up to the mailbox on the fence post at the entrance to Chantry Farms. His battered old Ford would rest half in the ditch and half on the one-lane macadam road.

"I could see down to the end of our lane from the front porch. He knew I was always waiting for him and he would wave the weekly copy of *Life* magazine from his window and then push it into our box. It was as though he were shoving half of Hollywood and most of the world into that box. By the time I ran the quarter mile down the hill and snatched it out, he would be out of sight. I'd run back up the lane to the house and my room so I could read it before anyone else touched it. I can remember the smell of a

234

fresh *Life* magazine to this day, and it is dearer to me than the smell of clover or lilacs or warm puppies. You see, Annie, nature, to me, isn't sweet. It's brutal. I grew up around a lot of animals. I wasn't under the delusion they were created by Walt Disney or had zippers in their tummies for you to put your jammies in. Ann, animals *eat* each other. They sever heads from bunnies and eat their young. Brood mares go berserk halfway through giving birth and drag the foal for yards and then kill it. Geese shit great green puddles that reek, then they bite you. I once saw a docile horse kill one of the hired hands with its hooves, and a chicken peck out another chicken's eyes. And worse than the brutality is the confinement of being in the country. You'd think a country child is a free child. Wrong. If you are a girl, there are constant reminders you aren't a boy, that you aren't allowed to be free. And all around you everything's free unless human beings shackle it or pen it up. A hunger to be free, to run as fast as I could and never come back, was with me since I could walk. It wasn't so much running away from something, as it was the ache to run *toward* something. I was in my teens before I realized that what I wanted to run toward was *people, humans.*" Jane squinted at the schooner that was now tacking around and heading north.

When she was twelve, Jane learned to drive an old Jeep that her brothers had fixed up. She had no idea how to shift the gears, but she knew she could steer it. One long hot afternoon when no one was around, she got in it and took it out on the main road to Leesburg—with much jerking and grinding of gears. She swerved past other cars, cutting in front of them, pushing the accelerator to the floor. There had been all hell to pay when she returned later that day. But she had taught herself to drive.

"My punishment lasted for one month. I was not permitted to ride my horse, Dumpling, or to leave the farm at all except to go to school, and to church on Sunday morning. The Saturday after the Jeep escapade, from my perch on the porch, I saw my mother reign Weather Prophet up at the mailbox. My heart stopped when she took the *Life* magazine from Mr. McCabe and put it under the front of her saddle. It never came again. 'Too worldly,' I was told when I protested and cried.

"After that things were never the same. I took to small transgressions, like sneaking out of services on Sundays and wandering around town. I used to walk over to the A.M.E. Baptist Church, which was for Negroes only, of course. Only Negroes were Baptists. I could hear them singing, 'Free at least, Free at last, Good God Almighty, I'm free at last.' I didn't know they were singing about freedom from oppression—from us and the Pughs and the Chewnings and the Kincaids—I thought they were singing about getting the hell out of Loudoun County."

On a very clear night in the summer, from the top of the far ridge, Jane could see the lights of Washington reflecting against the sky fifty miles away. To her it was Oz.

On Easter morning the spring Jane was sixteen, her mother called her into the little office off the kitchen. Grace Connor held a familiar blue slip of paper in her hand.

"Sit down, young lady." Her mother gestured toward a Hitchcock chair beside her desk.

"Yes, ma'am."

"Miss Gwalthney has forwarded your grades for the first part of the semester," she said, tapping the blue paper with her index finger.

Jane's heart thumped. She knew she wasn't doing well in school. She didn't care about school. The work was too easy and too boring. She preferred causing trouble in the dorm, or organizing the other girls to complain about the rules. It was more fun to find ways to beat the system than to go along with it. Fun that had resulted in two suspensions in the last eighteen months.

She had seen the blue letter on Miss Madiera's stationery the day she came home for the spring holidays. It had been reposing on her mother's desk for one solid week, and only now was she getting called on the carpet about it. That probably explained her mother being more tight-lipped than usual. Not that she ever needed a reason. Now, she was finally bringing it up after Easter services.

"This simply won't do. I see here a D in Latin, a C in algebra, a C minus in civics. Further, this." She pulled a typed report from the envelope.

"What's that?" Jane's hands were sweating.

"This is a deportment report from the headmistress. I won't read it to you. It is too upsetting to me." Her mother replaced it in the envelope.

"But I'd like to know what she said. I'd like a chance to defend myself."

236

"There is no need. I can tell you, however, Jane Carleton Connor, that the school feels that you most definitely will not graduate unless your grades improve radically. And it is highly possible that you will be asked to leave if your conduct does not improve significantly." Her mother's voice was completely level, free of inflection of any kind.

So that was it. She was going to be expelled.

"Under the circumstances, I think it is pointless for your father and me to continue to spend the exorbitant amount of money required to keep you in a proper school. You obviously do not appreciate the opportunity to be in the company of girls from fine families, or to avail yourself of the educational privileges such a school provides. I see no need for you to finish out the year. We will have someone pack your things and send them on here."

"But what am I supposed to do? Stay *here?*" The thought of staying at Chantry Farms, isolated and under her mother's constant supervision, made her temples throb and her breath come in short, little pants.

"I see no alternative, do you?" her mother said, not expecting an answer. "With the boys away at school we can use a hand. Not that you've ever been much good at any kind of management."

"But, Mother, I have one of the leads in the spring play. I'm editor of the paper. I need to . . ." Jane began to stammer for the first time in her life.

"That is enough, Jane."

"Mother, please . . ."

"You are excused." Grace Connor swiveled around in her chair and began to shuffle papers on her desk.

Jane walked through the kitchen and out onto the back porch. High on the ridge that ran along the back of the outer pasture she could see a flock of crows swirling up in the wind off the river. She walked to the barn where Early was brushing out Dumpling's tail. Her flanks glistened in the spring sunlight.

"Mornin', Miss Jane. Sure good to have you home for a spell." Early wiped sweat from his mahogany forehead with an arthritic hand.

"Morning, Early. Will you tack her up for me?"

"But, Miss Jane, I just got her all cleaned up. You gonna go splash mud all over her again."

"Early!"

He sighed and took a saddle from the rack.

"And put the Pelham bit on her, please." Jane went to a locker and pulled out a scuffed pair of boots. She slipped off her penny loafers and pulled the boots over the bottom of her jeans.

"She don't like a Pelham bit, Miss Jane. It's too hard on her mouth."

"Early," she said impatiently, "I've never been hard on a horse's mouth in my life. I'll have her out for some time and I want her to pay attention."

"Oh, Lordy. Your mamma find out she gonna jerk you ever way but loose, girl. You know how she feel about you riding these horses hard."

Early was slow about tacking up the mare and Jane paced the barn. Finally, Dumpling was ready and Early led the horse out into the yard. Jane was on her in an instant. She kicked her up and the horse bolted through the gate, through the walking ring, and, in seconds, past the last outbuilding and up toward the ridge.

She rode at a full gallop until she reached the top of the hill, where she pulled Dumpling up and swung off her back beside a giant oak tree. Jane threw the reins over the horse's head so that she could graze in the thick, moist grass. Then she lay down under the tree.

I just don't think I can stand it, she thought. I just can't stay here with her and nothing besides her except trees and grass and horses and boredom.

The public high school was full of hicks and hoodlums with their hot rod cars, and girls making fools of themselves over them. At home every single thing she did would be picked over, poked at and criticized. She pondered her choices and realized she had only one. She would leave. But how? She was only sixteen and her total assets consisted of an opal ring, a Parker pen and pencil set, an old Smith-Corona typewriter and an autographed picture of Alan Ladd. The opal ring, which had belonged to her grandmother, had been given to her on her twelfth birthday with the instruction that it was too valuable to be worn.

But there was hope. She also possessed the ability to type fifty-eight words a minute and her brother Tom's phone number at the Sigma Nu house at the University of Virginia.

The pressure of Dumpling's soft muzzle at the back of her neck brought her instantly to the present. She stood and brushed herself off.

"Come on, Dumps, let's fly!"

For hours Jane rode along the river, into the thick pine woods that began the foothills of the Blue Ridge. She rode until the sun was far below the tops of the trees. She was plotting her escape.

Four days later, while her mother was in the kitchen, scolding Alma, as usual, for not mashing the stems of the fresh-cut flowers before putting them in vases, Jane slipped down the back stairs with a small suitcase and her typewriter.

Tom had arrived at Chantry the day before from Charlottesville. He said he had been delayed by basketball practice, but Jane knew he had been playing poker for fifty-six hours. From his winnings he lent her a hundred dollars.

She knew Early would be going into town for feed at ten. She was crouched on the seat of the pickup when he opened the door.

"Miss Jane! What you doing?" The old man's eyes were round with surprise.

I'm going into Leesburg with you, Early. And if you say a word I'm going to smack you," she said with real menace.

"What you doing with them things?" Early looked down at the floor where she had stowed her typewriter and suitcase.

"Early, get in. Let's get going."

"Miss Jane, you is up to something and you mamma goin' to skin you alive. *Me,* she goin' to kill." He groaned into the driver's seat.

In Leesburg, Jane asked to be let off at the Greyhound bus terminal. She had checked the schedule and knew that the bus from Winchester would be there by eleven. She could be in Washington before 1:00 P.M. That would give her the afternoon to look for a place to live. The next day she would start looking for a job.

The wind off Rehobeth beach had picked up and was whipping the ocean into whitecaps, sending sailboats skittering toward shore. Jane pulled the collar of her work shirt up around her neck and buttoned the top button.

"Want to go inside and hear the end of this? Unless I've put you to sleep, that is." She smiled at Ann.

"Good God, you can't leave me hanging!"

Ann gathered up the ashtrays and glasses and made for the door.

Del had emerged during Jane's monologue and had made directly for the refrigerator. Billie Claire had come running up from the beach when the sun had begun its descent and joined Del in the kitchen. It was there that the decision to drive over to the bar at Bobby Baker's Carousel had been made. Ann had made no move to protest. She had barely acknowledged Del's presence. She just continued to sip her drink and listen to Jane. Jane had waved "hello" without interrupting her story. This was the first time she had ever told it. She wanted to finish it, get it all over with.

Del had laid a fire and lit it before he left, probably as a nonverbal peace offering. Jane and Ann took opposite ends of the long couch and shared a big beach blanket. The half-full bottle of Virginia Gentleman reposed on the coffee table.

"So, there you were." Ann tucked the blanket over Jane's feet and squirmed down into the pillows. "Sixteen, and with only one hundred dollars. And homeless."

"Those were the minuses, Annie. The plusses were that I was tall, blond and I could type. It didn't take me long to find out that I had two other assets as well. And equally valuable."

"What?"

"Tits."

"You didn't take to the streets! Come on!" Ann laughed.

"Of course not. But I'm dead serious. Tits and innocence. They're a powerful combination. When you are young and innocent and have a good figure you say and do a lot of things out of sheer dumbness that you wouldn't dream of doing ten years later. Annie, I had gone to a girls' school all my life. I never really knew any boys. Just the local creeps and my brothers. I wasn't permitted to have anything to do with boys—except the doctor's son. Ha! When I got to Washington, I went straight to the YWCA, which must have been crawling with dykes, but how would I have known? I lied about my age, got a room and walked over to the *Herald,* thinking the way to get a job was to put an ad in the paper. The old lecher at the classified counter took one look at my chest, asked me if I could type and sent me up to the personnel department. The next day I had a job on the dictation bank."

"Didn't your family come looking for you?"

"Not very hard. Tommy knew where I was, and eventually they got it out of him. My father called once and gave me a long, pedantic lecture, but he never once said, 'Come home.' My mother, I learned through Tommy, simply shrugged and said, 'She'll come home when she finds out what the real world is like.'

"Well, I found out, all right. I found out that the real world is *real,* and full of very real people—almost every one of them wanting something from you. The nice ones remembered a favor and paid you back. The mean ones didn't, so you avoided them. I was immediately drawn to the newspaper business because of the constant action and the lack of any sort of delusion. Things happen every day, all day. They're facts. People observe them and write them down. You know this, Annie. One of the basic rules is that you don't fuck around with facts, you report them exactly. A reporter calls in and tells me through the headset that the murder victim's widow wore a polka-dot dress and I typed down, 'polka-dot dress.' That was that. Then I learned that a columnist could write, 'cotton, dotted two-piece suit' and get away with it. Later, after I made staff, I learned that a *reporter* wrote, 'The President refused to comment,' and a columnist wrote, 'stern-faced, the President showed no emotion.'"

"Welll, that's pretty much the case. But, you and I know that even reporters aren't all that selective. Can't be. We all do a bit of picking and choosing." Ann poured more bourbon into their smeared glasses. "I already knew you'd been a reporter, but how did you do it with no college? I arrived in town with *some* previous experience—such as it was."

"Oh, I got the college. It wasn't easy, but the paper helped with a scholarship. A program Seth set up after he became publisher. I took second jobs between classes—waiting tables, typing students' themes, whatever I could find. People were very kind to me. I guess they sensed I was alone and determined. I never minded being alone, because I was free, and accountable to no one but myself, as long as I did my job. There were a few boyfriends, but nothing serious until I met Sean. Then when I found myself pregnant with his baby, I finally needed someone else. I couldn't handle it all, all by myself. So I went back to Chantry Farms. I hadn't seen or spoken to *them* for years. All I wanted from them was a place to lie down until whatever was going to happen happened. I suppose I hoped my mother would have mellowed a bit. Boy, was

241

I wrong. It was as if I had never left. The minute I arrived, I could see that she thought I'd been leading a wild life—booze, men, sex orgies, you name it. I tried to tell her what I'd been doing. Forget it. There was no way she would believe I'd been putting in fourteen-hour days of work and study, the energy it took to stay alive, let alone eating. And, you know, Ann, it never once occurred to me that a girl who is clever and reasonably attractive doesn't really have to work. That's why women like Allegra Farr fascinate me. She never lifts a finger, lives in luxury and all she has to do is dance attendance on Seth Hathaway. Had I only known."

"Oh, come on, Jane. You say you want freedom. What Allegra has isn't freedom. It's a special kind of slavery." Ann studied Jane over the rim of her glass.

"I know, I know. But sometimes when I sit down to pay the bills that add up to more than my income, it looks like a great life."

"You're kidding yourself. I don't mean to be presumptuous, but maybe your mother isn't the tight-assed bitch you say she is. Maybe she's been hurting all along and hasn't the emotional equipment to express it."

"That's possible. But it sure as hell can't explain it all." Jane took two long swallows of Virginia Gentleman. "I won't bore you with the way I feel when I see my son." She shook her head. "So there you are, friend. Your golden girl is made of brass."

"Platinum is more like it, honey. Does Paul know about your son?"

"Of course not! I don't tell people. I think it's selfish to load people with heartache they can't do anything about. Besides, I don't handle pity very well."

"You sure had me fooled, girl" Ann eyed Jane's empty glass. "I'm just sorry I never took the time to know you better before."

"Would any of this have made a difference, Annie?"

"No," she said quietly, "no, of course not. One difference, maybe. It makes me feel shitty to be crying the blues to you about my own problems."

"There! You see? That's why I never tell people."

"Well, it's been some years now. Have you ever gone back? What's become of your folks?"

"My father is dead."

"I'm sorry. What from?"

"Boredom," Jane said flatly. "Boredom interspersed with unrelenting, never-ending harassment. From her. Like Chinese water torture. The drip, drip, drip of criticism, complaints, demands and wistful sighs of longing for what might have been, and how terribly her children have disappointed her."

"What happened to your brothers?"

"Well, Tom recently divorced his second wife. He had a pretty good real-estate business in Richmond with Brady and Leander as partners. They started fooling around with land speculation and got in trouble with the Federal government. When the two younger ones pulled out and moved to North Carolina, poor Tom was left holding the bag and flat broke. He came back to Chantry Farms without a dime. He's taken over most of the management now. I talk with him every now and then. We have nothing in common, now, other than our knowledge of each other from when we were kids, and even that's beginning to fade. At least it doesn't make for much of a phone conversation."

"Don't they care how successful you are? I mean, being on the White House staff is not, as my darlin' managin' editor says, 'exactly chopped liver.' " Ann tried a New York accent and failed.

"There is no way to know what my family considers successful. To this day, I still don't know what my father's 'work' was. For my mother, I suppose, the only success worth notice would be something she herself had attained, and she hasn't attained much that I can name."

"You're very bitter, aren't you Janey?" She spoke very softly.

Jane stared into the fire for a long moment, then turned to her friend. "Yes, I'm bitter." There were tears in her eyes.

Ann looked away, toward the fire. Her neck muscles seemed to constrict and she swallowed.

Jane grabbed the bourbon bottle. "God damn. This is depressing. How did we ever get into this garbage? This is supposed to be a party weekend!"

Ann continued to stare at the fire. "Janey, chile, somebody is goin' to love you somethin' fierce someday and make up for everything."

Jane smiled. "To quote your Ernie again, Annie, 'From your mouth to God's ear.'"

Ann stretched. "I guess none of us has much time for the past.

243

None of us ever talks about where we came from or who we were before we came to Washington."

"No reason to, is there? All of us carry around a lot of emotional mildew. Because that's what all I've been saying is—except for Nat. He's still here." She patted Ann's foot. "Thanks for letting me air mine out at your expense."

Ann pursed her lips and tilted her head. Then with a half-nod, half-wag, she said, "Yep, friend. Christ, I'm hungry." When she attempted to stand she hit her shin against the coffee table and pitched forward. "Shit!"

Jane caught her before she fell. "Hey, lady, you are crocked!" She laughed.

Ann righted herself. "You say that because you have made no attempt at tryin' to achieve this position."

She threw back her shoulders. The effort sent her backward onto the couch. Jane grabbed for her so she would not fall against the hard armrest, and pulled her upright again. "Come on, old girl. What do you want to do?"

"Old girl want to take nappy. Old girl smashed." Ann curled into the fetal position beside Jane.

Jane sat for a moment, stroking Ann's tangled hair, and gazed at the fire. If it were ever required, she thought, I would kill for this lady.

Chapter Fourteen

July 1963

It was 10:00 A.M. on the morning after the Fourth of July.

WTOP radio had just informed Allegra that the temperature was ninety-four degrees and the humidity was eighty-nine percent.

She was seated on the balcony off her bedroom in the handsome Georgian town house on N Street. She found it difficult to breathe comfortably. For almost five minutes she had been wishing she were the victim of some vice, like cigarettes or alcohol or pep pills. Even compulsive eating would be acceptable.

She had already finished a breakfast of chilled cantaloupe, unbuttered Melba toast and black coffee, and there she sat with nothing to do, no one to talk with and nothing to think about. Not a goddamned thing. Damn Seth.

The open balcony looked onto the back garden of her house. It had been carefully landscaped to maximize the available space, planted with miniature shrubs and pines. White tubs of geraniums and snowballs lined the high redwood fence that separated her garden from that of a South American ambassador on the right, and two gay priests from Georgetown University on her left. The air was almost visible as it hung moistly over the ground, stifling.

The city was absolutely dead. If you mattered, you had left. Even those who *didn't* matter found somewhere to go over the long holiday weekend, if it were merely a day trip to the Chesapeake shore. Everyone Allegra cared to know had taken off for the Delaware and Maryland beaches or to the seacoasts of Virginia and North Carolina. The previous day she had spent hours on the phone calling her family and friends who were vacationing on Cape Cod or the Hamptons to wish them a Happy Fourth and catch up on gossip. On the *fifth* of July she had no excuse for calling *anyone.*

She certainly had no intention of spending a *second* evening with Grant Langtry.

What an odd evening the night before had been. She had just stepped out of a long and curiously unsatisfying scented bath at eight thirty when the phone had rung. From the tone of the ring she had known it was Seth's private line in her dressing room. She had picked up the receiver, fully expecting to hear Seth's voice. Who else could it be? The few people who knew the unlisted number would know Seth wouldn't be there.

The caller was one Grant Langtry from New York, and he asked to speak with Seth. She curtly told Mr. Langtry that Seth was out of town and where he was, something she ordinarily wouldn't have done for a stranger. Then, while she was trying to determine whether she had divulged Seth's whereabouts because she was angry with Seth or just bored and lonely, the cultivated and resonant voice asked if he had the pleasure of speaking with Miss Allegra Farr. She said yes, realizing no one could have Seth's number unless Seth himself had given it. They chatted for a few moments and he said he knew her father. He had been a guest of Dr. Robert Farr's in Chicago, and wasn't the world indeed small? Allegra warmed to the voice.

"Please don't think me presumptuous, Miss Farr. I'm down from New York for a few days and I'm dreading a second dinner alone. Is there the remotest possibility that you could postpone your dinner plans and join me?"

"Well . . ." He sounded all right, and he did have Seth's private number. There could be no harm meeting him for dinner. Better than watching television and stewing in the heat. He was probably a boring millionaire lawyer who dabbled in politics; that would explain his knowing both Seth and her father. Oh, hell, maybe it would make Seth jealous.

Grant Langtry oozed charm. "Miss Farr, I'm delighted. If you have a favorite restaurant . . .? I *have* booked a table at the Golden Parrot for nine."

He hurried to greet her as she entered the door of the old mansion off Dupont Circle.

"Miss Farr," he beamed as he took her jacket, "you have just transformed a most tedious business trip into an enchantment. Had I known you were *this* beautiful I would have asked for a table by the door."

They followed the maître d' to a corner banquette off the main dining room.

"Mmm." Mr. Grant Langtry was a distinguished, if ordinary-looking man whom she judged to be in his middle fifties. He was immaculately groomed and she noted that his nails were professionally manicured and polished.

Over cocktails they discussed her father, whom Langtry had evidently known for some years. Langtry was too polite to ask why she was in town on the holiday weekend, but she wondered about *his* presence.

"I'm surprised you found anyone to do business with this weekend," she said as she daintily snapped a bit of bread stick with her even teeth. "Your family must be disappointed you couldn't be with them." Grant Langtry wore a plain gold wedding band.

"Oh, they are all up at Martha's Vineyard. One of my partners and I had adjoining summer homes there. We did until recently. He was killed, down in this area, incidentally. Plane crash last February up near Olney in a blinding snowstorm. You may have read about it; it was in all the papers. Allen was only thirty-six. A terrible tragedy for the firm of Prouty, Langtry and Boxer."

"Of course I remember! You mean Allen Boxer? I knew him! Good Lord, he was your partner? I met him in New York several years ago. Oh, I'm so sorry. As a matter of fact, a good friend of mine, a reporter on the *Herald,* covered that crash."

Grant gestured for another round of drinks. Allegra shook her head. "Nothing for the lady," he told the waiter.

"I'm really so ignorant of the law," she said. "What kind of firm is Prouty, Langtry and Boxer?"

The waiter arrived with their menus. "Oh, we are pretty much all over the lot. Some banking, some antitrust, some negligence. Our heavy suit, I suppose, is real estate and construction. My grandfather, William Langtry, founded the firm and was involved with the Roeblings in building the Brooklyn Bridge. Shall we order?" He handed her the large menu card as the wine steward hovered at his elbow.

"Excuse me, Mr Langtry." The maître d' stood beside the table, holding his hand up to silence the wine steward before he spoke. In his other hand he held a phone with a jack. "Will you take a call from Congressman Peck, sir?"

Langtry glanced hesitantly at Allegra, then turned to the maître d'. "Yes, I suppose I'd better." The maître d' pushed the jack into the wall over Langtry's shoulder and handed him the receiver. Langtry placed his hand over the mouthpiece. "Please forgive me, my dear, I won't be a moment. I know what this is about. Hello. Carson?"

Allegra nodded and touched her napkin to her lips. Hmm. The world gets to be *teeny*-weeny. First Boxer, and now Melon's old corn-pone playboy Congressman. And Langtry and Peck seem to be buddy-buddy.

She tried to listen through Melon's ears. Heaven knew she had spent enough time listening to Melon babbling about Peck to do her the favor of finding out what was up with him and Grant Langtry. Peck seemed to be doing all the talking. Langtry simply made humming noises into the phone and looked apologetically at Allegra. She could faintly make out a dense string of words. The speaker did not sound at all calm; his words were coming fast and close together.

"Yes, I certainly do understand. You are making yourself quite clear, Carson. However, you must understand *our* position."

More rapid talking from the earpiece.

"That's up to you, Carson." An edge of exasperation hardened the words.

More jabbering. A few audible damns and hells. Peck obviously was the odd man out in the conversation.

Langtry frowned and jabbed out his cigarette.

"You can reach me at the Shoreham until Monday morning.

The three of us can meet at your convenience any time tomorrow."

She could hear the Congressman shouting indecipherable words, punctuated by clear obscenities.

"That's completely up to you. Good night." He replaced the receiver and waved to the maître d' to remove the offending instrument.

"Please try to forgive this unpleasant interruption. The Congressman is a bit agitated." He dismissed the incident. "What would you find pleasing for dinner?"

After they had completed their orders and Langtry had discussed the wines, Allegra asked, "How do you know Carson Peck?"

"The firm is doing some fund raising for his Senate campaign. He's on the right committees and our clients like us to keep our Washington lines open. As I told you, we are all over the map." He smiled as the captain poured wine into their glasses.

Allegra was completely bored by politics. She heard far too much of it around her own table. She was, however, interested in any tidbits she might be able to pass along to Melon. Trying to stay on Melon Bowersox's good side was in everyone's best interest. Whatever this slick New York lawyer was doing in town he was doing it with Peck, and it seemed to be making the young legislator terribly angry. She knew enough about the balance of power in town to know that lawyers doing fund raising were doing it for a specific reason, and they were ordinarily not in a position to anger Congressmen. In this case, Langtry obviously had the upper hand. Well, she didn't understand this odd situation, but maybe Melon would.

The morning of the fifth was more oppressively humid than the Fourth. She awoke in a pool of sweat. The air conditioner groaned and strained against the accumulation of a night's water. Her head throbbed. After-dinner brandy always did that to her and she almost always declined it. Yet, facing the remainder of the boring weekend she had let Langtry order three. She rang for Chu. No response. Then she remembered she had given Chai and Chu the rest of the weekend off. Damn.

She padded down to the kitchen in a flowing peignoir. The

house was absolutely still. Chai had left bowls of fresh-cut flowers in the dining and living rooms, and had laid out a breakfast tray in the pantry. She sat down in the breakfast nook and waited for the coffee to brew. The only sound was the soft plop, plop, plop of the percolator and the ticking of the antique grandfather clock in the front hall.

God, how had she gotten herself into this trap? Why hadn't she made some plans for the weekend? Even Miles was gone. Melon and Billie Claire were out there with everyone. Jane, too. Crap! Damn Seth. Damn, damn, damn. He paid no attention to Jeannine in town, but let her have a little hysterectomy and he runs right out to Rehobeth to hold her hand. She probably had him running back and forth with cold compresses and mint tea night and day. Reading Keats aloud and stroking her temples.

She poured coffee into a china cup and sipped it, drumming her long crimson nails on the tabletop, then rose and began to pace the kitchen.

What in God's name am I going to do with myself for another two days?

She went back upstairs and out onto her balcony. After a few minutes she became tired of gazing down at her own and her neighbors' backyards and went inside.

She picked up the little Gucci phone book on the stand by her bed and listlessly turned the pages.

She could shop! Shopping was always helpful.

Three months ago, when Seth had gone off to some dreadful publishers' convention, she had laid waste to Garfinkel's. The spring *Vogue* had informed her that Mrs. John Barry Ryan's lingerie, sheets, towels and personal linen all matched. That information had cost Seth four thousand dollars and change.

That was out. Nothing was open on Sunday.

She leafed through the little book again. She flipped pages at random until her eye fell on a small card slipped in the Bs. "Millicent B. T. Bremer, Interior Design, 1350 M Street," the tiny raised script read.

Aha! That was it!

Allegra hurried downstairs and swirled through the first-floor rooms, examining them in turn. The living room, huge and elegant with its Persian rugs, old English furniture, silk lampshades and gleaming parquet floors was perfect. The dining room couldn't be touched. There the Chippendale sideboard reposed, laden with heavy silver. The gleaming table and silk-covered chairs, while over one hundred years old, had only belonged to Allegra for two of them. The Williamsburg brass chandelier with its tiny electrified candles gave both the furniture and her guests a color and gloss that could not be improved upon.

She pounded up the curved staircase and checked the library, Seth's favorite room. Then, the two guest bedrooms. Perfectly appointed.

Her own bedroom was last. Here again, everything was perfect. Flowered English chintz, an exquisite canopied bed, the quilted chaise . . . It had to go. Everything in it had to go. She picked up her phone and dialed Millicent Bremer's number, then held her breath, praying someone would answer.

She had met Millicent at a party after the screening of *Advise and Consent* last year and promptly forgot her. She could vaguely remember a plump, giggling woman, badly made up and wearing an imitation Chanel suit and imitation Chanel sling-back pumps. One of the things Allegra prided herself in was her knowledge of what was authentic and what was merely a copy. Allegra had gone to the party with Miles, and he had managed to persuade Henry Fonda to sit down for a short interview. She had been left to wander around alone. The older woman had attached herself to Allegra, fawning over her and asking pointed questions about her town house. The woman had called her several times afterward, asking her to lunch and tea at her home in Chevy Chase. Allegra had politely and firmly declined. She had already consulted with Valarian and Dandridge in Manhattan, and, of course, her mother; besides the work on the house was nearly complete.

On the third ring a breathless voice answered.

"Hello, is Mrs. Bremer in? This is Allegra Farr."

"Oooo, Allegra!" The voice rose close to genuine hysteria. "How marvelous! I was out in the garden! I thought I was going to miss the phone! This is Millicent! How are you, darling! My, my, my . . . "

"Ah, yes . . . Mrs. Bremer. I know this seems odd on a holiday weekend and all, but would it be possible for you to stop around for tea later today? I'm afraid I need some expert advice."

Allegra held the phone away from her ear.

Millicent could be there in an hour. She would just need to clean up a bit. "Mud and fertilizer, don't you know?"

Allegra thanked her and replaced the receiver. God, the woman was eager. Yuk. Under any other circumstances, she would never have let her in the front door. But these were desperate times.

She knew the price to Seth would be astronomical, and also the price to her, having that silly woman jabbering all over town about Allegra Farr's this and that. So what? Seth should have made *some* provisions for her this weekend.

Millicent Bremer was given a complete tour of the house before Allegra brought her to the bedroom. Allegra knew she was bewildering the poor thing. The house was perfect, and any decorator worth an A.I.D. card could tell it. Allegra flung open the door. But for the unmade bed, the room was also perfect.

"I want it completely redone." Allegra's arm swept through the air.

"But, this room is . . . it's, it's . . . " she stammered, overwhelmed. "I mean, why in the world? You can't change this room. It's utterly sublime."

"It is not sublime. It is boring. I want to change it as quickly as possible. From wall to wall, floor to ceiling. All you need concern yourself with, for the moment, is how fast you can complete it."

"Well . . . " The decorator's eyes began to mist. She ran her hand down the rubbed and buffed mahogany of the four-poster bed. "Perhaps French? That is often a refreshing change from English."

"You are not paying attention, Millicent. Everything must go. Everything. I want you to create a surprise environment. I want this room to be tactile, sensual, erotic. Nothing *froufrou* or silly, and certainly *not* French. Your head is in the wrong century. I want the twenty-first, not the eighteenth," Allegra gave the heavy silk drapes a deprecating tug.

Millicent sat down on the foot of the chaise, unconsciously shoving Allegra's Persian cat, Mütsy, off onto the floor. Allegra sat on the edge of the unmade bed, and, as she explained what she had in mind, Millicent's face slowly drained of color.

The room was to be done in Lucite and brushed chrome; there

252

was to be a king-sized bed placed upon an eight-inch platform with a shallow step surrounding it. Sheets, pillowcases, throw pillows were to be white satin, and a chinchilla throw was to cover the bed. Vertical ribbons of brushed aluminum would cover the windows facing the garden. The two facing the street were to be completely covered and indirectly lit from hidden spotlights in the ceiling. The dressing room was to be totally mirrored, walls and ceiling. There was to be one art deco dressing table in it. Nothing else. All lighting there was to be recessed as well. The bulbs pink, if obtainable; if not, glass filters of that color would need to be made.

"And, I want the walls, the ceiling and the floor covered in gray suede. Actually, more silver than gray. Yes, silver suede."

"Miss Farr!" Millicent's eyes contained alarm and confusion. "I've never run across *truly* authentic-looking synthetic suede. Particularly in that quantity. And you say the floors . . . but, my dear . . . "

"I don't want synthetic suede. I want *real* suede. The kind that comes from a cow or wherever. Nothing artificial."

"Good Lord! That will take *miles* of . . . "

"Now, about the floor."

"Well," the pale woman tried, "it might be more practical to find a broadloom to perfectly match the silver suede."

"Millicent, I want suede on the floor." Allegra was becoming annoyed with the denseness of Millicent Bremer.

"But, my dear, that would be completely impractical." She shook her head from side to side, eyes never leaving Allegra's face.

"Laminate it," Allegra said flatly.

"Suede? Laminated? To the floor?"

"Precisely. I want this room to be cool, sleek, almost shall we say, feline?"

"Feline." Millicent stared at the floor.

Allegra nodded. "Now, let's see. Today is the fifth. I'd like to see your sketches and swatches, and, of course, the estimate . . . ah . . . is the fifteenth too early?"

"The fifteenth?" Millicent spoke in a monotone. Her eyes were wide with panic.

"Fine. Then, I'll expect you here . . . say, three?"

"Yes. Certainly. Three on the fifteenth." Millicent rose to go. Allegra showed the rubber-kneed decorator to the door.

She closed the door and leaned against it. Well, that killed an hour. She considered the remainder of the day. It lay before her, empty and endless as a de Chirico painting. A desire for contact with another human being welled in her. She wanted to be touched and crooned to as she imagined Jeannine was being consoled. She would even be willing to pay for it.

Petra Jensen?

Both the German Ambassador's wife and Eve Edstrom of the *Post* had raved about her. "She is the absolute best," Eve had said. "Expensive, and worth every cent. An hour with Petra is like a weekend at the Golden Door. She is the da Vinci of masseuses. Her hands are a miracle. She doesn't pound and hurt you the way so many of them do. Petra's Danish. You'd love her."

Allegra found Petra Jensen's number in the District phone book. She lived somewhere out off Kalorama Road.

She reached her apartment building switchboard and had to leave her name and number, as Miss Jensen was not in.

Allegra would have her in three times a week. At 10:00 A.M. That would be something pleasant to look forward to after her exercises and breakfast.

She sat down again in the breakfast nook and unrolled the morning *Herald* Chai had left. The front page carried a picture of the predictable Fourth of July beach scene taken at Ocean City. She found herself squinting for a familiar face among the thousands shown romping at the shore. Silly. Everyone was at Rehobeth. Everyone. Damn.

Her foot began to tap even before she became conscious of her plan.

What was she sitting here for? The party was over. Seth wouldn't be anywhere near Del's and Ann's. Ann had said it was to be an informal weekend. Just a lot of people dropping by. Wasn't *she* people? Why couldn't *she* take a leisurely drive out and, well, just drop by?

It would be futile to call Charles to bring the Lincoln around. He was off with that snarl of kids and the fat wife. She would take the Peugeot. Put the top down, lean back and relax. The three-hour drive would be diverting.

She packed a bag and filled a basket with jars and cans she found in the pantry. Aha! A large tin of pâté. Miles always fussed so about his pâté, and this was better. In the cooler by the wet bar she found three bottles of Moët. It would become warm during the drive, but what the hell? She tucked them into the basket.

From the narrow beach road, she could see the big house looming dark and deserted. She checked the slip of paper upon which she had jotted the house number. Perhaps the man at the gas station had given her the wrong directions. No. This had to be it. Ann had mentioned the big flag pole and the turnaround driveway.

As she entered it, a light went on and Allegra saw Jane walk past a large picture window.

"Ah, this *is* it!"

Allegra carried the basket up the steps to the deck and searched for a door. "Yoo-hoo! Anybody home?"

Someone in the house moaned.

"Hello, hello! It's me! Allegra!" She chirped.

Jane pushed open a door to her left. "For Christ's sake, where did you come from?"

Allegra could see that Jane was a bit drunk. "Surprise!" She held out the basket and followed Jane inside. "I was going bonkers in town and thought I'd drop by."

"Drop by! God Almighty, it's a three-hour drive." Jane's voice was not particularly hospitable.

Allegra's cheerfulness persevered. "Where's the party? I thought you were conducting a nonstop orgy out here? Is everybody dead?" She placed the basket that Jane had ignored on the bar top. She spotted Ann curled up on the couch, sound asleep. "And what is this? Our hostess flaked out already? Mind if I fix myself a little something to drink?"

Jane had fallen back into her chair by the fireplace. "Help yourself, Princess, if you can find anything. We aren't exactly in a receiving position, as you can see."

"I see that. Where is everyone?" Allegra began to poke around the kitchen looking for a clean glass.

"Del and Billie Claire are checking out the action at the Carousel. Miles took off hours ago with Billie Claire's brother. Melon's in her room, has been all day. Ann and I have been quietly getting plastered.

A gurgling sound came from the lump on the sofa. Ann sat up as Allegra put her drink down on the coffee table.

"Huh? Oh, hi, honey. Where in hell did you come from?" Ann's voice was slurred as she pushed her tangled hair back. "Brr. Did I pass out or did someone hit me?"

"Someone hit you," Jane said grimly. "Can I get you something?"

"Yeah, a room at St. Elizabeth's. If I ever get out, you can take me to Lourdes. Shit. My head," Ann moaned and collapsed again. "Fix me a drink, honey."

Jane shrugged and walked to the kitchen.

Allegra looked hesitantly at Ann. "I hope you don't mind my dropping in like this."

Ann propped her head on her hand. "Of course, not, honey. It *is* a bit of a drop-in, though."

"Well, I know. I really should have phoned, but I didn't. I just got in the car and drove. And, well, here I am," she said in her little girl voice.

"Anyway, welcome, darlin'. All the beds are full, but you are welcome to this here couch. That is, if I am ever able to remove my broken and pained body from it." Ann dropped her arm and fell back into the pillows. "I've never felt this terrible before," she said in a puzzled voice.

"Here, let me fix up some of the goodies I brought out. You people must be starved." Allegra scanned the room, stood and went to the kitchen.

As she began arranging artichoke hearts with four kinds of olives on a small platter, Melon shuffled into the kitchen and opened the refrigerator door. Allegra glanced over her shoulder.

"Melon! Hi! Oh, have I got a juicy bit of gossip for you. Last night I . . ."

Melon whirled around. "Jesus Christ! What are *you* doing *here*?" She appeared stricken.

"Well, I just got in my car and . . ."

Melon slammed the refrigerator door with such force that a basket of paper napkins slid off the top and fluttered to the floor.

"You are pretty fucking tacky, Allegra. Can't you leave your

256

great and good friend alone for twenty-four hours? I mean, considering he's a mile away with his *wife?*" Melon spit the word "wife" at Allegra and yanked off the top of a bottle of beer with an opener. The beer foamed onto the floor and the napkins.

Allegra was alarmed by Melon's appearance. She was without makeup, her nose was red and peeling. She was wearing nothing but an oversized man's shirt and bikini panties. There were dark puddles of mascara under her puffy eyes.

Allegra chose to ignore Melon's hostility and continue to arrange the platter.

"As I was saying, I had dinner with a friend of Carson Peck's last night and . . ."

"Big deal," Melon said without looking at Allegra.

"This lawyer, his name is Grant Langtry, seemed to have something rather important going with Carson Peck. And whatever it was certainly had your friend hot under the collar. He even called the Golden Parrot and yelled at this lawyer."

"What do you mean, 'yelled'?" For an instant Melon's eyes contained their usual spark of enthusiasm.

"Well, I don't know. The captain brought a phone to the table, and there was Carson Peck screaming 'shit,' 'son of a bitch,' 'goddamn' out of the phone so loudly I could hear it clear across the table. What surprised me was that they were both in town on this dreary, long, hot weekend, when anyone sane would be off somewhere else."

Melon was leaning against the bar, holding the beer in one hand, and a piece of chicken in the other. "You are easily surprised, Allegra." Melon tore off a large piece of drumstick with her teeth. "Besides, Carson Peck *eats it!*

Allegra blanched. "Well! I did think you'd be interested!"

"I'm not," Melon turned and walked toward the bedroom wing. A moment later, Allegra heard a door slam.

Jane had put on a Beethoven record and she and Ann were staring into the fire.

"Heavens! What's the matter with *her?*" Allegra set the tray of hors d'oeuvres on the coffee table. "I certainly hope I didn't set her off."

"It's not you, Allegra," Jane said. "She's not feeling well. Nobody is feeling well."

"I must say, this *is* a jolly little band." Allegra nibbled on a Spanish olive, after extracting the pimento and placing it in the ashtray.

"Sorry to disappoint you," Ann murmured.

"I thought you'd all be partying it up, and here Melon bites my head off, and you two are sitting around getting mean-drunk."

"Had you phoned ahead, darling, we would have had Lester Lanin in." Jane spoke with great weariness.

"At *least*." Allegra threw a Greek olive pit into the fireplace.

"What in the world enticed you out of the air-conditioned splendor of Chez Farr?" Ann asked.

"I was going crazy with boredom. I even had in a decorator to redo my bedroom. You know me when I'm bored. I simply have to spend money."

"Jesus, Allegra, your *bedroom!*" Jane perked up. "It's perfect. You really are something. You wouldn't be so bored if you had something to do with yourself besides looking beautiful for Seth and dreaming up ways to drive him to bankruptcy."

"Hey, what is this, Get the Guest?" Allegra wasn't used to being picked on.

"No, I'm serious," Jane said. "You've got marvelous taste, and all the time in the world. Why don't you get Seth to pop for some kind of little chicy boutique? Georgetown is full of them. You could be like one of those Victorian mistresses whose lovers bought them hat shops to keep them occupied."

"Hey, what a terrific idea!" Ann sat up, warming to the subject. "Allegra, you know how to do all that stuff yourself, anyway."

Within her espadrilles, Allegra's toes began to jiggle. "Hmmm," she said, "you know, you're right. That woman didn't suggest a single thing. I was the one who told her what to do. I'm going to redo the room in silver-gray suede and tons of mirrors. Very art deco, or should I say, decadent?" She giggled.

"Some decadent," Jane muttered over her glass. "Seth will shit a brick. I don't think he's the type to screw in a discotheque."

Allegra ignored her. "Girls, you are marvelous! What a wonderful idea! I'm going to ask Seth just as soon as I see him. I can see it all now. I'll rent space on Wisconsin, somewhere. I'll do it in pastels, indirect lighting, piped-in music. Nothing but classical, of course."

"Now we've done it," Ann wailed.

"Done what? She would be terrific. She knows everyone in town, anyway." Jane tried to retrieve an olive, but couldn't quite reach the coffee table and gave up.

"Well, it's on your head when the great Seth Hathaway finds out you put her up to it!"

Allegra was standing in the middle of the room. "I'll get Laura Gold to get me a marvelous Mucha print, something huge. The ambience should be very *fin de siècle*. Then, I'll . . . "

"Then Ann can come to work for you," Jane yawned.

"Ann?" Allegra stared at her.

"Yes, Ann. Because Ann's going to be out of work when Seth sells the paper to pay for all this."

Ann winked at Jane. "Anyone use a refill?"

Allegra's smooth brow was creased with lines of concentration.

The minute she returned to Georgetown she would call her mother and discuss the idea with her.

Chapter Fifteen

November 1963

When Ann seated herself before her typewriter the adrenaline began to pump, and, through an exercise of will, she began to concentrate totally. She was never able to explain what happened during those first three or four minutes, before she began to type. A rapid examination of every aspect of the event and people, dismissal, selection, then the structure and emphasis. At the moment when she was filled by a sense of certainty and power, she placed her fingers on the keys and began to create.

She was oblivious to the dense clatter of typewriters, ringing phones and conversations conducted at every level, from mono-tone-bored to imperative bellow. She stopped only to gulp down an entire cup of lukewarm coffee and light another cigarette. Ashes from the cigarette dangling from her lips occasionally dropped into her old Remington noiseless, the smoke encircled her head and fanned out from beneath the drooping brim of her magenta cartwheel hat.

Her story was a follow-up to a longer piece she had written the day before on the collapsing District of Columbia public school system. Several of the system's top administrators had called, angry and demanding an opportunity to present their position. Ernie had told Ann to go hear them out. After three takes she was finished.

"Copy!"

A smiling young man hurried to her desk.

She handed him the three sheets and smiled back.

"Thanks, *Annie*," he gave her a big grin.

"You new here?" she asked from under her hat.

"Yes. Ken's the name. Ken Fuller. Columbia 'J' School, M.A. in economics, Penn State. Handsome, single and headed for the big time."

"Well, pardon me for botherin' you with this little old piece of copy, Ken. On second thought, maybe you want this here job." She began to put her gloves and cigarettes in her hand bag.

"Actually, I think I'd prefer the foreign desk to city side," he said, his expression suddenly serious.

"And may Jesus want you for a sunbeam, Mr. Fuller. Until then, why don't you just hustle this deadline copy over to the desk before your mama finds you are out of your playpen."

"Yes, *ma'am*. Excuse me all to hell!" Ken Fuller stalked off.

Cute, she thought. She shouldn't have snapped at him that way. Fifteen years ago a good-looking, brash young man like that hanging around at the end of the day would have been a diversion. But now is now. She sighed and reached to retrieve her notebook. A sudden rush of fatigue moved up through her legs and stomach and back. She felt herself sag.

Now what? A cab home? Open the door and end the suspense: discover today's condition of Del Porterfield. Will he be drunk, sober, angry, depressed, up, down, sideways or not there at all? Gone out the window, the drapes blowing in the winter wind, leaving a beautifully crafted suicide note offering her permanent guilt? Gone off to a bar? Gone to an A.A. meeting?

Life between them had been strained for four and a half months, since Del had made such an ass of himself and ruined the big party out at the beach last summer. The remainder of the summer had been a succession of tense periods of sobriety, ended by what Ann described to Jane as days of Del being "knee-walking, commode-huggin' drunk."

The worst time had begun around the end of August, after Ann's coverage of the massive civil rights march down Pennsylvania Avenue.

She had met the buses arriving from Northern cities as they pulled into Washington before dawn. She marched with the exuberant, singing, chanting people, her high heels twisting and nearly snapping as she tried to stay near the front of the largest crowd she had ever seen. She clawed and elbowed a sliver of space for herself on the steps of the Lincoln Memorial. She listened to Dr. Martin Luther King tell the upturned faces of his dream, and twice dropped her notebook, only to have it handed back up to her by a friendly colleague on the steps. She made it back to the city room in time to make the second edition deadline.

It was not until she flopped into a booth at Bassin's that she noticed the blood on her ankles and the shredded stockings hanging from her legs. Her hand trembled as she raised the first of many drinks to her lips.

Del's hands jerked and shook the next morning when he held the *Herald* and tried to read her bannered story that ran across the front page. Five days earlier his second column in a row had been killed; they had both been analyses of the civil rights phenomenon. That very morning his usual space in the upper-right-hand corner of the editorial page of the Hartford chain's flagship paper had been filled with the Drew Pearson column that usually ran on the comics page.

He went into a sullen, childish pout which Ann tried to walk over and around. By the Wednesday after Labor Day his rage worked itself to the surface and the scene Ann knew was inevitable took place in the East Lounge bar of the Press Club. Del launched into a nasty attack on Mary McGrory's work. Ann told him to shut up. She did not see his fist coming, but when it connected with her nose, in an explosion of white, red, purple and black, she knew he had driven it with the remaining strength he did not require in order to stay vertical.

Merriman Smith got to her first and pressed his handkerchief into her hand. The last she saw of Del before Smitty hustled her into a taxi headed for George Washington University Hospital was an ashen-faced man being restrained by two grim-faced club members.

Del reappeared four days later. His face was puffed and the color of a diseased oyster.

Ann was in bed holding an ice bag over her nose. She had tried

263

several combinations of makeup to conceal the damage. She gave up because the process had been too painful.

Del sat on the foot of their king-sized bed, his head down, his body slumped, his hands clasped between his legs.

Cynthia Hartford was dropping his column entirely. She was picking up David Lawrence to replace him. He was to remain in Washington as bureau chief.

As he related Cynthia's brusque words of dismissal, Ann experienced a far deeper pain than she had when his knuckles struck the cartilage of her nose.

He did not need to explain how degraded and shamed and remorseful he felt. Del could count upon her to grasp fully the dimensions of his mortification.

Her own emotions were more complex. How was she to regard this man, her husband who had once been one of her professional exemplars?

She rose, pulled on a robe and pensively walked out of the bedroom. A few minutes later she reappeared with a glass of Jack Daniels in her hand and crawled back into bed. Del had not moved.

"Well?" he said, looking across the bed at her.

"Well, what? Did you expect me to make you a drink while I was up?"

"Ann, goddammit! I need you to say something about what Cynthia's done to me!" He watched her sip bourbon.

"Okay, Cynthia Hartford is a damn smart lady and a keen judge of her personnel. She knows what a drunk can produce and what he can't."

"Annie!"

"Oh, shit, Del. Don't look so stricken. What did you think she'd do after these past months? Recommend you for a Nieman Fellowship so you could spend a year drying out in the groves of academe?"

"Annie, I've tried, as God is my witness. Don't do this to me. I *need* you.“

"You need me to tell you to take a shower and shave. You reek of Scotch and B.O." She downed the rest of her Jack Daniels. "You look like one of those bums who sleep in Dupont Circle."

Del's chin dropped to his chest and his body heaved in a great, gasping sob. He buried his face in his hands and rolled over onto his side on the foot of the bed.

Ann watched him for a few minutes before she put on her robe again and left the room, glass in hand.

So much for the aristocracy, Momma, she thought. You were right all along. There are the givers and the takers. You and me, we both got takers.

Now it was the second week in November and the cute copy boy was bearing down on her desk.

"Miss Hutchins is asking for you, *Miss* Adams," he said pointedly and hurried off toward the morgue.

Ann waved halfheartedly toward Billie Claire, who was seated six desks down along the wide aisle that bisected the city room. She was stacking papers. Ann walked over.

"Are you finished?" Billie Claire asked.

"Finished. Over and out. Thirty." Ann managed a smile.

"You're dating yourself. I haven't written thirty at the bottom of a story since a high-school journalism class."

"I feel dated, honey. Tonight I'm looking up to see bottom."

"How about a quick pick-me-up at Duke's ? Do you have time?"

Ann took a deep breath to put down the queasiness that had begun to build when she was typing the last page of her story. "That sounds good. Ready?"

They took stools at the far end of Duke Ziebert's long, dark bar. The few stragglers who were still hanging around were mostly lobbyists. Billie Claire ordered a martini and Ann asked Mac for a brandy Alexander.

"Miss Adams," he said, wiping the bar before Ann could lay her cigarettes on it, "why are you ordering a toy drink? The Communists haven't poisoned the bourbon supply yet."

"Old dog, new trick," she shrugged, then turned to her friend. "What's new in Camelot today, Billie?"

"Well, Jackie's back and contrite about her fun and games in the Aegean. Tomorrow she's having a swarm of poor kids over for cocoa and cookies on the lawn, for God's sake. I'll bet someone in Jane Connor's operation dreamed this one up. Guess who gets to cover and file on that meaningful event?"

"Goes with the territory, kiddo. You want hard news? You can always ask Ernie to switch you to State." Ann sipped the creamy drink Mac had poured into a long-stemmed glass.

"I know, I know. But I'm really getting fed up with this Jackie crap. It's like working for the *Hollywood Reporter*."

265

Ann pressed both hands against the rim of the bar, her fingernails almost piercing the soft leather to the foam rubber beneath. She stiffened and tried to let her body go loose so that Billie Claire wouldn't notice. "Why, Billie, Fels Naptha on your tongue! Shame on you!" She laughed. The wave of nausea was now under control. She wiped away the tiny droplets of sweat with a cocktail napkin.

"I know, Ann, a bolt of lightning is about to come through the ceiling and strike me for speaking ill of our queen. But I feel so sleazy trying to squeeze copy out of what are really 'picture opportunities,' as the TV guys call them."

"Honey, you knew it would be all gloss and butterfly wings over there when you took the assignment." Ann swallowed the last of her brandy Alexander and waved her glass at Mac.

"Me, too," Billie Claire told the bartender. "Dammit, though, I *did* think, forgive my naiveté, I did think I'd be doing something of some journalistic importance. I feel as though I'm writing for a fan magazine. Why most of the time I'm simply filing thinly veiled gossip for a Jackie-adoring and insatiable world. It's tiresome, useless, bullshit journalism."

"It happens to be your *job*, Billie. And it's one most reporters would kill for."

"My beat is doo-doo, and you know it."

"No, I don't. You're covering a symbol. And that symbol means a great deal to an awful lot of people. Try to be more objective." She slumped a little, just a little. She felt tired the way her grandmother must have felt tired when her man came home with his pail, all sooty from the mines. The same soot on his bucket that she tried to scrub from their pillowcases. Especially on the night when her grandfather had come home and said, "We're closing them down. We're striking. God help us all." Ann, twice removed from those hills, sipped her second brandy Alexander in a bar that served ladies. She was known by name and title to everyone in Duke's. Everyone there also knew her husband's name and his current status. "Billie, no one at the White House *invented* Jackie."

"I suppose you're right." She munched on her second olive. "But sometimes it scares me when I think about all those Jackie gluttons 'out there.'"

Ann was becoming bored by the topic. The brandy Alexanders,

while shaving off the spiky burrs of the day's professional problems, brought the creases and sagging jowls of Del's present face into sharper focus. Eventually she would have to go home and gaze upon it. But not yet. "Anything else new?"

"Oh, yes. But before I go on to that, Ann, listen to this. You know that Bart Ramsey, that free-lance writer for the sleaze tabloids? He sold a piece for fifteen thousand dollars that contained just one single, solitary new little piece of information about Jackie. Just one line! He padded it out with the same old stuff. Now that's sick. Can you imagine what would have happened if JFK had actually married Grace Kelly? The nation would be paralyzed. Okay, on to other matters of import."

For another hour and a half the two women sat at Duke Ziebert's bar and gossiped. Ann did most of the listening, sitting facing straight forward in case another wave of nausea crept up on her. Billie signaled Mac for their check and slid a twenty-dollar bill on it while Ann was searching through her purse.

"I've got to run, Annie. I'm meeting Miles for dinner. It will be so good to see him. We haven't gotten together for months, not since your party at the beach."

Ann winced. "That particular pigsticking has been erased from the social archives." Ann thought she knew what Miles had been doing, and with whom. Evidently Billie Claire didn't, and she did not intend to be the one who filled her in. "Melon's been more flaky than usual lately," Ann said as they waited for the change.

"I've noticed that, too. Remember that crazy BBC correspondent she had a thing with? The one she said had the Wexford hounds in full cry tattooed down his back with the brush of the fox disappearing into his . . .?"

"Yes, yes!" Ann hooted and clapped her hands. "She was crazy about him. What's happening?"

"Well, he was in town on some kind of assignment for the entire month of September. Melon wouldn't even see him. Remember, she was going to take an overdose of birth control pills when she found out he was married? I can't figure her, ever. I had lunch with Allegra last week and she says Melon phones her constantly, and with nothing to say, really. Allegra seems to think Melon's fishing around for information of some kind."

"Hmm." Ann hadn't heard that one. Melon had been phoning

and cornering her, asking odd questions about Jeannine Hathaway, of all people. Well, there was no way she was ever going to second-guess Melon Bowersox.

As they walked to the street, Billie Claire said quietly, "Ann, I heard Ernie's going to nominate you for the Pulitzer."

Ann did not answer right away. "He mentioned it, yes," she said finally. "For that King march piece." She knew she was blushing. Ernie had told her a week ago and she had chosen to shove it to the back of her mind, because she couldn't cope with the possible complications it presented. "The promotion department probably called him when he had a hangover and his brain wasn't functioning."

"Come on. You deserve it. That piece literally had me weeping. I can still remember the lead, 'They came in waves, all colors, all . . .'"

"Please, Billie, don't quote my leads to me. It gives me the creeps."

"Sorry." Billie Claire looked bewildered. "Let's split a cab, partway.'

After she dropped Billie Claire off at 2500 Q Street, the taxi moved up Massachusetts Avenue past the stately mansions that housed embassies and consulates. Ann's stomach began to roll again. God, let him be sober. It's been seven weeks now. Please, God, let him be sitting in his beat-up recliner with his fiftieth cup of black coffee.

But she no longer trusted Del and his good intentions. Better to assume the worst, keep up the defenses; that was far less painful than the roller coaster of optimism and disappointment.

Ann didn't permit the sound of Del's old portable, audible as soon as she stepped from the elevator, to raise her expectations. He could type stone-drunk as well as he could cold-sober.

"Hello there, Del. Writing the great American novel?" She went directly to the kitchen and got out ice. These past weeks she had made no attempt to hide the liquor. Del's A.A. friends insisted that it wasn't necessary. She doubted if she would even if it were. "Say, why don't you do the whole Kay Summersby story once and for all?"

"Just a moment." He continued typing, ignoring the heavy sarcasm until he had completed the page. He pulled it from the machine and laid it facedown on top of a pile of others.

Ann listlessly examined the contents of the refrigerator. She wasn't hungry, but she knew she should eat or the nausea would become worse. She removed the leftover meatloaf and a package of potatoes au gratin from the freezer compartment. She was reaching for a can of green beans when Del appeared in the kitchen doorway.

"Ann, I'd very much like to talk with you for a few minutes."

"Shoot." She pushed the can of beans under the electric can opener. The whir drowned out his voice for a moment. "What?"

"Could you wait a bit on dinner and come and sit down?"

"Sure. I can wait for dinner." She picked up her drink, broke off a chunk of cold meatloaf and chewed it as she followed him into the living room. She sat down on the couch and placed her drink on the glass coffee table within easy reach. Del took a straight-backed chair from the dining area and set it directly across from her. He sat, very tense and square-shouldered, looking directly, and, she noticed, soberly at her.

"Ann," he began very deliberately, "I am on to the story of my career."

"Justice Douglas has joined the Mouseketeers?" She continued to chew the meatloaf.

He ignored her. "I have what I think are the leads to a story which, if they continue to fall in place, will blow this town wide open. It is Pulitzer material. His hands, tightly clasped on his knee, were white-knuckled and trembling. She had not seen him this serious since the morning they were married in Judge Bryant's chambers.

"Why are you out chasing stories? You're a bureau chief. Aren't you supposed to send out your troops?"

"This one is too hot. I'm going to track it myself. Also, I don't trust anyone else with it."

"Does Cynthia Hartford know what you're doing?"

"No, not yet. And I don't intend to tell her until I have everything absolutely solid. I've got to keep this tight for now. Play it close." He stood and began to pace.

"God, you sound like a character from *Front Page*. Keep it tight. Play it close. What the hell *is* this story?"

"Well, for openers, it involves some big names, headline names. People on the Hill, people downtown. But, get this, there may very well also be a murder. Perhaps two."

269

Ann couldn't prevent the long sigh. "You're investigating a murder?"

"Look," he stopped before her, "you have every reason in the world to assume I'm hallucinating or experiencing walking DTs. The murder, if it was a murder, is almost incidental to the major thrust of the story."

"Which is?"

"I'm truly reluctant to spell it out until I've pieced together more of it."

"Because I'd be in danger from *'them'!*"

"Quite possibly," he said tersely. He was struggling to maintain self-control. "I wouldn't be telling you any of it if I didn't need your help."

"Well, okay, Del. But before you tell me how it is I can be of help to you, let me sweeten up my drink." She felt queasy *and* dizzy when she stood. Damn it, she felt close to being drunk. How many nights in a row had it been now, this queasiness? Then there was tomorrow morning to deal with. And, what was this maniac tangent Del was off on? She slopped bourbon over ice, wishing she had some cream in the apartment. The brandy Alexanders had gone down easier than the straight whiskey. She walked back to the couch. She did not sit, less pressure on the stomach, but leaned her hip against the corner of the back. She was not at all sure she would be able to get up again. "All right. I'm all ears."

"Last week I was casually, and I *mean* casually, watching the AP ticker up in the club. They moved a short item on an FAA official whose car went off the road out near Glen Echo. The driver was alone, and dead, when the Maryland cops got to him. Ann, that dead man's name was *Clarence Quackenbusch.*" He was intently watching for her reaction.

"Wasn't he part of the dance team of Muckenfuss and Quackenbusch? Very big during the thirties?" She was trying hard not to weave.

"Stop it, Ann! *Clarence Quackenbusch!*"

"Sorry. I'm drawing a blank."

"Don't you remember him?"

"Obviously not."

"Clarence Quackenbusch was the FAA investigator who was out going over that plane that crashed near the Olney Inn last winter. The one you ran out in the snow to cover."

"Now how in the hell would you remember a piece of nothing information like that? About the only thing I recall from that evening was that you got drunk and passed out."

"But the next day I came *to*. And I remember you were complaining about your ruined dress and your ruined boots and you were wondering if the FAA was going to buy its investigator a new tuxedo. Quackenbusch is not a name one easily forgets."

"I forgot it."

"You used his name in your story. He was the FAA man in the tux, who just happened to be in the vicinity of a plane crash. The tux part wasn't in your story. I just remembered that when I saw the short wire story moving, and it rang a bell. I didn't have much else to do, so I came back here and checked through your clip file in the bedroom. Sure enough, there it was. FAA inspector, *Clarence Quackenbusch*. I've already checked, and the man who died last week is the same man you interviewed in the snow."

"Then, are you saying, Mr. Quackenbusch of the tuxedo was killed in a car wreck, and it's all part of a murder plot?"

"No, that is not what I am saying. Ann, please pay attention to me." He gave a significant glance toward her glass. "Two men were killed in the plane crash, according to your story. Do you remember *their* names?"

She slowly shook her head. "People from New York?"

"Yes. At least one was. His name was Allen Boxer. A lawyer. The other man was the pilot. He was from New Jersey."

"That's right, one was a lawyer." The walls were beginning to undulate. God, she should try to eat something. Coat the stomach.

"Now. Do you remember the July Fourth weekend?"

Ann moaned. "I'm trying to forget that, too."

Del was so rigid with determination he was beginning to quiver. "Annie, how often do I have to tell you I'm sorry as hell about what happened on the Fourth? Listen to me, *please!* The important part has to do with what happened the next day. Don't you remember? Everyone was hung over and tiptoeing except Allegra. She was following Melon around trying to tell her about a wheeler-dealer from New York she'd had dinner with on the Fourth. She couldn't understand why Melon wouldn't turn cartwheels when she told her her ex-boyfriend, Carson Peck, had phoned the big-time attorney at their table at the Parrot. Melon was in one of her screaming green moods."

271

"I remember that, vaguely, I suppose. Melon told Allegra to do something unnatural to herself and then locked herself in her room. Billie Claire couldn't even get in, and it was her room, too." Shit, maybe a Dramamine would help stop the wallpaper from sliding around.

"But just before Melon holed up in her room, I was on the deck nursing my hangover, and Allegra was in the kitchen with Melon. I only heard part of what Allegra was saying because I felt like hell and simply wasn't interested. Ann, I did hear a snatch of what Allegra said before Melon blew her cork. She said something like, 'I don't have it exactly.' Something like, 'Don't you think it's odd that Carson was in town on the Fourth of July yelling and swearing at a senior partner in a firm like Prouty, Langtry and Boxer?' A few seconds later, Melon slammed her door so hard it almost broke the windows."

"Del, do you think you could stop racing around the room? I have put in a most tiring day with the District school administrators. I don't have the energy left to follow either you or what you're saying."

"Please, Ann, hear me out! I'm almost finished."

"If you are expecting to write a Pulitzer story based on anything Allegra Farr said, you are one desperate man."

" *May I finish!*"

"I don't seem to be able to stop you."

"I began to repeat over and over, like a nonsense rhyme, in my head, 'Prouty, Langtry and Boxer, Prouty, Langtry and Boxer.' The names had a vaguely familiar ring but I forgot about it—then."

Ann sighed. Her glass was empty, but she did not feel steady enough to make it to the kitchen. "Will you freshen this up for me?"

"Yes. *After* I finish."

"Shit."

"After I read your clip on Quackenbusch and the plane crash I saw the name, Allen Boxer. It said that he was a partner in the firm of Prouty, Langtry and Boxer. That's when I remembered the incident on the deck and what Allegra had said to Melon, or tried to."

"Goddammit, Del! I want another drink."

He grabbed her glass, hurried to the kitchen, threw ice cubes into it and splashed bourbon over them. "Here!" He thrust the overflowing glass into her hand. "I have, since then, checked out several facts. One: Quackenbusch was the FAA inspector on the scene of the airplane crash last February. Two: Congressman Carson Peck was responsible for the Quackenbusch appointment to the FAA. Three: this part I got out of Allegra over the phone, without her realizing it. Four: the big New York lawyer she had dinner with on the night of the Fourth was one Grant Langtry. She never forgets an important name. Five: Carson Peck was in Washington on the Fourth, phoned Langtry at the Golden Parrot, and he and Langtry were planning to meet the next morning. Six: the man killed in the plane crash was Langtry's partner." He sat down on the edge of the chair a few feet from Ann and looked at her expectantly, triumphantly.

Ann could think of nothing to say. She tried to pull a placating or encouraging phrase from among the words spinning in slow motion through her mind: poor, desperate Del, grasping at straws, making an even bigger fool of himself. Finally, she managed, "Del, honey, everyone in town has some connection with everyone else. That plane crashed in a blizzard. It was a certified accident."

"Will you concede that the connections between these people sounds fishy?"

Ann nodded twice.

"And their reason for *being* in Washington that weekend was to meet with each other?"

One slow nod.

"And that Congressman's appointee sealed off the site of a plane crash in which his holiday weekend buddy's partner died? And now the *appointee* is dead in a crash I have some reason to believe is considered improbable, given the road and the weather, and so forth."

She shook her head. "This all seems a little thin for a Pulitzer."

"I've gone over your clips." Del stood. "I would like to look at the notes you made at the crash scene and everything else you have from that story." His lips were drawn tight. They appeared bloodless.

"Be my guest."

"Where are those notes, Ann?"

She lurched toward their bedroom. "See, now. Olney Inn notes. Cold, cold night notes." Ann pawed through a metal file drawer. "Here you go. February." She dropped a notebook onto the bed. "There's your Pulitzer, Del. Wear it in good . . ."

She tottered into the bathroom, knelt on the tile floor before the toilet and began to vomit.

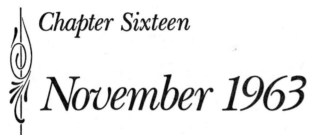

Chapter Sixteen

November 1963

Rain streamed down the thick panes of the glass-sided phone booth. Heavy morning traffic splashed great vertical sheets of water onto the side facing K Street. Melon pressed the receiver to her ear and intently listened to the seventh ring. She could barely hear it.

Finally, an almost inaudible, "Hello?"

"Hi, Allegra?" she shouted into the phone, cupping her hand around the receiver in order to be heard, and because she was having difficulty hearing. "It's me, Melon."

"Melon. Yes. Ah, Melon, you've caught me at a bad time."

"What are you doing?" She tucked her earlobe into the opening of her free ear and squeezed her eyes closed.

"Oh, the usual."

"What's that?"

"Good heavens, Melon! My morning routine. Do you want the details again? Where are you? I can hardly hear you."

"I'm in a phone booth on K Street," she yelled.

"A phone booth! At nine o'clock in the morning in the pouring rain? Are you all right?"

"Natch, love." She tried to sound cheery and offhand.

"I'm on my way to the office and knew I wouldn't have a chance to call once I got there. You free for a little lunchy?"

There was a short pause on the other end of the line. "I'm so sorry. My schedule today is absolutely frantic. Maybe later in the week?"

Melon chewed her lower lip. "What's up? Anything exciting I should know about?"

Even through the buzzes and clicks and the splatter of rain and the whoosh of passing cars, Melon could hear Allegra's sigh.

Tough shit. Let her sigh.

"Listen, Allegra, can't you just hop a cab and meet me for lunch? The maître d' at the Jockey Club has the warms for me. He'll comp us for lunch."

"No, I'm sorry. I just *can't.*"

"Well, how about a drink later? The National Association of Manufacturers is giving a bash at the Sheraton Park. Great food. We could swing in there and check the action."

"Melon . . . darling. I'm having people over. I already have lunch plans and a fitting after. Honestly, it's one of those days."

"Who are you having over?" she persisted. "I mean, besides Seth, of course?"

A pause and an even louder sigh. "Jesse Unruh is in town on some business. Seth asked me to ask him to dinner. John Bailey, Larry O'Brien. A bunch of Kennedy people. It's a late buffet. Very simple, but it does take some planning. My couple can't possibly handle it alone."

"Hey, Allegra, I've got it! Why don't I come over and give you a hand? I could wear a maid's uniform. It would be a kick." She giggled.

"Really, Melon! Now wouldn't Seth just *love* that! I'll see you later in the week. Okay? Bye, now." The click was clear.

Melon slammed her receiver into the cradle.

Goddamn snot. Goddamn bitch.

She stared out at the rain for a moment. "Wouldn't Seth just *love* that," she repeated, imitating Allegra's exasperated tone. "You bet your sweet ass he'd love it, lady. He loved it out on that sand dune last summer, Miss La-de-da," she said to the telephone. Allegra had said a "late buffet." That could mean that Seth might be going somewhere else before he went to Georgetown. She had

276

checked the city wire the night before for all the available parties in town. The only thing really big was the do at the Sheraton Park. Would Seth drop in there? Possibly. That group had a lot of clout. She certainly had no intention of hanging around a big, boring cocktail party alone without a good reason.

Maybe she could find out from Ernie Prescott if the *Herald*'s publisher would be attending. If anyone might know, it would be Ernie.

Melon yanked open the door and popped open her umbrella. Three stays were broken and it hung down on one side, dripping rain onto the sleeve of her raincoat, the one with staples in the hem.

As she made her way to her cluttered desk in the back of the city room, she heard Ernie bellow, " *Miss* Bowersox! If you don't *mind!*"

She swung around and walked over to his desk. "Hi, Bright Eyes. How's the handsomest city ed . . .?"

"Cut the crap. Where the fuck have you been?"

Melon's eyes flared. She did not like frontal attacks. "What do you mean, 'where the fuck'? Don't talk to me like that!"

"Melon, I'm sorry. I got no breakfast this morning. My ulcer ate it all." He tenderly placed a hand on his belt. "Anyway, you are almost forty-five minutes late."

"Ernie, a dear friend of mine was leaving for Europe this morning. One of her children is very, very ill at a school in London. She couldn't get a cab in all this rain and she asked me to drive her out to the airport." She looked straight at her weary editor.

He sighed. Melon had forgotten that only a week ago she had been complaining to him because she did not own a car. "Okay, Melon, forget it. I've set you up to interview Margaret Chase Smith at ten thirty, sharp. I was just about to give it to Patricia Roberts, but I want you to do it."

"Ernie," she wailed, "give it to Pat. Please. Who needs another piece on Smith, anyway?"

"I need it, that's who. She's getting pushy with her Armed Services Committee stuff and I want to find out her thinking."

"So, pick up the *Congressional Record*. It's all there."

"No, *you* pick up the *Congressional Record*. Ask the morgue to give you anything she's said about defense appropriations in the past three months. You can look through it in the cab up to the Hill. Unless you want to drive your *car*." He lowered his voice as he made his point.

Melon refused to acknowledge it. "Shit on a shingle, Ernie! Margaret Chase Smith!" But she knew she was licked.

"Just do it!" he shouted and reached for a ringing phone.

She stopped at the long counter that separated the morgue from the city room and asked the clerk for the pertinent background material. It came to quite a bundle. She jammed it into her bag.

She entered the elevator and glanced at her watch. It would make her late, but she pushed the fifth-floor button anyway. She swung through the company cafeteria as though looking for someone. The large, low-ceilinged room was empty but for three women from classified and some salesmen from advertising. No reporters. Not one executive, not even an executive secretary.

That's all right, that's all right, she reassured herself. She could finish off the old bat in an hour and then do some nosing around on the Hill. Bobby Baker rumors were popping all over town. She had heard Ernie talking about putting someone on the story full time, and she wanted the assignment. It would be an attention-getter. Money, broads, pay-offs. Bobby was going to be a wonderful story and she wanted it.

Melon had been in Baker's company on many occasions. Whenever Bobby was involved with a function she was certain there would always be plenty of booze, laughs and good-looking lobbyists to flirt with. Further, she had found him to be an excellent source for material on the Hill. But Melon did not like the man. She held a vivid memory of the day she put Bobby Baker at the top of her personal Shit List.

Two years before, she had been having a perfectly harmless little fling with one Ogden Forrest. She knew Ogden was married and she had no intention of breaking up his marriage, or anyone else's. He was handsome and rich and enjoyed elegant dinners and dancing afterward. His father was, she knew, the influential and controversial syndicated columnist, Cameron Forrest; she also knew Ogden's wife was the daughter of a Senator Bobby Baker boasted of "having in his back pocket." Three times Ogden had come back to Melon's for a nightcap. And there he had sat, each time, on the edge of her bed in his jockey shorts and penny loafers and cashmere socks, tears running down his cheeks saying his wife " . . . didn't give me enough . . ." and, " . . . I'm only a man . . ." The third time had been enough. Melon didn't need *that*.

She was relieved when she didn't hear from Ogden for almost a week. And then she received a call from Bobby Baker while she was at the desk in the city room. At first the conversation was just bantering chitchat. Startled, Melon suddenly became aware of the reason for his call. He was warning her to stop seeing Ogden Forrest, and he wasn't kidding.

After she hung up, she was slitty-eyed angry. Ogden's wifey must have complained to Daddy or Daddy-in-law, and one or both of them had given Bobby a call. How *dare* he presume to tell her who not to see! She was tempted to call Ogden and ask him to take her to the Shoreham that night. If she did, though, they'd end up at her apartment with him sitting there in his shoes and socks crying. Crap! It wasn't worth it.

That day Bobby Baker made number one on the list.

Quite a few people around town had heard about Melon's Shit List. She was even asked if, because she limited it to ten people, when a new person made it, someone else was moved off to make room? "That's right," she had said. "But a couple of bastards are on it for life." Bobby was one of them.

Bobby had been making a lot of people's lists of late. For some months there had been rumors around Washington that Lyndon Johnson's protégé, a man about whom the Vice President had said, "If I had a son, he would be the boy. Bobby is my strong right arm." Bobby Baker, secretary to the Senate Majority Leader, was a young man of enormous influence on Capitol Hill, and downtown as well. The rumors about him concerned some financial shenanigans that Melon and most of her friends believed, but about which no one had enough to print, no solid proof.

By fall, the scandal broke wide open. A suit was filed in Federal court charging Bobby with influence peddling in the Senate to procure huge defense contracts for a vending machine company that he secretly owned. That was just the tip of the iceberg. Within a few weeks, stories began to flood the press concerning Baker's wheeling and dealing, partying and other general no-nos for a highly placed government employee.

Because he was known to be close to the Vice President, the

press and the public ate up every little detail. By now the Baker story was up for grabs and any journalist who could dig up a new lead was virtually guaranteed front-page space across the country. Melon dearly wanted to come up with *something* new, but the *Herald* had already assigned two reporters to the story full time, and it didn't look as if she would get a shot at it.

"Unless," she muttered to herself, "unless I come up with something they *have* to let me write." Meanwhile, there was her current dreary assignment to cover.

The distinguished lady Senator from Maine was most informative, if one understood what the hell she was talking about. Melon hadn't cracked the background material in her bag, so her questions were necessarily limited. Fortunately, the woman liked to talk. Melon took copious notes. She would worry about how she was going to write them up later. "Wing it," she muttered as she flipped shut her notebook and thanked the Senator for her time.

Rain splattered against the white marble facade of the Old Senate Office Building. Melon splashed across the street to the Carroll Arms Hotel, then down the half-dozen steps that led to the entrance to the restaurant. It was just beginning to fill up with Senate-side staffers in for early lunch.

She instantly spotted Scotty Peake and Layte Bowden from Senator Smathers' office sitting at the bar. Now there were a couple of Bobby's chums. "Hi, Scotty. Hi, Layte. How's everything?"

They barely acknowledged her presence, mumbling, "Hello," and "Hi, Melon," before turning back to their drinks.

"Rat finks," she mumbled under her breath. She scanned the room. Brian Cocoran was having lunch with Johnny Solters from Scoop's office. Nothing there. Matty Matthews from the Democratic Campaign Committee . . . hmm. He might be a source. Matty knew everything, but he was incredibly partisan. Not likely he would give her any tidbits on the secretary to the Majority Leader.

Aha! Pay dirt! Standing at the door waiting for a table was Carol Tyler. She was the woman all of Washington was saying was Bobby's mistress, but couldn't prove or print. The woman saw Melon and immediately said something to the man escorting her and turned back toward the door. Melon pushed her way through the bodies lined up to be seated and into the revolving door, just in time to see Carol Tyler and her escort entering another door to the hotel farther down the street.

The Quorum Club! That's where they're going! Crap! It's private. Then she remembered Matty Matthews inside and went back into the public restaurant.

Fifteen minutes later she emerged chattering provocatively with Matty, who happened to be a member of the private eating and drinking club hidden away upstairs in the hotel. The Quorum Club was rumored to be financed by lobbyist money and unofficially run by Bobby Baker. It was only twelve fifteen.

Matthews led her to the unmarked door and pushed it open. Melon was hastily trying to make out faces in the dark room when a voice at her elbow said, "Sorry, ma'am, this is a private club." His fullback's body was covered by a navy blue tuxedo.

"It's all right, Eric," Matty said. "The lady is waiting for a member." He gave her a quick kiss and departed.

"Of course, ma'am." He immediately became respectful, almost too respectful. "I'm so sorry. Would you like to wait at the bar?"

"Thank you." Melon swept past him and headed for the small bar on the right wall of the windowless room.

Eddie, the bartender, worked nights at the Monocle Restaurant down the street from the hotel, and he had frequently seen Melon in action. "Hey, Melon, what are you doing here?" He looked rather uncomfortable.

"Shhh," she hissed and eased herself onto a stool.

"You bet your ass, shh. You better drink up quick, honey, before someone spots you. Reporters make these guys nervous."

"What are they going to do, Eddie, throw me out? I hope so. I haven't got a thing to write yet." She ran her fingers through her short, curly hair and placed her breasts provocatively on the rim of the bar. "The usual, Eddie."

"How can you drink that thing? Olives in whiskey . . .? Christ." He reached over his shoulder for a Manhattan glass.

Melon's eyes were becoming accustomed to the darkness. She scanned the room. No sign of the Tyler woman. "Shut up and pour, Eddie," she said around the filter tip of a Marlboro.

"There's a friend of yours over there." He indicated a candlelit alcove in the farthest corner of the room. In the dim light she could make out the gleaming waves of Congressman Peck's head bent attentively toward a striking redhead who was nestled close beside him on the banquette. Yuck!

Jack Williams, a lobbyist for a group of dairy farmers in the Midwest, slid onto the stool next to hers. She had met him at parties, usually in the company of Bobby's entourage. Williams was given to wearing pastel suits and pointy-toed shoes and laughing very loudly at anything Baker said, after a slight pause to see if anyone else was laughing.

In the time it took them both to finish two drinks, Melon learned that his nickname was "Ain't Been Wet Yet!" Williams because of his expert ability to barbecue meat on his outdoor grill in Bethesda in a driving rain, that he had three boys, "all jocks, yessiree," and that he had a wife who really knew how to please him.

Melon endured it all, waiting for the chance to cross her legs toward him and ask "Jack, you sound like a home-loving man. How come I see you with Bobby and his gang so often?"

"Oh, you know how it is. Gotta make the contacts around the Hill," he said, never taking his eyes from the space just above Melon's left knee, the one closest to his thigh.

"I see Bobby with a lot of pretty girls. You get any of the fallout? Surely he can't handle them all?" She gave him a little sideways look.

"You got him wrong, little lady." He was now staring at a point on her blouse where a button had somehow come unbuttoned, revealing the slight, but definite curve of her breast. "Bobby's true-blue."

"True-blue to who?" Melon asked, bobbing her head to the deliberate rhyme.

"True-blue to Carol, of course."

Melon looked across the bar into the smoked glass mirror and pulled at the tight curls over each ear. "Who's Carol?" she asked in her most disinterested voice.

"Carol Tyler. Crazy about her, and keeps her in style, I must say."

Bing! Melon's mental tape recorder clicked on. Boy, was *this* guy dumb! He must know who she was, yet he was just blabbering right along.

"Keeps her? Oh, come on. How do you know that?"

"'Cause I've been to her place, that's how."

"I don't believe you."

"Whadda ya mean?" he said, rising to the bait.

"I mean, I think you are making this up. Besides, he's married."

"Listen, girly. Anybody who's been down to that town house in Southeast . . . Purple wall-to-wall carpeting isn't something you're likely to forget."

Hot damn!

Melon pushed a five-dollar bill across the bar to Eddie and grabbed her bag. "Mr. Williams you are a darling man. I do hope I have the pleasure again. Bye, now." She turned toward the door, but not before she caught the bewildered look in the man's eyes.

Melon stood in the middle of the street outside the hotel. The cab either had to stop or hit her. She could see a passenger leaning forward anxiously as the car screeched to a halt, inches from her knees. She pulled open the door and hopped in, explaining breathlessly that she was a reporter for the *Herald* and would they mind? They did not.

Ernie Prescott was on the phone when she reached the front of his desk.

"Ernie, hang up," she hissed, still breathless.

The editor glowered at her and continued to talk rapidly into the phone.

"Ernie, for God's sake! I've got to talk to you!"

He slammed down the phone. "Shit, woman! What is the *matter* with you?"

"Ernie, I've got a lead on Bobby Baker's mistress. Her name is Carol Tyler. He keeps her in splendor in a town house in Southeast, complete with wall-to-wall purple carpeting! Can I check it out, Ernie?"

Prescott blinked up at her. "Melon," he said, very slowly, as though talking to a six year old, "we are holding space for your feature on Senator Margaret Chase Smith. We have already pro-moed it for tomorrow's paper. Now, I would like you to go to your desk and write your little story. And get off my back!"

"Ernie . . .!" She was almost screaming, tears popped into her eyes. "Ernie, please! I know I'm onto something! Let me check it out! I'll write the damn Smith piece as fast as I can. Then can I . . . ?"

"NO!"

"Pleeese," she whined, "I'll stay late. On my own time. Sarah McClendon has had all the good stuff on Baker up until now. We haven't had anything but follow-up stories in the paper. This could be a blockbuster. I know it! If it doesn't check out completely, I'll never mention it again." The tears had now reached her chin and were dropping onto the front of her blouse.

Ernie sighed. "All right, Melon. You win. Go ahead. But, and I mean it, on your *own* time."

Melon whacked out her feature on the Senator in record time. It wasn't particularly newsworthy, but she felt it gave a nicely rounded portrait of the lady. Even if it didn't shed much light on her position regarding defense appropriations. She slapped the copy on Ernie's desk within forty-five minutes of writing her lead, and then rushed back to her desk and began to telephone.

In mid-July she had persuaded Ernie to let her turn her desk to face the entrance to the city room. Her eyes seldom left that door, because, through it Seth Hathaway would occasionally walk. At the sight of him her entire body would tense and a ripple would wash through her stomach and down her inner thighs. The phone receiver would then require an extra tight grip because of the perspiration on her palms. Long after Seth left the city room, previously passive and manageable muscles, tendons and nerves remained coiled in taut spasms. This had been going on for four months now. She had become conscious of her body in a panicky new way, and it frightened her.

It was as if her mind and body possessed but one intention, even asleep: to be where Seth Hathaway was. She could place him almost minute by minute when he was in the *Herald* Building. From Ann, she was able to form a general timetable of his life with Jeannine. By phoning Allegra at least once a day she could piece together the remainder of his schedule. Seth was a very busy man. And he was an encapsulated man.

There had not been one moment since she had returned from Rehobeth in early July when she had been able to arrange to be alone with him. He hadn't avoided her, not really. It was his life, his schedule. It was as if he were a royal person—always accompanied, every minute arranged for him. There were hundreds of large and small necessary events, beyond his daily agenda at the *Herald.*

Melon had attended three parties at Allegra's, for two of which she had virtually coerced invitations. She had been escorted by a recently divorced Under Secretary of Commerce, one of the recently chosen bachelor astronauts, and an absolutely beautiful single Congressman from California with a deep cleft in his chin. She had chosen carefully; each man was handsome and intelligent, with the possible exception of the Congressman, but his chin made up for his brain. They were all socially poised men who would not be ill at ease in the company of the famous publisher and his peers.

Naturally, Seth was unable to single out Melon for special attention, to say nothing of anything more intimate. On the three social occasions, he had greeted her warmly, but with reserve, and had twice stood in the same circle as she as they drank their predinner cocktails. Never once had he even brushed against her nor had their eyes met and held. Melon would watch Allegra watching him, circling like a buzzard, seeing to his drink, graciously extricating him from anyone who lingered at his side too long.

Melon had phoned him from time to time with the choicest morsels of gossip she had culled from her conversations with dozens of sources each day. The most she had received from him had been an amused chuckle, followed by a brisk, "Thanks, Melon. That's most helpful information."

Miss Wilton, his streamlined mother-tiger of a secretary, didn't like putting Melon through to him, but did it anyway. Seth must have said something to her about taking Melon's calls. That knowledge was reassuring. She didn't call often.

Then there was his appearance. He was always immaculate. Unlike the editors and reporters around her, she never saw him with his shirt unbuttoned, tie loosened, sleeves rolled up, not even in the unbelievably oppressive days of a Washington August. He seemed to wear a coat of armor, a uniform, that set him apart from the rest of the men at the *Herald*.

In mid-October, *Life* magazine had carried a photograph of Seth with President Kennedy and the Attorney General in Palm Beach. The three men were sitting on lounge chairs on some sort of terrace overlooking the sea. Each had been wearing Bermuda shorts and open, short-sleeved polo shirts. They had been tanned, and laughing the way physically strong and confident men laugh—without inhibition, eyes crinkling. As Melon had studied the picture her mouth had become dry and her palms moist. *That* was Seth! The Seth she remembered from Ann's deck at Rehobeth. The Seth who had gently put his open palm under her elbow and led her to the beach, to the sand dune and to the period of ecstasy that still haunted her. Then, he had looked the way he did in the *Life* photo; his body was not camouflaged beneath vests and button-down shirts and knotted ties. If she looked very carefully, she could make out the faintest of contours where his Bermudas were stretched against his crotch. She kept the torn-out color photo in the jumbled top drawer of her desk and looked at it morning and evening and in the middle of the night after she awoke from dreaming about him.

After two hours on the phone she had convinced herself that her Carol Tyler lead checked out. It might be another matter to convince Ernie.

During those two hours there had been no sign of Seth Hathaway. She could usually count on him stopping in around 5:00 P.M. to go over the front page for the next day's paper. It was now close to six. Then she remembered her conversation with Allegra that morning and walked toward Ernie's desk.

"Who's covering the NAM dinner tonight, Ernie?" she asked as nonchalantly as possible.

"Hildy Bornstein."

"Oh. Maybe I could drop over for the speeches."

"Suit yourself. But Hildy's covering. Didn't know you were interested in boring business speeches."

"Well . . . if our esteemed publisher is attending, maybe it's a bigger deal than Hildy can handle."

"Melon, you've got to be kidding! I told Hildy she could probably write it from the press releases. She didn't even need to go up there." He tilted his head. "Where on earth did you get the idea Seth was going? He's not."

"You're sure?"

"Melon, for Christ's sake, go home."

"Okay. But first I need to stop up in promotion for something."

She went to the ladies' room and checked her hair and makeup, then rode the elevator to the tenth floor. Fortunately, promotion and the executive offices both occupied that floor. Melon had carefully cultivated the friendship of a layout artist in promotion,

286

a young man with whom she "shared an interest in batting averages." Months ago she had found a seat next to him in the cafeteria and observed he was intently reading the sports section. It had taken a little baseball research to keep up her end of the conversations, but it had paid off as a valid excuse to drop by promotion and chat. From the chair beside the baseball nut's drawing board she could see directly into the reception room of the executive offices, and beyond to the double doors of Seth's office.

She stood beside the drawing board and listened to the artist rattle on and on about the Senators' chances for the next season, stuttering a bit under the attention of the pretty reporter—whose interest in him was as bewildering as it was flattering. She clutched her raincoat and purse, ready to make a fast exit when and if Seth appeared in the outer office.

Melon tensed the second she saw him. He was hurrying through the double doors talking rapidly to Miss Wilton, who was trotting behind him trying to take notes on her pad. Blowing a kiss at the confused layout man, Melon moved rapidly toward the bank of elevators down the hall. She had let two cars pass when she heard footsteps behind her.

"Oh, hello there, Melon. What brings you up to the thin air of the tenth floor?"

She looked around, prettily startled. "Oh, hi. Just an errand in promotion." Her hands were sweating again.

He stood aside to permit her to enter the elevator first. The doors slid closed and the elevator began its slow descent.

Melon was alone with Seth Hathaway and his briefcase. Truly and at last alone.

"Oh, Seth!" She shoved her arms under his, held him as tightly as she could and pressed her face against his raincoat-covered chest. "Hold me. It's been so long"

The elevator came to a stop at the eight floor. Gently and firmly, Seth pushed Melon away.

A silly, stupid, hateful, ugly woman Melon had never before seen stepped in.

I'll kill her! The rat-faced bitch! Melon bit down hard on her lower lip. Oh, joy! The bitch pressed the sixth-floor button.

"Good evening, sir," she said to Seth.

"How are you, my dear?" he said to the awed woman.

287

Slowly, slowly, the paneled box moved downward. Damn can't the creep walk down two flights? No one spoke. The woman's eyes were carefully aimed straight ahead, and when the doors opened on six, she left without a word.

Seth firmly punched the first-floor button again, and when Melon clutched his arm and laid her cheek against his shoulder, he drew away.

"But, Seth, we're *alone!*" Melon looked up at him, baffled by the annoyance in his eyes and the set of his mouth.

On three the elevator doors opened to a darkened hall. The classified department had left for the night. Seth pressed the hold button and held the door open. He spoke quietly.

"Melon, I'm afraid I don't understand."

"Don't understand!" her voice rose. "I love you, Seth. You know that."

"Now, Melon . . ."

"Don't 'Now, Melon,' me, Seth. I'm not a child. You asked me to trust you. I did. I do."

"We had a little interlude. It was delightful. You are a delightful lady and we should do it again sometime."

"*Interlude!*" she yelled. Seth's face showed concern, then a touch of panic. "What the fuck are you saying? *Interlude!* I dream of you every night. I know how busy you are, so I've simply waited. I'm not a naive child. We had something beautiful together. Extraordinary. You felt it. You must have."

"Melon, calm down. I know you are not a child. You are an attractive, full-grown woman. Attractive, full-grown women have momentary relationships with men who desire them. It is nothing to build your life around."

"But we were different! Oh, Seth, hold me. Just for a minute. I know you have to rush, so I don't expect you to . . ."

Still pressing his finger on the hold button, he reached for her. He took her shoulder in his large, free hand and held it. Hard. There was no consolation in his grip. It hurt.

"Seth . . ."

"Listen to me very carefully, Melon. It has been obvious to me that you've been more than a little interested in my activities during the past months. I don't want to be brutal, but this is for your own good. What you have been doing is hounding me. Spying on

288

me. I don't like it. Everywhere I look, there you are watching me, like a love-struck adolescent. My secretary notices it, other employees notice it, Allegra has even mentioned it. Melon, you are making a fool of yourself and I want you to stop it."

"Fool?" A great buzzing began in her head.

"Yes, by every definition of the word. It is embarrassing both to me and to the woman I love. I'm surprised that a woman with your rather . . . celebrated experiences with men isn't in more control of her emotions."

"Seth, don't . . ." This time, her tears were real.

"Now. Just so you can get it all in perspective, I will tell you that our little . . . session on the beach meant nothing to me other than a pleasant release of tension. I had had a long week and quite a few drinks. You were prancing around in that see-through thing you had on just looking for a poke, and I obliged. Have I made my position clear?"

The buzz in Melon's head shifted abruptly to a painful throb. She could hardly make out his face. He took his finger off the hold button and the car began its final descent to the lobby. As the door opened Seth pushed by her and strode out and across the lobby, his free hand jammed into the pocket of his trench coat.

Melon stumbled after him for a few steps, then stopped. Her large eyes were wide, and her thick lashes stuck together in little starry points, formed by tears. She couldn't see the two sportswriters who walked past her, glancing at her with open curiosity.

She pushed blindly through the revolving door in time to see Seth pulling shut the door of the waiting limousine at the curb. She quickly turned in the opposite direction and headed west. The rain plastered her hair to her head and poured down the collar of her coat.

The self-pity that had welled up in her became transformed into stony rage.

"Release of tension!" she muttered. "Just getting his rocks off!"

She could still feel the pain of his grip on her shoulder.

"What did you need me for, you bastard! Could have jerked off in the john! Son of a bitch!"

A scholarly looking middle-aged man who had just emerged from the National Geographic Building glanced at her, then looked hurriedly away.

"I embarrass *Allegra!*"

By the time she had crossed Seventeenth Street, the ringing in her ears had stopped. She was suddenly filled by a vast, black calm, a void. Seth had used her. Using her body, she might forgive. He had used her *head*. He had known how she felt for months, and he had let her go right ahead and make an ass of herself. Let her go on suffering.

She jabbed at the bottom of her raincoat pocket and extracted a crumpled tissue covered with lipstick and God knew what else. She made an attempt to wipe her eyes. Great streaks of mascara came off on the tissue.

So the great Seth Hathaway didn't like to be hounded. Well, sir, little Melon, here, doesn't like to be *had*.

She walked faster, turning up the collar of her coat against the downpour. And she began to plot the first move of her revenge.

Seth Hathaway would pay. His pain would not be cheap.

Chapter Seventeen

November 1963

Jane paced back and forth in front of the long counter while a sullen girl in an aggressively perky uniform computed her car rental bill.

"Miss Connor," the clerk slurred, "in going over your bill I see we gave you our *weekly* rate, and you only kept the car for five days. That means we'll have to charge you the *daily* rate. If you would like to keep the car for an additional two days you will only have to pay . . . "

Jane sighed. "Just tell me how much I owe you."

"But, you see, if you keep the car . . . "

"Miss, I don't want to keep the damn car. I want to pay up and get out of here. Now!"

"Well, pardon *me*! I was only trying to . . . "

"I'm sorry," Jane squinted at the plastic badge pinned to the orange polyester lapel, "Norma. It's been a long five days."

On the floor beside her feet rested one small suitcase and one half-full paper Hutzler's shopping bag. The suitcase contained a tumble of clothes and essentials she had thrown into it one hundred and ten hours before, after she had received the call from the Adela Whelan Home in Baltimore. The shopping bag held the entire earthly belongings of Nathaniel Connor: one partially bald stuffed koala bear, one plastic milk bottle containing four large, colored clothespins, one pair of bedroom slippers with beagle puppy heads on the toes, three pairs of cotton pajamas and one flannel bathrobe.

With a wounded sniff, the clerk shoved an itemized bill across the counter for Jane's signature.

Jane's hand dragged a pen across the form. Her signature was unrecognizable. The in-time punched on the indecipherable form read, 11/17/63, 1:12 P.M. It didn't say Sunday. At that moment, if the piqued clerk had asked Jane the day of the week she would not have known. She had slept only twelve hours since she had picked up the car at the F Street Avis office.

Jane stuffed the receipt in her purse. "Thanks." She picked up her suitcase and the shopping bag.

"You're welcome, I'm sure," the clerk pouted, as her eyes took in Jane's expensive linen suit and Gucci bag. They were very close to the same age.

"Fifteen hundred Mass," Jane told the taxi driver and sat back. When she closed her eyes they stung from days of chain smoking, fatigue and withheld tears.

"Not yet, dammit," she muttered and opened them.

"What's that, lady?"

"Nothing. Talking to myself."

She watched the familiar buildings flash past and wondered why so few people were about in the middle of the day. God, how sterile and empty the place was. Washington was just one great marble combination file cabinet and dormitory. For a moment, she fantasized a day when the sheer pressure of megatons of paper would explode and cover the city in a mile-high pile, suffocating and killing every dull and colorless bureaucrat in it. The paper stayed. The people flowed through its apartments, hotel rooms, restaurants and mansions in a steady, endless stream. Washington was nobody's hometown; they were either just arriving or getting ready to leave.

Jane was almost stupefied with fatigue. She should be feeling *something*. She probed through her numbness to find an appropriate emotion. Nothing.

Remorse? Sadness? Relief? Guilt? Nothing. Just a dull ache that seeped through the emotional armor she had been fabricating and polishing over the years. Against this day?

On the preceding Wednesday, the Adela Whelan Home's staff

292

physician had phoned. Nat's cold had suddenly developed into pneumonia. He was being taken to the hospital by ambulance. Dr. Rita Silverstein did not think the prognosis was favorable. "Mrs." Connor (Jane had let the home's staff assume she had been married and was uncomfortable about the deceit) should, if possible, come to Baltimore Memorial as soon as she could.

"Mrs." Connor made it to the hospital in a little over an hour.

Over the years, Dr. Silverstein had spent many hours with Jane, explaining Nathaniel's condition after there was nothing left to explain. Dr. Silverstein had ridden in the ambulance with the boy and was waiting for Jane at the pediatric nurse's station. She led Jane to the end of a long ward filled with children, to the side of the crib containing her ten-year-old son. The pneumonia had so weakened him, he was completely calm and manageable.

Jane looked down at him. His face was almost beautiful. The fever had given color to his pallid cheeks, and his ordinarily expressionless eyes seemed to sparkle up at her. One fragile arm was extended, strapped to a padded board, a needle inserted in a vein in its soft underside. Extra-large diapers encased his lower torso.

This was not the first time Jane had sat beside Nat's bed in Memorial Hospital. When he had become ill with chicken pox, measles, several cases of the flu and one unbelievable bout with hepatitis, she had stayed beside him, holding his little claw-like hand, humming tunes, wiping the spittle from his upturned face. The boy had been afflicted by every secondary infection and reaction in the annals of pediatric medicine.

Now his unfettered hand lay in Jane's. Occasionally his eyes blinked open, taking in Jane's face, the nurses and doctors who slowly moved around him, his koala bear, the ceiling, the windows. His large blue eyes contained no reaction, no recognition, no response.

For ten years this helpless, infuriating and sometimes beautiful boy had lived in a physical world to which he was oblivious. He smiled, now, in his sleep, and his fingers twitched against Jane's palm.

Are you dreaming, Nat? In your deepest sleep, do you experience some kind of joy?

Once, long ago, out of self-pity, she asked him aloud if he forgave her, and then, ashamed and angry with herself, retracted the question, again aloud. She had not done this to Nat. The Tooth

Fairy had, the Wicked Witch of the West had, maybe the Easter Bunny. She never let herself consider the idea that God had done this to both of them. She remembered a hymn the field hands used to sing at the A.M.E. Baptist Church so many years ago in Leesburg. "You are my cross and my salvation." She didn't believe it, not really, but humming the tune helped drown out confusing conjecture.

From time to time she dozed, her head against the crib's railing, her fingers resting on Nat's hand or arm. Doctors and nurses padded in and out on their thick rubber soles, listening to his chest and back, measuring his blood pressure and temperature, refilling the bottle that hung over the side of the crib, swabbing a patch of skin and injecting the contents of a syringe into his flesh.

At three thirty Friday night Nat stopped breathing. Jane watched his last breath and waited for the next. She rang for a nurse, her eyes never leaving his face. Nat looked no different dead than he did alive, except the high fever-color instantly receeded and left him almost translucent in the darkened room.

She remembered that for a time, as a child, she had believed that when children die angels come to take them away. A white-haired nurse answered her ring. The nurse swiftly examined Nat and mumbled a prayer in Latin, crossed herself and whispered, "It's a blessing." Then she reached down into the crib and closed Nathaniel Connor's eyes for the last time.

"I'm sorry, Mrs. Connor, he's gone."

"You are quite sure?" Jane looked up at the older woman, her face devoid of any expression but curiosity.

The nurse laid the boy's limp hand gently on the blanket. "Yes, quite sure. I'll call Dr. Silverstein."

Jane slowly lifted herself from the straight-backed chair beside the crib. Every muscle and tendon ached. She lowered the side railing, leaned down and kissed Nat's forehead. "Bye, Nat." She straightened and stared down at him for a moment. "See you later." She meant it.

Jane walked from the room, head high.

There were forms to be filled out, questions to be answered, decisions to be made. The funeral service? Selection of a casket? Which cemetery? Which undertaker? Dr. Silverstein offered to take care of most of the details if Jane would "just sign these forms please."

Seated across a desk from a matronly hospital counselor in a windowless office on the main floor, Jane could feel the numbness taking over her body. "There will be no funeral service. If someone will call my hotel with the details about where and when he will be buried . . . "

It was seven thirty Saturday morning. She hadn't eaten since noon the day before. Her head pounded as she lit the last Marlboro in a pack she had opened after midnight.

"As you wish, Mrs. Connor. Surely you have family or friends . . . someone who could be of some assistance, comfort to you at a time like this . . . ?" The woman's words trailed off.

"Yes," Jane took a long drag on the cigarette, "at a time like this." As opposed to a time like graduation or a wedding or having a baby. A time like getting a raise or falling in love or winning something or losing something. A time like this. "No, thank you. No. I shall undoubtedly seek comfort from several very dry martinis and the first man who blows in my ear."

The counselor twitched with shock, then composed herself. The dead boy's mother wasn't to be held responsible at such a time.

Shortly after nine Jane walked back to the tiny hotel room where she had dropped her suitcase before she realized she would not be sleeping there. She fell on the bed without undressing. The arrangements had been made. Her son was to be buried at ten the next morning.

Someone of assistance. The counselor's words throbbed through her head. She wasn't quite sure she would know what to do with someone of assistance. Friends? What in the world would she say to friends? "Hello. I have had a seriously retarded son for ten years and he just died. Never told you? Must have slipped my mind. Want to drive to Baltimore and stand beside his little grave with me? Want to speak to me in hushed and pitying tones? Want to feel helpless and useless, friends, friends of mine?"

No.

She rose on her elbow. There *was* Paul.

Although she had never told him of Nathaniel's existence, he knew she was burdened by a personal problem which entailed a large financial obligation. The unstated guiding rule of their relationship was complete acceptance of the other's privacy. No questions asked. Personal information only on a voluntary basis.

Right now, she *wanted* to share her feelings with him. She reached for the phone beside the bed. She was kidding herself. She didn't want to share. She wanted to scream. She wanted to wallow in self-pity and helplessness. To be lifted and carried and permitted to cry and to be told everything would be all right. She wanted her hair stroked back from her wet cheeks and the cooing sound of someone strong telling her how brave she had been, how brave she was, how hard she had tried to do the right things.

No.

She dropped her arm.

It was Saturday morning. Paul would be at home with his wife in their Park Avenue apartment. How would he explain her call to his wife if she answered? He certainly would feel constrained about anything he said to her, with his wife standing at his elbow. It would be awkward, and worse, unfulfilling. No, Paul couldn't give her what she needed right now.

The only people who knew about Nat were her mother and Ann. But Ann was going through her own private hell, and she didn't need a cry of help from Jane.

Mindlessly, rapidly, Jane grabbed the receiver and then realized she had forgotten the phone number at Chantry Farms. She reached Leesburg Information, hung up and signaled the hotel operator again.

The phone rang three, four times. "Hello?" the familiar voice intoned.

"Mother, it's Jane."

There was a long pause on the other end of the line. "Yes? Hello? Jane? Where are you?"

"I'm in Baltimore, Mother."

"Baltimore? What on earth for? Baltimore is the most dreary place."

"Mother, Nathaniel died last night."

She listened to Grace Moncure Connor thoroughly clear her throat. "What? What is it?"

"I said, Nat's dead. Pneumonia."

"Pneumonia?" Her mother sounded incredulous. "There is absolutely no reason for anyone to *die* of pneumonia in this day and age."

"I think that is rather beside the point, Mother." Wearily, Jane lowered her voice. There was another long pause as the line

296

crackled between them. "He's dead and I'm here in Baltimore to bury him."

"Hmm. Yes. Well, am I supposed to come up there for some sort of service?"

"No, Mother, I just thought you should know that my son is dead."

She carefully replaced the receiver, without listening for her mother's response, if indeed there had been any.

She sat on the edge of the sagging bed. She was angry with herself. What a stupid, masochistic thing to have done. She eased back against the chenille bedspread and fell asleep. She slept a few hours and awoke and smoked, then fell again into fitful sleep.

Sunday morning dawned gray and bleak. The rain had started again sometime during the night. The sandwich Jane had ordered up to the room lay half eaten on the night table, its edges curling over a piece of darkening lettuce.

Sometime during her restless sleep the phone had rung and someone had told her what to do in the morning.

In the hotel lobby she met Mr. Dalmas, the undertaker. He brought along a Pastor Hobbes. At the grave site he recited the Lord's Prayer and the Twenty-third Psalm under an enormous black umbrella. The cold rain turned the waiting mound of freshly shoveled earth to black mud that oozed down one side of the small, raw rectangle. Then, as an impassive cemetery laborer scraped the mud onto the simple fruit-wood coffin, Pastor Hobbes launched into Chapter Seventeen of the Book of Revelations, his voice booming from beneath his umbrella.

Jane turned away from the grave and the bellowing minister. Why in the world was the man going on about abominations of the earth at a child's funeral? Before he was finished, she shook her head and walked up a slight rise to Mr. Dalmas's black limousine, her high heels sinking deep into the soggy ground.

Now, three hours later, she was seated in a Washington taxicab that smelled of urine and cigar smoke. Poor Nat, she thought, staring out the window, poor little boy. You never even had a shot at it.

She stopped at the desk for her mail and telephone messages. There were piles of each. Before going to the elevator, she went to the janitor's office in back of the front desk and knocked.

"Why, hello, Miss Connor," the wiry black man said, with a tired smile. "Lot of people been lookin' for you this week. Dessy Seymour at the desk says you got a pile of mail and things."

"Thanks, Horace, I got them. I've been out of town." She handed him the shopping bag. "Would you please dispose of this for me?"

Horace peered into the bag. "You want these things thrown out, Miss Connor? Somebody might could use them."

"I'd rather you just threw them out, please, Horace. They belonged to a relative of mine, who," she paused, "outgrew them." She turned to leave and hesitated for a moment. She reached over and plucked the bald koala bear out of the bag and shoved it into her purse.

Her phone began to ring before she got her key in her door. She let it ring while she shed her wrinkled raincoat and dumped the contents of her suitcase on the double bed.

"Yes?" she sighed into the receiver on the eleventh ring.

"Jane? Thank God I've found you. Where have you *been*?" It was Melon, of course.

"Look, friend, I just this minute walked in. Give me a chance to pee and read the mail. I'll call you back."

"But where have you *been*?" she persisted. "I even called at the E.O.B. asking for you. God, *they're* a friendly bunch. I finally got someone to tell me you were on annual leave. What's up?"

"Melon . . . "

"Were you with Paul? I know! You had a face-lift. An abortion. It's a new man, isn't it? Jane? You've found Mr. Right and have been holed up in a motel all week! Tell me, tell me, tell me," Melon pressed, curious about any or all possibilities that might explain Jane's absence.

"Melon, I am not going to tell you, tell you, tell you, because whatever I've been doing might wind up in the paper, paper, paper."

"Then, you *were* doing something I could . . . "

"I am about to burst a kidney, my front door is wide open and the neighborhood mugger is standing there exposing himself. Let me off the goddamn phone!"

"Wait. I've got to tell you something. This is terribly important, and it's something I can only tell you."

Jane sighed and leaned back across her bed. "Can you give it to me in ten words or less?"

298

As Melon chattered, Jane extracted the hospital bill from her purse and was consciously acknowledging the numbers on it for the first time. Then there were the doctor's bills and the funeral charges. She assumed Pastor Hobbes was included in those. This meant another big bank loan on top of what Paul had lent her last summer.

Melon was talking so fast the words ran together. Something about Seth, as usual. Today she was furious with him because he had slighted her in the *Herald's* elevator, or some such nonsense. "Mmm. Mmm-hmm," Jane periodically mumbled as she added figures in her head.

Suddenly, she became aware of silence. I'm sorry, Melon. You were saying?"

Melon began to sob. "You haven't been listening to one word I've said, Jane Connor. I honestly thought you were the one person in the world who possessed . . . empathy. I'm in *pain*, dammit, and you aren't even *listening*. You've been off screwing your brains out on some tropical beach somewhere. You're just sitting there not listening to me with a goddamn *tan*. Well, fuck you, *friend*!"

Jane winced when Melon slammed down her phone.

She laid down the bills and walked to the john.

Monday morning Norm Franklin called her into his paneled office. "Family problems taken care of, Jane?"

"Completely."

"Okay, then here's where we are." He got his pipe going, swung his feet onto his desk and picked up the legal-sized sheet from Salinger's office giving the President's schedule. "Today, the President is in Tampa. Chamber of Commerce speech on the tax bill. Thursday he's in San Antonio with the Johnsons. Then it's Houston and Fort Worth. Friday, Dallas. That's to be a full blowout motorcade, little children with flags, Governor Connally riding with him. The whole bit."

"Think that will smooth the ruffled Texas Democratic feathers?"

"That's the idea. The kicker is Jackie. This will be her first really important political appearance with him. That's where you come in. We will get a lot of play on this; I want you to watch all the coverage and keep me informed. Be thinking about how it could be done better, if possible. This won't be her last trip; she's going to

299

be more and more visible as we get closer to the sixty-four campaign."

"Okay. Incidentally, do you have the press list of who's going?"

Franklin nodded and pulled two stapled sheets from under the pile on his desk. He handed it to her.

Scanning the second page she found Billie Claire's name. "Ah, good, Billie Claire Hutchins of the *Herald* is going. She might give me a little fill-in on everyone's mood. Let me give her a ring and get some sort of a preliminary reading."

Franklin pulled on his pipe and nodded. He really was a bit of a jerk. The White House job was as close to God as he had managed to get in his career. His wife even sent thank-you notes to people on little White House embossed memo slips he swiped for her.

She rang Billie Claire's extension. Billie Claire came on the line breathless. "Hi, Jane, can't talk. On deadline. American Women in Radio and Television cocktail party at the Press Club at six. Wanna go?"

"Sure," Jane said, suddenly realizing that she had spoken to few familiar humans for a week. A party would be good. "See you there."

The party was in full swing as she pushed through the double doors of the East Lounge. Billie Claire waved from the end of the long bar and Jane joined her and a circle of familiar faces. With one exception.

Sam Kazin was a bear of a man. He stood exactly the same height as Jane, but was half again as wide. And it wasn't fat; more, solid muscle. He seemed coiled, as if ready to spring, like a well-conditioned athlete. She smiled and acknowledged Billie Claire's introduction by extending her hand. She had heard his name before, but couldn't place it.

"Sam is with *Newsweek* in New York," Billie Claire chirped. "He's down here doing a cover story on McNamara." She leaned close to Jane's ear and whispered, "And, he's single."

Jane gave her a little push and Billie Claire turned to speak to Vera Glaser.

"May I buy you a drink, Jane?" Sam moved to her side at the bar. Benny had already slid a Scotch and soda in front of her. She smiled at one of her favorite bartenders and turned to Sam, who was openly staring at her. "You are the most beautiful woman I've ever met," Sam Kazin said matter-of-factly. "I work at *Newsweek.* What do you do?"

Jane shook her head to clear it. She didn't know which remark to respond to. "Well, thank you, and the White House."

"Jesus, the first *really* smashing thing JFK's done so far. What do you do there?"

"Speechwriter," she lied. No way was she going into detail with a stranger.

"You're kidding! Which ones did you write?"

"Well, several of my *words* made it. Let's see. Remember 'ask not what your country can do for you'? Two 'ands' and one 'because' in that speech were mine."

"You are very cute," he said, not smiling. "In fact, you are the cutest person I have ever had dinner with."

"What?" She blinked at him.

"Oh, spareribs, maybe. A steamship round of beef. You must know all the good places in town. You have a coat?"

"Well, the jacket I'm wearing. The rain's stopped . . . "

"Come on, while everyone can see me leaving with you. Good for my ego." He placed a firm hand under her elbow and propelled her toward the door. "Don't worry, I'm paying."

"Now, wait a minute, Mr. . . . "

"Sam. Just plain Sam."

Jane decided not to protest. She had a feeling it would do her no good. The man had simply taken charge, and before she realized it, she was out on the curb on Fourteenth Street with his hand still on her arm. With his free hand he hailed a cab.

"The Rotunda," he told the cabdriver, "and as rapidly as possible. I have this condition."

"I thought you didn't know Washington? You give orders as if you lived here."

He leaned back into the seat and grinned at her. "Ah, I have done it. I have captured and now hold prisoner a member of the White House staff. A beautiful blonde from whom I shall extract information most highly prized."

"I think you are absolutely batty," Jane said, studying his face.

Sam Kazin's face conveyed a series of unsettling contradictions. His dark brown eyes fixed one with intense, probing directness, while the heavy brows arched or drooped in perplexity. Meanwhile, his forehead folded into creases of surprise or concentration, and his mobile mouth drew into a taut line or relaxed and turned up in a gentle smile. His hands were broad and rippled with veins and he moved with a grace startling in a man so large. His presence made Jane feel somehow smaller, protected.

After they were seated on a back banquette at the Rotunda, Jane finally caught her breath. The man had refused to tip the cabdriver until he had endorsed the statement that Jane was "the most beautiful woman in the world." He had then tipped the hatcheck girl on the way in, telling her that he was sorry they didn't have any coats to check, but perhaps "this will take care of it." He then asked the captain his first name, how he voted and if the food was any good. He must also have slipped something to the captain, because the flurry around their table was instantaneous and continuous.

"Now," he said, turning to her on the padded leather seat, "start at the beginning. You were born so-and-so, raised so-and-so. Bring it all the way up to why you lied to me about what you do at the White House. I love it when women lie to me. Means they're on the defensive."

Jane felt the blood rush to her face. She was both flattered and furious. How dare he accuse her of lying? Worse, how dare he know for sure that she was? She had been sensitive about the White House job since she had taken it. She knew she was to tell no one what she did there, and while she could accept that as a political and public relations expedient, it still made her uneasy. No one had ever really bothered to quiz her about it, except Melon, who quizzed everyone about everything, so that almost didn't count. One simply didn't question members of the White House staff. Now, here was this outsider, this *New Yorker*, brazenly poking into something that wasn't his business.

"I'm not going to tell you anything about my job," she said simply and quietly, hoping their evening wouldn't be ruined by getting off to an argumentative start. She liked this odd, self-assured man. He was vastly sure of himself, but he was also funny and brusque. In addition, he was slightly wacky, and Jane found herself responding to him in a far less guarded way than with every other man she knew.

"Okay," he said, waving for another drink, "we will drop the subject for now. But I intend to bring it up again as our relationship progresses."

"Progresses? I'm only here for a good, hot meal, 'Just Plain Sam.' I was in the mood for hot food and strange company and you happened to come along."

"Now," he settled himself more comfortably, "let's talk about me."

Jane's mouth fell open.

"Here's what you need to know about the next man in your life. I'm a former reporter on the *Mirror*, and now an overpaid *Newsweek* editor. Graduated NYU and Columbia 'J' School in the Year One. I'm thirty-five, single, Jewish with an explanation and I can't swim. I think JFK is overrated, Harry Truman was a genius and Alger Hiss is guilty. My father was a CPA, may he rest in peace, and my mother lives in Brooklyn waiting out her days for me to marry Sheila or Shirley or Rona. If she saw me out with a girl like you she would plotz. Her heart would attack her. By her, I lead the life of a wasted person. From this aggravation I get two phone calls a week, always at the most embarrassing moment, and every Friday, a CARE package of chopped liver and kreplach is left with my doorman. I let him keep it. I figure, let *him* get the heartburn. If she knew how much food I've left under the seat of the D train in a greasy paper bag . . . "

In spite of herself, Jane was laughing. She managed to push a piece of fish around her plate, but the constant stream of stories and anecdotes issuing from Sam so captured her attention that most of the meal was eventually whisked away by the ever-attentive waiters.

Over espresso he suddenly interrupted a long and utterly hilarious story having to do with two ridiculous years in the Army on Guam. He stared at her. "We have a problem."

Good Lord, she thought, he can't pay the check. "What's the matter?" She tried to remember whether or not she had her American Express card with her.

"You are going to hate my apartment," he said flatly.

"Your apartment? You live in New York," she said, bewildered. A state to which she had grown accustomed during the past two and a half hours.

"Smart girl." He tapped his head. "Smart. But not so smart that you like Formica."

"Formica." She nodded.

"That's what my apartment is. Wall-to-wall Formica. A lot of books and a *lot* of Formica. Coffee table, dining room table, end table, platform for the bed. All Formica. I even have a big Formica plant on the windowsill. At least I think that's what it's made of. It goes 'clink' when you tap a leaf and it's an interesting bluish-green—the leaves. My mother left it with the doorman before he knew to keep her stuff. You'll hate the rest of the apartment. I haven't cleaned it since forever. Someone once said that a place doesn't get any dirtier after the fourth year. Mine is living proof."

"Wait, wait," Jane waved her hand helplessly. "I live here in Washington. You don't have to worry about whether or not I like your Formica forest or not. It's academic. Right?"

"You are probably going to want to change everything around. Probably even want to get a larger apartment. Look. That's fine with me. We'll get rid of all the Formica; got to keep the plant though. Oh, jeez! I've got all this junk around that Natalie left. Never mind. She was some free-lance lunatic I got involved with. Anyway, we can . . . "

"Stop!" Jane cried.

"What's the matter?" He looked at her as if she were in some physical danger.

"Just stop for a minute. You are absolutely nuts. I have no intention of rearranging your Formica, which, incidentally, I loathe. Nor do I care about whoever Natalie is nor am I ever leaving Washington, D.C."

"Wrong. You will leave Washington because you will have no choice."

"What in God's name are you talking about?" Her voice was beginning to rise. Wait until I get my hands on Billie Claire. This man is single? He's a psychopath!

"I'm talking about the rest of your life. Washington is too small for you. Sooner or later you will realize that, and then you will come and live with me and be my love. You simply won't have any choice."

"That's it! Now I know you are cuckoo and I'm going home. This has been a particularly trying week and I need some rest." She picked up her bag and made a move to push the table away.

He grabbed her arm and pulled her back, gently, and looked

304

directly into her face. There was laughter and determination dancing in his eyes. "Listen to me for a minute, Beautiful."

"Don't call me Beautiful." She tried to twist her arm out of his grasp. He held tight.

"That's a conceited thing to say. Should I call you Pigface? You *are* beautiful, don't fight it. Now. This town is dull and dreary and tasteless. It has been the same town for the last one hundred years; only the faces change. Washington is the sticks. It's just a sleepy little Southern town with delusions of grandeur. If you would stop and think for a minute, you would realize that you are living in a cultural and intellectual vacuum here. A Gobi of creative thought, a . . . "

"Sam, what are you talking about? This is the most exciting city in the world. This is where the *decisions* are made!"

"Perhaps," he said evenly, "but the decisions as to what you read, what you will hear and perceive in the arts, in music, in the theater, even what you wear, the decisions on things that will enrich your life are *not* made here. You've got inexpensive taxicabs and a clean zoo. That about wraps it up. Beyond that, this is Kansas. You've got a political job, obviously, and if you play it cool you can probably keep it up for the next Kennedy Administration. Then what? You'll have the mark of Zorro on you. After Kennedy's second term, what if the Republicans get in?"

"I can always go back to newspapering," she said defensively.

"Ahh. That's the word, 'back!' Regression. Back to square one. One doesn't go *back* in life, one moves *ahead*, grows. Now. When are you coming to New York?"

Jane sighed. "Sam, I *will* be in New York in two weeks, but I'll be with a friend. A man."

His eyes twinkled, then creased at the corners. "Great! You have two weeks to dump him before the Formica attack."

Jane sagged. For a week that had started so badly, it was ending on a zany and hopeful note. Sam Kazin was not going to be easy to discourage. She wasn't sure whether she really wanted to.

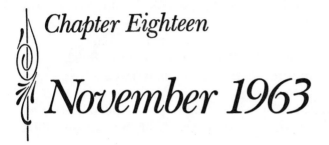

Chapter Eighteen

November 1963

"Oh, sweet Jesus, you must be a witch." Seth Hathaway lay flat on his back, eyes closed, breathing heavily.

Allegra knelt on the white satin sheet, her knees several inches from his lax right hand, and looked down at him. Then, after a few moments, she bent and made slow designs on the palm of his hand with the tip of her tongue. "Mm, you taste good here, too."

He groaned. "For God's sake, stop!" With effort, he lifted his hand and stroked her cheek. "Any more tonight and I'll have a coronary." Slowly his eyes opened and he smiled up at her dreamily. ·

She knew exactly what he was seeing: a nimbus of golden hair above flawless peach-pink shoulders and breasts, the face partially obscured by shadows. "Are you as happy as I am, darling?"

"Happy doesn't quite cover the way I feel, Allegra. You are heaven. My angel. My treasure." He drew her down beside him and held her tenderly against his chest.

"My darling, darling Seth," she murmured against the curly mass of red and gray hair. "My only love. My world." As she spoke she was able to see that two crimson nails on her right hand were slightly chipped. She made a mental note to call her manicurist first thing in the morning.

Putting the condition of her nails out of her mind for the moment, she began to graze his belly with her fingertips, circling slowly, moving her hand lower and lower. She could feel his skin tighten and she was several inches above his pubic hair. "You aren't finished yet," she hummed into the cavity of his chest.

He firmly clasped her wrist. "I will most surely *be* finished if I don't stop you this minute." Seth turned away from Allegra and sat up. "Dammit, I've got to go. Why can't I sleep here? You'd think Jeannine could read the morning paper by herself after all these years. But, oh, no. Love, make a drink for the so-called road."

Allegra slipped into a pale green velour robe and moved toward the second-floor den. "Come, darling, I'll poke the fire."

"Yes, do that." He glanced about. "This room doesn't encourage thoughts of going out in the rain. What an inspiration." Seth shook his head. "Only you could have dreamed up floor-to-ceiling suede. Ah, well."

Seth's study was leather and dark wood, lighted by parchment-shaded lamps. She laid cherrywood on the embers in the fireplace and set glasses, crystal decanters and a silver ice bucket on a tray before the fire.

Tieless, and wearing his smoking jacket and suit trousers, Seth made himself comfortable beside Allegra on the brown corduroy Lawson facing the fireplace.

"How was your day, darling?" She poured Cutty Sark over carefully shaved ice and handed him the glass.

"Exhausting. Too much to do and not enough time. Sam Kazin from *Newsweek* is in town. I wanted an hour or so with him. He's doing a cover on McNamara. Jack called me about it the other day. Seems he wants certain points made in that story, and obviously he can't make them himself. Asked me to sort of grease the wheels. Dammit, Kazin had only an hour, and by the time I got to the Press Club he had taken off. He hadn't waited for me. That man is tough. No one's been able to soften him up. Well. Eventually, we'll get to him. Now, then, what happened in your beautiful life today, my love? And what is it going to cost me?"

"Darling! Don't even joke about that! You know how I try to economize." She snuggled next to him.

"Umm, yes. I noticed daisies on the entry table instead of your usual birds-of-paradise. You are *trying*, love." He brushed his lips

308

against her forehead. "After these last hours, how could I deny you anything?"

"And the rest of your day?"

"Oh, the usual. Constant phone calls. Sometimes I feel as if the damn thing is grafted to my ear. Oh, here's something that will interest you, my lovely. We are nominating Ann Adams for a Pulitzer."

"Wonderful." Allegra stifled a yawn. "What for?"

"Her coverage of the Martin Luther King march last summer. A quite remarkable piece of work. She's a consistently excellent writer. You must ask her here very soon."

"Of course. I worked on the list for next week's dinner party today; I'll simply add her name to it, if you'd like. But should it be Mr. and Mrs., what?"

"Hmm. Tough question. I think you had better make it just to her and send it to the paper. I should have gone over the list with you. I'm sure you were discreet?"

"Seth, I'm *always* discreet. And I certainly know enough not to invite any Texans. I thought for a bit that Bill Moyers might be all right, but then I had second thoughts. Darling, you know I always do what you tell me to do. Here, I'll show you." She rose and walked to Seth's huge rolltop desk to the left of the bay windows. "Look. Miles and I looked at that space on Wisconsin Avenue this afternoon as you suggested. Here's the floor plan. It's absolutely gigantic. Just perfect for . . . "

"Allegra," Seth took the piece of paper without unfolding it, "I have been having some second thoughts about this boutique idea of yours."

"Darling, you can't be concerned about *Miles!*"

"The day I begin to worry about you and a screaming queen like Miles Buford I'll turn in my jockstrap. No. I'm really worried about your getting involved with the business side of this thing. You have exquisite taste and original ideas, no doubt about that. But you know nothing about keeping books and taxes and all the paperwork involved in a business. I have the feeling that you picture yourself sitting at an adorable antique desk, dressed to kill, chatting up some ambassador's wife about her drawing room drapes. It wouldn't be like that at all."

"But, Seth," Allegra sat up very straight, "how can you say that?

309

I'm wonderful with details. Look how I run this house. The parties, the dinners, the help. It's all very complicated. You don't appreciate it because you don't know what goes on behind the scenes. I deliberately do not trouble you with the details I have to deal with. Frankly, I don't think that's what's worrying you."

"Oh?" He ran his hand down her rigid back.

"I think you're jealous of anything that would take me away from being with you."

Seth continued to rub her back. "You are right, perhaps. Maybe my concern *is* more for myself than for you. I want you every minute. I don't want to have to wait for you while you snip up some old bag's chintz."

"Seth, darling . . . " Allegra whirled and took his face in her hands, "you wouldn't be jealous of what I do in a little *shop*. During the *day*. And think of the scrumptious bits of gossip I'll pick up."

He laughed. "I have Melon Bowersox for that, love. Really, the point is that I think it will just be too much of an undertaking for you."

"*Please*, Seth." Allegra's hand slipped inside his loose smoking jacket; her thumb and forefinger deftly slid down the zipper of his trousers. Instantly her hand was inside. "Pleassse!"

He laid his head back on the couch pillows and took a deep breath. "God, woman." He was becoming rigid. "If you want a little shop in Georgetown, then you shall have a little shop in Georgetown. But one thing, Allegra."

"What?" she murmured, her head now in his lap.

"Promise," he said, assisting the zipper on its downward course, "promise you won't stop what you're doing."

"Oh, how marvelous this is. Mmm."

"You are the most sensitive in the feet and calves," Petra Jensen noted briskly. "I told you that the first time, *nej?*"

"Ouch!"

"*Selvfølgelig,* but of course. Your Achilles tendons are irritated this morning. I can feel the tension. It is better, *nej?*"

"Mmm."

"You are not getting enough sleep, my dear."

"That couldn't be helped, Petra." Allegra felt like a slowly melting candle. The source of heat was Petra's hands. "Mr. Hathaway didn't leave until three in the morning."

"It is more important that you be beautiful for him than to satisfy him more than once. A man his age! He can have his pleasure well before midnight if you are well organized."

"Mmm. Sometimes, sometimes not. So much depends on his mood. Mmm. That's heavenly. I've got to pick it up the moment he walks in the door. Everything I do must seem spontaneous, and that takes concentration."

"*Tak.* Did you try the little trick last evening?"

"It was marvelous. He almost went mad. I must have been doing it right." Petra was now working on the small of her back and the flesh just above it. When her sensitive fingers encountered the smallest tension, she explored the area and gently worked over the muscle until it was soothed.

"Good. Just remember. Relax your upper torso, tighten your buttocks and automatically the vaginal muscles constrict. It takes practice. Actually, it achieved great refinement in the court of Louis the Thirteenth. The competition among the courtesans was quite fierce. Now, *hurtigt,* quickly, roll over please. Your back, *du er ferdi,* you are finished."

Allegra rolled over onto her back, dragging the sheet that covered her. "You are the most amazing person, Petra. Do all Danish women know as much about sex as you do?"

"Ah, it is an attitude, Miss Allegra. Everything that is accomplished in this world starts right here." She gave a sudden playful tug to the golden tuft between Allegra's legs.

Allegra defensively pulled up her knees and giggled. "Do you really believe that? Don't women also get things done with their brains?"

"Ah, *selvfølgelig*! But brains in a woman are terrifying to men. One must use her more obvious attributes, and use them well. Ha!" She was now working on Allegra's silken inner thigh. "What is this! Bruises? You must not let him make a mark on your skin."

"It's all right. No one will see that but Seth."

"That is not the point. Your body is a temple! It should not be abused! Now." Petra placed moistened pads on Allegra's eyes and began to work on her chin and neck. "*Du er en engle.* You are an angel," Petra murmured.

"Please don't let me fall asleep, Petra. I'm having an early lunch with Miles."

"*Ja.* Your friend, Miles. He is still in love?"

"In a daze is more like it. A fog. He can't think straight. I don't know where it will all end."

Miles arrived at one, bearing a tiny antique silver pillbox he had discovered in a junk shop, black with soot and time. He had polished it and had a jeweler fix the broken clasp.

Allegra adored it and kissed him on both cheeks. "Miles, you are such a love. Come have a glass of wine while I finish my makeup and we'll run to lunch. I booked the Carriage House for one thirty."

Miles sat on the end of Allegra's bed while she applied another coat of mascara.

"Did you get a chance to call the rental agent on that empty shop?" She licked the mascara wand and swooped it across her lashes.

"Yes, I did. I asked some pertinent questions and got the right answers. I think you should grab it before it gets away. The price is right. He even offered to apply the first year's rental against the purchase price if you decide to buy. I don't think you can do any better." He put down his wineglass and stepped up behind Allegra. He picked up a tortoiseshell hairbrush and began gently to brush her long, wheat-colored hair. "Do you mind?"

"Oh, darling, of course not. Please." She was now outlining her mouth in crimson with a tiny sable brush. "Then I should lease it?"

"My advice is, do it." He continued to brush her hair. After a long pause, he said, "I didn't call Billie Claire."

"Oh, Miles. You promised! It's really not fair. She is so hurt and bewildered. I told you she was practically in tears on the phone last week wondering why she hasn't seen you, why you haven't called. She thinks it's something she's done. Really, Miles, you simply must."

"I know, I know. I just can't get up the courage right now. I'm too fragile. This Nicky thing has completely thrown me. I realize I promised you I would straighten things out with Billie but give me some more time."

312

"Why don't you just tell her about you and Nicky? That would solve everything."

Miles gasped. "Oh, Allegra! How could I? I have no right. No right to hurt her, no right to hurt Nicky."

"But you are hurting her right now. Not speaking to her. How does that help anything?"

"I *can't*! Nicky has me walking around in circles. He is all I think about. Most of the time he treats me like shit and I keep coming back for more. Don't you think I would just blurt it out if I were with Billie Claire for more than five minutes? Oh, the things I am longing to ask her about him. Anything that will give me clues that will help me hold onto him. How I can make him love me as much as I love him. And, besides, Billie doesn't know about Nicky and he'd kill me if I told her."

"Miles," Allegra reached around and took the hairbrush from him, "the longer this goes on the worse it is going to be."

"Darling, give me a little more time." Miles sat back down on the bed and passed his hand over his eyes. "Let me try to figure this thing out. Right now, I can't concentrate. I can't sleep. I've lost eight pounds. Look at me," he extended his right hand, "I shake. For no reason. My hand shakes when I even talk about him."

"My poor darling." She put her arms around his hunched shoulders and pulled his head to her breast. "Miles, I need you so, and to see you this unhappy breaks my heart."

He looked up into her exquisite face. "*You* need *me*? But, why?"

"I need you because, very simply, this boutique means everything to me right now. Without *you* I won't be able to make a go of it. Seth expects me to fail. Even while he is agreeing to let me have it, he is telling me I'm going to botch it."

"You mustn't listen to him. You are a genius. This boutique is perfect for you. He's just jealous. You can do it."

"I can't do it without you, Miles."

He disengaged her arms from his neck, stood up and looked down at her. "You are such a love. You're trying to keep my mind off Nicky and I adore you for it."

"Please believe me. I'm being very selfish in this. Between the two of us Designs by Farr can be a smash. I *know* it."

He encircled her waist and waltzed her around the bedroom.

313

"Oh, Allegra!" He sang the first few lines of "Ain't We Got Fun," as they swirled around the room until they slipped on the laminated suede floor and fell across the bed laughing and clutching each other.

They both sat up at the same time.

"Now," Miles said excitedly, "I see the entrance. Those windows! We'll smash out those monstrosities that are there and make two huge bays with those tiny, leaded glass panes. We'll do a double door. Red lacquer, I think, with two enormous brass lion's head knockers. The outer look will be Federal, but, inside . . . look out! Outer space! Mauve. You've always loved mauve. We will drown you in it!"

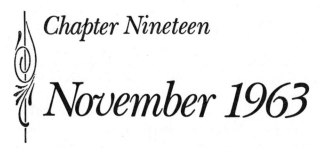

Chapter Nineteen

November 1963

Billie Claire wearily hung her raincoat on a padded hanger and placed the hanger on the shower curtain rod to let the coat drip. She undressed and rinsed out her bra, panties and hose, which she hung over two wire hangers.

"Crap!"

She had done everything in the wrong order. She transferred the hangers to the bathroom door frame, turned on the shower and stepped in. After she was clean and shampooed, she replaced the hangers and set her hair in rollers and applied three different night creams to her face, knees, hands and elbows.

Dressed in a nightgown, quilted robe and large, fuzzy red slippers, she pulled her small suitcase from the closet shelf and slowly began to pack it.

The clock on her desk read eleven forty-five. She had finished Michener's *Caravans* the night before, and a brand-new copy of Eisenhower's *Mandate for Change* lay beside the morocco leather address book Miles had given her for her birthday two years ago. In his beautiful script he had written in the private addresses and phone numbers of Richard Burton, Gregory Peck, Burt Lancaster, Rex Harrison and a dozen other gorgeous men. One evening she had dialed Burton's number, and when she realized that she was actually speaking to him, she hung up, embarrassed and giggling.

Billie Claire did not feel like reading Ike's memoirs, she felt like talking to Miles.

The last she had heard from him was a short, apologetic phone call after he had stood her up for dinner well over a week before.

For months she had been aware that Miles was involved with someone. Obviously, a lover. She had heard rumors, and she could tell from the excited, distracted edge in his voice. He had been in love before, though, and had still found time for her.

She sat down and reached for the phone in one motion.

"Oh, Miles, it's me, Billie Claire," she said in a small voice.

"My precious!" Miles shouted, overjoyed. "When are you having me to dinner? Better, let me take you out so you will forgive me for being so rude. Tomorrow? Lunch, let's say?"

His jubilant response took her completely by surprise. "I can't tomorrow. I'd like to, honestly, but I can't. I've missed you, Miles."

"Then, let's do something special tomorrow evening."

"Miles, I mean, I won't be here."

"Darling Billie, where are you off to now?"

"God help me, Texas, until Sunday sometime."

Miles moaned. "Oh, you poor dear. You got stuck with *that* trip? Can't Helen and Fran cover for the wires and let the poor dailies stay home? You could get captured and eaten down there."

"I have no choice. Jackie's going, so we're all in the soup, except Helen; Smitty will cover for UPI.

"I can't bear it for you. Texans are such . . . primitives."

"Hopefully, I won't have to mingle with the primitives. Just follow Jackie around and try to pick up *something* to write about. I probably won't even come within fifty feet of her. Believe me, I'm not looking forward to this one."

"Well, maybe she will do or say something marvelous or outrageous right in front of you and you'll be able to scoop everyone. There's always hope."

"Miles?"

"Yes, love?"

"Can I ask you something?"

"Anything."

"What's up with you? I though we were buddies, I mean, *real*

316

buddies. You never call. You're never home when I call. Have I done something?

She waited and listened to a Mozart piano concerto playing on Miles's stereo. She waited for several heartbeats until he answered very slowly.

"Billie, Billie, my sweet, my life is a mess right now. Don't ask me to explain. I will soon. It's very complicated and has nothing to do with you. But, I do have some fun news for you. Ready?"

"Ready," she said, feeling somewhat relieved, and choosing to believe Miles when he implied there was nothing she had done.

"Allegra is definitely going to open her decorator design shop. She has the place on Wisconsin Avenue. And, she has asked me to be her partner."

"That's fantastic! The two of you will be a smash. What good news. I knew Allegra was thinking about doing something like this, but I never thought Seth would actually let her go ahead with it."

"Well, she worked her wondrous charms on him and she's just signed a lease with an option to buy. I would have told you before, but I didn't want to say anything until we had ironed out the details."

"Oh, Miles, I'm so excited for you both. What are you calling it?"

"Designs by Farr."

"Catchy."

"I think so."

No *wonder* I haven't heard from you. You must have been running around like mad. Will you quit your job? Would that be wise, now?"

"I won't be able to yet. Some things are still up in the air." Miles voice trailed off and she could hear the music again. "If it looks as if we can make a real go of it, then, I guess I'll be able to afford to quit the *Herald*."

"Of course you'll make a go of it. God knows, you deserve to."

"God may know it, but these days, I have a feeling he is lolling around listening to Herb Alpert and the Tijuana Brass. I don't think His eye has been on this sparrow."

"You sound down again."

Immediately, Miles perked up. "Not at all, darling. Top of the world. I'm going to name my yacht after you."

"Let's have dinner after I get back from this boring trip, okay?"

"You're on, my love. Call me when you get in Sunday and we will do something très chic."

Billie Claire turned down her spread and was asleep in minutes. The gnawing anxiety she had felt about Miles had vanished. Now she understood. She had been silly and selfish to think she had offended him. He had simply been getting his life together. It was nice to have him back in hers.

She called a cab at 5:30 A.M. and was one of the first reporters to pass through the guarded gates at Andrews Air Force Base. She stood around the apron of the runway for a few minutes balancing on one foot and then the other, trying to keep warm in the cold, damp morning air. The sun had just begun to break through the gray sky for a brief moment, when she was joined by Pete Lisagor and then Hugh Sidey from *Time*. They all greeted one another and moaned about the early hour and the predictable boredom of the trip and the questionable night life in San Antonio, Fort Worth and Dallas.

Over Lisagor's shoulder Bille Claire could see the Presidential helicopter swooping in to land near Air Force One. The press plane had dropped its steps and they were now free to board. More than two dozen reporters shambled onto the field in various stages of wakefulness, lugging portable typewriters and overnight bags. They climbed the steps to the welcome warmth and comfort.

As soon as the press plane was airborne, Bloody Marys blossomed. Members of the press moved up and down the aisles and made room for two girls from Salinger's office who squeezed through the narrow aisle passing out the advance text of the President's speech that day. Some looked it over, making notes in the margins; others simply folded it and put it away for the time being.

The two-and-a-half-hour trip was uneventful. Marianne Means stopped for a few minutes and leaned against the back of Billie Claire's seat to inquire about Ann. They discussed the Del situation for a while and both agreed that things looked rather hopeless. They both commented on the absence of both Helen and Fran.

Billie Claire began to relax, even to look forward to the trip. There might not be much to cover, but she enjoyed being among her peers. At least she hoped they thought *she* was a peer. She loved the gruff good nature of her fellow journalists. The unspoken rules of gentlemenly behavior, the lack of cutthroat competition among the elite corps that covered the President of the United States, made her feel safe and special. They were all there for the same reason. They were hurtling through the sky in pursuit of the most powerful man in the world, in order to chronicle his words, his actions and the actions and words of those around him. She refused the second offer of a Bloody Mary from the stewardess and leaned back to count her blessings.

The first day Kennedy stuck close to this schedule, Jackie, beautifully dressed and coiffed, at his side. Whatever internal political problems the Texas Democratic party was embroiled in certainly weren't being made worse by a visit from this glorious man and his exquisite and stylish wife.

She spent the evening with a group of Secret Service men. Two of them had been "friendly" with Melon Bowersox, as they put it, and wanted to pump Billie Claire about her.

She enjoyed the company of Secret Service men. They were, to a man, good-looking. They were carefully selected for their appearance. As square as Billie Claire felt she was, around a Secret Service man she felt like the world's most sophisticated woman. They were mostly Irish Catholics from small towns, who, had luck not been running their way, would have been cops or Marines. Sometimes Billie Claire liked a night on the town with a group of them more than sitting around chewing over the day's events with a group of tired, half-smashed reporters. There was also the chance that one of them would take a shine to her. And an out-of-town fling with a Secret Service man was a lot less complicated than one with a man she would run into in the White House press room.

As it happened, she regretted what she had drunk, as she sat on the plane from Fort Worth to Dallas the next morning. And by the time she boarded the first press bus to follow the Presidential motorcade, her hangover had reached a very specific position in her frontal lobes. She eased herself into the second seat back, grateful to get a spot where she could see. Not that there was much to look at but the rear of the photographers' truck directly in front of them.

The warm early afternoon sun had been beating down on the parked bus, turning it into an oven. The President's open car was about ten cars away. If she had felt more energetic she would have chanced a quick run to the front of the motorcade before it pulled out to check the occupants' seating positions in the automobiles. She knew the President and Jackie were riding with the Governor of Texas. She wasn't clear about the Vice President's car, and who was riding with him. She assumed the press pool car was among the first four.

What's the difference? she thought, holding her throbbing head and cursing whoever it was who had suggested switching to margaritas at 2:00 A.M.

The bus finally got under way and moved slowly down the street. A few people were scattered along the curb waving. The reporters waved back. She dozed off for a moment and awakened with a start. Jim Mathis of the Newhouse syndicate was standing in the front of the bus, although she thought she had seen him take a seat about halfway back.

"The President's car just sped off," she heard him say to no one in particular. "Really gunned away."

Odd, she thought, craning to see around a bus that had moved in between them and the photographers' truck. She slumped back into her seat and reached into her purse for a crumpled copy of the speech the President would be making in a few minutes at the Trade Mart. Her eyes wouldn't focus. She put it back.

After the bus crept up to the Trade Mart and parked, Billie Claire stepped out into the boiling sun and fished helplessly through her purse for her sunglasses. A man ran past her, then another. Tom Wicker was right in front of her and she saw a man grab his arm and ask him something. Wicker shrugged and kept walking.

Billie Claire and the other reporters moved unhurriedly through the huge hall, each casually following the person in front, until they all arrived at the pressroom on the second floor. She always marveled at the efficiency with which Presidential traveling pressrooms were handled. They seemed to pop up overnight.

She remembered having to wait two weeks for the Chesapeake and Potomac Telephone Company to install her one little phone when she moved into 2500 Q Street, while an empty hall anticipating the traveling White House press corps could be completely vacant at sundown and by dawn be bristling with hundreds of telephones, all hooked up and connected to the outside world. Magic.

She looked out across the room. Long tables in neat rows covered with tablecloths sprouted instruments like mushrooms. By each phone was a chair and a typewriter, some of rather uncertain vintage. The Trade Mart pressroom would easily accommodate all the traveling journalists. Billie Claire dropped her handbag onto a chair, scribbled, "Hutchins /*D.C. Herald*" on a sheet of paper and snapped it under the paper guide of the old Remington. No telling how many "locals" would show up to cover the event and leave her without a machine or phone.

She had just begun an in-depth search for her sunglasses when she saw Marianne Means run over to a group of reporters who were standing by the back wall. She said something to them and they turned as one and started to run toward the door.

Instinctively, Billie Claire grabbed her bag and moved into the pushing, shoving pack that was trying to get through the door. As they ran down the long hall, she remembered Eddie Folliard's words when she first got the White House assignment. "Stay close to the man, B.C. Stay right up his tail. That's what you're here for. You never know what's going to happen."

It was now obvious that something *had* happened to him.

She came abreast of Doug Kiker of the *Herald Tribune*. Doug was tall and rangy; he was taking one step to her three.

"What the hell is going on, Doug?" she gasped. "Where is everyone going?"

"The President has been shot," he puffed, leaving her behind. Then, over his shoulder he yelled, "He's in Parkland Hospital. Get on the bus if you can." He sped away from her down the hall, his coattails flying.

She ran as fast as she could. Suddenly she saw a waiter rounding a corner carrying a large tray of food. The waiter saw the thundering pack bearing down on him, but he was unable to move out of the way. She could see that the waiter and Kiker were on a collision course. Kiker hit the man full force, spraying food into the air and off the walls.

Everyone kept running.

Adrenaline burst in the back of her skull with such force her breath came in uncontrollable gasps. Oh, shit! Oh, merciful God! Oh, please, goddammit! No, no. Stay with the man, Eddie had said. It hasn't happened. It *couldn't* happen! Some red-neck Bircher's taken a potshot. He's just nicked and the Secret Service is overreacting. He's okay, he's okay. Shit, my notebook. She instinctively reached around and pulled her shoulder bag close to her side. The underarms of her thin cotton blouse were great, dark, wet rings that clung to her bra.

She crawled aboard the press bus as it began to move. From inside, men were yelling, "Move it, move it! Go!" Some people tumbled into seats and others simply held on to anything stationary they could grab when the bus screamed out of the parking lot in low gear. Everyone was talking at once, many were swearing loudly. Some stood silently, trembling.

Within minutes they pulled into the emergency entrance of Parkland Hospital. The bus braked to a neck-wrenching halt, but not before reporters began to fling themselves out the open door. It came to a dead stop only feet from what Billie Claire knew was the Presidential car. From the window of the bus she could read the familiar license plate: GG300 District of Columbia.

Several sponges lay beside the plastic bucket by the rear bumper of the empty car. In a daze, Billie Claire hurried from the bus and ran to the car and looked down into the bucket. It was full of bloody water.

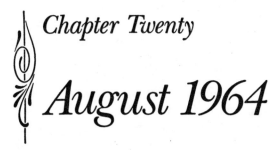

Chapter Twenty

August 1964

Allegra Farr's rented limousine made the trip to Atlantic City in just under three hours. As it pulled into the entrance of the Haddon Hall, the thick, hot August air of the seaside resort had already begun to ruin her hairdresser's careful work. The doorman snapped to attention and then broke into a trot when the huge black car glided to a stop.

He opened the door and Allegra stepped from the air-conditioned interior carrying her handbag and a matching makeup case. She vaguely gestured in the direction of the trunk. Two bellhops descended on the rear of the car and assisted both the doorman and the driver with her luggage. All four men were needed.

Allegra strode to the front desk and asked for the manager as the men made a return trip to the car for two hang bags full of long gowns, a four-foot trunk, several smaller cases, a circular box containing falls and hairpieces, a large duffle bag which held a collapsible professional hair drier and a valise the size of a man's two-suiter that contained daytime clothes. Each bag was covered by the tiny interlocking *G* pattern of Dr. Aldo Gucci.

As the pile of luggage was loaded onto two dollies, Allegra's beautiful straight nose was accosted by the smell of mildew. *That* she had *not* expected. She hated traveling alone, as it was. *Mildew?*

She hated the whole business of registering at a hotel, and, worse, the grubby act of tipping. She realized Seth could not arrive with her for the Democratic Convention, but she did feel that arrangements should have been made for someone, anyone, to meet her and take care of details.

The massive lobby was none the better for a fresh coat of paint. The faded reminder of once splendid decor and times was quite evident in the patched carpeting and dingy lighting and ancient chandeliers high above. Mr. Tash, the manager, came scurrying from some recess in back of the front desk, obviously fully aware that Miss Allegra Farr's arrival demanded his personal attention. His greeting fell just short of a slavish grovel.

Atlantic City had been a madhouse ever since the announcement had been made that the 1964 Democratic Convention would be held there. The faded old resort, once the epitome of society summer vacation spots, with its mammoth old hotels and access to a sweep of the Atlantic Ocean, had fallen upon hard times as the Federal highway system and air travel passed it by, making other Eastern resorts more accessible and more chic. With limited funds, the Atlantic City hotels had done the best they could during the past months. The inexperienced, hastily hired staffs could do little but try to cope with the demands of thousands of worldly people who planned to attend the convention. And, while each guest felt himself to be more important than the next, there were some things money simply couldn't buy, and the old city reeled under the onslaught on its inadequate hotels, restaurants and public facilities.

Seth had warned her. He had been dumbstruck when she announced her intention to go to Atlantic City for convention week. There had been a scene as he had tried to explain to her that the idea of entertaining with any style during the convention was out of the question. Nonetheless, as usual, Allegra had persevered, insisting that she could handle it. She only wanted to arrange a couple of parties. One small cocktail-buffet for some members of the President's Club, the exclusive group of political movers and shakers around Lyndon Johnson. The thousand-dollar "dues" the members paid would guarantee them certain privileges during convention week, and also, after Johnson was elected President in his own right. The buffet party, she was confident, the hotel staff could arrange.

324

The second party a day later was to be on a grander scale. For that Allegra told Seth she could call in caterers. And then, Chai and Chu would be there to take care of basics, and she couldn't imagine how things could *not* work out. Besides, she had no intention of missing the fun. Nobody who was anybody would remain in Washington when a Democratic Presidential Convention was being held so close by.

During the days of arguments Seth had tried to point out that he would not be available until late each night, that his presence would be required elsewhere. He was quite close to LBJ now, and there were many political matters to be seen to. Allegra countered with the argument that the entertaining would be good for her new business, provide new contacts for her, let people know she was serious about it.

Finally, he gave up and told Miss Wilton to make whatever arrangements she could: find Allegra the best suite in the best hotel and warn the staff to stand by.

Three days before she left, Chai announced that his daughter's baby's birth was imminent and the doctor expected complications. Chu must leave immediately for Baltimore to be with her daughter and she wouldn't go without Chai. Allegra told Chai and Chu that, of course, they must go, and she didn't tell Seth. She would be able to manage in Atlantic City, somehow. Surely the hotel would have people who could come in and set up a bar, for heaven's sake? The place was a beach resort, after all, and people would be much more informal and less demanding of social detail. She was serenely confident she could make do.

Mr. Tash led Allegra's entourage into the elevator and down the musty dark corridor to the top floor of the Haddon Hall. As she watched the seat of his blue serge suit shining ahead of her, her nose again crinkled with the smell of mildew, now accompanied by the smell of cleaning fluid and Lysol. New lighting fixtures, waiting final installation, hung lightless from naked wires in the walls. Indications of incomplete renovation were everywhere.

Mr. Tash unlocked the door and led her into a huge room with floor-to-ceiling windows that overlooked the sea.

Allegra was appalled.

Just possibly, the carpeting might have once been beige. Now it was bald and stained. There were water stains on the walls and ceiling, and from the door she could see paint chipping and curling around the window frames. She could also see a spring projecting from under an overstuffed chair.

"I don't believe this," she said to the bellman who was trying to push a dolly laden with the matched cases over the doorjamb. Another bellman scurried about the room, switching on lamps, two of which did not respond. He turned on the window air conditioner. It whirred, groaned and then heaved back into silence. She moved through the other rooms. A long hall separated the two adjoining bedrooms that contained only single beds and indifferent furniture from the thirties. One bedroom, as large as the living room, led out onto a wraparound terrace. The tile floor rattled as she walked to the outer railing. She glanced at the Atlantic Ocean and then stormed back inside.

"Impossible," she said flatly. "This simply will not do! Here . . . " She gestured toward the bellman who was unloading her bags. "Don't put them down. I'm not staying."

Mr. Tash was standing by a large television set with two missing knobs. "But, Miss Farr . . . "

"A prisoner of war wouldn't stay in a place like this. It is abominable. How much did you say these rooms rent for?"

Mr. Tash had suddenly gone gray under his yellowish tan. "Ah, well . . . During convention week this suite goes for five hundred dollars a day."

"Good Lord! Well, let's go. I will simply have to change my accommodations. Please show me what else you have."

Mr. Tash did not move. "Miss Farr, this is the Buckingham Suite. The very best we have."

"I don't care if it's Buckingham *Palace*. It must be the tackiest, most repellent place I've ever seen. Now, surely you have other suites?"

Mr. Tash looked as if he were about to cry. "Miss Farr, the hotel has been sold out for months. We have the Governor of Texas registered here. We have four Senators and the Italian Ambassador, all in quarters less . . . ah, less desirable than this suite. I'm afraid you will find the same situation at any hotel in the city. We are all doing the best we can."

Allegra sat down on a rump-sprung chair. "Could you at least try? Surely there is something. I mean, I do have some contacts in Washington who could perhaps . . .?"

"Miss Farr, Henry Luce tried to get this suite only this morning. We held it for you. We are well aware of your contacts."

Allegra was beaten and she knew it. She reached into her bag and extracted a sheaf of singles. She passed them out to the bellmen as if she were dealing a deck of cards. In seconds she was alone.

All right, you got yourself into this, now get yourself out. Even though Allegra was seldom confronted with a make-do situation, after a few minutes of panic she became quite calm.

First she threw open, or attempted to, every window in the suite. Might as well get some fresh air in here, if nothing else. She walked to the closest bath, undressing as she walked. As she stepped into the shower she turned the knob. One second, two seconds . . . a thin dribble of tepid water escaped from the shower nozzle, wetting her feet, and then receding. Nothing.

"Oh, dear God, what *next*?" she wailed, pushing back the shower curtain, which came off its rusted rings in her hand and dropped to the floor.

Wrapping herself in a threadbare hotel towel, she padded to the master bedroom and sat down on the single bed by the phone to think. On the scratch pad under the lamp she wrote HELP in large, balloon-shaped letters.

She spent the next hour on the phone. It took five minutes to get the hotel operator to answer her ring. There was no florist in the hotel, but she could give Allegra a number to call. No, she did not think the hotel had catering facilities available, and anyway, the staff was already putting together six receptions in the next three days. Allegra managed to reach Mr. Tash somewhere in the bowels of the building, only to be informed that he was terribly sorry, he was not aware that Miss Farr had plans to entertain such a large number of people, but, yes, they could send up ice and liquor. Food, of course, would have to be ordered a week in advance.

After the conversation with Mr. Tash the panic returned. She would look like a fool. She had mailed out invitations two weeks ago from Washington. She had invited the President's Club first, and then the next night was to be the reception for over a hundred! *Everyone* would be coming. What could she do? Turn them away at the door? Have them standing around in the shabby suite with no one to bartend or serve?

Maybe Miles? She reached for the phone and then realized that he had told her he would be taking in some shows in New York through the weekend. They had agreed to close the boutique for the week.

Oh, Lord, what can I *do?*

The sweat began to pour from under her arms and down her sides and back. The suite was sweltering. Not even the damp sea breeze could cool the top rooms at midday.

She reached for her address book on the foot of the bed. Another five-minute wait for the hotel operator, who was by now almost hysterical from the overload of calls. A mob must be milling around the desk, checking in. And once in their rooms, everyone wanted something from the one-woman switchboard. Why in God's name couldn't the hotel have at least put in dial phones?

"Hello, Petra?" She heard the note of panic in her own voice.

"Why, Miss Allegra! Haven't you left yet?" came the calm Scandinavian voice.

"Oh, Petra! I'm already in Atlantic City and it is a disaster! They've put me in a suite that should be condemned. There's no air conditioner. It smells so terrible I'm breathing through a towel. I can't get any help. I've got all those invitations out and I'm desperate."

"Oh, my dear! What will you do?"

"Petra, please help me!"

"But, my dear, how can I help you? I'm here in Washington."

"Petra, can you come up here? *Now?*"

"Miss Allegra, why? What could I possibly do for you there?"

"Petra, you've got to help me out. I'm going to look like a total fool. Seth warned me not to come, but I insisted. I *can't* lose face. Not with him. Not with all these people. How will it look? Washington's most glamorous hostess entertaining in a fleabag. No food, no help, no flowers, no ice. The gossips will have a field day. I'll die. I'll simply die of humiliation." She began to cry.

"Now, now, don't cry. Petra will come. I come now."

Allegra bounced up and down on the bed. "Oh, Petra, you are an angel. You *will* come? Right now? Hire a taxi. I'll pay for it. Anything. Rent a plane!"

"No. Petra will take a car. I drive. I will be there in a few hours. Everything will be okay."

"Petra, I love you. I will make this up to you."

Allegra hung up the phone and fell back on the one lumpy pillow. It smelled, too, but thank God Petra was always so sure of herself, so knowledgeable. She would fix everything. Somehow.

She glanced at her Piaget. Two P.M. Odd that Petra would be home at that hour. She usually had appointments until well into the late afternoon. Allegra dismissed it. What's the difference? She's coming. Allegra walked hopefully to the second bathroom. She turned the shower handle and a slow stream of water came from the nozzle. It was even warm.

She got through the night in the lumpy single bed and slept until nearly eleven o'clock the next morning when she heard voices from the living room, things being pushed about. Over it all she could hear Petra Jensen's commanding voice giving orders.

The older woman had arrived just after dark the evening before. She had insisted that Allegra have a long, relaxing massage and take a little yellow pill "for your nerves," and go right to bed. From somewhere in the hotel Petra had summoned hot soup and a bottle of chilled rosé. Allegra was asleep before ten.

She walked to the master closet where Petra had hung her gowns and daytime clothes. Her evening slippers and shoes were in a neat row at the bottom of the closet. Her makeup and beauty supplies were in neat rows on the dresser. She pulled on a caftan and walked toward the commotion in the living room.

She could not believe what she saw. Petra was only a few inches taller than Allegra, and was certainly no muscle-bound Amazon, yet there she was, lifting one side of the worn sofa. A man in gray work clothes was lifting the other side. Between them they got it out into the hall and stepped aside for two men carrying in a long modern sofa covered in a fresh floral print. Matching chairs were already in the room, as well as other furniture Allegra had not seen before. Another man crouched beside the air conditioner, tools from a metal box strewn about him on the floor.

The room was awash with flowers.

"You like?" Petra asked, returning to the room, her face red from exertion and pride.

Allegra stood with her mouth open. "Where in God's name did all this come from?"

"I rent," Petra said as she started to tug at the ancient television set.

"Here, let me do that." The workman took over and hauled it

out into the hall. "We'll have a new one up here before noon, Miss Jensen."

"You *rented* all this?" Allegra slowly looked around the room. Except for the worn carpeting, it looked almost livable.

"*Ya.* I call furniture company in Ventnor. Got it from Yellow Pages. They come right away."

"But the flowers? There isn't a florist in the hotel."

"Oh, yes. And more are coming for your other rooms. I get from Yellow Pages, too. Bartenders coming. They will be here by five, and some maids, also, they say. Good, no?"

"*Good?* Petra you are a genius!" Allegra squealed, still unable to believe it all. "How did you find *them?*" She nodded toward the workmen.

"When you go to sleep, I talk with the assistant manager. I gave him a bribe to help me," she said matter-of-factly. "He introduced me to the headwaiter in the restaurant downshairs. I tell him we pay fifty dollars an hour for help, and he got me six young men and two maids. From the union, he say." She winked. "They come for both nights. Food, also. I call from Yellow Pages. Restaurants, *ya?* I order all the food. Some Italian, some Chinese, some French, some hot dogs, even. Lots of food."

Allegra sat down on the new sofa. "Petra, this is a miracle. You have saved my life."

With a whoosh the air conditioner came to life. The workman stood back proudly and surveyed his work.

"The bedrooms, now," Petra commanded. "They're broke, too. You fix, *ya?*"

The workman nodded and picked up his tools.

"And how did you find *him?*"

"I go to the basement and find that one last night. He say he come for hundred dollars."

Allegra rose and walked to Petra and threw her arms around her. "Petra, thank you. Thank you so *much.* I hadn't *dreamt* of all this when I called you."

Petra pushed her away good-naturedly. "It is nothing. Mr. Hathaway wants things to be right for you. You must have place right for people, to give nice parties. Now. You go get ready for hairdresser."

"Hairdresser?"

330

"*Ya.* I call. He come to make you pretty for tonight. The salt air. Very bad for hair."

"Oh, Petra." Allegra felt like a little girl who was loved and cared for by someone who took complete charge and made everything come out happily ever after. She lounged for a long time in her bath.

People began to arrive shortly after seven. The convention opened at that hour, and while the official delegates and the television press milled around on the floor of the arena, the people on Allegra's guest list had no need to be present in the convention hall this early in the proceedings.

Petra's put-together staff, mostly local college boys, had arrived by five. The bars were quickly set up, one in each of the larger rooms and one on the terrace. Petra had even found a man to come in and somehow glue down most of the loose tiles that might trip a guest.

As two Senators and their wives were shown into the room by one of the college boys wearing dark trousers and tie and a white shirt, Allegra stood by the tall windows, cool and serene. Her thin white caftan barely showed the outlines of her lovely body. The hairdresser had arranged her pale hair into a high French twist and tucked one white orchid into the swirl at the top of her head. Her only jewelry was the enormous carbouchon emerald earrings Seth had given her for her last birthday.

She greeted the Senators and their wives and then moved regally toward the next couple entering the suite. She kissed Scooter and Dale Miller, who were longtime Texas friends of the Johnsons and then greeted the people behind them and introduced the Millers. She had heard the rumor that Dale Miller very much wanted to be Chief of Protocol. She knew it would be wise to be especially nice to him.

The evening proceeded without a mishap. The air conditioners worked, the bar was bountifully stocked and the food was excellent and plentiful if somewhat eclectic. It was not until the last group of guests had seated themselves before the television set to watch the convention that Allegra realized that Petra had not been in evidence for at least an hour. Petra had moved quietly and unobtrusively around the suite during the early evening, seeing to the tables and the bars, checking supplies and quietly giving orders to the help. She had changed from her pants suit into the white uniform she always wore when she came to give Allegra her massage. She neither mingled nor spoke to the guests, but simply went about her work. Anyone who noticed her would have assumed she was the supervisor of some local catering service.

Guests thanked Allegra profusely as they left, raving about her minimiracle, and the fact that *only* Allegra Farr could have put together such an evening in this impossible place.

The last people to leave were Texans. There had been an almost total Texas atmosphere to the party. It was noisy and boisterous. A lot of food was dropped on the carpet and on the terrace, and several glasses were broken.

"Now I know Camelot is gone forever," she said to her reflection as she began to unpin her hair in front of the bedroom mirror.

"Here, let me do that," Petra said, as she suddenly materialized behind her.

Allegra turned, startled. "Where have you *been?*"

"I sit in kitchen," Petra said, gently pulling the orchid from Allegra's hair and plucking out the silver hairpins.

She had completely forgotten the tiny hall-like room next to the master bathroom. "The *kitchen!* Oh, Petra, why on earth would you sit in there?"

"It was your party, Miss Allegra. You heard what they all say when they leave? You are the most perfect hostess."

"No, not me, Petra. You did it. You did it all. If only Seth could have gotten here. What a bore having to have dinner with the Connallys. He would have been so proud of me . . . and of you."

"You do not tell him about me." She began to brush Allegra's hair. "He will hear from *everybody* that you do this. It should be that way. You like me to brush your hair?"

"I love it, Petra. Miles always does it, but I like the way you do it better."

Allegra lay awake for a long time marveling at how beautifully the party had gone and how Seth would react when he learned of it. She knew Jane would mention it to everyone she spoke to. She would tell Seth somehow. Jane was so thoughtful.

She felt a little uneasy taking total credit for the success of the evening. Petra had actually done it all, but she seemed so insistent that no one know. How wonderful it was to have someone so organized to lean on and to trust. Petra had met and overcome what could have been a major disaster. And the success of the big party the next evening was completely assured, with Petra overseeing every detail.

Surely there must be something she could do for that incredible Danish woman, that saving angel who, hardly knowing Allegra, had swooped down into her life and smoothed out lumps and swept away the crumbled pieces? The party and its arrangements would cost Seth a small fortune. But that didn't matter. What mattered was showing Petra, in some unique and appropriate way, how sincerely grateful to her she was.

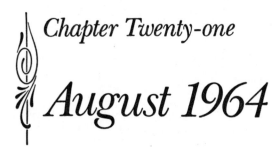

Chapter Twenty-one

August 1964

Jane checked into her seedy room at the Dennis an hour before Allegra's party at the Haddon Hall was to begin. She took in the amenities. Essentially, there were two: a firm double bed and a recently reappointed bathroom.

She shrugged. From what she had heard in Washington about Atlantic City, she was grateful.

A message had awaited her at the desk. Paul would pick her up at seven. That did not give her much time to unpack, shower, completely redo her makeup and dress.

She was trying to pull up the zipper of the new shantung cocktail dress she had bought the day before at Garfinkel's when Paul called from the lobby.

"Darling," she said, struggling with the zipper, "come up and zip me up."

"Instantly," he replied and hung up the house phone.

After five minutes in Allegra's large suite, Jane realized that everyone in every room was "someone of consequence," and that Paul knew them all. He escorted her from Congressman to Senator to news executives from both Washington and New York, to LBJ favorites and JFK holdovers, introducing her to every man and a few women. She already knew many of the people, but that did not stop Paul Hyram Sayer. His determination that she become a successful independent "consultant" was only a little less than her own.

It had been Paul who had suggested she open her own office after she had told him she could no longer bear to remain at the White House.

The days after John Kennedy was killed in Dallas she had remained in her apartment, drapes drawn, the only illumination coming from the flickering television set. Along with millions of other people, she stared at the screen with horror and disbelief.

Paul phoned that terrible Friday afternoon, but Jane did not want to talk. Not with him, not with anyone. By the following Friday, he was so concerned about her emotional state, he insisted she come up to New York for a few days to sort things out. She consented, caught the shuttle and checked into the suite he had reserved for her at the St. Regis.

During their last dinner together in Manhattan before she flew back to confront her future in Washington, Paul broached the subject of just exactly what did she plan to do?

She told him she was convinced President Johnson would be bringing in his own people for staff jobs, and the chances for Kennedy holdovers at her level were precarious.

"I could use you in Washington myself, Jane," he said offhandedly.

"Use me? Good heavens, how?"

"Well, the firm represents a great many people who need representation in Washington. Information, introductions."

She laughed. "I'd never thought of myself as Jane Connor, Lobbyist, before." But she could see he was quite serious.

"Is that such an uncomfortable idea? You know very well that the Federal government is an amorphous swarm of people and agencies and committees to people outside Washington. My God, the amount of red tape to be cut through for the smallest transaction is awesome. Corporations, law firms, individuals with business before Congress or the regulatory agencies are in perpetual need of someone who can pick up a phone, have a few words with a contact and get done what they want done."

"Hmm. But do I know enough people, Paul?"

336

He nodded. "You know all of the Kennedy people and a lot of the Johnson people. Where do you think all the Kennedy men are going to go? Back to Harvard or Wall Street? No. They will be setting themselves up right there in Washington. Johnson will be bringing in new men very few people will know. He'll eventually reshuffle the whole system. You'll be able to tell outsiders who to talk with at Interior, and how much clout so-and-so has at the FCC. Knowing the names and the men is enormously valuable to out-of-towners."

"Yes, I do know a lot of people. But I'd never before thought of using it that way."

"Well, try," he smiled. "Now, let me make you a business proposition that has nothing to do with my lust for your long blond body."

"Paul, you shock me," she said with mock horror.

Within the month, Jane resigned from her job at the White House. In another month the little public relations pocket operation in E.O.B. 240 would self-destruct anyway. But she felt a resignation was good manners. After all, the entire Cabinet had offered to resign when Lyndon Johnson became President. Much to her surprise, he asked most of them to stay on. For the appearance of continuity.

Paul set up a commercial account at Union Trust Bank and saw to the incorporation papers so that she would be, as he put it, "legitimate." She rented a small two-room office suite in the Press Building and had stationery printed in dignified black, engraved type which read, "Jane Connor and Associates, Inc., Consultants."

When Melon asked Jane who her associates were, Jane laughed: "Anyone I care to associate with," and swiveled around in her new high-backed leather chair behind her new polished desk.

Immediately, Paul introduced her to several of his clients. One was the manufacturer of industrial equipment who needed to be kept informed about the activities in the Department of Labor, as well as several Congressional committees. The other was a strange little man who had made a great deal of money in real-estate speculation and who now wanted to "acquire things."

The little man was a passionate right-winger who wanted to gain control of radio stations, magazines and small newspapers. Jane was retained to keep out her antennae for media properties he could purchase "blind" and then attempt to impose a different editorial "slant."

Jane shrugged. For her services to just the strange, rich little reactionary, she received a monthly retainer and billable expenses that amounted to more than twice what she had made as a GS-15.

After four months she had nine clients.

She was able to pay all of Nat's hospital and funeral bills, the loan from Paul was repaid and she began to enjoy an affluence she had never before known. She could walk into a store and buy Anne Klein suits and blazers, retail, cash.

She reveled in being her own boss and was astonished by her success. She did, though, find it difficult to explain, simply, what her job was to unsophisticated non-Washingtonians. But those who knew, immediately understood what she meant when she said she was a "Washington rep." They did not blink and say, "For whom?" They realized that for people who made their living peddling influence, the question was definitely bad form. It was rather like asking a doctor who his patients were.

Jane didn't know where it would all lead, and she didn't especially care. For the first time that she could ever remember, she was having fun and being paid for it.

By the time of the Democratic National Convention in August she could "case" a social gathering as well as any lobbyist who had been "consulting" in Washington for a quarter of a century. She could tell, two minutes after her arrival, if there was any business to be done in the room.

At Allegra Farr's party at the Haddon Hall there was nothing *but* business to be done. No one, it seemed, came to a national convention without a deal to be put together, an action to be instigated or a score to settle.

She watched Paul talking with a Johnson crony, Representative Homer Thornberry, and realized she felt deeply grateful to her distinguished patron. She knew better than to confuse gratitude with love. She did not love him. She was comfortable with him and he with her. Paul was accepting of her; he was amusing and amused. They had been together for so long she had forgotten what deep, mindless passion felt like. For the present, life was pleasant, and certainly not emotionally complicated.

They remained at Allegra's until the last guests, after bestowing the most sincere compliments on their hostess, lurched off. Jane and Paul took dinner at an unpretentious seafood restaurant on the Boardwalk.

The thick and humid sea air, the good food and the crowded party left Jane exhausted. As she turned back the bedspread on the firm double bed, she hoped Paul would simply fall asleep and not reach for her in the darkness.

He began to caress her the moment he came to bed, and they made love in the quiet way of lovers who have ceased to surprise each other.

Paul had a breakfast appointment with some civil liberties lawyers in the restaurant of his hotel. He was showered and dressed before Jane realized it *was* the next morning.

He slipped into a crisp seersucker jacket and leaned down to give her a light good-bye kiss. "I've called room service for you. God knows when they'll be up with it, though."

She thanked him and blew a kiss toward the closing door.

Over the sound of the running shower she heard the rattle of a room service cart in the bedroom. She pushed open the sliding door several inches and called, "Who's there?"

"Room service, ma'am."

"Christ, don't you knock?" she yelled, looking frantically for something to cover herself with.

"Sorry, ma'am," came a disembodied voice with an odd Southern accent, almost like a white man trying to imitate a black man, "the door was unlocked."

Through the rippled glass of the shower stall she could now see a figure standing in the door of the bathroom.

She mustered her most indignant voice and tried to quell the panic that had welled up in her throat. "I'll thank you to leave the check in the other room." Christ, why hadn't she checked the lock, or at least closed the bathroom door?

"What are you doing in there?" The voice had changed to a kind of little-boy quizzical whine.

"I beg your pardon!" She was now crouched as far back in the corner of the shower as she could get, holding a ridiculously small hotel washcloth against her stomach. "Get out!" she shouted at the cloudy figure three feet from the glass. "Get out of here, *now!*"

"But I don't want to. I want to come in and play with you."

Suddenly, she recognized the voice.

"Sam! Sam Kazin! Is that you?"

"Can I come in and play now, please?"

"What in God's name are you doing in my *bathroom?*"

"Delivering your breakfast," he said, pushing the shower door back two inches farther and peering in.

"Get out of here, you rat," she said, laughing from relief, and in spite of herself.

"No, I want in," he said and reached for the faucet. A blast of cold water hit her square in the face.

Before she could locate the faucet with her eyes squeezed shut, he had stripped and was pushing his way into the shower with her. The stream of water hit his neck and was diverted away from her. He put one arm around her waist and reached for the soap tray with the other hand. He began sudsing her back and arms and buttocks with the tiny sliver of hotel soap.

"Come to make Missy *clean,*" he said, imitating a B movie retarded servant, his eyes rolling. "Missy need Igor. Igor like way Missy feel. Missy very slippery now."

Jane almost gagged when she choked with laughter as the water poured into her mouth. "This is insane. This is ridiculous. Rape!"

"Oh, Missy want rape, too?"

Suddenly Jane stopped laughing. He was kissing her and his hands were sliding over her body with an intensity and ardor she had not experienced since San Antonio and Sean. When he entered her, she clung to him and gasped. She gave herself up to the slippery grace of their bodies moving together and apart, the pulse of the water streaming about their heads and shoulders and backs.

Sam had bribed the hall porter as her breakfast tray was being pushed toward her room. He couldn't believe his good luck when he found the door to the room unlocked. He hadn't planned to greet her in quite the way he had, as he explained,

"Opportunity is something I have learned to adapt to rather quickly." He was leaning against the side of the bathroom door, a bath towel wrapped around his middle.

"I'll say." Jane ran a comb through her dripping hair and twisted it up onto the top of her head. "You are going to get yourself killed one of these days, you nut."

"And for what better cause?" He moved toward her again and pulled the towel away from his waist. "Umm." He nuzzled her damp neck. "Igor want more."

Exhausted and tingling, Jane raised herself on one elbow and looked at her travel alarm clock. "Sam, it's nearly noon! I have a lunch date!"

Sam Kazin raised his head from where it had been buried in two pillows, but left his arm where it was, tightly holding her to him.

"With whom?" he asked matter-of-factly.

"Sam! That's none of your beeswax, as we used to say."

"None of your cute Sayings from the Goyim, if you don't mind. What idiotic phrases you people have. Let's see, there's 'Golly gee whiz,' and 'Heavens to Betsy.' Beeswax! Arghh!" he moaned and covered his eyes. "What are you going to have for lunch? A salami and mayo on white bread with some Fig Newtons?"

"How can you make hasty generalizations about me like that?" she laughed, and swung her legs over the side of the bed.

Sam rolled toward her and tried to pull her back down onto the bed. "I've always felt that hasty generalizations are one of the real pleasures of civilized discourse."

"But you don't really know anything about me."

"I know everything I need to know," he said, sitting up and reaching for the phone. "Room service? Room 1227. Two bottles of Moët, chilled, please. Not frigid." He paused. "As soon as possible."

"What are you doing?"

"Ordering champagne, obviously."

"But I said I have to leave."

"You don't have to do anything you don't want to do."

"I have to honor my social and professional commitments."

"Bullshit. You now have a better offer."

"Life isn't quite that simple, Sam."

"Yes, it is. Now, who are you not having lunch with?"

"I *am* having lunch with my *lover*," she said angrily.

341

"Correction. You are *not* having lunch with your *ex*-lover. Your ex-lover is that old fart you told me about, right?"

"Goddammit, Sam. Paul Sayre is a very prominent and influential Wall Street lawyer."

"Who, I bet, wears slipper socks and says things like, 'insofar as,' and 'notwithstanding.' Further, he probably laughs at your jokes whether they are truly funny, knows two positions in bed and wears a Cartier watch *over* his shirt cuff. You are well rid of him. You don't need to go out for food. We have plenty right here." He gestured toward the breakfast tray resting beside the bathroom door where he had left it three hours before.

Jane walked toward it naked and lifted the warmer covering one plate. "Yuck! It has all congealed to slime. I wouldn't eat that mess if it were the only food on earth."

The phone rang several times during the afternoon, and all but once, it fell silent and unanswered. Looking back, Jane remembered no meal more delicious than congealed scrambled eggs, stale croissants and warm champagne.

The next morning she swore she would never see Sam Kazin again. The intensity of their time together frightened her. Jane now realized Sam was an all-or-nothing man. She did not intend to *be* all for any man, nor see a man as *all* for herself. Not with the good life she was living, for the first time.

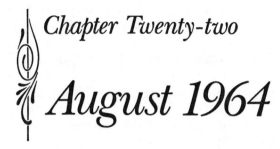

Chapter Twenty-two

August 1964

Jesus Christ, he's going to kill us all.

Billie Claire reached inside the neckline of her sleeveless linen shift and frantically yanked at a bra strap that had begun to slide down her arm. She was soaked through. Just ahead of her she could see circles of sweat spreading through the fabric of Rufus Youngblood's baggy, brown, storebought suit.

The President's "personal" Secret Service man trudged on and Billie Claire trudged after him. It was eighty-nine degrees. The air hung over Washington in a moist yellow haze that coated her skin with a film that felt like mucilage. The searing pavement burned through the soles of her open pumps as she marched with the pack of other reporters around and around the White House oval driveway.

She was too far away from the tall, rangy President to hear whatever in hell he was saying as he happily strode along. May Craig had his right side covered and Marianne Means was on his left. Three dozen other sweating White House reporters were bunched behind them. President Johnson increased his pace. She broke into a stumbling trot and muttered curses.

Shit! The man could be declaring World War III and she couldn't hear it. Some beat. Thanks a lot, Ernie.

Lyndon Baines Johnson was full of beans today. Thirteen laps around the oval drive, well over an hour of puffing and sweating. Up front, his two little beagles, Him and Her, were yapping and pulling on their leashes.

"Lord forgive me for ever complaining about Jackie," she said within earshot of Pete Lisagor.

He gave her a weak smile. A ring of sweat darkened the collar of his light blue shirt.

"Goddammit," she said loudly when someone clipped her arch.

For a moment she stopped and hopped on the uninjured foot. After the pain lessened a little she hurried to catch up.

And she had been thrilled when Ernie had told her she was being assigned full time to cover the President! No more teas and beautification stories on the First Lady. Only hard news now. Presidential news. Front-page stuff. But she certainly had not figured on Lyndon Johnson. When he had been Vice President she had hardly noticed him. Now he was the thirty-sixth President of the United States, and he was dynamic, driving, imaginative and infuriating.

These walks had been dubbed Death Marches by the White House press corps. The President delighted in their discomfort. With no warning, he would bolt from his office and yell through the West Wing at the scatter of reporters who were lounging and chatting, "Y'all want to take a walk today?" Then he would move smartly through the outside doors. In the mad scramble that followed, Secret Service men and reporters leaped up and tumbled over each other in order to keep up. Anything the man said might be copy, instant and hard news.

Today's topic was the Democratic National Convention. LBJ was to make his triumphant appearance at the Convention Hall in Atlantic City at an as yet undetermined hour that night. No one had been able to find out when.

This was a typical Johnson tactic, Billie Claire had discovered early on in his Administration. Never telegraph your shot. Never tell anyone what you're going to do ahead of time. It saved explanations if he changed his mind. He kept as many options open as he possibly could, and, she was convinced, one of his goals was to keep the press off balance and drive them mad with uncertainty.

Also, LBJ could not bear to be second-guessed. Billie Claire had heard that after word leaked out that he was going to appoint a prominent man to an important post, Johnson appointed someone else. The leak had cost a good man a high position. *Nobody* second-guessed LBJ.

His appearance before the convention tonight *(whenever* that was to be) would be the closest the country had yet come to a coronation. Billie Claire had been hearing stories all week about how Johnson had choreographed the entire extravaganza in Atlantic City. About how he had been torturing poor Hubert and even Tom Dodd with the second spot on the ticket, dangling it and then pulling it away. It was coming down to tonight and he wanted his presence before the delegates to achieve maximum drama. The only remaining suspense was his choice of a running mate.

The pathetic band was now halfway through the fourteenth lap of the driveway. That came to nearly four miles in the pressing August heat, someone calculated. Everyone scribbled down the information.

Billie Claire was becoming increasingly annoyed. For hours before the "walk" began, she and everyone else in the press corps had been asking anyone they could collar *when* the President was leaving for the convention. No one knew.

She had made an appointment with her hairdresser for five thirty. She could just get in a quick set and comb out and be able to make it to Andrews before eight, depending . . . depending on this maddening man.

She had already missed at least one of Allegra's parties, and the word that had come back was that she was bringing off miracles at the Haddon Hall.

Then there was her brother. Nicky had been elected an alternate delegate from New York. He was very much excited about his first public venture into national politics, and his firm considered this an excellent opportunity for his career's advancement. Nicky was a very ambitious man. Billie Claire had been looking forward to at least a lunch with him. He was invariably full of gossip, and relayed it in her view far more wittily than Melon.

The weary, sweating group of reporters marched onward. Out of the corner of her eye she saw the *Boston Globe* and the *Philadelphia Inquirer* stumble off and collapse under a shade tree farther west on the broad lawn. She persisted. The President was saying something about Speaker McCormack's performance as convention chairman. He was chuckling away and speaking only to those in his immediate presence.

One helluva way to inform the Free World, she panted to herself.

After ninety-five minutes and fifteen full laps around the driveway, the Death March ended. The President turned to the purple-faced people who managed to cross the finish line with him and, singling out the women, handed each a newly struck medal the size of a silver dollar and bearing his profile.

"Ah'm going to give you a medal," he drawled as he dropped one into Billie Claire's wet hand.

Stunned, she slipped it into her bag and joined the rest of the band as it trooped back to the pressroom.

At four that afternoon the word was passed to the pressroom that the President would emplane for Atlantic City within the hour. Senators Humphrey and Dodd would be on the plane with him. That was the very first word.

She immediately phoned Ernie. He told her he was cutting her loose from the White House press corps while she was in Atlantic City, because he had enough floor coverage. He wanted her to do feature material at the convention. That meant she did not have to sit up in the press gallery high above the convention floor, or camp in the lobby of the Pageant Motel across from Convention Hall, where the Johnson entourage had set up its command post—in all one hundred and twenty rooms.

When Billie Claire walked onto the floor of Convention Hall, Governor John Connally was making the first nominating speech for Lyndon Baines Johnson. She stood transfixed for several moments. She had seen national political conventions on television and in films, but those had not prepared her for the spectacle and immediacy of the actuality. She was still in a daze and blinking from the brilliant lights when she watched California's Governor, Pat Brown, take the podium. Suddenly the thundering strains of "Happy Days Are Here Again" exploded from a huge pipe organ.

The demonstration for Lyndon had begun. On cue, the delegates went berserk. The smoky air was filled with the sound of klaxons and cheering, the sight of tiny parachutes bearing Ameri-

346

can flags, bobbing sunflower posters from Kansas, gold-foil sunbursts from California and real stalks of corn from Iowa.

The press pass and total-access floor pass that dangled from her neck permitted her to move wherever she wanted, without restraint. Theoretically. For the moment she was only able to move her elbows a few inches away from her sides. She braced herself against a metal chair as screaming, chanting, joyous LBJ delegates shoved and danced past her.

Ernie had yelled into the phone that he wanted her to get an interview with John Connally. "Just get to him, Billie. He'll be happy to talk to the *Herald*. I want an in-depth feature." He had then told her LBJ had caused a memorial film on John Kennedy to be moved forward and shown *after* the nominations. Lyndon did not want emotional delegates to become overwhelmed by the moment and do anything rash—like decide Bobby should be the Vice Presidential nominee. John Connally, though, would make a good tie-in between the Kennedys and the cowboys. The handsome governor had narrowly missed assassination himself in John F. Kennedy's open car in Dallas.

Billie Claire climbed up on a chair and tried to see who was on the platform. She could see only a small part of the bunting-draped stage.

Terrific! Go find John Connally in all this and request a quiet, sit-down chat. Now she couldn't even climb down from her chair. She realized she was deep in the Iowa delegation and trapped. Helplessly, she searched the crowds for someone else with dangling press credentials who could help her escape. No one in sight. Just a sea of polyester suits, straw hats and corn.

She braced her calves against the back of the metal chair as the delegates roared their approval to nominate Johnson by acclamation. Up on the platform she caught sight of Lady Bird and Lucy and Lynda Bird standing beside the tall President. Lyndon Johnson stepped to the microphones and "suggested" the delegates select Hubert Humphrey as his running mate, and, evidently, stepped back. She couldn't see.

Billie Claire managed to climb down from the chair and shove through bodies into what seemed to be an aisle. A mass of people was slowly flowing in one direction, and she hoped the flow would move past an exit from the main floor.

347

Suddenly she was grabbed from behind and lifted off her feet. She screamed and twisted until she could see who was holding her. She looked down into the handsome, smiling face of her brother.

"Gotcha!" he shouted above the music and cheering.

"Nickeeee!" She squealed, threw her arms around his neck and held on. "Oh, Nicky. Save me!" She was laughing now.

"Absolutely. Come on." He put her down, grabbed her hand and, like a football blocker, battered through the happy throng to a relatively unpopulated corridor at the edge of the floor.

"What are you doing down *here?*" She straightened her clothes and beamed at her brother. She was proud of her necklace of press credentials, happy he could see her in the act of being a reporter.

"Don't ask. We alternates are supposed to be up there in the peanut gallery." He gestured toward a bank of seats high above the floor. "I didn't have much trouble wangling a floor pass. Let's get out of here. The big moment's over."

"Nicky, I'm supposed to be working. My editor wants me to track down Governor Connally."

In this zoo? He's probably already back at his hotel, soaking in his bathtub. Come on, let's grab something to eat. You can look him up later."

"But, Nicky, I'm on *assignment!*"

"Move." He gave her a little shove toward the long ramp that led out of the hall.

The main dining room at the Claridge Hotel was jammed. People were waiting ten deep in front of the maître d's post at the door. Billie Claire watched her brother slip through the dense crowd to the head of the line, bend his silver-blond head toward the harassed maître d, speak intently and then flash his enchanting smile.

Watching him, she thought, God, he's a beautiful man. And he didn't just sit back and *use* it. He was thoughtful and hardworking and cultivated. He always acted as if he were unaware of his natural looks and charm and their effect on the most worldly men and women.

Never, even as a child, had she been jealous of her brother, had she wished him to be other than he was. Sometimes, though, in the darkest, most private hours of night, she permitted herself to resent her own plainness. She did not resent her brother's attractiveness. She did wonder about God's whimsy. In a world that treasured and rewarded physical beauty in women, why had *Nicky* been given skin like Carrara marble, teeth as even, white and straight as a Cossack captain's? They had both been formed in the same womb, why were they so different? Why couldn't God have doled out something to her? Long lashes, maybe? Would emerald eyes with a few tiny flecks of gold have upset some universal master plan? Shit. Maybe the day she was conceived He was fresh out of emerald eyes with gold flecks and long lashes. At least *one* Hutchins had not been overlooked.

Sometimes when she was feeling sorry for herself and wishing she looked other than she did, she recalled one of Jane's stories. Job was angry with the Lord for his condition and crying out to Him in anguish, "Why me, oh, Lord? Why me?" Job received an answer from on high. "I don't know. Something about you just pisses me off." The corners of Billie Claire's mouth involuntarily curled up in a small, sad smile.

She became aware of the maître d's arm. He was holding it straight up and he was nodding toward her. Nicky, of course, had managed a table.

They squeezed into a small curved booth in the back of the huge hotel dining room. The place was packed with press people, lobbyists, Congressman, Senators and delegates. Before the waiter arrived to take their drink orders, several very beautiful women stopped at their table to say hello to Nicky. They barely acknowledged his introduction of his sister, her press credentials still hanging from her neck.

Nicky was finally able to order their drinks. After the waiter hurried off, he took both of her hands in his. "Now, Sweet Pea, tell me what you're up to."

"I've already told you, I'm on assignment."

"Listen, Pearl Mesta is throwing one of her huge things out in some mansion in Ventnor tonight. Wanna go?" He released her hands, reached into his coat pocket and flashed a heavy, cream-colored card at her.

"Nicky, you've got to be kidding. At this very moment I'm supposed to be interviewing the Governor of Texas. If Ernie knew I was sitting here with you, he'll kill me."

"Come on, love. Nobody really *works* at these things. This is a joke, a show. The only departure from the script has been the ruckus about the Mississippi delegates."

"Well, I work, dammit. And if I don't find John Connally before tomorrow morning, I won't have to worry about working for a long, long time."

"So, what's the big deal about Connally."

"Some people see him as a kind of bridge between JFK and LBJ. His being shot also, and all. Anyway, now he's become a kingmaker for his old pal, Lyndon. Christ, I don't know. Ernie wants me to interview him and see if he'll say something that will indicate which people will be in and which people . . ."

"I don't know that yellow is the best color for you, Billie."

"What?" She stared, startled, at him over the rim of her old-fashioned.

"That dress. It doesn't do a lot for your skin."

"I don't understand. What does the color yellow and my skin have to do with Governor Connally and the last of Camelot, for God's sake?"

"Nothing, really, I'm sorry. I was just looking at you and wondering about your life. Are you happy, Bees?"

He hadn't called her that in years. It was his kid name for her, just as she used to call him Nicko. "Why, yes, I am. I'm excited about my work. My God, I'm covering the President of the United States, and this is a promotion."

"But, are you *happy*?"

She shrugged. "I haven't thought about *happy*. Right now I feel pretty good about myself. If you mean, am I in love, no. Does someone love me? No."

"Probably just as well. Sometimes loving and being loved gets to be a pain in the ass. Especially when you have five or six loves going on all at the same time."

"I wouldn't object to just *one*. By the way, are you aware of those two women three tables to your right? I think they're trying to catch your attention."

He glanced at them. They were with a party of seven. Five male delegates and the two women. "Them? They are very high-priced New York hookers, darling baby sister."

"Oh, cut it out, Nick. They're models or actresses. Look at them. The blonde's clothes must be worth a thousand dollars. Not counting *jewelry* ."

350

"So? Hookers don't get paid in chopped liver."

Then you've seen them before? Don't tell me you've begun to *pay* for it?"

"Hardly. If I've lost the magic touch, I'm not aware of it."

"Indeed. I saw that picture of you in *Women's Wear Daily* with the Countess What's Her Name."

"Good God—*her*," he laughed. "Can you imagine the following combination—thirteen million dollars, a doctor of philosophy from the Sorbonne, a graduate of Cordon Bleu"—he raised his brow—"you've seen her picture, also gorgeous? Charlotte, in addition, happens to be insecure and an utter nymphomaniac." He shook his head. "*Nothing* satisfies that poor woman."

"She *is* gorgeous."

"That was a particularly unflattering photograph."

Billie Claire sipped her drink and wondered what a *flattering* photograph of herself would look like. "Between parties in the Hamptons and the tug and pull of the jet set, when do you find time to practice law?"

"It's all part of the same game, B.C." He sighed wearily. "Just like being an alternate delegate. The backroom boys in Manhattan got together and pointed their collective cigar at me and said, 'You, boy. Get yo tail to Atlantic City and act enthusiastic for Lyndon.' A useless exercise in principle, and very helpful, in fact. I manage to shuffle papers at the firm and also get my picture in *Women's Wear Daily*."

Billie Claire tried not to look self-conscious and graceless. Unlike Nicky, she had not been adored since Breath One. "Don't you ever fall sincerely in love with any of those beautiful women?"

"Dearest, one doesn't fall in love with women like Charlotte. One *wears* women like Charlotte."

"Well, *one* doesn't fall in love with women like me, either." She realized, unhappily, she was permitting her momentary dejection to show.

"Now, now." He touched her cheek, very briefly, then withdrew his hand. "You have many wonderful qualities. Stop putting yourself down. You are smarter than most, you are good and . . . kind to others."

"And plain. Right?" He wasn't able to come up with even a "nice-looking," or a "pretty." He probably had no idea how much worse his "good . . . and kind . . . " made her feel. He was accustomed to women who took their beauty for granted. "I'm sorry, Nicky. Let's discuss something other than my appearance."

He shook his head. "No. You must be fair to yourself. I think you have a tendency not to try quite as hard as you might. I mean, you should try for a little more polish, a touch of glamour. *You* know what I mean. It wouldn't hurt, would it?"

It hurt.

Her throat tightened. Goddammit. I will not cry. God and her hairdresser knew how hard she tried. She had enough jars of skin treatments and cosmetics in her apartment to keep all four Gabors going for the next decade. She spent what she was able to on clothes, but trying to find something drop-dead chic when one has a forty-inch bust was not easy. She *did* try, dammit. There was no way she could ever begin to look like any of the women in her brother's life. They all seemed like aliens from another planet.

She turned away from his intense, appraising gaze. If only he wouldn't *inspect* her the way he sometimes did. He did it, the intent inspection, for a part of every time they were together, and then he would stop. She hated this little period during which his disappointment with her as a woman was naked in his eyes. She probably looked, in his mind, like a grotesque caricature of their exquisite mother. Billie Claire had been bearing this for years—Nicky's attempt to understand the vagaries of genetics. Their mother was a majestic scarlet tanager and she was a timid brown wren. It was that simple, and she wished he could understand.

"Who is your current wearable lady, Nicky?" She said hoping to deflect his scrutiny.

"At the moment, Danya Harlow-Hughes. She may be coming down tomorrow. If she can pry herself off the deck at her house at Montauk. You'll like her."

"Oh, I'm sure I will," she said in a try at enthusiasm. Fortunately, she didn't have to try to *like* many of these women from *Vogue* and *Town and Country*, because he seldom brought them around. "But I don't think I'll have time to be meeting anyone this time. I'll have to leave when the President leaves. Meanwhile I've somehow got to find the Governor."

"You want a governor, I'll get you a governor," a disembodied female voice announced from behind Nicky's head.

Nicky jerked his head around and Billie Claire peered at the plastic plants that framed their banquette. They both saw a well-manicured hand part the greenery, and then Jane Connor's smiling face.

"Janey! You're here, too!" Billie Claire squealed. "Jane, you remember my brother, Nicky. From Rehobeth."

"Sure. Nicky, nice to see you again. Forgive me for eavesdropping. Who are you trying to track, Billie?"

"Oh, Christ, Jane. Ernie pulled me off the regular watch to do a feature on John Connally. I haven't made much of an attempt to find the man. I suspect it's a lost cause. LBJ will probably roar off at some ungodly, unannounced moment and I'll be stuck with nothing for Ernie."

Jane was now on her knees on the adjoining banquette. "That's a snap, kid. When you're finished here, tag along. I'm headed for Allegra's suite at the Haddon Hall. She's promised to have everyone who either gets bored at Pearlie May's party or couldn't get in. I'm certain Big John will be there."

"You are an angel of mercy. Can Nicky come, too?"

Nicky waved his hand as if to dismiss the thought. "No, you gals go ahead. I've got to get back to the floor and mingle."

"But you weren't going back there," Billie Claire said.

"I've reconsidered." He pulled a twenty from his wallet. "Your everlasting conscientiousness, as usual, has made me feel guilty as hell." He laid the bill on the table. "Why don't you join your friend here and her party, and I'll go do something useful."

"Oh, no, Nicky," Billie Claire wailed. "Please don't. You haven't even eaten yet."

"I can get a hot dog or a piece of fried chicken." He stood. "Nice to see you again, Jane. I'll give you a buzz if I don't see you again while I'm in Atlantic City, Billie."

She watched him dodge nimbly between the closely placed tables. Halfway across the vast dining room, he was stopped by a distinguished-looking white-haired gentleman who looked vaguely familiar to Billie Claire. Nicky smiled warmly and acted suave as hell. After a moment, when the spectacular brunette with the older man extended her hand, Nicky took it, bent at the waist and kissed it. The three of them talked a few minutes longer. Then Nicky nodded, glanced at his wristwatch, pulled the cream-colored card from his pocket and rapidly wrote something on it. When he strode off, the brunette's eyes followed him.

"Hey, Billie," Jane said softly. "Come sit with us. No one's ordered yet."

"That's okay. I'm not very hungry now."

"Billie, don't. He's not what you . . . "

"Yes, he is, Jane. He's as perfect as he looks."

Jane sighed. "Yes, I know. Look, you can't sit there by yourself. At least come around and have a drink with us."

"All right. Just one more."

"Good," Jane said to Billie Claire, then, over her shoulder, "Make room for an important Washington journalist, everyone."

One who will never make *Women's Wear Daily* in *this* life, Billie Claire thought to herself, as she slid toward the edge of the padded seat.

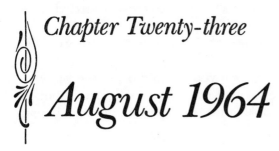

Chapter Twenty-three

August 1964

Everyone passing through the corridors formed by the make-shift partitions in the press area of Atlantic City's Convention Hall heard it. It was quite a remarkable sound. Half-scream, half-wail of pain. The sound was followed almost immediately by a rapid, hysterical stream of profanity, punctuated by throat-tearing sobs.

Allen Wachtel of KKGT-TV Atlanta, heard it; his camera crew trudging behind him heard it. The five men stopped and peered into the doorway of the twenty-by-fifteen-foot cubicle that housed the *Washington Inquirer's* convention staff. A woman, who appeared to be in her mid- to late twenties, wearing a too short skirt and a half-tucked-in blouse, was throwing a fit. She stood in front of a desk, behind which stood three shirt-sleeved and bewildered newsmen. She had taken off her belt and was attempting to whip one of the men across the chest, but her rage and hysteria affected her aim. The thin belt simply whipped the loose papers on the desk into a flurry.

"This paper *eats* it!" she screamed, slashing the belt in a sideways motion that knocked over a big jar of rubber cement. The contents began to ooze over the edge of the desk and onto the floor.

The television newsman smiled, shook his head and motioned

to his crew to follow him away. "I tell ya, fellas, you let 'em out of the kitchen and they'll corner ya." The crew chortled and marched on.

"Now, now, Melon," said one of the newsmen in the cubicle, "calm down. Let me explain."

"You've got nothing to explain, you asshole! I get the picture! You're not running a paper, you're running a comic strip. Look at these assignments!" She shook a piece of paper at him, then began to read it. " 'Bowersox:

10:30 Interview Convention Hall pipe organist
12:00 Interview fireworks coordinator for LBJ birthday party
1:00 Cover Congressional wives' luncheon, Dennis Hotel'

Jeesus Christ! I'm not up here to do this Mickey Mouse crap. Get some copy kid to do it."

"Melon, *please*." Tom Howell, her editor, looked very weary. "That's the kind of stuff we *need*."

"Don't give me that horse manure. What's the matter with the feature I filed last night?"

"Melon," he said, trying very hard to be patient, "that's *pure* gossip. We had to spike it. You can't run a story naming by name half the drunks in Congress and their condition yesterday, for God's sake!"

"What do you mean? They were all there at that party. Most of the better call girls in New York were there with their skirts up over their heads! I saw, with my very own eyes, the Chairman of the House Committee on Finances and three White House aides so drunk they could barely stand up. It was a hell of a party and a lot happened. I wrote it the way I saw it."

Tom Howell groaned and sat down in the rickety typing chair behind the desk. The two other men in the group moved away and resumed their typing, watching the argument through the corners of their eyes.

Melon was fed up with the *Inquirer*. She knew she had made a terrible mistake after her first week there. The reaction of the other reporters and staffers in the city room to the arrival of the rival paper's most controversial reporter was wary and cool. People reacted to Melon with downcast and embarrassed eyes, or open, envious wisecracks to each other within her hearing. She had tried to make the best of a bad situation. She had no choice. There was no going back to the *Herald* after the way she had behaved. Particularly after the very nasty scene with Ernie Prescott. She really hadn't meant to quit, just shake him up a bit and make him come crawling, full of apologies and promises. He hadn't.

Seth's no-nonsense rejection of her had sent her into a deep depression. She stopped showing up at work for days at a time, and when she did, she spoke to almost no one but Ann and Billie Claire. She did as little work as possible and left the city room to walk home and sit in her apartment alone and drink. Miles had even brought her some marijuana. It only further depressed her.

From the abyss of desperation Melon called North Hollywood for the first time since the preceding Christmas. One of Charlie's few chores was answering the phone. There her brother was, a man in his early twenties, who wore dark glasses when he sat before a huge color television set ten hours a day. He told his sister he was helping a lot with meals, now that their mother was so busy with her job as Southern Regional Director for the California Service for the Visually Handicapped. Their father? He was still working for West Valley Plumbing and still saying, "One of these days . . ." whenever he said much of anything. Charlie said their father had begun to switch from beer to bourbon. "Bourbon smells terrible, and it makes him lose his temper with me. Melon, when are you coming back? When you were here life was more interesting." She mumbled an excuse about important assignments and asked Charlie to say hello to everyone. When she hung up she wondered what would have happened to her if she hadn't received the scholarship to Smith. Her mouth became cottony, and she shivered.

After two and a half weeks, she pulled herself together enough to walk into Duke's one evening after a fierce argument with Ernie. She found the *Inquirer's* editor, Tom Howell, in his cups and feeling horny. Before the evening was over, Melon had been made a feature writer on the *Inquirer*. It had seemed like such a great idea. It wasn't.

She had insisted on going to Atlantic City to cover the convention and they had given her the bottom of the barrel, assignments that the *Herald* wouldn't even have bothered with. She had done her best. She felt that one sure way to get attention was to track down stories that would be *different,* stories Melon considered real news, and real news to her was news about people. She had done the story on the drunken blast at one of the hotels on her own, and now she was getting jerked around for "celebrating trivia, violating privacy."

When she walked into the *Inquirer's* cubicle that morning, she fully expected to be ridden around the room on the shoulders of her co-workers. But, no. They had spiked the story and delivered a lecture on journalistic ethics. That's when she, looking desperately for a weapon, had whipped off her belt and tried to strike Tom Howell across his smug, tight-assed face. Nothing she did or said could persuade him to run the story, and after screaming and crying and swearing at the top of her lungs, she knew it.

Tom stared at her for a long, silent moment. "Melon, what do you want me to do?" he asked helplessly.

Melon picked up her bag and turned toward the doorway. She lifted her right hand and formed a fist, extended her middle finger skyward, and said, very, very slowly, looking directly at him and shaking her finger menacingly, "Perch and twirl, Tombo."

A row of newly installed phone booths stood along the back wall of the basement level of the hall. Melon slid into one and fished around in her bag for her address book. She remembered Jane Connor had told her she would be staying at the Dennis, and if anyone knew where the action was by now, it would be good old Janey. She glanced at her watch. It was twelve forty-five. *Maybe* she could catch her dressing for a late lunch.

It took several minutes to get Jane's room number from the operator at the Dennis. The name Melon called the operator did not speed things up.

The phone rang four times.

"Miss Connor's suite, Ramon speaking," a male voice said.

"Jane? I mean, is Jane there? Jane Connor?"

"Who eeez calling Meese Connor?"

"Paul? Is that you?" Melon was bewildered.

"No, Mr. Paul. He ees dead."

"What the fuck is going on over there? Let me speak to Jane Connor, please." She could hear Jane giggling in the background, then a rustle of the phone being moved about on cloth.

"Hello. Who is this?"

"Jane, it's me. Melon. What are you doing, banging the bellboy? Who was *that?*"

"Ah, a friend. What's up?" Jane sounded impatient.

Something was going on and it annoyed Melon not to know what it was. "Well, I just walked out on that rat's ass job of mine, temporarily. I'm free for the rest of the day. What's happening? Where's the party?"

"I haven't the faintest. I'm tied up right now, and . . ."

"Yeah, it sure sounds like it. Is he cute? He's probably sixteen, you dirty old lady."

"Melon, I honestly can't talk now."

"Come on, what's on for tonight?"

Jane sighed. "All I know about is *another* thing at Allegra's, but this one is very private. I mean, it's a sit-down thing and all. Impossible to get into. I guess you're on your own. You shouldn't have any problems. Bye, Melon." The phone went dead.

Shit! Melon sat in the phone booth for five minutes watching people hurry by. Headed toward her was Haynes Johnson from the *Star.*

"Haynes!" she shouted and jumped off the phone booth seat and dropped her bag, spilling its contents on the floor. "Where's the action today?"

At midnight Melon was in the hall of a hotel. Which hotel, she could not remember. She was leaning against the wall several feet away from the open door of a suite in which a party was still grinding on.

Three people rounded a corner fifty feet down the hall. Two of them were men wearing wrinkled seersucker suits and straw hats with red, white and blue bands that read, "All the Way with LBJ." Melon almost wept with joy when she recognized the third person.

"Billie Claire!" she shrieked. "Billie, old buddy, old honey, old girl."

She pushed herself away from the hall wall and started to run long the strip of carpet toward Billie Claire and the two men. After five uncertain steps, she tripped and sprawled to the floor.

"Owww! Shit!" Melon grabbed her ankle. "*Now* I've gone and done it."

Billie Claire told the two men she would see them in the morning and knelt on the rug beside Melon. "God, Melon, it's beginning to swell already."

"That's okay. Now I won't have to interview the people who're running the fried chicken concession tomorrow. Fuck it, this hurts like hell."

Billie Claire frowned down with concern. "I don't know how I can get you to your hotel." She struggled to bring Melon upright. "But, if you can kind of hobble, I can get you to Allegra's suite. It's on the next floor up."

"Why not?" Melon laid her arm over Billie Claire's straining shoulders. She didn't care where she slept. She felt dizzy and her ankle was throbbing.

A sleepy young man in a wilted white shirt and black bow tie eyed them with bloodshot eyes.

"We're friends of Miss Farr's," Billie Claire said. 'Miss Bowersox here is a reporter with the *Washington Inquirer.*"

"Miss Farr went to bed well over an hour ago," the young man said uncertainly. "I can't wake her. We just finished cleaning up and I was just leaving."

"So leave," Melon said. "I'll just flop on the couch over there."

Still, the tired waiter hesitated.

Shifting Melon's weight, Billie Claire fumbled with her purse. "Here, *my* credentials. *I* work for Mr. Hathaway's paper."

That seemed to mollify him. "Well, okay, I guess."

Billie Claire laid Melon on the couch and removed her shoes. "You'll probably feel better in the morning"

"Christ, the *morning!*" Melon curled up and closed her eyes. "The morning *after* tomorrow. Night."

Melon heard Billie Claire and the waiter leave the suite together. She fell into a fitful sleep. The couch was too soft and her ankle hurt.

She lurched to full and miserable consciousness five hours later. The drapes in the living room were drawn and the room was only dimly lit by sunlight that shone in between a few openings. Her ankle was still very sore, her tongue felt as if it had begun to grow fur and her bladder was painfully full.

She slowly sat up. Just as she was about to utter a full-throated groan, she heard voices and other noises. Allegra and someone.

360

From the sound of Allegra's voice, it was quite clear, even to Melon, that she was in the midst of making love.

Melon forgot her ankle, her mouth and her bladder, and silently hobbled toward the sounds. From two rooms away, she could tell that the door to the room Allegra was in was, if not fully open, ajar.

The opportunity of a lifetime! To catch Allegra and Seth going at it. What a tale this would be! A description of Allegra's legendary sexual hold over Seth Hathaway!

Or, maybe, at the big moment, she could fling open the door and shout, "Ta da! So that's how it's done!"

Seth and Allegra would be mortified.

Melon silently approached the door and peered through a four-inch opening.

Allegra was most definitely in the act of making love. But that wasn't Seth Hathaway in bed with her. Melon watched for a full minute.

Then she silently backed away and limped across the living room to the entrance to the suite. She was fully awake, the adrenaline pumping. Only when she was well down the Haddon Hall's corridor did she dare breathe. After she rounded a corner, she blew out her breath. She slowly shook her head once and smiled.

"Oh, man! Holy *shit!*" She leaned against the corridor wall. "I'm gonna tell," she hummed in her best little girl voice.

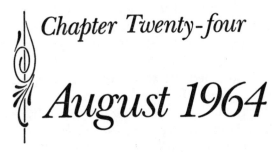

Chapter Twenty-four

August 1964

The blast of hot, humid air that poured over the two women when they stepped onto the sidewalk from the small Italian restaurant on L Street was almost overwhelming. Ann blinked against the dazzling sun as she peered down the street in search of an empty cab.

"Now, are you sure you have it straight?" Ann asked the slender woman at her side. "Let's run through it one more time, okay?" Her companion nodded nervously and bit her lower lip in concentration. "There are only four copies. One is with your lawyer and one with mine. One is in a safe-deposit box at Riggs Bank. The manager has the key, and I've got one in my purse. I have an appointment with Mr. Hathaway the minute he gets back from Atlantic City in the morning. I will give him my copy."

"But, I'm still scared," Joan Quackenbusch said. "God, it seems as if this has been going on forever, Ann. A year and a half of this is just too much." She shook her head. "I can't live this way any longer."

"Well, after tomorrow you won't have to. You can send those two beefy brothers of yours home to the Tennessee hills."

"Can't say as I'll miss cooking for them, but I've surely slept better with them in the house," she sighed. "Ann, you haven't said anything, so I guess there's no change in your husband?"

"There's no change," she answered curtly. Ann spotted a cab making the turn off Vermont Avenue and shot her hand into the air. She handed Joan Quackenbusch some bills. "Just stay put. Let those mountain men answer the door or the phone. I'll call you as soon as possible tomorrow."

Ann stood on the curb and watched the woman's taxi merge into the afternoon traffic headed east on L Street.

Of all the people involved in the tangled mess that was carefully documented on the sheaf of papers in her purse, Joan Quackenbusch was truly the only innocent and the one suffering the most.

Ann flagged down another taxi for herself.

She sat back and stared straight ahead.

No, Del was also an innocent. And she was a very nervous and frightened thief. Tomorrow, before noon, she would lay the stolen goods on Seth Hathaway's desk and watch him read and absorb their full significance. She had not received a Pulitzer for her Martin Luther King piece, but she knew without a doubt that the *Herald* and Ann Hawkins Adams would be awarded one the following April.

Ann triple-locked the apartment door, walked across the untidy living room and turned on the air conditioner. She threw her broad-brimmed straw hat on the sofa and went to the kitchen to make herself a double brandy Alexander.

Tomorrow afternoon she would call the maid and ask her to please come back. The apartment and her laundry were in terrible shape. Hattie had been baffled and hurt when Ann called to tell her she wouldn't be required until further notice. The same day Ann had hired a locksmith to install additional locks, a jimmy-proof deadlock, a steel anti-jimmy plate that ran down the side of the door and a new cylinder in the old lock—on both the main door and the service entrance off the kitchen.

Ann sat down beside her hat and looked across the room at Del's genuine leather recliner.

"Tomorrow I'm gonna march into Seth's office and do it, Del, honey," she said to the chair.

The chair's arms were furry with dust. No one had sat in the chair since April, since the afternoon in April when Del had fallen from his stool in the Tap Room of the Press Club and been taken in an ambulance to Sibley Hospital. He had been unconscious when he was admitted. The doctors had informed Ann that they expected him to remain so. In layman's language, Del suffered from acute brain damage and cirrhosis of the liver, as the result of alcohol poisoning.

Ann held up her glass in a toast to the empty chair. "We're one helluva team, you and me, honey." She sipped and stared into space, waiting for the brandy to ease the pain.

After the night last November when Del had told her, or tried to, about his story of a lifetime, he had not said another word about it.

Ann assumed he'd given it up. All of Washington was immobilized by shock and sorrow after Kennedy's assassination. Some people, like Jane Connor, left one job and took another, no longer able to cope with life as it had once been and would never be again. Del had become withdrawn and secretive and uncharacteristically finicky. Ann assumed his new demeanor was the result of a combination of horror over John Kennedy's death and his own total abstinence. When he went out in the evening without a word of explanation, Ann supposed he was off to another A. A. meeting. She never asked.

During that period, from November to April, they made love more frequently than they ever had before. It was as if both of them tacitly agreed that this was the only way left for them to communicate. Many times, afterward, Del clung to her, sweating, until he fell asleep. Ann attributed this to drying out and anxiety about his work. His work seemed to be at a dead standstill. The title of bureau chief meant almost nothing after having been a star columnist. He was indifferent to his work.

Hank Leader, a public relations man who practically lived at the Press Club, had been with Del when he fell. Hank rode in the ambulance with Del to Sibley. It was Hank who called her from a pay phone at the hospital. He did not sound sober himself.

"Annie," he slurred, "I'm at Sibley with Del. He's had a . . . an accident, kinda. Pretty bad shape. Better get the hell over here, hon."

By the time she reached the hospital they had wheeled Del out of Emergency and put him in a room with one other man and two empty beds. He lay, eyes closed, mouth slack and utterly still. His face was nearly purple, the broken capillaries around his nose and under his lower lip looked like red secondary road markings on a fuzzy map. The doctor told her he was in an advanced state of dehydration. His liver was badly distended and his blood pressure was extremely high. Two months later, and now affixed to three different plastic tubes, he was exactly as he had been in April at Sibley. Only his color had changed from purple to an oyster gray. More doctors told her the brain damage was irreversible.

As late June began to roast the capital, Ann finally accepted the doctor's solemn words. She took a week's vacation and set to work on the jumble of papers on and in Del's desk. Sandwiched between the overdue statements from the insurance company and back bills for Lewis and Thomas Saltz shirts, she found an accordion file stuffed with yellow copy paper. As she glanced through the pages she saw the name "Carson Peck" scattered through the copy.

She gathered up the pages, seventy-two in all, and sat down to read. By page seven she realized what Del had been up to. He had carefully documented every item with a numbering system. She reached for the accordion file again and found another sheaf of papers toward the back. These pages showed the names, dates and backgrounds of every source for the story. She closed her eyes for a moment before she turned to the last pages. The final page was dated April 16, the day he had walked into the Press Club for a celebratory drink and ordered Scotch for the first time in seven months.

She was sure he had never shown these pages to anyone. Convinced of it. On the last page he had euphorically scribbled, in his fine patrician hand, a note to himself which read, "If this doesn't get me back my balls, nothing will. Hallelujah, I'm born again!!!!"

Ann carried the pages and her drink into the bedroom and propped herself up on their big bed. She began again from page one, carefully reading each line and double-checking the numbered references.

"Lordy," she said after the second reading, "what a helluva piece of work!"

She visualized poor, determined Del, plodding, digging, going through committee reports, old files, checking and cross-checking every fact like some driven cub reporter showing the boss he was good enough for the police beat. The story itself was foolproof, exact, immediate, one that would explode official Washington.

She stacked the papers and suddenly began to sweat. Droplets ran down her face, her back, between her breasts.

The last entry had been on April 16. This was June 7. The day before she had seen Carson Peck, along with two other Democratic senatorial candidates on *Face the Nation,* looking fit and cheer-`ul, very much a man who was sure he had an election in the bag.

The pages she held in her sweating hands proved that Carson Peck was, among other things, deeply involved in a multimillion-dollar kickback scheme and a murder, all engineered by his A. A. Marshall Austin. Not a word had leaked. Not once had she heard even an oblique reference around town to Carson Peck's involvement with anything more treacherous than an occasional redhead or pneumatic blonde. From the way the piece was carefully cross-checked she could tell Del had done his interviewing blind, talking around the subject to people, picking up a tiny piece of information here, a scrap of a lead there. No one had any idea what he was after. It was obvious to Ann, from his careful documentation, that he was afraid, personally, of repercussions, should any of those involved find he was on the trail. It was a masterful piece of detective work. Ann was more than impressed. She was dumb-founded.

It made sense now. The secretive sliding out into the night. His growing obsession with locked doors, lowered blinds, calling her from different phone booths around town. His early suspicion that Clarence Quackenbusch's death in the car crash was not an accident had proved itself out. The one source he apparently had not been able to develop fully was Quackenbusch's wife, Joan, whom he had located in suburban Maryland. To Ann's experienced eye, Joan Quackenbusch obviously had more to tell than Del had gotten from her. Perhaps, she, too, had been afraid. And she had every reason to be.

The dangling story, the story without the final, firm, end, mesmerized her. It wouldn't take much to put the last piece in place. Del had done the hard part. All someone would have to do would be to . . . She stopped her mind from spinning to pace around the apartment. She couldn't stop thinking about those pages in the accordion file, fantasizing how she would handle it were it handed over to her to complete. She paced faster. She hadn't felt so alive in months. Her whole body tingled the way it used to when she was hot on the trail of a story that would crack wide open with just one more phone call, one more question placed in the right way to one more source. She still felt the sting of losing the Pulitzer for her civil rights coverage. She could take this story to Seth. He would see the ramifications of it immediately. Seth deserved this story. Cynthia Hartford, the bitch, certainly didn't. And she knew nothing about this story that Del had dug with his bare hands.

Ann made her decision stretched out on the king-sized bed. In order to make it work she would have to start from scratch, using Del's story and notes as a road map. She couldn't take a chance that he had actually done it perfectly. The most valuable source was obviously Joan Quackenbusch. Ann was certain the reason Del had not gotten what he wanted from her was that he had approached her in his usual courtly manner. Ann knew that wouldn't work. She knew her method would. She would simply scare the shit out of the woman. Tell her she would probably be murdered to keep her quiet and only Ann could prevent it by bringing out the *full* story. That would be her plan.

If Del had discussed the Carson Peck–Marshall Austin–Clarence Quackenbusch story with her, she would have helped him. She certainly had more experience dogging civilian sources than he did. Did. Had. Never would again. The man was breathing, but no longer alive.

She sat up and crossed her legs. If there was the smallest chance he would ever again open his eyes and be capable of reading a line of print, she would not have considered what she was about to do. She would have gone after Joan Quackenbusch, typed up the complete story, and, gritting her teeth, given it to Cynthia Hartford to run under Del's byline. Ann moved her free foot in nervous little circles. She had never before stolen a sentence from another journalist. Now here she was plagiarizing an entire series.

She set both feet firmly on the floor. "But that's the way it's going to be." Honest Ann was about to become a determined thief.

The next morning she told Seth she was "on to something big." Seth's confidence in her had been touching. Few publishers would have given her such a free hand. He had told her to take all the time she needed. He would see that her work load was greatly reduced to allow her time to work without daily pressure. She had blessed him for it and set to work.

As the summer dragged on and she worked eighteen-hour days, the nausea and the pain in her middle increased. She had no time for a doctor. She gobbled Dramamines and aspirins and forced herself to eat what she could of a can of soup at night and an occasional poached egg on toast in the morning. Every bartender in town knew by now unquestioningly to serve her brandy Alexanders, rather than Jack Daniels on the rocks.

The morning after her lunch at the Italian restaurant with Joan Quackenbusch, she rode the *Herald's* elevator to the tenth floor. She wore a jade green silk shift Del had been especially fond of.

Miss Wilton greeted her with great courtesy. Miss Wilton had long been aware of her boss's fondness and respect for Ann.

"Mr. Hathaway will see you in a few minutes, Miss Adams. He's sorry to keep you waiting."

Ann sat down on a pale orange plastic chair and lit a cigarette. "I'm sure his desk is neck-high after a week away."

"Mmm. I do think there is only one place worse than Washington in August, and that's Atlantic City. Poor man, he looked exhausted this morning."

"Maybe coronations bore him," Ann grinned.

Miss Wilton, an old-line Republican, gave Ann one of her rare smiles from under her Mamie Eisenhower bangs. She picked up her intercom receiver a split second after a soft buzz sounded. "Yes, sir? Thank you." She replaced the receiver and said, "You can go right in, Miss Adams."

Ann stubbed out her cigarette and walked to the high double doors of Seth Hathaway's private office.

"Ann, my dear," He stood and came around his desk to shake hands and buss her on the cheek simultaneously. "Are you well?"

Ann nodded unconvincingly and took the wing-backed chair he guided her to, gently holding her elbow. "Tolerable, Seth, tolerable." She placed the large manila envelope she had been carrying neatly on her lap. "How was that pigsticking in Atlantic City?"

Seth sighed, in a deep, slow gesture of fatigue. "Pigsticking it was. My poor friend, Hubert, got some runaround. Don't know how the man takes it."

Ann smiled. "Well, Seth, you remember what Ol' Lyndon's always said, 'You got to go along to get along.' I guess Hubert took that to heart."

Seth shifted in his seat and carefully began to arrange the objets d'art on his desk top. "Annie, we're not here to talk politics this morning, are we?" he asked softly.

"No, sir."

"I take it that envelope you are carrying like the crown jewels is something you'd like me to see?"

She leaned forward wordlessly and handed it to him across the expanse of his desk. He did not seem to notice the slight tremor in her hand.

"Is it all here?"

"Every drop. I've done a covering sheet that explains it all. It's there on top." Seth had pulled the stack of papers out of the envelope and laid it down on his desk. "The memo's only a couple of pages, if you want to just run through it, I've got time."

Seth buzzed Miss Wilton for coffee and motioned Ann toward the long, low sofa near the window of his spacious office. They sat side by side as he read Ann's memo, which tersely described the story. Before either had finished their first cup of coffee, Seth put the pages down on the coffee table and turned to Ann, his face unsmiling and tense.

"I don't have to ask you if this all checks out, do I, Ann?"

Ann stared into his pale blue eyes. "No, Seth. You know it does."

He nodded. "Yes," he exhaled wearily. "This is pretty heavy stuff, Annie. There is no way we *can't* run with this. I think I better get Ed Bennett Williams over here. Better have the in-house counsel here as well. Then we will have to have the top brass. We'll have to make it as airtight as possible. I can't afford to have any of this leak."

"Whatever it takes, Seth. I'm glad you like it."

"Like it!" he boomed, jerking his big frame up from the sofa. "Like it? Woman, this is the most sensational stuff I've seen in a long, long time. My God, woman, don't you realize what you've put together?"

"Yup," Ann said, her eyes intent on the match she was holding to her twentieth cigarette of the morning. She coughed raspingly.

"Put out the goddamned cigarette, Annie," he said absently. "Damn things will kill you."

She paused for an instant, looking at him, and then continued to draw on the cigarette. She placed the burned-out match in the ashtray and crossed her legs.

"I'm no lawyer, Seth, but I don't think you are going to have any trouble with this. What you have here is the bare bones of what I see as maybe a four-parter, maybe five. I have mountains of documentation—tapes, notes, you name it."

Seth returned to the sofa. "We're going to need every bit of it to protect ourselves, Annie, my girl."

Within the next three days every employee at the *Herald* knew that something big was brewing on the tenth floor. The managing editor was nowhere to be seen in the city room, nor were Bob Basting, the *Herald's* Congressional reporter, Phil Maltby and Fred Wilson, political experts and most of the editorial board. No one was talking and nothing leaked. The tension was almost palpable. All anyone knew for sure was that Ann Adams was involved, and, good or bad, so were their jobs.

Seth planned to break the story in the Sunday paper, with a front-page banner running over the logo in red. The lawyers had suggested minor revisions and deletions, and two rewrite men from city side disappeared into a windowless room on the tenth floor for three straight days.

Seth invited Ann down to the composing room on Friday night to see the story after it was set in type for the Sunday paper.

"Like it?" he asked, holding up a copy of the front page. He had to shout over the clatter and din of the huge Goss presses.

The banner headline read: THE STRANGE CASE OF THE MISSING CASES.

"Love it!" Ann shouted back.

"Come up to the office and we'll have a celebratory drink. Take the paper with you. You can read it over while I make some calls."

They rode the elevator to the tenth floor in silence, both completely exhausted from the previous week. Ann sat on Seth's couch and began to read.

The ultimate corruption of Carson Peck had begun long before he ever considered running for the U.S. House of Representatives. He had permitted himself to be a puppet for individuals who found it extremely profitable to have a U.S. Congressman at their command. His campaigns were lavishly financed and his position on important committees were mined for the opportunities they provided to funnel contracts to favored construction firms represented by the New York law firm of Prouty, Langtry and Boxer. With his administrative assistant, Marshall Austin, pulling his strings, Peck became the conduit for millions of dollars in graft. When Peck occasionally complained about being manipulated, he was thrown a bone. One bone was the inconsequential appointment of an old Marine Corps buddy, Clarence Quackenbusch, to the Federal Aviation Administration.

When a small private plane crashed in a snowstorm outside Washington, killing the pilot and Allen Boxer, Marshall Austin put in a call to Quackenbusch and ordered him to close the site and retrieve two aluminum cases from the wreckage. Quackenbusch did as he was told. The cases, transported to his home in the trunk of his car that night, were pried open by a nervous Clarence. They contained $950,000 in one-hundred-dollar bills. Quackenbusch was told to hide the cases and await further instructions from Austin. Quackenbusch panicked. He called his wife Joan to the garage where he had the opened cases. Joan Quackenbusch panicked. It was obvious to both of them that that kind of money had to be tainted, and they argued into the night over whether they should turn it over to the police or the FBI or, as Clarence decided, to steal it. Joan disagreed, but Clarence prevailed.

During the ensuing months, Austin, Peck, Langtry and Quackenbusch were locked in a tense struggle for possession of the money. In August the Quackenbusch house was burglarized and ransacked. In September, their dog was poisoned just outside the boxwood hedge that ran along the front lawn. Soon after that, Joan began to get strange phone calls asking her what school her children attended and how often she used the car. She was beginning to crack and so was her husband.

In October, according to his wife, Quackenbusch became virtually paralyzed by fear. Joan did everything she could to persuade him to return the two cases, which by then were in a hiding place unknown even to her. Her husband refused. "He just became sort of crazy, ranting around about corruption and criminal politicians," she had later told Ann. "All the while I knew he had almost a million dollars of dirty money hidden someplace. I didn't want the money, I wanted my life back. But, somehow, in his mind, he felt that keeping it was some kind of weapon against the forces of evil. It was madness."

On a rainy day in November, after returning from a trip to the supermarket with a neighbor, Joan Quackenbusch had gone to check the water heater in the basement. There, against the back wall, she saw that two cinder blocks had been removed, revealing a hole approximately four-by-four-feet square dug from the earth beyond the wall. She knew then where her husband had been hiding the cases. Their car was gone and so was Clarence.

There was no one to call. Nothing to do but sit and wait. At three that afternoon she opened the door to two tall and very serious-looking Montgomery County policemen. Her husband had gone off the road near Glen Echo. He was dead. Could she answer some questions?

In the course of their interrogation, she was able to ascertain that there had been nothing in the car except the driver, and the policemen wanted to know about the rather deep dent in the right rear fender, the one with fresh, light blue paint on it. There had been no dent that morning. She asked for the return of some "packages" she had left in the trunk and was assured the trunk contained nothing but a spare tire and a jack. Did her husband have any . . . enemies? Someone who may have held a grudge? Joan shook her head in terror. That was when she knew her husband had been murdered.

Del had put the rest of the story together. All he lacked was Joan Quackenbusch's full story. Ann had been able to make her talk. Del had already determined that the trail led straight to the Congressional doorstep of Representative Carson Peck, Democrat of Tennessee, and his merry band. All the *Herald* had to do was print the story and let the chips and the FBI fall where they would. With a story of this magnitude and documentation, grand jury indictments would be only weeks away, if not sooner.

Seth hung up the phone, after spending a half hour in a heated argument with the Lowater Paper Company in Canada concerning an overdue shipment of newsprint. He walked to a small bar in the alcove behind the big double doors and poured them both a drink. Ann said nothing about the glass of Jack Daniels he handed

373

her. She simply put it down on the coffee table and looked up at Seth.

He sat across from her in the wing-backed chair and raised his glass. "To you, Ann."

Ann raised her glass but did not drink. She set it back down on the coffee table. "May the ghost of Willie Randolph roll over."

"What's the matter, Annie? Don't you want bourbon? Can I get you something else?" Seth looked concerned.

"No. That's all right. Maybe later."

"Ann Adams, I've never known you to refuse a drink!" He leaned toward her. "Annie, don't bullshit an old bullshitter. You're not feeling so red-hot, are you?" When Ann started to speak he raised his hand. "Things get back here pretty fast. I've known about your health for some time. You may be a good actress, but not that good. I haven't spoken until now because I'm selfish."

"Selfish? What does that have to do with anything?"

"I wanted you to finish this story even if it put you in the hospital."

Ann laughed. "I always knew you were tough, Seth, but that's *real* tough."

"Toughness had little to do with it. I knew you had to do that story for a very special reason."

"What's that?" she said, finally taking a little sip of the bourbon. It burned her throat and when it hit her stomach, it exploded in a tiny spasm of pain.

"Because it's Del's story."

She stared at him as the spasm intensified. She was certain she was going to become ill.

"I'm right, aren't I, Annie, old girl? It's Del's story." He lowered his feet from the edge of the glass-topped coffee table.

Hot tears boiled up in Ann's eyes. Their presence was mortifying. She never let anyone see her cry. "Seth, help me," she said softly, crumpling the page of newsprint in her lap. "Help me, please."

Seth rose from his chair, towering over her. His anger colored his face a ripe persimmon. "Stop it! Stop that goddamn blubbering! Now!" He shouted as he paced the floor.

She covered her face with her hands. "Seth, I can't. Do you know, do you have any idea how I feel? How in God's name did you guess? Nobody knows!"

Seth continued to pace. "No, I don't think anyone else knows. I pray to God that no one else knows. I'm going to take that chance on Sunday morning."

Ann's body crumpled in anguish. "Don't. Don't do it, Seth. It's one thing for me to take the risk, it's something else for you to."

"You were willing for me to take the risk up until a minute ago. Your balls shrink pretty fast, lady."

"Your knowing makes the difference, Seth. I can't go ahead with it now."

"Now, listen to me, Adams, and listen once because that's as many times as I'll say this. I knew this was Del's story after the first day of checking it out. There was simply too much legwork here. There were people in this story you couldn't possibly have had the time to get to. I don't miss *anything* around here, Annie. I know how goddamn sick you are. I know you couldn't have covered this kind of ground in a few months by yourself. Then there was Del Porterfield Third, ace newsman gone to booze, sitting around the Hartford office doing shit for work and trying to dream up a way back. The night of the first day the editorial board combed through your backup material, I made a few phone calls. One was to my old friend, Cynthia Hartford in Chicago. I fucked her once a hundred years ago. She's still grateful. Seems Del had told her he was onto something big around the first of the year. She told me enough for me to get the picture. I was even suspicious when you came in here asking for time to put together a blockbuster. You are a lot of things, Annie, but long-range *investigative* report-er is not one of them. I've never seen you dig so hard and run so fast. I knew something was up. And, honey, when something is up with a woman, invariably it has to do with a man."

Ann listened to Seth. She had never before heard him so exercised. She was as fascinated as she was sick with fear. For herself, for Seth, for the paper that had been her home for most of her working life.

She involuntarily took another sip of her drink. "Why a man, Seth? Couldn't I have another motive? Isn't it possible I saw a goddamned good story going to waste and simply picked up the pieces? This story never would have been published if it had been up to Del. He's a vegetable now and you know it."

"There are a million stories in the big city, if I may be corny, Ann. You could have gone after any one of them. Why this one? Granted, it's sensational, and you did one hell of job. Why this one?"

"I never respond to someone who already has the answer, Seth. Don't set me up."

"That's what I like. Some *fight!*" He roared. "Look, my friend, I'm no shrink, but *I* know why you did it. *You* know why you did it. No one else has to know. I'm going to run with it and take my chances. Stealing a drunken husband's story is not a Federal offense. I'm running a newspaper, not a court of law. You deal with your own personal demons and let me run my paper."

Ann rose to go. She felt a desperate need to be alone. "Seth, I don't feel too good about this at the moment."

"You'll feel better next spring, Annie."

She frowned at him as she pulled her shoulder bag over her arm. "Spring?"

Smiling, Seth held the door for her. "That's when they give out Pulitzers, babe."

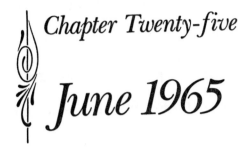

Chapter Twenty-five

June 1965

Hardin and Weaver, the capital's Bob and Ray imitators, were working their way through their usual early morning silliness.

The sound of their voices floated into Allegra's consciousness from the radio-alarm-clock combination hidden in the headboard of her enormous bed. She stretched her legs down between the white satin sheets, and for several moments tried to identify the reason for the excited buzz of tension just above her stomach.

Time magazine!

Today was the day she was to be in *Time!* She was to be a sliver of history. The idea made her skin tingle. Think of it! One of Washington's influential women! The housewife in Biloxi, the banker in Seattle, the thousands of patients in dentists' waiting rooms around American would never know she was actually the mistress of Washington's powerful and very much married publisher, Seth Hathaway. But everyone in Washington would. Delicious.

Allegra propped herself up against three oversized goosedown pillows and tried to guess what Seth's gift would be. Last night he had said the event certainly called for something special. He would have a time topping the necklace of floating opals and diamonds he had given her at Christmas. Perhaps earrings to match the necklace? He told her the opals were extremely rare and exquisitely matched. Perhaps there weren't anymore. "Not to worry," she murmured jauntily. He was an ingenious gift-giver. He'd think of something.

She buzzed the kitchen intercom. Chai's flat Oriental voice answered, "Good morning, Miss Allegra." He persisted in making it sound like "Aregra."

"Good morning, Chai. I'll be ready for breakfast in five minutes, please."

"Yes, Missy." The speaker outlet clicked closed.

Five minutes later her bedroom door opened and Petra, rather than the expected Chu, entered, carrying a white wicker bed tray.

"Petra! You're an hour early!"

"*Ja,* and I've brought you a surprise." Petra set the tray over Allegra's legs. Tucked into the open compartment on one side was a neatly furled copy of *Time.* Petra stood by the edge of the bed and beamed.

"Oh, goody!" Allegra squealed. "Let me see! Let me see!" She snatched the magazine and pushed the tray away to provide room. She patted the space beside her on the bed. "Come, get here beside me and we'll read it together."

Petra eased herself down onto the side of the bed. "Miss Adams. She looks nice, no?"

Allegra stared at Ann's smiling, freckled face on the cover, beaming from beneath a huge, lime-green cartwheel. She felt a surge of gratitude to Seth. She knew he must have selected the photograph and insisted that *Time* use it. It was at least two years old. Ann hadn't looked that well since the summer at Rehobeth. Now her skin was more the color of the hat she was wearing on the cover.

Streaked across the corner of the cover, obscuring about a quarter of Ann's hat, was a banner reading, WASHINGTON'S WOMEN OF INFLUENCE. Just under Ann's lime-green linen shoulder were smaller black letters reading, "Pulitzer Prize Winner Ann Hawkins Adams."

"I'm so excited!" Allegra bounced on the bed. "You find it, Petra. I'm too nervous. What if I look like death warmed over? They never showed me any of the pictures they took, you know."

Petra took the magazine and began deftly flipping through the pages. "You went to see Miss Adams?" she said as she searched for the right pages.

"What? Oh, yes. Yesterday. I spelled Jane Connor. She's always with Ann in the early evening, although I don't think Ann has any idea what time of day it is lately."

Petra continued to turn pages. "Your friends are very nice to Miss Adams. Always visiting and taking her nice flowers. Too much company for someone so sick."

"Well, we kind of want to be with her in case she starts to talk about . . ." Allegra caught herself.

During the past weeks Allegra, Jane, Melon and Billie Claire had managed to nip in the bud the vague rumors about Del having a part in Ann's series. They were almost certain they had been successful. But, as Ann's pain increased, so did her medication. And now their fear was that Ann herself, in a morphine haze of guilt, would tell the truth.

"Talk about what?" Petra stopped flipping.

"Petra! Do find the right page, please! You're driving me crazy. Here, give it to me." She snatched the magazine from the woman's hands.

"Go ahead yourself, then."

"Here it is! Here it is!" Allegra gasped as the page fell open to show a full-color picture of her standing beside her drawing room fireplace. That day flooded vividly back to her. She had tried on a half dozen gowns before Wally Bennett, the *Time* photographer in Washington, had arrived at ten in the morning. She had settled on a burgundy satin de la Renta her mother had insisted she buy the season before. She was delighted with the choice of photograph. Wally had taken pictures of her in the dining room; the table had been completely set with a service for twenty by a bewildered Chai at seven in the morning. Wally had also taken several pictures of her wearing a linen shift, standing and sitting in the small, but exquisitely landscaped back garden. The picture they used was by far the most dazzling, she was certain.

"Look, Petra! I'm in a picture all by myself. Oh, poor Billie Claire. Just a head shot along with Helen Thomas and Fran Lewine. And, look! My picture is bigger than Mrs. John Sherman

Cooper's *and* Scooter Miller's. I can't *stand* it! Seth will be so proud! What do they *say* about me?" She was so excited she couldn't read the print.

"Here, I'll read." Petra pointed to the long paragraph next to the picture.

"No, *I'll* read!" Allegra grabbed the magazine back. It was becoming quite wrinkled. "'Allegra Farr is the dazzling daughter of Chicago surgeon, Robert C. Farr. Her father's considerable wealth has assisted both the Democratic party and his beautiful daughter's Georgetown salon, where she presides over one of Washington's stellar dinner tables. Allegra Farr has raised the formerly tedious art of private entertaining in the Nation's capital to new and elegant heights in an Administration known more for its chili and twang than the tinkle of crystal and the crackle of wit.'" Allegra couldn't finish reading. She hurled the abused magazine across the bedroom where it landed on a sleeping Mütsy. The cat leaped up and streaked into Allegra's dressing room.

"Shit and goddamn!" she sputtered. "Those jerks make me look like an *idiot!* It sounds like *Daddy* foots the bills around here. Crap!"

"Shh, shh." Petra stroked Allegra's arm. "I think it's nice the way they write about you."

"Damn it, Petra. Everybody from the President on down knows I'm Seth Hathaway's mistress. My father has nothing to do with my quote, success, unquote. People will just be hysterical when they read this."

"But they not put in the magazine about Mr. Hathaway!" Petra was shocked.

"Well, they can't come right out and *say* it, Petra. Jane said they always say 'great and good friend' when they mean mistress. Couldn't I have at least had *that?*

"I not write magazine, Allegra. I say it's nice what they say. They say how beautiful you are, right?" She laid her hand on Allegra's stomach and began to move it very slowly.

"Oh, Petra. My God, you know what that does to me."

"*Ja,* I know." She rose and started to undress. Her body was as perfect as Allegra's, but on a far grander scale. Petra was two inches taller and her breasts were larger, but as high and firm.

There was no fat, just large, strong limbs and lines. "Junoesque," Seth had called her indifferently.

Allegra watched her, her teeth lightly holding her lower lip. "Hurry, Petra. Hurry, please. I'm almost there already." She slipped out of her nightgown and set the breakfast tray on the floor.

"But we have time. We have time for many, many pleasures, my angel." Petra threw back the light blanket and top sheet. She lay against Allegra; her hands and mouth began to move over her.

Allegra gasped.

"*Ja.* You are so ready. Now then." She shifted to a different position.

Allegra was reaching her second climax and Petra her first when Seth Hathaway opened the bedroom door. Allegra's eyes were closed, as were Petra's. Neither of them heard his leather soles on the laminated suede. He stood, with one foot in the room and the door fully open, immobilized.

He must have made a sound. Later, Allegra could not remember. All she knew was that her head was tilted back when she opened her eyes. Standing, Seth's thigh was at her eye level. She could see the pin-striped fabric of his trouser leg, the tailoring at the crotch and the large bulge of an erection beneath the fabric.

A second later she felt the blow. With one swift movement of such force that her head slammed against the back of the bed, he struck her once with the open palm and then again with the back of his large hand. Petra jumped from the bed, scrabbling to gather her clothes and bag. She was dimly aware of Petra bending down, nude, to search for her clogs, and then pushing past Seth toward the door.

His voice was low and menacing. He stared down at her and spoke through clenched teeth. "So this is what my Ice Princess has for breakfast?"

Allegra was so dizzy from his blows, she had difficulty bringing him into focus.

"So this is why my beautiful one is so famously loyal?" He was holding her chin in his hand so tightly she could not move her head. "What's the matter, gorgeous, don't I do it enough? Don't I do it right? You've got to have a woman work you over? How long has she been warming you up for old Seth?"

He released her face with another slap and she buried her face in the pillow, unable to speak. An instant later he was on top of her with his clothes on. He held her down with one hand and tore his pants open with the other.

"Seth, please! Don't! Please!" She was being raped. He was ripping at her flesh and mouth and groin with great fury and force; the pain was so great she almost lost consciousness.

With each thrust he growled and then shouted, "Slut!" "Cunt!" "Bitch!"

It didn't take him long. His passion subsided soon enough, but not his rage. He withdrew from her and swung his feet to the floor. She tried to speak, but he held his hand over her mouth. She wrenched free.

"Seth, darling, please listen to me." She was crying. "She seduced me. She came in here this morning and forced herself on me."

"Fucking lie!" he roared. "Fucking perverts, the two of you!"

"Seth, you know that's not true. She attacked me, Seth. You've got to *believe* me."

He reached toward her and grabbed her left breast so hard she felt the pain rush up through her shoulders and neck. He would not let go.

"Listen, bitch. Melon Bowersox tried to tell me you and that Danish dyke were going at each other. She had seen you in Atlantic City. I put her down as drunk and crazy, as usual. Now I see for myself what you two have been up to." He released her breast and stood up, pulling his shorts and trousers into place as he rose.

"Seth, I love you," she whimpered into her clenched fists.

"Shut up!" He was standing in the middle of the room. "How many other broads have you had up here in Sugar Daddy Seth's playpen? Ever give Melon a taste? How about Ann? She has a kind of butchy edge to her."

Allegra screamed, clutching the satin sheet to her breasts. "Stop it! Stop it, goddamn you! How dare you say something like that! How dare you! Petra is the only woman I've ever touched in my entire life!"

Seth exhaled, patted his mouth with his crisp handkerchief and deftly refolded it into his breast pocket. He appeared his usual poised self.

"Allegra," he shot his cuff and glanced at his wristwatch, "it is nine fifteen. You have until six this evening to clear out of this house. Take what you can carry. That's all. Is that clear?"

Her eyes were round with fear. She shook her head.

He reached into his inside pocket and withdrew a small shiny red Cartier box and tossed it onto the rumpled bed. "You can hock this if you wish." He reached for his briefcase and extracted a copy of *Time* magazine. "And this you can shove." He threw it on top of the Cartier box. "Now, get out."

She listened to his rapid footsteps on the stairs.

"Seth!" she screamed, frantically trying to untangle herself from the damp sheets. The footsteps did not slow. She heard the solid bang of the front door, and then silence.

She was trembling as she stood naked in the open door of the bedroom.

"Missy? You okay?" she heard the voice of Chai from the foot of the stairs. She could not answer him. "Missy?" he called again.

Somehow, she found her voice. "It's all right, Chai. Go away." She turned back to the room.

Goddamn Melon Bowersox! That meddling, big-mouthed little sneak!

She ran to her dressing room and rummaged around in the drawer of the art deco dressing table. She had put a bottle of Librium in there somewhere. She found the bottle and shook out two fat black and green capsules.

Through the confusion and numbness she felt at what had just happened to her, she knew that Seth meant exactly what he had said. In their almost four years together he had never really lost his temper with her, and certainly never been physically rough. Through the buying sprees, the huge bills she had rung up on clothes, the house, the decorators, he had remained constantly loving and paternal, as though it pleased him to indulge a beautiful and incorrigible child. It seemed, in retrospect, that there had been nothing she could do to anger the man.

"Well, you finally found something, lady," she sighed.

She walked, nude, to the window of what had been their love

nest and looked out over the little back garden. She felt some remorse at this abrupt change in her life. But, she could still have
Petra. And . . . my God, the boutique! Miles! She sprang to the
white phone beside the bed and dialed his apartment.

Miles would have to quit his job at the *Herald.* They would both
have to work at the boutique full time. She knew, was certain, he
would want to become her *full* partner.

He did not answer. She tried his desk at the *Herald.* Not there
either.

Allegra tried to calm herself. She read the rest of the *Time* cover story. When she finished, she smiled. Jeannine Hathaway's
name had not been mentioned.

Allegra began to thumb through her address book.

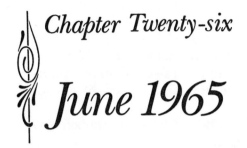

Chapter Twenty-six

June 1965

Billie Claire finished her two poached eggs beside the open window of her apartment. The day glistened. A slight breeze turned the leaves of the big oak trees across Q Street along the edge of Rock Creek Park.

She planned to buy ten copies of *Time* at the newsstand in the Statler lobby before going to the office. Two people had already called to read to her from copies they had picked up the night before. But she asked them not to. She wanted to savor the words herself, in private. And more than anything, she wanted to know if the picture was okay. "Do I look like a dog?" she had asked, and had been assured that she looked "terrific."

As she gathered up her bag and light summer sweater to leave, the secretarial service rang from the lobby. She picked up the phone and turned the button on the bottom in order to hear the man at the desk.

"Yes?"

"A Mr. Buford to see you?" came the voice of yet another new Nigerian student clerk.

"Oh! Send him right up."

Miles would be bounding in momentarily to surprise her with a copy of *Time*.

She went back to the kitchen and turned on the flame under the coffee.

At his knock she hurried to the door and opened it. She gasped. "Miles!" She stepped back. "What's *wrong!*"

He wore a two-day stubble, his hair was matted and his clothes were wrinkled and dirty, as if he had been sleeping in them outside. There was a rip in his blazer pocket. His eyes were bloodshot and his face was swollen.

"Everything is wrong." He fell on Billie Claire and sobbed into her shoulder. "I'm going to kill myself."

"Miles, what in the *world* . . . ?"

He held her for a moment, then pushed away, lowered himself onto the couch and buried his face in his hands.

Billie Claire was stricken. She eased herself down beside him on the couch. "Miles, honey, please tell me what happened. I can't bear to see you like this." She put her arm around his shaking shoulders.

Finally, his sobs subsided and he fumbled for a handkerchief. "Billie, he left me. Just walked out, the bastard. He told me I was *old!*" He collapsed again into body-wrenching sobs.

Billie Claire had no idea who he was talking about. She knew he had been having a very serious affair, but she had no idea the relationship had gone sour. She rushed to the kitchen and poured a steaming mug of coffee. She grabbed a box of tissues from the kitchen shelf and returned to his side.

"Do you want to talk about it, darling?" She placed the coffee down on the table by his knee and handed him the box of tissues.

Miles took a deep breath that caught in his chest. He exhaled and then blew his nose into three wadded-up tissues. "Billie, I thought I had found it at last, what we all look for. I thought we had *it*. We were going to live together. I was going to move to New York. I was up there last weekend and put security and a month's rent on a place in Murray Hill. I'd even talked to Jake Walker on the *Journal-American* about doing some free-lance until I got settled."

She stared at him. She had no idea he was making all of these elaborate plans to leave Washington, and she felt a twinge of hurt that he had not told her.

"Oh, Miles, I'm so sorry. Maybe it isn't over. Maybe he'll change his mind."

386

He got up, jammed his hands into the pockets of his wrinkled chinos and began to pace the floor. "No, it's over. I haven't told you what a scene it was. It went on for hours Billie, hours. He brought one of his tricks home. Some faggo he found in a bar around Georgetown. Brought him to my apartmen and was sitting there with him when I walked in. Bastard!" He slammed his fist into the palm of his left hand. "Do you know what he said to me?"

Billie Claire blinked.

"He said he was 'disposing' of me. He said, 'I do the disposing.' Like a piece of garbage, a piece of trash. Jesus, after two years. Two years together and I still don't understand him. Billie, you know him, you grew up together. Help me understand." Miles was kneeling in front of her, holding both her hands, the tears welling up again in his bloodshot eyes.

Billie Claire felt a little ping in the back of her neck, like something snapping. Her chest suddenly tightened and she choked. "Grew up together? Do you mean *Nicky?* Her eyes were wide. She pulled her hands away from his as though they were diseased. "You mean . . . *Nicky?*" The room began to swim around her.

He pounded his fist onto the sofa. "The bastard."

"Oh, my God." she said softly. "Oh, my God. You and Nicky. Two years? You mean you two were . . . lovers? Last August during the convention?"

"Yes?" he shouted, then he quieted. "I thought . . . Do you know how many suicides, at least attempted suicides, he's responsible for? He's only thirty-two and he's responsible for mayhem."

Her mouth felt gummy and her arms numb. "Then, those men who've called me weren't outraged husbands? They were Nicky's lovers?" She searched Miles's eyes for an answer and saw only pain and fury. Her brother was responsible for the agonized man beside her.

"Come on, Billie Claire, deep down you've known about Nicky."

"No, Miles, I didn't know. He always talked about his gorgeous *women.*" Her voice was heavy with defeat and disgust.

"You *didn't* know? Christ, I'm sorry. He said he'd kill me if I ever told you about us. I couldn't understand why."

"Then why are you telling me now, Miles?"

"Because I hate him. I don't care if he *does* kill me. I *want* to die. Oh, Billie, I need *you* so."

"So I see."

The phone rang.

"Don't answer it!" Miles said and shook his head.

"I've got to." She slowly rose from the couch.

The caller was an agitated Allegra Farr. "Billie Claire, do you know where Miles is? I've been trying everywhere to find him and no one has any idea where he is."

"He's right here."

"He's there? Oh, thank God. Let me speak to him."

"Ah, Allegra, could you call back?"

"No, I can't call back. This is a crisis, Billie. Please!"

She held her hand over the mouthpiece. "Miles, it's Allegra. She says she has to talk to you."

"Crap," he snapped and wiped his eyes with the damp tissue in his lap.

Billie Claire brought the phone to him.

She could hear the agitated sound of Allegra's voice, but not the words. At first Miles look horrified. That modulated into a frown of concentration which ended with a deep sigh.

"Darling, I'm stunned." He paused. "No, of course I understand. I'll be over in half an hour. Don't fret, love, everything is going to be all right."

He slapped the receiver into its cradle. "Billie, I must fly!"

"What's happened?"

"Seth has thrown Allegra out. She's got to be out of the Georgetown house by six this evening. She's panicked. I've got to go to her."

"*She's* panicked?" Billie Claire returned the phone to her desk. "Terrific! You walk in here and dump this information about my brother on me and then skip off to Allegra because *she* needs you. Miles, we've got to talk."

Miles walked toward her. She was afraid he would touch her and quickly moved away.

"Billie, I'm sorry. Please forgive me. I'm as torn up as you, you know that. But Allegra is my future."

Billie Claire sighed. "Okay, Miles, go on. I guess there isn't much to say after all." She slumped into a corner of the sofa. She had no intention of walking him to the door.

"I'll call you tonight. And, Billie," he turned at the open door, "thank you. Thank you for everything."

"Sure," she said flatly.

He quietly closed the door.

All these years Nicky had been lying to her. All those great and elaborate lies to poor, stupid Billie Claire. Poor, naive, bumpkin Billie would buy anything he said. From high school, through college and after. All the beautiful women had just been a cover. All those times he compared her to them, criticizing her for not being like them, he had been a lover of *men*. He *must* have realized the effect his stories about his alleged women was having on her.

She felt herself shiver. All those years of simply taking it from him. Fully accepting Nicky as the beautiful one, and she was the plain brown wren. Good old second-best B.C. Keep her from ever feeling she was truly worthy, possessed of grace and style. Always keep her just a bit off balance, give her the sense of being ever so consistently, *slightly* clumsy and awkward. She wasn't unnerved by Nicky's being gay, but she was furious that he had lied to her to enhance himself at her expense.

"He is a bastard," she said to the empty room where the morning breeze had quickened and was stirring the curtains again.

Ever since she had been little she had played a game with herself when confronted with a crisis. She would say to herself, "How do you feel?" and then wait for the answer to come. Riding down on the elevator, between the third and second floors, she whispered, "How do you feel?" When the lobby door opened the answer came. She felt humiliated and numb.

A Yellow Cab had just dropped two blue-haired ladies at the front of her building, and she slid into it. "Sixteenth and K streets, please," she told the driver.

Billie Claire rested her elbow on the armrest and stared at bright green leaves and blooming flowers.

If she felt humiliated and numb, how did *Nicky* feel? Not about her discovery of his relationship with Miles; he couldn't know about that yet. How did he feel about his life? She was bombarded by what must be the fears, compulsions and confusions of his days and nights. What if his sedate law firm discovered he was homosexual? How had he managed to keep it from them *this* long? Why did he need to hurt the very people he loved?

All along she had felt Nicky had been blessed with everything she had not been given—beauty, grace, wit. And the adoration of their mother. Billie Claire felt her body sag. Exquisite, always unpredictable, self-centered Consuela Grenville Hutchins had maimed her son. She had made him her pet, played seductive games with him, teased him as if he were one of her suitors. But, while Nicky had been a diversion for Consuela, Consuela became an obsession for her son. Billie Claire remembered her brother's intense, almost desperate spying through keyholes, his listening on extension phones, his reading of their mother's mail. Why? She sadly shook her head. The great love—and hate—of Nicky's life was their mother. Beneath his perfect facade raged a pathetic, crippled little boy who would never grow up.

"But *I* damn well will," she murmured. "Beginning today."

She walked through the Statler Hotel lobby clutching ten copies of *Time.* The powder room off the lobby was empty. She went into a stall and leaned against the closed door. Ann's freckled and smiling face grinned out at her, reminding her of the way Ann had looked during her visit to George Washington University Hospital two days earlier. She winced and then flipped through the pages. She found herself in a head shot at the top of the page. An overline read, "Covering the Great Society." Her picture was between Helen Thomas of UPI and Fran Lewine of the AP.

She was identified in a caption as "Billie Claire Hutchins, White House Correspondent, the *Washington Herald.*"

"Not much, but something," she whispered.

She closed the magazine, and with dispassionate objectivity studied the face of Ann Hawkins Adams.

Someday, she thought, I will have a Pulitzer of my own and I won't have to steal it. I will be the best reporter in this town—man *or* woman.

The numbness was replaced by a knot of cold, hard purposefulness.

She slid back the door latch to **the** toilet stall and walked to the large mirror on the opposite wall. She studied the ordinary brown hair that never took a decent curl. The ordinary face and the ordinary eyes.

"That's it, old buddy," she said to her unsmiling face. "From now on, no more Miss Good Guy."

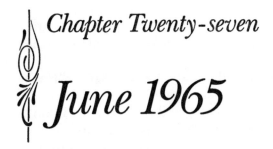

Chapter Twenty-seven

June 1965

Tom Howell, the *Inquirer's* second city editor in two years, took a sip of his coffee from a paper cup, made a face and looked out across the city room. Approaching him at a near run was Melon Bowersox, her high heels snapping, her breasts jiggling. She slowed to make the turn in front of his desk.

"Here's our star now!" he called. "Guess we can't fire a celebrity for simple lateness."

"Cut the crap," she snapped and swerved back toward his desk.

"Well, you finally made the big time, Melon. How does it feel?" He tossed a copy of *Time* toward the front of his desk. "Ask me when I'm not hung over," she said, ignoring the magazine.

"Poor baby. Another big night?"

"Another boring goddamn night, you mean. Tommy, if you ever again give me another crap assignment like that, I'll quit."

"Not again. What's the matter, Melon? Isn't the National Association of Freight Forwarders exciting enough for you?"

"I said that was a crap assignment, and you know it. I got one interview on how they feel about pending legislation and six hours of Blackie's House of Beef and a sing-along at some shithouse bar somewhere in Southeast."

"Nobody said you had to socialize, Melon." He reached for his coffee and then pulled back his hand, evidently thinking better of the idea.

"Come on, Tom. You give me a four o'clock assignment and you know goddamn well I'm going to have to drag ass out to drink with people."

The editor sighed and gestured toward the magazine. "Have you seen it?"

"No. But someone called this morning and read it to me. I don't think I want to see it." She desperately wanted to see it, but she wouldn't give him the satisfaction. Besides, her head was pounding. She turned and headed toward her desk.

During the next half hour reporters, copyboys and phone operators stopped at her desk to congratulate and tease her about making *Time*. A tired Alex Wilson, who covered the Municipal Building, Washington's city hall, swiveled around from his desk immediately in front of hers. He had another copy of *Time*.

"Really ironic, isn't it, Mel?" he said as he stared at the cover.

Melon was making a sharp, dark red line across her upper lip. She snapped shut her compact. "What?"

"Ann Adams on the cover of *Time* and too damn sick to even appreciate it. Del out of his gourd in the loony bin. Some timing, huh?"

"Yeah, I saw her after lunch day before yesterday. She's all doped up and in pain. I could cry."

"You ever regret leaving the *Herald?*" He placed both elbows of his frayed shirt on the front of her desk.

"You bet your ass."

The reporter laughed. "That's what we love about you, Melon. You're so *delicate*."

Mornings had never been Melon's favorite time of day. Her hangover and her disgust at the type of assignments she had been getting didn't add to her good humor. "Listen, Alex, this rag has never seen the likes of a reporter like Ann Adams, and it never will."

He shrugged. "Maybe you're right. Never will see one as good as her husband, either."

"Oh, yeah?" She leaned toward his face. "Please note who won the Pulitzer." She jabbed a fingernail into the cover of the magazine.

Her colleague looked menacing. "Del Porterfield could have had a Pulitzer if it weren't for certain circumstances . . . "

Melon's hands began to sweat. Jesus, she thought, what does *this* jerk know?

". . . like the booze that rotted his brain."

Melon let out her breath. She had awakened that morning wondering how Ann would react to the cover story. She had decided to cancel her lunch date and drop in on Ann. See if she was continuing to hold up, as far as the truth was concerned. Thank God the hospital switchboard had stopped putting through calls, even before her phones had been removed. On a day like today she would have been swamped with requests for interviews from all the networks and newspapers all over the country. No telling what she might let drop. Melon was reaching for the phone to cancel her date when it rang. She snatched up the receiver and impatiently barked, "Bowersox."

"Melon, please don't say my name." She listened to Seth Hathaway's familiar deep voice.

"Yes?" She squinted her eyes in concentration.

"How quickly can you get across town?"

"To where?" she asked, trying to keep her voice level.

"To my office."

"Ah, about fifteen minutes, I suppose. What's up?"

"I'd rather see you in person," he said firmly.

"Right." She slammed down the phone and grabbed her purse. "Alex," she shouted, "cover my phone. I'll be back in an hour."

She ran toward the main entrance to the city room. Tom Howell looked up as she raced by.

"Melon, I've got you down to interview Carol Lynley at the Mayflower at twelve," he called after her, exasperated.

"Fuck movie stars," she yelled as she pulled open the large plate-glass door to the corridor.

"Why should I when I've got one on my staff," he shouted and shook his head.

Miss Wilton looked frazzled and immediately ushered Melon into Seth's office. Her former boss, and brief lover, looked terrible. She had never seen him so pale. He looked like an old man.

Wearily, he gestured for her to take the chair beside his desk. She sat down on the edge and stared at him.

He rubbed his great hand across his chin and gazed out the office window for a moment.

Melon was out of breath from the trip. "Seth, is something the matter? Is there something I can do?"

He turned back to her and leaned forward. She could see a large vein pulsing along his left temple.

"Melon, we've known each other a long time."

She nodded in response.

"You know I am a man who despises injustice. I would not go out of my way to hurt someone."

"Yes, Seth."

"I want you to know that you were right about Allegra and that Danish woman. I know you had your own reasons for telling me but that no longer matters. You were right."

"Oh, shit! What happened?"

"I caught them." He closed his eyes for a moment. "This morning. At the house." He opened his eyes and looked at the small vase of flowers Miss Wilton placed on his desk each morning before he arrived. "I have asked her to leave."

Melon was stunned. Well, at last. She tried to sort out whom she truly felt sorry for. Not Allegra, she had it coming. "I don't know what to say, Seth."

"I loved her very much, you know. It was almost like . . . an obsession. She drove me absolutely mad," he said wistfully to some point beyond Melon's shoulder, as if memories of better times were flooding his mind. "She was always something perfect to me, in all ways. And then to see her there abandoning herself to her masseuse like that . . . It made me sick." he choked and fell silent.

"Wow," Melon said softly. "I'm sorry as hell, Seth. Really I am. Is there anything I can do?"

"Yes. Would you mind listening to me for a few moments? You are the one person I feel I can speak to about my feelings right now."

"Sure. I mean, you know I'll listen to whatever you want to say." Jesus, the *one* person!

"When I left Allegra's house this morning I was beside myself with rage. I almost asked my driver to turn back—I wanted to kill her. After I came here, I told Miss Wilton I did not want to see or talk with *anyone*. All I could think of was Allegra writhing in ecsta-

394

sy with that woman. I watched long enough to see that the ecstasy Allegra was experiencing was quite genuine, and of an intensity that astonished me." He smiled ruefully. "As I calmed down, here in the silence, I recalled the hundreds of times we had made love. The variety was infinite; each time was more incredible than the last." He paused. "For *me*. I simply assumed her pleasure was as deep as mine. I suppose the measure of her skill is just that—I *assumed* she was feeling as much pleasure as I was. And then I thought of the times when we weren't in bed. Melon, for almost four years Allegra has devoted herself to my comfort and gratification, and that of the guests she's entertained. Her reputation as a hostess is fully deserved."

Melon nodded. "She is the best."

"Allegra Farr is a genius, in her way, a very great actress, and not just for three or four hours a day. She is on from the moment she wakes until she falls asleep. What I witnessed this morning, though, was not acting. And now that my anger has subsided, I realize Allegra has apparently needed someone to do for her what she did for me."

"But she wasn't exactly operating in a state of *poverty,* for God's sake!"

"No." Again the rueful smile. "I've spent a medium-sized fortune on Allegra. And it was worth it while it lasted."

"I guess so," Melon said dubiously. She found the man's gallantry astonishing.

"Yes. But I've also looked at other areas of my life since I walked into this room. I've treated you shabbily. I've subjected my wife to enormous pain and humiliation. I will deal with her later. Now, I want to set things right with you."

"Seth, don't. It's not necessary. I love you. I always have. Since my freshman year in college."

He nodded. "Yes, I know. I don't know quite how I feel about you, Melon, except that I miss you around here. Isn't that crazy? You brought something unique to this paper. To me. In a funny way, I think you and I are alike in some odd way." He reached out his hand to her and she laid hers in his. "Are you happy at the *Inquirer?*"

His hand was cold and dry, and that frightened her almost as much as his intensity.

"No," she blurted, "it's a zoo. I get the crap assignments and there is so much dumb jealousy and backbiting it's like being with a bunch of school kids. They act as if they're doing you a big favor to even give you a by-line. And I was supposed to have gotten a promotion by now."

He gave her hand a squeeze and released it. "Then I have a proposition to make to you."

He smiled for the first time. "I want to publish a column that will set this town on its ear. A column that no one but you, in my opinion, is qualified to turn out."

She laughed nervously. "I know! You want me to serialize the *Kama Sutra*."

"Don't be flip, Melon," he said. "Or maybe I shouldn't say that. Yes. With this column I want someone who *is* flip. I want you to come back aboard and do an honest-to-God gossip column for us."

She gaped at him. "Seth, you've got to be kidding. They don't *do* gossip columns in this town. Oh, I know, Betty Beale at the *Star* or Don McLean, maybe. But not *hard* gossip. Washington is too hicky to take it."

"Not true, Melon. Not anymore. The Kennedys changed all that. We've finally got some sophistication here. I think this town is ready for a column by you now. I just have to make sure our libel lawyers are."

She beamed at him. "Hot damn, I'm coming *home!*"

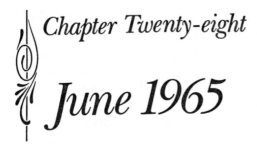

Chapter Twenty-eight

June 1965

Ann watched the slow sweep of the second hand on her bedside clock. Thirty-five more minutes until the afternoon nurse would appear with her needle. Every three hours one of them appeared with a syringe on a towel-covered tray.

The drugs were never enough. Never ever enough.

Were they afraid she would become addicted? With so little time left to live, why were they so stingy with those injections? It took twenty minutes for the drugs to take effect, and even then the medication wasn't strong enough. The pain was slightly lessened and her ability to endure it slightly increased. She counted the seconds as she waited for the fix that, at the most, enabled her to suffer with a little resignation. Why in hell couldn't they simply blast her into euphoria? What difference could it make now? She knew the cancer was beyond treatment and so did the doctors and nurses.

She followed the second hand and plotted an article on the cruelty of the treatment of terminal cancer patients. Why did the doctors make their patients cry out, beg for relief? Do they think we're kidding? Playing sick for attention? Saying it hurts when it doesn't? An article on the Big C and what it *feels* like. She could see the front-page feature, filled with quotes from the dying.

There would be interviews with their families, nurses, doctors, sociologists.

Ann turned her head away from the clock. The effort almost caused her to lose consciousness; sweat popped out all over her body. She was hooked up to so goddamned many machines that moving any other part of her body was out of the question. But the only needle that mattered was the one on the tray under the starched white towel borne by the RN.

Two new doctors were in today. One was young and intense, the other man was white-haired, calm and gently courteous. The younger man seemed determined, the older one was resigned. She trusted the white-haired one.

The top of the big tree outside her window was thick with leaves. Was it really already June?

Her room was changed. The bar and sofa and the easy chairs had been removed. They had been replaced by machines that gurgled and clicked. A woman in white nylon usually sat on a straight-backed chair and read, or quietly moved to the side of the bed to take blood pressure and pulse measurements, and monitor all the dials on the machines.

Ann had not given up her furniture without a fight. Having friends in for visits helped to deflect some of the pain, and she wanted her friends to be comfortable. Then two men had removed the television sets and her roars of rage brought in every staff member on the floor. But the worst was when she reached full consciousness after a drugged nonsleep and found her phones were gone. She was weaker, but still able to muster a few furious outbursts at the nurses and then the doctors. The doctors, of course, had won. Now she was completely cut off from the outside, life-sustaining world.

So, Momma, this is what it all came to in the big city. This is where the push and hustle and trying to "get it right" got me. Dammit, Momma, why couldn't it have been fast and dignified? Not this putrid garbage crawling through me. So, this is the way it ends, smelling of oil and rubbing alcohol and the sweet stink of my own body rotting from within. Oh, God, I want to smell black-eyed peas simmering with onions and ham hocks. Real life smells, like garlic or sweat or exhaust fumes from cars, the cigarette-whiskey-beer smell of a serious bar. Momma, Momma, I guess I'm finally coming to you. I just didn't ever think it would be this way.

She could not let go of her pain enough to doze. The pain and the second hand were now the only reminders that she was still alive.

Those fuckers. They took away my phones . . .

"Annie?"

She had not heard Jane come into her room.

"Annie?" Jane's sweet face materialized through the pain-fog. "I brought you something. Can you hear me, love?"

"Mmm? Jane?" The words were slurred. She felt a faint smile flicker over her face and fade. She hated for Jane to see her the way she must be looking. But her presence was almost as welcome as the nurse's needle. She felt Jane's cool and reassuring hand on the arm that wasn't connected to one of the dripping bottles strung overhead. They'd given that arm a rest. Collapsed veins, or something. "Hi, hon."

"Hi, yourself, old pal. You look like a pincushion. What is all this shit?" Jane said softly, gesturing toward the new apparatus. "See what I've got?"

Ann blinked and tried to raise her head. Jane seemed to be holding a rectangle of color about two feet from her face. "Let me try to focus for a minute, hon. These damn drugs could blind a body." She squinted. "Good God Almighty, they used the lime-green hat. That's one of Del's favorites."

"Your freckles show," Jane smiled. "And I think it's terrific! I've never known a cover girl before." She pulled back the *Time* magazine and reached for the metal chair next to the bed. "Do you want me to read it to you?"

"Yeah, I guess so, honey. Maybe there's a good line for the gravestone."

Even in her pain and drug daze, Ann could see her friend's large blue eyes widen. They shimmered with tears.

Jane coughed and started flipping through the magazine. "Okay, kiddo. Page forty-three. It begins, and I'm quoting, Annie: 'A ring of blue smoke seems to perpetually hover over the seventh desk in the long line of metal desks in the front row of the metro staff section of the Washington *Herald*. Beneath the smoke,

399

hammering nonstop on an old Remington noiseless typewriter she refuses to relinquish after almost twenty-five years in the business, sits Ann Hawkins Adams, Washington journalism's most colorful and competent local reporter.

"'A tall, rangy redhead with the salty tongue of a mule driver in her native Tennessee, Ann Adams is considered by her peers to be one of the most thorough and dedicated reporters in a city where the press is considered a second government. Adams is the first local reporter of either sex to win a Pulitzer Prize. Two years before, her coverage of civil rights demonstrations earned her a Pulitzer nomination, however . . .'"

"Mrs. Porterfield, are you ready for your injection?"

"Am I *ready!* Good Lord, woman!"

"Ahem." The nurse pointedly cleared her throat for Jane's benefit.

"I'll be right back, Annie. Don't go away."

The door whooshed shut.

Ann was swabbed and injected. She wanted to bite in half the thermometer the nurse placed under her tongue. What, at this point, did her temperature have to do with anything?

Before the nurse left, Jane returned. The drug began to take effect. Ann sighed.

"Okay, Janey."

Jane resumed her reading of the article.

The words sounded crisp and punchy, typical *Time* style, Ann thought drowsily. From the details, they must have interviewed everyone but her dry cleaner.

When Jane got to the description of her series on the Peck kickback scandal and the murder connected with it, Ann made a small gesture with her free hand. "You can stop now. I'm having a hard time living with the honest facts of that series. I'm not proud of what I did. Hearing about it in print only compounds the lie."

"Okay, hon." Jane closed the magazine. "Your shot going to work yet?"

Ann nodded. "As much as it ever does." She turned her head toward her friend. "Hold my hand?" She felt the gentle firmness of Jane's soft, strong hand. "I always was so proud of my work, you know. It was all I ever knew in life that gave me joy, except the first times with Del. I was good, Jane."

400

"*Good?* You are the *best!*"

"It all turned to shit in the end. Del down the drain, this nasty business with the Peck series . . . my plastic Pulitzer . . ."

"Forget that. It's not what's important." She held the magazine before Ann's face. "*This* is what's important. Your entire life, the good stuff."

"I've got to make it up to Del, somehow . . . before I go." She felt her friend wince. "You understand better than Melon and B.C. and Allegra. I mean you understand why I stole his story and why I need to make things right. I never should have done that. I spent months sneaking around lying. God, how I need to feel honest again."

"No one can get through to Del anymore, Annie. I told you how he was last week when I saw him out at Chestnut Lodge. He's gaga. Gone. The way he's been ever since he arrived there. No one can give that man any information."

"I can give him back his good name."

"Ann, remember Elizabeth Taylor's Oscar for *Butterfield Eight?* That was a lousy movie. It was for her work and life up to that point. This cover on *Time* isn't just for the Peck series. It's for years and *years* of great reporting."

Ann's face was almost the same color as the pillowcase beneath her head. The red Dynel wig, too large and too bright, made her look grotesque and pathetic. The only noticeable effect of the chemotherapy was total loss of appetite and partial loss of hair. She sighed and closed her eyes. "Del was brilliant," she said, as if she had not heard a word Jane had said. "We both drank a lot before we fell in love. I'm the one who pushed him further into the bottle, and I know it. Competition, it's a vicious thing between a man and a woman. It kills everything good. It's killing him, and . . . Who knows? Maybe it gives you cancer." A sliver of a smile passed across her pale face and disappeared.

"Stop it, Ann!" Jane said softly.

Suddenly the pain ground through her with a new and different intensity. She clutched Jane's hand. The spasm took her breath away and she began to gasp for air.

"Annie, what is it?"

"Terrible," she moaned, thrashing her head from side to side. "Call nurse. Terrible. Call doctor."

Jane thrust her hand under the pillow and held her thumb steadily on the call button. Within seconds Ann's caretaker nurse and two others raced through the door.

Ann felt strong, warm hands pry hers from Jane's. There were women's voices, then men's voices. She felt herself being examined, being palpated. The pressure of the doctor's fingers was beyond endurance. She screamed. No one told her to stop. A needle was pushed into her hip.

Almost instantly the pain flowed away, like a receding wave on a distant beach. She waited for the next wave to gather momentum, curl and break. No. The ocean became a quiet lake, unrippled, with the stillness of early evening in the late summer.

She dozed and dreamed of being in Mexico with Del. Del was tan and lean, his hands were tender and they did not quiver. He was caressing her as they watched a great orange sun slide into the turquoise waters of Acapulco Bay.

Her eyes opened and she made out the features of Jane's face. "Hello there, Good Lookin'. I've been on the beach with Del."

"What a marvelous idea. You needed to get away."

She was having trouble keeping Jane's face in focus. "What a friend you've been. *I* sure wouldn't visit me. Visiting me would give me the creeps."

"I'm here because I love you. How could I *not* be here?"

"I think about my momma a lot. Mostly dreams, now. All the drugs play tricks." The words were slurring badly. "When was the last time you talked to your momma, Janey?"

"Oh, not for a long while. A year and a half. When Nat died."

"You ever going to make your peace with her? You should, you know."

Jane picked up her hand. "I suppose. I've got to let go of the hurt sometime."

"It's the only way any of us grows up, honey." Jane pressed Ann's hand against her cheek. Ann cupped her chin and drew Jane's face close. "Make me a promise," she whispered.

"Anything."

"Forgive her. Whatever you're holding in your heart against her, give it up."

There was a long silence before Jane said, "Okay, Annie. For you. I promise."

402

She dozed off and when she awoke Jane was still there. "Mmm. I'm awful tired. Think I'll take a little nappy."

The last thought she had before she fully lost consciousness was of that Fourth of July morning out at Rehobeth. She was washing strawberries. There was going to be a wonderful party that evening.

Chapter Twenty-nine

June 1965

The midafternoon sunlight startled her. Jane had been sitting in Ann's semidark hospital room for over three hours. Twice she had gone into the corridor and waited, pacing and smoking. The second time, Ann's screams had raised the hair on her head and the backs of her arms. Abruptly, they had stopped.

When the doctor had come out he had looked grim. "I've given her as much morphine as I can. Miss Connor, I know you are practically family for Mrs. Porterfield."

"Yes, Doctor?"

"We will keep her going as long as we can."

The fluid that suddenly filled Jane's mouth tasted like bile. Her whole body stiffened with rage. "Keep her *going*?" She could hear herself shouting. The heads of passing nurses and attendants swiveled in her direction. Her anger virtually obscured the doctor's features. "Jesus wept, Doctor! Where did you go to med school? The University of Marquis de Sade?"

The doctor jerked away from her. "Now, now, Miss Connor, I am only . . ."

"Don't use that patronizing she's-crazy tone of voice on me! The woman wants to die, dammit. Let her go, you creep. Let her *go!*"

"Miss Connor, you are alarming the staff and other patients."

"Well, I hope to *God!*" She was now three inches from the doctor's flushed face. "You people keep loading her up on dope. You know what they call that stuff on the street? Shit! Shit! And that's what it is. You give her just enough to stay alive, so she can have another attack of pain that rips out her guts and then you give her a little more shit."

Two burly attendants moved up on either side of her. Jane knew she was yelling. She also knew she was outnumbered.

"Miss Connor, we will have to ask you to be quiet or leave," the doctor said, placing his hand on her shoulder, not unkindly.

Suddenly she was calm. Weak and calm. "Okay, I'll be quiet." Her body slumped. "But please, in the name of God, give that woman some peace." She started to move toward Ann's door, but paused and turned. "You see, she wants to be with her mother."

The doctor nodded and looked down at his stained white shoes.

A vast sadness filled Jane as she rode in a taxi to her office in the National Press Building.

So this was the great day? A great lady finally achieves recognition. All of it empty, joyless, too late. She realized that her sadness, her pity and anger were mixed with guilt and self-pity. She felt cheated. Her friend would no longer be a part of her life. It, Them, whatever, were taking her friend away.

What do men do when they feel overwhelming grief and rage? she wondered as they passed the front of the Executive Office Building where she had spent three nonproductive years of her life. They go get laid or drunk or hit somebody. What are we, the historical bearers of the world's grief, supposed to do? Cry, she supposed. Cry and keen and rend our garments. She wouldn't cry. Not yet.

Her secretary, Beth, beamed at her when she entered the little anteroom to her office. An enormous, expensive and completely tasteless floral arrangement almost bowed the legs of the coffee table in her private office.

"Hi. The phone has been ringing nonstop. Everyone in the country must have called. I was going to phone the hospital with messages, but I sort of thought you wouldn't . . ."

"What is *that?*" Jane gestured toward the flowers.

"Oh, they came this morning. From Mr. Sayer. He's phoned

406

twice this morning and left another message with the service while I was out to lunch. Incidentally, congratulations!"

"Thanks, Beth."

"I loved the picture of you. But Melon Bowersox will die when she sees hers. She looks like Betty Boop with all that makeup. Did you show it to Ann?"

"Yeah." Jane started toward her office. She didn't want to talk about Ann. Not now. "I'll start returning some of these." She scooped up a handful of pink phone message slips from Beth's desk. Beth was sullenly looking out the window that framed the Washington Monument. "Hey, kiddo. You okay?"

Slowly, Beth turned back to her desk. "Yeah, yeah, sure," she sighed.

Jane pulled a straight-backed chair up to the front of her secretary's desk and eased herself down. "You're not convincing me, hon. I'm sorry I've been so swamped lately I haven't even asked you how your life's going."

Beth shrugged. "It goes, so to speak, Jane. It's just that sometimes I think I should pack it in and go home."

"And do what? Marry the local plumber? Come on, Beth. Nobody ever goes home once they've seen Pennsylvania Avenue. They just talk about it. You've got man troubles, right? Who is it, that intense young man I saw you with in the East Lounge?"

"Intense is right! In a coma practically. He finally got his permanent Civil Service status at Commerce. Now he can clearly see the next thirty years of his life stretched out in front of him. You know what his idea of fun is? His idea of beating the system? He spent a month testing different ways to get to Annandale. Down Shirley Highway one day, down Route One the next, then Columbia Pike. He was able to cut three minutes from the commute by cutting through Arlington, so now he wants to buy a house in Annandale. Live there forever and wait for retirement. Is that a dream, Jane? Is that living life to the hilt?"

"No," Jane said flatly. "But then again who says you have to sit in Annandale, Virginia, for the rest of your life?"

"If I marry him I do." Beth leaned on both elbows and gazed intently at Jane.

"Well, that's simple, chowderhead. Don't marry him."

"But he wants a home and babies, and he loves me."

"Do you want a home and babies . . .? Better yet, do you love him?"

"There're two answers. Yes, and what else *is* there?"

"The *world* is what else, Beth." God, she felt tired, and very, very sad.

"But, you see, I'll never be like you. I'll never be like your friends, your women friends. I don't kid myself. You women have somehow turned yourselves into celebrities—today." She held up a copy of *Time.* "I mean, *who* you are is as important as what you do. If you weren't lobbying you'd be doing something else interesting, because someone would pay you to be *you.* Am I making any sense?"

"More than most," Jane said, smiling into the eyes of this plain, sweet young woman. "But there are friends and there are friends, Beth. There are the friends you love, and there are the friends in high places. The survivors here know the difference. They never confuse the two—that's fatal."

"Why?" Beth blinked.

Jane stood up and stretched. Already, it had been a long and difficult day. "Because highly placed friends can make you important if they are carefully cultivated. Friends you love keep you from feeling guilty about it."

"That seems so cold. If you had your choice, which of the two would you choose?"

Jane was now standing in the doorway of her office, still smiling. "Now, isn't that a silly question. You've been in Washington for over nine months."

Suddenly, Beth looked like a very young, very disillusioned schoolgirl.

Beth had picked up a dozen copies of *Time* and placed them on Jane's desk. Her clients would no doubt be impressed. But the idea of sending anyone a clipping seemed a bit tacky. She tossed the stack of magazines onto the long table behind her desk as the phone rang.

"Miss Bowersox herself, on one," Beth called through the open door.

"Is this 'spunky, aggressive and highly individualistic' Miss Mary Ellen Bowersox?"

408

"The very one. Couldn't you just crap, Jane? I mean, *really.*
Spunky! Is that too cute for words? Who wants to be *spunky?*"

"Oh, I don't know, Melon. You've been called a lot worse."

"Thanks, chum. Listen. How is Ann? Beth said you've been
over there all day. Did she say anything?"

"Don't sweat it." Jane was annoyed. It was so typical of Melon to
be worried about her own hide instead of whether Ann was alive
or dead.

"Jane, I've got a flash for you."

"A flash?" Her voice was flat and dull. She was used to Melon's
flashes. They occurred daily. "How intense a flash? I've had a
rather hairy day."

"Big department. Big, big flash department."

"Okay, I can handle it. Shoot."

"Seth wants me to come back to the *Herald.*"

Jane could tell that Melon was whispering into a hand she had
cupped around the mouthpiece of her phone. "They must be
running low on spunk over there, Melon."

"No, I'm not kidding. He's done a complete turnaround."

"Well, this publicity will work wonders for all of us, I suppose.
Everybody but Ann, of course."

"Come on, Jane," Melon whined.

"Look, I just came from George Washington Hospital. Someone I love very much is in such incredible pain I threw a fit and
begged her doctor to kill her. I've rather had it for today. Okay?"

"Jeez, Janey, I'm sorry. I mean, I'm so excited about this Seth
thing, I wasn't thinking straight. I hate it over here at the *Inquirer,*
and . . . I thought you'd be happy for me."

Jane sighed. "I'm happy for you. It's just that it's been a rough
day."

"But I still haven't told you what he wants me to do. He is going
to give me my *own column.*"

Jane knew that she might as well hear Melon out. If not it would
only mean another phone call later. "What kind of column?"

"Would you believe *gossip?*"

"Oh, come off it, Melon. This town's never had an out-and-out
gossip column. A lot of the stuff the *Post* does in their women's section qualifies. But gossip is a dirty word here and you know it."

"I know! That's why the idea is so exciting. He says as long as I

409

cover myself, you know, document stuff, and if I can't, I can run blind items. The old 'what Senator will have to declare bankruptcy if he doesn't stop picking up the bills for what glam Public Works Committee staffer.' That kind of stuff."

"You'll get the crap sued out of the old boy."

"He doesn't think so. Admit it, Jane. It's really a brilliant idea. Think what it will do for circulation."

"Um-hmm. Edward Bennett Williams will *love* this. Look, Melon. Let's have a drink tomorrow and we can talk about it. I just got in and there're about four hundred call-backs on my desk."

"Wait! I have another goody for you. I've been saving it."

"I don't think my heart can take much more."

"Well, wait until you hear this." Melon was speaking very slowly, one word at a time. "Seth—has—thrown—Allegra—out."

"*What?*" Melon had finally succeeded in capturing her attention. "Melon, are you drinking?"

"No. I mean it. He has kicked her out."

"A man like Seth doesn't *kick* someone like Allegra out of a hundred-thousand-dollar town house. I mean it simply doesn't happen in real life."

"Janey, believe me."

Jane did. One thing about Melon, she knew Melon lied like a pawnbroker about relatively meaningless things. Big items, she got dead right. "All right, give me the details."

"Allegra is having an affair," she said, stating the facts in her usual headline style.

"An *affair?*" Jane was incredulous. "Who in God's name would Allegra be having an affair with? She may be light-headed, but she's loyal."

"She's having an affair with her masseuse."

"Melon, your French is a little shaky. Masseur is masculine, masseuse is feminine."

"Right. I said masseuse, and I mean masseuse. Don't pull that boarding school shit on me."

"Wait a minute, wait a minute." Now Jane was fascinated. "You mean that tall Danish woman? The one who looks like something out of Wagner?"

"The very one. And she's been doing more than sing over Allegra's flawless body."

"Holy shit!"

"Seth got so excited when he saw the *Time* article, he jumped into his limo, whisked over to her house to surprise her. And there Allegra was rolling around in that satin playpen she calls a bed, playing kiss face, or whatever it is two women do, with Petra Jensen."

"Melon, I wouldn't dream of asking an ace reporter like you who your source is, but if I guess will you tell me?"

"You don't have to guess. Seth and Miles both told me. Allegra is staying with Miles until things settle down. I'm going over tonight to hold her hand."

"Ah, Melon, if you are going back to work for Seth, I wouldn't push my luck like that. If he's angry enough to throw her out—and he adored her—you know that he's likely to make you part of the clean-up process in his life."

"For Christ's sake, Jane. Allegra didn't do anything to *me*. Besides, she and Miles are going to have a really terrific shop, and I'll be able to use her as a source. She knows everybody."

"You never miss a beat, do you, Melon?"

"I try not to. Ciao."

Jane hung up the phone and shook her head. She was genuinely astonished by Melon's news, but before she had a chance to digest it, she noticed Beth signaling another call.

Paul Sayer's elegant voice purred onto the line. "Darling, I've only a minute. We're taking depositions today in a complicated antitrust case. Just wanted to say I saw the piece. You certainly came off well, and I hope it makes you millions."

"Thank you, Paul. Wasn't too bad, was it?"

"I'd say it will get you American Motors, Continental Oil and the National Basketball Association by Friday."

"Thank you for the flowers, but I thought you refused to represent mobsters."

"I do. Why?"

"Well, whoever picked this thing out either has a connection with a Mafia funeral parlor or a racetrack. It's enormous."

He chuckled. "I told my secretary to do something spectacular. I hope it's not *too* spectacular."

"It is, but sweet. Thank her for me. Paul, when are you coming down?"

411

"Darling, I won't be able to make it Friday evening. Eleanor invited people for the weekend and I simply must be around."

"Wonderful!" She hoped he heard the sarcasm.

"I know I promised to get down Friday, but . . ."

"It's okay, Paul. I understand." Her voice was soft and flat.

"I hope so, darling. I'll make it up to you, of course."

"Um, Paul, my other line is ringing," she lied.

"All right. I'll phone you tonight, if I'm able." And he was off the line.

Damn it! "Why me, Lord?" she asked aloud.

"Oh, I don't know, something about you always . . ." Beth called from the other room.

"You are fired, Beth Hanson."

Her secretary poked her head around the corner and grinned. "You can't fire me. I'm the only secretary in Washington who will work for a woman. Damn. Here comes another call."

Jane reached for the receiver and started to push the button. Beth answered first. "You are right, Beth. You're not fired. Who is it?"

Beth stood in the doorway. "George Washington Hospital." She looked grim.

Instantly, Jane knew what it was. She inhaled deeply and pushed the blinking button. "Yes?"

It was the doctor with the dirty white shoes. "Miss Connor, Mrs. Porterfield died at four twenty this afternoon. I'm sorry. I knew you would want to be informed."

She felt a stab of pain under her left breast. Her hands began to sweat. "Yes, of course. Thank you, Doctor. If there are any personal details I can attend to, please . . ."

"Thank you, Miss Connor. We'll be getting back to you."

She set the receiver back in its cradle.

Beth slowly walked into Jane's office and sat down on the edge of the sofa. "She's gone, right?"

"Right. She's gone." Jane paused. "Bethy, honey, could you go back to your office and close the door for a bit?"

"Sure."

Jane got up and paced the floor for a few minutes. Then she decided not to fight it. She sat back down at her desk, put her head on her arms and wept. For her friend, for herself, for the obscene waste of it all.

Finally the sobbing ended. It had been a release, and she felt better. She went to the little sink behind the screen in the corner and splashed her face with cold water. That helped, too.

She sat and stared out the window for a long time.

Beth's timid knock on the door startled her. Poor kid. She wanted to be of comfort, but Jane didn't want to be comforted. And Beth understood this.

"Come."

"I hate to bother you, but there is something very strange coming through the door. I thought you might want to talk with the delivery men."

"What are you talking about?" With a sigh, Jane rose and walked out into the outer office.

Two men in gray work coveralls were struggling with a lumpy package that stood about five feet high and was wrapped in brown paper. Tied around the paper was a huge red ribbon and bow. Her name and address had been printed on the brown paper in letters a foot high.

Mystified, Jane asked the men what it was, and then realized how stupid her question was. How would they know?

"You wanna take delivery or not, lady? We got other stops to make," one of the men said as they all stood around staring at the thing.

"Ah, well . . . I'd like to know what it *is*. How did it get here?"

"Lady, it's Air Express, and you'll have to sign for it."

"Let's see what it is first." She stepped over to it and began to tear off the paper. Beth helped her rip away enough wrapping to reveal a preposterously unnatural plastic philodendron. A layer of dust coated its bluish-green leaves. An envelope was stapled to a leaf a third of the way from the top.

Jane tore it open.

King Formica is on the six o'clock shuttle and he loves you.

Jane stared down at the note and then at Sam's "Formica" plant,

413

his treasure. She felt the tears working their way back into her eyes and throat.

"I don't blame you, lady. Pretty horrible thing to send somebody."

The delivery man's sincere sympathy brought her back to the present. "Ah, well, yes. Ah, let me sign for this."

"You're gonna *keep* it?"

Jane looked at him in astonishment. "Why, of course I am going to keep it. It's the most beautiful thing I've ever seen."

She turned to Beth. "Honey, if you're on the way home, take that big bouquet in there. It's for you."

Epilogue

December 1965

Seth Hathaway sat in a vast leather chair wearing silk pajamas and a monogrammed velour robe. He sipped coffee as he browsed through a thick stack of Sunday newspapers.

Jeannine sat opposite him in a wing-back chair upholstered in crewelwork. Her own copies of the same papers were neatly stacked on the candlestick table next to her chair.

Both chairs were arranged before a fireplace in the library of the Georgetown mansion that had been built by Jeannine Magnuson Hathaway's ancestors five generations before. For all but the first four years of their marriage, Seth and Jeannine had lived in the beautiful house.

Beyond the library, through the arched doorway leading to the entrance foyer, the soft glimmer of Christmas-tree lights reflected against the high polish on the black and white tiled hall floor. Evergreens were entwined through the banister of the great curved staircase. Little velvet red and white birds were affixed to the Williamsburg chandelier that hung over the center hall.

Jeannine smiled across at her husband. "More coffee, dear?"

"Yes. I'll get it while I'm up. That fire could use a little help."

Seth rose, tossed two small logs on the fire and poked them into place with a brass poker. He poured coffee from the silver service on the long table by a wall of books. He set his cup and saucer on the table beside his chair, then walked the few steps between his chair and his wife's. He bent, took her chin in his hand and gently kissed her mouth. For a moment, she gazed up at him and rested her slender hand against his cheek.

They smiled at each other the way two people do who have sat long beside a sick child's bed, terrified their child might die, and then seen the little one yawn and ask for cinnamon toast.

Seth had never apologized to Jeannine. His open and full-time resumption of their life together had been apology enough for her. Her acceptance, without words and without recrimination, of his return, had said, "Your apology is noted. I hereby forgive you the years of my pain and humiliation. Now, let's get along with the rest of our lives, shall we?"

At no time did she, by the most subtle intonation, say, "I knew all along I would win." But she knew she had.

With Seth, she was as gracious with her contentment as she had been during her years of humiliation and discontent. Only once did she mention Allegra. That had been in mid-November. She had said, over after-dinner brandy, "I understand Miss Farr and Mr. Buford are opening a branch of their shop over in Alexandria."

Seth had cleared his throat.

"Miss Farr's success is well earned," she had continued. "That shop's prosperity is the result of imagination, hard work and intelligence. Precisely the qualities required of a mistress."

At that, Seth had roared with laughter. "Goddamn you, Jeannine!"

Now, in mid-December, they basked in the scent of burning logs and steaming coffee.

"Have you read Reston's column yet?"

Jeannine shook her head. "I've become bogged down with Betty Beale. Big doings at the British embassy Friday night. Isn't she the one who once used the headline, 'Parties and Picnics and Balls, Balls, Balls'?"

"Hm." Seth smiled. "Yes. Possibly the most amusing words she's written. Ah, how are your plans for the Billie Claire Hutchins dinner coming along?"

"Well, I've asked twenty, and somehow twenty-two have accepted. I really must sort it out. And that doesn't include Jane and Sam Kazin. She sent a delightful and amusing regret. She says her morning sickness simply wouldn't permit the shuttle trip down from New York. I'm so sorry. I do enjoy both of them."

Seth folded back *The New York Times* editorial pages and settled himself farther into his chair. "Mm. Yes. Billie Claire will be disappointed, too. Our new White House chief of correspondents has become most imperious."

"She's earned that position, Seth. Her work is consistently excellent, and you know it." Jeannine sipped her coffee and gazed at her husband over the rim of her cup. "Or you wouldn't have given her the position."

He laid down his papers. "It's a pity Ann Adams didn't live to see Billie Claire where she is."

"Yes. I was very fond of Ann. Everyone was. Ann and I went through a lot together. More than anyone will ever know." He hunched around in his chair, uncomfortable, as always, when he thought of the Peck series.

"I am glad," Jeannine continued, "that Ann was spared the nasty little spate of gossip some of Del Porterfield's friends began just before and just after she was honored by *Time*. Why, the very *idea* that Ann would resort to plagiarism. Or," she smiled, "that you would publish it. That was for me personally insulting. For the *Herald*."

They sipped coffee.

"About the Billie Claire Hutchins dinner," Seth said. "You did invite Melon Bowersox, didn't you?"

"Why, of course. You asked me to, did you not?"

"I just wanted to be sure. She always livens up a party."

"Umm, if you say so, my dear. But, frankly, I think Miss Bowersox needs careful watching."

Seth nodded, smiled and went back to reading his paper.

4

THE EVIDENCE OF
WASHINGTON

BY WILLIAM WALTON

PHOTOGRAPHS BY EVELYN HOFER

HARPER & ROW, Publishers | 18 17 | New York

Photographs and text protected by copyright under the Berne Convention.

Printed by Conzett & Huber in Zurich, Switzerland, for Harper & Row, Publishers, Incorporated, 1966.

Produced in association with Chanticleer Press, Inc., New York.

All rights reserved.

For information address Harper & Row, Publishers, Incorporated,
49 East 33rd Street, New York, N.Y. 10016.

Design by Janet Halverson

First edition

Library of Congress Catalog Card Number: 66-20747

I

A hill and a river. The two together are the reasons for Washington. And Washington is first of all a reasonable city; not frenetic, like New York, but accustomed to the slow processes of argument, delay and decision reached by at least the semblance of reasonableness.

The Hill is a low, tree-covered eminence where the Capitol of the United States stands. As hills go it is small, only eighty-eight feet above the river, but those eighty-eight feet are of considerable importance. They serve to lift the Capitol above the city, a declaration of its intention that nothing shall be more important. Long ago this rising ground had another name, Jenkins Hill. Now it is simply "The Hill." Any Washingtonian, no matter how divorced from politics—and a few are—knows what "The Hill" means. In that name all the power and complexities of Congress are gathered. It is the meeting place for the 535 men and women elected from fifty states to govern the nation. The city's principal avenues radiate from The Hill. All streets and houses are numbered outward from The Hill. Power emanates concentrically from The Hill, out across the city, the nation and the world.

Yet The Hill might be only a shady grove were it not for the river, the other reason for Washington. The river is a great geographical borderline, a source of power and of beauty. It affects the climate, soothes the senses, rests the eyes and saves the city from feeling trapped and landlocked. Without it, The Hill never would have been chosen for a meeting place. The river's Indian name sounded to English ears like "Potomac," and ever since it has been so called, a name that has burrowed deep into history and language. "All quiet along the Potomac" recalls the critical situation of the capital during the Civil War. "Potomac fever" describes

The Jefferson Memorial

a political disease familiar to all those exposed to its symptoms. The country's South and North are computed from the Potomac's shores. True, a string of survey markers, the Mason-Dixon Line, was meant to show the nation's division, thus making Maryland a southern state. But by sticking with the Union, if only narrowly, Maryland returned the north-south line to its true position, the Potomac, exactly as George Washington had perceived when he picked the site for a new capital in 1791.

The Potomac, twisting a broad course south from Washington to Chesapeake Bay, proclaims this area to be Chesapeake country. As the crow flies, the Chesapeake, only twenty miles east, determines the character of these coastal lands. Only one other estuary, the St. Lawrence, cuts a bigger gash into North America. The Chesapeake is, geologically speaking, an extension of the Susquehanna River sunk into the sea many eons ago, causing the Potomac to sink, letting in sea tides as far as the place where Washington was to be. The rest of the Potomac, above the tidal zone, is a different river, at first cascading wildly over rocks and falls, then winding domestically through the rich farmlands of northwest Maryland to receive the waters of two big tributaries, the Shenandoah and the Conococheague. Finally, growing ever smaller, it twists to its Appalachian headwaters high in the mountains of West Virginia. For two centuries the river was the main route of commerce; now it gives Washington a bountiful water supply, a magnificent recreation region and a setting of haunting beauty. The river dominates the physical environment just as The Hill dominates the political scene. Together they are the reasons why.

The first visitors came by river. Broad and slow, the Potomac was an inviting entrance to an unknown land, deeply forested, heavy with greenery ranging up over the low hills. For thousands of years, Indians had owned these forests, paddled the river and its tributaries, beaten a network of

Right
The white man's friend

Next two pages
The upper Potomac

4

Push ma ta ha was a warrior
of great distinction—
He was wise In Council—
Eloquent in an extraordinary
degree, and on all occasions,
& under all circumstances,
The White man's friend.

trails through the woodlands, cleared cornfields and built small villages of grass-matting huts where stream and trail met. Rich with game and fish, the region supported an easy primitive life, its peace broken only by the warfare even primitive people invent. Nowadays, standing on ancient Fort Washington, five miles below the capital, a visitor looks out on a great sweep of river and dense foliage, extraordinarily like the scene that awaited explorers more than three centuries ago. Farm clearings are wider, a few smokestacks poke up in the distance, red of brick glints here and there through leaves, and a highway cross-river hints at civilization. Still it is an unchanging, placid scene.

Below Washington, the Potomac is slow and majestic, its currents deflected by the tide, its movements measured, predictable and inviting to man. The first men to accept the invitation, according to ancient archives in Madrid, were probably Spaniards, in the year 1563 or even earlier—well ahead of John Smith, the legendary first visitor. The Spaniards, then the zealots of Christendom, came as missionaries and were slaughtered, a compliment which others later returned to pay in kind. Frenchmen followed, bent not on a spiritual errand but on business, which, according to Francis Parkman, was good for several years—as many as three thousand fur pelts came down-river each season, to be shipped up the coast by undesignated means. Only tantalizing remnants remain of the first white men in these parts; if further records were kept the documents have not survived. It remained for the persistent English to keep a toehold in this part of the world and to write about it in the endless diaries Englishmen are prone to keep as they stalk the world.

In June, 1608, John Smith, a tough adventurer, visited an Indian village where Bolling Air Field now spreads out in Southeast Washington, and he seems to have gotten as far as Chain Bridge above the site of Washington. A few other explorers, probing up from Jamestown, gave the area a gingerly inspection, traded for Indian corn and sailed away. Not until 1632 did an explorer record his impressions of the place, pin-

The first secretary of the treasury

5

pointing them so precisely that we recognize the site of the future capital of the United States. Captain Henry Fleete, part reprobate, part daring explorer, had spent years as an Indian captive, spoke the local tongue and knew the nearby terrain. "On Monday the 25th of June," Fleete wrote, "we set sail for the town of Tohoga. When we came to anchor we were about two leagues short of the falls." (They were at Georgetown, the first of a good many white men to come.)

> This place without all question is the most pleasant and healthful place in all this country, and most convenient for habitation, the air temperate in summer and not violent in winter. It aboundeth with all manner of fish. The Indians in one night will catch thirty sturgeons in a place where the river is not above twelve fathoms broad. And as for deer, buffaloes, bears, turkeys, the woods do swarm with them, and the soil is exceedingly fertile.

Now the sturgeon have departed, victims of river pollution. The woods swarm, not with bear and wild turkey, but with real-estate developers. Now the river flows tawny with silt from the ravaged land. But it still remains the principal geographic feature of this spot where a new nation built a new capital.

Carefully and cunningly the site was chosen, fittingly by the man for whom the city was to be named. George Washington knew the area well, only some fifteen miles north of his beloved Mount Vernon, a region broken into patches of timber and cornfields set in a bowl of low hills where the river spreads out after tumbling down the last rocks of the Fall Line. In New York a new and struggling Congress, riven by conflict, turned the final decision over to the man who had made so many judicious decisions during the arduous Revolution. The Father of his Country would know best. He chose the place where he had crossed the Potomac by ferry, on journeys north to lead his tattered armies. Modern travelers must look sharp to see the site as it really is, the surrounding hills, the green cleft river, the arching skies. Bemused by his own works, modern man tends to see only the buildings that have risen, the highways and the bridges that have scarred the landscape, and the unending suburbs of creeping monotony. But the land survives, and the wisdom of Washington's choice endures beyond the later works of man.

Horticulturally, it was a meeting of North and South. This was the northern practical limit for many of the natural treasures of the South, of boxwood and camellia, and they mixed well with the evergreens and hardy trees that crept down from the North. Almost everything would grow here except palm trees and their like. The climate was salubrious, as Fleete boasted, mainly mild in winter, in summer pleasant except for those awful attacks of humidity. But then what East Coast site was free from such attacks? At this altitude—seventy-five feet—and this latitude—thirty-nine degrees—humidity is a natural occurrence. Even New York, which boasts a superior situation, swelters in humidity intensified by encompassing masonry. The river seemed the greatest token of future greatness. It was second to none on the Atlantic, second not even to the mighty Hudson in drainage area and possibilities for transport. Here the Father of our Country erred. But why could we expect him to foresee that the Mohawk Valley and the Erie Canal would be the principal route west? He believed he had chosen a conjunction of all things, a conjunction of North and South, just as nature indicated, and of East and West as the Potomac seemed to foretell. George Washington's motives were also political, and nothing could have better foreshadowed the character of his city than this political beginning. The North-versus-South conflict worried the Founding Fathers, as it has generations of their successors. The northern colonies already were oriented toward business, the southern ones toward agriculture. Business meant free yeomen, and agriculture, in those days, meant slaves. The theme recurs forever in American history. George Washington, man of thought as well as of action, foresaw the problem. Every relevant letter that he left behind, every order and note, bears on the primacy of choosing a site balancing North and South to unite a country then only lightly tied together, a new country of ill-knit states, frightened of independence and sharing little except residence on the far side of the Atlantic.

A dinner party in New York settled the site of the future capital. Thomas Jefferson described how he had found Alexander Hamilton pacing nervously one day outside President Washington's quarters. The new nation, Hamilton told him, was in crisis. Would the new federal government assume the debts run up by various colonies during the late Revolution? Without Assumption, the nation could not establish with foreign bankers the credit needed to launch the nation; and the Southerners were holding out against Assumption. He asked Jefferson's help. Newly back from years in France, Jefferson demurred on the ground that he was not yet abreast of domestic issues. Finally he agreed, however, to invite a few members of Congress to dine that night with Hamilton. At that dinner the compromise was worked out—the Southerners would back Assumption in return for getting the capital where they wanted it, on the Potomac. And the deal stuck. By act of Congress, President Washington was given authority to choose a site anywhere on the Potomac between the East Branch, now called the Anacostia, and the Conococheague, high in Maryland, near the Pennsylvania line. Until the compromise, Wright's Ferry, Pennsylvania, at the falls of the Susquehanna, had been the Northerners' principal candidate for a site. Others in the running were Annapolis, Trenton, Baltimore and Germantown.

George Washington set to work quickly, lest the deal come unstuck. Congress would meet in Philadelphia for the last decade of the eighteenth century, then remove to the banks of the Potomac. His decision must already have been made, because there is no record that he gave serious consideration to locations other than the one between Georgetown and the East Branch. From that locality he chose three men to be the future city's commissioners, and a man to design a city. There was no competition for the job, no far-ranging search for the best brains and skill for such an important commission. The President, accustomed to command, simply picked his man—an eccentric Frenchman, Pierre Charles L'Enfant.

AYSH-KE-BAH-KE-KO-ZHAY.
(FLAT-MOUTH.)
A CHIPPEWA CHIEF.

II

Alas, poor L'Enfant, he served us well. In his own time he was neglected, a pauper on his deathbed. L'Enfant's fame, nonetheless, has long outlived that of most of his contemporaries. How account for the persistence of the L'Enfant Plan in Washington and for the constant recurrence of his name? Some 175 years have passed since he drew his city design, and a different civilization has emerged to inhabit his city, yet his name still has magic. A new plaza is named for him, new streets; speakers invoke his name; a few knowing tourists visit his grave and turn to look across the slow Potomac at the panorama of his work. Perhaps his name recurs because "planning" has come into a new vogue, the reverse of New Deal days when a favorite vituperation was to call one's enemy a "planner," intimating him to be socialist, un-American, doubtless loyal to Moscow. In the current lexicon a planner is a man with vision, skill and guts. A whole suburb (Reston, Virginia) gets planned on a single drawing board. Social workers collaborate with economists and architects to plan a huge section of the city (Southwest Washington). Highway builders make the biggest, and usually the most destructive, plans which other planners then must modify. Planners are everywhere, and with them has come a new birth of interest in Pierre Charles L'Enfant, who started it all in Washington.

L'Enfant was crotchety and vindictive; George Washington finally fired him, and he spent the balance of his days badgering Congress for money he felt, with considerable justice, was his due. Yet despite all negations, this strange, semi-educated man laid down a plan whose bones still show through a modern, bustling city after almost two centuries. The bones are good; the structure serves. And with occasional surgery

West parlor, Mount Vernon

9

here, a grafting there, it should serve the city for a long time, perhaps forever, insofar as cities can be said to live "forever."

Son of a Gobelin tapestry designer, L'Enfant was born in Paris in 1754, studied at least briefly at the Royal Academy, and was a French Army lieutenant in 1776 when he volunteered to join thirty other French soldiers in helping the American Revolutionists. That is the sum of the records he left behind in France. Miraculously, some records have survived of his service with the Revolutionists, enough to make one feel that L'Enfant fought a good war: Valley Forge; the siege of Savannah, where he was wounded; capture by the British and exchange for a Hessian soldier. L'Enfant emerged a major with a commendation from General Washington himself. In fact, L'Enfant somehow managed to keep quite close to the Commander in Chief, and though his principal duties were in the Corps of Engineers, he impressed on Washington his abilities as a draftsman and as a man of many talents. He was called on for all kinds of creative chores—to sketch a portrait, to design a banquet hall, to draw a fortress, and finally, after the war was over, to design a city. Perhaps L'Enfant's ubiquity and eagerness made it natural for Washington to turn to him. Certainly it indicates the paucity of creative manpower in the states, for L'Enfant was almost entirely self-taught in architecture and city planning.

Jefferson, as usual, was able to reach into his own cultural baggage and provide L'Enfant with some of the materials he needed. In one bundle, Jefferson sent him the plans of Amsterdam, Strasbourg, Paris, Frankfort on the Main, Karlsruhe, Orléans, Bordeaux, Lyons, Montpellier, Marseilles, Turin and Milan. An incredible list, but then Jefferson collected everything—scientific instruments, books on science, art, agriculture, seeds, trees, furniture. Why not city plans? By the spring of 1791, L'Enfant set to work along the Potomac, armed with Jefferson's maps, a compass, surveying instruments and little else but a remarkable mind. On foot and horseback he crisscrossed the hills, swamps, woods

Right
Deputy commissioner for Indian affairs

Next two pages
George Washington's house

10

and cultivated fields that stretched east from the little port of George-town. This was the site General Washington had chosen; and L'Enfant, learning every contour with amazing speed, roughed out his plan by June of that year. George Washington found it attractive, and by December it was being exhibited proudly in the halls of Congress. How simple and effortless it seems. Yet this man, working in a raw, ill-defined landscape, had imagined a city plan of considerable sophistication.

What L'Enfant proposed with such speed is the essence of the city as it stands today. The Capitol he placed on Jenkins Hill—a "pedestal," he called it, "waiting for a monument." The president's house was assigned a favorable spot looking down the river toward Alexandria. Between the two buildings he drew an elegant diagonal—Pennsylvania Avenue. He allotted a broad open space for the Mall, then extended a grid pattern out from the main public areas, a grid relieved by diagonals and circles. They were, he said, aimed at pleasing the eye and providing "pleasant prospects," as well as quick transportation between various points. They are there today, where L'Enfant put them—Dupont Circle, Scott Circle, Logan and Washington Circles, all imparting a grace to the city which an ordinary rectangular system never would have achieved. The avenues yield vistas and hasten intracity communication, just as he planned. The accomplishment is L'Enfant's. He had nothing to do with execution of the plan—in fact, he was dismissed before another year was out—but no one has been able to subtract one iota of credit from him. He did it single-handed. Poor L'Enfant! One can only conclude that he was a genius. The rest of his life was trouble.

From the beginning, the three district commissioners had found Washington's engineer and city planner a thorny, high-handed employee. He declined to submit to their authority, constantly tried to deal with the President over their heads, was careless of finances and, finally, extremely laggard about producing the master drawing for the engravers. But L'Enfant had a case for his own side; his principal oppo-

Capitol gatepost

11

nents were land speculators, and he had a running battle to keep the great site open for his vaulting imagination. Matters reached a crisis when L'Enfant, hard at work driving actual stakes and cutting trees where his great avenues were to be, found that a local burgher, Daniel Carroll of Duddington (a house that stood near the present site of the Capitol), was building a new residence athwart an avenue. L'Enfant, to the horror of the commissioners, had the house torn down. Writing to Washington about the matter, Thomas Jefferson reported, "The Major says he had as much right to pull down a house as to cut a tree," and went on to observe that a jury, however, would award "much greater damages for destroying a house than a tree." With this as one big mark against him, the commissioners promptly found L'Enfant guilty of complete insubordination and told Washington they wished to fire his engineer.

Instead of making it easier for the President, L'Enfant behaved so haughtily to Washington's aide that the President felt himself insulted and broke with L'Enfant forever. It was a sad moment, nobody behaving very well, the proud, insolent designer perhaps worst of all. The matter of pay came up immediately. Washington thought his services to date worth $2500 to $3000, suggesting that the commissioners might, as an alternative, offer L'Enfant 500 guineas and a choice lot in the new city. They chose the latter, but L'Enfant turned it down as too niggardly. The matter rested there until 1800, when he presented to Congress a claim for $9500 just as that august body was moving into the new city L'Enfant had designed. Congress rejected the claim. Ten years later, after constant badgering from a man on the edge of privation and hounded by creditors, Congress voted to L'Enfant the princely sum of $1394.20. Before L'Enfant could refuse again, his creditors closed in and took the pittance. Still he had one more chance to turn down something from the federal government—an appointment as professor at West Point. True to form, he declined that, too, in 1812.

At last poverty engulfed this strange, neurotic, talented man. His final decade was spent as the dependent of well-to-do landowners living just outside the city. At his death in 1825, aged seventy-one, the pitiful estate he left behind was this:

3 watches	$ 30
3 compasses	12
Surveying instruments and books	2
1 lot of maps	1
	$ 45

Did those maps include, one wonders, the incredible bundle Jefferson had given him? What they would be worth today!

Two men could scarcely have been more unlike, Jefferson and L'Enfant, the one so thorny, obstinate, gifted in creativity but wanting in ability to deal with his fellow men, the other cultivated, philosophical, an intellectual, able to cajole men into carrying out his loftiest ideas. Both left an imprint on the city they helped found, an imprint visible a century and three-quarters later. L'Enfant's mark is largely physical; Jefferson's is spiritual and of such depth that the two men should not, of course, be considered on the same par.

Jefferson was, to all intents and purposes, the first president in Washington, though John Adams, with his doughty Abigail, did spend a few months in the unfinished White House just as his term ended, long enough for Mrs. Adams to hang her famous wash in the East Room and complain about the lack of firewood and adequate servants. It remained for Jefferson, first president to take his oath in the city, to set the style of the presidency in its new setting and, most of all, to establish a relationship between the presidency and the city.

Jefferson's Washington was a strange little settlement that boasted just 599 habitable houses, a handful of government buildings, a few dozen stores, warehouses, inns and other business places connected by unpaved roads branching out through the clearings L'Enfant had started.

First snow

To the civic problems of this unfinished town Jefferson devoted infinite time and thought, establishing the President as de facto mayor, a state of affairs that has continued ever since, with minor variations.

A basic problem was to attract private capital to the new city, so that it would not be dependent solely on federal expenditures. Jefferson tried to do it by encouraging new banks, by giving priority to principal streets and by river-wharf construction. His often-stated predilection for Greek Revival architecture influenced private builders, as well as those operating with government funds. So strong was the influence that even today one can still find old houses or even a few rows of early structures that bear the Jeffersonian stamp, mostly three-story red-brick houses with dormers, white trim, classical motifs incorporated in the design, uniform in concept but individual in detail. As city dwellings they are still pleasantly habitable.

The height of buildings was an early Jeffersonian concern, and there again he left a distinctive stamp upon the city. No building, he said even before removing to the capital, should be allowed to rise above three stories and thus compete with the Capitol. Such foresight is all the more remarkable since no American city had yet become vertical. Though Jefferson's strict three-story rule has been relaxed over the years the principle has not been abandoned. Washington has remained a horizontal city. Jefferson's concern with outdoor beauty led him to plant quick-growing poplars along Pennsylvania Avenue, to give it the definition which later planners have constantly re-emphasized, and to order further plantings of slow-growing oaks and elms for permanence. Trees, houses, wharves, stonework on the new Capitol—nothing seemed to escape his broad-ranging attention, despite his necessary musing over deeper matters, such as citizen participation in the affairs of an expanding and complex republic.

The style Jefferson gave the presidency was unstudied, a style that flowed easily and naturally from the man himself, his philosophy, his intellect, his attitude toward his fellow men. His predecessors had invested the presidency with a touch of regality, formal levees and receptions reminiscent of court life. Jefferson turned away from such practices toward an informality that delighted his fellow citizens, though it shocked some diplomats, notably the British minister, who complained about being received by a president in house slippers and rumpled coat. His house, instead of repeating the adapted English customs and decorations current among American gentlemen, took on a French flavor, resulting, no doubt, from his long sojourn in Paris. Quality of food and drink took precedence over elaborate protocol. Equally novel, the quality of conversation that occurred while food and drink were dispensed was of even higher order.

In the Jeffersonian pattern of life the President's informal entertainments in the White House became more important than the formal ones. The White House became a curious yet comfortable blend of home and palace, where senators and representatives could be invited for a meal and conversation, where private citizens might mingle with the official guests to the mutual advantage of all. Jefferson made the presidency an intimate part of the city, an intimacy that flowered into an affection so deep that when he retired in 1809 the local citizenry addressed him an extraordinary farewell:

> The world knows you as a philosopher and philanthropist; the American people know you as a patriot and statesman—we know you in addition to this as a *man....* It is to you we owe much, very much of that harmony of intercourse and tolerance of opinion which characterize our state of society...we pray you may be happy and if... [you receive] but a portion of the felicity you have conferred on others, our prayers will be fulfilled.

Much moved, Jefferson responded to the citizens of Washington that he was happy to lay down the burden of office, "...but it is with sincere regret that I part with the society in which I have lived here. It has been the source of much happiness to me."

From Monticello, he kept close watch on developments in his beloved city, and when disaster struck only five years later he was quick to proffer help. Jefferson's Washington was the city scarred by British torches in the War of 1812, and while he branded the entire incendiary attack as "vandalism," he was most angered by the burning of the Library of Congress. Brick and stone could be restored, but not books. The destruction of a library, the repository of man's learning, was an attack on human dignity.

Only three weeks after the British attack Jefferson wrote offering to give to Congress, as a replacement, his dearest possession, his personal library. "I have been fifty years making it and have spared no pains, opportunity, or expense," he said, counting it as between nine and ten thousand volumes and describing the collection's vast scope in philosophy, religion, science, law, politics and many other fields, as well as the richness of the bindings. Humbly, he asked only to keep a few books for pleasure during his remaining years, promising that on his death they, too, would join what became the nucleus of a new Library of Congress and finally one of the great libraries of the world. That gift, better than any words, explains Jefferson's feelings toward the city, the government and the nation he helped create.

Right
Tombstones by Latrobe, Congressional Cemetery

Next two pages
The Rotunda

THE HONORABLE
J. PINCKNEY HENDERSON
A SENATOR IN THE
CONGRESS OF THE
UNITED STATES
FROM THE STATE OF
TEXAS
BORN 31 MARCH 1808
DIED 4 JUNE 1858

III

Jefferson's gift came at a time when American morale was lower than at any time since Valley Forge. The nation was invaded, the capital captured, the government scattered and the White House a smoldering ruin. One can only imagine what this must have meant to a new and uncertain nation. Militarily the damage was not very grave but the psychological scars were deep. How else explain the persistence of talk, even to this very day, of "when the British burned Washington"? A cabdriver whose knowledge of history is, to say the least, sketchy will lecture his fare about which sections of the modern Capitol were actually burned, and every professional guide includes a lurid description in his spiel. Visiting British statesmen and newly arriving ambassadors inevitably make some reference to the event, usually with arch jocularity. This curious persistence in the city's consciousness, a century and three-quarters later, is a recurrent reminder that invasion is, after all, possible. Ironically the one invader was the nation destined to become, in time, our closest friend and ally.

For an understanding of Washington one must go back to the crudely blended comedy and tragedy of August 24, 1814, the Battle of Bladensburg. If it were not for the fact that brave men died there, the battle would have been little but a farce: army officers, jealous of command, arguing with each other instead of preparing defenses; politicians galloping hither and yon or hurtling about in carriages, frantic but futile; a small redcoat force marching off from their ships, anchored up the Patuxent River, uncertain what they were heading into.

The War of 1812, "Mr. Madison's War," was an unpopular one with most Americans. British naval power had brought commerce to a stand-

A Senate staircase

17

still. New England seethed with separatist talk. Only Maryland responded to Madison's call for help in defending the capital, and Maryland's assistance was meager; the bulk of her troops was kept for defense of Baltimore, a much more likely target. Washington seemed scarcely worth a battle. A dozen or so government buildings stood along the avenues L'Enfant had designed. Houses, taverns and shops clustered here and there among the trees. A small navy yard had been built up the Anacostia. Otherwise, it was a capital in name only. Still, Admiral Sir George Cockburn, sailing with orders to harass the coast and punish the Americans, found it worth a thrust inland from the Patuxent, a little estuary of the Chesapeake. Cockburn, instead of sailing up the Potomac, was attacking the back door, as any moderately astute military man might have foreseen. Aboard his ships was a well-trained body of troops under command of Major General Robert Ross, a forty-eight-year-old Irish veteran of the Peninsular Wars. The troops were put ashore August 17 and for the ensuing five days marched leisurely through the woods and fields of Maryland, unchallenged by a single shot, harassed only by heat and bugs. Not until they were nine miles from Washington did they meet a soldier. There an outpost was encountered, but it hastily withdrew.

Horsemen bringing news of the British landing plunged the capital into fresh orgies of panic. The records left behind by cabinet and army indicate that nothing practical was done to defend the city until an aroused citizenry offered to build earthworks at Bladensburg, obviously where the British must cross the Anacostia. Newly appointed by Madison to organize the defenses, Brigadier General William Winder accepted the offer, and digging started while the British marched. A vacillating type, Winder insisted the British might head for the Navy Yard Bridge instead of Bladensburg. At ten o'clock Wednesday morning, August 24, Winder received word the British were nearing Bladensburg; only then did he believe it.

Right
Lafayette Square

Next two pages
The Queen's Birthday Party

"In the utmost haste he started for the same point, preceded by Monroe and followed by the President and the rest of the cabinet and the troops," wrote a later historian, Henry Adams. Just the thing to help the situation—a president and his cabinet on the battlefield! But there they were. And there were 2000 men sent from Baltimore, another 1000 assorted soldiers whose officers were trying to form a battle line. The British were already in sight when Winder and some 2000 more soldiers arrived breathless, assembling into line wherever they could. They had no cover, and the hastily built entrenchments were never used.

A British soldier wrote later that the Americans "seemed country people who would have been much more appropriately employed in attending to their agricultural occupations than in standing with muskets in their hands on the brow of a bare, green hill." These were not gimlet-eyed frontiersmen, accustomed to tracking bear and Indians, about to give a lesson to European soldiers; these were farmers and small tradesmen whose bravery was all the more touching because they lacked both training and leadership.

In suffocating August heat, the first British light brigade, without waiting for rear troops to arrive, dashed across the bridge into the face of hot musketry fire that checked them for a moment, but they pressed on and quickly brought their Congreve rockets into play. The rockets, rather like fireworks pieces but with exploding cases, struck terror into the American lines. Within a half-hour, the lines wavered, then broke. One unit retired in an orderly manner toward Washington. A band of 400 sailors held out briefly along the road. The rest was panic: disordered soldiers walking, running, riding off westward through dusty heat toward Georgetown, Rockville and safety. The great battle was over. Quick though it was, the British lost 64 dead, 185 wounded. American casualties were 26 killed, 51 wounded. For this price, a capital fell.

Two hours of rest, then the British marched on. About sunset, sweaty and thirsty, they appeared over a small knoll at Second Street, North-

Chauffeurs

east, a block from the partly finished Capitol. By eight o'clock Admiral Cockburn and his men had piled books, desks, chairs and carpets in the House of Representatives and mocked the proceedings of democracy. "All in favor of burning this nest of Yankee——, say 'Aye,'" the legend says Cockburn shouted. There were no dissenting votes, and torches were applied. By eleven, the White House was in flames. The War Department Building, a hotel, the ropewalks near the Arsenal, all were set afire—and the following day, the Treasury.

President Madison, as soon as fighting started, had retired from the battlefield and soon was surrounded by retreating soldiers as he hastened back to the terrified capital. At six o'clock he slipped across the Potomac in a small boat from the White House grounds and, by carriage, fled into Virginia. The next night the President, alarmed by rumors that were groundless, hid in the woods, fearing he too would be captured—which must be counted the nadir of the presidency.

How small it all seems now, in times when the burning of a capital would be a holocaust enveloping millions of persons; how tiny the Battle of Bladensburg, involving only a few more than 10,000 men in all, less than an infantry division. In perspective it was merely a brief raid. The damage was slight because there was so little to burn—never to be compared with the great fire of London or even Chicago's disaster. But the memory persists because the act was symbolic, as so much in Washington is.

Jefferson's Washington was restored and enlarged in the ensuing years, but progress was a good deal slower than he had optimistically expected. When Jefferson retired, the city population stood at 8000. Forty years later, on the eve of the Civil War, there were close to 60,000 inhabitants. The steady population increase, instead of solving problems by attracting skilled artisans and men with bank accounts, had only multiplied them; Jefferson's successors failed to demonstrate either skill or vision equal to his in the struggle to create a great city.

Right
Washington Monument at night

Next two pages
Detail, monument to General Grant

20

Diplomats and foreign travelers had, for two generations, ridiculed Washington, its "magnificent distances" leading nowhere, its muddy streets, poor lighting, crude plumbing and, most of all, its provincialism. The discontent was not limited to foreigners. Congressmen and government officials complained aloud, and scarcely a year passed without a new plan to move the capital elsewhere, north or west, anywhere just so it was away from the miasmic swamps along the Potomac, anywhere with better rail connections, anywhere with better-developed city facilities. The government's investment in real estate was still small enough so that proponents of change felt a shift could be made without insupportable loss. The Capitol, with two new wings by Thomas U. Walter, was nearing the shape we know today, although the dome was not yet complete. A handsome Treasury Building had been erected—across Pennsylvania Avenue, unfortunately—and was of suitable grandeur. James Renwick's Smithsonian had added a novel note to the heavily forested Mall. But there were still no great complexes of government buildings. Small Georgian structures still dominated a city which lacked grand houses, theaters, great churches, schools, intellectual institutions, a stylish life, all the things one associates with great capitals. The atmosphere remained palpably southern, a little sleepy except when Congress was in session.

What the city had achieved, in a positive way, was much harder to define than its deficiencies. Looking back, with the superiority of time, it is apparent that Washington had achieved something greater than massive buildings. Within sixty years Washington had become the political center of the nation, not yet dominant, to be sure, but still the meeting ground, the debating hall, the center stage in a great struggle moving inexorably toward a bloody denouement—the struggle which decided that the Union should be preserved and that the capital should remain fixed in Washington.

More than any other single event, the Civil War gave Washington a

Lincoln Memorial

new physical look, a new importance. A decade after the war, a little-known writer, Mary Clemmer Ames, analyzed perceptively what happened to America when Abraham Lincoln summoned the states to send troops for the defense of their capital.

> How many an American boy, marching to its defense, beholding for the first time the great dome of the Capitol rising before his eyes, comprehended in one deep gaze, as he never had in his whole life before, *all* that that Capitol meant to him and to every free man. Never, till the capital had cost the life of the beautiful and the brave of our land, did it become to the heart of the American citizen of the nineteenth Century the object of personal love that it was to George Washington....

Mrs. Ames had lived long in Washington and had watched the raw, sunburned troops as they bivouacked across the city, moved out to battle, and then came back to fill the hideous temporary hospitals with their sufferings. Beyond the swirling action of every day, she perceived something deep happening in the hearts of Americans. "Washington city," she wrote,

> was no longer a name to the mother waiting and praying in the distant hamlet; her boy was camped on the floor of the rotunda. No longer a far off myth to the lonely wife; her husband held guard on the heights defending the capital. No longer a place good for nothing but political schemes to the village sage; his boy, wrapped in a blanket, slept on the stone steps of the great treasury.
>
> Never, till that hour, did the Federal city become to the heart of the American people what it had so long been in the eyes of the world—truly the capital of the nation.

Democracy was creating the symbols every nation needs. Myth and legend and symbol are necessary, if a system of government is to survive. In authoritarian regimes, the symbolism is easy: a crown, a wreath, a hammer and a sickle. But democracy finds the search slow. Freedom and equality are hard to symbolize, and no one, not even General Washington himself, could have foreseen that the dome of this strange, slowly accumulating Capitol building would emerge as a symbol to rank along with the flag in its ability to move the hearts of men. True, myth and

The second inaugural address of the sixteenth President

IF WE SHALL SUPPOSE THAT AMERICAN SLAVERY IS ONE OF THOSE OFFENSES WHICH IN THE PROVIDENCE OF GOD MUST NEEDS COME BUT WHICH HAVING CONTINUED THROUGH HIS APPOINTED TIME HE NOW WILLS TO REMOVE AND THAT HE GIVES TO BOTH NORTH AND SOUTH THIS TERRIBLE WAR AS THE WOE DUE TO THOSE BY WHOM THE OFFENSE CAME SHALL WE DISCERN THEREIN ANY DEPARTURE FROM THOSE DIVINE ATTRIBUTES WHICH THE BELIEVERS IN A LIVING GOD ALWAYS ASCRIBE TO HIM. FONDLY DO WE HOPE ~ FERVENTLY DO WE PRAY ~ THAT THIS MIGHTY SCOURGE OF WAR MAY SPEEDILY PASS AWAY · YET IF GOD WILLS THAT IT CONTINUE UNTIL ALL THE WEALTH PILED BY THE BONDSMAN'S TWO HUNDRED AND FIFTY YEARS OF UNREQUITED TOIL SHALL BE SUNK AND UNTIL EVERY DROP OF BLOOD DRAWN WITH THE LASH SHALL BE PAID BY ANOTHER DRAWN WITH THE SWORD AS WAS SAID THREE THOUSAND YEARS AGO SO STILL IT MUST BE SAID "THE JUDGMENTS OF THE LORD ARE TRUE AND RIGHTEOUS ALTOGETHER·"

WITH MALICE TOWARD NONE WITH CHARITY FOR ALL WITH FIRMNESS IN THE RIGHT AS GOD GIVES US TO SEE THE RIGHT LET US STRIVE ON TO FINISH THE WORK WE ARE IN TO BIND UP THE NATION'S WOUNDS TO CARE FOR HIM WHO SHALL HAVE BORNE THE BATTLE AND FOR HIS WIDOW AND HIS ORPHAN ~ TO DO ALL WHICH MAY ACHIEVE AND CHERISH A JUST AND LASTING PEACE AMONG OURSELVES AND WITH ALL NATIONS ·

legend had been evolving in the nation's first eighty years—legends such as those about noble Pilgrims, so pure of heart; legends of bravery against the forest savage, the British oppressor and the foreign invader. Washington himself was taking on a mythological character. He seemed so much a figure of Providence. The genius of his military campaigning, his strength of character in holding the ill-assorted colonies together, and his wisdom in turning the presidency into a viable office that could be handed on to his successors, all sustained the myth.

His was a persuasive legend but still lacking the greater mystical quality that a new nation needed, and finally found, at the same moment the Capitol dome itself emerged as a national symbol. The miracle was Lincoln. Millions of words have been written to explain the mystique of Lincoln. None, finally, has succeeded. About him we know almost everything—his wisdom, his inner strength, his humor, his religious faith, his sense of destiny—everything but the final mystery. Here was autocratic power wielded with compassion, political mastery combined with some unprecedented occult quality, a religious mysticism which ignored orthodox theology. Father Abraham was called thus by his soldiers long before psychologists came to talk of father figures. The mystery is as triumphant as the miracle he performed. By the end of the Civil War a supreme figure had joined the Pantheon, and the capital had taken on a new symbolism.

From that moment forward, Washington was a different city. Though physical development was halting, the city never again was a sleepy southern village stirred to action only during the months Congress was in session. Too much history had engulfed the capital, too much depended now on the actions of the government, first in coping with Reconstruction of the ruined South and then in keeping pace with the rampant industrialization which was changing the face of the land. Looking around after the Civil War, Washington began to recognize its inadequacies—the poorness of the streets, the lack of sanitation, the

Boss Shepherd

23

desecration of L'Enfant's plan—and set out to rise by the bootstraps. What followed was a brief, sometimes hilarious period of violent activity, most of it directed by Alexander (Boss) Shepherd. Under his enthusiastic direction, miles of streets were paved, sidewalks built, 60,000 trees planted, an adequate sewer system created and reservoirs dug, all in a ruthless, high-handed manner worthy of Baron Haussmann at his best. But President Grant, Shepherd's patron, was no Napoleon III and never gave Shepherd the powers that had enabled Haussmann a few years earlier to change the face of Paris by imposing the uniformity of height and façade which turned the French capital into the Paris we know. Both Shepherd and Haussmann achieved, however, one common end—bankruptcy, the fate which so often befalls the imaginative and the creative, the men whose ultimate beneficiaries are the tightfisted and the shortsighted. Without Shepherd's openhanded spending, the city would never have been able to move on to further glories, nor would it have been ready, thirty years later, for the third wave of planners who would again change the face of Washington. The third wave was the McMillan Commission, who took the stage in the time of Theodore Roosevelt. But before they came, Washington and the nation went through a strange and not altogether edifying period, the days of the Robber Barons—voracious expansion, building of railroads, corruption, boom and bust.

Boss Shepherd, as he ripped up Washington streets, rooted out the sewers and ran up colossal debts, was a figure typical of his time. When the municipal and congressional outcries grew too great, President Grant vacillated, as another, later military president was to do, and Shepherd lost his job. With poetic justice he ended his days developing Mexican gold mines that never quite paid off, and though he came home to unexpected honors from a forgiving citizenry, Shepherd never made the fortune that he had sought.

Shepherd's flamboyance fits with the age of Jay Gould and the others, but an atypical figure teaches us most about those tumultuous

Tomb in Which Andrew Jackson REFUSED to be Buried

This Roman sarcophagus, of about the 3rd Century and mistakenly believed to have contained the remains of the Roman emperor Alexander Severus, was acquired in Beirut, Syria (now Lebanon), by Commodore Jesse D. Elliott and brought to the U.S. in 1838 aboard the U.S. frigate *Constitution.* Elliott offered the sarcophagus to the National Institute, a forerunner of the Smithsonian Institution, in 1845 with the suggestion that it be offered to former President Andrew Jackson for his final resting place. Jackson, then in retirement at the Hermitage in Tennessee, thanked Elliott for the honor but emphatically declined, saying that his republican principles forbade his burial in a "repository prepared for an Emperor or King".

JACKSON'S LETTER TO ELLIOTT
March 27, 1845

I cannot consent that my mortal body shall be laid in a repository prepared for an Emperor or King — my republican feelings and principles forbid it — the simplicity of our system of government forbids it. Every monument erected to perpetuate the memory of our heroes and statesmen ought to bear evidence of the economy and simplicity of our republican institutions and the plainness of our republican citizens, who are the sovereigns of our glorious Union, and whose virtue is to perpetuate it. True virtue cannot exist where pomp and parade are the governing passions. It can only dwell with the people, the great laboring and producing classes, that form the bone and sinew of our confederacy.

I have prepared an humble depository for my mortal body beside that wherein lies my beloved wife, where, without any pomp or parade, I have requested, when my God calls me to sleep with my fathers, to be laid, for both of us there to remain until the last trumpet sounds to call the dead to judgment, when we, I hope, shall rise together, clothed with that heavenly body promised to all who believe in our glorious Redeemer, who died for us that we might live, and by whose atonement I hope for a blessed immortality.

I am, with great respect, your friend and fellow citizen,

(s) Andrew Jackson

decades ending the nineteenth century, a man who never occupied the White House nor any governmental office, a man who stood on the sidelines, watching, commenting, disapproving, never participating, remembering everything—Henry Adams.

One of the stranger figures in American history, Adams seems to grow rather than shrink in importance as the years go by. Despite his own sense of rejection, Adams managed to be on the edge of great events, to stay near the seat of power and to know intimately most of the great political figures of his time. Adams' great-grandfather, John, was the second president. His grandfather, John Quincy, was the sixth. His father, Charles Francis, was Lincoln's ambassador to London. To an Adams the presidency seemed close to a family prerogative and the White House a normal place where one might expect someday to live. In his early twenties Henry Adams went as his father's private secretary to London, where he played a role in the great struggle to keep the Britain of Palmerston and Russell from recognizing the Confederacy as a nation. In his brilliant *Education,* Adams shows some guilt qualms at not having served as a soldier, along with all of the young men of his generation, but finally he came to feel that his role in London was of sufficient importance to merit absolution, a stand with which one is inclined today to agree. He came back to America expecting to do what an Adams naturally would do—participate in the governing of the nation. As a journalist he wrote a bit, making frank use of the high sources open to him as an Adams. But somehow, slowly, he began to realize that there was no great demand for his services in government, that his friends fresh from military service were finding the same thing true, that they were in fact a lost generation—the first of several the nation was to produce.

The final blow was the election of Ulysses S. Grant. Adams had, of course, met Grant. He met or knew everybody. What he knew of him didn't impress Adams much, but he was willing to wait and see. What

A president's letter

25

he saw horrified him. Years later, writing his *Education,* Adams reported:

The progress of evolution from President Washington to President Grant was alone evidence enough to upset Darwin.

At Washington, in 1869–70 every intelligent man about the Government prepared to go.... The administration drove [Adams] and thousands of other young men into active enmity, not only to Grant but to the system or want of system which took possession of the President.

Turning his back on these horrors, Adams retreated to Cambridge and the Harvard faculty for seven years, but the pull of Washington was too strong. Government intrigued him more than pedagogy, and some of his friends were trickling back to Washington, now that Grant and his sycophants were leaving. Among those friends was John Hay, who had returned to be assistant secretary of state and to work on his life of Lincoln with his fellow secretary, John Nicolay.

Soon Adams found a niche he was to occupy the rest of his life. He described it himself as "stable-companion to statesmen." They exchanged cozy visits, had tea or dinner, walked across Lafayette Park to the White House, all in a tight little world. "Lafayette Square was society," Adams wrote:

Within a few hundred yards of Mr. Clark Mills' nursery monument to ... Andrew Jackson, one found all one's acquaintances as well as hotels, banks, markets and national government. Beyond the square the country began.

A tight world, but in reality Washington was beginning to change in character and looks. Adams and Hay jointly commissioned Henry H. Richardson to build them a double house alongside Lafayette Square, more original in style than any architecture the capital had seen until then, with the exception of Renwick's Smithsonian. Richardson's double house was typical of his work, massive, romantic, combining much rough stone with carved details. At least it was a new look. And across the park A. D. Mullet was creating the new State, War and Navy Building, tiers of gray granite columns piled up row on row. The strictly Georgian look of Washington was disappearing, the look which Jefferson had cultivated and which had left a late-eighteenth-century stamp on the city through its first decades.

The streets and circles of L'Enfant's plan were beginning to fill out. Larger houses were going up. Wealthy western senators, some with copper fortunes, others with silver, chose to announce new riches with fine houses. Congressional families began to establish headquarters in the capital city and ceased to patronize hotels and boardinghouses.

Society spread beyond Lafayette Square as the embassies moved up Connecticut Avenue toward Dupont Circle. The city was changing, growing along with the nation it ruled. More important, the people in Washington were changing. They no longer seemed predominantly direct descendants of the high-minded, dedicated men of the Federal period. New men were appearing along with new styles of architecture, rougher, more aggressive men, men bent on using government to improve their fortunes and the fortunes of their friends. The gentlemanly atmosphere yielded to the dominance of business. The red-brick houses with white trim were giving way to bolder, more ornate and ostentatious structures which would have saddened Jefferson. Men were changing along with the architecture. Or, perhaps, vice versa.

IV

Reading the stones of Washington is scarcely as complicated as reading those of Greece or Egypt, but for all the newness of the American capital, it has accumulated, in a century and three-quarters, a vigor and complexity of its own. From the touchingly simple Greek Revival buildings of the earliest days to the reinforced concrete of the latest era, the city can be read as a brief essay on the development of American architecture, even though certain pages are missing and not all the illustrations are in sharp focus. Beyond a mere architectural record, however, the stones of Washington speak other messages—about the foibles of men, the workings of democracy, and even the ideals of the republic. A record, coldly cataloguing changes of taste, would be of only antiquarian interest. When buildings begin to say more, like the churches and palaces of Florence or the Cathedral in Chartres, when they begin to reflect aspirations as well as pretensions, then buildings, particularly in groups, are worth a close perusal. Such testaments in stone may say more than the writings and orations of the times in which they were built.

By sheer bulk, the Capitol and the obelisk soaring above the Mall are insistent images in the mind's eye, so dominating they are hard to view in any analytical or comprehending way, so overwhelmingly symbolic that their intrinsic qualities seldom are noted. The Washington Monument and the Capitol dome together form a symbol as universally recognized as the Eiffel Tower, or, more aptly, the Acropolis. Democracy builds by fits and starts, and very slowly. So it was with the monument and the dome. The Capitol was begun in 1792, and the tenants are still making major alterations every time they can get the money. The monument was begun in 1848, and thirty-six years later its capstone was set

Right
Small rotunda, Latrobe, the Senate

Next two pages
Washington Monument, winter

in place. The fitful course of construction includes quarrels over design, charges of incompetence, changes in plans, new concepts, shortage of funds, occasional disinterest and endless, endless debate. This, it seems, is the democratic pattern. One wonders how it is possible for anything of merit to emerge from such a process.

But indubitably something fine has emerged in both cases. The monument, being simpler, is easier to admire, a great shaft rising clean-lined for 555 feet, tapering slightly until the last twenty feet, when it veers in sharply to the aluminum capstone. The entire surface is un-broken except for four pairs of windows, two to a side, which pierce the masonry near the apex, opening a view for sightseers. The stone is smooth, the only interruption one of color. At a height of about 155 feet, a shift in color marks where construction stopped in 1854 for twenty-five years. The long delay was a boon in one major way. Original plans for encircling columns at the base and for heroic sculpture of Washington driving a four-horse chariot were never realized, to the ultimate benefit of mankind. And a later scheme, by the McMillan Commission in 1901, to create terraced and formal gardens in the best Beaux-Arts manner around the base, came to nothing. Which is also all to the good.

The monument rises unhindered from a strong symmetrical grassy mound. Nothing interferes with its purity, a great abstraction, memori-alizing less one man than the early republic itself. The debates, delays, struggles for money, the changes and the committee system seem to have worked. Out of such fire some purity has been forged, a purity that speaks of idealism, nobility of aim, the simplicity of aspiration, perhaps the central reason why the American democratic experiment has sur-vived. It is far and away the nation's greatest monument.

The Capitol is quite another matter. Many hands and many minds have fashioned it. It has been altered, added to, revised, enclosed, until, like the nation itself, little remains that the Founding Fathers would recognize. Its conglomerate character yields more answers to the ques-

Corncob column, Latrobe

29

tion about democracy and architecture. It becomes apparent that democracy seldom makes use of the major talents available among its people, at least for its official building. The safe, mediocre professional is preferred, never the innovator, whose contribution must be tested and catalogued until it is safe. Perhaps this is as it should be. A Capitol by, say, Frank Lloyd Wright might now be as ready for demolition as is his once-respected Imperial Hotel in Tokyo. Besides, the safe, mediocre talents are better geared to work with the committee system which is endemic to democracy—and even those talents seldom find it easy to work with a committee.

The work of the earliest architects, William Thornton and Benjamin Latrobe, is now visible only on the west façade of the Capitol, so extensive have been the alterations and additions. There one can see the two cube-shaped sections, one on either side of the central part which supports the dome. The two sections, topped by cupolas designed by Latrobe, are much as Thornton first pictured them in his design, which won the $500 prize so generously offered by Congress. Thornton, an amateur architect from Philadelphia, was a man of more taste than skill, and his working drawings were so deficient that grave construction troubles developed. Benjamin Latrobe, who took over from him under the aegis of Jefferson, was forced to make several changes—a development which did nothing to smooth relations between the two architects. Latrobe was a considerably more sophisticated designer, with true originality, a subtle sense of proportion and a touch of genius. Latrobe completed the two matching cubes to shelter House and Senate just in time for the British to burn them in 1814. There were those who wished the British incendiaries had done their work more thoroughly; then a fresh start could have been made without the limitation of Thornton's underpinnings. As it worked out, Latrobe restored the buildings, changing as he went, and eventually Charles Bulfinch linked them by a central section and a low dome, somewhat as Thornton had pictured the plan.

Latrobe added to the Capitol graceful arches, skillful surface details and an inventive design for columns. Hoping to replace the Doric, Ionic and Corinthian orders with something more American, he designed two new column-capitals, one incorporating ears of corn, the other tobacco leaves. What could be more American? The two principal American crops, learned from the Indians, were woven into the new temple of government where only acanthus and lotus had been thought of before. Jefferson, his patron, was delighted. And Latrobe sent him sample columns for his garden at Monticello. Such chauvinistic tampering with the classics might have resulted in something grotesque, but Latrobe's skill was such that his corn and tobacco columns are quite beautiful, much admired by knowing visitors who search them out in the Capitol's lower reaches.

The Capitol which these men built was a simple one, graceful, small and unpretentious. The spirit was Greek Revival, with all it entailed of admiration for Greek ideals. The pervading influence was Jefferson's. A modern-day chief executive can hardly imagine how the third President was able to keep such a firm rein on anything congressional. The Congress submitted, though sometimes churlishly, to Jefferson's directions, on the basis of the Washington precedent. The first President had been given the task of creating the Federal City and suitable buildings to house the government. The tradition carried on through Jefferson's time and a bit longer. But after the first builders came the deluge. First a larger dome, wooden with a copper covering. Then, in the 1850's, new wings were flung out on either side for House and Senate, wings that gave the first touch of pomposity, turning more toward the Romans than to the Greeks. The architect was Thomas U. Walter, who proved again the affinity democracy has for hiring the mediocre. Giant flights of steps, heavy Corinthian columns, elaborate interior detailing contributed to a new concept of the Capitol of the United States. All that remained to complete the grandiosity was to top it off with a dome of proportions suitable to the huge new wings. Walter did it, using cast-iron construction rising above tiers of columns, the whole recalling St. Peter's in Rome and St. Paul's in London. Perhaps it seems too demanding to compare this political capitol with two of the world's great architectural masterpieces, but comparison is inevitable. The Capitol's very size makes it so, and the commanding dome immediately calls to mind those works of Michelangelo and Christopher Wren. In both latter cases the domes were raised over vast interior spaces designed for religious ceremonies, and the domes, vaulting toward heaven, gave ultimate expression to the purpose of the buildings. Wren's dome seems lighter, more delicate than Michelangelo's with its strongly emphasized ribbing and heavily accented support detail. Wren's building was, of course, 200 feet shorter than Michelangelo's, which aspired frankly to be the greatest church of Christendom. An Englishman would find it difficult to avow such an aim, so Wren, building long before the zenith of empire, made his dome a trifle more modest, even delicate, carefully related to his church, and the result seems most spiritual of all.

In such high company, the Capitol, though handsomely assertive, can achieve only third place because the dome will always look just what it is—an afterthought clapped atop a structure far too small. Of far greater interest, though, is the concept itself. The kind of building other nations had erected as their greatest religious temples was chosen by democracy for a new use, secular rather than religious, a temple for a republic. The separation of church and state is a cardinal tenet of the American system, but the reality goes even farther than separation. Church and state are not equal, the American system is a secular system, and the Capitol emphasizes this fact by employing a religious symbol for secular ends.

There has always seemed to be something mystical about the fact, apparent in old photographs, that the dome was half-finished when Lincoln made his first Inaugural in the time-honored spot on the east

Right
The President's Room, the Capitol

Next two pages
Capitol dome

steps. By the time of his second Inaugural appealing to "the mystic chords of memory" to bind up a reunited nation, the great dome was, at long last, completed. The Capitol grew as the nation grew.

Thornton's design, Latrobe's improvements, Bulfinch's additions, Walter's wings and dome, all of it was there. Simplicity and elegance were gone, but it housed a legislature that had lost those qualities itself. The scars of a bitter civil war, the turbulence of a dawning industrial age, the stresses of growth and change—these were the new problems of the nation governed from these halls. For two generations only minor changes were made in the Capitol, which gradually had found acceptance and finally a kind of unquestioning veneration.

Ninety years after the dome was finished, the old section of the Capitol, the Thornton-Latrobe section, received a death blow. Under the direction of Speaker Sam Rayburn, in the time of Eisenhower, a new front was built across the east side, thirty-two feet out from the building line and completely enclosing the old structure. The result is hideous. With great fidelity the architects reproduced the old columns, pediment, window frames, lintels and cornices in a harsh gray marble, which tries, but fails, to reproduce the feeling of the old weathered stone shored up by paint and preservatives. No one believed that Thornton and Latrobe had produced anything rivaling the Parthenon. What they had achieved was a graceful and beautiful façade, now lost forever behind tons of cold marble. The one favorable thing to be said for the new façade is that by moving it forward thirty-two feet, lining up with the huge Walter wings, the central section now is in scale with the dome and looks better able to support that massive weight. Unfortunately there is no vantage point from which the spectator can enjoy such a view; trees and buildings across the street block the view. One can only surmise, and that seems too little for the price paid—the loss of a beautiful old façade.

While Capitol and monument demand first attention because of sheer massiveness, the third in the city's triumvirate of greats is, for

Pages

many reasons, the White House. Politically the White House and the Capitol are co-equal, balancing executive and legislative in the American scheme. Aesthetically the White House gains first place with ease. Elegantly simple, the White House as the residence of the president of a great power is a wonderful understatement, depending on beauty of setting and perfection of detail to assert itself in the urban landscape. The White House, according to L'Enfant's plan, anchors the cross-axis of the Mall and succeeds in doing it even though startlingly small. Few European travelers, seeing it for the first time, fail to exclaim over its smallness and unpretentiousness, two characteristics that we owe as much to Jefferson as to the Irish-born architect James Hoban. Jefferson's concept of the presidency was egalitarian. He wanted his house to be comfortable, beautiful and utilitarian. In all but the latter he succeeded.

James Hoban, during his student days in Dublin, undoubtedly knew Leinster House, the apparent model for his White House drawings. The engaged Ionic columns, the main North pediment and the alternating curved and triangular over-window pediments all seem to come direct from Dublin. Leinster House, of course, had its own antecedents, among them the Château de Rastignac in Périgord, with a portico strikingly similar to the South Portico on the White House. Whatever Hoban's sources, he drew a chastely simple residence, so satisfactory that it has withstood fire, renovation and restoration and today stands essentially as he designed it, except for the addition of two inspired wings. Those wings, necessary for office space as the presidency expanded, could have been the undoing of a late-eighteenth-century building. Instead they have enhanced it.

Under the presidency of Theodore Roosevelt, McKim, Mead & White were commissioned to design the West Wing, housing a new office for the president himself. Depressing the façade as much as possible below the Pennsylvania Avenue ground level, they linked the offices with the main house by a simple, low structure and a covered arcade.

Capitol crypt

34

A similar plan was used when the East Wing was added by President Franklin Roosevelt. Both wings are so inconspicuous that the main White House seems to stand alone in a parklike setting, with arching elms framing the north façade and a rolling lawn stretching south toward the Ellipse and the monument grounds with Jefferson's Memorial terminating the cross-axis. By all standards the White House is the most beautiful of Washington's public buildings. Democracy, having achieved something of grace and beauty, has at least had the good sense to let well enough alone.

These earliest buildings of the republic have in common a simplicity and grace that were expressed again and again—by the talented George Hadfield when he built the Old City Hall (1820), by Mills in his classically satisfying Treasury Building (1836) and by the several architects who contributed to the handsome tan sandstone Patent Office (1836), now being converted into the National Portrait Gallery. Until the Civil War the architecture of democracy was restrained, harmonious and reposed. The war proved to be as much a watershed for architecture as it was for politics.

A new postwar age found expression in such strange and grandiose buildings as Mullet's State, War and Navy Building and Meigs' Pension Building. The only precedents for such a leap away from Jeffersonian classicism had been provided in 1849 by Renwick when he built the fanciful turreted Smithsonian of red sandstone along the Mall. Renwick's fancy was a romantic one, understandable in an age that breathed hard over the novels of Sir Walter Scott, and besides, the Smithsonian Institution, entailing government support for science, was such a new concept for the federal government that a fresh approach seemed justified. The buildings by Mullet and Meigs were a more alarming matter. Mullet took the classic pediment and column, reduced their size, and piled them, one after another, up a six-story façade, then topped it all off with a mansard roof embellished with dormers, medallions and heavily clus-

Brumidi ceiling

tered chimneys. Fashioned of gray granite and of massive scale, the building all but overwhelms its simple next-door neighbor, the White House. Even in the materialistic Grant administration such boldness drew angry outcries. Henry Adams termed it "Mullet's asylum," and despite the spacious comfort of its offices, succeeding generations have debated what to do with it. The city's foremost historian, Constance McLaughlin Green, sidestepping an aesthetic judgment, gives the building a major historic role. When several million dollars were appropriated for its construction in 1871, she says, it "laid to rest the last fears of losing the capital to the Mississippi Valley." She documents her statement by charting the sudden increase in real-estate transactions and prices that ensued. As an anchor to the capital, it was assuredly heavy enough to do the job. In contemporary times, a decision finally was made by President Kennedy to preserve and restore the building as a part, for better or for worse, of the nation's architectural heritage.

Just as Mullet's State, War and Navy Building was being completed, a fiery Army engineer, with a good deal of architectural training, produced another daring addition to the federal landscape, the Pension Building. General Montgomery C. Meigs had served as Lincoln's quartermaster general and supervised construction of the city's remarkable aqueduct system. In neither role was there more than a hint of his capacity to conceive the red-brick and terra-cotta Pension Building which in 1884 rose on Judiciary Square. Drawing its main façade direct from the Farnese Palace in Rome, the building goes on to incorporate ideas and innovations that make it one of the most interesting in Washington. Meigs introduced double-paned windows, the sheets of glass separated, to cut down summer heat, precursors of much later insulation. Elevators and fireproof materials also made it something of a design landmark. By using galleries around a vast center court, Meigs achieved a remarkable ratio of usable floor space, about eighty percent. The eight great interior columns are of brick, painted to simulate Siena marble, and the interior court is of such elegance that it became the scene of inaugural balls from Grover Cleveland to William Howard Taft. The exterior of Meigs' building is equally unusual. Detailing of window pediments, lintels and cornices is done with terra-cotta carefully matched in color to the warm red-brown of the bricks. Most remarkable of all, around the building's entire 1200-foot exterior stretches a buff terra-cotta frieze that must be among the longest in the world. A three-foot band between first and second stories, the frieze depicts the Union forces, infantry, artillery, cavalry, support units, sailors, all in meticulously correct detail, marching eternally around the handsome building. The sculptor, a Bohemian-American named Casper Buberl, deserves enshrinement as the grandfather of all Pop Art sculptors. And those circling soldiers were more than an architect's fancy. They were symbolic, some said, of the Civil War veterans circling the U.S. Treasury, seeking bigger and better pensions. In fact, during the forty-one years of its tenancy, the Pension Bureau paid out more than eight billion dollars in pension benefits to the veterans, or veterans' widows, from all American wars. The Pension Building, though a trifle outsize, is a handsome structure, so well designed that it could still be a useful one if the filing cabinets and temporary partitions marring the great central court were removed.

Not even the wildest partisan of Mullet's State, War and Navy Building could ever claim that form followed function, that harmony and repose resulted from his piling of column atop column. Still, other buildings of that era were vulgar, ornate, actively ugly. Mullet's building is none of these. Neither kitsch nor camp, it tells, like carved black furniture, of the taste of the times. Together the two buildings, for all their eccentricities, enrich the Washington scene; and though they depart, as the country had, from the Jeffersonian ideal, they are of enduring interest and in many ways express more individuality, more creativeness, than did the Noble Romans who were to follow.

Though the Romans of Architecture were late in stamping their Imperial mark on Washington, their influence is by far the most pervasive in the city, surpassing in scale of construction and quantity of stone the work of both the Greek Revivalists and the later Romantics. The Romans bore such names as Daniel Burnham, John Russell Pope, and Charles McKim, Arthur Brown, Cass Gilbert, Delano & Aldrich. In the first third of the twentieth century they built so many new structures in Washington that the city would be unrecognizable to Henry Adams or any of the other nineteenth-century citizens who loved their capital in its rambling, unplanned days. Eclectic, neoclassical, call it what you will, the Roman style borrowed the columns, architraves and pediments of the ripest Imperial periods and put them together for new purposes. The result has been roundly abused by later critics as sterile, pompous and provincial. In truth, Washington's Roman period is too close in time for a final verdict. The question is as big as their work. Their largest monument is a massive group of buildings known as the Federal Triangle, filling the space bounded by Pennsylvania Avenue, Fifteenth Street and Constitution Avenue, an area nine blocks long. Here beats the bureaucratic heart of government, if such a thing exists, for here are housed the departments of Labor, Commerce and Justice, the Interstate Commerce Commission, the Internal Revenue Service, the FBI, the Post Office Department, the Federal Trade Commission and the National Archives. Truly an impressive concentration; and the Romans, as they went about designing these buildings, spared no effort to give the impressiveness an architectural embodiment. Scattered about the core of Washington are many other examples of the Romans' period—Union Station, the Supreme Court, the National Gallery and the Jefferson Memorial. Altogether they add up to a strong assertive statement which, in a sense, has been the architectural image of the government. Their construction, from 1901 to 1938, was the great splurge of building that L'Enfant had envisioned as he laid out the city. The splurge was a century late, and the builders were a different breed from the Thorntons and Latrobes of earlier days.

Right
Bureau of Standards

Next two pages
Meigs' Pension Building

THE ORIGINAL WRIGHT BROTHERS AEROPLANE, 1903
SEE LABEL BELOW

The new architects were far more sophisticated, as was the country. Of them all, Daniel Burnham was the most Roman and also the most influential, not in originality of design but in the powerful role he played in molding Washington. Burnham was a tycoon-architect, a new type produced to match the tycoons of other fields in an era when Big Business was achieving its bigness. His was a world of private railway cars, of rich dinners with fellow tycoons in New York, of big deals and bold plans. His friends were on the same scale, the railway presidents, corporation chiefs and big manufacturers who were shaping America. Burnham had first helped Chicago rise from its ashes and then had become a national figure when he put together the Chicago World's Fair in a way that profoundly affected American thinking about city planning and architecture. The fair was a boldly beautiful arrangement of buildings around lagoons and canals, gleaming white, a new kind of borrowed classicism that brought ancient Europe to America in a new way. The borrowing was frank and open. Its designers made no bones of their admiration for the past and little attempt to add to it. They merely adapted. Most Americans were charmed or awed, but one of them, a man who thought deeply about architectural matters, entered a violent dissent:

The virus of the World's Fair caused a violent outbreak of the classic and the renaissance in the East which slowly spread westward contaminating all that it touched... thus Architecture died in the land of the free and the home of the brave... thus did the virus of culture, snobbish and alien to the land, perform its work of disintegration; thus ever works the pallid academic mind.

The man who said it was Louis Sullivan, the greatest architect of those days.

Though it was true that individual creativeness received no stimulus from the fair, the idea of improving urban landscapes did get a boost, and by 1900, Washington's centennial, the idea reached the capital.

In the Smithsonian collection

The Senate Committee on District Affairs, headed by Senator James McMillan of Michigan, appointed a commission to consider how the city's park system could be improved and the city made more beautiful. Daniel Burnham, quite naturally, was chosen to head the commission; his fellow members had worked with him on the Chicago Fair—Charles McKim, Frederick Law Olmsted, Jr., a noted landscape architect, and Augustus Saint-Gaudens, the sculptor. They set about their task in the highest style. Here was a rare chance, they obviously recognized, to remake a national capital, and if they worked well, their place in history might be assured. History, in fact, was uppermost in their minds. First they toured the great houses and gardens of Tidewater Virginia and Maryland, then wandered through Annapolis and Williamsburg to see how our colonial forebears, working on a smaller scale, had solved the problems of creating capitals. Then the entire commission, except Saint-Gaudens, who was ill, took off for a Grand Tour of Europe to immerse themselves in the great creations of the past—the gardens, parks, squares, avenues, palaces and public buildings of the old world. What they visited is of great interest to anyone looking at the plan these Grand Tourists finally created. In Paris they strolled through the Tuileries, visited the Beaux-Arts and then spent a day in the Bois de Boulogne. Another day was spent at Versailles, Fontainebleau, the Luxembourg Gardens; then Rome and Venice. On the steps of a circular temple at the Villa Borghese they discussed the location for Memorial Bridge in Washington. The Vatican Gardens, Hadrian's Villa, the Villa d'Este and then the incomparable Piazza San Marco; after that, Vienna (Schoenbrunn), Frankfurt, Berlin and finally England, where they spent an afternoon at Oxford, then to Bushey Park and Hampton Court, Hatfield House and Westminster Abbey. For seven weeks the commission members stuck close together, looking and studying, making notes and Kodak shots, referring often to the tin map-case of Washington maps they had brought along.

The Court

40

There is something grand about the way they worked, with great seriousness and confidence, and certainly without thought of personal gain, except for what history might accord them. Burnham, the tycoon-architect, was obviously the dominant figure on the tour, according to all notes and diaries which have survived. But McKim and Olmsted played important parts too. Olmsted in particular was useful and creative as he snapped photographs and analyzed the parks and gardens. As the son of the first Olmsted who had laid out Central Park, he had truly grown up in the atmosphere of landscape architecture and could give valuable insight to the others more oriented to the architecture of stones. McKim, long before this European jaunt, was a dedicated classicist, a course that one of his partners said had been determined by a New England sketching trip in 1876. So his touring with the commission did nothing more than add to his great store of architectural knowledge and serve to weld the commission together in their ideas and concepts.

The great program they evolved came to be known as the McMillan Plan, in honor of its senatorial sponsor, who unfortunately died soon after the paper work was completed. With considerable imagination, the commission recommended stripping away much of the nineteenth-century muddle cluttering the central capital and going back to the fundamentals which had attracted both George Washington and L'Enfant. The city's natural setting and the great stretch of river would be brought back into the picture. First the commission recommended creation of landscaped parkways on either side of the Potomac as far north as Great Falls and as far south as Mount Vernon. Numerous other small parks were also designated to carry further the program L'Enfant had first suggested to provide green oases throughout the city.

In the monumental heart of Washington the commission decided to push further the Mall scheme, which L'Enfant had drawn only between the Capitol and the Washington Monument. By pushing the Mall west-ward to the river, the plan would provide a site for another great monu-

Associate justice

ment, this one for Lincoln; and the newly reclaimed swamps of the area would provide hundreds more acres of parkland. The Mall itself must be a minimum of four hundred feet wide, the commission decided, in order to give a setting proper in scale to the soaring Washington Monument and the big Capitol sprawled atop its hill. To emphasize the shape of the Mall, each side was to be planted with four straight lines of elms, two great bands of greenery as daring as the brush strokes of a well-disciplined but highly imaginative painter. All this was the heart of the McMillan Plan, as we remember it, because these were the parts which slowly came into being. Other parts, such as elaborate formal gardens around the base of the Washington Monument and numerous fountains along the Mall, have been forgotten because they got no farther than the drawing board. But the plan, as it turned into reality, and as the elms grew to give the desired definition to a new great Mall, was brilliant. It changed the looks of Washington for the better and provided a strong foundation for latter-day improvers.

Congress, as might be expected, was not impressed; and the Speaker of the House, old Uncle Joe Cannon, was definitely unfriendly, in his case because the Senate and not the House had sponsored the plan. The local press, with something less than enlightened zeal, called the plan crazy, dead-duck and un-American because it drew so heavily on the formal precepts of the French landscape architect André Lenôtre and his followers. Despite such potent opposition, the plan was soon off and running, due primarily to Burnham's tycoon connections. He had been commissioned by old Alexander Cassatt, president of the Pennsylvania Railroad, to design a new station in Washington. The railway tracks in those days crossed the Mall just below Capitol Hill, and the B & O Station, where Garfield had been assassinated, stood just where the National Gallery now rises. Removal of the tracks was a prime requisite of the McMillan Plan, and Burnham persuaded Cassatt that his railroad would be acting in the public interest if the new station were built farther

Right
Stradivari, the Library of Congress

Next two pages
The Mall

42

north and the tracks tunneled under the Mall. After a good deal of backing and filling, and a healthy appropriation to reimburse the poor railroads, the scheme was adopted and the B & O joined in to make it a Union Station. With that bold stroke, the way was open to develop the Mall along the chaste lines Burnham and his associates had envisioned. Another kind of man, a less worldly one, one less well-connected, could not have launched the plan so successfully. He was able to carry impressive weight with various congressmen. He is owed a great debt even though Union Station and the adjoining post office he designed are of a pompous style more reminiscent of the Chicago World's Fair than the Rome he adored.

After Burnham, who went on to be the first chairman of the Federal Commission of Fine Arts in 1910, the Romans who contributed most to the changing city were John Russell Pope and Charles McKim. Pope designed the National Archives Building, the National Gallery, the Jefferson Memorial and a half-dozen rich mansions around the city. McKim contributed the beautifully arched Memorial Bridge linking the Mall with Arlington Cemetery and designed the Army War College on Buzzard's Point. Their classicism was more refined than Burnham's. So was the architecture of others who contributed buildings during the great construction splurge from 1925 to 1937. As a result the Federal Triangle, for all its massiveness, lacks the heavy vulgarity of the Chicago Fair.

The dozen designers of the Federal Triangle made another, highly unusual contribution: they managed to suppress themselves. In the architectural profession this is a rarity, especially when one receives a commission for a prominent public spot. Then most architects are prone to write their egos across the landscape, even at the cost of an inharmonious building. A supervisory committee directed development of the Triangle, imposing regulations, such as a common cornice line, which kept the various buildings closely related to scale. The committee also saw to it that designs, though all in a similar Roman idiom, varied enough to prevent the façades from becoming nine long blocks of monotony. In the process, some truly beautiful areas developed, such as the graceful semicircular façade of the Post Office Building by Delano & Aldrich. In comparing the Triangle buildings with others in Washington, one other quality shines forth—the superb workmanship that American architecture had at hand. Limestone and granite are cut with tremendous skill; the detailing is beautiful. After three decades the buildings look even better than when they were completed. This was a great advance over the day when inept workmen limited the architects of the Capitol; it went hand in hand with the other technical advances in the nation. The Federal Triangle, though ignoring the architectural experiments which had long been afoot, succeeds in its intent—to speak with harmony and dignity of the permanence of government.

After the Romans, not exactly Goths and Vandals, but certainly a fumbling decadence of taste and direction. All building, except temporary wooden structures, stopped in Washington during the Second World War and started again only fitfully afterward. The less said the better about the buildings of the first postwar decades, the vast ill-planned State Department addition, the cold marble Federal Aviation Building, the tasteless office building next door. No administration will ever point with pride at these exercises in construction without principle. Other cities rejoiced in a wave of brilliant new buildings as a new generation of architects, taught by Wright and Gropius, by Mies and Corbusier, experimented and created structures unlike anything America had ever seen before. Not so the federal government. As was its wont, the government took the safe route of mediocrity with the single exception of the commission to Eero Saarinen to design a new airport and that, of course, was safely out of town in Virginia. The faceless buildings of the Eisenhower years correctly reflect the atmosphere of Washington in those days. The nation had survived, but barely, a convulsion of

Right
Detail, Rayburn Building

Next two pages
Saarinen's air terminal

44

McCarthyism which brought government itself into disrepute among thinking men. Then a retired general in the White House spread a mantle of mediocrity and middle age over the city. Vice-presidents of Quaker Oats, General Motors and the soap industry took over key government posts. No self-respecting architect for a moment thought of competing for commissions from the federal government. Not until the inauguration of President Kennedy brought a new life and vigor to the capital did architects get a chance to express, as had the Greek Revivalists, Romantics and Romans, the spirit of the times in which they lived.

Democracy's ways in architecture are slow and ill-directed and frustrating, but sometimes a nation tries to make amends. So America did when it became clear to members of the McMillan Commission and others that the L'Enfant Plan had, after all, been a brilliant one. In 1909 the bones of the almost forgotten French engineer were disinterred from the roots of a gnarled cedar in Maryland. His coffin was carried to the Capitol, there to lie in state as only Lincoln's and a few others had done. Then, with the highest officials of the land attending him, L'Enfant was buried in Arlington on the lip of a hill overlooking the city he had designed, the design marvelously apparent in the street pattern across the river and repeated on a bronze tablet on his tomb.

L'Enfant's tomb

V

All of the monuments are not marble; many are flesh and blood; they live on in Washington, sometimes in careful privacy, sometimes well chronicled by the press. Some were great themselves. Others are the sons or daughters of the great, or at least lineal descendants. Some were mere bit-players in great moments of history, but all remain part of a history-laden landscape.

Though George Washington left no children, his wife did, by her first marriage, and her descendants still inhabit the austere yellow plaster house, Tudor Place, which William Thornton built on a Georgetown hill. In a less conspicuous house on P Street lives a white-haired woman whose name, Jessie Benton Frémont, recalls long-ago events. Her grandmother was the daughter of the great Senator Thomas Hart Benton of Missouri. Her grandfather was the dashing John C. Frémont, who played a role in the winning of the West and who ran, fruitlessly, for the presidency. Alice Roosevelt Longworth still reigns in a slightly crumbling mansion near Dupont Circle. Though Mrs. Longworth's historical credentials are matchless—daughter of a president, widow of a Speaker of the House, cousin of another president—she needs them less than most. Armed with a wide-ranging intellectual curiosity, a phenomenal memory and a wicked wit, she could have made her way alone to the eminence she occupies. For more than six decades the capital has quoted her epigrams and laughed, or shuddered, at her barbs; the victims, like as not, being later residents of the White House. Other Roosevelts, of course, are tucked about the city because the Roosevelts, like the Adamses, have been a prolific clan. There are always a few of both families in residence, their numbers only slightly less than the Lees of Virginia.

The daughter of the twenty-sixth President

U.S. Grant III, grandson of the General-President, still lives in Washington and, until recent years, the three spinster daughters of Grant's great colleague, General Philip Sheridan, lived together quietly near Sheridan Circle where they could see papa's equestrian statue every time they left home. Mrs. William E. Borah, widow of the Idaho senator, still lives on in Washington, as does Mrs. Mitchell Palmer, widow of the attorney general who engineered the notorious raids on political radicals after the First World War. If you are lucky at a Washington party you may run into the wise and urbane Francis Biddle, FDR's attorney general, or Miss Grace Tully from the same administration. President Wilson's grandson, Francis Sayre, is dean of the Washington Cathedral. Two former secretaries of state, Dean Acheson and Christian Herter, live three blocks apart on P Street.

Many other houses around the city can boast of presidential occupants. Monroe's red and white Federal House is now the Arts Club. Madison and Dolley lived in the Octagon while the White House was being rebuilt. The Tafts and the Hardings both lived on Wyoming Avenue in solid, unimaginative red-brick houses that still stand. The young Franklin Roosevelts filled an R Street house with their bouncing family during the First World War, when Franklin Roosevelt was Assistant Secretary of the Navy—but not many remember them at that address. The Roosevelt family aura clings closer at another address, 1600 Pennsylvania Avenue. They lived here a little over twelve years—longer than any other family in history.

The list goes on and on. Grandsons of Civil War generals, veterans of the Spanish-American, widows from the First World War, admirals and generals from the last war, cabinet members, former senators, administrators, congressmen—all played a part, however minor, in history, and then lingered on in Washington, held there by friends, long associations and by the titillation of nearby power, spoiled for Boise or Dubuque. New administrations come and go; new figures rise in power, some by

The dean of the Washington Cathedral

sheer seniority, some in a more yeasty way; new power centers coalesce and dissolve. History accumulates, layer on layer, and lingering figures from the past add an historic flavor to the city's changing pattern, a feeling of continuity, a sense that the past is not, after all, more than a moment away.

The bench marks of the past are quite apparent. Wandering through the Capitol, one sees the old Senate Chamber where dark-browed Webster debated Hayne, a forensic landmark of an age when lung power and rhetoric were requisites of political primacy. There on Tenth Street is the theater where Lincoln fell, mortally wounded by Booth's bullet, and across the way a simple boardinghouse where, next morning, he breathed his last, surrounded by his weeping cabinet. There is the spot where Franklin Roosevelt stood, erect in his steel braces, and summoned a faltering nation to put aside its fears, the same spot where John F. Kennedy, twenty-eight years later, proclaimed: "Let the word go forth from this time and place, to friend and foe alike, that the torch has been passed to a new generation of Americans...." There the British applied their incendiary torches in 1814. There Walt Whitman nursed Civil War soldiers and heard "America singing." That magnolia was planted by Andrew Jackson himself behind the White House. Its leaves were woven into the wreath placed, before dawn one somber morning, on the coffin of John F. Kennedy when he came back to lie in state where Abraham Lincoln, Franklin Roosevelt and William McKinley had rested before him.

There is the Blair House window where Harry Truman, wakened from a nap in his underwear, peered out at assassins trying to storm the entrance. There, the old Court Chamber where the Dred Scott decision was handed down in 1857, and across the street a newer, more august chamber where the school desegregation decision followed a century later.

These are the bench marks that recall a man or an event. In some

Right
Painter and his wife

Next two pages
Tidal basin and river

48

parts of the city, a whole area or a street serves the same end. Who can walk up S Street, above Sheridan Circle, without thinking of Woodrow Wilson pacing his closing years in the square, red-brick house with Palladian window? His high-topped Rolls waited in the drive to take the frail, stubborn intellectual on rides through the countryside. As he lay dying, two years after leaving the White House, crowds knelt in S Street praying for his high-minded soul.

His strong assertive wife, Edith Bolling Wilson, kept the memory alive through almost four decades of widowhood, the Edith Bolling who first had been married to a Washington jeweler and then ascended to the White House by marrying a widowed president. Edith Wilson made a considerable impression on Washington, not all favorable. Gossip flew when the President courted her. Ripe beauty, a head held high. Often they were seen driving together, always carefully chaperoned, but still she seemed a trifle dashing, and he *was* the President. Would they or wouldn't they? Finally they did, and the marriage seemed a happy one. Then, after the President's tragic stroke, while valiantly campaigning for his beloved League of Nations, Edith Wilson came closer to control of the presidency than any other woman ever had. Even cabinet members were barred from Mr. Wilson's presence for weeks at a time. Little notes with orders and ideas—in whose hand?—came out to Mr. Tumulty, the secretary. Whose orders? Whose ideas? Gossip mounted ever higher— was Mrs. Wilson really the Acting President? Tabloid writers have played luridly with that thought ever since. Now serious historians try to penetrate the mystery. Washington, seething with curiosity and frustration, never knew for certain. By the time the congressional representatives got into his bedroom the President was better, smile a bit crooked, Edith hovering nearby. Ever afterward there seemed something a bit enigmatic about her, even as she grew stouter in widowhood and more and more respectable. A bit of the grande dame, conservatively dressed, gracious, going occasionally to weddings and small parties,

House majority whip and his wife

49

dignified and conscious of a role in history, playing bridge with other widows in her high-ceilinged S Street house, until she, too, died there, and was taken up Massachusetts Avenue, past the embassies, to the Cathedral for burial in the crypt beside her husband. Her presence, forceful, assertive, secretive, is still on S Street.

As S Street evokes Edith and Woodrow Wilson, so N Street recalls a more recent, more tragic presidential couple, Jacqueline and John Kennedy. As far as traffic is concerned, N is a quiet street paralleling the river in Georgetown, one of the oldest streets in town. But the quiet is broken by laughing, hurrying university students, bound for the Jesuits' Georgetown University at the end of N Street. The Kennedys brought their own liveliness when they moved to one of a series of houses rented in the first years of marriage. The young Senator, lithe and vigorous, organized touch football games that surged up and down the block between Thirty-third and Thirty-fourth. His brother Robert came from his house around the corner on O Street, and sometimes passing students joined the fray. Caroline ran in or out with Miss Shaw, her nurse, bound for the park or a friend's house nearby. An easy street for children. Then they made a brief try at country living; but Mrs. Kennedy didn't like it, so they finally bought 3308 N Street, a tall, deep pink brick house with a walled garden behind it.

The tempo of their lives was increasing in the late 1950's. The Senator was running for the presidency, at first an unacknowledged race, then an open one. Traffic surged in and out of the pink house, where Mrs. Kennedy had transformed the lofty twin drawing rooms, off-white, tall mirrors, deep, comfortable chairs and the red and purple splashes of her favorite anemones. Senator Kennedy left to campaign in primaries, first in Wisconsin, then in West Virginia, and came home the victor. On spring and summer evenings that year, the N Street house saw a succession of small dinner parties where the talk ricocheted, arms were twisted, delegates promised, plans shaped. Once John Kennedy was the

N Street, Georgetown

50

nominee, and then elected, N Street was chock full of reporters, camera-men, television crews. They stayed until the snowy January day when the shining young couple drove away to the White House. Now tourists occasionally idle on the sidewalk, read a plaque left across the street by newspapermen, remember the high excitement of those moments.

Finally it was to N Street that a poignant, black-clad young widow came back in sorrow. First she borrowed a house from Averell Harriman, then bought one across the street, screened by ancient magnolias, a house where she thought she could hide herself away from prying eyes.

The Kennedys' own house had been sold while they were in the White House. The President had thought it would be too small for them when his term was over—too small and lacking in privacy. He did plan to live in Washington, however. "Not at first," he said to me once. "Wilson made a great mistake in settling down nearby after being presi-dent. It isn't fair to your successor to be so close, looking over his shoulder. We may spend a couple of years in Cambridge. Maybe travel some. But then we'll come back here when the heat is off." He asked me to watch for a suitable house and if it came on the market we would buy it secretly.

John Kennedy's feeling for Washington was probably deeper than that of any president since Jefferson. He had lived here most of his adult life. He knew the streets, the parks, the surrounding countryside. He treasured the city's beauties, deplored its ugly areas, and schemed, as president, to help make the capital a far more beautiful city than he had found it. With eager interest he plunged into plans for rebuilding La-fayette Square in a manner suitable for a White House neighbor. He watched with fascination as the commission he appointed began to hammer out plans for rebuilding the north side of Pennsylvania Avenue. He schemed to get the ugly "tempos," emergency wartime buildings, removed from the Mall and other areas where they scarred the city's beauty. These and many other plans were afoot.

Trash man

Then his widow and his children were back on N Street, in the magnolia-shielded house Mrs. Kennedy had bought. It didn't work. Not Washington people but out-of-town tourists came driving slowly by, thousands of them. They packed the sidewalk, waited hours for a glimpse of any Kennedy. No longer could Mrs. Kennedy stroll down the street to shop on Wisconsin Avenue, take Caroline to school, do any of the simple things she had done before. Sadly she moved away to the privacy of New York. Even after she was long gone, the tourists still came struggling up N Street, gaped at the house, stood awhile and slowly moved on.

S Street and N Street are relatively minor streets, for all their associations. The city's greatest street, perhaps the greatest in the nation, is richer than any other in history and memories. Pennsylvania Avenue, the mile between White House and Capitol, was one of the first marked out by L'Enfant, and on it have moved almost all of the major characters in the nation's history. Presidents ride up it to yield their power at the Capitol. And newly inaugurated presidents ride down it in triumph to their new home at the other end. Soldiers returning from the wars receive acclaim along the historic route. Visiting kings and presidents follow the same path. So do the slow-marching steps of mourners following the coffin of a fallen hero.

Of course, if you live in Washington, Pennsylvania Avenue is merely the route to the office, but even those who traverse it twice a day cannot ignore the accretions of history. After Jefferson's poplars grew old and died, mud and dust plagued the avenue until the 1870's, when a new wood-block paving was inaugurated with a street carnival, outdoor dancing and Japanese lanterns. Jefferson rode the historic mile on horseback to his second inauguration, and all his successors made the journey by carriage until Woodrow Wilson acknowledged the coming of the Automobile Age by driving up in a clumsy, high-seated Pierce-Arrow.

The avenue down which Lincoln's funeral procession moved was

Right
Resident, Eighth Street

Next two pages
Capitol Hill

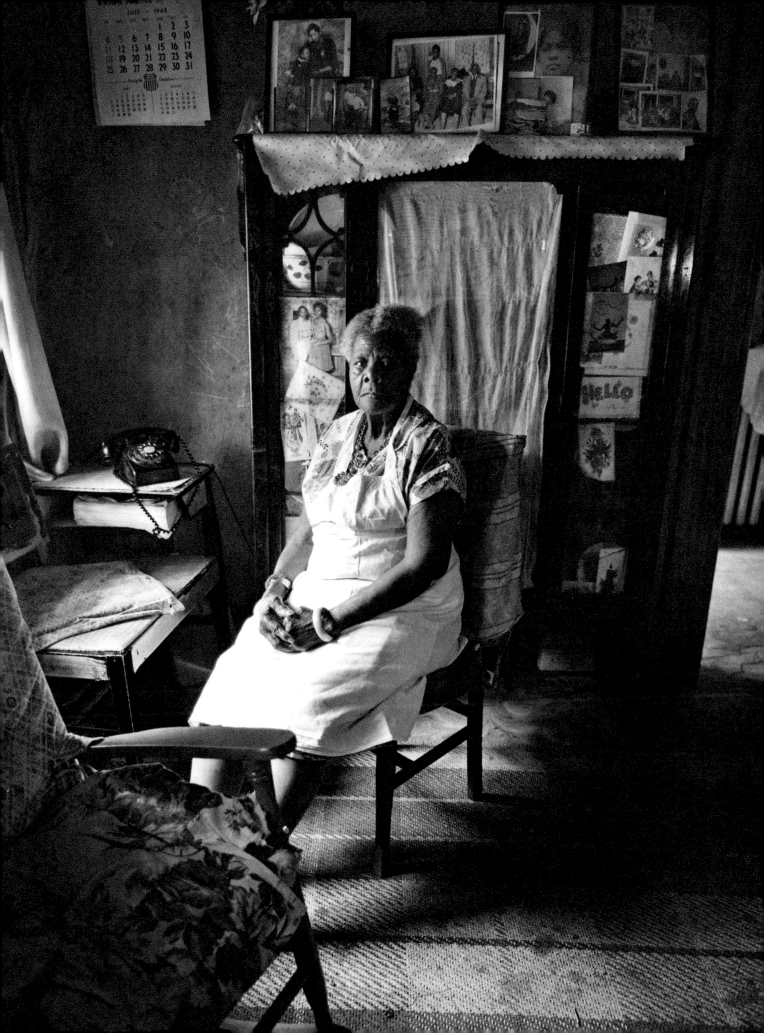

lined with low buildings, almost the height Jefferson had prescribed, buildings inhabited by hotels, saloons, produce stores, hardware stores and bookshops—a nineteenth-century commercial street. So many carriages were in the procession that the hearse had reached the Capitol at the moment some cabinet members were leaving the White House. One cabinet member recorded his own emotions and his deep sympathy for the thousands of Negroes who wept and prayed along the avenue as their emancipator's body was borne slowly away in the April sunshine. Along the same avenue, only six weeks later, marching men moved in a two-day victory parade the like of which has never been seen before or since. The Grand Review of the Union Armies lasted two days, bringing into the choked city men from the Army of the Potomac, the Army of Tennessee, the Army of Georgia. Hour after hour they poured up the avenue, some flushed with youth and victory, some hobbling on crutches or waving a blue-uniformed stump, the victors, the survivors who had left their brothers and friends buried in a hundred battlefields across their own country. But they had won and the Union would stand. The city of Washington would remain its capital. President Johnson, the first President Johnson, stood in a reviewing stand with his cabinet and generals Grant, Sherman, Sheridan, and all the rest. Everyone was there.

"But Abraham Lincoln was not there. All felt this," was the touching entry Gideon Welles put in his diary that night. The poignancy was one that was to be repeated eighty years later—sorrow tempering victory; Franklin Roosevelt was missing when his soldiers came marching home.

The grave of the thirty-fifth President

VI

Because public Washington is always under such merciless scrutiny, private Washington guards its inward existence with considerable jealousy. Walled gardens, houses that present noncommittal façades, a delight in bringing off some small piece of business that the press doesn't find out about—these are evidences of the urge for privacy that continues alongside the acknowledged duties of public life. Special delights are treasured, delights the ordinary tourist has not discovered—the eloquent sculpture by Saint-Gaudens in memory of Mrs. Henry Adams, in Rock Creek Cemetery, the ancient and seldom-visited Congressional Cemetery, the view back toward Washington from St. Elizabeth's Hospital, where Ezra Pound was incarcerated so many years, little streets like Duddington Place in Southeast, Philip Johnson's elegant pre-Columbian museum, the Old Navy Yard, the magnificent gardens of Dumbarton Oaks, the Phillips Collection, the new and fascinating Afro-American Museum—these are but a few of the treasures that Washingtonians cherish and display to perceptive visitors.

Though the great public buildings, the monuments and avenues all combine to give the capital a certain magnificence, there is one simpler, less dramatic place that for Washingtonians sums up their city—Lafayette Square, where public figures lived privately. Other older cities of the eastern seaboard have their counterparts—Boston's Louisburg, Philadelphia's Rittenhouse, New York's Washington Square—but with a difference. Both Louisburg and Rittenhouse have an aura of faded snobbism and one is given to believe, on visiting either, that the rich and wellborn have always frequented these purlieus and just possibly might still be there. New York's Washington Square, as Edith Wharton elo-

Executive Secretary

54

quently recorded, once had just claim to such pretensions, though now an encroaching university, waves of Italian settlers and finally barefoot guitarists have swept away that square's last vestige of such distinction.

The appeal of Lafayette Square is first political before being either aesthetic or social. The men and women who have lived here since the founding of the city have left the aura of their power, their fame and their accomplishments to this simple, informal park that faces, appropriately, toward the source of power, the White House. Great names stud the roster of residents—Daniel Webster, Clay and Calhoun, Martin Van Buren, Henry Adams, Mark Hanna, Dolley Madison, James G. Blaine, Stephen Decatur, and scores of others, the cabinet members, the diplomats and generals who shaped the city's history and at the same time the nation's. Only a dozen houses have survived, all now in the process of restoration and none as a private residence. Otherwise, the old inhabitants, could they return, would find the place quite as they left it. St. John's Church, mellow and beautiful, is still there. So is Decatur House. The paths circle, just as Andrew Jackson Downing, the great New York landscape architect, laid them out in the 1850's. Many of the trees are still there, too, elms grown more stately, magnolias twisted into magnificent glossy old age, beech and yew, tall statues of patriots at each corner and, in the middle, Andrew Jackson, dressed not as president but as the hero of New Orleans, rides his rearing bronze hobbyhorse and tips his bronze bateau eternally.

The squirrel and pigeon population seems often to outnumber the human, except on a summer noon when government secretaries by the score sprawl in the shade consuming Cokes and sandwiches, idly watching the tourists clambering back into their buses after a visit to the White House. Quiet has descended on a square that, in its day, saw high drama, political and personal, watched the flaring political torchlights, heard the muffled funerary drums, witnessed a crime of passion, a hundred intrigues, the comings and goings of the republic's rulers for a

In Rawlins Park

55

century and three-quarters. Over there at the southeast corner, Daniel Sickles gunned down his wife's paramour, Philip Barton Key, in a scandal that shook the antebellum capital. Key, a noted lawyer and son of the author of "The Star-Spangled Banner," had for months been romancing the beauteous Mrs. Sickles, sometimes boldly walking her around Lafayette Square inside the iron fence which then enclosed the park. Fate, in the shape of a wronged husband, caught him just outside the famous Rodgers house, site now of a courthouse entrance. Key was carried, dying, up a few doors to the still surviving Tayloe house where he expired among members of his family.

The Rodgers house, built by an 1812 war hero, seems to have been a magnet for violence. Though it jogged along peacefully for several decades as a club, where Clay and Calhoun both boarded, the house later became the home of Lincoln's secretary of state, William H. Seward, and it was here that an assassin gravely wounded Seward and his son at the same moment that Booth was shooting Lincoln. Across the park that dark, fateful night, another cabinet member slept in a dwelling where part of the Hay-Adams Hotel now stands. Gideon Welles, Lincoln's secretary of the Navy, was roused from an early slumber by voices calling under his window. In his voluminous diary he recorded how he stuck his head sleepily out the window, heard the incredible news and then hastily dressed. Just as he emerged from his doorway, a mysterious group of men standing under the street lamp suddenly extinguished the light. Welles, knowing that assassins were abroad, plunged on into the darkness in anguished terror, crossed to Seward's house and found the Secretary of State lying on a blood-soaked bed. In a room above him, Seward's son lay unconscious as a doctor worked over him. Now believing the awfulness of the night, Welles drove away in a carriage to Ford's Theatre.

Most nights on Lafayette Square were not as terrible. More often the lights blazed, the carriages stood in line and the world of politics and fashion mingled in these ancient houses. On the northeast corner the

Pew number 54, St. John's Church

ebullient Dolley Madison reigned off and on for almost half a century. She and her little husband, the wizened Jamie, moved into the house soon after 1801 and were still living there when, after their own inaugural, they received the retiring President, Thomas Jefferson, within these walls. Years later, Dolley returned a widow, rotund, overdressed and laden with charm, to live out her days as the grande dame of the capital, no matter who was First Lady. The political world made it a custom to call first at the White House on New Year's Day and other ceremonial occasions, and then to rush right across the park to call on Dolley and presumably have more fun. Poor though she was, her house ranked as the second most important in the city. After her death in 1849—President and cabinet of course packed St. John's for the funeral—her house served as headquarters for General McClellan in the Civil War and passed through the hands of many distinguished residents.

The list is so long one must touch only briefly. Across from Mrs. Madison, the fiery Charles Sumner of Massachusetts lived and died, bent and broken by the caning he received on the floor of the Senate. Next door was the home of Senator Samuel Pomeroy of Kansas, the house from which Grover Cleveland departed to take the presidential oath. In the Tayloe House, Mark Hanna later made his headquarters and frequently had his protégé, President McKinley, in for breakfast. On the north side of the square all the houses but one are gone. Alone remaining is Ashburton House, now the parish annex of St. John's, a solid mansard-roofed structure, once the British legation. Here Daniel Webster, secretary of state for Harrison and Tyler, negotiated the treaty settling the northeast boundaries of the United States. Next door, St. John's provides the square's principal architectural distinction, the finest work left by Benjamin Latrobe. Pale yellow plaster, high-sprung arches that are characteristic of his work, a graceful tower—all conspire to make a pleasing whole, and in springtime the side yard bursts with crocus, blue chinodoxa, snowdrops and daffodils, starry early magnolias and japonica.

Eighth Street

All the early presidents and all the late ones, too, have worshiped in St. John's, so that one battered pew, number 54, is forever reserved—just in case the man across the park takes a notion to drop in.

The western half of the square is equally distinguished, though only half the houses survive. Gone is the elegant house that Daniel Webster's admirers presented to him (long before we worried about gifts creating a conflict of interest). Gone, too, is the double house built by the brilliant H. H. Richardson for John Hay and Henry Adams, a pair that in their day dominated the square as much as Dolley Madison did in hers. When Henry Adams wrote that Lafayette Square was society, he referred, of course, to the tight little world of his cronies. But those cronies happened to include the Secretary of State, other sometime cabinet officers, a few senators and a couple of carefully culled diplomats, the Camerons, the Lodges, the Hays, Clarence King and a few others. Though the Hay and Adams houses have succumbed to the wreckers, the oldest, and perhaps the most beautiful, has survived. Decatur House was first to appear on the square, and oddly enough was also the last to be used as a private dwelling, continuously occupied from 1818 until 1956. A severe red-brick block, Decatur House presents an austere façade to the square but inside it is all grace, well-proportioned space, with finely preserved woodwork by Latrobe. It was built by a hero of the War of 1812, Stephen Decatur, who allegedly used prize money won off the Barbary Coast in suppressing piracy. Decatur, alas, did not survive long to enjoy his elegant mansion. A proud and belligerent man, he was challenged to a duel by his one-time naval sponsor, Commodore James Barron, in 1820. From the dueling ground at Bladensburg, Decatur was brought back to die on Lafayette Square. His house passed through many hands. Three secretaries of state lived there in succession—Henry Clay, Martin Van Buren and Edward Livingston—giving the house a head start on all the others springing up around the square. A vice-president, George M. Dallas, followed. So did Judah P. Benjamin, who was to win his greatest fame as secretary of state in the Confederacy.

Blair House

58

The list went on through the years until finally an elegant, trim widow, Mrs. Truxtun Beale, reigned for the first half of the twentieth century as the last private resident of Lafayette Square. To the end Mrs. Beale, though far from stuffy, maintained some of the square's traditions. Only candles lighted her drawing rooms on festive evenings, and but for the changes in dress, her soirees must have been much like those of a century earlier. Like Dolley Madison, she entertained on the same nights as the White House; the more favored diplomats were invited to supper at Decatur House after they had paid their respects to the president at his annual diplomatic reception. Many a newly arriving ambassador, immediately after presenting his credentials, would call next on Mrs. Beale, who would receive him kindly and start him off with a little tart advice, product of long experience in the social jungles.

Tomb by Saint-Gaudens

VII

For all its sense of history, Washington is also as acutely contemporary as the problems pouring daily across the desks of government. The fact that power resides here forces Washington to be sensitive to happenings everywhere, not just in Vietnam, the Congo or other international hot spots, but to damaging floods along the Mississippi, a drought searing Texas and Oklahoma, racial outbreaks in Rochester, an epidemic in Atlanta. Washington reacts; one result is a feeling of being in touch. Whatever shortcomings Washington has, a feeling of isolation is not one of them. Here is, one feels, the main current—perhaps not the source of everything, not the only fountainhead; but the mainstream is surely passing through, and the manifestations are many. Comings and goings are one sign. The man and his family next door may be just back from Nigeria, where he was a crop consultant for two years. Around the corner another young couple has just left for India to work for the World Health Organization. One friend phones that he is in town for two months, between assignments in Tokyo and Rome. Another will leave soon to work on the poverty program in Detroit. The comings and goings are constant. The State Department naturally has always been sending its men everywhere; the armed services, too. But nowadays everybody goes everywhere: labor experts, agronomists, scientists, teachers, artists, everybody is out trying to help solve the problems which daily pour in on Washington. Dinner-party conversation is another index. A newspaperman, just back from California, discourses at length on the latest guerrilla outbreak between South and North politicos. A British M.P. is willing to discuss British election probabilities just so long; then he wants to hear the latest backstairs White House gossip. A scientist from Scripps in La Jolla, here to advise about a new aquarium, gets a full

Right
Springtime

Next two pages
Summertime

report on a Senate water-pollution hearing. A half-dozen talkers each contribute evidence on a matter of perennial interest—who is in favor at the White House? To whom does the President really listen? Washington is forever talking, listening, gathering information and passing it on. Events in other places have reality here because many of the participants pass in and out of Washington. The decision to make New Orleans a hurricane disaster area is made here. The steps carrying out the decision are superintended by a Washingtonian dispatched to the scene. A State Department officer cancels your dinner date because of new trouble in Panama. Events are not newspaper headlines. Events are intertwined in the lives of secretaries, assistants, chauffeurs, teletype operators, messengers and writers, as well as the top echelon of the town.

Essentially Washington is three cities. Best known is the political one, occupying roughly the area first laid out by L'Enfant and also the surrounding part of the District of Columbia. Here, in terms of action, is the city's heart, with a population numbering some 800,000, almost exactly the figure L'Enfant envisioned for his dream capital. No one in his right mind should ever think of living in Washington without an abiding interest, either primary or secondary, in politics. Politics is the city's reason for being, main industry, way of life, perpetual topic of conversation and lifeblood. Politics, of course, has many manifestations and disguises. There is the common garden variety of Hill politics, wherein senators and representatives debate and negotiate and connive to promote legislation and improve, at the same time, their own position. There is military politics, involving matters of high policy and low matters of personal advancement. There is economic politics, pertaining to dimly understood theories and sharply understood practices. The politics of industry, of science, of the arts, of city and country, state and county—all abound. The politics of foreign nations, of major powers and minor satellites, of foreign regimes in power and cabals out of power —all have their place in Washington. The city seethes or simmers, or just goes placidly along politicking, according to the moment.

Springtime

61

The second Washington is much larger, stretching deep into the Maryland countryside, spilling across the Potomac into Virginia, growing by leaps and bounds, so that the current headcount, 2,300,000, is only temporary. This is what the local press likes to refer to as Greater Washington. Greater than what? Greater than anything L'Enfant foresaw, greater than the highways and sewer systems and buses can bear. Greater Washington has gobbled up surrounding towns, Bethesda and Silver Spring and Wheaton in Maryland, Arlington and Fairfax, Clarendon and Falls Church in Virginia. Dozens of smaller ones, too, so that all must be considered part of that rather frightening concept, a greater Washington, and they are in truth parts of the city, lacking much centrifugal force of their own, providing sleeping space and living places for the hundreds of thousands who pour daily into the central political city. These hundreds of thousands, if not involved directly in the government, are at least engaged in the supporting services, operating the restaurants and beauty shops, the clothing stores and printing presses, the utilities and transportation, the department stores and gin mills, the barbershops and trucking companies, all the manifold operations necessary to a city of such size. The third Washington is even bigger: tourist Washington. In 1965, its population was a staggering, choking, suffocating nine million people. The growth rate is so great that even the Board of Trade, which ordinarily would be dancing with glee, gets a bad case of jitters contemplating traffic and other problems of the imminent future.

Nine million people sweep annually into the smallest of the three Washingtons because nearly everything that tourists want to see is concentrated in the small political city. It is as though the entire population of New York City had decided to engulf Washington. Fortunately they don't all come at once. The tide is highest in summer, and many a humid June morning the downtown area, especially around the White House, Washington Monument and the Smithsonian, looks as though Tourist Washington has won a total victory. The natives have fled. The tourists are in full control, their long lines, three abreast, snaking around the

Right
Capitol police

Next two pages
Capitol

White House grounds, across to Seventeenth Street and beyond. Their buses line the Ellipse and screen the view into Lafayette Square. They surge, determined and sweating, up the low hill to the monument, where more queues form. For a breather, they escape the scorching sun into the Smithsonian, where they can wander for hours until other attractions beckon. Tourist Washington, biggest numerically, is a world unto itself, as though some strict law of separation were in force, separatism based on purpose and on ways of life. Tourists are easily discernible (camera, colorful shirt, shorts and canvas shoes), usually ignored, except by guides, souvenir salesmen and police, and soon gone. The two worlds, the world of tourists and the world of Washingtonians, almost never mix. They pass almost unseeing and certainly uncomprehending. Each might as well be wearing blinders for all they see of one another.

The White House itself is a good example of how it goes. Each morning, in preparation for the invading hordes, White House attendants roll up the carpets in the main rooms and the ground-floor corridor where tourists enter. A huge screen is trundled into position, blocking the corridor so the President can, if necessary, reach the elevator to his private apartment unobserved. At ten the doors open, and for two hours the triple line is shepherded through, first along the corridor from the east entrance, up a marble staircase to the first floor, through the East Room, the Green, Blue and Red rooms, the State Dining Room, and out the front entrance. Chatting, gaping, lagging, pushing, shuffling, the crowd engenders a low buzzing noise that penetrates far into other parts of the White House, destroying any illusion of privacy the occupants might have. The President, safe in his West Wing office, goes on about his affairs with little disturbance. His wife must stay upstairs or slip out the back entrance. Her secretaries, with offices in the East Wing, are temporarily cut off from the main house or must push through the throng. There is no other route. But somehow the intricate affairs of government go on, even while the tourists, as many as 13,000 on big days, pass through on the other side of an invisible boundary. The two worlds are shoulder to shoulder. But they do not meet; they do not see one another. Each is intent on his own affairs. At twelve noon this intimacy ends. Doors close, the carpets are put back in place, floors mopped, guard ropes removed, screen taken down. The house reverts to its tenants who, for a while, have allowed the landlords to look over their property.

Politics, by one definition, is the struggle for power. Everywhere in Washington are the evidences of power. The Hill symbolizes it most vividly but The Hill is not alone. The President, in his person and in his office, holds more power than any other single man, power strong enough to counterbalance all the group-powers of The Hill and the group-powers of the third element in the American governmental system, the Supreme Court. The President *is* the power of the whole United States of America. Men operating within the presidency learn that limitations do exist, that being president does not mean being Louis Quatorze, that finally The People, if they use it, do have the ultimate power. But that does not detract from the powerfulness of the position. To get a glimpse of that source of power is the cherished dream of nearly every tourist who comes to Washington. Few do. Some may catch a hasty view of the President entering or leaving a governmental building. Or some may see a flash of long black limousine, flags flying, motorcycles thundering; or, if they are very very lucky, a few tourists may catch an extroverted President walking his dog inside the iron fence and even share a smile and a handshake as the flashbulbs explode. The odds are long against such luck, and the tourist must settle for other evidences of the power which has magnetized him irresistibly to Washington.

The pull of power is strengthened, deepened and enriched by the sense of history which is Washington's other most persuasive characteristic. History, like power, is everywhere, palpable in the noted buildings which have witnessed great events, the streets familiar to the great men of other times, the warp and woof of a political, historical city. This sense of history draws the tourist, to be sure, but few Washingtonians themselves are immune to it—a sense differing from that pervading older

Souvenirs

64

American cities such as Boston and Philadelphia. Theirs seems a history of long ago, of brave colonists and founding fathers. The simple red-brick and white-trim buildings are shells of ancient glories. Current history there may be a hunt for corruption, a plan for urban renewal. Necessary events, no doubt, but not ones to stir the blood. New York, on the other hand, overbuilt, overcrowded, struggles with daily existence, remembering only sporadically the early heroes and the later giants. It lives constantly in a shifting present. For a brief time it appeared that the United Nations would enhance New York with a new history-making power. But the wielders of power remained in Moscow, in London, in Paris, Delhi and Cairo, and sent out instructions to their UN delegates, just as the United States delegation receives its instructions from Washington.

The special historic sense of Washington is of power being used, of history in the making; and because additions are being made every day, the history of the past is more readable and more pervasive. The traditions of Henry Clay, Uncle Joe Cannon and Sam Rayburn hover close behind the chair of austere, colorless John McCormack as he presides over the House of Representatives. The Treasury Building is bracketed fore and aft by statues of Alexander Hamilton and Albert Gallatin, financier of the Revolution, to remind the secretary presiding within, be he Douglas Dillon or Henry Fowler, that he must remember all the decisions of his predecessors before he strikes off on his own.

Somehow history, in Washington, is more reassuring than inhibiting. A president, looking out through some of the same trees Andrew Jackson looked through, takes solace from remembrance of his predecessors' troubles. So may a senator, harassed to support some special bill, remember that, in this selfsame lobby, great men have agonized over great issues from the republic's early days. This feeling is the special sense of Washington. From Hill to White House, the avenues, buildings and monuments all speak eloquently of a past which, far from being embalmed, pulsates with the new history accumulating day after day in the same streets, the same offices, the same legislative halls.

Tandem columnists

VIII

Among the things that Washington isn't is industrial. No industrial smoke darkens the sky, no humming factories sprawl into the suburbs, no armies of workers troop through plant gates at dawn. This alone makes it unique among American cities of such size. It accounts, too, for the cleanliness of the Potomac air and the cleaner-than-average look of the city as a whole. That is the characteristic which first strikes the traveler reaching Washington. Cleanliness, and then "horizontalness," another rarity in the American scene.

Viewed first from National Airport, the city across the Potomac is a low-lying mass off to north and east, with only one monumental thrust of masonry needling into the sky, and farther east the Capitol dome rising from its stately hill. The general color is pale, all buff and gray and off-white, with generous interstices of green. Toward the northwest the land rises gently, and its lower slopes are red with the elderly bricks of Georgetown, the old riverport which was here before the federal capital. The Northwest hill mounts to a Gothic cathedral spire, denting an otherwise regular horizon, while to the west rise the tree-clad Virginia hills and Arlington. Seen from across the placid Potomac, the city looks inviting, calm and classical. The first approach is equally favorable. The highway into the city is a tree-lined park skirting the water. Sailboats jam a nearby marina; a few fishermen squat along the bank. Nothing more important than a scow in tow or an oil barge will pass because the channel, silting constantly, is very shallow. Across a long bridge, and the traveler passes immediately into the monumental heart of Washington, trees stretching in serried ranks toward the obelisk and the Capitol; a glimpse of marble monument through the green; farther off, govern-

Washington family

66

mental façades, circles, squares and parks. The effect is intensely recognizable as one unmistakable city. The horizontal impression is quickly reinforced in the center of the city. The average building height is ten to twelve stories, a restriction imposed with the specific aim of preventing any architectural competition with the Capitol or the great monuments. The result is, to some eyes, monotonous; but to most it is harmonious and certainly it succeeds in letting in the sky in a most dramatic way. In every part of Washington you are always conscious of the weather, of the changing light and of the shifting sky, which seems to arch higher because man has chosen not to compete with it. With poetic insight, Robert Lowell has observed that in summer Washington's "green statues ride like South American liberators above the breeding vegetation." Those infamous summers, which in times past gained for British diplomats a special "hardship post allowance," continue from mid-May until early October, the lushness emphasizing Washington's southernness. Winter Washington seems another city, crisper, more active, more northern, particularly when one of a half-dozen expectable storms dumps several inches of snow on the boxwood and magnolias, which were not designed for such wintry assaults.

The Capitol, proud on its eminence, dominating the city, is the cornerstone for marking the city into four quarters, Northeast and Northwest, Southwest and Southeast, each with a distinctive character. Smallest is Southwest, between the Capitol and the river, an area once covered by two- and three-story red-brick relics of the mid-nineteenth century. Most have now been torn down, and Southwest is the scene of the capital's most ambitious urban renewal project, where apartments, private houses and public housing spring up in profusion.

Southeast Washington looks just about as it did three-quarters of a century ago, only shabbier. Row on row, the houses are generally red brick, attached to one another or having tiny yards around them. Many neighborhoods are populated by Negroes, but most are middle- and

State Department official and his family

lower-class whites. At the corner grocery or the neighborhood chain store, the shoppers wear hair curlers, and the predominant accent has a hillbilly sound. The Anacostia River cuts through Southeast, providing a site for the old Navy Yard, numerous docks and naval installations, and a few service industries. Across the Anacostia, the quality of housing improves, the look grows a bit more proper middle class, before blending into the Maryland suburbs.

The four quarters of the city do not have clearly defined color lines, but Northeast Washington is predominantly a black city. Here are the real slums, but interrupted by long shopping streets that could be in any undistinguished city, except for the distant silhouette of the Capitol dome. Here is a Negro world as varied as the white one. Slum streets give way to better-kept row houses, row houses give way to homes of the well-to-do and even the rich. Schools, churches and stores are almost exclusively Negro, except for a few enclaves where white residents have held on. The architecture starts with post-Civil War near the city's center, then grows more modern as it reaches toward the suburbs, but it is a quarter without distinction. The best that can be said for it is that some neighborhoods, lined with ancient trees, provide better housing than most cities do for their Negro citizens. The worst that can be said is that such slums are an anachronism and a disgrace.

The largest quarter of Washington is Northwest. This is the city most people mean when they refer to Washington. In it are the White House, the Federal Triangle, most other government buildings, the embassies, fine residences, the Connecticut Avenue shopping district, downtown business section and such residential areas as Georgetown, Spring Valley, Wesley Heights and Cleveland Park, as well as many blocks of Negro residences. The great hotels, four universities, the art galleries, theaters, clubs and principal churches are in Northwest. So are such landmarks as Lafayette Square and Dupont Circle, the Protestant Episcopal Cathedral and Catholic St. Matthew's Church, Walter Reed Hospital and

Civil servant

68

the Carter Barron Amphitheater, the Naval Observatory and the new Kennedy Center for the Performing Arts. Winding through Northwest is Rock Creek Park, one of the city's great distinctions, rugged, heavily forested, full of scenic delights and surprises, bridle paths, picnic places, a winding stream, a zoo, an old mill. On hot summer nights, citizens lucky enough to live along its borders can feel the cool air welling up from the woods, a natural air-conditioning system.

Contemporary Washington, aware of history and aware of events current everywhere, is a city of contradictions and distinctions. Having grown cosmopolitan, it retains just enough of a Southern air to give a sense of old-time leisure. The green spaces are lovely and the vistas beautiful, but though devoted to improving man's lot everywhere, Washington itself is scarred by appalling slums, mostly inhabited by Negroes, and by poor schools attended by both black and white. Center of a great democracy, the city does not govern itself—it is not allowed to—nor, as a result, does it have much civic conscience. Washingtonians leave civic conscience to the federal establishment. Theirs is a city of careful privacy and constant publicity, a city of accomplishments and deep frustrations—statistically, in terms of people, somewhat more black than white, physically, in terms of place, very green and very white.

So many people have had doubts about Washington. Henry James, pernickety as ever, found the city "overweighted by a single dome and overaccented by a single shaft." Earlier, Charles Dickens poked mild fun at "the city of magnificent intentions"; and other inveterate European commenters, such as Harriet Martineau and Mrs. Trollope, etched sad descriptions of the capital's provincialism. Most Americans were content to accept the evaluation of Europeans. Washingtonians, for their part, seldom rise in defense of their own city. Something about Washington fails to stimulate the kind of fierce civic pride which in Dallas or Denver is considered to be typically American. Perhaps it is because Washingtonians are prone to think of the city not as a personal possession but as

Civil servant

one in which they share co-tenancy with the federal government, and thus with the rest of the nation. Washington is, in a sense, everybody's city, or at least his second city.

An urbane contemporary writer, Russell Baker, sees this finally as a virtue, observing that Washington is "notably free of the small-town chauvinism of New York or San Francisco. The Washingtonian is unruffled by New York's insistence on being thought the most thrilling city on earth or by San Francisco's claim to be the loveliest." Certainly Washingtonians look on their city as something of a freak, unlike any other of the cities which have grown up along the Atlantic coast. A trifle bland, the city lacks any of the special quarters devoted to Italians or Irish or Poles which could give a cosmopolitan flavor. The foreign-born residents of Washington are still citizens of their own countries. They are here as diplomats or students or trade representatives—and there are thousands of them. The black-and-white balance, the presence of many foreigners, the absence of industry, these are all substantial elements in Washington's character.

Until the summer beach crowd starts coming home after six, the Sunday traffic on Washington streets is provided mainly by churchgoers and families out for an afternoon drive. Then the underlying and dominant quality of the city shows through. Washington, for all its world position and power, is a very middle-class city, and middle class means family. On Sunday, families come out in full force in the quiet streets. The men and women who on weekdays are government workers hurrying to the office appear on Sundays in the familial role, taking the brood to the neighborhood church and afterward piloting them on a leisurely drive about town, or maybe to a picnic in Rock Creek Park. The pace is unhurried, unexciting, very middle class. The reason, according to Russell Baker, lies in the fact that Washington is "perhaps the last great city in which middle income can afford a house, a tomato patch and a canopy of dogwood within fifteen minutes of the office."

Right
Presiding Bishop of the Bible Way Church and his wife

Next two pages
Southeast

70

Another reason lies in the absence of industry. In other American cities, such as Pittsburgh and Detroit, industry has produced a society of sharp contrasts between industrial workers and industrial managers. Government and its supporting services create no such contrasts. There are areas of cruel poverty, but little ostentatious wealth. Government employment is a leveler, providing security, a steady job and regular advancement, even if no high pinnacle is available—which fits the middle-class mind to the T.

Play it safe. That is what the vast majority of Washington's 250,000 government workers are doing. Of course, among them are exceptions— creative minds, ambitious doers and dedicated workers. Otherwise the government service would have sunk long ago into a bottomless morass. But the prevailing mood is: don't stick your neck out; do enough to keep your supervisor happy; don't let Eager Beaverism get you into trouble. Bureaucracy, the world over, behaves thus; and Washington, far from being an exception, proves the rule.

Washington is the Illinois State Society having an annual dance in a hotel ballroom attracting government girls and men from congressional offices, each hoping that the other is "important," or at least romantically inclined. Washington is a newly arrived ambassador from a young African nation, rather frightened, terribly lonely, hunting for a place to live. Washington is the splashy overphotographed party, given mirthlessly by a self-styled great hostess, fooling nobody, not even the newspaperwomen who try to make it sound glamorous. Washington is the rock-and-roll music joints flowering after dark along Fourteenth Street and populated mostly by servicemen in civilian clothes. Washington is a government girl living in a Twenty-first Street roominghouse, having her TV dinner alone in front of the boob tube. Washington is the middle-class Negro family, spick and span in their Sunday best, riding sedately around the city on a Sabbath afternoon. Washington is a garish Cherry Blossom Festival, staged annually by the Board of Trade to attract

The District commissioners

tourists who don't need attracting because they already come by the millions.

Washington is the obituary of an elderly spinster who came from North Dakota in 1917, worked in the Bureau of Engraving for forty-three years, and spent her retirement in a Takoma Park nursing home. Washington is an embassy dinner party where the ambassador, over the brandy, finds out more from a newspaperman than he has learned in weeks of asking the State Department. Washington is winter skating on the Reflecting Pool, the skaters creating the pattern of a Brueghel painting. Washington is a summer-evening concert at Watergate, where canoes with close-locked couples tie up along the bank and musicians compete with Eastern's nine-o'clock shuttle from National Airport to New York. Washington is jam-packed bus stations and an empty railroad station. Washington is lunch at the Cosmos Club, where most of the members look like retired geology professors, or at the Metropolitan Club, where the lunchers seem to have just stepped out of an investment company's Washington branch office.

Washington is Rawlins Park in the springtime, long-limbed secretaries chattering together under lush, waxen magnolias. Washington is long bus queues at rush hour, hopelessly snarled traffic in the season's first snowstorm, and cafeterias downtown serving dinner at five thirty every afternoon.

Of the middle-class Sunday drivers a surprisingly large percent are Negro. Perhaps this should not be a surprise, since Negroes comprise fifty-eight percent of the District of Columbia population. What is surprising, I suppose, is their affluence. A large number of the Negro populace are card-carrying members of the middle class. Their clothes, automobiles, houses and way of life proclaim it; and that, no doubt, is one of the more significant developments of the late twentieth century, both socially and politically. For the Negroes of Washington, such gradual

The president of Howard University

72

escalation in status has been a long time coming. Negroes have participated in Washington life from the very beginning. When Andrew Ellicott
made the first survey of the city's swampy site for L'Enfant, his assistant
was Benjamin Banneker, described condescendingly in the local press as
"an Ethiopian." In the first decade, Negroes, living mostly in shanties,
made up one-fourth of the young city's population. The Civil War caused
a sensational jump in the size of the Negro quarter and created grave
problems because so many were ill-educated, newly freed slaves. Though
conditions were generally miserable, Negroes have found Washington a
haven compared with other northern cities. For at least a century, certain government posts have been open to them; mostly menial ones, true,
such as messenger, janitor and scrubwoman. Still, living conditions were
better than in some of the industrial ghettoes, and a certain freedom
existed, enough so that Negroes developed their own newspapers and
built some of the city's finest churches. A Negro elite grew up in the late
nineteenth century and expanded as the newly founded Howard University began to graduate doctors, dentists, lawyers and teachers. Negro
businessmen made fortunes, some from real estate, others from ordinary
trade, and the Negro world, separate and *un*equal, was swelled by a
constant emigration from the South. In those days Washington, without
a moment's soul-searching, practiced all the evil regulations of Jim Crow.
Not as blatantly as the South, perhaps, but the restrictions were all
there, in hotels, restaurants, trolley cars and public rest rooms. Anti-
Negro sentiment was so strong that when President Theodore Roosevelt
invited Booker T. Washington to lunch in the White House, a storm of
criticism resulted. Just as in the rest of the country, the status of the
Washington Negro was worst in the years from 1890 to 1933. Then, with
the coming of the New Deal, a few glimmerings appeared, partly because Franklin Roosevelt brought with him such high-minded and progressive assistants as Frances Perkins and Harold Ickes, who were, in the
phrase of Constance Green, "color blind." As secretaries of Labor and

Howard University students

73

Interior, respectively, Miss Perkins and Mr. Ickes were able to make a dent in Washington's segregation policies. The most dramatic moment came on Easter Sunday, 1939, when Ickes arranged for contralto Marian Anderson to sing on the steps of the Lincoln Memorial after she had been refused use of the DAR's Constitution Hall. An audience of 75,000 massed around the Reflecting Pool, symbolic of a new age coming, spurred on by the Second World War and its social upheaval. After the war the Thompson restaurant case forbade segregation in public eating places, and the city's schools, under pressure both from militant blacks and progressive whites, quietly ended segregation soon after.

It had been a long time coming. Now in thirteen agencies of the District government, half the employees are Negro. In the federal government, Negroes have gained more and better jobs during the Kennedy and Johnson administrations, until finally a Negro has reached the Cabinet. To assume that true equality has been achieved would be ignoring some harsh realities, however. The bulk of Negro employment in government is still in the lower echelons; positions of power are still held mostly by whites. Though the old school segregation has ended, a new kind has taken its place. Middle-class white families have joined the suburban exodus apparent in every city, leaving many public schools totally Negro again.

Washington's black and white citizens are beginning to mix in the ordinary affairs of the city. One of three District commissioners is a Negro. The school board and other branches of civic government are mixed, and some of the self-consciousness of relations between the two races is beginning to wear off. The *Post* and the *Star* occasionally print pictures of Negroes on their society pages, even when the subject is not an African diplomat. Negro names appear on guest lists without discrimination. White students enroll at Howard University, and white professors teach there too. Negroes in evening clothes no longer are greeted with stares as they walk through the Mayflower lobby to dinner or a reception. In the last twenty-five years such progress has been made that when President Johnson was host to an all-day symposium on the arts, it did not seem strange, only just, that Marian Anderson presided at one of the sessions in the White House.

IX

"Washington is like those exquisite Chinese boxes that contain another box and then another and another," said the tall dark-haired woman sitting in her shady Georgetown garden. "Each one you open is, you're sure, the last one, but then you find there's still something else, something more inside. You can feel it. I've lived here almost twenty years and I still keep opening new boxes. I begin to wonder if I'll ever open the final one—or if there is one." The dark-haired woman, slim and elegant, is like a heroine from fiction. In fact, like a very specific heroine, the leading lady Henry Adams created in his first novel, *Democracy*. Adams called her Mrs. Lightfoot Lee and endowed her with all the graces—beauty, breeding, intellect and the ultimate one, a comfortable income.

My friend has all of these and, like Mrs. Lightfoot Lee, came to Washington because she thought life here, amid the political leaders and diplomats, would be more interesting than in New York. Her many gifts enabled her to open box after box of the city's life. She became a hostess, meaning that she drew pleasure from bringing people together for dinner or for tea or drinks and that her entertaining was so artful people enjoyed going to her comfortable house, knowing the food and drink and conversation would all be good. Unlike her fictional prototype, who flirted with but did not marry a Western senator, my friend fell in love with and married a senator. I'm not sure why I tell her story, even this briefly, but probably it is to indicate something about the city of Washington, some quality that draws such people into its orbit and holds them. Others, hearing of the city's charms, have tried, failed and moved on to more salubrious places. Perhaps they did not possess my friend's endow-

A senator's wife

ments. Certainly Washington is no place for the idle rich, for anyone seeking madcap gaiety or a feverish pace. Washington, giving considerable rewards, also exacts a price from those who would become a permanent part of its life. Intelligence combined with an interest, more than skin deep, in things political is one requirement. Which is not to imply that Washington is an intellectual Parnassus, reeking erudition, a center of abstract thought and pure learning. Far from it. Intelligence rather than intellectualism is the requirement. And intelligence, in this case, does include a reasonable amount of learning, an acquaintance and perhaps involvement with ideas as well as actions, on the assumption that politics, the city's all-consuming activity, is based on ideas as well as on pragmatic considerations.

While the Idle Rich find little to amuse them in Washington, the Working Rich, an entirely different breed, have a significant place in the city's structure, both social and political. For a man of independent means, ranging from merely a comfortable income to a great fortune, there are real opportunities for public service. If he has had some experience, he may become undersecretary or assistant secretary of the Army, Navy or Air Force. He may become a roving ambassador if, by working hard at lower-ranking diplomatic assignments, he has shown a gift for such matters. He may even become undersecretary of state; it has happened. There are places for him in various agencies—Central Intelligence, the regulatory agencies such as Interstate Commerce, Communication, Federal Trade and a dozen others. The careers are real, not token, and the limitations are chiefly those of a man's talents. The wives of the Working Rich, less interested in bridge and golf than their more frivolous sisters, are likely to participate in worthwhile charities, to support the activities of museums and educational institutions, thus enriching the city's civic life in a way that many of the older residents have failed to do. The possession of riches enables this special group to add a certain restrained opulence to Washington life. They can acquire the

Roving ambassador

handsome old Georgian houses, fill them with fine furniture, Fortuny fabrics and Lowestoft, build swimming pools, hire staffs of servants, serve good food and wines. More than any other group they have enabled Washington to take its place with other capitals of the world in offering the amenities of life along with political action.

The Working Rich came on the scene first during the New Deal. Their appearance was one of the lesser manifestations of the deep-seated revolution that occurred in American life during the Great Depression, a watershed of history second only to the Civil War. Again one finds Washington reflecting the nation, a city severely shaken, the government completely reorganized and the capital never to be the same again, its responsibilities graver and acknowledged, the scope of activities infinitely broadened, the scale assuming worldwide proportions. The Second World War emphasized all these characteristics and, of course, attracted the services of even more of the Working Rich—such men as Robert Lovett, John J. McCloy, James V. Forrestal and Frank Knox, and a host of others who gave many years of dedicated public service. The prototype of all was W. Averell Harriman, who came the earliest and stayed the longest—from the early days of President Franklin Roosevelt, through the Truman and Kennedy administrations and well into the administration of President Johnson. First with NRA, then on special missions for FDR in England, then ambassador to Russia, chief European administrator of the Marshall Plan, secretary of commerce, a roving ambassador and finally undersecretary of state for President Kennedy— the list is an incredible one. For more than thirty years Mr. Harriman has given himself to the federal service, with the exception of the Eisenhower era, and those years he whiled away as governor of New York. In the process he became one of the nation's most skilled diplomats, able to cope with the wiles of Stalin, Molotov and Khrushchev, an intimate of Winston Churchill, a friend of Charles de Gaulle.

The war and its aftermath kept many of the Working Rich in service,

Reporter

such men as David Bruce, Gordon Gray, Paul Nitze and Dean Acheson. A younger generation has followed them; and so has another important segment of society, the academic. The first professors who joined FDR were such a phenomenon in American political life that they attracted attacks of unparalleled bitterness in those revolutionary New Deal days. Looking back a quarter of a century later, it is hard to fathom the depth of the suspicion elective officials felt for men who had devoted their lives to intellectual pursuits. All of the anti-intellectualism, from both province and city, centered on these professors, who, along with a group of enlightened lawyers and other recruits, were indeed making changes in the government, just as suspected, but changes no doubt necessary and even late in coming.

The New Deal professors, Rexford Tugwell, Adolf Berle, Jerome Frank and George F. Warren, had their counterparts in the Truman administration: Leon Keyserling and Edwin G. Nourse. The longer they stayed, the more permanent became the role of the academic in government life and therefore in the city. By the time of John F. Kennedy there were no outcries, except joyous ones, when his appointments included the most brilliant assemblage of brains ever to desert campus for capital— John Kenneth Galbraith, McGeorge Bundy, Arthur Schlesinger, Jr., David Bell, Walter Heller, Jerome Wiesner. The academicians brought much-needed intellectual fare to Washington's social life. While dinner at a professor-in-government's house may consist of tunafish casserole, salad and a bottle of California rosé, the conversation can make up for the absence of splendor; and with any luck, dinner next night may be with the Working Rich and will establish a gustatory balance. Both Working Rich and professors have, after many years, achieved a remarkable degree of acceptance from the real proprietors of government, the members of Congress. No longer is it fashionable at congressional hearings to attack professors just because they are professors. An intellectual working for the government is likely to be treated no better and

Professor, Howard University

79

no worse than any other witness appearing to defend an appropriation or a policy. It was not always thus. And congressmen have even gotten accustomed to meeting the intelligentsia after hours, to share drinks or a meal and engage them in civilizing conversation.

That matter of conversation is an important one. Henry James, who in his long life of writing and traveling became familiar with many capitals, called Washington "the city of conversation," and though he made the observation more than sixty years ago, it is still germane. Conversation is the basis of Washington's social pattern, which distinguishes Washington from New York and likens it to London or Paris. A small dinner party in a small Georgetown house is perhaps Washington's most typical social occasion. And conversation, from the first cocktail at eight o'clock until the guests start leaving at eleven, is the party's motive power. Big charity balls, embassy cocktail parties and such well-publicized occasions command the attention of the society-page writers, who also dwell lovingly on entertainments given by one or two rather comical professional hostesses. Such antics are out of Washington's mainstream and would pass unknown, except for carefully arranged publicity. Depending on the host's taste and pocketbook, the small dinner party can be simple or elegant or both, if he is clever, with more attention paid to mixing guests than to mixing drinks. An ambassador, an assistant secretary of state, one of the more loquacious CIA officials, a newspaper columnist and a senator might be mixed on one evening with suitable wives or extra women guests. The mixture need not be of elements that agree politically; in fact, one hostess is known to prefer antagonists at her board, depending on her own skill to prevent mayhem and keep the conversational pot boiling. When Richard Nixon was vice-president and conducting a blood-feud with his fellow Californian, former Senator William Knowland, she gave a dinner in honor of them both and sat back in amusement to watch the result, which was acrid. On another occasion one of her more formidable female guests turned to me at the

Before the annual ball

80

dinner table saying, "Young man, our hostess tells me you are the only Democrat present, and that I may do with you as I will." Usually the political-party balance is better maintained, Republicans and Democrats thoroughly mixed, but for many years it has been a well-acknowledged fact that it is much harder to round up a literate, articulate Republican of reasonable attractiveness to fill a dinner-table slot than a similarly endowed Democrat.

One Washington woman, a veteran of many political and social occasions, even goes so far as to claim that she can distinguish between feminine Democrats and Republicans by simple physical means. "Very easy," she says. "Lady Republicans have big fronts and lady Democrats run to big behinds." There are, of course, exceptions, but my researches have thus far confirmed her conclusion as a generalization. And the DAR, in annual spring convention in Washington, bring fresh evidence, and even add orchids to the part of their anatomy which proclaims their predominant Republicanism.

With Republicans and Democrats intermingling, Washington society, instead of being a thing apart, is essentially an extension of the city's main business, politics. A few enclaves are apolitical, but even the noted cave dwellers have been swept by political winds. Cave-dwelling describes the action to which old-line Washingtonians resort when they feel menaced by the brash political newcomers who arrive in fresh waves with every newly elected Congress. By withdrawing, they presume themselves the guardians of tradition, revered social customs and carefully manicured pedigrees. Some of their pretensions are laughable, such as those of a certain lady who complained bitterly to me because President Kennedy had not chosen a lineal descendant of hers to commission a warship named for her ancestor. He had chosen, instead, the wife of a governmental official who was instrumental in getting the warship built—which is just the kind of choice cave dwellers can't understand. But silliness is not the complete picture; some cave-dwelling families,

Butler

81

whose forebears have been in these parts for a couple of centuries, have managed somehow to keep their bloodlines vital, and they do play a part in civic life, raising funds for hospitals and schools, directing church and charitable activities. Some even have dipped their toes in politics. Their most positive contribution is a sense of stability in a city that changes rapidly.

In the strange mixture which composes Washington society—cave dwellers, government officials, foreign emissaries, military figures—a distinctive flavor is added by the fact that the press, unlike other cities, is an integral and important part of the social scene, not just an observer. The balanced dinner party, goal of most successful hostesses, nearly always includes one or two working journalists, a term that covers a broad field—political pundits who write only two or three columns a week, reporters scrambling for daily hot news, radio and TV performers, cartoonists, even sometimes the lowly photographer. Journalists and what they write have become a weighty factor in governmental checks-and-balances, a truism that is recognized by their acceptance as equals in all social as well as political activities of the capital. Of course, a hostess merely wanting newspaper publicity will ask a society reporter to her dinner, but the more serious and respected writers, Walter Lippmann, Joseph Alsop, James Reston of *The New York Times*, Marquis Childs and their ilk, are asked for different reasons—because they are well informed and in the conversational give-and-take of a good evening will add immeasurably to the party. And the range of the Washington press is great, including such a perceptive stylist as Mary McGrory, a wit like Art Buchwald, a trenchant cartoonist such as Herblock, the newly rising reportorial team of Rowland Evans and Robert Novak, and numerous others including some distinguished foreign reporters.

The foreigners, both press and diplomatic, have increased in numbers enormously since the Second World War, to such an extent that they have added more boxes-within-boxes in the city's intricate structure.

Columnist

82

Creating their own small worlds, some of the foreigners are inclined to stick close together, African diplomats seeing other Africans, Arab seeking out Arab, or Latin American engrossed in the company of Latin American. Not surprisingly, the largest of the foreign colonies, and by all odds the most important, is the British.

Legend has it that every prospective British ambassador to the United States is asked two questions before his final appointment: What happened August 24, 1814? Who was Sir Lionel Sackville-West? On his ability to answer both questions, preferably with wit, may hinge the success of his mission. He will use the information, over and over, in replying to toasts, addressing luncheon clubs and staving off importunate newspapermen. To the first question, the correct answer is: the British troops burned Washington. The second answer: British Ambassador to the United States in 1888, when he made an egregious error, interpreted by Americans as interference with domestic politics, leading to his recall. Sir Lionel, asked by a Californian how he would vote if he were an American, replied ingenuously that if he had the chance, he would vote for President Cleveland, in the belief that he would be a better friend to Britain than Benjamin Harrison. The outcry was sharp and quick. Harrison's supporters dubbed Cleveland "the English candidate." Particularly in New York City and Boston, with their heavy Irish, anti-English population, the issue carried great weight and may have been decisive. Cleveland lost New York, and the presidency, by a narrow margin.

But no matter the errors of the distant past, the British occupy a very special place in the American capital. For one thing, there are so many of them. The official mission lists 600 employees ranging from Her Britannic Majesty's Ambassador down to footmen and chauffeurs. The actual British colony is even bigger, including World Bank officials, the military, retired civil servants, newspapermen, and many more. But mere size cannot account for the British position in Washington. Obvi-

Cartoonist

ously the British-American alliance is a keystone in the affairs of both nations and finds expression in a constant shuttling back and forth between the two capitals. In Washington one feels as in touch with London as though it were an American city. Gossip, political and social, travels fast between the two. A Briton who lunched in London can easily turn up that night at a Washington dinner table. My neighborhood drugstore regularly carries *The Times, Manchester Guardian, Observer, The Economist, New Statesman, Encounter,* and a half-dozen other British publications. What Debo Devonshire said about Harold Wilson is quickly repeated on the Washington circuit. This cozy relationship has been growing for a long time. Ever since the days of Sir Lionel Sackville-West, the British have paid Washington the compliment of sending rather distinguished men as ambassadors. Cecil Spring-Rice, James Bryce, Lord Halifax, Lothian and Inverchapel all were top-drawer, so well-connected at home they could reflect their government's policy with quick accuracy. The British ambassador has therefore always held a dominant position in the Washington diplomatic corps, even though he seldom has stayed long enough to become dean, a rather empty position based solely on length of tenure. The British Embassy's annual Garden Party, celebrating the Queen's birthday the first week in June, is the city's most important social event except for certain White House doings.

The ultimate intimacy in exchanging ambassadors was reached when Prime Minister Harold Macmillan allowed President Kennedy to name his own choice for the Washington post. It was done informally, of course, but the President sent word to London that he would be pleased to receive an old friend, Sir David Ormsby-Gore, who later became Lord Harlech. The choice was a brilliant one. Of President Kennedy's own generation, Lord Harlech was broadly educated, knew the London political scene intimately and achieved a deep understanding of America. His rapport with the President was complete, and David Harlech probably knew more about the inner workings of the American government

Dean of the diplomatic corps

than any other British ambassador in history. The uniqueness of the British position stems also from the fact that the Commonwealth ambassadors, from Canada, Australia, New Zealand, India, Pakistan, Ceylon and so forth, tend to stick together even though their empire is no more. In many matters their interests seem identical, or at least close, and together they wield more authority than any would separately. After the British ambassador, the Russian is most important, for reasons of power. In the tense days of the Cold War, the Russian ambassador and his staff lived mostly to themselves, participating in only the more formal diplomatic social life of Washington. With the Khrushchev thaw, however, came a great change. Russians entertained more easily, accepted more invitations, mixed into the ordinary life of a foreigner in Washington.

On the surface, the presence of so many diplomats, missions from more than a hundred countries, adds a stylish glitter to Washington's social life, but the contribution is of a sturdier quality well below the surface. At the second or third levels of rank the foreigners are woven more closely into the city's life, worshiping in Washington churches, buying in supermarkets, their children attending local schools, themselves participating in many aspects of civic life, a give-and-take of infinite benefit in eroding the provincialism innate in most Americans and giving the city reason to claim cosmopolitanism.

Ambassador from the U.S.S.R.

X

Being middle class and modest and bemused by politics, Washingtonians are disinclined to think of their city as having great intellectual weight, certainly not in the sense that both London and Paris dominate their nation's intellectual life, nor even to the lesser extent that Cambridge and New Haven and Berkeley spread a glow far beyond their academic confines. Content with political pre-eminence, Washington has enjoyed entertainments and let it go at that, entertainments such as pre-Broadway tryouts for two weeks at the National Theater (which is not national, but privately owned), concerts by the touring Philadelphia and Boston symphonies, an occasional Hurok ballet. The slowly accumulating distinction of the National Gallery and the city's other art collections have gained appreciation as treasures worthy of a great capital. These and a few others have been looked on principally as pleasures, not as evidences of a world beyond the political. But that world, the world of the mind, has made an almost sensational growth in the middle decades of the twentieth century, a growth unheralded by promotional fanfare and neither planned nor analyzed.

Future historians are likely to mark October 4, 1957, as a crucial one for America, the day that Russia lofted Sputnik. Across the national consciousness, and particularly in the recesses of some previously unpenetrated congressional minds, dawned the possibility that perhaps the American system was not the unchallengeable best, the most ideal and most fruitful in the entire world. Just perhaps, great feats of science and engineering and accomplishment could be achieved by others, others marshaling their brainpower and national resources in a better way, or at least a way more immediately productive of concrete results.

Right
The director of the National Gallery of Art

Next two pages
Renwick's Smithsonian

The normal congressional reaction to such a situation, like any other crisis, is to appropriate a few billion dollars for its correction. And that was done, but miraculously the matter did not rest there, nor could it. The ensuing years have witnessed a good deal of soul-searching, both public and private, about the quality of American education, about the aims and support of science, about the government's role in intellectual enterprises. Even to carry on such searching and debate, the government found that it must bring in battalions from the intellectual community; and many of them came to stay in various branches of the federal establishment, the Space Agency, the Defense Department, even the White House itself.

The way of the intellectual in government has always been a stony one, but this time the path had been traveled more recently, by FDR's Braintrusters and by the intellectuals assisting government in wartime. Other changes had occurred in Washington, some of them almost unnoticed, such as the extraordinary number of learned societies and academic organizations which have transferred their national headquarters to Washington, another manifestation of the centralization of power in the capital. The atmosphere had become palpably more friendly to intellectuals.

Such institutions as Brookings, the Carnegie Foundation, the Johns Hopkins Institute for Advanced Studies and the Dumbarton Oaks Center for Near Eastern Studies, to name a few, have given Washington life a flavor that was missing in Henry Adams' day. The National Institute of Health, because of its research orientation, and the National Bureau of Standards have both become magnets attracting more brainpower into the city; but the giants of them all are of course the Library of Congress and the Smithsonian Institution. These two, unlike in many aspects, share a common problem in being government supported and therefore rooted in politics but planted to nourish the life of the mind. Between root and branch there should be no conflict; and the two

The secretary of the Smithsonian Institution

institutions, in their own often odd ways, have solved the situation admirably. The Library of Congress still provides members of the legislative branch with bales of research annually, but that function long ago became a minor operation compared with the other multiplying services and functions that have accrued.

From the nucleus of Jefferson's precious volumes, the library has grown to include 43,000,000 items, a figure staggering to the mind but nonetheless necessary to indicate something of the library's scope. Among its possessions are such treasures as a Gutenberg Bible, Jefferson's draft of the Declaration of Independence, the papers of twenty-three presidents, L'Enfant's original plan for the city, five Stradivarius musical instruments, Alexander Hamilton's touching last letter to his wife, 10,000 Mathew Brady negatives, thousands of other rare and fascinating items. Special richness in Americana is matched with extraordinary collections of Chinese and Russian books and documents. The private papers of hundreds of political notables, of artists, writers and musicians, all add to the attraction the library has for scholars from all over the world. The library, surpassing its congressional function, has become a truly national library, comparable only with the Bibliothèque Nationale in Paris or with the British Museum. The mere presence of such a formidable institution could not help but enrich the city's cultural life, and the library assiduously cultivates this area of activities with chamber-music concerts, poetry readings, lectures, exhibitions and a profusion of other events, making it a community as well as an international scholarly enterprise.

In the world of the mind, the Smithsonian occupies far greater geographical territory, lining the Mall with museums, even though its intellectual position is not of such unchallengeable purity. The Smithsonian's history has been more checkered, its acquisitions more helter-skelter, its directions more ambiguous than those of the library. What finally assures the Smithsonian a top position, however, has been an undeviating loyalty to original scientific research in its 120 years of existence. A legacy to the

Co-founder of the Phillips Collection

American government from an eccentric British chemist, James Smithson, illegitimate son of the Duke of Northumberland, provided funds in 1835 for establishment of an institution dedicated to "the increase and diffusion of knowledge among men." After eleven years of congressional debate the gift was finally accepted, due a great deal to the tireless sponsorship of John Quincy Adams, who, after his presidency, was serving in the House of Representatives.

With such a broad objective, "the diffusion of knowledge," the Smithsonian could have become anything from an agricultural college to a school for orphans, both of which were proposed during the long debates. What it did become, however, was a coalition of twelve bureaus ranging through a broad scientific spectrum from astrophysics to anthropology, a repository for great scientific collections, antiques, mementos, paintings and plain junk, and finally it also became a center for mass education of Americans. Such diverse responsibilities have blurred the Smithsonian's image so much that tourists know it chiefly as the scene of endless displays of old airplanes, automobiles, steam engines, costumes, precious stones, bird skeletons, dinosaur bones, Indian relics and the like. Washingtonians are prone to treat the museums merely as a convenient place to take the children on a rainy Saturday morning. But the Smithsonian has played a formidable role in developing American life by, for instance, sponsoring some of the key expeditions to explore the Far West, the Arctic and the once-vast Indian territories. Frontiers of the mind have received even greater attention from the Smithsonian. One secretary of the Institution, Samuel Langley, was an important aviation pioneer who managed to put an unmanned aircraft into flight for half a mile along the Potomac as early as 1896. The list of the Smithsonian's accomplishments is long and continuing, thus attracting to Washington another group of intellectuals to leaven the political pudding.

Amid such giants, the city's five universities seem pygmy. Georgetown University, the eldest, founded in 1789 by Jesuits, has the highest

Benefactor, Dumbarton Oaks

reputation because of its law school and a well-developed School of Foreign Service. Neither American University nor George Washington University has achieved much academic distinction, nor has Catholic University; but the fifth of the group, Howard University, is unique and rapidly growing in importance. Chartered in 1867, for the education of Negroes, Howard is largely dependent on federal funds and was quite naturally desegregated years ago; white teachers teach there and white pupils are enrolled, though Negroes are predominant. The university's importance stems from the fact that it has become a mecca for foreign students from all over the world, especially the newly emerging nations. From Tanzania, Vietnam, Mali and Ceylon, students of all skin colors and ethnic origins have been attracted by the fact that here, at last, they can study abroad without the campus dominance of a white majority. Looking at the variety of faces and costumes, one wonders how many future presidents and prime ministers are being trained on this red-brick campus only a mile from the White House.

Washington's art treasures, instead of being assembled under one vast roof like the Louvre or Metropolitan, are fragmented among a half-dozen galleries, a system that has considerable merit. Instead of searching through confusing corridors and wings to find, for instance, Oriental painting, a visitor knows that he must go to the Freer Gallery on the Mall to study the great screens, prints, jade, ceramics, and other elements of that superb collection. To look at American painting of the past he can go to either the Corcoran Gallery or to the Smithsonian's National Collection, an ill-selected group of paintings that in the near future will have a new home and arrangement alongside the newly established National Portrait Gallery. To look at contemporary painting, he must go to either the Washington Gallery of Modern Art or the unsurpassed Phillips Collection, both near Dupont Circle. To look at great European painting, he will make his way to the National Gallery, where the Mellon, Kress and Chester Dale collections have been joined into one of the most important

The Corcoran Ball

90

galleries of this hemisphere even though only a scant twenty-five years old. In importance to the capital, the National Gallery ranks alongside the Library of Congress and the Smithsonian in contributing to the life of the mind. In music and theater, the city offers less, but does support, somewhat grudgingly, the National Symphony and a thoroughly first-rate repertory company, Arena Stage, which occupies a handsome new theater-in-the-round on the Southwest waterfront.

The city's literary life is a different matter, less institutional, somewhat erratic, but with quite a history. Literature, by one sweeping definition, is merely "printed matter," and by another definition, in the same *Oxford Concise,* is "writings whose value lies in beauty of form or emotional effect." The literature of politics most often is the former. Rarely does beauty of form come from the political hand, yet in our own time, two men, President Kennedy and Adlai Stevenson, have reminded us that it can happen. They are of a small company in a city where literary quality is more apt to level out into the prose of the *Congressional Record* or *Advise and Consent.* But a strange collection of literary figures have mixed in the Washington scene, if only briefly, and added luster to it. Sorrowing for Lincoln, Walt Whitman wrote "When lilacs last in the dooryard bloom'd…" at a time when he was also working in Washington on a new edition of *Leaves of Grass.* Certainly that moment had greater literary merit than that spent by Frances Hodgson Burnett, who, dipping her pen in molasses, wrote *Little Lord Fauntleroy* in her house on K Street. The story made enough money for her to build a grander house on Massachusetts Avenue, to write another perennial seller, *The Secret Garden,* and live out her days in comfort.

One of Washington's longest staying literary transients was Ambrose Bierce, who worked here more than a decade for William Randolph Hearst, and it was from Washington that Bierce went off on his mysterious trip to Mexico whence he never returned.

Tom Paine visited Jefferson, to the scandal of the city's more con-

The Library of Congress

91

servative citizens. Washington Irving came to visit friends. Ralph Waldo Emerson came to preach. Edgar Allan Poe came to get drunk. Poe's performance was the more remarkable in Washington eyes because he came over from Baltimore for his alcoholic outing; Washingtonians usually reverse the process. Louisa May Alcott nursed Civil War soldiers in a Georgetown hospital. John Burroughs came to sit at Whitman's feet and to start his career as a naturalist. Sometimes sentiment more than intellect stirred the city's writers, and some of their creations have had remarkable durability. Francis Scott Key, a Washington lawyer and poetic dabbler, wrote "The Star-Spangled Banner," anxiously watching Fort McHenry outside of Baltimore. John Howard Payne, languishing abroad, thought of Washington as he wrote "Home, Sweet Home." In the twentieth century Elinor Wylie and Paul Laurence Dunbar both lived and worked in the capital. Washington's literary figures are of a motley crew, no common thread tying them to this political city.

The true literary giants are, logically enough, also the political giants—Jefferson, Lincoln, Theodore Roosevelt, Woodrow Wilson. The rough-hewn, little-educated man who became president in the nation's greatest crisis, Abraham Lincoln, was a writer who inspired Edmund Wilson to say:

Alone among American presidents, it is possible to imagine Lincoln, grown up in a different milieu, becoming a distinguished writer of a not merely political kind.

Citing the Gettysburg Address and the Second Inaugural as merely two examples of his literary art, Wilson found that Lincoln's "own style was cunning in its cadences, exact in its choice of words and yet also instinctive and natural." By his exertions, Lincoln became a man of true education who found it perfectly natural to read aloud a scene from *Macbeth* to his cabinet as they boated down the Potomac. But Wilson is a bit too stringent in ruling out other presidents; some had very marked literary abilities.

Right
The Folger Library

Next two pages
Rotunda, National Gallery of Art

Theodore Roosevelt's career started with much more conventional beginnings than Lincoln's, but he did not stop with Harvard. The moment he finished formal schooling he started scratching out books that increased in quality. First came a slim naval history of the War of 1812. *The Winning of the West* became a classic and, finally, his best work, handwritten in Africa, describing his explorations and observations. TR's writings had beauty of form and often emotional effect as well. Woodrow Wilson, the former professor and president of Princeton, must be ranked among the literary men, at least to the extent that *A History of the American People* is still readable, and his speeches showed a gift for phrase. But strangest of all to be considered a literary figure is Ulysses S. Grant, a leading contender for title of the nation's greatest general and worst president, though there are several competitors for the latter honor. Grant's *Personal Memoirs,* printed now in a paperback edition, have reached out to a new generation whose vision is not befogged by vapors of his odiferous administration. His lucid thought, the form and style all combine to create a literary work of prime importance. Grant's genius on the battlefield, which Lincoln had appreciated, appeared in a new guise as he struggled to finish this massive work before approaching death. He had waited more than two decades before evaluating the men and battles of his command. Perhaps that is why his judgments are so reasoned, so serene, and perhaps he has a lesson for contemporary figures who rush their memoirs to us the moment a calendar page is turned.

Political Washington, with such diarists as Harold Ickes, Gideon Welles and Henry Morgenthau, and a vast company of memorists, has produced a flood of political literature which lives chiefly on its historical merits. The closest that Washington ever came to producing a Bloomsbury was in the time of Henry Adams and his circle. Since then, journalists have held undisputed sway and currently have fallen prey to a curious delusion that novel-writing, instead of being art, is a spare-time occupation. The result has been a spate of shockers, such as *Seven Days in*

Arena stage

May and *Night of Camp David*, which have added little to the capital's literary reputation.

In world literature, Washington's most eminent figure is one of its least publicized residents, Alexis Léger, who as Saint-John Perse, the French poet, won a Nobel prize for *Anabasis, Eloges, Winds* and other writings. He has chosen Washington as his home for many years, and by his very rareness proves the truth of the conclusion that Washington, whatever else its virtues, is not the Left Bank. Perhaps Cyril Connolly put his finger on the problem when he wrote: "Washington has immense charm, the streets of Georgetown with its ilexes and magnolias and little white box-houses are like corners of Chelsea or Exeter, but a political nexus offers few resources to the artist."

XI

Such a nexus, such a political connection, is just what almost everyone in Washington is seeking, a connection that wires him somehow into the power circuit. The power lines converge in many places, in the White House, in the Pentagon, in the Supreme Court and certainly with great concentration in Congress sitting dominant on The Hill.

From the very first mud-spattered days, Congress has dominated Washington in a practical way. The hours it keeps, the months it meets, the political complexion, the mood and temper of Congress, these all regulate the city's warm heartbeat. A congressional debate lasting far into the evening will disrupt scores of dinner parties throughout Washington, change ticket reservations, throw off the next day's schedule for thousands of people. Whether a long congressional session ends in July—as seldom happens any more—or runs on to the end of September affects household leases, apartment rentals, plans to change jobs or when to take a vacation. A sharp shift in the political balance of Congress has a deep effect on the city. New congressmen rent houses, bring new constituents into jobs, shake up all the arrangements that have been made by the previous congressman. These are but the physical aspects of congressional dominance. More important is the political climate emanating from The Hill, a condition hard to define, but Washingtonians are intensely aware of its existence and its importance. Any doubter needs only to look back on the turbulent postwar years when Senator Joseph McCarthy was riding high, mocking the White House, insulting colleagues, harassing the armed services. Washington quivered with anger, shame and fear. Uncertainty stalked through every department of the government and every cranny of the city. No one knew what outrage the next day's hearing might bring. Not until the Senate's own censure motion started McCarthy down the road to oblivion did the city begin to recover. The recovery was long and slow. The damage had been deep. Confidence in Congress had been severely shaken, for the climate of Congress in those days was harsh, set not by McCarthy alone, but also by other congressmen following his evil example. Fortunately such hurricanes are rare on The Hill. Usually the weather is pleasant, with only passages of turbulence.

The Congress is complex, contradictory and confusing in its shifting moods and styles, sometimes seeming to hold a mirror to American life, sometimes seeming to turn inward on its own quarrels and usages and preoccupations, unaware of the nation's distresses and desires. But great men have walked these halls; and moving through the soaring rotunda, past Latrobe's columns, up the staircases and elevators, into the galleries looking down on legislative chambers, one is aware that despite the littleness of many individuals, despite sham and obfuscation and delay, there is something deeply exciting about being in the Capitol of the United States, where Congress has met and legislated for 165 years. The names of great leaders spring to mind from distant past as well as recent years, John C. Calhoun and Robert Taft, Norris and La Follette, Platt and Quay, Tom Connally and Champ Clark, Webster, Clay, Lodge, Cannon and Reed. It goes on and on. Some are memorialized by sculptures, mostly bad, which line Statuary Hall, where every state is entitled to enshrine two of its heroes and a hilarious hodgepodge of shapes, sizes and sculptural skills has resulted. Forgotten politicians stand on equal footing with peerless leaders, suffragettes, poets, priests and Indian chiefs, the last reminding us that before Europeans and Africans settled this land these were the true natives who, in the opening centuries, were a thorny problem to their conquerors. These effigies along with the moving, breathing men and women down on the legislative floor imply a panoramic view of America—and that perhaps is the key to the excitement latent in this massive building on The Hill.

Within the Capitol the legislators live in a separate world like a small medieval state, with all the services and comforts self-contained. The Capitol has its own police force, its own subway, its own bank, barbershops, restaurants, gymnasiums and steam rooms, its own airlines and railway ticket offices, its own daily paper, its own physicians, architect and post office. The House has a doorkeeper and the doorkeeper has a secretary. There are twenty-four doormen. There are file clerks, bill clerks, enrolling clerks, stationery clerks, tally clerks, reading clerks. The Senate's door is kept by a sergeant-at-arms who has an assistant and *three* secretaries. In addition to all the clerks, superintendents and administrative assistants, the Senate also has an official upholsterer. So much sitting is tough on the furniture.

Small wonder that Senators and Representatives find it an absorbing world. However, they no longer stick together, as they once did, living in boardinghouses clustered along Pennsylvania Avenue, patronizing the same hotels and saloons, seeing little of the remainder of the city and its inhabitants. Nowadays a congressman, knowing that long sessions will keep him in Washington, is most likely to bring his family with him and set up full-time residence—and he usually brings along his own pattern of life. If he has a ranch-type Rambler back in Racine, he is likely to rent a similar one in Parkfairfax or Wheaton Hills. If he has an apartment in Kansas City he is likely to rent a similar one on Sixteenth Street or perhaps at the Shoreham. Some live in hotels. A few lease handsome old houses in Georgetown. A few still manage to commute. The commuters are principally from New York and environs within easy reach of the hourly airline shuttle service, a development that has brought New York and Washington into close community.

The longer a member of Congress stays in Washington, the deeper he penetrates the city's life. At first, congressmen and their staffs huddle rather close together, their social life centering around the various congressional clubs and state societies created to stave off loneliness. Gradually, however, they branch out, and as their committee assignments become more important, so does their status in Washington life. Status, to a congressman, is measurable by many things—how big and attractive his office space, the size of his staff, the frequency with which the White House consults him, the amount of newspaper space he commands, the license plate on his car, the rank of his seat at a dinner table. All these and other signs add up to a specific status rating. Committee assignments are of prime importance. To be a member of the committees on Ways and Means, Foreign Affairs, Rules, or Appropriations carries far greater esteem than being a member of Merchant Marine or Post Office. Least of all is the poor District Affairs Committee, which handles Washington city matters; and congressmen avoid it like the plague.

Being majority leader of either House or Senate carries enormous weight. So does being minority leader or whip. The men who hold these jobs are frequent White House visitors, called in for consultation on pending bills, on international crises or ceremonial occasions such as the signing of a bill or the swearing-in of a new official. The rest of governmental Washington is acutely aware of all these gradations in status and the power they indicate. A cabinet member or a bureau chief must keep such niceties in mind; how else would he evaluate the phone call from a congressman or his administrative assistant demanding a report on some program or requesting information about a newspaper rumor, or suggesting an appointment? Letters, phone calls, personal visits, or a summons to appear on The Hill—these are the ways congressmen make their presence felt in every part of official Washington.

Technically the three branches of the federal government—legislative, executive and judicial—are separate and distinct. Actually their powers, instead of being clearly distinct, are often overlapping so that power becomes a shared commodity. The President cannot legislate, but

Right
Doorkeeper of the House

Next four pages
Heroes

he does propose legislation and then lobbies for it with all the formidable powers at his command. Congress cannot execute its own mandates—that is the duty of the executive branch—but Congress can press for action by such means as giving or withholding appropriations and, by other methods, seek to have its will carried out. The Supreme Court can neither legislate nor execute; still it has and uses powers which at times smack of both legislative and executive action. The school-desegregation decision, for example, has been a more potent weapon for civil-rights reform than any single piece of legislation. Similarly, the decision ordering certain states to reform their election districts in closer conformity to population will probably create deep changes in future Congresses, ending rural domination and creating a House more nearly representative of an America grown largely urban. These shared powers, flowing back and forth among the three great branches of government, are of deep intricacy, and so are the relations between the two bodies of the legislative branch itself. The byplay between House and Senate has been a source of fascination and amusement to Washington for 165 years, the Senate with 100 members each rejoicing in a six-year term and considering itself exclusive, powerful and pre-eminent, the House acknowledging that its larger membership, 435, and shorter terms, two years, make it more formless and transitory, nevertheless boasting that its very size and frequency of election make it more truly representative of the will of the people. Between the two chambers the struggle is unceasing.

In certain periods the stature of individuals—giants like Henry Clay or Thaddeus Stevens or Henry Cabot Lodge or James G. Blaine, and even constellations of giants—has made one or the other of the two chambers pre-eminent. Strong personalities, ones with an affinity for power, have exerted tremendous influences on these parts of government. One need only examine the autocratic power with which such men as Czar Reed or Uncle Joe Cannon wielded the speakership to realize how much one man can shape and color the position of the House in the intricate intragovernmental balance. Thomas Reed, a Maine Republican who became speaker in 1889, was a superb debater and a sharp wit. Having been a troublemaking minority leader, he came to the speakership with a firm belief that minorities should not be permitted to block the will of the majority; and from the august speaker's chair he made rulings that reinforced his power, which already included the authority to appoint all committee chairmen. He became a legislative czar, indeed, and gave the House a cohesion which enabled it to surpass the Senate, at least for a time. The speaker's power was enhanced further by a profane, tobacco-spitting Illinois politician, Uncle Joe Cannon, who ruled ruthlessly until a rebellion clipped his wings in 1910.

By the time of "Mr. Sam" Rayburn, who served as speaker seventeen years, longer than any other, the speaker's powers were less autocratic and, in his case, were based on a network of personal relationships, favors done and promises kept. The power to appoint committee chairmen, a key one, had been passed on to the Democratic caucus and its Committee on Committees, where the seniority rule now holds sway— and thereby hangs a sad tale of declining prestige and efficiency. Because of seniority, the majority of committee chairmanships in a Democratic-controlled House are held by Conservatives, most of them Southerners whose safe districts send them back repeatedly to Congress. The result is that the House of Representatives, despite Democratic majorities in twenty-eight of the last thirty-four years, has become the most conservative element in the governmental complex, more conservative than the Senate, the presidency or the Supreme Court.

A perceptive insider, Representative Richard Bolling of Missouri, in his book *House Out of Order,* concluded that this state of affairs was due simply to the fact that the House is no longer responsive to its own majority, a negation of all democratic ideals. The Conservatives, mostly southern, are able as committee chairmen to bottle up legislation of which they disapprove. The prime example is Representative Howard

Senator

100

Smith, mournful-looking octogenarian Virginia judge, who is chairman of the all-powerful Rules Committee. No bill can reach the floor unless his committee gives permission, and the issues he opposes are many, commencing of course with civil-rights reform and continuing through the broad spectrum of social legislation, medical care for the aged, higher minimum wages, aid to education, better housing, and even home rule for the District of Columbia. At the beginning of the Kennedy administration, Speaker Rayburn made a small dent in the problem by enlarging Smith's Rules Committee from twelve to fifteen men, thereby giving northern Democrats a slightly better representation. President Johnson, by some alchemy known only to himself and Judge Smith, has succeeded in shaking loose a surprising number of key bills, but the problem itself remains, with the power of Judge Smith and his cohorts unbroken.

A slight counterbalance to such entrenched conservatism is provided in the House by the Democratic Study Group, a loose association of about 140 Democratic congressmen, nearly all northern and mostly of urban orientation. Their "study" includes not only an analysis of the issues they think important to the nation but also, and perhaps more importantly, methods of circumventing the Conservatives in both political and parliamentary strategy and tactics. Bolling himself, a onetime protégé of Mr. Sam, is a leading member of the Study Group, as are such vigorous and hard-working members as Frank Thompson of New Jersey, Edith Green of Oregon, James Roosevelt, John Brademas, and John Blatnik of Minnesota. After sixteen years in the House, Bolling has come to believe, sadly, that reform must come from outside pressure because the Conservative power structure's grip has become too tight to be shaken loose by any internal coalition of reformers. He proposes that, in addition to ending conflicts of interest, reforms should center in restoring power to the speaker, power to nominate committee chairmen, subject to ratification by the Democratic caucus, and thus end seniority as the sole determinate of chairmanships. In addition, he is a strong advocate

Senator

101

of redistricting on a strict population basis, so that the House, still lurching along as though America were a rural nation, will become more representative of the urban areas, which comprise two-thirds of our whole.

Reform has its advocates on the Senate side of the Capitol as well, but in the Senate the matter, like most things senatorial, is different. The conventional picture of this august body, and a rather accurate one, is startlingly close to one's conception of the Union League Club, whose members, neatly groomed and polished, rest their haunches in leather chairs to exchange ideas amid the aroma of fine cigars and the best bourbon. Just enough of this atmosphere exists to give the picture veracity, but the similarity blurs when the Senate's full membership is considered, a membership which, from time to time, has included wild-eyed western Populists, untrimmed southern radicals, demagogues as well as statesmen, men of working-class origins, and nowadays an increasing number of much younger men, who for all their well-tailored sophistication do not treat their Senate seats as memberships in a well-bred bankers'-and-lawyers' club. The two Kennedy brothers, along with Frank Church of Idaho and Birch Bayh of Indiana, to name a few, are investing the Senate with a new undercurrent of vitality that may create changes in an institution which prides itself on being unchanging, traditional, the guardian of the sacred flame of the American government.

In truth, the Senate does stand, more than any other elected group, for continuity. The voters have an opportunity to turn the president out of office every four years, and the entire House can be replaced every two years, but no more than one third of the Senate can be ejected in any one election because their six-year terms are staggered, only a third coming up for election at any one time. This system alone does provide continuity, which is reflected in many aspects of its organization, such as its rules. The Senate's rules are continuing, have continued with only infrequent changes since the first session in 1789, whereas the House must adopt its rules with the beginning of each new session. A six-year term provides a senator with something extremely rare in political life: a sense of security and even independence. At its worst, such tenure makes it unnecessary, at least technically, for a senator to reflect his constituents' views, but, at its best, it allows a senator to rise above petty pressures and to consider ideas on their own merits, to vote accordingly and thus to behave as a statesman. Senators represent states rather than particular groups of voters, as do representatives, or rather than all the people, as does the president. By representing states, the senators provide the element of federalism which was a prime goal of the Founding Fathers as they searched for ways to create a new system of government, one of checks and balances that would provide stability but not inhibit the growth of freedom.

With federalism as its cornerstone, the Senate was the natural battleground for the great struggle of the nineteenth century, the struggle for preservation of a Union which is federal in character. The great debates and the great debaters, Clay and Calhoun, Webster, Hayne and Benton, established the Senate as the nation's greatest forum, an image that persists long after the Age of Debates has passed. When such nation-shaping agreements as the Missouri Compromise could be worked out in the Senate, then political power was certain to reside with that arm of the government, and reside there it did, until debate and compromise were no longer possible, war became inevitable, and power passed, as it always has in wartime, into executive hands.

A great portion of the Confederacy's civilian leaders, Jefferson Davis and Judah P. Benjamin and their like, had served in commanding Senate positions. Their defection en masse left the Senate weak and shaken, a state that was repaired only slowly. But the South, with its one-party system, kept sending back the same senators so many times that they climbed back into the committee chairmanships after the war, and once again took power even though a numerical minority. One wry observer has called the southernness of the Senate, particularly its elite inner club, "the South's revenge for Appomattox." Certainly the atmosphere is predominantly southern, the veneration of tradition, of courtly manners, of gentlemanly agreements, even of bourbon and branchwater. In fact, the very clubbiness of the place is southern. In the past one hundred years, clubbing together has been the predominant characteristic of the South, clubbing to exclude the outsiders, the Negroes first, but also Poor Whites, those who don't belong; clubbing to assure that government rests in the hands of the chosen few; and in the process the South has become the only section of the country where a doctrine of aristocratic government-by-the-few has won open and predominant support.

The Senate's aura is just that. The inner club is largely southern. Its will is exerted by negotiation, accommodation, private conversation and persuasion. A senator who is powerful in the club can achieve position of great political potency without becoming a national figure or drawing together massive political backing. Such a man today is Senator Richard Russell of Georgia. In headline or TV terms he is little known outside the South, but his power within the Senate is second to none, a deep-rooted member of the hierarchy that sees presidents come and go, the passing of senate majority leaders, and through it all remains one of the few who decide what the Senate shall do. "Dick Russell says" is one of the most important phrases that a senator can use in swaying a colleague or passing on an order. The phrase is not used carelessly; thus it does not get debased. Curiously, such currency is of little value outside the Senate, as is demonstrated every four years when political parties choose their presidential candidates. Often as not, Senate tycoons stand by helplessly while their party chooses exactly the candidate opposed by the senator. Dick Russell, for instance, had little stomach for Adlai Stevenson but was bent on preventing the domination of Estes Kefauver, a southern senator who, by Russell's standards, had not played the Senate game, was not a member of the inner club. Russell could block Kefauver but could not choose the nominee.

Senators, once they have achieved such eminence, are first of all members of the Senate, and only secondarily members of political parties. Time and time again, this distinction is illustrated by a majority leader who shapes his program to fit Senate rather than party needs, for example, when Senator William Knowland, as Republican Leader of the Senate when President Eisenhower was in the White House, repeatedly ignored the President's wishes for Senate accomplishments which would help him in the 1956 campaign.

As the Age of Debate passed, more and more Senate business, like that of the House, came to be transacted in committee, so that average Senate sessions, to the perpetual disappointment of tourists and other visitors, are dry, colorless affairs, only a handful of dutiful members going through the necessary forms, with the exception of roll calls and extraordinary floor fights when the full membership turns out. The Senate's majesty, its style and atmosphere find more frequent expression in hearings held by one of its more prestigious committees, of which that on foreign affairs is the undisputed leader.

With headquarters in the Capitol itself, rather than in one of the Senate office buildings, the Foreign Affairs Committee meets in a setting of rococo ebullience, the small chamber itself of great dignity, the anteroom a florid display of Constantino Brumidi's mural decorations, gilding, carving and furniture preserved intact from the era of General Grant. Here the present chairman, Senator J. William Fulbright of Arkansas, presides with a quiet scholarly air that is in contrast with the manner of some of his predecessors, men such as Senator William Borah of Idaho, who, at his zenith in the 1920's, truly controlled American foreign policy. Such power frequently has been gathered into the chairman's hands, sometimes because the White House occupant was weak or more interested in domestic affairs, sometimes through the sheer weight of Senate prestige, which in some periods, such as the close of President Wilson's second term, has gravely outweighed the president's.

Congressman's wife and son

Principal source of the committee's power is its constitutional authority over treaties and a long list of presidential appointments which can be made only with "the advice and consent" of the Senate. Appropriations, Judiciary and a few others rank almost as high, but a seat on the Foreign Relations Committee is the ultimate goal of most senators, who, once they become members, are wooed by presidents and secretaries of state and ambassadors and a vast company of others anxious to influence high policy.

For all its Borahs and Vandenbergs, its Norrises and La Follettes, the Senate is not all dignity, power and responsibility. The roster has also included a strange, varied company, Cotton Ed Smith and Ole Gene Talmadge, Boies Penrose and Huey Long, Bilbo and McCarthy, clowns and villains as well as statesmen, a fact of which it is sometimes necessary to remind senators bemused by the glamour of their own institution. Traditionally the Senate has not considered itself a training ground for presidents. In fact, it has put great store by its separateness and power over foreign affairs, which, in the Senate view, is almost co-equal with that of the president. But in recent years a change has occurred which may, in the long run, have a deep effect on relations between Senate and White House. Four of the last eight presidents have come directly from the Senate to the White House. Nothing like it had happened earlier, and Senate aficionados are not quite sure it is the best thing for their revered institution.

A president who knows all the ins and outs of Senate politics, the pressure points, the special interests, the strengths and weaknesses, is a much more formidable opponent than a man who comes to the presidency from a state capital. Both President Truman and President Kennedy drew on a backlog of Senate training to meet their higher responsibilities. But theirs was minor compared to the experience which President Johnson brought when he made the transition. Behind him were many years not just as a senator but as a majority leader who had demonstrated consummate skill and talent for the job. What that meant for Congress—the voice calling from the White House was the same that a few years earlier had called from the majority leader's office—is clear when one looks over the long, dramatic list of domestic legislation, much of it highly controversial, which President Johnson pushed, shoved and cajoled through Congress in 1965. The climate for such social change had, of course, been created in part by President Kennedy; the legislative skill of President Johnson put such changes into law; and the senate, pretty much obeying its old leader, never had seemed less formidable. No one in Washington who has seen the Senate in both lean and fat years would dream of considering the Senate's current position a permanent one. Like the Supreme Court, the Senate has in the past demonstrated remarkable, even miraculous, recovery powers.

The Senate's method of operation, by negotiation and accommodation in private, brings up one of Washington's fascinating diversions, analyzing the visible and the invisible. So much is visible in the operations of Congress, the White House and the numerous governmental departments, yet there are always unanswered questions. How did that particular event occur in just that way? What were those missing links? Who provided the impetus for this or that sequence of happenings? No doubt there are persons who hold considerable power and still manage to be invisible to the public gaze; but it is doubtful that there are many or that their ultimate power is very great. There are, however, agencies and areas of government where invisibility cloaks some rather important operations. Neither the Central Intelligence Agency nor Mr. Hoover's Federal Bureau of Investigation could be classed properly as invisible; both are too thoroughly and constantly publicized. The CIA, inhabiting a huge Harrison & Abramovitz building on a wooded hill up the Potomac, is probably the only intelligence agency in the world which advertises its whereabouts with a large roadside sign directing motorists to its heavily guarded gate—and though the activities of both agencies are pretty well disguised, Washingtonians are always conscious of their presence and of their power. Much less visible are the Defense Department's own intelligence operations and particularly the vast and mysterious National Security Agency, where lights, even when no apparent crisis exists, burn all night in a huge complex of buildings midway between Washington and Baltimore. Certain aspects of Space Agency research, nearly all of Atomic Energy, as well as the intelligence operations could truly be classed, without being sensational, as a part of invisible government.

Some other areas, much less sensitive, as the Defense Department would define sensitivity, are also invisible for other reasons, mainly because people don't know about them. The Bureau of the Budget is a perfect example. Sounding like the most pedestrian and boring of activities, the Bureau actually is somehow involved in almost every phase of government. Its power, little recognized by outsiders, is immense, since it finally controls departmental expenditures and, by such means, can and does shape policy. Presidents of the past three decades, recognizing that power, have kept their Budget Bureaus close beside them for constant and quick communication.

Oddly enough, one of the three major branches of the American government, the judicial, is in an important way invisible. The Supreme Court, quietly majestic in the marble temple designed by Cass Gilbert, appears highly visible, its decision days covered by the press, awed tourists watching briefly the nine justices—there to be seen and heard as they question lawyers pleading constitutional cases. But for all such visibility the justices, as far as Washington is concerned, are an invisible quantity, seldom appearing at social or political occasions, taking little part in community life, their presence felt rather than seen. The great ones of the past, such as Oliver Wendell Holmes, Benjamin Cardozo and Louis Brandeis, have perforce led intellectual lives, the imprint of their great-

Right
Document Room

Next two pages
The Bench

ness left behind by their thought and writings rather than their actions. Such is the essence of the highest court's position.

A few justices have managed some extracurricular activities, such as Justice William O. Douglas's constant and effective campaigning for conservation and the preservation of our natural resources. Single-handed he has saved Washington's C & O Canal and its adjacent woodlands by leading well-publicized hikes along the Tow Path. By mountain-climbing expeditions and resulting books, he has helped focus attention on the need for conserving wilderness areas. Activities of this nature are the exception rather than the rule, however. Justices, for the most part, seem to enjoy their invisibility. This is far from true of other members of the legal profession, who form one of the larger cadres of the city's population.

Washington is a kind of heaven for lawyers, the multiplicity of departments and bureaus and regulations and rules providing an ever-mounting source of business. Many a congressman, retired by his constituents, has settled down to a lucrative Washington practice, aided by the knowledge he gained while serving in the government. Every law-school graduating class seems to send to Washington a fresh wave of eager young lawyers, a chosen handful to serve as law clerks to the justices, the rest to gain experience in some of the big firms which have risen up to dominate the legal scene. Only a Mandarin mind could guide the reader through the complex strata of Washington's legal world, explain why some types of lawyers have more prestige than others, when lawyering verges into lobbying, why one stratum looks down on another.

Likewise drawn to the city by the processes of government is another huge group, the members called by many names, such as Industry representative or legislative analyst or congressional consultant. The plain name is lobbyist, and they are usually quite visible. How many there are in Washington no one can say. They are everywhere, under many guises,

Associate justice

sometimes posing as sedate representatives of a nationwide committee, sometimes frankly emblazoning their purpose on letterhead and office door, oftentimes as lawyers with an industry or a foreign nation as a client. Some lobbyists achieve positions of great influence due to the political power or wealth of the forces they represent. The AFL-CIO is one example, the NAACP another, and the mass industries such as automobiles, oil and steel are still others. A lobbyist can also be an ex-newspaperman, in shiny-bottomed suit, eking out a living with one typewriter, a mimeograph machine and a Congressional Directory. Whatever the extent of their numbers it is safe to say that the second biggest industry in Washington is the industry of influencing government, or trying to.

Sometimes the title of a lobby is so euphemistic you would never guess its content. Who, for example, would know that the National Highway Users' Conference was not made up of little old ladies who like to go out driving, but instead is a potent association of truckers, auto manufacturers and oil interests lobbying constantly for more massive highways across the landscape? You could guess the purpose of the Associated Third Class Mail Users, Inc., but what would the American Meat Institute be? Or the National Broiler Council? Or the National Ice Association? The lobby gamut is a great one, from the American Hot Dip Galvanizers Association, Inc., to the Association of Regular Army Sergeants, each with its special cause to plead. Most are legitimate, some a touch shady, some very worthwhile. The lobbyists are everywhere, in the Statler bar, flashing their credit cards in Trader Vic's or Paul Young's, buying a drink at the Press Club, waiting in a congressman's outer office, which is how many pass a great deal of time. But sometimes they do open battle. When a change was proposed in the Taft-Hartley law not long ago, some forty-five representatives of the AFL-CIO were counted as lobbying for the change, while an equal number, representing the

U.S. Chamber of Commerce, the National Association of Manufacturers and the Farm Bureau, were drawn up in battle array against them. Usually the confrontations are not so dramatic, their pressures exerted in quieter ways, working through a congressman's constituents or, if he is friendly to the lobbyist's cause, by helping him gather information and political support. Since even the President himself must be a lobbyist, lobbying is a perfectly legitimate occupation and, in an odd way, adds variety to the Washington scene.

XII

More than anything else, Washington is the presidency. The Hill and the river are the reasons for Washington's being where it is. The presence of the President gives Washington focus, establishes its style, concentrates in one person the government of the United States. Washington is not only the home of presidents; it is the creation of presidents. Named for the first one, who chose the site, shaped by the third president, the city has been molded by all the succeeding presidents as they added their own institutions and embellishments and characteristics, the imprint of their ideas of government, the reflection of their attitudes toward man and society, their concepts of how to behave and how to live. President Andrew Jackson could make his office, his home and his person so available to the citizens that a new feeling arose about the presidency, reviving Jeffersonian intimacy between city and White House. Lesser men such as John Tyler added personal distinction to the manners of the office as did some women, for instance James Buchanan's niece and hostess Miss Harriet Lane, who brought her own paintings and objets d'art and a graceful presence into the executive mansion. Minor additions, to be sure, but the house and the office soon received the great, fundamental additions that Abraham Lincoln made as he, of necessity, gathered into his hands undreamed-of powers, political and economic, to prosecute a war that preserved the Union. Lincoln's accumulations were of a concrete kind and also of a myth-making nature, combining to give the whole nation an image of a true capital, small though Washington was.

His successors for the rest of the century shaped the capital and the presidency in their own image, war veterans such as Garfield, Benjamin

Harrison and McKinley, who built the huge Pension Office and argued more over the ethics of political patronage than over the social-industrial changes in progress. None read or cared to acknowledge what Lincoln had taught of the presidency and its powers, none until Theodore Roosevelt ushered the presidency and the United States into the twentieth century and into the company of great powers. So it has remained ever since, with only one brief nostalgic excursion, in the 1920's, back to a no longer tenable theory that such trivial men as Millard Fillmore and Calvin Coolidge were worthy of this great office. As shapers-of-the-capital, the presidents have behaved variously and sometimes unexpectedly. Between them, President Coolidge and President Herbert Hoover, neither exactly radical in his political approach, made one of the most radical physical changes by laying out the vast Federal Triangle of buildings along Pennsylvania Avenue. Those plans matured in the Franklin D. Roosevelt administration, whose own planning was far more bent on social and political reform than on changing Washington's face. By the time of President Franklin Roosevelt, however, all of the characteristics that we now observe of Washington and the presidency had become clearly defined, the city's sense of history and of history in the making, the sense of power and its many manifestations, the feeling of being in touch and of government reaching into all classes for its servants. All these were palpable, as well as the way all the strands of government, no matter whether legislative, judicial or executive, passed through the presidency to give the national capital cohesion and centrality.

Small wonder that the office of the presidency, occupied thus far by only thirty-five men, has come to be looked upon with awe. Not all of the occupants have inspired awe, of course. Chester Arthur in his elegant tailcoats was scarcely awesome. Neither was dour, penurious Calvin Coolidge, nor Rutherford B. Hayes, nor bumbling James Buchanan. The ones who did inspire such feeling—Franklin Roosevelt, Woodrow Wilson,

White House staff

113

Abraham Lincoln—were ones who seemed a true embodiment of the power of the office, embodied because they used the power. The feeling of awe is coupled with one of respect. Even though the president happens to be of another political faith, an American is inclined to respect him and, above all, to respect the office. Respect is tempered by still another feeling, a warmer, cozier emotion which amounts to possessiveness. Americans are extremely proprietary of the presidency. It is the one office, along with the vice-presidency, which all the people have a voice in filling. Therefore their stake is personal and direct. "Is he in his office?" asks a camera-slung tourist at the White House gate. As the guard nods understandingly, the tourist is apt to relay this information to his family. Then all stand silently staring a few moments, drinking it in, drinking in the fact that there behind those white walls, so near, sits the man who is their president.

Nor is it just the visiting outlander who gets a charge from the nearness of the president; the whole city vibrates to him. When a president goes off for a weekend in Hyannis Port or to his Texas ranch, there is a noticeable lessening of tension, a relaxing, as though you too can afford to take it easy if *he* can. Washington is constantly aware of the presidential presence, the action going on around him, the rumors and reports that seep out of the White House, the hourly bulletins on his thoughts, ideas, temper, health and humors. The physical manifestations are, of course, most apparent. A helicopter sweeping low past the Washington Monument is heading for the presidential landing pad just below the South Portico. He must be aboard. A long black car followed by a bigger black Secret Service car announces that he has just departed for a visit to The Hill—but the presence is felt without these outward signs.

The tone of Washington is set by the occupant of the White House. If he is a kinetic, highly charged type like Theodore Roosevelt, he produces similar activities in the capital. The tone of Franklin Roosevelt's opening years was tumultuous, with new ideas and new personalities being woven into government service. John F. Kennedy set his own distinctive tone, vibrant youth, a bright beckoning future, younger men bringing vigor to the government. The Kennedy tone penetrated both government and city, even into the city's gymnasiums. This matter of tone involves emulation, to a degree, but also it is expressed through the kind of men a president attracts to his service. The tone can be dull, or worse. For example, the days of Warren G. Harding were, by all accounts, degraded; the Ohio Gang ruled Washington. Corruption in high places spread cynicism and despair far down into the lower ranks of government; poker and whiskey, innocent enough pleasures, were invested by Harding with a sinister coloration that really stemmed from the darker doings afoot.

Of all Washington's power lines, the hottest is between White House and Capitol. Congress, while intensely jealous of its powers and often at odds with the president, is intensely aware of the occupant of the White House and his doings, and of him as the greatest single power generator of all. The men who occupy The Hill are prone to refer to the White House as "Downtown."

"The opinion Downtown is thus and so," a Hill man is likely to say. The tone, sometimes a bit condescending, may imply that "The president proposes; Congress disposes." That sometimes is true, but the president's powers are many and varied. Within his domain are many things a congressman wants: help with a potent constituent, favors for another, federal appointments in the district back home, a hundred different things, some big, some little, and it is a brave or untutored congressman who breaks completely with the man in the White House if he is of his own party. The favors go both ways because a president, as earlier noted, can only propose legislation, then lobby for it. He needs votes, and some of the best brains of his staff are engaged in the constant search for the "ayes" to put across a legislative program. When the president is a man of Lyndon Johnson's legislative background, then he is his own chief lobbyist, but most presidents are dependent on the support and skill of the majority leaders in both houses. They and the various whips must do the behind-the-scenes cajoling and accommodating to achieve legislative action. By this cooperation the president shares with them some of his power, for in the process of negotiation the president can be committed to some course of action as a countermove. The president's relations with the Supreme Court are a good deal more distant, at least in a technical sense, but neither is unaware of the other or his needs and wishes. The classic example of conflict between the two was provided, of course, by FDR's attempt to pack, or enlarge, the Court when the Nine Old Men constantly overturned the New Deal's key statutes. President Roosevelt lost that battle, but won his own war; within a few years, retirements and shifts gave him the majority he needed, and since those days, less than thirty years ago, the court has developed into one of the more liberal forces in the federal system.

Dominant but sharing its power, symbolic but intensely practical, the American presidency, in the long run, defies exact description or final analysis or complete understanding. Qualities exist beyond the presidency's expressed and implied powers, beyond the historic legitimacy of the line of descent, beyond concentration of executive authority in the hands of one man. The American people have created the presidency and shared it and refined it in a thousand ways. To their own creation the people turn their eyes and attention, forever watchful, approving, mistrustful, questioning, deeply committed and involved, as they are in no other single institution of the land. The involvement explains their unappeasable hunger for every detail of presidential life and thought. By such concentration of emotion and aspiration, the people have endowed the office of president with an aura apparent to any man who steps into the presence of the President of the United States. Yesterday he may have been a senator or a governor or merely a friend; today he is the President. Sitting behind his flag-flanked desk, the quality

The Red Room

is obvious. It is still there as he sits up in bed reading late reports, a glass of milk and a bottle of pills on the night table beside him. And a bit of it stays forever, clinging long after he has passed the actual presidency on to his legitimate, elected successor.

The presidency encompasses so many roles that it is no wonder men of average talents have had profound difficulty in fulfilling their responsibilities with any distinction. Commander-in-Chief of the armed forces, leader of the dominant political party, spokesman on the intricate relations with all other nations of the world, guardian of the national wealth, planner of the national future, teacher, negotiator, ceremonial figure— even, in one sense, leader of matters spiritual as well as temporal—all these a president must be. Other capitals are acutely sensitive to what the American president says, does, and thinks. So is the stock market. And so, in varying degrees, are most of the other sectors of American society. A hint of changing economic policy or even of presidential ill health can send market values plummeting.

As far as Washington is concerned—Washington as a city to live in and not just the seat of the federal government—one of the most important aspects of the presidency is its relation to the District of Columbia. In essence, the president is mayor of Washington, there being no elected city government, the mayoral duties performed by three District of Columbia commissioners, all appointed by the president. Such local appointments are one of the ways the president creates the ambience of his capital.

Even more crucial is the character he gives his cabinet and his own intimate White House staff, which, like the court of a monarch, reflects his tone, carries out his orders and becomes the operative organ of the presidential ego. His cabinet members may be classifiable as "men around the president," but not necessarily close to the president. It all depends. Many a cabinet secretary has found himself in splendid isolation, far outside the inner circle, with no direct access to the president,

Place setting

and thus a nonparticipant in major matters. That can happen when a president, activated perhaps by regional or ethnic politics, appoints a cabinet member without knowing much about him. He may find the secretary totally unsympathetic, or ill-suited or any number of things. More generally the president uses cabinet appointments to add luster to his administration. If he pays a political debt along the way, or adds to the political balance of the administration at the same time, so much the better, but his principal motive is to have his work done well and enhance the regime. Conflicts with cabinet members seldom are to a president's advantage. Lincoln, at the outset of his administration, found that he first must tame his secretary of state, William H. Seward, who thought Lincoln was an inferior and manageable type. The president with great skill achieved his goal but left behind in his cabinet one member who was almost to cause the downfall of his successor, Andrew Johnson. Secretary of War Edwin Stanton did everything but seize final power after Lincoln's assassination, and historians are still plumbing the depth of his part in the machinations which led to President Johnson's impeachment. That event, in which Johnson's position was sustained by the margin of only one vote, provides a footnote on one other interesting aspect of the relations among the branches of government. The House has the power to impeach a president, but only the Senate, sitting as a judicial body, has the power to try such a case.

Presidents putting together cabinets approach the matter many different ways. President Kennedy thought of his as a cabinet of talents. President Harding, probably sensing his own inadequacy, obtained the services of Charles Evans Hughes, Andrew Mellon and Henry C. Wallace to bolster the prestige of his administration. Cabinet posts are one of the best ways of enlisting the services of wise and skillful men who have never braved the election process.

Such men as Elihu Root, Henry L. Stimson and Dean Acheson thus have been able to make great government contributions by sharing the

presidential power in appointive posts. Sometimes the president's administrative assistants are far more important than cabinet members. Since the days of FDR, administrative assistants have formed the nucleus of the White House inner circle. Originally men "with a passion for anonymity"—Mr. Roosevelt's phrase—these are the workhorses who share presidential confidences and sometimes, by controlling access to the president, wield immense power. That anonymity faded as the power of their positions became more and more apparent. In the Kennedy administration, Ken O'Donnell and Larry O'Brien achieved notoriety as the Irish Mafia and became the most assiduously sought-after men in Washington. Later, in President Johnson's administration, Jack Valenti and Bill Moyers, to name but two, have occupied similarly intimate positions.

To say that they are sought after is something of an understatement in a city where society is composed of hunters and the hunted. Newspapermen wanting information or at least guidance, congressmen and politicians seeking favors or support, hostesses yearning for the cachet of entertaining important men, all dog the trail of White House assistants with dinner invitations, requests for appointments, phone calls and mail. An O'Donnell or a Valenti has an extremely vital role in the complex interplay of Washington where supper parties and quiet cocktail meetings are often as meaningful as legislative lobbies and committee sessions. After hours, he is the president's representative, stopping first perhaps at the Metropolitan Club for a drink with an American ambassador home on leave, then at home for a quick change and off to Georgetown with his wife, for dinner.

The dinner ritual in Washington is precise—arrive at eight, leave at eleven—admirably suited to men who work hard and must have their wits about them next day. A presidential assistant is likely at dinner to spar with an unfriendly columnist, listen attentively to a senator's ideas, plant a presidential suggestion in return and perhaps learn a few tidbits

Presidential assistant

119

of juicy gossip. His wife, who has been doing her part by collecting information on her own, may show no sign of wanting to leave; the assistant gives her a signal or a more positive nudge, and off they go. She doesn't know it yet, but her husband has promised they will drop in at Joe's for an after-dinner drink. Joe's sounds like a beer joint, but it isn't; Joe's is an elegant columnist's elegant residence where presidents, generals, ambassadors and cabinet ministers are such frequent visitors that police and cab drivers treat it like a public building. At Joe's the presidential assistant may be in for a sophisticated news-pumping, or he may be given a dressing down, or he may even plant an idea of his own. Whatever goes on, the assistant is there as the presidential representative, just as he is every time he shows up on The Hill or anywhere else in town. Disseminating the president's ideas as he goes about, the assistant serves also as the president's eyes and ears; no president ever has enough of either.

The president himself appears infrequently at private houses. President Kennedy was an exception, finding relaxation in small private dinners at the homes of old friends. Those occasions, private though they were, never succeeded in being secret. A president is watched too closely to have a secret life. Even if the press fails to discover a date in advance, someone is bound to spill the secret, maybe a neighbor noting extraordinary dinner preparations next door, maybe a policeman assigned to special Georgetown duty, maybe a child babbling on the morning school bus.

Once Rowland Evans, a newspaper columnist friend of President Kennedy, found his private dinner had become public knowledge because an overeager city sanitation department, tipped apparently by the precinct police, sent a crew to shovel snow from his sidewalk. So assiduous were their attentions, clearing even the front steps while leaving the rest of the block piled with snow, it was obvious that a most important guest was expected. In Washington there is only one such person. Presi-

Right
Statesman

Next two pages
The President's car

dent Kennedy's propensity for visiting his friends revived in Washington a feeling of presidential intimacy. Residents came to feel that if they kept their eyes peeled they might see him, not just on state occasions, but hopping from his car, swinging jauntily up the steps of a house just down the street. Once he took a friend, Chuck Spalding, down to the White House gate at night to help him hail a cab. Traffic continued heedless down Pennsylvania Avenue until a late-evening stroller stopped, flabbergasted.

"What's the matter, Mr. President?" he asked. "Won't they stop for you?" With that he put two fingers in his mouth, gave an ear-splitting whistle, and got the attention of a passing cabbie.

Most presidents are not glimpsed so informally, although all make their presence felt even if unseen. At certain historic periods, the city, sensing deep change, becomes acutely conscious of the president, as when the Chief Executive yields the White House to a new president of the opposite political party.

Those who witnessed the change-over from Herbert Hoover to Franklin Roosevelt have never forgotten the dramatic shift in atmosphere which transformed Washington that chilly gray March morning in 1933. "The icy aloofness that had enveloped 1600 Pennsylvania Avenue," wrote Constance Green, "gave way to heart-warming friendliness." The head of the Secret Service, in a position to see it all from inside, remembered that in a few hours the White House was "transformed" into a gay place, full of people "oozing confidence." And that confidence seeped out all over the city. With the new President came new men to cope with the terrible economic disaster which had overwhelmed the Hoover administration. Washington was openmouthed at the audacity of men like Rexford Tugwell and Raymond Moley and the other Braintrusters as they attacked the problems, perhaps not with solutions but certainly with self-confidence, a quality the city had almost forgotten. The new President, equally audacious, soon had the newspaper corre-

White House press

spondents clustering around his desk in an informal give-and-take press conference that was to become a ritual, just one of the Rooseveltian innovations. Historians such as Arthur Schlesinger, Jr., have only lately been putting together the evidence of the deep, very permanent changes the New Deal wrought in those first hectic days. Many of the participants played their parts and then departed, but a goodly number can still be found in Washington, among them one who first arrived in that vintage year as a Texas congressman's assistant—Lyndon Baines Johnson.

On the moment in November when a new man is elected president, the Secret Service immediately begins addressing him as "Mr. President," even though technically he is only Mr. President-elect. That custom is symptomatic of all Washington's attitude toward the new man. The king is dead! Long live the king! The retiring president is of waning interest. All thoughts, all talk, all action focuses on the new man who, in the strange interim period before he is inaugurated on January 20, starts to guide Washington's destiny.

The last time such a change-over occurred, in November, 1960, the popular vote margin was tiny, but Washington awoke next morning vibrating to a new dynamism. An elderly Republican was giving way to a young Democrat. The Republican and his wife had occupied the White House but had not used it much. The Democrat and his beauteous young wife gave every sign of bringing back to it the buoyancy, the exuberance that had enlivened the administrations of both Roosevelts.

Suddenly the Kennedys' red brick house on N Street was the center of the nation's capital. Newspapermen and TV camera crews clogged the narrow Georgetown street. Who went in and who went out was chronicled in minutest detail, what they ate and what they wore, Caroline's behavior and the latest rumor about who would be secretary of state, all were devoured with an appetite that only Washington in the throes of such a transformation can enjoy. New faces and new names appeared in the news. Robert McNamara. Who had heard of him?

A few people in Detroit—or on Wall Street. The Defense Department started boning up. Would Senator Fulbright be secretary of state? Or Adlai Stevenson? Who was Dean Acheson pushing? The air was thick with rumor and counter-rumor, and reporters by the score trailed the President-elect when he went calling—once to see Walter Lippmann, the wisest newspaper writer in town; once to see Mr. Acheson, the former secretary of state. The Kennedy telephone line, supplemented by many extra lines, was impossible to dial, even if one was lucky enough to know his private number.

Washington relished every moment, every rumor, every hard fact that finally emerged. For Washington, all of the city's special characteristics seemed to be summed up and intensified in that brief interim before a new presidency started—the sense of history, the feeling of contemporaneity, the fascination with power, the love of politics. All were distilled anew as December changed into January, as a new Congress met, as the politicians and soldiers and professors and plain citizens began gathering from every state in the Union to inaugurate the new president—until it all climaxed that bright snowy noon on the Capitol steps.

For the republic, of course, an inauguration is a great act of renewal, the regeneration of an ancient and honorable governmental system, of reaffirmation of principles and ideals. For the city it is all that and something more besides. Such moments are Washington's special treasure, shared with the nation and with the world, to be sure; but still possessed, savored, experienced and enshrined by the city alone.

But Washington sees such drama only a few times in a century. Other sights and sounds bespeak the special qualities and characteristics and functions of the usual Washington, sights such as the extraordinary concentration of long black limousines around an embassy at cocktail-party time and around the Capitol for the opening of Congress; the way sudden glimpses of Washington, a line of trees along the Mall or the façade of a 1910 apartment house, signal a reminiscence of Paris, and strangely enough how one view, looking back from up-river, makes Washington look in late afternoon like a pale-washed Mediterranean city. Sounds as well as sights: the sound of clangorous sirens announces the passage of an African president on a state visit; above the traffic noises of Massachusetts Avenue a Muslim call to prayer wails from the Islamic Center's minaret; in the sunset stillness "Taps" echoes across the river, cool and sad, from Fort Myer above Arlington; along a red-brick Georgetown street a scissors grinder, probably the last of his calling, shuffles in tempo to the rhythmic one-note of his hand-bell.

Archives Building

WHAT IS PAST
IS PROLOGUE

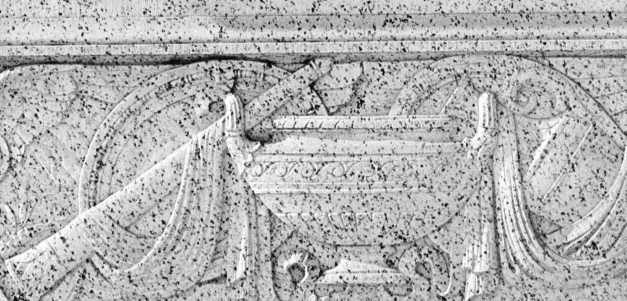

KEY TO PORTRAITS

INDEX

(Page references in *italic* denote illustrations)

127

129